I0710440

First printing edition 2024.

ISBN: 978-1-962891-14-1 (eBook)
ISBN: 978-1-962891-01-1 (Paperback)
ISBN: 978-1-962891-27-1 (Hardback)

Library of Congress Control Number: 2024900224

Seeking Elvyra, book one of The Great King and the Seer
Published by Vellichor and More
www.vellichorandmore.com

Seeking Elvyra

The Great King and the Seer
Book One

Jessica Pietro

Vellichor and More

This book is dedicated to all the people who have helped make it possible, encouraged me on this journey, and supported my family for years. There are so many of you, but I would like to specifically thank the women who read this book first and have been helping me work out the kinks ever since: Kim Shank, Rebekah Wyman, Shandy Perlman, Alaina Tobias, and Julie Helms.

I would also like to add a very special thank you to my husband, Jeremy, who has been my biggest, most loving supporter, not only through the creation of this series, but in our everyday lives.

Through my highs and lows, my ideas and projects, my adventurous spirit, and all the other oddities that make me—me, you have endured with the most exquisite kindness, love, and encouragement.
Thank you, Baberz, for being my best friend.

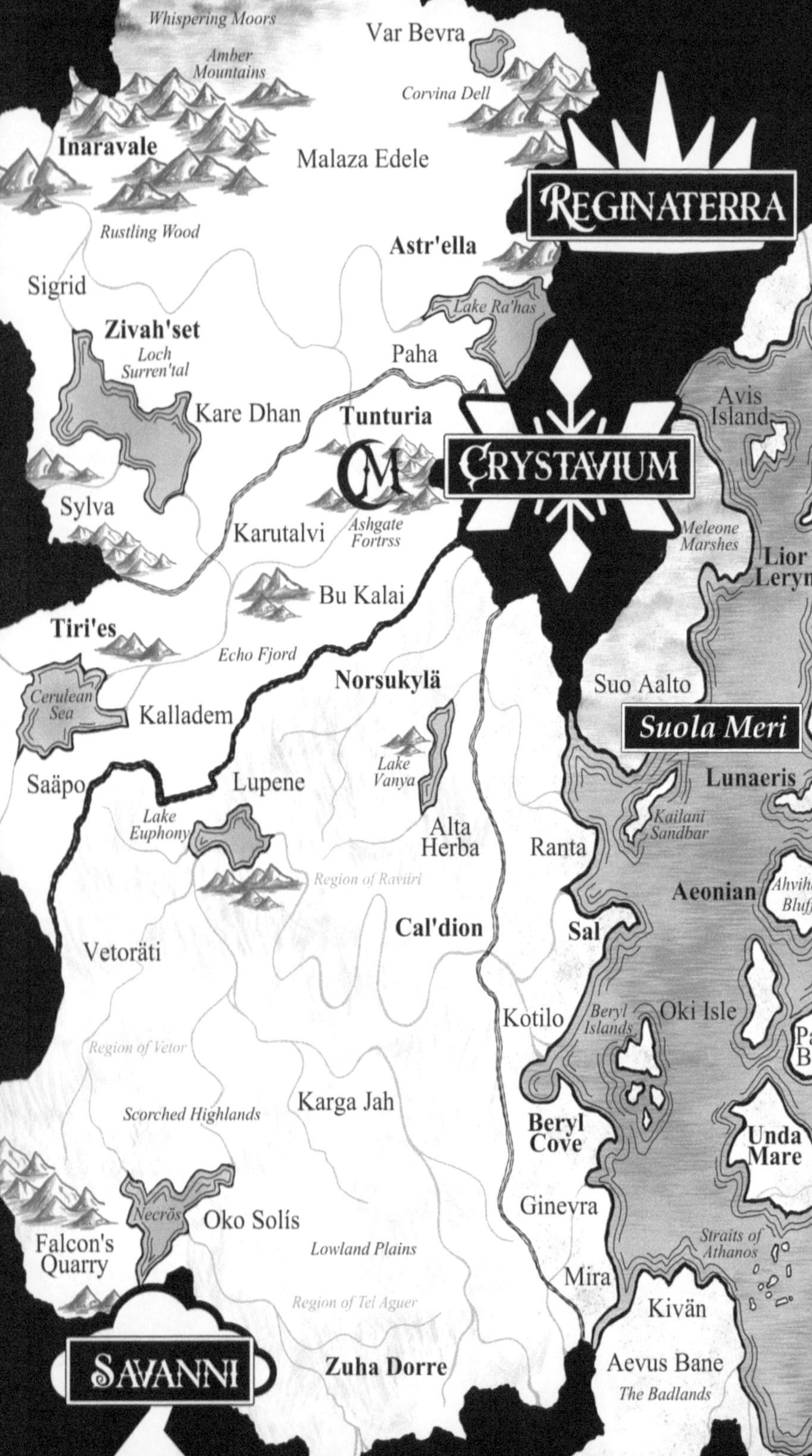

Whispering Moors
Var Bevra
Amber Mountains
Corvina Dell
REGINATERRA
Inaravale
Malaza Edele
Astr'ella
Rustling Wood
Lake Ra'has
Sigrid
Paha
Avis Island
Zivah'set
Loch Surren'tal
Tunturia
CRYSTAVIUM
Kare Dhan
CM
Ashgate Fortrss
Meleone Marshes
Lior Leryn
Sylva
Karutalvi
Bu Kalai
Tiri'es
Echo Fjord
Suo Aalto
Cerulean Sea
Norsukylä
Suola Meri
Kalladem
Lunaeris
Lake Vanya
Saäpo
Lupene
Kailani Sandbar
Lake Euphony
Alta Herba
Ranta
Aeonian
Ahvihae Bluffs
Region of Raviiri
Cal'dion
Sal
Vetoräti
Kotilo
Beryl Islands
Oki Isle
Pal Be
Region of Vetor
Karga Jah
Scorched Highlands
Beryl Cove
Unda Mare
Necrōs
Oko Solís
Ginevra
Straits of Athanos
Falcon's Quarry
Lowland Plains
Mira
Region of Tel Aguer
Kivän
SAVANNI
Zuha Dorre
Aevus Bane
The Badlands

CORDILLERA
GRIM WILDS
METSA SATEEN
ALUNDA
Kamari Ravine
Aurora
Jericho
Kovae Saam
Peregrine
Elowen
Mountains
Lunalakota
Mountains
Lake
Lyall
Skull's
Gate
Lake
Tas'kare
Koen
Orchards
Lacuna Kaput
Lagoon
Uvelyen
Obscura
Katutaan
Neoma
Dell
Vertice
Dellalune
Visk'arus
Region of Sadella
Bujarshuri
Werifesteria
Region of Vastitas
Petrichor
Gorge
Celeste
yä
Ruins of
Nefel Ibata
Dysmaa
Villa
Montis
Ky'uso
Ame Hana
Ruins of
Neoma
Umi
Ochrana
Lasskon
Region of Vallemortis
Kesken
Ala
Region of Imber
Seigan
Palace
of Sateen
Caritas
Eunoia
Region of Pluvium
Sena
Ferus Basah

PROLOGUE

Six years ago, in the port of Ranta on the banks of the Suola Meri, two sisters awoke to the sounds of booted footsteps. Creeping from their beds, they cracked the door of their room and peeked out to see soldiers dressed in crimson, onyx, and ashy gray.

The girls watched in petrified silence as intruders tore through every cabinet and drawer. They had no idea what the King's Legion searched for, but their distinctive attire matched the regimentals of their father.

More than two weeks had passed since he'd disappeared, leaving them alone with the promise of a quick return.

Despite Iris' protests, Foxxglove knew they were no longer safe awaiting an absent father who might never come home. Avoiding detection, they slipped through the back door and hid beneath the deck facing the waves of the sea.

Long after the Legion finished their ravaging and dispersed, the sisters mustered the courage to tiptoe back inside to face the havoc left behind. Knowing they might never again find sanctuary there, each packed a bag and abandoned their home for the wilderness of Arkaemor.

Foxx and Iris traveled Alunda, learning to hunt, live off the land, and protect themselves, all the while wondering if they would ever see their father again. They returned to Ranta every so often but were met each time with little more than the slow deterioration of a home left uninhabited.

C

Half a year ago, the sisters crossed the barrier from Alundan beaches into the grasslands of Savanni. They happened upon a village in the southern farmlands where a woman approached them and introduced herself as Maeve. Maeve claimed to have known their mother long ago. She also knew of her death and of their father's disappearance, and she even speculated as to where he might have gone. With knowledge of things past and things to come, she told them to follow in their father's footsteps and shared with them snippets of the destiny awaiting them.

Alongside her premonitions came a warning: Should they embrace the path before them, tides would change, sands would shift, and the world as they knew it would be forever transformed.

Foxx found the drama of her words annoying and possibly delusional, but Iris felt elated with the idea of a hope-filled adventure.

Before their departure, she gifted them a carnelian stone, calling it a vital ingredient of the journey laid out before them. Half an inch thick and just big enough to fit in the palm of Iris' hand, the chiseled stone resembled the silhouette of a flat-topped acacia tree.

Departing the village, they returned to their cottage one last time, knowing their paths may never lead them back. By then, their childhood home sat in a state of disrepair. Ruptures in the roof gave access to the elements. Invasive foliage tore its way through the walls. Once abandoned, it stood rotting on the beach as a ship run aground, left to erode away in the assault of the high tide.

Rifling through the house, they hoped to unearth any clues to aid in their quest. In the top drawer of their father's desk, they discovered a map of the desert territory to the east known as the Grim Wilds. On the map, a star and a note scribbled in their father's hand read: *You will know it when you see it.*

They traveled south to the city of Sal and from there caught a boat across the Suola Meri. When they hit land, they proceeded on foot against the rising sun until they reached the eastern edge of the territory.

They camped along the border for several nights, still insecure in their decision. If Maeve's predictions were to be believed, there would be no turning back once they progressed into the Wilds.

After three days and four nights of debating, they rose at dawn and crossed the translucent barrier into the desert. If either of them felt the strain of a destiny accepted, neither spoke it aloud.

Part One

Wilderness Grim

When they fell, it shook the world.
One land divided in two.
A deviation cut a passage through time
woven into the intricacies of what once was
and what would someday be.
He mourned them.
But He had known their futures all along.
Nothing surprised Him. Nothing ever would.
He saw the cords of time and how they twisted and turned.
Like a leaf on the surface of a river.
Like the wind shakes the trees.
He bound them together.
Created a new, so the old could be dealt with.
To guide them. To restrain them.
To break them, if necessary.
A trail forged at the beginning of the ages.
The stepping stones of time forever set in place.
Nothing could alter them.
Nothing could sway the path.
Not even them. Not even the others.
Not even the fated Great King of Arkaemor.

~An excerpt from Jumalan Sana.
Found in the book of Jaeho the navi.

CHAPTER 1

THE GRIM WILDS

Paws pounded holes in the sand as they hastened across the desert, but the beast stood no chance against the arrow whizzing on its trail. It plunged into the middle of the brute's shoulders, piercing to the left of the vertebrae climbing its neck. The animal shuddered and collapsed to the ground.

Seconds later, the archer halted her sprint and peered down at the heap of fur. She toed its muzzle before kneeling and setting her weapon at her side. The bow's limbs were crafted of hickory, and the frequent pull of her fingers had darkened the center of its string.

She prodded a fang and ran the tips of her fingers over the triangular plates that shrank in succession as they descended its spine. Horns sprouted from the wolf's cheekbones, curving skyward. These were too small to repurpose, but more menacing horns flanked each ear, large enough to make utensils and other tools.

Lycanox were double the size of their relatives, the timberwolves, and those of the desert reflected their home territory with sandy fur. The only contrast in pigment came from a maroon stripe running from the tip of its nose to the end of its tail. Diverse breeds of lycanox populated many territories in Arkaemor, but none grew as ferocious as those of the desert.

Blotting sweat from her brow, she recovered the arrow with a swift tug. Blood sullied the tip, and she wiped it across her shorts before returning it to the quiver strapped to her back.

Her name echoed from the distance, shattering the silence.

Moments later, a young woman pushed her way through crinkled brush and jogged into view. Black hair whipped around her shoulder from its high ponytail as she stalled in front of the beast. A thin section hung free in her face, white as the bubbling crests of ocean waves. "You got him!"

A smirk twisted the archer's lips as she plopped onto a large rock and flung her bow over her shoulder to free up both hands. "He was fast." Scorching rays beat down on them from above, and again Foxxglove wiped away sweat.

"It seems you were faster." Iris winked at her sister.

Crossing her arms over her chest with eyebrows raised, Foxx accused, "Yeah? And where were you?"

Iris replied with doe eyes. "I guess I'm slower than you."

"Not *that* much slower." Foxx massaged her temples with the heel of her hands.

Iris joined her sister on the rock and nudged her shoulder. "I was gathering dinner. There's an undressed jackrabbit hanging in the cave and a stockpile of prickly pear cactus pads and fruit."

Foxx chuckled and nodded with approval. "Wow, you've been busy."

"While you were chasing away our intruder, I too made good use of my time. Now, let's scavenge this beast!" She grinned and pulled a dagger from her scabbard belt.

Though Foxx had grown partial to the bow, Iris favored a pair of sister blades she'd purchased in Aeonian in exchange for the last of their mother's pearls.

Thorn, a double-edged dagger measuring a foot from tip to end, had an obsidian handle. The pommel displayed a rosebud, and thorny vines climbed the grip before spreading out in two directions to wrap the deeply curved quillon. Silver, and two inches wide where it met the hilt, the blade tapered symmetrically into a point.

She called her shortsword Bloom. Ornamental roses covered the dark ruby handle and sprouted leafy vines that wove up the grip to the crossguard. The design continued into etchings on the blade, which measured twice as long as Thorn. Nearly three inches wide at the hilt, it thinned briefly as it extended from the crossguard and ballooned wide again before tapering to a point.

Foxx laughed and shoved Iris from her perch. A scorpion scuttled away from the disturbance. "Even in this heat, we won't have time to dry the hide before departing in the morning. Take the horns if you want, but leave the rest for the birds. It will soon be dusk."

C

Their cave sloped into the earth deeper than their eyes could see, but they trusted the fire to deter any dangers lurking in its depths.

While Foxx built a fire, Iris gutted and cleaned the hare. She sliced through the skin on its stomach to remove the innards and separate the meaty parts from the scraps.

Once the fire blazed and the heavy smoke from the brush and kindling subsided, Foxx dismantled the cactus fruit. The maroon skin of a prickly pear indicated its ripeness. After chopping off each end, she slit it from top to bottom. Using only her fingers, she stripped away the thick rind, preparing one for each of them and placing the others into her pack.

Before their expedition led them to Savanni, the only knowledge they had of the diverse climates, creatures, and traditions of the territories outside Alunda came from their mother. Born in Metsa Sateen, she'd spent much of her youth adventuring throughout all seven territories of Arkaemor. Though Foxx and Iris had only explored parts of three territories so far, they'd learned enough to survive and even thrive in the wilderness.

After setting the meat to roast, Iris disposed of the waste about 10 *sylis*, or 60 feet, outside the cave entrance for another predator to chew through. On her way back to the fire, she retrieved a leather-bound journal from her pack and opened it to the page on the lycanox. Her mother had given her the journal long ago, and as an avid note taker, Iris enjoyed documenting their adventures.

When they first left home, she undertook the challenge of cataloging everything their parents had taught them. She noted stories and song lyrics, details regarding the different territories of the Five Kingdoms, and whatever other information she thought could be important someday. As they traveled, she created pages for predators they encountered and anything else she found interesting.

Each documentation of a predator had a sketch of the animal and information regarding its size, coloring, strengths, weaknesses, and level of danger.

Since they'd fought lycanox before, she already had an entry for them. A detailed illustration of a lycanox spanned two pages. In a free patch of parchment near the beast's physical characteristics, she added: *Grim Wilds - tan fur, red stripe. Five back plates. Faster and larger than others. Foxx took down with one arrow between shoulder blades. Lucky shot.*

Watching her sister over the roasting meat, Foxx wondered when she'd gotten so grown up. Twelve to eighteen in the blink of an eye.

Iris returned her journal to her pack and retrieved their cutlery, handing one of each to her sister. "Do you think we'll find it tomorrow?"

Foxx passed her a pear and divided the meat. "Hard to say." She dug into her meal. Her hair, daisy-petal white, whipped back and forth across her shoulders as she shredded meat from bone. "If the map is accurate and I've interpreted it correctly, then yes."

Iris devoured her dinner. "I'm a little nervous. What do you think we'll find there?" A breeze entered the cave, rustling the flames and causing a glowing ember to burst free, spewing cinders in her direction. An orange flake landed on her forearm, stinging momentarily before darkening to ash.

Her eyebrows and shoulders lifted as she bit into her pear. "Another clue? Another piece to the puzzle? A dead end? Who knows really, when we're basing this entire expedition on the ramblings of an unhinged, old woman and a dusty, abandoned map."

Iris hated her sister's skepticism and had faith in their journey. Foxx understood the very real possibility of Maeve's lunacy and that their efforts may amount to nothing. She had faith in herself and her sister but not much else.

"Sometimes it feels like we're searching the whole world to find a dead father in a place that doesn't even exist." This was a point Foxx often made when they discussed the logistics of finding the otherworldly kingdom their mother had always raved about.

Iris bit into a tender piece of meat and replied with a full mouth. "Don't talk like that. We're going to find Celestelvyra, and we're going to find Father." Taking a sip from her water sleeve, she realized the importance of finding water soon. If they didn't, their hopes and their skepticism would be irrelevant. "Father isn't dead. He found Celestelvyra and has been trying to find a way back to us. He just hasn't made it here yet." She wiped her mouth with the back of her hand.

Foxx sighed. "It's been six years, Iris. If he did find it, trust me, he doesn't plan on coming back." Peeling off her knee-high boots, she set them on the ground next to her. They were the best boots she'd ever owned—sturdy but breathable and dyed the color of a dark plum—though currently coated in a chalky layer of garnet dust.

"He misses her. He left because that house constantly reminded him of her absence, and staying with us, mirror images of her, would have killed him. He didn't just leave to find some mysterious realm, he left to get away from us." Pain flickered in the depths of Foxx's heart. The ache of abandonment cut deep, ingrained into her core.

Iris' brow exposed her fury, though she reigned it in before Foxx noticed. "That isn't true. He wouldn't do that." She picked at the meat between her fingers and stared into the fire. "Besides, Mother used to tell us stories about Celestelvyra. It was her dream to leave Alunda in search of it. She used to paint pictures of it, remember?"

"She painted a lot of things, but Father never believed it was real. He thought her crazy for believing in fairyta—"

Iris shot to her feet. "Our mother was not crazy!"

Foxx matched her sister, standing in outrage. "Just because you bought into every romantic notion and fantastical whimsy she ever spewed at us doesn't make them true. You can write about them all you want in that book of yours, but it doesn't prove anything other than your desire to believe in wild delusions!" Her yell reverberated throughout the cave, disturbing a cauldron of bats sleeping within the tunnel. Chirping and screeching in a frenzy, they escaped in a cloud through an opening above.

Iris' anger diminished into discouragement as she blinked back tears.

A sudden loss of appetite had Foxx casting her meat into the fire. Coals scattered about the cave like shooting stars. After stomping out the biggest embers, Foxx let the others fade on their own.

Iris unfurled her bedroll and faced the wall. "You know, I've always tried to trust you, to follow you." She sniffled. "I'm asking you to trust me. Father is alive and Celestelvyra is real. I can feel it, and I know we can find them." Wiping the lone tear from her cheek, she curled up and fought her way to sleep.

Foxxglove cleaned up the remnants of their dinner, her anger already waning. Then she unrolled her own bedroll and placed it along the wall opposite her sister. Laying down facing the fire, she found herself entranced by the motion of its vermillion flames. Mesmerized, drowsy, and drained, she laid awake for only a short while before entering into dreamland herself.

C

As the invisible moon set in the west, the sun rose in the east.

Foxx awoke first, and after a stretch outside the cave in the early morning sun, she began packing. She tied her bedroll to her bag and extinguished the dwindling embers of the fire. Her movements soon stirred Iris into consciousness, and together they removed all traces of their stay.

Neither mentioned the dispute from the previous night.

With packs shouldered and weapons adorned, they lifted their eyes to double-check their direction.

They'd traveled the desert since the first day of the Petal moon, crossing the barrier from Alunda in search of the starred location on their father's map. Yesterday, the month of Petal had slid into Susi, and soon litters of arctic wolf pups would be emerging into the permafrost of Crystavium.

Hiking southeast, they searched for anything that might be significant. So far, they found the land notably bleak. Only a few towns lay scattered throughout the Wilds, though most were within a two-day journey of Alunda or Metsa Sateen. Wells dug by nomadic tribes made the trek across the territory's center achievable, and sparse wildlife provided nourishment if one knew where to look. It had taken time getting used to the environment of the desert, so different from the abundant lands of Alunda, but they'd learned long ago to cope with hunger and dehydration.

Foxx scaled a rock formation to better survey the landscape. Iris opted to stay below and watch over their packs. Though slighter than her sister's and not as muscular, years of hunting and travel were evident in Iris' frame. Foxx had wider hips to match her shoulders and toned biceps in pristine condition for climbing.

Iris groaned as she scraped her dirty fingernails with the edge of a blade. "Does it seem particularly scorching today, or is it just me?" Tucking hair behind her ear, she spotted Foxx fifteen *sylis* up in the stone cliffs.

"It's just you," Foxxglove chided, continuing her ascent. When she reached the top of the mesa, she brushed her hands on her shorts and took in the view. Nothing but dunes and tall plateaus; sand and red clay; and a few crispy cacti lie on their path as far as she could see. She kicked a stone from the edge of the cliff and began climbing down.

Back in the sand, she pulled the map from her pack and opened it between them. Iris pored over the topography, shielding her face from the sun with her hand. "We need to travel a little farther south, I think."

"But what are we looking for? That's what I don't understand. There isn't a picture or symbol on the map besides his scribble."

Iris pointed to her father's written note. "Hopefully we will *know it when we see it*, as the map suggests."

Foxx rerolled the map and turned south. Iris scurried to catch up. When the sun peaked in the sky, Iris munched on prickly pear and jackrabbit jerky to satisfy her growling stomach. As their shadows began to lean left, a woman's scream pierced the silent wilderness. They looked around, listening closely. Another scream told them the direction of the cry, and they ran off in search of it.

A sand dune came into view and they sprinted toward it. They saw a woman and a young child standing next to each other atop the mound. Crouching down with one arm wrapped around the child, the woman waved at them. Not in summon but in warning.

Iris' boot sank into the sand, and they slammed to a stop as she yanked it from the pool of liquid earth.

"It's a shiver of sandhaier!" Foxxglove shouted, dragging her sister away from the danger. Gray dorsal fins protruded from the vibrating surface at sharp angles.

"The Wilds have them, too?" Iris drew her sister-swords and scanned the area for evidence of how wide the pool had spread.

Foxx let an arrow fly, striking sandpaper skin below a visible row of fins. The crest of its body disappeared beneath the surface, taking her arrow with it.

Iris darted around the outer rim of sand shifting like waves of crystalized water and leapt onto the dune, placing herself between the sandhaier and the strangers. Over her shoulder, she greeted them with words of encouragement. "You're doing great! We'll handle this, okay?" The woman bobbed her head, her eyes wet with fear. "Climb up there." She pointed higher up the dune, and they obeyed. Iris returned her attention to the pulsating sand, Thorn and Bloom at the ready.

Dorsals from three more sharks cut through the surface, sliding effortlessly through the pool. A single shark breached the sand and snapped at her, its jagged teeth stained with dried blood.

Foxx shot an arrow, but it missed its mark as the monster dove back into the sand. Another rose in front of Iris and she slashed it above its eye, splattering bluish-green blood across the ground as it dropped into the sandy waves.

Foxx stood three *sylis* from the shifting pit, waiting for another to jump. She gleaned a pebble from the ground and whipped it at the shark closest to her, hitting it above its would-be gills. Enraged, the shark leapt from the sand. Muscular legs unfolded from beneath it like the back legs of a frog and hugged either side of its wide abdomen. It landed with a thud on the outskirts of the pool, and elongated pectoral fins stabilized the front half of its body.

On solid ground, it sized her up before leaning forward in preparation to charge.

Iris yelled her sister's name, but Foxx's bowstring was already pulled taut against her cheek. The sandhai lunged, pectoral fins alternating as they sliced through sand, pushed forward by the talons of its back feet. Jaws gnashed and chomped as its tapered head whipped from left to right, and a caudal fin trailed behind, sharp enough to cut through bone.

Foxx's arrow plunged between the fish's beady eyes, and it collided with the ground, skidding to a stop at her feet. Her boot mounted the beast's lifeless body. "Two down."

The injured shark, sliced above its eye, leapt from the sand again, its maw targeting Iris. Planting her feet, she swung her sword in a wide arc, knocking the sandhai backward and leaving another bloody gash below its mouth. Before the shark could sink beneath the surface, Foxx's arrow struck its head, causing it to drop into the sand.

"Show off," Iris called across the pool. "I had him!"

"The last time you tickled it with that dwarf sword, it didn't take. I figured I would make sure it stayed dead this time."

Iris growled.

The last sandhai vaulted from the sand, landing on two feet and hastening toward Foxx. It closed the distance between them quicker than expected, and she stumbled back, pulling her bow string taut. Before her release, a hollow thud reached her ears and the beast tumbled forward, crashing into her legs and knocking her over.

She scrambled away as it flailed. Blood sprayed the ground, marring the sand with teal ichor as the shark fought to reach her. She grabbed at the hilt of the blade at her hip but failed to pull it free of its sheath.

Iris appeared and shouted a fierce battle cry as she plunged Thorn into the top of the shark's head, holding it in place until the beast stilled. When she yanked the blade free, she offered Foxxglove a hand. Grinning, she toyed with one of the tiny throwing knives from the sheath strapped to her chest. "How's that for a dwarf sword?"

"Stroke of luck," Foxx chided, though she beamed proudly as she wiped sand from her legs. Tugging the first knife from the sand-hai's leathery skin, she handed it to Iris, who returned it to its home. The sand around them, previously shifting like a pool of water, had returned to its motionless state. Foxx turned Iris toward her and searched for concealed injuries.

Chuckling, she swatted her away and spread her arms as she spun in a circle. "I'm fine, Foxx."

The woman approached them with a hand over her heart and eyes bright with relief. A saffron scarf framed her face and matching robes covered all but her caramel colored hands. The child peeked out around her mother, staring at them with round, chestnut eyes. Her magenta garments trembled as her fingers clutched her mother's robe.

Stepping closer, the woman took Iris' hand in both of her own and touched her forehead to the backs of her knuckles. "*Shutohan.* Thank you, thank you." Spoken through her desert accent, the *th* in *thank* came out sounding like *ze*. Releasing Iris' fingers, she did the same to Foxx. Then she reached into the satchel hanging from her shoulder and retrieved a flat loaf of bread wrapped in linen, holding it out to them.

Foxx held up her hands, denying the offer. "No, no. There is no need for that."

Persistent, the woman pushed the bread closer and placed it in Iris' hands. She spoke again in Bryä, the language of the Wilds.

Iris held it, not wanting to accept the offering, knowing full well the scarcity of food in the desert, but also not wishing to seem rude.

Her eyes met the young girl's, and she knelt down, placing one knee in the sand. The girl clung tightly to her mother's hip.

Slipping her hand into her own bag, Iris pulled out one of the bright, red pears she'd collected the day before. "For you."

Cautiously, the child took one step away from her mother without releasing the death grip on her robes. Iris extended it closer, and the girl reached for it. Now in her hand, she considered the fruit for a moment before pulling it close to her chest. "*Shutohan*," she whispered.

"You're very welcome." Iris dipped her head and stood. "You be safe out here, all right?"

The woman and the girl smiled. Bowing again, they turned from the sandhaier corpses and walked off together into the afternoon sun.

CHAPTER 2

VISIONARY

Foxx and Iris watched the mother and daughter disappear into the distance, both remembering the feel of being led around by a mother's loving hand. Neither spoke of this reminiscence as they passed their water between them, conserving what they could.

"I hope we come across a well soon." Iris screwed the top back onto their sleeve and slung it over her shoulder.

Foxx lifted her pack away from her back for a few seconds to cool herself. "We will. Are you ready to get going?"

Iris fist-pumped the air. "Southward!"

Leaving the sandhaier corpses to shrivel in the sun, they rounded the dune and discovered it not simply a hill of sand but the remnants of an old building. The mound rose up at its back, but the front remained mostly unobstructed.

"Have we been here before?" Iris squinted to expose the building's hidden mysteries. Foxx blocked the sun with her hand and sifted through her memories.

Fractures in the sandstone blocks revealed the passage of time. Two pillars supported an awning over a doorless entrance, and sand poured down through the opening.

Iris moved closer to get a better look. The top of the doorframe rose to her chin, proof the building had sunk into the ground at least two feet, and the pile of sand blocking the way peaked about thigh level. She bent forward to glimpse the inside, trying to judge the hole big enough to climb through.

Light spilled into the room from two square windows cut into the front wall and from the doorway, now impeded by her silhouette. In the shadows, Iris could see a table at the center of the room and clutter lining the outer walls but not much else.

Knowing her sister all too well, Foxx watched her scouting the doorway with concern. "We shouldn't go in there. It could collapse."

Iris pushed against the walls on either side of the doorframe to test their stability. The blocks stood firm. "I think it'll be fine. It's clearly survived here for a long time."

"I don't know that *survived* is the word I would choose." Foxx took a few steps back, hoping a bigger picture might jog her memory.

"It's still standing even with all this sand piled on top of it. If it wasn't structurally sound, there wouldn't be an inside to crawl into."

Foxx crossed her arms, not thrilled with Iris' logic. Knowing the near impossibility of preventing her from doing something she'd already determined to do, Foxx didn't argue but tried a different approach. "Iris, I think this reminds me of a painting of Mother's. Come and see what you think."

Iris left the doorway and joined her sister, taking in the entire scene.

"Imagine two trees on either side, wrapped in layers of curling bark and crowned with huge palm leaves." Foxx motioned toward the trees she envisioned in her mind's eye. "Steps leading up to the stone patio. Potted ferns on both sides of the door."

"And a water oasis there!" Approaching the long-gone pond at the base of the missing palm, Iris tapped the ground with her boot. "What could have happened to the trees? There isn't even a stump here."

Unsure, Foxx asked a followup question. "Why would Mother have painted this?"

"We have to go in and check it out." Iris returned to the lost patio and peered through the door.

Foxxglove deliberated, joining Iris below the awning and rubbing her hand along the stone pillars. They were smooth, polished by years of sandstorms. "I think you might be right. This must be where the map intended to lead us. We knew it when we saw it."

They widened the entrance, dragging away handfuls of sand until it was large enough to crawl through. Foxx went first, sliding down the opposite side of the hill and landing on the stone floor below. Iris followed.

As Iris had seen from the doorway, a plethora of debris lined the outside of the room. They picked through broken desks and disheveled bookshelves. Sand blocked windows on the eastern and western walls, and two doorways stood on the wall opposite the entrance: one entirely clogged by sand and scraps, and the other leading into a dark hallway.

A table covered in a thick layer of dust sat at the center of the room. As Foxx inspected it, Iris moved to examine the corridor. A shiver tickled her spine as she peered into blackness. She whistled. "It sure is dark back there."

Foxx blew a gust of air across the table, spraying dust in a wide arc. A carving lay hidden beneath the filth, and she bent to get a better look. Before she spoke Iris' name, her sister beat her to it.

"Foxx, get a load of this." She'd abandoned the scary corridor to more thoroughly investigate the outskirts of the room. Something hanging on the eastern wall caught her attention.

Foxx moved to join her, and when she realized what Iris discovered, her hand flew to her mouth. "Oh my! What is this doing here?"

On the wall hung a beautiful painting on a large canvas. Brought to life by immaculate brushstrokes and bright colors, the artist's style was unmistakably their mother's.

Recovering before Foxxglove, Iris stepped closer and fingered the outer edge of the painting, inspecting the wooden frame behind the canvas. Giving it a soft tug, she tested it to see if it would move.

"What are you doing?"

Iris lifted the painting from the wall and held it in the light peeking through the doorway. It depicted a tree towering over a cliff. Though nothing like any plant they'd seen in Alunda, the tree was obviously tropical, with spotted bark and giant roots that stretched toward the water below. Water streamed through the root system, cascading into a teal lagoon. Emerald foliage sprouted from the walls and dotted the shore surrounding the pool.

In the bottom right corner of the painting, scripted words read:

A gift to the Monastery,
Lacuna Kaput, Metsa Sateen
Amaryllis Wild

"This is unbelievable," Foxx uttered, her face a reflection of complete awe. "What do you think it means?"

Iris laid the painting down on the table. She ran her fingers over the textured brushstrokes embedded into the thick paint. Touched the tree's branches and roots. Slid her fingers down the crystal waterfalls. "There's something we're missing."

Inspiration struck, and Iris turned the painting over, laying it facedown. Canvas stretched around a wooden frame. Another piece of wood spanned the middle, attaching the top of the frame to the bottom. Tucked within the wooden ridge in the bottom corner lay a flat, turquoise stone carved into the shape of a skull.

She picked it up and held it to the light, turning it over in her hand. Then she gave it to Foxx, who whispered with tentative excitement, "Iris, that's like the stone Maeve gave us. Look." She pulled the other stone from her bag and let both sit flat in the palm of either hand.

Though not cut from the same type of rock—one green like lichen and the other dark red—both measured half an inch in thickness and fit perfectly in the center of her hands. "This one matches the symbol on this table." Foxx adjusted the painting to show Iris the skull carved into the tabletop.

"But what are they for?" Iris took back the skull and let light shine through the holes representing eye sockets and nostrils. An etched line zig-zagged down the center from the top.

"I don't know." Foxx analyzed the series of events, thinking it impossible they weren't connected. She flipped the canvas back over to dissect it further. "Metsa Sateen is the territory east of here where Mother grew up. Lacuna Kaput might be the name of this waterfall." Foxx stared into Iris' eyes, pursuing the hope alive within her sister and longing desperately to feel it, too.

"Why is it here, Foxx? Is this what the map wanted us to find?"

"What else if not this? I think this waterfall could hold the next clue." She pulled out their map, hunting the best place to cross into the Metsa.

Iris left Foxx to read the map and returned to the corridor. She felt drawn to it, as if something in the darkness beckoned her to step from the light and follow the path into the unknown. Foxx said her name, and Iris sensed frustration in her tone, like it hadn't been the first time she tried to get her attention. Dragging her gaze from the shadow, she turned to her.

"What are you doing?" Foxx's fist pressed into her hip.

"Sorry." Iris shook away foggy distraction. "I don't know. That corridor feels weird."

Foxxglove walked over to it and peered down the hall. Then she shivered, took two steps backward, and refocused on the map. "It'll be another two days at least until we can get to the Metsa. There's a village on the barrier, Kesken Ala. We can head there and resupply before venturing into the jungle."

Iris put both stones in her pack, took one last glimpse at the dark hallway, and headed for the door. "But how will we know what to search for once we're there? Metsa Sateen is a huge territory!"

"I'm not sure." Foxx pushed against her sister's back as she climbed the hill of sand. After Iris made it through the doorway, she reached back to help pull her sister out. Once outside, Foxx brushed the sand from her clothing. "Maybe someone in Kesken Ala will have heard of it? Or maybe we will know it when we see it."

C

They traveled northeast for the rest of that day and the next, with the village of Kesken Ala as their destination. On the morning following the second moonrise, the girls awoke high on a rock plateau. After packing their bedrolls and eating the last of their jackrabbit jerky, they trekked on.

Foxx had the map in her hands. "We should reach the rainforest by sundown." She pointed to the location she assumed them to be. "So only one more sunny day roaming the desert. Once we leave Kesken Ala, we'll be under the cover of the canopy."

"Fantastic. Then we'll get to experience the loveliness of soggy, humid heat rather than skin-cracking dry heat." Iris had one of her throwing knives between her fingers. She let it slide through them, caught it before it slipped from her grasp, and flipped it over to let it slide down again.

Foxx chuckled. "Soak up the sunshine while you still have it."

Iris shielded her face with her hand, admiring the clear sky. A few tufts of white clouds dotted a hydrangea-petal backdrop. "I definitely prefer the sun to the rain, but does it have to be so *sweltering*?"

"Are you ever satisfied?"

"Not as a general rule, no." Iris slid her knife back into its sheath and tapped her sister's shoulder. "Race you to that cactus!" Before Foxx had a chance to respond, she bolted.

Foxx sprinted after her. "Cheater!" she yelled, but it only took seconds for her to catch up and overtake her. Zipping past Iris, her hair blew behind her in a wild mess. Sandy clay rattled beneath their feet, spewing a cloud of red dust in their wake.

A dull ring pierced Foxx's ears, and she winced. Her stomach whirled with nausea that made her brain fog. Then her feet tangled beneath her. She lost her grip with the ground and tumbled forward, colliding hard into the sand.

Iris skidded to a stop and dropped to her knees at her side. Foxx's eyes fell closed, but her body continued to quiver. Crying her name, Iris shook her shoulders to rouse her. She tapped her cheeks until Foxx's eyelashes twitched. "Are you okay? Foxx, what happened?"

Her eyes fluttered open. Disoriented and confused, she tried to sit up and found the world spinning in a dizzying loop. She leaned into Iris and closed her eyes again. On the edge of consciousness, Iris' panicked whispers were too muffled to comprehend. Then foreign images forced their way into her mind.

Suddenly in the dark, terror raked through her. Fingers restrained her mouth, silencing her. Someone gripped her from behind, holding her in place despite her squirming. His body was warm against hers, and he smelled of ale and sweat. The air was thick with moisture. Rain splattered nearby trees.

Another dose of horror washed over her as Iris whimpered from somewhere out of sight. Again she struggled, trying to wiggle free of her assailant, but he held her firm.

She screamed.

And found herself again in the light of day. Tears blurred her vision. She tried to blink them away.

Iris leaned above her where she'd fallen into her lap. "Foxx, talk to me. What's going on?" She tried to soothe her tremors, rubbing her arms and combing her hair with her fingers. When their eyes met, Foxx burst into sobs and buried her face in Iris' lap. Blood trickled from her nose and down her chin.

Iris slid her hand down Foxx's back. She tucked her hair behind her ear and wiped tears and blood from her face. Then she wiped away a tear of her own before it could fall from her chin. Foxx ceased crying and stilled, her breathing stabilizing.

Two turkey vultures appeared above them, lingering as they rode the updraft. Iris monitored their shadows on the sand.

Incoherent murmurs pushed their way through Foxx's lips.

"I'm here, Foxx. I'm here. We're safe." She rocked, consoling her.

A man cleared his throat, and Iris started. She looked up into the blinding sun to see the silhouettes of two men standing above her.

The closest man asked, "Anything we can help you ladies with?"

Iris didn't answer, squinting as she looked between them.

"We heard a commotion from our shelter up over that hill." He pointed north. "Thought we would come see if everything was all right." Crouching and no longer blackened by the sun, he smiled. "So, is everything all right?"

Without instruction, the other man stepped to the side to make himself visible, though he didn't acknowledge her. Instead, he stared off into the distance with a bored expression.

"Did she hit her head?" The crouched man leaned closer, tilting his head to get a better look at Foxx.

"She tripped." Iris looked down at her sister, trying to figure out what to do. She scrutinized their appearance, but found little to indicate their nature or intentions. Both carried a pistol. One wore it strapped to his belt. The man standing behind him had his arms crossed with a gun gripped in one hand. Neither dressed in the customary robes of the desert but instead wore pants tucked into boots and dirty tunics. The one holding his pistol had a jacket slung loosely over his shoulders. "Who are you?"

"My name is Orion, and this strapping young man behind me is Declan." Declan's eyes flashed to her but quickly returned to the distant location holding his attention. Orion glanced over his shoulder and then smiled at Iris as though they shared a private joke. "Don't mind him. He's just moody."

Iris couldn't be sure, but she thought she saw Declan tolerantly roll his eyes. "I'm Iris, and this is my sister, Foxxglove."

"A pleasure to meet you. Now, why don't you let me carry her to our shelter? We have fresh water and shade. She may fare better in the cool of a cave until she's well enough to move on. What do you think?"

Iris tried to analyze the situation the way Foxx would, previewing all possible outcomes. Trusting these men would remove her sister from the heat. If they turned out to be dangerous, she felt confident she and Foxx could handle them, or at the very least, manage to flee.

Her eyes scoured their physiques. The man in front had a brawny build and looked to be several years older than her. The other appeared younger and leaner but muscular nonetheless.

Drawing her attention back to Orion, she eyed his corded biceps. He noticed and grinned, clearly assuming her perusal the result of his dazzling appearance and not because she was sizing him up. Thorn and Bloom had never let her down before, though they would do little to ward off bullets.

"So, may I take her off your hands?" A genuine smile lit his eyes, like two bold sapphires.

At last, Iris surrendered and lifted her hands away from her sister, giving him permission to take over. Orion hoisted Foxx effortlessly into his arms. Iris shimmied off her pack and bow as he supported her weight. Declan had already begun walking when Orion nodded north and said, "This way. It's not far."

☾

Foxxglove blinked into consciousness. The room spun, and her pulse throbbed in her ears. Something hit her cheek, startling her. Slowly, requiring tremendous effort, she lifted her hand to wipe the nuisance away. Another drop hit her face, and she bolted upright, her head screaming at her for such a hasty movement.

When she heard her sister call her name, relief momentarily melted tense muscles. Iris appeared, but anxiety lingered. In the fringes of her memory, she thought the sun had been shining, but now she sat covered in shadows.

"I'm so glad you're awake. The sun is already high in the sky. I was so worried." Iris brushed her sister's hair out of her face and handed over a freshly-filled bag of water.

Still blinking her way further from dreamland, Foxxglove pushed the bag away and whispered aloud the questions whirling through her thoughts. "What happened? Where are we?"

"You had some kind of fit, Foxx. We were running, racing to the cactus." She paused, studying Foxx's expression. "And the next thing I knew you were on the ground, crying… afraid. Don't you remember?"

Foxx shook her head to dispel the fog from her mind, wishing to recall the events of the morning.

Iris threw a thumb over her shoulder. Two unfocused figures stood near a dancing fire. "Orion and Declan heard us and came to our rescue. Orion carried you here, and Declan added some of his water to our sleeve, see?" She held up the bag again, encouraging her to drink.

Foxx accepted the bag with Iris still clinging to it in case her limbs lacked their full strength. The water revitalized her systems, and she took in her surroundings. She sat on a bed of fur inside an unfamiliar cave. Their packs rested against the wall to her left, and to her right, two men stood in deep discussion. Past the fire lay the cave mouth and their gateway to freedom.

Iris stood with hands outstretched. "Do you think you can get up?"

Foxx placed both hands into her sister's and rose to her feet.

"The lady has arisen!" Orion moved toward them, and Declan followed a few paces behind. "How are you feeling? You've been through quite an ordeal."

Foxx gazed at the men, still trying to acclimate to her surroundings. Though the one who'd addressed her had said little, something in her didn't trust the undertones of his voice. Residual fear of strangers lingered in her heart, left over by her recent nightmare.

Her eyes widened as she realized it might not have been a dream at all. She'd been running, not sleeping, and it had overtaken her.

Iris introduced the man as Orion, and Foxx noticed her beaming. She wondered what she'd missed while unconscious and how long her sister had been left in the care of strange men.

"Very nice to meet you, Foxx." Orion's smile mirrored his shady tone.

"And behind him is Declan."

Foxx looked past Orion's shoulder and met Declan's gaze. He dipped his chin in greeting, but didn't smile.

The cave remained silent for a long, awkward moment.

At last, Foxx took a steadying breath, and her face awakened into a soft smile. "Well, thank you so much for assisting us. I'm sorry to have caused such trouble." She attempted to straighten any out-of-place hairs. The close proximity of men, no matter how untrustworthy they might seem, had her feeling the weight of the scar on her face. A thin gash stretched from her right brow to her chin, running the length of her jaw. An injury from years long passed. "I don't really remember what happened, but I'm glad my sister didn't have to handle it on her own."

Orion bowed in a gentlemanly manner, and Foxx noted the telling maneuver. "It was no trouble at all. I'm glad we happened to be in the area and were able to serve."

Declan remained silent and aloof behind his companion. Foxx wasn't sure which bothered her more: Orion's kindness or Declan's avoidance.

Iris bobbed up and down on the balls of her feet. "I'm so grateful to you both!"

"Where are you ladies headed? It isn't safe out here alone in these Grim Wilds, and we would be more than willing to escort you anywhere you wish to go."

Foxx didn't miss Declan's slight flinch. "We aren't alone."

In the same instant, Iris said, "We're traveling to the Metsa."

Foxx's eyes shifted to her sister, and Iris looked back at her with a furrowed brow.

Orion brightened. "Ah, as are we! Perhaps we could—"

Foxx interrupted. "We really should be going. We've traveled on our own for a long time. I think we can handle whatever is thrown at us."

"Well, that clearly wasn't the case today."

For a moment, everyone paused, taking in Orion's words. His smile remained, but the kindness ebbed from his eyes. Declan's brows lifted, the left one disappearing behind a tuft of tawny hair.

Foxx sucked in a breath, and her lips puckered, accentuating the high cheekbones framing dark, narrow eyes. Most of the time, they were alluring, watchful, and identical to her mother's. Now, mistrust sharpened her pupils. Iris felt the tension and took a step toward her sister, her arms lifting slightly from her sides as she braced herself.

Leveling her nerves, Foxx spoke with forced calm. "A misfortune that won't be repeated. We're already behind in our anticipated timeline so we really should leave immediately. This incident has already held us up enough." She glanced around the cave. "And you still have packing to do before you're ready to go anywhere."

Though his face darkened with disappointment, Orion dipped his head, conceding.

"How can we repay you for your assistance and the water you've provided? Would you accept payment in coin? We could spare a few *aeses* or even a *faeru* or two if that seems fair." Foxx glanced sideways, and Iris understood her request. She turned from them and retrieved their bags.

A genuine smile returning, Orion peered at Iris wistfully before dragging his eyes back to Foxx. "That won't be necessary. It really wasn't a problem. I'm happy we could help, and I wish you the best of luck on your travels." Iris rejoined them, and he caught her gaze. "Perhaps we will meet again." He extended a hand to her, and she accepted the gesture. Dipping his head, his intense gaze never left hers as he placed a kiss on the back of her knuckles. Goosebumps trailed up her neck as heat flooded her cheeks.

Orion stepped back, indicating their freedom to leave. Before exiting, both women reached around to wave farewell. "Thank you again." Foxx made visual contact with both men before stepping out into the sun.

"Thank you, Declan," Iris said. Surprised, his hand lifted and stalled in the air, a hint of a smile upturning his lips. Her eyes shifted to Orion's, and another blush colored her cheeks. "Thank you, Orion. Perhaps we will meet again."

CHAPTER 3

KESKEN ALA

They arrived in the village of Kesken Ala just after dusk. A small but eccentric town, Kesken Ala sat directly on the border of the Grim Wilds and the rainforest territory of Metsa Sateen.

As they approached, Foxx and Iris caught a glimpse of the translucent barrier that cut the town in half, leaving one side in the dry desert of the Grim Wilds and the other in the lush, green Metsa.

Though the throng of trees concealed the houses on the jungle side, distorted by the blur of the barrier, the houses in the desert were constructed of wood and clay bricks and faced each other in long rows.

In defiance of the bleak landscape, Kesken Ala stood splashed in color. Doorways wreathed in flowers and fabrics of poppy, tiger lily, and cerulean, and buildings adorned with cloth banners that hung from second-story windows, were but a fraction of the striking pigments on display. Along with lines of brilliantly dyed clothing, streamers festooned the roofs, zig-zagging back and forth atop the main street. A few blocks in, tents and tapestries in an array of extravagant hues shaded the merchants of an outdoor market.

After walking a few paces up the main road, Foxxglove and Iris saw an elderly woman sweeping the steps in front of her home. Draped in a scarf of silken fabric the color of honey and bejeweled with jade and spessartine gemstones, the woman greeted them and introduced herself as Rossnetta. Her long robes fell to the ground in loose folds, embroidered with fanciful designs. Golden wrinkles gave evidence of the woman's age, though her inviting eyes sparkled with youthful adventure.

Recognizing their need for hydration, she instructed them to wait while she hustled inside. The water Declan added to their skins hadn't lasted long in the unbearable furnace of the Grim Wilds. It'd been almost two hours since they last tasted water on their tongues.

Rossnetta returned with a mug in each hand, and they accepted the pottery with extreme gratitude. As they sipped their water, the woman chattered about the town, the shops, and all they could expect while staying there.

The outdoor bazaar visible from her front yard was impeccably named the Myriad Market. Vendors offered tropical fruits and flowers, dyed fabrics, fresh spices, and an assortment of other commodities.

An attractive young man, whom she described in great detail, owned the indoor grocery on the corner across the way. Up the street and one block north, they'd find a blacksmith well known for crafting exquisite weaponry and unique household items. Though he'd be out of their price range, she insisted his business worth visiting if such things interested them. Two blocks east of him lived the village tailor, an unpleasant crone they should keep away from unless absolutely necessary.

After directing them to the Briar Tavern, the town's only dryside inn, Rossnetta wished them a merry night and invited them to join her for tea the following day. By the time they left, darkness had settled in thick and heavy, with hardly a sliver of the Susi moon brightening the cloudless sky. The street lanterns cast a flickering glow, scattering light across the colorful village and making everything shine with firelight.

As they entered, a bell chimed above the tavern door. Patrons filled nearly every seat and talked cheerfully amongst themselves. Many held discussions between tables, clearly well acquainted. Paintings hung around the room, decorating the otherwise plain interior.

Across the back wall, a man with a shaggy beard stood drying clean tankards behind the bar. When he saw them, he offered a friendly smile. "Merry evening! How can I help ya ladies?"

Foxxglove and Iris crossed the room. "We're just passing

through and were hoping you might have a room available for a night or two."

"And some food!" Iris leaned against the bar, her shoulders heavy with exhaustion.

The jolly man's cherry-shaped cheeks rose above his beard. "Lovely. Seth here will walk ya up to your room so you can get settled, and when ya come back down we'll get yous some food. How does that sound?" He gestured to a young boy, aged ten or eleven years, sitting on a stool at the bar drawing on some loose parchment.

At the sound of his name, Seth leapt to attention, hurried over to them, and bowed at the waist. His black hair toppled forward, and when he rose, a toothy grin lit his eyes. He rushed to them, loose pants swaying, and began eagerly removing Iris' pack from her shoulders.

Startled by the action, she sputtered, "Oh! I can carry my bag up!"

The boy persisted. "No, no, miss! This is my job, and Mr. Magpie requires that I work for my dinner!"

Iris heeded the man—presumably Mr. Magpie—and saw a proud smile etched into the fair creases of his face. Though the relationship between them was unclear, his expression warmed her heart, and a deep yearning for her own father sparked in her gut.

After winning Iris' pack, he rushed to Foxx, who removed her own without pause to avoid the debacle her sister endured. "Why thank you, Seth, that is a huge help to us. We've traveled such a long way."

Seth beamed, loaded both packs onto his shoulders, and led them up the stairs. His sandaled feet struggled with each step. When they reached the top, he gestured to an unlit oil lamp sitting on the floor and requested one of them to grab it. Then he guided them to an open door on the left side of the hallway. "It's in here, misses. Right this way." Bryä seemed to be his native tongue, but he spoke to them in Arkaen. The charming way he rolled his r's had Iris feeling a motherly desire to squeeze his adorable cheeks.

Seth practically dragged the packs across the floor, but the weight did not deter him from placing one at the foot of each bed. Taking the lantern from Iris, he set it on the tiny table against the wall between the beds and lit the rope. Then he bowed and scurried to the door.

Iris called his name before he vanished and pulled an *aes* from her pack, flipping it toward him. He caught it with glee, bowed again, and disappeared through the doorway.

Flooded with exhaustion, the sisters collapsed into the comfort of actual beds. They'd only intended to rest a few minutes but woke to find the lantern burned out.

Iris yawned and relit the wick. "I'm starved."

Foxx smelled herself. "I need a bath." She rummaged around in her bag for cleaner clothes and headed for the washroom down the hall.

Iris stood with a tall stretch. A peek out the window indicated they'd slept well past highmoon, though noise continued to echo up from the pub.

When she reached the bottom step, she surveyed the room, standing there for a moment to take in the jovial chatter of the remaining patrons.

Seth appeared in her line of vision, and she heard him exclaim, "Mr. Magpie! It's one of those girls! Look!"

Magpie waved her over. "Come here, girl, ya must be starvin'!"

Iris made her way to the bar and stopped next to Seth's stool.

The jolly barkeep placed a tankard of ale in front of her. "Expected ya down here hours ago, we did, but ya must have been wiped out from yer travels, eh? This one's on the house. Now what'll ya be having to eat?"

"At this point, Mr. Magpie, I think I could eat anything. Why don't you surprise me? I'm Iris by the way, and my sister's name is Foxx."

"Iris, then." He turned to fill two more tankards from the tap, and Iris took that moment to observe him. He didn't wear the traditional attire of the desert but instead had on a cotton tunic and trousers shielded by a dirty apron. Though Seth clearly hailed from the Grim Wild's with his Bryä accent and dark skin, Mr. Magpie's cadence and pale features alluded to origins outside the territory.

After delivering the drinks to the men down the bar, Mr. Magpie returned. "Now how about we get that hot dinner for ya both, eh? I'll send Seth up with it as soon as it's ready. Or yer welcome to eat down here if'n ya wish."

"Upstairs sounds excellent, Mr. Magpie. Thank you so much. Seth, there's another *aes* in it for you if you bring us two more ales along with the food." She looked at Mr. Magpie. "And some fresh water if you have it available?"

"Certainly, my lady. You go on and rest now, and we'll have it all up to ya shortly." With the dip of his chin, he disappeared into the kitchen.

Iris stepped out around Seth's stool and claimed the seat next to him. "Shouldn't you be sleeping, Seth? It's awfully late!"

Seth shook his head. "I always stay up and help Mr. Magpie run the pub." A cackle echoed from the kitchen. Iris smiled as Seth's cheeks flushed. "Well, I sort of help."

Chuckling, she looked at the parchment on the bar in front of him. "What do you have there?" His face blossomed into a deeper, tulip red as he pushed the drawing closer. Her eyes widened. "That's a nieda. Wow, Seth, it's incredible. Have you ever seen one in real life?" She immediately realized he must have for his drawing to be so detailed and precise.

A shadow spread across his features and curled the corners of his lips toward the floor. He lowered his head, peering at his hands in his lap and fiddling with the apron that covered the clover tunic hanging past his knees.

Iris placed a hand on his shoulder. "I've seen them before, too. It was horrible."

He wouldn't return her gaze. "They live in the forest of Sateen. Well, all over really, but they get really big in the forest." He paused and sniffled. "My… my mother…" His chin dipped closer to his chest.

"My mother isn't with us anymore, either. And my father… well, he's the reason we're so far from home."

Seth lifted his eyes and pulled a ratty piece of fabric from the pocket of his apron to blow his nose.

Iris smiled. "She must have been a pretty amazing woman if she taught you to draw like that." It was only a guess, but a spark of life returned to him, and he sat up straighter on the stool. "My mother was a talented artist, too. She loved to paint."

Seth's face brightened, a dose of his whimsical energy returning. "My mo-mother was a painter, too. She painted all of the pictures you see hanging here in the tavern. A bunch of shops in Kesken Ala display her work."

Iris glimpsed the exquisite pictures hanging on the walls and again felt a pang of grief in her stomach. "These are extraordinary,

Seth. Truly." His cheeks reddened again as he studied the sketch in front of him. "Your drawing is really great, too. I'm sure you'll be just as good as your mother as long as you stick with it and keep practicing."

The moment of sadness passed, and his chin lifted with a grin. "Thank you Miss Iris." He reached out and placed his hand on hers, appearing ages older than seemed possible. "Now go back up to your room and rest, and I will be up soon with your dinner."

Iris grabbed her tankard and headed for the stairs. Turning back to the bar, she watched Seth admire his drawing. He beamed again and bounced on his stool before returning to the kitchen.

C

Not long after Iris returned to their room, Foxx came through the door with wet hair. Iris had relit the lantern and sat down within its glow. "You look refreshed. Seth will be bringing up food and drink soon."

"Wonderful." Sinking onto the bed, Foxx dried her hair with a towel. After a dunk in warm water, the ragged scar spanning the length of her jaw bloomed bright like a strawberry. Though Iris knew of Foxx's insecurities regarding the harsh blemish, she'd never thought it marred her beauty. Instead, it added a ferocity to her already attractive features.

Foxx let the damp towel fall to the floor. "I was thinking we should stay tomorrow night too. It will give us a short reprieve and time to resupply. Then we can begin our venture into Sateen."

"Sounds like a plan to me." Iris handed over the ale.

Foxx closed her eyes and let the drink's tingling warmth spread relaxation through her body. Then Iris said her name and reawakened her attention. "Yes, Iris?"

Iris fumbled over her words. "I was wondering if you were worried that your scare earlier might…"

Foxx finished her sister's stammered thought. "… have something to do with the sickness that took our mother?" Iris remained silent, and Foxx let out a long breath. "I really don't know, but either way, it doesn't change our plan."

A knock at the door alerted them of Seth's arrival with their food. As Foxx opened the door, the smell of cooked meat smothered in gravy wafted into the room.

"Here you go, misses." After setting the tray of food and drink on the table between the beds, he slid a water bag from his shoulder onto the floor. "Mr. Magpie said to give you this. He said to tell you to keep it free of charge!"

Foxx said, "That was very kind of him, Seth. Be sure to tell him we say thank you."

Iris agreed and grabbed a plate from the tray, immediately digging in. "We recently lost our second bag and planned on getting another one, so that's a big help."

"Lost?" Foxx's eyes shifted suspiciously toward her sister. "Is that the story we're going with?"

Iris' head sank into her shoulders. "Well, we *did* lose it."

"Because you threw it at a coyote who then snatched it and fled."

"It was a very scary coyote! And coyotes are no joke!" She looked at Seth who was grinning at their banter. "Seriously, you do *not* want to mess with a coyote."

Seth chuckled. "You guys are funny."

Iris took another swallow of ale, brows raised in a taunt. "At least I've never accidentally shot someone."

Foxx scoffed. "Oh, you had to bring that up? My arrow barely nicked him!"

"He bled all over the place."

"Some people bleed more profusely than others."

Seth tilted his head, brow wrinkled skeptically.

Iris mirrored his expression. "Three people had to carry him to the town medic!"

"Because he was a huge baby!"

All three were laughing now. When the giddiness settled, Iris said, "Seth, I'm glad you're here. I wanted to show you something." From her pack, she dug out her leather journal and placed it in his outstretched hand. "I thought you might enjoy flipping through this."

Letting the book fall open of its own accord, Seth's eyes widened.

A drawing of a krikettirapu, more commonly called a cricket crab according to Iris' notes, filled the page in front of him. The sketched krikettirapu resembled a fiddler crab, with one claw bigger than the other. It had three swimming appendages on each side and two back legs separated into three segments: two longer segments able to bend like a hinge and one short segment for maneuvering the claw at the end. These legs gave the cricket crab the ability to leap high into the air like a cricket or bend its legs in the opposite direction and attack from above with its sharp claws.

Seth read out loud. "Cricket crabs are native crustaceans of Alunda and are typically only dangerous in large groups. Sometimes during low tide, a cast of hundreds will invade the shore causing a lot of injury and damage." Closing the book, he looked at Iris. "I will give it back tomorrow! Thank you for sharing it with me."

"I hope you enjoy it." She reached again into her bag, this time handing him two *aeses* and a *mett*. "Those are for you." He clutched the coins and book against his chest. Then she held out a silver *faeru*. "Be sure to give this one to Mr. Magpie, okay?"

Seth sprang forward and swung his hands around her neck. "Thank you, Miss Iris." Then he hurried away.

C

The next morning, Iris woke to find Foxxglove sitting in bed reading a novel titled *Across the River*. A typical romance, the book starred a handsome prince with a dreadful queen for a mother. Contrary to her pessimistic and skeptical disposition, Foxx loved it. She hoped to finish it before entering Metsa Sateen and planned to hunt for a new title as they shopped the market later in the day.

Iris went for a quick but refreshing bath, and when she returned, they headed downstairs for breakfast. Mr. Magpie stood behind the bar, and Seth sat on what seemed to be his regular barstool. Noticing their arrival, he squealed Iris' name, dropped his pencil on the bar, and rushed over. After hugging her around the waist, he grabbed her hand and dragged her back to his seat. "Look what I drew!"

Iris' mouth fell open, her fingers rising to her lips. "Seth! It's wonderful!" She lifted it to get a closer look at the exquisite illustration of a flower. Specifically, an iris.

"It's for you." His eyes found the tile beneath the bar, his finger tracing the grout lines.

She hugged him tightly around the shoulders and ruffled his hair. "Thank you so much, Seth. I absolutely love it." Releasing him, she handed the drawing to Foxxglove, who also commented on its beauty.

Mr. Magpie grinned proudly. "Seth, why don't ya take the ladies to a table so we can serve 'em a nice breakfast. Hows'ome eggs and wild pig bacon sound?" Foxx and Iris concurred and followed Seth to a table in the corner of the pub.

"I'll get you something to drink. Be right back!" He scurried off.

Foxx watched until he disappeared into the kitchen. "He seems like a great kid."

Iris agreed. "Sad about his mother though. Killed by a nieda."

"No! That *is* sad. Is Mr. Magpie his father?"

"I don't know actually. He calls him Mr. Magpie, so I would think not." She gestured to the walls surrounding them. "These were all painted by his mother." Foxx observed the art exhibition with interest. Seth returned with two cups of water, each with its own floating wedge of citrus, and they thanked him, causing a blush to bloom. Then he darted off again, returning to his barstool to draw.

Mr. Magpie arrived at their table carrying two hot plates of food. The aroma drifting from the plates awakened their stomachs. Each plate held two eggs—sunflower yellow in the middle with perfectly white edges—four thick slices of the most scrumptious smelling bacon, and a pile of golden-brown fried potatoes.

Iris lowered her nose to the food and sniffed deeply, allowing the tasty scent to fill her nostrils. "This smells delicious. Thank you Mr. Magpie."

"You're very welcome misses. Enjoy."

Before he walked away, Iris stopped him with his name. "I was wondering… Seth isn't your son, is he?"

He smiled. "No, no lass. I knew 'is mother. Tragic what 'appened to her. She was a grand woman. Raised him up 'erself, she did. His father was nev'r around. Esther, that was her name, Esther, and Seth used to come in 'ere and bring me vegetables from 'er garden, or pies and other sweets they made together. Flowers they'd pick in the forest to set on my tables. When she—" He paused, strong emotion seeping into his voice. "When Seth come running in that day crying and alone, blood and ick all over 'im, I had ta keep 'im. He had no one else. We got their house all sorted, that's where these paintin's come from. Beautiful paintin's. Hung 'em to honor her.

Seth's been here ever since. He helps me out, getting old ya know. Never gets in the way. A good lad."

Foxx nodded. "You're a good man, Mr. Magpie."

"Nah. It's nothin any man wouldn't a'done."

"It is definitely not nothing." Iris wiped damp lashes.

His eyes fell to the floor. "Well, you ladies enjoy yer food." He bowed his head and left the table.

The girls dug in, the delicious smell making them ravenous. They didn't mind eating campfire food, but they hadn't eaten anything so appetizing in ages. Through a mouthful of savory bacon, Iris suggested, "We should visit Rossnetta this morning, then do some shopping."

Foxxglove shrugged, not willing to stop eating long enough to respond.

Iris watched Seth slide from his stool. Catching her eye, he waved before striding out the door.

After they finished their meal, Foxx paid the tavern owner, and they returned to their room. Assembling all the supplies on the beds, they took inventory of their possessions.

Each owned several sets of clothing, most verging on tattered. Their bedding was in good shape, as well as their utensils and cookware. Foxx recited the list of items to track down in the market as they returned the acceptable belongings to their bags. "I would like to get some jerky and dried fruits, maybe some nuts. Our flint and steel is rapidly meeting its end, so we should look for another one. And honestly, I could do with some new clothes."

Iris held up an old shirt and wrinkled her nose before discarding it on the get-rid-of pile between them. "We should see what they're selling arrows for. I know you can make them, but it may be tricky to do in the damp jungle. If we can afford them, we should at least grab you a few."

"You're only suggesting that because you want to check out the throwing knives at the weapon shop."

"Mine are getting so beat up!"

Foxx grinned and shook her head. "We have some things to trade: two pelts and the horns from the lycanox."

When they felt confident in their needs, they made their way downstairs, waved at Mr. Magpie, and headed out onto the street.

They found Rossnetta in her yard pruning garden flowers and

greeted her with a *merry morning*. Thrilled to see them, Rossnetta ushered them into her tiny home for a mug of hot tea, as promised.

Her front door, framed in rosemary bundles, opened into a quaint kitchen. The inside had floors cloaked in woven rugs and walls mantled with detailed tapestries and paintings. The kitchen had a fireplace built into the wall, lidded with a cast iron flattop. Coals beneath still glowed with heat from earlier that morning.

Rossnetta had them take a seat at a table barely big enough for three and pulled some dishes from a cabinet painted with leafy vines and delicate flowers. Humming to herself as she moved about the room, she placed a pot of water on the flattop and stoked the warm coals until a small patch of flames reignited. She set a mug in front of each of them and put the third before the empty chair. Then she moved a glass jar of dried leaves to the table and relaxed into the seat across from Foxx.

Iris caught a whiff of the scent permeating the jar even with its lid on tight. "Are those mint leaves?"

"My own special blend, dear. A little of this, a little of that." She gestured to the bundles of dried herbs hanging throughout the room. Opening the jar, she pinched a clump of leaves and dropped some into each of their mugs. "So you're staying with Mr. Magpie, yes? Such a sweet man, Mr. Magpie. Reminds me of my late husband. He was such a sweetie, too. And so handsome!" A giddy squeal escaped her lips as she stood and retrieved the hot water, tipping some into each mug.

"How long have you lived alone, Rossnetta?" Foxx asked.

"Oh, it's just over ten years, I believe. Yes, ten years." She stirred golden honey into her own cup and offered the crock to the girls.

Iris took a sip of her tea, swishing it around in her mouth and allowing her tastebuds to explore the herbal flavors. "Oh, this is tasty!" Its flavor matched the smell of the dried leaves, as well as another spice she recognized but couldn't place. Foxx sampled the tea and immediately went back for more.

"Where are you young ladies from?"

"We're from Ranta in Alunda." Foxxglove held the warm cup between both hands and allowed the aroma to waft up her nose.

"Ah, the land with the magical sea. Such a charming territory." Her gaze drifted as if reliving a pleasant memory. "I have some pearls from Ranta. Are you traveling anywhere in particular or just adventuring?"

"We aren't really sure. For now, we're heading to Metsa Sateen in search of a waterfall."

"Any old waterfall or one waterfall in particular?"

Foxx set her cup down and leaned an elbow on the table. "The one we're looking for has a giant tree standing on top of it and pours down into a gorgeous lagoon."

"Ah, I see. Lacuna Kaput, I believe, is the one you must mean." In response to their surprised expressions, she added, "Oh, yes dearies, I am a very old woman as you can see, and I know of many things you would scarce believe! I have seen the waterfall myself, you know. Oh, it was magnificent! Atop it sits the biggest, most spectacular kapok tree, and the water below is the prettiest turquoise you could ever gaze upon."

Foxx glanced at Iris, who smiled. "Do you remember how to find it?"

"It's somewhere in the northern region of Sadella. If I had an old map, I would give it to you. Perhaps you'll find one when you're shopping. If I'm correct, it lies on the eastern side of Sadella. I do remember that it was a bit off the trail. You'll hear it before you see it. The water drops so far to reach the pool, and the sound echos grandly throughout the deep cavern."

"Where else have you traveled, Rossnetta?" Iris pulled her feet up in the chair and folded her legs beneath her.

"Why, I've been all over Arkaemor. When I was a young woman, I traveled through all the territories and saw many great things. This is a truly amazing land we live in, would you not agree?"

Both nodded. Foxx added another drop of honey to her mug. "So if you've been all over, why did you choose to end your journey here? In the Grim Wilds of all places?"

Rossnetta threw her head back in laughter, the palm of her hand smacking the top of her knee. "Love, of course! I fell in love. A grizzly man, but oh, how I loved him. He was from the Wilds, from right here in Kesken Ala, to be precise. He traveled with me a bit in the beginning—he did adore me so—but I could see it wearing on him. He wasn't the wanderer I grew up to be. So we bought a home here, and this is where we stayed."

"And you never wanted to travel again after he passed?"

"It wouldn't have been the same without him I'm afraid. Once you find your life partner, your perception changes. It's not that I wouldn't enjoy seeing the wonders of the world again, of course I would, but it wouldn't be the same if I couldn't share those special moments with my someone." She smiled sweetly. "Perhaps someday life will force me elsewhere, but for now I'm at peace in Kesken Ala."

The conversation subsided as the women contentedly sipped their tea.

Iris tipped back her mug, gleaning the last few drops of sweet liquid. "Rossnetta, what do you know about Seth?"

"Little Seth! Such a sweet young man! Horrible what happened to his mother. He witnessed the whole thing you know. Good of Magpie to take him in. He would be on the street or dead if he hadn't."

"Mr. Magpie seems like a very good man," Foxx said.

"Oh, the best! He and my husband were great friends. Little Seth comes over and helps me in the garden and inside with the cleaning. He even gets groceries for me when I need him to. Delightful boy."

A child's howl flew through the kitchen window. Iris leapt to her feet. "That's Seth!"

Rossnetta turned toward the sound. "I bet it's those older boys. They're always picking on him!"

Iris' hand grasped the hilt of her sword, ready to slide it from its scabbard if necessary, and raced out the door.

CHAPTER 4

HUNTED

I ris bolted toward the sound of the intensifying cries as Seth's tormentor ignored his pleas. Rounding a corner between two storefronts, she skidded to a stop to find him lying on the ground against a wall. Three boys towered over him, one kicking him in the stomach and another pinning his hand with his shoe. They wore cruel expressions, taunting with teasing words.

Oblivious to Iris' arrival, the largest boy spouted, "Is your mama going to save you, Seth? No? Are you going to cry?"

Iris crept up behind him, grabbed his shoulder, and swept his legs out from under him. By the time he realized what happened, the boy lay on his back with the tip of Iris' shortsword an inch from his nose. His hands flew up, framing his pale face. The other two boys backed against the wall on either side of Seth, not brave enough to fight for their friend but too terrified to flee.

"What exactly is going on here, gentlemen?"

All three boys trembled. Seth took slow, relieved breaths, wiping sweat from his brow as he sat up.

Iris watched him, not looking away until he met her gaze. "Seth, are you all right?"

"We were just playing," stammered one of the two boys against the wall. The other nodded his head in agreement. The boy behind Iris' blade did not move a muscle. Sweat poured from him, already soaking parts of his shirt and dripping down his face.

"It doesn't seem like playing when one boy is on the ground

being kicked and three others are standing above him doing the kicking." She shifted her blade without necessity, spooking the boy beneath it. "That to me looks a good bit like bullying."

The boys against the wall talked frantically over each other. "No, no! We weren't bullying. We were just having a little fun!"

Seth stood, moving to stand beside Iris and attempting to brush away the red dust marring his pants.

Iris motioned for the boy beneath her sword to rise and join his comrades on the wall. He scrambled backward until he stood between them. Iris kept her blade aimed at his chest. "And you? What do you have to say about all this?"

He stuttered, trying to get the words out through his terror. "I'm… I am sorry m-m-missus."

"I'm not the person you should be apologizing to."

Foxxglove entered the alley and took in the scene. Crossing her arms, she stood several paces away, allowing Iris to handle it but still presenting a united front against the little brats.

The biggest boy looked at Seth, his eyes plump with tears. "I'm s-sorry, S-seth." The other two echoed him.

"Listen here boys. I am leaving town tomorrow, but I will be stopping back to check on my friend." She gestured to Seth, who smiled. "If I hear about anything like this happening again," she pulled her knife away from the boy's chest and pretended to slice her own throat with it. "In fact, you three are going to make sure that no one else bullies Seth either. I am officially knighting you as his protectors while I'm away." Placing her blade on the leader's right shoulder, then lifting it over his head to rest it on his left, she knighted him formally. The sword being so near his head brought on a new wave of trembling. "Is that understood?"

They nodded frantically. Her eyebrows lifted, waiting for more. "Ye-s miss. We w-will make s-ure."

Iris returned Bloom to her scabbard. "Very good, boys. Now, off you go." She shooed them away. When they disappeared around the corner, she put her hands on Seth's shoulders and bent down to his height. "You all right?" She inspected him thoroughly. His swollen cheek had darkened with a bruise, but if any injuries existed beneath his clothing, he kept them concealed.

"Oh, yes, Miss Iris! Thank you so much!" He jumped at her, wrapping his arms around her neck and squeezing her tight.

"You're welcome." Standing, she hung an arm over his shoulders and ruffled his hair as they joined Foxx at the mouth of the alley. "Now Seth, what did we learn?" He thought for a moment, searching for the answer that would please her. "Something can be learned from every rough situation. So what did we learn from this?"

"I learned that you're a lot scarier than you look!" he exclaimed with raised eyebrows.

Foxx laughed. "He's not wrong."

Iris rolled her eyes at her sister. "The lesson here is that even the worst bullies can be taken down by someone brave enough to stand against them."

Seth's chin dropped to his chest. "I wasn't very brave."

Iris looked him square in the eye. "Lucky for you, today's trial comes with a second lesson. The truth is, sometimes we need other people to be brave for us until we're able to do it ourselves. Sometimes we need others to teach us, like Foxx taught me. When we come back to Kesken Ala, I'm going to teach you."

"Do you really think you'll come back?" He tried to conceal the longing beneath his words.

Foxx shot a disapproving look at her sister, but Iris ignored or didn't see it.

"Without a doubt. I don't know how long it will take, but when my journey is finished, I will definitely come back to see you." He hugged her around the waist as they wandered down the street toward the Myriad Market.

The market bustled with people, and Foxx found it hard to believe any place could be so busy in a town as small as Kesken Ala. Vendors lined both sides of the street calling out their wares and enticing customers to visit their booths. Many knew Seth and greeted him personally.

"Let's find the weapon shop first," Iris suggested. Foxx eyed her with playful accusation.

"Daniel sells weapons." Seth pointed to a middle-aged man two booths down from where they stood. "He's very nice."

Iris' eyes brightened. "Let's see what he has in store."

As they approached the booth, Daniel addressed Seth directly and extended his hand. The boy's tiny hand nearly drowned in the man's large one, but Iris could see how Seth responded to the manly gesture and decided she liked Daniel already. "Daniel, these are my friends, Iris and Foxxglove."

"A pleasure to meet you ladies." Daniel dipped his head. "What can I help you folks find today?" His eyes followed Seth as he scanned the blades laid out on the table.

"I'm looking to possibly purchase a few arrows." Foxx's eyes shifted to Iris who gazed at her expectantly. "And my sister would be interested in exploring your throwing knives." Iris squealed.

The shop owner grinned. "I think we can help you with those items. Let me hop back in the shop for a minute and bring you some options." He turned from them and strode toward the building at his back, calling out to someone in Bryä.

A gorgeous woman appeared in the doorway, and Daniel kissed her cheek as he passed by. She wore an outfit of plum harem pants and a snug top supporting her curves. An exotic scarf bejeweled with golden gems covered her head, and a ring circled through the left nostril of her slender nose. Crisp onyx lined her eyes, which turned their way as she glided into the booth. "Merry morning ladies. Seth, my young friend. It is good to see you." Her voice rumbled from her throat, low, like distant thunder; her accent thicker even than Seth's.

"Hi Lakshmi." His cheeks darkened like a blooming dahlia, and Foxx thought the woman's smile would make any man faint.

Lakshmi observed his shyness with gentle humor. "Who have you brought to us today?" Her eyes glanced between Iris and Foxx. Seth introduced them and explained what they were searching for. "My husband seemed very excited. He should return any minute with some items for you to look through. Feel free to explore what we have out on the table while you wait."

Foxx and Iris thanked her and continued perusing. Lakshmi gave her full attention to Seth, asking him about his morning thus far.

As they surveyed the decorated blades, Foxx felt her breath quicken and a sudden fogginess cloud her head. She touched her sister's back, drawing her eyes. When Iris looked at her, she pointed toward the closest alley. "I'll be right back."

In response to Iris' concern, Foxx shook her head to assure her. Iris smiled, mouthing *love you* before returning her attention to the blades.

Foxx rounded the booth and stepped into the narrow alley between the weapon shop and the indoor grocer. Leaning against the wall within the shadows, she laid her palms flat against the cool stone at her back. A blossoming tightness gripped her chest, similar to what she'd experienced before her episode in the desert. Closing her eyes, she breathed through her nose. The thought that another vision might come so soon after the first—and so close to a crowd—sent a rush of panic through her. She fought to restrain it.

Her mother's attacks often happened at home where she spent the majority of her time, but Foxx had a few memories of public incidents that set her nerves on edge.

Opening her eyes so she could find something to distract herself, she looked toward the market. She watched the townsfolk shop the booths, engage with friends, and generally live happily in their tiny village on the border.

Like Daniel's weapon shop, the indoor grocer had a booth set up out front. She could see bags of baking flour and salt, as well as fruit, vegetables, edible plants, and long, thin slabs of jerky.

A man approached the booth, reviewing the dried meat options. Studying him from a distance, her eyes trailed his sharp jawline, following its edge up to disheveled hair. With a hue like the skin of pecan nuts, it shined in a shaft of sunlight cutting through the tapestries above.

Sensing her stare, the man's head turned in her direction. The shadows of the alley failed to conceal her with the sun blazing from high in the sky. His gaze bewitched her so she couldn't look away. An unfamiliar flutter tickled her chest. Frozen against the wall, she watched him watching her.

His lips parted into a smile. He lifted a hand.

A wave of nausea crashed over her, and she tore away the roots strapping her boots to the ground. She launched herself from the wall and darted to the end of the alley, freeing herself from the encounter with the beautiful stranger.

C

That evening, after a mouthwatering meal of roast pork stew with a side salad of rainforest greens, Foxx and Iris stood between the beds in their room and took a final inventory of their supplies. They had all of their belongings, old and new, splayed out on the beds to make sure they hadn't missed anything.

"I am loving my new knives," Iris cooed. They were thin and

shiny and sharp. She had struggled with trading in her old ones, but it didn't make sense to carry extra weight.

Foxxglove filled her quiver with her new arrows, replacing the ones lost to the sandhaier and a few worse for wear. She ran her fingers across the fletchings, admiring the additions.

A shy rap at the door prompted Iris to invite the knocker in. The door cracked open, and Seth poked his head through, saying her name like a question.

Iris waved him in, and he crossed the room, sitting next to her on the bed and handing over her journal. "Thank you for letting me look at your book." His face turned beet red, and he looked up at her with hooded eyes. "And thank you again for saving me today."

Iris ruffled his hair. "No need to thank me, Seth. I hope they leave you alone now."

He shrugged and stood up. "So you're leaving tomorrow?"

"We will be sure to see you in the morning before we go," Iris promised.

He dipped his head and wished them a *merry night* as he scurried from the room.

Iris changed out of her sleeveless shirt and replaced it with one she'd purchased. With straps two fingers thick, the fabric hugged her torso. She hoped the forest green color would help her blend in as they ventured through Metsa Sateen. Twisting and bending her upper body in weird angles, she tested its flexibility. "So comfortable."

Foxx had also bought a new, sleeveless tunic that hung to her thighs. Crafted of lightweight material, it was reputed to be durable, breathable, and quick drying.

"It would be nice to get some kind of water-resistant jacket to combat the heavy rain."

"Good idea!" Iris stuffed her belongings into her pack. "So, wake up, have breakfast with Seth, grab the last few things we need from the market, and then we're off to the Metsa."

"Sounds like a plan to me." After everything was packed and ready for the morning, they crawled into bed. Foxx put out the lantern to darken the room. "Love you, Iris."

Iris curled into a ball with her knees to her chest, hugging her pillow. "Love you, too, Foxxglove."

C

Ripped from sleep by a lantern blinding her tired eyes, Foxx held up a hand to block the glare.

Mr. Magpie stood over her, an expression of worry filling the crevices of his face. "Miss Foxx! Miss Iris! You need to wake up, lovies." He shook Foxx's arm until she sat up. Over his shoulder, she glimpsed Seth standing in the doorway clutching his own lantern. By the way the light shivered around him, she thought he must be trembling.

Hearing the commotion, Iris sat up. Her throat rough from dry air and her brain still fogged in a sleepy haze, she asked, "Mr. Magpie? What's going on?"

"You 'ave to go now, misses. There are soldiers looking for ya. They came round askin' for two young women. One with hair as dark as ebony and the other's whiter than ivory stone. Says your father's in trouble with King Pollux, and they need ta bring ya in. I said to them, 'no such women like that been 'round these parts,' I says. But they said they had orders to check e'ry room in e'ry inn, anyway!"

The girls gaped at each other, fear momentarily immobilizing them.

"Foxx, what do we do?"

Mr. Magpie answered for her. "You've got ta run, Miss Iris! I put some hot food and ale in front of 'em. Convinced 'em to fill their bellies 'fore takin' a look 'round. But ya haven't much time. You have to go!"

Leaping from their beds, they rushed to slide on their boots, tying them as quickly as stiff fingers would allow. Then they gathered their weapons and threw their packs over their shoulders.

Mr. Magpie motioned for Seth to enter. "Bring that here, Seth." Removing the satchel thrown over Seth's shoulder, he handed it to Foxx. "I packed a few extra things for yer journey. I know ya had a chance to go shoppin' but figured ya may not have gotten it all finished. I hope this here fills any of the gaps. All the shops'll be closed down with it being so early, and I don't want you hangin' round until they open. Just get going on yer way."

Foxx's chest filled with love for the sweet, old man they barely knew. "Mr. Magpie, I don't know how to express my gratitude for the kindness you've shown us." Iris felt tears brimming behind her lashes as Foxx attempted to hand him a small handful of coins.

He pushed it back, unwilling to accept it. "No, no, Miss Foxx.

Yous 'ave already given us too much. You take this as a gift. Just promise to stop back 'round and see us if yer ever in Kesken Ala again, ya hear? Now, let's go!" He passed Seth in the doorway, gesturing for them to follow.

Instead of turning right from the door in the direction of the stairs, Mr. Magpie led them left and deeper into the house: down the hallway, past the washroom, and through a door on the right leading to a different set of stairs. At the bottom of the steps, Mr. Magpie held the door open into the pale night. "Take this alley to the right and follow it 'long to the back street called Straight. Follow Straight all the way into the Metsa. And stay out'a sight!"

Seth stopped in the doorway and called after them, prompting both women to turn back. He paused for a sheepish moment before asking, "Do you think our mothers are painting in the After together?"

Iris looked at Foxx, shocked by the question and hoping she would have an answer. When she didn't, Iris said, "I think if they aren't, then when we finally see them again, we will have to introduce them."

Joy lightened his big, brown eyes as tears streamed down his face. He waved fervently as the women turned north in search of the street called Straight.

C

The soldiers lounging in the Briar Tavern were not the only King's Legion in town. As they crept through the shadows with the stealth of burglars, Foxx and Iris glimpsed several pairs of scarlet-clad soldiers knocking on doors. Many nailed up sheets of parchment, but the girls hadn't been able to get close enough to see the declaration.

One thing they knew for certain: far too many soldiers filled the streets for their arrival to be random. Somehow, the King's Legion had known they would find the sisters in Kesken Ala and had come to retrieve them. Foxx and Iris hadn't the slightest idea how they could have known, or more importantly, *why* they hunted them in the first place. Mr. Magpie had helped them flee, so something about the way the soldiers inquired after them must have scared him enough to risk defiance.

The callousness of the Legion was apparent, even from a

distance. Not one seemed apologetic for disturbing the citizens before the sun. Several sat tall atop decorated horses, barking orders to those on the ground.

Foxx and Iris paused at the corner of Straight and Westover, hoping to overhear the pair of soldiers speaking to the irritated grocer. One held a piece of parchment in front of the shop owner's face. The man shook his head, speaking out of range for them to hear. His furious demeanor didn't deter the soldiers in the slightest, and when he finished his rant, one of the two addressing him shoved the parchment against his chest, holding it there until he accepted it. He turned and pushed it onto a nail sticking out from the doorframe, then proceeded to slam the door in the soldier's face.

As the men moved on to the next establishment, Foxxglove whispered, "I wish we could see what's on that paper."

Quick as a sparking flame, Iris shot forward, bolting up the alley until shadow gave way to moonlight. She surveyed the area, ignoring the whispered yells at her back, and snuck to the door. Swiping the parchment from its nail, she sprinted back to Foxx, feeling mighty pleased with her covert heist.

Foxxglove glared furiously. "What were you thinking? Are you crazy?"

"We needed to see what it said. Now we can." Iris shoved the rolled up page into her pack. "Let's keep moving. I know Mr. Magpie said to follow Straight Street, but I think we should head to the outskirts and follow the edge into the Metsa instead. The soldiers are expecting to find someone harboring us in town. They won't anticipate us fleeing along the town border." Foxx agreed, and again they turned north.

When they came to the northern edge of Kesken Ala, the vast Grim Wilds stretched out to their left, and to their right lay the verdant Metsa. The sky lightened with the dawn's morning glow, though the sun had yet to make an appearance above the jungle's trees.

The territory barrier separating the Grim Wilds and Metsa Sateen flickered within their sights. After a quick glance of silent communication, the sisters ran for it, skidding to a stop when they reached the wall. Past the translucent barrier, the sky pelted rain onto lush, green grass.

Iris looked at the sand beneath her feet, comparing it to the ground on the other side.

Foxxglove reached for the wall of rain. Pressing the tips of her fingers through the tangible barrier, she touched the humidity and moisture of the other side.

Iris glanced behind them, her head responding to the sound of footsteps. "Are you ready?"

Foxx took a deep breath and smiled. "I love the rain."

Shouts called out at their backs, alerting them they'd been discovered. Three soldiers charged their way, one mounted and two on foot.

"Foxx, it's time to run!"

They launched themselves forward. Passing through a territory barrier felt like suddenly dropping face first into the surface of a lake, even when there wasn't a downpour on the opposite side.

The wall stretched around them and time seemed to slow as the density of the barrier caressed every cell of skin. Sudden moisture shocked their nerves the moment their hands and knees broke through the other side. As their faces followed their limbs, they experienced a few seconds of complete oxygen deprivation. When their mouths escaped the captivity of the wall, their lungs sucked in a huge gasp of humid air.

Then they ran.

Though technically in the Metsa territory, trees had been cleared out to build the eastern half of town. Before reaching the safety of the overgrown treeline, they had to run the length of the village. Until then, the sparse grove exposed them, offering little shield from the Legion's pursuit.

As they sprinted along the edge of Kesken Ala, Iris glanced over her shoulder to see both foot soldiers crossing the barrier. The men held rifles but didn't attempt to shoot. Then the soldier on horseback burst through the wall, the hooves of her steed thundering above the reverberation of the rain as it galloped across the field.

More soldiers joined the chase, the shouts of their comrades alerting them to the girls' presence.

Rain drenched Iris and Foxx's clothing and mud sprayed their boots as they ran as fast as their feet would carry them. When she noticed her sister's teeth-baring grin, Iris yelled through staggered breaths and splattering rain. "Foxxglove, what could you possibly be smiling about?"

Foxx looked back at the soldiers, then ahead at the treeline a few paces away. Glancing at Iris to confirm she maintained speed, she screamed, "I love the rain!" This admission seemed to propel her forward even more quickly than before.

A soldier darted out from around the corner of the final building and slammed into Iris' side. The unexpected impact had her hurtling toward the ground. She rolled and landed in a crouch with Thorn already in hand.

Foxx laced her fingers together behind the soldier's head and smashed his face into her knee. Stunned and feeling the pain of a potentially broken nose, the man cursed and stumbled away from her. In two steps she attacked him again, lifting her leg high and slamming her boot across his jaw. He slumped to the ground, unconscious.

"Geez, Foxx!" Iris exclaimed.

The soldiers behind them were close to catching up. Foxx grabbed Iris' hand and hauled her toward the jungle.

They burst through the treeline, leaping over rocks and felled branches and dodging bushes and trees in their path. Crossing over trails carved through the forest, they agreed without discussion to keep running through the thick foliage.

The soldiers fell behind, unable to keep up with the agility and swiftness of two experienced travelers as they dodged the obstacles of the rainforest. Finally far enough ahead, they slowed their sprint to a fast jog and scoured the land for a shelter.

Crossing another trail, they paused. A tree with enormous roots grew alongside the trail. They spotted a rotted out cave in the trunk well hidden by the root system and began scaling the intense tangles anchoring the tree to the earth.

When they reached the hole, they found the base nearly flat and big enough for them both to fit comfortably until the soldiers gave up their chase. Getting as low as they could to avoid detection, they laid down without removing their packs in case they needed to flee.

Neither sister had realized the fires burning in their lungs, but now at rest, their chests heaved as they gasped for air. They were soaked from rain and sweat. Blood pounded in their ears. Their eyes met, and they shared a look of relief. Iris bit back the laughter threatening to escape as she thought over the bizarre series of events.

When the blood ceased pulsing in their ears, the timbre of the wilderness sharpened into focus. Pitter-pattering raindrops broke through the canopy; birds cawed and chirped; bugs skittered and screeched. A breeze whisked through the trunk, cooling them from the oppressive humidity.

The sound of movement on the trail had them sharing another glance. They couldn't be sure if it came from pursuing soldiers or a creature who called the jungle its home, but they were hidden well enough not to check.

After nearly an hour of waiting in silence, they removed their packs and got comfortable, hoping to get a little more sleep before the sun fully rose.

C

The King and Queen of Arkaemor resided at the center of Inaravale in a fortress known as Castle Solís. Located along the western edge of Reginaterra, the royal city sat wedged between the hills of the Rustling Wood in the south and the Amber Mountains in the north.

Castle Solís was a fortified palace built within the confines of a deadly moat and high external walls. Watchmen from the King's Legion stood sentinel at the castle gates all hours of the day and night, as well as throughout the entirety of the grounds.

The Thrones of Arkaemor dwelt in the grand throne room, quite accurately named the Hall of Sunsets. Watchmen lined both sides of the crimson rug spanning from stained glass doors to dais. Dressed in the cardinal, charcoal, and dark gray of the King's Legion, they stood at attention with exactly one *syli* and two feet of space between them. The only modification in their uniform was a golden pin in the shape of a setting sun attached to their left breast.

As the Commanding officer of the King's Legion entered the Hall of Sunsets, he endeavored to conceal the tension between his shoulder blades. Exposing it revealed a weakness, and in the King's Legion, weakness tempted malevolence.

Hector Kayvan walked the length of the rug, receiving a mixture of respectful nods and indignant scowls as he passed by the other soldiers.

Being younger than most High Legion officers and the youngest commander in Legion history had earned Hector hostility within his ranks. Many would prefer to see another man commanding the King's forces, but as long as they served him faithfully without question, he gave little heed to their personal regard. To not serve him meant directly defying the sovereigns, so rebellion among the troops wasn't a common occurrence.

One of the Watchmen, a young soldier named Johnathan, shot him a glare as he walked past. When Hector dipped his head in return, the soldier snapped his eyes away. Despite his heartless lack of concern for insurgency with those below him, Hector felt a pang tighten his chest. Nothing could remedy the soldier's valid resentment. Hector had played his hand long ago, and the consequence of those choices remained his burden to bear.

Reaching the end of the carpet, Hector lowered himself to one knee at the foot of the dais. "Your Majesties, I have come to share the progress we've made in the eastern territories." He stared at the steps before him, the weight across his shoulders threatening to drag him the rest of the way to the floor.

King Pollux and Queen Sirena Aldrich sat side by side in twin thrones atop the gold staircase. Embedded within the gold, a mosaic crafted of daffodil, sienna, and crimson tiles shimmered in the light from chandeliers hanging high above. Behind the thrones, a large window showed an extravagant view of Inaravale and the land beyond its borders. As the setting sun shone through the window each day, its beams ricocheted off the tiles, creating brilliant sparkles throughout the hall.

"At ease." The King waved his hand in the air, encouraging Hector to stand and face them. Pollux wore a decorated military uniform converted into fanciful attire fit for a king. No longer the lean, muscular man of his youth, he still made a formidable impression in his fur-lined cape and jewel-encrusted crown. He wore black, spit-shined boots laced with gold bands that matched his buttons. Standard Legion regalia like Hector's had scarlet buttons and black laces rather than gold.

Her Royal Majesty the Queen wore a glorious gown the color of nearly dried blood. Blonde hair dappled with flecks of white hung in heavy curls pinned behind her ears. Atop the curls rested a crown similar to the King's but more delicate and housing twice as many jewels. Below her crown, a penetrating gaze rimmed in dark ink scrutinized her own fingernails.

When Hector straightened and locked his hand over his opposite wrist behind his back, King Pollux asked, "What is the news you would like to share, Commander?"

Queen Sirena retrieved a flat stone from the plate held next to her by a servant in royal attire. She brushed it against her nails one at a time, sharpening each so they tapered to a point.

Hector cleared his throat. "I sent men into the Grim Wilds, instructing them to visit every town in search of the traitor and his daughters. Three days ago, Captain Amar's unit heard of a possible sighting of the daughters near Kesken Ala."

Sirena sat forward with an elbow on her knee, her eyes blazing into Hector's. Her thin face and sharp chin added a severity to her wicked beauty. A vicious expression crossed her features for a brief moment. Then, she repeated, "A *possible* sighting, you say?"

Hector had anticipated this, knowing the Queen would not be pleased with anything less than concrete, but also knowing too well the danger for anyone caught supplying false information, unwittingly or not. His fingers fidgeted with his wrist. The Watchman to his right stifled a grunt. "That's correct, Your Majesty." He offered a slight nod in her direction. "Amar's team arrived in Kesken Ala early this morning. Not long after their search began, two young women were spotted sneaking around the outskirts. The moment they were discovered, they fled. The unit gave chase but eventually lost them among the trees of Sateen." His breath caught in his throat as he awaited her response.

"I see." The Queen sat back and again filed her nails, speaking to him without affording him her full attention. "So how can you be sure that these are the daughters of Sawyer Belamour if your soldiers were unable to encounter anything but their backsides as they ran away?" Another quiet chuckle escaped the Watchman. Sirena paused her filing mid-stroke and looked at Hector over long fingers.

Hector shifted his weight. His gaze slid to the King before quickly returning to the Queen's glare. "The two women were of the correct age. One had long ebony hair, and the other's was shorter and white as Cordilleran snow." The Queen shuddered almost imperceptibly, revealing a mysterious crack in her veneer. He pretended not to notice. "One of the soldiers claimed to have seen them up close, running into them at the edge of the forest. However, they managed to escape him."

Sirena threw her head back, mocking a laugh. "And where is this soldier who allowed them to slip from his grasp? Has he been punished for his impotence?"

Hector knew what the punishment for the soldier's *impotence* would have been and had not allowed the man to join him for the meeting. "I am told he received a broken nose and a boot to the jaw, Your Majesty."

The Queen looked unimpressed. "Is that supposed to be funny, Commander?"

"No, Your Majesty."

"So, the word of an incompetent imbecile and some matching hair. That seemed crucial enough information to interrupt our day, Commander?"

His chest tightened, squeezed from afar by her cutting stare. "Yes, Your Majesty."

"What I want to know is… Where. Are. They. *Now?*" Boiling over, she whipped the stone file past Hector's head. He blinked for a fleeting moment but showed no other signs of flinching.

The servant who'd presented the file to the Queen crept down the dais and over to the fallen instrument without a sound. Bending to pick it up, he placed it back on the plate and returned to his original position behind the throne.

Hector continued. "I ordered the majority of the search party into Metsa Sateen. We will have men stationed in every city throughout the territory as well as along the barriers. I also sent General Wraith to investigate another lead in Kesken Ala so we can remove any doubt regarding the womens' identities."

The King interjected before the Queen could speak more daggers. "Very good, Commander. I appreciate your persistence in this matter." Sirena scoffed and placed her hands into her lap.

"Thank you, Your Majesties." Holding one hand across his stomach and the other behind his back, Hector bowed. He turned from the thrones, making eye contact with the insubordinate Watchman as he did so, but the King addressed him again before he could take a single step.

"Oh, Hector? One more thing." Pollux sat forward in his seat and fidgeted his fingers against his knees. "Has there been any news on—"

"No!" the Queen interrupted, slamming her palm on the arm of her throne. The servant standing behind her winced and almost dropped the plate. Ungracefully, he regained his composure and rebalanced it on his palm before the Queen witnessed his digression. She glared sternly at her husband. "No, there will not be any news on that subject, Pollux. We've discussed this. You must let it go." Placing her hand over his, she allowed her features to soften. "It is time to move on, my love." An expression of defeat seeped into the crevasses of his face. Sirena turned again to Hector. "Thank you for your report, Commander. Now leave us."

Hector peered at King Pollux apologetically, bowed to them both again, and left the Hall of Sunsets.

Chapter 5

A Chance Meeting

Iris awoke to the harmonious melody of birds—a luxury she hadn't experienced during their month-long trek through the desert. Sweat coated her entire body despite laying motionless in the shade of the tree—another contrast to the dry territory they'd fled in the night.

Rays of sunshine sliced through cracks in the deteriorating trunk, illuminating air particles slipping in and out of each sliver. For the sun to be shining on them in the understory, Iris knew it must be late in the morning. Possibly even early afternoon.

Her stomach rumbled, a further indication they'd slept later than intended. She sat up and stretched her muscles, sore from the run and awkward sleeping position, and reached into her pack to grab a hunk of dried boar.

The grocer had named boar a favorite of his, second only to python jerky. After a sample, they'd purchased several bundles. Along with the meat they'd bought dried fruit, nuts, hard cheese, and yucca root, which he explained could be cooked and eaten like potatoes or turnips.

Foxxglove stirred, peering sleepily through the slits of her eyelids. She greeted her sister, who acknowledged her through a mouthful of jerky, then sat up and took a drink of water. Her leggings and tunic had soaked through in the night, but it seemed futile to change into dry clothes. At the moment, the rain had ceased, but sultry air encompassed them regardless.

Foxx removed her tunic, exposing the undershirt that did little more than conceal her breasts. She didn't anticipate running into many people along the trail, and if they came upon a town, she could slip it back on. After attempting to wring it out, she slid it into a pocket on the outside of her pack.

Iris tossed her a chunk of meat. "How did you sleep?"

"Surprisingly well. You?"

"Also well. I think that sprint wore us out."

Sitting in silence for a few minutes, they consumed the jerky and took in the foreign surroundings, allowing their bodies to awaken. Foxx twisted her shoulders, stretching the muscles along her spine, and pulled her knees beneath her to stand.

Glimpsing a passing shadow outside the trunk, she locked eyes with Iris and held a mute finger to her lips.

The *crack* of a snapping branch accompanied the shadow's movement, and it occurred to them simultaneously that the boisterous noise of jungle dwellers had ceased. A soft thump rattled the tree, triggering a plume of dust. Foxx scrutinized their surroundings as the inside of the trunk darkened. Grabbing her pack, she situated it between her shoulder blades and nocked an arrow.

Iris shouldered her own pack, drew Thorn and Bloom, and crouched into a defensive stance facing the opening. "What do you think it is?"

Another rumble vibrated the trunk, and several pieces of bark dropped past the opening from somewhere above. It clapped against the roots on its way to the ground, sending sharp echoes into the silent jungle.

"I don't know. I'm going to peek out and look around." Foxx stepped toward the entrance, the tip of her arrow following the trail of her vision. Chittering reached her ears, and she glanced back at her sister, who gulped. She lifted her gaze up the trunk's speckled bark, squinting past her arrow to confirm her suspicions. From five *sylis* up, hidden amongst leaves and branches, a creature crept toward her. Foxx said her sister's name, and Iris could hear the terror in her voice.

"What is it? Foxx, what do you see?"

Then the creature dropped, covering the distance between them in an instant. It landed less than a foot from the tip of Foxx's arrow and roared, exposing a maw of long teeth like those of an angler fish.

Foxxglove fell into a crouch and scrambled back.

Bigger than their room at the Briar Tavern, the nieda had eight spindly legs, each with three claws the size of an eagle's talon. A shorter leg cleaved below the femur revealed a weakness. Crusty, cyan blood marred its tip.

The nieda stood at the entrance, trapping them. Claws latched onto the bark and yanked, tearing away rotting wood and enlarging the hole.

Primed to strike, Foxx and Iris regarded the creature. "Ready?" Foxx asked. Iris signaled agreement at the edge of her vision. Foxx's arrow sailed through the air, hitting its mark: one of the many teal eyeballs scattered throughout its spherical body. Stumbling back, it lost its grip on the doorway, creating an exit.

Iris shot forward, slicing its injured leg with Bloom and slamming Thorn into the flesh beneath its grotesque mouth. Foxx ran through the opening, and Iris snatched the dagger before following her sister down the root system.

They bolted up the trail. Foxx turned and let another arrow fly, striking the nieda as it descended the tree. It tumbled to the ground. The spider launched into a chase, taking less than five seconds to catch up to them. It hurdled over their heads and blocked the trail, releasing another shrill scream. Blood spewing from fresh wounds, it withheld its attack, waiting to see what they would do. Taking their measure, it stomped the ground.

Iris asked, "What do we do? We can't outrun it."

"Kill it."

Iris used the hand holding Thorn to wipe sweat from her brow. "Fabulous idea, Foxxglove, but how? It has two arrows sticking out of it, and I stabbed its... head? Face? Whatever. I stabbed it. It doesn't seem too concerned by the holes we've already poked in it!"

"Then we keep poking holes."

The monster's stomping escalated, becoming more erratic. Then it lunged. One clawed leg grabbed Iris around the middle and lifted her from the ground. She tried to slash it and dropped one of her swords. Foxx's arrow penetrated its side, but the beast continued to shake her sister, dangling her upside-down before flinging her off the trail into the vegetation.

Foxx screamed her name, but no further movement came from the spot she'd landed. Another arrow struck the monster above its mouth. Taking a step backward, Foxx sprung over a root only to catch her heel on another. She stumbled and fell. The nieda leapt on top of her. The tips of its hair scratched the bare skin of her stomach and arms as she attempted to block its attacks.

She swung her bow, smacking the wood against the monster. This did little damage and only served to anger it further. It wrenched the weapon from her hand and tossed it aside.

More chittering preceded a piercing scream aimed at her face. The cyan blood peppering its body dripped onto her cheeks and poured over her hands as she held them out in front of her to shield herself. It pulled back to gain extra momentum for its final strike.

Before what would have been a devastating blow, a gunshot rocked the woods. Struck, the nieda halted, and a fresh wound spewed more ichor. It dripped down Foxx's cheeks and into her nostrils, poured into her ear and stained her hair the color of blue spider-guts.

The nieda backed away, though it quickly regained its composure and scuttled forward, bellowing again. Instead of directing its many eyes at Foxx, it locked onto something on the trail behind her.

A man's voice crowed, "Hello, my beautiful Beastie! I've come back for our final round!"

The nieda became even more hostile. Wiggling the previously injured leg, it raged. Chittering. Sputtering. Fuming. Stomping. Foxx tried to barricade her body from its volatile movements with little success.

"That's right! Let's finish this where we left off." Another bang blasted the creature backward. A third shot and it stumbled away, leaving Foxx free to scramble to her feet. The man stopped next to her, flashing a dazzling and oddly familiar grin. "Katutaan?"

Foxx blinked. "Oh. No, I speak Arkaen."

"Brilliant. I'll be right with you, my lady. I've got some unfinished business to settle with Beastie over there." He pointed his rifle at the nieda, winked like a madman, and raced off after it.

Foxx shook away her stupor as Iris rose from the brush and rejoined her on the trail. Neither spoke as they observed the fight between the man and the nieda. After wiping her hands on her pants to cleanse them from the goo, Foxx retrieved her bow from the foliage along the trail and nocked an arrow. She let it fly and struck another of the creature's eyes.

"Nice aim!" The man didn't turn to face them. Another two

gunshots blared, followed by a thud as the full weight of the monster collapsed to the ground.

Relief settled in, and Iris turned to Foxx, throwing her arms around her. "Foxxglove, I was so scared! It was on top of you, and I didn't know what to do. Nothing seemed to be hurting it and I—"

"It's fine!" Foxx interrupted, squeezing her. "We're okay, we made it. We're safe now." Considering their surroundings, she amended, "Well, relatively."

Iris pulled a rag from her bag and wet it before handing it to Foxx. It helped, but only a real bath would clean her completely. Scratches on her arms and stomach continued to bleed, though none looked deep enough to require stitches. Dumping more water on the rag, she dabbed them as clean as she could. Once she found a stream and rinsed off, she could decide if any were severe enough to require curavenum.

A whistle of relief blew from up the trail, prompting them to turn and face the stranger sauntering their way. His rifle rested on his shoulders, and rolled up sleeves cut across thick biceps. A poorly-tucked shirt revealed a tanned chest beneath three unclasped buttons.

Foxx surveyed his shaggy, unkempt hair and sharp jaw. Her gaze landed again on his smile, and she realized why it felt familiar. A flush of embarrassment rushed over her as she remembered the man she'd seen at the Myriad Market and her cowardly bolt out of sight. She then recalled her immodest attire and glanced down at herself in shock.

He drew closer, and his smile widened as he bowed to each of them. "Sorry you ladies had to witness that. I've been after that Beastie for a while now. She got me good with one of her claws when last we dueled." He pulled down his collar to reveal a healing wound on his neck that disappeared beneath his shirt. "Nearly killed me. Figured I ought to return the favor."

Despite attempted avoidance, Foxx's eyes caught his, and she discovered them even more beautiful up close, especially with the matching verdant jungle in his backdrop. Her lips parted as if she meant to speak, but when she didn't, Iris interjected for her. "You really saved us!"

Foxx's head cleared marginally, and she managed, "Yes, thank you, sir. You showed up just in time."

"Happy to help." The man handed Foxxglove the arrows he'd

retrieved from the felled nieda. "I thought you might be wanting these back." A tattoo inked into the bottom of his wrist portrayed a perfect circle encasing an uncentered crescent moon. Drawing her eyes from his body art, she accepted the arrows and thanked him again.

He ran a hand across the top of his hair, discovered a glob of goo, and grimaced at the corpse of the nieda. "The name's Asher, by the way."

"I'm Iris. What are you doing here anyway? It was so lucky you came along when you did!"

"I was out here several nights ago. That's when I last skirmished with her. I managed to escape her clutches and have been recovering at the Raindrop back in Kesken Ala ever since."

Foxx thought it strange for him to offer information about being in Kesken Ala and wondered if the shadows of the alley had hidden her better than she realized.

"There was some kind of commotion last night and when I woke this morning, the entire village was overrun by soldiers. I figured today was as good a time as any to hit the road." He shrugged. "Chalk it up to good timing." Then his focus shifted to Foxx, and his beguiling grin widened. "I still haven't been gifted your name."

She cleared her throat, swallowing the ripples in her stomach. "My name is Foxxglove. Foxx." Her fingers tightened around her bow where it hung at her side.

"Foxxglove and Iris, huh? Two divine flowers in an enchanted wood." He lifted a hand to the jungle, emphasizing his poetic words.

Iris smiled, unable to contain the glee she often displayed when they interacted with handsome men. Though usually unaffected by such things, Foxx found herself having a difficult time pulling her gaze from his radiant irises.

Asher motioned behind him with his shoulder. "Up the path is a little clearing. I was on my way there to have a rest and enjoy my luncheon as I waited for Beastie to reappear. Since that task has already been handled, you ladies are welcome to join me if you'd like." Though he clearly intended to address both of them, his eyes remained on Foxx, an action she found unnerving.

Iris gave Foxx a subtle nod indicating her consent, and after a moment of contemplation, Foxx agreed.

"Sitting down for a rest sounds lovely. Lead the way, Asher." As his name left her lips, a tingle of nerves made her shiver.

Asher clapped his hands together and grinned with all his teeth. "Fantastic." Then he turned on his heel and headed up the path with the girls trailing behind him.

C

The clouds reopened, sending showers into the jungle, but the clearing Asher led them to lay shrouded beneath a cluster of understory, allowing only a few splatters to slip through. Slabs of rock protruded from the forest floor, perfectly positioned for sitting.

As they ate their luncheons, they sat in the semi-awkward silence often shared by strangers. Each lingered inside their own minds, unsure how to converse now that the adrenaline of battle had settled. Iris met Foxx's eyes. Foxx looked at Asher, who stared down at his boots or up into the trees. Then Foxx looked back at Iris and shrugged or sighed or studied her own boots.

Hating the stillness, Iris sorted through the bag Mr. Magpie gave them before their flight from Kesken Ala. She discovered several food items, a spool of rope, a leather pouch containing a piece of flint and a rod of steel, a portable lantern and a jar of oil, and a hat with a floppy brim.

Tugging on the hat, Iris tightened the strings around her chin. Then she pushed both fists into her sides and jutted her hip out. "How do I look?"

"Like a true resident of Sateen," Asher said.

"Ridiculous," Foxx countered, shoving a piece of hard cheese into her mouth as she scanned the items Iris laid out.

Iris took the hat off and whipped it at her sister. "I can't believe Mr. Magpie gave us all this. We didn't overpay him that much."

Asher took a bite of his sandwich made of thinly sliced meat and soft, yellow cheese. With a full mouth, he asked, "Who's Mr. Magpie?"

Iris swiped a cube of cheese from Foxx's stash and stacked it atop a piece of jerky. "He owns the Briar Tavern on the dryside of Kesken Ala."

Foxx shot her a warning glance. Asher might have saved them, but if he'd been in town that morning and learned who the King's Legion hunted, he may have tracked them down with the intention of turning them in. Divulging too much information about Mr. Magpie and Seth could incriminate their rescuers.

The parchment Iris swiped during their escape remained rolled up in her pack. As far as Foxx knew, they hadn't provoked the King in any way. They rarely came in contact with Legion soldiers, and though their father had worked for the King, it didn't seem plausible for that to be relevant since he'd been missing for more than half a decade.

Remembering Maeve's warning about things being set in motion, she wondered if accepting their supposed destiny had somehow placed them at the end of a Legion sword. Though eager for answers, Foxx thought it safer to wait until they parted ways with Asher before unveiling whatever the parchment contained.

Asher scratched his chin. "So, why exactly would the owner of the Briar Tavern give you that bag of equipment?"

Foxx broke free of her musings as her words came out in a rush. "We overpaid him for the room and there was this little boy who took a liking to Iris. I guess they wanted to help us out."

Asher nodded slowly. "Ah. I see." The girls held an anxious breath as he took another bite of his sandwich and cracked a smile. "Do you break hearts every time you leave a town, Iris?"

Iris exhaled a chuckle. "Only the lucky ones." Seeking the release of nervous energy, she drew Thorn and Bloom and began practicing the movements her sister had taught her. Though partial to the bow, Foxx had become a talented swordswoman since leaving home. She'd been determined to protect them in the wilderness and trained countless hours to perfect her skills. Then she'd tutored Iris to do the same.

Even though their father had been a soldier, he hadn't taken the time to teach them to hunt or fight. They'd never needed such skills. Their mother taught them to use knives in the kitchen: how to clean a fish and keep their blades sharp, but she hadn't been a hunter or a fighter.

While Iris practiced, Foxx redirected the conversation. "So, Asher, why are you traveling through Metsa Sateen?"

His gaze met hers and dimples threatened to poke through his cheeks. "I am certain you will laugh when you hear it."

Intrigued, Iris turned to face him. "Oh, you definitely have to tell us now or we might die of curiosity!" She badgered him playfully, pretending to jab at him with her shortsword. "Well?"

Asher crossed his legs at his ankles and his arms over his chest. His hair had begun to curl, dampened by the humidity, and he flicked a strand away from his eye. "Okay. For the sake of your lives, I suppose I can tell you." Foxx leaned closer, anticipating his answer. Asher continued to hesitate, his eyes sliding back and forth between them as he cleared his throat. "The truth is: I am on a quest to find Celestelvyra."

Iris froze mid swing. Foxx's mouth dropped open.

Asher laughed and leaned back in his seat. "Yes, that's generally how people respond and why I'm often leery of sharing. Thank you for confirming the question of my sanity." He ran his hand over the top of his head, and though he chuckled, his eyes let slip a flash of insecurity.

"A quest? That's mighty pretentious sounding, don't you think?" Iris smirked.

"Well, searching out the unfathomable land of stories and legends is a mighty pretentious intention. I think *quest* suits it perfectly."

Foxxglove regained her composure and stood. Searching his eyes, she sensed his sincerity. "You're truly searching for Celestelvyra? Seriously?" When he didn't answer her question, she asked another. "Why are you searching for it?"

His chin dropped, and his eyes shifted down before returning to her. "I am absolutely serious about looking for the Sacred Realm, yes. Though I would rather not share my reasons at this time, if you don't mind."

Foxx tapped a finger against her bottom lip. "I didn't mean to pry. It's just that…"

Iris picked up where she left off. "We are also searching—or rather, *on a quest*—to find Celestelvyra."

Asher got to his feet, meeting them where they stood. "Truly?" They nodded. He looked up, resting his hands on his head as he teamed with energy. "Well, that's great! I mean, what are the odds of that? We should go together, don't you think? Three heads are certainly better than one or two."

Overwhelmed with information, Foxx said, "Asher, would you mind if I had a moment alone with my sister?"

Disappointment showed, but he agreed. He swung his rifle over his shoulder and bowed deeply before walking a ways up the trail.

Sheathing her blades, Iris returned to her seat and criss-crossed her legs. "This is really weird, isn't it? What do you think?"

Foxx paced, her boots scuffing a trail in the soil. "I don't know what to think." She tried to work through all possible outcomes, weighing each choice.

"He did save us." Iris' fingers tapped a symmetrical pattern on her knees. "It might be nice to have another person in our party. Safety in numbers and all that. Plus, maybe he knows the way."

"Or maybe he'll lead us astray. Or! Maybe he works for the King and Queen and will gut us in our sleep. Or worse, turn us over to the Legion the next chance he gets." Foxx's mind spun with so many questions and even more potential answers.

Iris cocked her head to the side and crossed her arms. "You don't really think that though, do you? I can tell. Something in you wants to trust him. You never would have agreed to eat with him if you didn't."

"No." Foxx didn't meet her sister's gaze. "Honestly, I don't know why I agreed to eat with him."

Iris studied her in the way only a sister can. Foxx was unfailingly cautious about who they interacted with, especially when it came to men. Even more so with attractive men, a category Asher fit securely into without question. She'd never allowed them to be put in a situation like this. Never even considered the possibility of traveling with someone else, male or otherwise. It only took minutes for her to separate them from Orion and Declan when she awoke in the cool of their cave, despite how kind they'd been. Yet within minutes of meeting Asher, she'd agreed to dine with him.

Rather than pointing this out, Iris offered another factor to consider. "Why would he save us if he planned to kill us?"

As a brand new fear spawned into existence, Foxx's eyes turned cold. "The King's Legion didn't shoot as they chased us from Kesken Ala, even though they easily could have caught us if they had. So it's possible, though I can't fathom why, that we're worth more to the King alive than dead."

CHAPTER 6

ARMS LENGTH

As the King's Legion passed into Metsa Sateen, the Briar Tavern filled with patrons seeking comfort food and pints of ale.

Seth lounged on his usual stool drawing a picture of an ivory dove perched next to an ebony raven with a single white feather. He leaned back to admire his work just as two men in crimson, black, and gray triggered the bell above the door. A hush fell over the room as the soldiers approached the bar.

Mr. Magpie greeted them with his ever-present jolly demeanor. "Merry luncheon, gentlemen. Didn't know there was any soldiers left in town. Ya must be famished from yer hunt. What can I get for ya fine lads? How's 'bout the Sausage Special?" He pointed to the board on the wall behind him.

The stockier of the two men spoke. "I am General Dagon Wraith of the King's High Legion. This is Captain Amar." He threw a thumb over his shoulder. "We're here about the two women sought by His Majesty. Rumor tells they were seen entering your tavern yesterday around highsun."

Seth's eyes widened, but he kept his head down, pretending to ignore the men standing next to him.

Mr. Magpie glanced his way and winked—a silent promise things would be okay. "We have quite a few ladies and gents comin' to the tavern all the time. You will have ta be a tad more specific about the ones yer trying to find." Magpie leaned forward with his elbow on the bar and his chin in his hand.

The soldier slid a piece of parchment in front of him and tapped the page. "They look a bit like this. One with long, dark hair, and the other's white as snow. Would be hard to miss that scar. Surely you've seen these pictures already. My men posted them up all over town."

Seth's heart pounded as he gaped at the black and white birds in his picture. Knowing it might spark suspicion if he tried to remove it, he leaned over as if continuing to draw and covered it with his body. Captain Amar stood at his back, and Seth couldn't tell if the soldier was gazing over his shoulder to glimpse the drawing or if his fear was making him paranoid.

"Like I told the soldiers this morning, I think we may 'ave seen two ladies like ya speak of. Stopped by yesterday askin' fer directions ta the Metsa. I told them to head left out the pub and follow the road 'til the rain hit them. They'd be sure ta find it. Then they was gone." He pushed the parchment back across the bar.

Dagon scrutinized Mr. Magpie before looking back at Amar, who studied the young boy on the stool next to them. "You didn't serve them anything?"

Magpie shook his head. "They could not ha' been here more than a few minutes. I asked 'em if they needed a room, but they was in a hurry to get going. Seemed nice enough girls to me."

Dagon pushed Seth's shoulder out of the way and yanked the drawing from beneath his arms. Seth cried out for him to leave it alone. The general ignored him and held the picture in front of Mr. Magpie's face. "So, you expect me to believe they were in your establishment but minutes, yet your boy has drawn their likeness here?"

For the first time since the soldiers entered, a cloud of panic flushed Mr. Magpie's features. He straightened, pulling his nose away from the parchment. "That's a drawing of two birds, my good lad. Not two ladies."

Dagon set the drawing on the counter next to the parchment depicting the two women. He pointed to the white feather on the black bird and the white streak on the woman with dark hair. "Coincidence, Amar?"

"Per'aps he saw the poster and found inspiration," Mr. Magpie suggested.

Amar examined both images. "I would bet not, sir." Suddenly aggressive, Amar latched on to Seth's collar and wrenched him off his stool. Seth screamed and tried to fight his way out of the man's grip. Mr. Magpie leapt around the side of the bar with more agility than seemed possible for his hefty frame. Dagon's palm shot to his chest, stopping him in his tracks.

"You leave Seth out of this, ya hear? He 'as nothing to do with it."

With a gesture from Dagon, Amar released Seth's tunic. Dagon stepped up to the tavern owner, chest to chest, matching his height and ferocity. "Magpie, is it?"

Mr. Magpie stood unflinching, his face a portrait of cold stone.

"Well, Magpie. Let's say we go outside and discuss this issue further. Wouldn't want to scare the boy anymore than necessary. What do you think?"

C

As the rain died down, only breaking through the canopy in splatters and drips, the air settled into a humid mist like a low-hanging cloud resting amongst the trees. Birds chirped louder in the reprieve, and a hidden animal swung through the branches above, rattling the leaves.

Grabbing the stolen parchment from her pack, Iris unraveled it and held it between them. Three faces stared back at them: their father's first, and their own in two individual boxes below his. Across the top, bold, capital letters spelled out the word *Wanted*. Beneath the pictures, it read:

> *By order of King Pollux and Queen Sirena Aldrich of Arkaemor: Sawyer Belamour is a criminal wanted for treason. Anyone with information regarding his whereabouts or the whereabouts of his daughters, Foxxglove and Iris Belamour, pictured above, should report immediately to the King's Legion. A reward will be granted to any individual who assists in the capture of these fugitives.*

Below it in smaller font, the paragraph was repeated again in Vetoräti, Bryä, and Katutaan. Mystified, Iris' voice cracked. "I don't understand. What did we do? What did *he* do?"

"I don't know." Foxx reread the parchment again before returning to her pacing.

"But it's been six years."

"I know." Six years since their mother died. Six years since their father abandoned them. *Six years.*

"What crime could be so treacherous that he would still be hunted after six years?" Iris asked.

"I. Don't. Know. They must have been hunting him all along." The Legion had torn their house apart searching for their father. It would seem they never gave up, but Foxx couldn't imagine what he could have possibly done to spawn such extensive efforts.

Iris let the parchment rest in her lap as she lifted her eyes to the trees. "Remember what Maeve told us? Once we started our journey, the tides would be changing. Somehow, the King learned we were searching for our father, so he added us to the list of the hunted. It's the only thing that makes sense."

"None of it makes sense. How could he possibly know? I doubt Maeve told him, and she's the only person who knows anything about our journey." Foxx tried to replay their interactions with people since meeting the mystic, but nothing stood out.

"There has to be more to this journey than we yet understand," Iris said.

Foxx nodded, her eyes scanning the ground. "Then a mystery man shows up to save us and just *happens* to be searching for Celestelvyra too?"

Iris held up the parchment. "Do you think Asher has seen this? He was in Kesken Ala this morning. Though it mentions nothing about Celestelvyra."

"Maybe he's a soldier? Maybe he knew our father? He looks old enough to have served with him if he joined young. Maybe he's hunting him for the King and opted to take a more casual approach, appearing to us as a civilian to gain our trust."

"He doesn't seem like a soldier."

Foxx stopped pacing and pinched her bottom lip. She had to decide their fate. Iris relied on her to keep them safe. "You're right. He doesn't seem like a soldier, but that doesn't mean he isn't." Taking the parchment, she rerolled it and stuffed it into her pack. "The only option is to keep moving forward. We have a plan. Let's stick to it and do our best to avoid the Legion at all costs."

"What do you want to do about him?" Iris pointed in the direction Asher had walked.

Foxx looked at her sister before turning her attention to the trail. They hadn't allowed invaders into their circle of trust for years. They'd made that mistake early on, and it had been a lapse in judgment they'd paid a hefty price for.

Now, with a royal target on their backs, they risked not only themselves but every person they came in contact with. She thought of Kesken Ala and the roots they'd planted there in promising Seth they'd return. They'd never done that before. Allowing Asher to travel with them put him in danger, too.

On the other hand, Iris made a good point about safety in numbers. Foxx feared the jungle might be a different kind of monster than anything they'd yet faced. Having a third and obviously skilled companion could be the difference between life and death.

If his intentions did turn out to be nefarious, they might be able to escape him. They'd survived much worse than a battle against a single man. Though he might have others waiting nearby for the opportune moment to strike. She scoured the treeline, but if someone lay camouflaged amongst the foliage, they remained hidden.

Another thing to consider was the possibility of crossing paths with him regardless. With them heading in the same direction—allegedly—it might be more prudent to keep their eyes on him so he couldn't catch them unawares, as the old adage about keeping enemies close suggested.

Foxx sighed, displeased with feeling such uncertainty. "I don't trust him. However, having an extra with us could prove helpful, at least until we get out of the jungle. I sure wouldn't mind having him around if another nieda crosses our path."

"Brilliant!" Asher's voice erupted behind them, causing them to flinch. "Those are my thoughts exactly." He raised his fists in a miniature cheer for good decisions.

Foxx scrutinized him as though she could determine how much he'd overheard purely by the creases in his expression or the contour of his lips. Still, the decision had been made. They would travel together, but they would keep Asher at arms length and remain on guard to flee—or fight—if necessary.

Foxx extended her hand between them. "Okay, Asher. On to Celestelvyra?"

Asher accepted her hand, and a pact of understanding passed between them. "On to Celestelvyra." Shafts of sunlight drew sparkling flecks of gold to the surface of his emerald eyes. Foxx thought she detected a sensation of relief hidden behind his smile—a notion both confusing and troubling. She filed it away for future examination. Asher rubbed his palms together with newly ignited energy. "So what's the plan?"

Iris and Foxx exchanged a look as they shouldered their packs. They hadn't discussed anything further than allowing him to join their team, and neither knew what to divulge and what to keep to themselves. It didn't make sense to keep him entirely in the dark. If they intended to work as a team, both sides needed to share what they knew.

Foxx slid her bow over her shoulder. "Well, what was your plan?"

Asher blinked. "I have a few ideas."

"You strode into Metsa Sateen with nothing but a rifle and a *few ideas*?" Foxx asked.

"Plus this winning smile." He pointed to his own face.

"A smile won't help you in the jungle."

"I'm thinking it already has."

Foxx scowled, and Iris tried to cover the giggle bubbling up her throat. "Well, it won't help you find an impossible realm."

Asher tilted his head. "If you truly believe it impossible, then why are you searching for it?"

Foxx held his gaze, unsure how to answer his perfectly reasonable question. In truth, she asked herself the same thing nearly every day. "I have my reasons."

"And I have mine." He seemed utterly delighted by their raillery. "So, what trail of breadcrumbs are we following now?" Foxx grumbled at his evasion, and he laughed. "I think we've successfully waded through our very first argument, love. It went swimmingly in my opinion. Wouldn't you agree?"

"I have some notes."

Iris had yet to remove her hand from her lips. Asher heard another giggle escape and sent a playful wink in her direction.

Foxx sighed, yielding her resistance. "Our mother once painted a picture of Lacuna Kaput. Have you heard of it?" Iris choked on the water she'd lifted to her lips, a failed effort to stifle her amusement.

Asher startled at Iris' reaction but recovered quickly. "Lacuna Kaput? I may have heard of it. What is it?"

Foxx tucked the thicker section of her side-part behind her ear. "It's a waterfall."

"There are many waterfalls in Sateen." Asher readjusted his pack so it settled between his shoulders with his rifle hanging next to it.

"We think it's in the region of Sadella, on the eastern side. That's where we're headed. Unless you had a more solid plan?"

He mulled over her words, smiling, and she wondered if she'd somehow given away more than she'd meant to or if he was simply very perceptive. Or perhaps he was merely skilled at making himself *appear* perceptive. It was nerve-racking.

"Maybe someone living in the Metsa will be able to give us more accurate directions," he suggested.

Foxx's line of sight slid to her sister. Neither cared for the idea of running into civilians, though it seemed impossible to think they wouldn't. As long as they avoided the Legion, things should go smoothly. Sateen was a huge territory. It didn't seem likely for them to run into someone who would recognize them from a sketch.

Unless soldiers up ahead had plastered their pictures on every available surface, which was a definite possibility.

"Are there any towns nearby?" Like her sister, Iris hoped to avoid places the Legion might be searching.

Asher scratched his chin and lifted his eyes to the canopy, thinking it over. "Ky'uso and Werifesteria are north of here. Seigan and Eunoia are southeast. If we stay on the trails, it stands to reason we'll run into someone who knows where the waterfall is. I wouldn't worry too much about it."

Iris pulled the hat Mr. Magpie had given them from her pack and tugged it back onto her head. "I say we head northeast and see what we find."

Foxx agreed. "If we need to adjust our course at some point, we can discuss it then."

Asher perused her face as she tried her best to appear impassive against his penetrating stare. "Do you think the waterfall has something to do with finding the Sacred Realm of Celestelvyra?"

Iris held her breath as she waited for her sister to respond.

Foxxglove took a minute to think it over. "I don't know for sure, but I can't get it out of my head. I think it's worth checking out."

Asher shrugged and moved toward the trail. "That's a good enough breadcrumb for me, love. Let's go find Lacuna Kaput."

C

Hours passed on the trail with little conversation. Asher took the lead, with Iris walking behind him and Foxx at the back. Whether the lingering silence felt comfortable or not went unnoticed as each of them remained preoccupied by their own musings. Iris thought of Mr. Magpie and Seth, and wondered if the King's Legion had departed Kesken Ala in peace. Foxx reconsidered their confidence in Asher and fretted over potential pursuing soldiers. Neither knew what went on inside Asher's mind as he swaggered along the trodden footpath ahead of them.

The narrow but well-defined trail meandered tenderly through the rainforest. The diverse landscape of the Metsa exploded with more variations of green than they'd ever seen: chartreuse, juniper, turquoise, seaweed, spring onion, sage, olive, and jade, to name a few. Other dramatic hues burst through the greens in a riot of ruby, mango, violet, cobalt, and pineapple.

Foxx and Iris had been raised in the tropical landscape along the shores of the Suola Meri, but the enormous leaves of Alunda's indigenous palms couldn't compare to the sheer size of Sateen's leafy plants. A few were so huge, Iris could have rolled herself up in one and used it as a blanket.

Though some sections of the trail became tricky to maneuver, much of it remained flat and free of debris but for a few scattered stones and roots requiring a high stride. Locals built bridges to span the streams intersecting the trails. Some had elaborate staircases or archways crafted from wooden planks and stacked stones, while others were as simple as flat rocks protruding the water one after another.

In a matter of hours, the company glimpsed vibrantly decorated birds, an obsidian snake with morning glory diamonds running up its back, troops of monkeys high up in the understory, a flying beetle whose open wings exceeded the size of a human head, and a fluorescent lizard scurrying up the trunk of a tree on six legs. Croaking frogs and chirping insects serenaded the jungle in constant melody, embellished with the warbles, howls, and tittering calls of animals out of sight. Camouflaged movement rustled nearby vegetation more than a few times with no sign of the source.

Jarring the girls from their contemplative states, Asher held his arm out to halt their hiking. "Look at this." He crouched, sitting on the back of his heels and waving for the girls to join him.

Iris dropped next to him. "Oh my gosh, amazing! Teeny frogs!" Unable to curb her curiosity, Foxx bent down on Asher's opposite side to find tiny pops of vivid color speckled atop a collection of mossy rocks and shrubs.

Most were no bigger than Asher's thumb, which he held up as a comparison. "Poison dart frogs, to be exact."

Foxx found the mixture of hues astounding and couldn't help trying to identify the variations in each species. There were black frogs with fern spots. Some shined bright as a chili pepper with cerulean legs and feet. Several shared the hue of a daffodil with assorted black freckles, while others were dressed in sapphire instead of yellow.

Foxx said, "They're incredible. Did you say they're poisonous?"

"They secrete a deadly poison from their skin when defending themselves. People have been using them to poison weapons for centuries." Asher watched Foxx out of the corner of his eye, beaming at her interest and seemingly very pleased with himself for being so knowledgeable.

The feel of his eyes skipped her heart like the smack of a flat stone across water. Her defenses kicked in, questioning how this seemingly good-natured man might be so educated on the uses of frog poison. Freed from her amazement, she stood abruptly. "We should probably keep moving." Iris sensed her sister's mood shift and rose to her feet.

Asher watched the tiny frogs for another minute before standing to join them. Looking up at the canopy, he said, "Foxxglove is right. We'll soon lose the light. Finding a place to hunker down for the night should be our next objective. Once we make camp, I'll hunt something fresh for dinner so we can save the dried food for daytime travel."

"I can hunt," Foxx said, reasserting the notion that his traveling with them wasn't a necessity. They were perfectly capable of taking care of themselves.

"I wasn't suggesting you couldn't. Only offering my services. If you prefer to handle dinner, I can help Iris prepare a fire."

Foxx realized she'd begun to loathe his friendly smile for no reason other than the prickle in her stomach that accompanied it. "Fine. Shall we move on?" It didn't surprise her to find him wounded by her hostility. A sharp pain in her chest escorted the guilt she strived to bury.

Nodding without meeting her eyes, Asher turned from them and started up the trail.

Iris didn't immediately follow, allowing him time to travel several paces before facing her sister. "What's wrong?"

"Nothing is wrong," Foxx replied without conviction.

The sound of footsteps had both girls turning to find a different man walking their way. Fear rendered them speechless, and they stepped backward off the trail, allowing him room to pass. As he approached, he smiled at them from beneath a flat-brimmed hat made of straw. His olive skin wrinkled on either side of thin and angled eyes, common for those born in Sateen. The girls' mother had passed similar features along to Foxxglove, though Iris looked more Alundan, like their father. Shuffling slowly along the trail, the man placed his palms together at his chest and bowed to them before continuing on his way.

The sisters exhaled relief. "That was mildly horrifying." Iris' heart raced. "I hate having such anxiety about running into people now." Foxx nodded in agreement, and Iris tilted her head to one side, crossing her arms. "So if nothing is wrong, why are you being so mean to Asher?"

Adrenaline from seeing the stranger had reduced her anger, and her gaze shifted to the forest floor. "I'm not being mean. I'm being cautious."

"You *are* being mean."

"Fine, I'm being mean."

Iris' amused expression seemed to indicate knowledge of a secret Foxx wasn't privy to. "Well, okay then."

"Don't give me that look," Foxx grumbled, frustration resurfacing.

Iris' smile grew. "I'm not giving you a look."

Foxx growled and pushed her sister forward. Iris laughed and jogged ahead, bridging the broadening distance between them and their new companion.

C

Asher found shelter beneath the roots of a large tree. While he and Iris gathered kindling, Foxx trotted off to hunt. The forest grew boisterous as the sun went down and nocturnal creatures ruled the night. Their constant calls kept her alert as she crept soft-footed amid the trees.

Darkness came quickly beneath the canopy despite the first quarter moon making its way into the sky. Scattered among the shadows, thin beams of light sliced through the trees, reflecting off wet foliage and sending a slight illumination across the forest floor.

Foxx let her mind wander as she scoured the land, patiently awaiting her prey to reveal itself. Her vision in the desert resurfaced, and she allowed herself a moment to digest it. Memories of her mother's erratic behavior plagued her thoughts when she let herself think back on it, so she'd put a great deal of effort into ignoring it completely. If that first vision indicated Foxx would suffer the same sickness as her mother, she wondered at the possibility of preventing the slow tumble to insanity before it consumed her.

Shivering, she shoved those thoughts back into the depths of her heart and slammed the door.

Foliage rustled up ahead and halted her steps. Pulling back the bowstring, she honed in on the swishing leaves to see an animal emerging. Standing more than two feet tall on four legs, it stepped from its hiding place and scanned the surrounding area. Foxx counted backward in her head, her stare fixed down the arrow's shaft as she assessed the perfect moment to let it fly.

The animal looked back and another appeared, much smaller than the first. The baby nuzzled its snout into the larger animal's side, and Foxx paused, feeling a dull ache in her chest. She'd killed mothers before without a doubt, but never had she done it in front of the young.

At last sensing her presence, the mammal's eyes flickered toward her.

Foxx retracted her arrow and let the bow drop to her side. Backtracking to avoid startling them, she signaled that the mother and her pup were free to go in peace. On her third step back, she bumped into something and shrieked as flashes of being accosted from behind reemerged. She spun on the assailant and aimed an arrow at his face.

"Blimey!" His accent thickened in surprise, and his hands flew up to block her attack.

Relief flooded her senses, followed quickly by profound fury. "Asher! What are you doing? I almost killed you!"

His accent diminished as he regarded the arrow's tip. "I'm concerned you still might."

Foxx released the tension, slid her arrow back into her quiver, and swung her bow over her shoulder. "You shouldn't sneak up on someone in the middle of a hunt."

"It seemed the hunt was already over when I arrived." His chin lifted toward the plant where the animals had cleared off.

Foxx's brows knit together. "What is that supposed to mean exactly?"

"I'm not insulting you. I just meant: when you saw the young capybara, you decided not to leave it motherless. It was an honorable response."

"It was dinner. I shouldn't have hesitated."

"Perhaps on another night we won't have the luxury of being decent humans, but we aren't so desperate for food tonight we need to be making orphans."

Foxx remained silent, her gaze scanning the trees, foolishly hoping another animal might appear. It amazed her how different the jungle looked after the sun slid beneath the horizon, as though it were a separate territory all its own.

Much like with the jungle, the shadow of the night heightened Asher's intensity, transforming it into a living thing with breathtaking tentacles and intimate sparks. When their eyes met, the tip of her tongue tingled with caution and curiosity, like the feel of apprehension before tasting something new. "Will you stop staring at me, please?" she choked out, not sounding nearly as harsh as she'd hoped. "Let's go back to camp."

That insufferable smile spread across his cheeks. Foxx rolled her eyes, though her heart beat so fiercely within its cage, she thought it impossible he couldn't hear it, and she wondered how she had allowed herself to become so reactive to a man she'd known less than a day.

He surprised her by saying, "You don't like me, do you."

Foxx scoffed. "I have no opinion of you. I don't know you."

Asher's smile faltered, no longer present in his eyes—a candle extinguished by the breath of her hostility. Again, she felt something like guilt at the thought of hurting him. "It's not that I don't like you. I just don't trust anyone. We've been burned before by misplaced trust and have learned the hard way that not everyone is as nice as they appear."

"You trusted Magpie though?"

More than ever she wished Asher hadn't heard that name and hoped they hadn't doomed their friend by exposing it. "That was different."

"How?"

Taking a step back to cool her blood, she thought she'd never known darkness to feel so constricting. The trees walled her in on all sides, and he blocked the exit. Her fingers curled into fists, and a bitter cold like shards of ice cut into her palm.

Asher's voice drew her eyes back to him.

She shook her head to clear away the panic and stretched out her freezing fingers. The rest of her body was slick with sweat. She squeezed her upper arm, confirming her strength and coaching herself not to fear the darkness or the man in front of her. "It's different because he was a friendly, old man we met running an inn and not—" She sputtered to a halt, realizing the words about to spill from her lips in her distraction.

"Not a charming and utterly attractive hero who saved you from the monsters of the jungle?" His smile returned.

Foxx exhaled, feeling the tightness in her chest disperse. A smile played at her lips without her consent. "Something like that." Then she lifted a brow. "And it was only one monster."

"Fair enough. I suppose I'll have to prove I'm worthy of your trust then, won't I? And possibly slay a few more monsters along the way."

"I'll try not to be too disappointed when you fail."

This prompted a laugh, and she echoed his amusement with laughter of her own. An unexpected lightness settled between them.

"Ready to head back?" Asher motioned toward their camp. Foxx nodded, and when he turned to walk away she followed close behind him.

CHAPTER 7

MANDRILL

Hector strode through the halls of Castle Solís in the direction of the warroom. Hearing General Dagon's gruff voice, he glanced back to see a Watchman pointing at him, indicating to Dagon where he could find his commander. Amar stood at his side, but as the general turned to Hector, his captain walked the opposite way. Hector clasped a hand over his opposite wrist and waited for Dagon to approach.

Despite the simplicity of Dagon's mission, sprays of dry blood stained his face. His almond skin, made darker in contrast to the bright reds in his uniform, hadn't been washed clean to hide his transgression. He wore his brutality proudly, like a badge of honor.

"Commander." Dagon dipped his head, and dirty blond hair fell into his face. He kept one side shaved to display tattoos on his scalp that disappeared beneath his collar.

"What news have you from the Wilds?" Hector asked, all business. He'd never much cared for Dagon. His ferocity made him a fine general, but Hector had always been leery of trusting his cold-blooded and sadistic nature. The Queen, of course, adored him.

"It was definitely them. They stayed at the Briar Tavern for two nights and the proprietor, a man named Magpie, helped them escape."

Hector's heart sank, but his face revealed nothing. "And what has become of this Magpie? Have you brought him back with you?"

"No, we did not."

80

Hector had known this would be his answer. "Understood, General." He turned and continued his walk down the hall. Dagon fell into step next to him, his heavy boots scuffing the carpet. "Any idea where the sisters are now?"

"Amar's unit lost them to the Metsa, but we have all the main exits guarded, as you commanded, and we've sent soldiers into the settlements as well. Amar and I returned to report our findings so you would have something solid to offer the King, but we'll be rejoining the hunt tomorrow. If it suits you, I would like to take a few more soldiers back with us."

"Yes, that's fine. I trust your judgment on who."

"Thank you, Commander. According to the captain, the sisters were more skilled than we anticipated."

Hector dropped his chin to the Watchman Thomas as they passed each other. Thomas responded in kind. "Two young women bested the trained soldiers of the King's Legion?" Hector lifted a brow, and Dagon nodded, his expression mirroring Hector's disbelief. "I guess if they've been on their own in the wild since Sawyer left as we now believe might be the case, it stands to reason they've learned how to survive."

"We may need more than a couple soldiers at the exits to collect them. You heard what happened to Faber, I'm sure. One of them managed to break his nose and knock him out cold with little effort."

"Yes, I heard."

"Your orders?" Dagon asked.

They reached the door to the warroom, and though Hector's fingers grasped the handle, he didn't push it open. "Progress as you have been. I have a feeling they'll head through Sateen rather than backtrack to the Wilds. I'm not sure of their destination, but it stands to reason they would press forward."

Dagon's gaze shifted to Hector's lingering hand. "I fear they may head to Jericho now that they know the Legion is after them. If they make it, we may have a hard time retrieving them. The Konungr protects those behind his walls."

"Then don't let them make it to Jericho. Set up extra men between Metsa Sateen and Cordillera, and catch them before they cross over. There's history between the Kirkavalls and the Belamours, so it would be best to avoid his domain entirely."

Dagon bowed and continued down the hall as Hector pushed open the warroom door, releasing a sigh as he closed it behind him.

C

As the Susi moon swelled from quarter to full, Foxx, Iris, and Asher fell into a rhythm. Despite her best efforts, Foxx found the constant battle to keep her guard up grueling. Asher had been nothing but helpful, kind, and respectful to both of them, and his overall demeanor slowly pried at the layers of resistance around her heart. Iris had bonded with him as well, which added an extra complication in keeping him at a distance.

Though his presence unsettled her, Foxx couldn't deny that having him join the party had been beneficial. A skilled tracker, he saw the forest through an altered lens, awakened to the secrets the veil of verdant terrain concealed. He easily spotted which shelters were uninhabited and what animals roamed close by. He toed his way through the trees, unheard and unseen as he crept up behind his prey and slaughtered it before it even realized it was dying.

Asher often walked at the front of the line, pointing out new plants they passed or sharing interesting facts about the different creatures they saw. Like how three-toed sloths almost never come down from the trees and how tapirs can grab things with their elongated snouts, like elephants. He taught them which plants were safe to eat and which would kill them where they stood. He knew when leaves were safe but berries would make them sick and which roots needed to be cooked rather than eaten fresh.

Foxx wondered if his extensive knowledge indicated a specific interest in Metsa Sateen or if his education covered a variety of subjects. When she questioned it, he made a flippant excuse about being gifted with a brilliant memory and said something about how he couldn't help being so magnificently intelligent. Foxx had thrown a piece of jerky at his face in response, and he'd snatched it up, devouring it with glee.

Soon they were deep in the jungle. Each day, they would begin their hike with the rising sun. When the night wormed its way through the thick vegetation, they would search out somewhere to make camp and settle down until morning.

The fire kept most creatures at bay as they slept, but on extra rainy nights with minimal shelter it was impossible to keep the fire lit. On the nights they kept a fire burning, the girls hoped the smoke wouldn't be visible through the trees or that the soldiers hunting them would not be as skilled a tracker as their companion. Either way, fire or no fire, monsters or soldiers, the constant concern for their safety began to wear on them.

When the guilt seeped in, they discussed informing Asher of their fugitive status. If they were captured, he could be arrested for helping them. Iris pushed to tell him the truth, but Foxx resisted, unwilling to completely trust him. It had been nearly a week since they fled the Wilds. Surely if the soldiers continued their pursuit, they would have caught up to them by now. Perhaps they worried for nothing.

Near relentless precipitation had also begun to take its toll, even under the canopy. Iris tried to contain her misery, but on occasion, her partiality to sunshine expressed itself in grumbles and whines. "I am so tired of this rain. My boots are soggy, and my feet have never been so blistered in all the years we've been traveling. And don't even say it Foxx. Even *you* can't enjoy rain this much."

Foxxglove shrugged. "I really don't mind it."

"But it's so sticky and muggy, and I feel like I'll never be dry again!" She stubbed her foot on a lifted root and almost tripped into a pit of mud. Yanking the edges of Mr. Magpie's hat down over her ears, she silently thanked him for his forward thinking. "I don't understand how a normal human—born on *land*—could stand being this sopping wet for days on end. Maybe you would be better suited as a mermaid."

Foxx reached up and ran her fingers along the edge of a leaf bigger than her head. The movement disturbed the droplets so they merged and trickled to the ground. "But can't you see how marvelous the world is when it glistens?"

Asher remained quiet but made no effort to conceal his amusement as he glanced back at them over his shoulder—an action Foxx noticed him doing often.

"Where there is water, there is life. Without it, this jungle could not exist. We couldn't exist. It is a gift that it falls so freely." Foxx held her palms out reverently, allowing the drops to splash against them.

"Leave it to you to find misery in everything *but* the rain."

Foxx's mouth dropped open. "I don't find misery in everything!

You're the one who complains constantly. *It's too hot. It's too dry. It's too wet.*"

Iris scoffed. "And you're like *Everything is hopeless. What's the point of it all? Never trust anyone. Father abandoned us. Mother was crazy—*"

"Iris!" Foxx stopped walking to stare at her sister with wide eyes. Asher looked back at them, pausing his steps without turning around.

Iris realized her harsh and revealing words, and her eyes flashed back and forth between them. "I'm sorry, Foxxglove. I wasn't—"

"It's fine." Foxx began walking, and Iris hurried to catch up.

Grabbing her hand, Iris threw her arms around her. "I'm sorry, Foxx."

Foxx sighed and returned her embrace. "Me, too, Iris."

Asher smiled and continued forward.

The sisters turned and walked side by side on the widened path. Foxx looked up into the trees. "Anyway, my point was: where there is water, there is life. The Wilds is like a grim death. Metsa Sateen is teaming with limitless life."

"The Grim Wilds has life." Iris counted with her fingers. "Lycanox, bats, scorpions, sandhaier, vultures, verivaras, cacti, shrubs, palm trees… to name a few."

"Yes, of course there are things surviving in the desert. I suppose I just cherish the rain. It's revitalizing. It makes me feel alive."

Asher rotated so he walked backward. "Pluviophile." His rifle lay across his shoulders, and both wrists dangled over either end.

Iris eyed him quizzically. "Define your terms."

"A pluviophile is a lover of rain. According to a friend of mine, at least. Though knowing him, he might have made it up to mess with me."

Foxx barely heard the end of his explanation, as she'd recently found herself ensnared by his handsome face shimmering in the rain as he passed through shafts of sunlight. Her eyes latched onto his lips, captivated by the way they moved to form the words she unintentionally tuned out.

This had become a recurring issue.

Shaking away her distraction, Foxx refocused. "You've been awfully quiet today, Asher."

He continued walking in reverse, expertly knowing when to step over the lifted roots on the path. "Just enjoying a peaceful walk through the trees, love."

Foxx's stomach clenched at the pet name, and she scolded it, thinking he probably called many women *love*. But she couldn't help noticing he hadn't used it in reference to Iris even once, and she felt utterly childish for the observation.

Iris said, "I like that. Pluviophile." Asher tipped an invisible hat before twisting around to face front. "I'm going to have to write that down. Though if I ever use it, it will probably be in insult." Iris stuck her tongue out at Foxx, who chuckled.

The day grew hotter as the sun roasted the canopy. Foxx had to keep detaching her tunic from where it clung to her skin in damp patches. Iris' attire hugged her body, so she didn't suffer the same issue, but she did continue complaining about feeling like she'd taken a bath fully clothed in dirty water.

After walking in silence for a time, Foxx said Asher's name. "So, it's been almost a week and you still haven't given us a single clue as to why you're trying to find Celestelvyra."

Asher cast a glance over his shoulder. "That's true."

"Well." She attempted to sound as casual as he did. "Are you going to at some point?"

"I might do."

"How can you expect us to trust you if you don't trust us?"

"You haven't told me why you're traveling to Celestelvyra." He lifted a brow, and her eyes found the ground. "Suppose I'm a nefarious pillager of remarkable and unique antiquities. I hope to find Celestelvyra in order to score some peculiar items to bring back to Arkaemor and trade for a substantial profit." He didn't stop walking or turn to face them as he spoke with total seriousness.

"Or perhaps the love of my life has been stolen away to the Sacred Realm by an evil aristocrat, and I intend to find it so I may be reunited with her, slay the dragon, and free my beloved." Another several moments passed. "Or possibly my mother is mortally ill, and the only possible way to save her is a potion made by a crafty wizard who resides—"

"Okay, okay," Foxx interrupted. "You don't have to tell us."

He cackled, and Foxxglove shook her head. Then he turned to face them, his intense expression aimed at Foxx. "Perhaps for now we can keep our reasonings to ourselves. That way, we will have no cause to lie to each other. What do you think?" She gulped, the vehement look in his eye sending her nerves into chaos.

A woman's scream ricocheted through the trees, followed by the discharge of a shotgun. Shocked into silence, they listened for more sounds of distress, immediately hearing screeching followed by another blast.

"This way." Asher veered off the main trail and onto a small path concealed beneath a layer of dense foliage. Following him, Foxx and Iris bounded over roots and pushed through vines and leaves as they rushed in the direction of the gunfire. More inhuman shrieks reached their ears.

Iris said, "That sounds like monkeys!"

Finally breaking through the trees, they found themselves in a clearing. At the back corner of the alcove sat a charming log cabin with smoke billowing from the chimney. Surrounding the cabin and terrorizing the yard was a horde of angry primates. A man and woman stood on the porch guarding their residence. The woman held a long rifle, and the man, a double-barreled shotgun.

Baboons swung onto the house from high up in the trees. With no obvious reason for their madness, they swarmed the porch, slammed their fists into the rooftop, and tore up the yard. Ripping chunks of wood from the roof and flinging the scraps to the ground, they howled and beat their chests with their fists.

Foxx, Iris, and Asher stood against the treeline taking in the scene. Many of the monkeys were the size of full grown men. Patches of sky blue framed their cherry-red noses, and tan fur surrounded their faces like a mane. When they cried out, their mouths displayed two pairs of lengthy fangs.

Foxx shielded her face from the rain as she gaped at the baboons. "What is happening? I didn't know monkeys behaved this way."

"They're mandrills, but they aren't usually aggressive like this. There must be more than fifty of them!" Asher regarded the sisters before drawing his rifle and entering the yard. Foxx and Iris flanked him with weapons raised.

The mandrills didn't immediately notice the intruders. The woman stayed close to the front door, and the man stood further out on the covered porch, shielding her.

Foxx saw a mandrill atop the awning preparing to pounce. An arrow already set in her bow, she shot it through the skull. It toppled forward, smashing against the ground in front of the porch.

At this, the man and woman spotted the strangers standing in their yard, as did the mandrills. Several split off from the pack and raced toward them.

Iris charged, blades outstretched. A mandrill advanced on her from the left, and she swung Bloom wide, slicing it clean across the throat. Another attacked from straight ahead, vaulting through the air. Iris planted her feet, bracing herself for impact, and plunged Thorn into the animal's chest. Dropping to one knee, she laid the creature on its back and removed her dagger from its carcass. Back on her feet, her ferocity propelled her forward through the muddy grass. Slaughtering the rabid monkeys in her path without pause, she bounded onto the porch. Her eyes lit with enthusiasm as she greeted the young couple. "Lovely morning, don't you think?"

Their shock only lasted a moment before they matched her smile and refocused on the forces swinging toward them. Iris spun to face the oncoming horde. One dropped in front of her, and she stabbed it between its ribs. Persevering despite the wound, the mandrill snapped at her face. Yanking Thorn from its ribcage, she swung Bloom in a horizontal arc and removed its head.

The woman gawked, but the husband's smile grew. "Nice one," he praised. Then he blasted a baboon ascending the steps. It toppled backward as he reloaded his weapon. Moments later, another charged the staircase in front of him. He pulled the shotgun up to fire but wasn't quick enough. The monkey tackled him, slamming his shoulder blades into the porch as it straddled his torso and roared in his face. Throwing its head forward as if to bite his shoulder, the mandrill was met with the barrel of the man's gun shoved horizontally between its teeth. He held the gun away from his body with all his strength, enraging the mandrill further. It screamed, shoving itself more aggressively against him and pounding the wooden planks on either side of his head.

Iris lunged, sliding across the slick porch on one knee and plunging Thorn into the side of the mandrill's head. It froze, stunned rigid, before its whole body slumped on top of the man in a dead heap. He thrust the mandrill off, disgusted, and Iris saw the thankfulness in his expression. As his gaze slid over her shoulder, his appreciation shifted into dread, and she realized she'd left herself open.

A loud bang exploded over her head, ricocheting into her

eardrums and making her drop to the deck. She glanced up at the woman with immense gratitude before hopping back to her feet.

Asher and Foxx stood back to back in the yard three *sylis* from the others. Foxx took out a mandrill running past her on its way to the porch, wondering how they would keep this up with limited ammunition. She didn't know how much Asher had on hand, but the number of monkeys was overwhelming.

Asher eliminated two charging in from the treeline and shot another diving from a nearby branch. Their bodies slumped to the ground, littering the yard with felled corpses. "I hadn't anticipated our first dance to be such a dangerous one, Lady Foxxglove."

Though Foxx couldn't see his face, she could hear the merriment in his tone. She released an arrow that shot through one mandrill and directly into another, causing both creatures to fall. "Clearly you have not been paying attention." A burst of laughter escaped him. "Do you always prefer to dance with women back to back? I'm wondering if I need to make note of it for next time."

"Only when the situation calls for it."

A group of three raced toward them in a triangular formation. Asher shot one through its skull, and it tumbled to the ground, but the others didn't slow. He cocked his rifle, shooting the right flank. When he tried to cock it again, he found the chamber empty. He'd already used the extra magazine in his pocket, so he said Foxx's name, compelling her to take over as he dropped into a crouch and dug through his bag. An arrow struck the last of the three through its left eye, dropping it right at Asher's feet. Blood splattered across his shirt. "Cutting it a little close, love, don't you think?"

"Next time I'll let it get you and call it a day."

"My hero." He stood, sliding the magazine into the chamber and rejoining the fight.

"Will you two please stop flirting during the mad monkey invasion?" Iris called from the porch, to which they both answered *no* simultaneously.

More monkeys fell, but their numbers seemed unending. No matter how many they shot down, more emerged from the trees in an endless swarm.

"There are too many of them," Foxx yelled. "It's as if every mandrill in the jungle has converged on this location!"

"We'll run out of ammunition before we kill them all. I think we need to scare them off." Asher shot two more emerging from the tree line. Foxxglove shot another tearing apart the roof. It rolled down the slope of the building and dropped into a flowering bush in the garden.

"How do you propose we do that?" Iris shouted.

The man on the porch asked, "Any ideas?"

Asher turned and shot a mandrill advancing toward them from the left. "I'm going to need you to cover me again, love." He fell to his knees, not waiting for her response, and rummaged through his pack. Foxxglove widened her arc, flinging arrows in all directions.

A small stack of freshly chopped wood was piled nearby in the yard. Rejects, Asher suspected, since they'd been left out in the rain. They would be soaked through, but he had an accelerant. Grabbing it from his pack along with his firestarter, he moved toward the wood pile.

"Any time now. I'm nearly out of arrows."

He stood holding two planks of wood, each with a ball of fire blazing at one end. Backing up to her with both torches in one hand, he reached into his bag again and pulled out a pistol. Foxx allowed herself a glance away from the yard for a split second to see what he held. Then she fired her last arrow, looped the bow over her shoulder, and grabbed the pistol in one fell swoop. Since she no longer needed both hands to shoot, she also drew the long dagger from the sheath on her hip.

"Do you know how to use it?" he asked.

Foxx cocked the weapon and fired it into an oncoming monkey's heart.

"Beautiful. It only has 6 rounds."

She felt his hand graze her hip as he slid something into her pocket. The unexpected touch made her shiver.

"That's the only other clip, so use them wisely. I'm heading to Iris. Keep covering." Calling Iris' name, he held out the flaming sticks. Before jogging away, he looked back at Foxx. Her face shone with sweat and mist, and her cheeks were pink with adrenaline.

She felt his stare and glanced his way, firing off another shot at a lunging mandrill. "What?"

"In case we don't make it, you should know how much I enjoyed sharing this dance with you." He winked at her, watching her cheeks bloom from soft pink to bright red, and darted toward the house.

Iris leapt from the porch, sheathing Thorn to free one of her hands and catching a flaming plank midair. Then Asher and Iris charged the mandrills, waving their impromptu torches.

Running into a group of four racing across the yard, Asher waved the torch back and forth, shouting raucously. Three of the four backed away in fear, but one leapt at him, fangs bared, and crashed into the end of his torch. Asher shook it to shoo the monkey away, but the flames licked its fur, and the creature caught fire. It squealed and flailed as the flame ignited across its body. Then it flung itself around the yard trying to put the fire out. It howled in agony, but no matter what it tried, the blaze grew bigger.

The other primates saw their comrade's calamity and reacted with trepidation. Noticing their increasing terror, Iris ran at them more forcefully, shouting at them as Asher had. They ran from her at top speed, fleeing the fire.

Foxx and the couple on the porch continued defending, but many of the mandrills had already bolted. The flaming mandrill disappeared into the jungle, leaving the rancid smell of its burning flesh hanging in the air behind it.

Iris and Asher chased the last of them away, and the property grew quiet but for the drizzling rain and heavy gasping as everyone recovered. The trio converged in the middle of the yard, and Iris returned the fiery stick to Asher, who extinguished both in the muddy ground. "Everyone okay?" she asked.

Foxx nodded.

Asher patted himself down as if to check for wounds. "All fine here. You?"

"I'm good." Iris waved her hand in front of her nose to push away the lingering smell.

The couple stepped off the porch, scrutinizing their land and the devastating graveyard of corpses. "Everyone all right?" the man asked, sticking his hand out to shake Asher's. He wore canvas shorts and a shirt with rolled sleeves. A kind smile wrinkled his bearded cheeks. "We may not have made it if you folks hadn't shown up. Seriously. You really saved us." He regarded the yard with repugnance. They all did, unable to pull their eyes from the evidence of the gruesome massacre.

"I'm glad we happened to be walking by. I'm Asher, and this is Foxx and Iris. I've never seen mandrills act that way. Any idea what provoked them?"

Foxx noticed the woman observing Asher curiously as he spoke.

She looked to be in her late thirties, with short spikes of blonde hair sticking out in all directions.

"We've lived here for years and have never been attacked by monkeys. My wife, Runa, was out here digging in the garden, and they swarmed her. I heard her screaming and rushed to her side, but there was no way we were going to get rid of them all without your help. The name's David, by the way."

"Mandrills are not usually hostile unless cornered," Asher said, proving, as always, his extensive knowledge of the rainforest. "I have never heard of them attacking like this before, but there are a lot of things happening in Arkaemor now that don't make sense."

Runa asked, "Would you folks like to come in and have some dinner? It's the least we could do."

Asher consulted his companions, who shrugged. "All right, yes, dinner would be great. Thank you."

David said, "Why don't you ladies head inside and help Rue with the food, and Asher and I will clean up this yard." He looked a question at Asher, wondering if his blatant bribery would take.

Grinning, Asher slugged from his water sleeve. "Sounds good to me, David." Foxx opened her mouth to protest, but he interrupted. "I'll collect your arrows for you. You girls head inside and wash up." He winked at her, prompting a smile in return, and watched them ascend the porch before turning back to David. "Okay, now what are we doing with all of these monkeys?"

CHAPTER 8

NEW DISCOVERIES

Bamboo piping drew rain from the roof into buckets by the front door. Runa dunked her hands and glanced back at Foxx and Iris. "Go ahead and wash up, then dump the bucket when you're finished. It will be full again by tomorrow." The girls followed suit while Runa drew fresh water from a pump at the bottom of the steps.

The inside of the cabin smelled like wildflowers. Removing their boots, they hung their belongings from hooks on the wall inside the front door. To their right, a living room with cushioned furniture, bookshelves, and a smoking hearth drew their attention. Handmade rugs decorated the floor.

The kitchen to the left reminded them of Rossnetta's. Small, but roomy enough, it had a round table at its center with four chairs; a stove with a fire smoldering beneath it; and a sink. A glass of fresh-cut flowers sat atop the table, and the walls had been furnished with bushels and wreaths of dried blooms and greens.

Runa reignited the fire under the cooktop. "David will bring in meat for us. I hope you don't mind mandrill for dinner?"

The thought of a home cooked meal thrilled them both. Iris crossed the room to the table, and Foxx followed after. "I've never had mandrill before, but it sounds fine. What can we do to help?"

"First, we can stew these vegetables. Foxx, take that pot down there and put it on the stove." She pointed to a shelf at the other end of the room. "Fill it with the water on the table and let it heat to a boil. Then take that cast iron skillet and set it next to the pot to warm."

It felt strange being ordered around a kitchen. Memories of her mother emerged: a young Foxx standing on a chair next to Amaryllis stirring soup on the stove. *Every husband needs a wife who can cook. Imagine what your father would eat if we didn't cook for him!*

Smiling at the memory, Foxx did as instructed.

Runa set a basket of vegetables, pungent herbs, and wild onions on the table in front of Iris and handed her a knife. "Iris, you work on chopping these."

When Foxx finished preparing the pans, she joined her sister at the table to ready the produce. Runa got out plates, cups, and utensils. Then she moved to the pot of water and stirred in seasonings from glass jars she kept in a cabinet by the stove. The aroma dispersed throughout the room in the rising steam.

Asher arrived with the meaty parts of two skinned mandrills. To avoid removing his muddy boots, he called to them from the doorway. "It smells delicious in here, ladies. Would someone mind coming to collect this meat?"

Runa rushed to the doorway to greet him, carrying a large bowl. "Ah, thank you, Asher. You can put them right in here." He thanked her and rejoined David outside. Runa made quick work of cleaning meat from bone. Iris and Foxx tossed the vegetables and herbs into the boiling water. Then Runa added the mandrill bones and dropped the meat in the skillet. As the fire died down and the meat began to sizzle, the ladies withdrew from the kitchen and settled themselves in the living room. Foxx and Iris sat next to each other on the two-person couch, and after Runa made sweet water with lemon for each of them, she sat across from them on a rocking chair.

"Should we go see if the men need any help?" Foxx took a sip of her water. "This is really delicious, Runa. Thank you."

"I'm glad you like it. No, the men can handle the monkeys. I'm sure they'll be joining us soon." The rocking chair seemed to swallow the woman, who was petite in every sense of the word. Her calm and pleasant demeanor reminded them of a patient mother, and both sisters wondered why they saw no evidence of children in the home.

Looking around the room, Foxx thought about what it might be like to have a small house of her own somewhere deep in the jungle.

She wondered what her mother's home had looked like when growing up in Sateen and if it had resembled Runa and David's.

She hadn't considered the idea of settling down in a house—or of motherhood—in a very long time. Before she and Iris abandoned their cottage all those years ago, she'd assumed that one day she would find a husband, have a couple of children, and live happily ever after, like the stories in the books she enjoyed so much. Now, the notion seemed almost unreachable. When she entered the wilderness, every day became hyper-focused around survival, and she no longer had the time, nor the energy, for dreaming.

She hoped Iris would have that life someday, if it's what she wanted. They rarely discussed plans for the future anymore, so she really couldn't be sure what her desires were.

Runa returned from stirring the food and interrupted Foxx's ruminations. "It was lucky you were close by today. Do you live in the Metsa?"

Iris shook her head. "No, we're from Alunda, but our mother was born here. She grew up outside of Werifesteria."

"Yes, I can see evidence of a Sateen heritage in you, Foxx. Alunda, you say? Very nice. I have never been, but I've heard it's glorious. A paradise of beaches, am I right?"

"Yes, it is pretty glorious, isn't it Foxx?"

"I miss it." Homesickness swirled in Foxx's belly as it hadn't in ages. Like with everything else that unsettled her, she shoved it away to deal with later. Sometime in the future when she had time for dreaming, perhaps she would have time for healing as well.

"Are you traveling for a particular reason or just to tour the Five Kingdoms?" Runa added another lemon slice to her drink.

Foxxglove answered, "Sightseeing, really. No particular destination in mind." Displeased with how comfortable she'd become lying about their plans, she steered the conversation away from herself and Iris. "Are you originally from here, Runa?"

"David is from the Metsa. I'm from the mountain region of Cordillera, one territory over." Runa pulled her feet up under her and relaxed into the chair. "I noticed your friend's tattoo. Is he from Cordillera as well?"

Foxx and Iris thought for a moment, trying to discern the connection. They knew little of Cordillera besides knowing it was a land of magnificent mountains and deep valleys. "Why would you think that?" Foxx asked.

"Jericho, the City of the Moon, is the royal city of Cordillera." She pointed to her right where a watercolor painting of the symbol tattooed on Asher's wrist hung on the wall. About the size of a hand print, the painting hung at the center of a wreath of dried flowers. "Jericho is where Vali and Ingrid Kirkavall reside, Konungr and Dróttning of Cordillera. I thought he might wear it as a symbol of his home city or territory, but perhaps he just likes the design."

Foxx pondered this. Her mother had taught her about the city of Jericho and the royals who lived there, but she hadn't considered a connection to the city could be the reason for Asher's tattoo. It didn't seem like him to so flippantly choose a design symbolizing a city he didn't hail from. Especially since he displayed it so openly on his wrist. "I'm honestly not sure what it represents."

"Though I wasn't raised there, I have visited the royal city myself a few times. It's enchanting."

"What's it like in Cordillera?" Iris asked.

"It's lovely. A lot of mountains, of course, and the most tantalizing valley with a river running right down the middle. I miss my home territory as well, Foxx, so I understand what you're feeling. It's hard to leave home, even if you do it for the right reasons. And snow! How I miss the snow. It's so much prettier than rain."

Iris eyed Foxx as if to say, *See? Normal people don't love rain.*

Runa went on, missing the playful exchange between the sisters. "I haven't traveled any further west, but I've heard each territory has its own special sort of splendor."

Iris set her empty cup on the table next to her seat and spied a bloody cut on her arm that must have happened during the mandrill attack. She inspected it but decided it was nothing to worry about. "We've gone as far as Savanni but no further west than that. And we weren't in the savanna for very long, so I definitely want to explore it more. They have elephants there!"

Runa chuckled at her enthusiasm. "We have elephants in the jungle as well. Much smaller than the ones in Savanni but still grand."

"I'm excited to see Cordillera. We've never encountered snow before. Maybe we will head there after exploring Metsa Sateen." Foxx didn't know if this was a truth or a lie, but it seemed plausible.

"You will love it. It truly is amazing. Though I might be slightly biased." Runa finished the last of her citrus water and set her cup next to Iris'. "You ladies are sisters, yes? I thought so. You look different but also the same. Know what I mean?"

Foxx said, "Yes, I definitely do. As you pointed out, I have our mother's Sateen traits, but Iris favor's our father's heritage—tanned skin, dark hair, fiery attitude."

"Hey!" Iris crossed her arms in exaggerated offense.

Runa chuckled. "I see. But where did you get that hair, Foxx? I don't know that I've ever seen hair as white as yours."

"We aren't sure about that one." Foxx twirled a lock of it around her finger, peering at it as though the answers to the mysterious color might suddenly make themselves known.

"Well, it's lovely. White as the snow that caps the mountains of Cordillera."

Foxx liked the comparison and grew even more excited to discover snow because of it.

"What about Asher? Not your brother, so… friend? Husband?" Runa glanced at both girls' hands, searching for a wedding band. "I noticed a touch of an accent, didn't I? Though it seems to have faded."

Foxxglove's cheeks brightened. "No, he's just a—" She gaped at Iris, hoping to find a word in the air between them. "Friend? I guess. We're traveling together. A traveling companion, I suppose."

"And yes, he does have a slight accent. It comes out more when he's frustrated, and it's adorable! Don't you think Foxx?" Iris turned to see Foxx's pink cheeks deepen as she mumbled noncommittally.

"Those eyes he has…" Runa gazed off into the distance, as if picturing his face and trying to place it somewhere.

"I know," Foxxglove agreed dreamily, though she recovered quickly, clearing her throat and adjusting herself in her seat.

Runa and Iris giggled. "So perhaps a husband someday?" Foxx shook her head and looked at the floor. Throwing a thumb at Foxx, Iris grinned. Runa laughed and continued to search her memories. "He feels so familiar to me, but I can't place how I recognize him."

"I just have one of those faces." Asher and David stepped into the room. The rain had picked up, and their clothing clung to them in damp patches. Asher's hair had drawn together in spikes that dripped streams of water down his face.

"Towels, Rue?" David asked, and Runa rose to retrieve them from the hall closet. "All the mandrills are taken care of. Skinned a few to cook up and threw the rest in the burn pile. Seems wasteful, but we have no way to preserve them."

"Did you count them?" Iris asked with curious excitement.

"Seventy-two," Asher answered.

"Seventy-two!" the women repeated back in unison.

Runa gaped as she handed them each a towel. "There are seventy-two dead monkeys in my yard?"

"Technically, there are sixty-three in the burn pile, seven hanging naked out back, and two in the kitchen." Asher wiped his face before tossing the towel over his shoulder.

Foxxglove surveyed his cheery disposition, even more pleasant than usual, and was curious as to what might have prompted it. Noticing her looking his way, he directed another wink at her, and she wondered if she would ever get used to his beautiful face. Her lips curled at the corners.

"I cleaned all your arrows and put them back in your quiver, love." He didn't break eye contact with her, as if they alone were in the room. "Not all of them survived, I'm afraid. Two were burned with the carcasses." He bowed his head, feigning mournfulness, accompanied by an overly dramatic sigh.

"Your outstanding consideration is appreciated." She chuckled while internally commanding her stomach to stop fluttering and willing the butterflies to die.

Jovial sadness disappeared, replaced with rascally arrogance. "You asked for slayed monsters, and so I give you slayed monsters." Asher wiggled his brows playfully, and Foxx shook her head at his ridiculousness.

"I think you may have enjoyed the monkey slaughter a little more than is entirely proper, Asher," Iris teased.

Finally setting Foxx free from his gaze, he looked at Iris. "Hey, I never claimed to be proper. And I had a fantastic partner, which made the endeavor even more enjoyable." His eyes flashed back to Foxx, and her cheeks flushed again.

David clapped him on the back. "It was mighty proper, you coming to our aid. And then remaining to help clean up the mess, at that."

"I was promised dinner, so that may have played into the second part."

"Dinner should be ready very soon." Runa scurried from the room to check on the food.

"Thank you dear. Now, Asher, let's finish getting washed up before the food is on."

Asher agreed. "After dinner, we should climb up and patch the roof. They seemed to have done a fair amount of damage up there."

"Do you have experience patching roofs, my friend?" Their conversation faded as they stepped back outside.

Now alone in the room, Foxxglove leaned closer to her sister and spoke low. "Do you think it's strange that Runa recognizes Asher?"

"I think you're overthinking things, as usual. People think they recognize other people all the time. What I'm curious about is whether or not he really does have experience patching roofs. I wonder how he made a living before he began searching for Celestelvyra."

Foxx didn't allow herself the distraction of her sister's tangent, even if she was also curious about that herself. "She mentioned his eyes though. How many people have those rainforest-green eyes?" Her gaze drifted again as she pictured the color: like the verdant leaves of the jungle speckled with golden rays of sunshine.

Iris snapped her fingers in front of Foxx's face. "You have a little drool." She tapped her own lip.

Foxx threw her hand to her mouth, felt nothing there, and realized Iris was making fun of her. "Very nice. All I'm saying is, it's suspicious."

Runa called from the kitchen, "Dinner's on! Come make yourselves a plate."

The men returned and stood barefoot on the rug in the entranceway. Their clothes remained damp, but their skin and hair looked far dryer than the last time they'd entered and they'd wiped away as much mud as the towels could manage.

They ate their soup in the living room, with David and Asher standing by the relit hearth until their clothing dried.

Runa and David asked more questions about their adventures so far and shared their own stories about their lives, how they met, and more about how much Runa missed Cordillera. When she questioned Asher's tattoo, he simply said he liked the design before turning to David and changing the subject.

Before the sun went down, David and Asher ventured back outside to patch up the roof, and when darkness fell, David offered for them to stay the night. "We don't have a lot of room in the house, but there's the barn out back. It'll keep you dry at least, and believe it or not, a cool breeze often blows through there at night."

Foxxglove thanked him for his generous accommodations, and Asher promised they would be leaving at sunrise. After a pleasant *merry night*, Asher led the girls to the small barn at the back of the house. Though more like a roof elevated on two walls rather than an actual building, it did provide a spacious tunnel for the promised breeze to flow.

"There's a fire ring." Iris stopped in front of it. "Do you think they'd mind if we built a fire?"

Foxx claimed her sleeping spot against the piles of dry palm branches lining the right side of the room. "Why do we need one? We've already eaten, and we'll be fairly protected from wildlife in here, don't you think?" Plopping down in the crunchy leaves, she set her bag and bow next to her and began removing her boots.

Iris shrugged. "I like sitting around a fire."

"Tie a rope across there, and we can hang our wet clothes up to dry overnight. I'll build a small fire." Asher situated himself next to the ring at the barn's center and began the process.

"Thank you, Asher." Iris sent Foxx a victorious look of defiance and received an eye roll in return. "I might hang all of my clothing up so everything in my bag is dry before we leave tomorrow. Though I'm not sure why it matters since it will all be damp after an hour of trekking in the rain anyway." Digging through her bag, she retrieved a rope, and Foxx stood to help her string it up.

The fire sparked to life, bringing light to the dim room, previously lit only by the small oil lantern Mr. Magpie had given them.

Asher dug through his bag for fresh clothing, and the girls did the same. Standing on opposite sides of the space, they changed into dry attire before meeting in the middle to fold the wet articles across the line. Iris hung up most of the clothing from her pack, but Foxx and Asher only hung what they'd been wearing that day.

Asher returned to the fire and Foxx to the spot she'd claimed. Iris meandered to the left side of the barn and stared up at the hanging mandrill corpses. She grimaced. "Gross."

"You skin animals all the time." Foxx leaned back against the palms, extending her legs and rolling her feet in a circular motion to stretch her ankles.

"I've never seen a skinless monkey though. Not as big as these, at least. It's not pretty. Too like a human." She gagged, sticking out her tongue in disgust.

Asher smiled as he stoked the fire.

Noticing, Foxx asked, "What are you over there grinning about?" His eyes met hers for a single moment, but he offered no reply. Iris left the dead monkeys and sat down next to him, nudging him playfully in response to something Foxx hadn't heard. She couldn't help feeling a shade of jealousy at how relaxed Iris was around him. From an outward perspective, they might have known each other their entire lives.

Iris held her palms out to feel the fire's warmth, finding the reflex comforting.

Foxxglove played with a dried palm branch in her fingers, her eyes following its long leaves as it spun between them. She said Asher's name, prompting him to lift his head. "Are you from Cordillera?" She didn't look his way as she continued fiddling with her palm branch, attempting nonchalance. Though since he'd already avoided a similar inquiry once that evening, she suspected it wasn't as nonchalant as she hoped.

He crinkled his eyes as if confused by the question. "What makes you think that?"

"Your tattoo. It's a moon, isn't it?"

Asher looked at the circular tattoo on his wrist, then back at her. "It is, yes."

"It looks like the one Runa has hanging on the wall. According to her, it represents the city of Jericho."

"Yes, I saw the picture on the wall."

"You're doing that vaguely cryptic thing again," Iris pointed out. He chuckled and went back to stoking the fire.

Foxx gave up the inquisition and instead mused, "That ordeal with the mandrills today was insane." She dropped the palm leaf and put her hands behind her head as she stared up into the wooden rafters.

"Things like this will continue to happen more and more as time goes on." Asher put down his fire poker, and Foxx noted that he seemed far more interested in this conversation than in discussing his body art. Though why get body art on your wrist if you didn't plan on discussing it?

"What do you mean by that?" Iris retrieved her journal and a pencil from her pack and began drawing a savage mandrill.

Asher reached into his own bag and pulled out a leather-bound book similar to Iris'. Holding it next to hers, he said, "Look at this. Proper close, huh?"

"Wow! They're so similar. You have great taste."

"Why, thank you." He grinned and dipped his head.

"What do you use yours for?"

"It's my diary, and you keep your hands off it." He grinned, but she thought he probably meant it, so she vowed not to touch it. "What's yours?"

"More of a journal, I guess. I like to keep track of things. So it's not so much a daily log of personal thoughts as it is a collection of information. Maybe I'll show you sometime, but right now, I want to circle back to what you just said." The smoke rolling off of the freshly lit fire blew toward her and burned her eyes. Holding her book in front of her face, she tried to block the fumes. Unsuccessful, she used the book to fan the smoke away until it dispersed, thinning out and lifting high into the rafters. "That is *so* annoying."

Asher laughed. "What I mean is… the animals of Arkaemor, many of them aren't what they should be, and as time goes on, they continue to degenerate."

"Explain *aren't what they should be.*"

Adjusting himself into a more comfortable position, Asher cleared his throat. "So it's like this: though many animals were created with the traits we think of as predatory: sharp teeth, venom, claws, et cetera, some of the creatures roaming Arkaemor weren't part of the original design for creation. They were born… altered. Mutated, corrupted, and monstrous. They essentially aren't real. Tangible, yes, but fake. False. A nieda is similar to a spider. A lycanox is a wolf that shares traits with a bull or an ox. Verivaras are human-sized bats. None of these creatures reproduce like all other living things, and though they're kindred to animals, they aren't actually members of what scholars would consider the animal kingdom. These monsters are in a category of their own. "

Foxxglove sat up, intrigued by the conversation. "And how could you possibly know what the original design for creation looked like?"

"Because I am ravishingly handsome, and as a result, very knowledgeable people tell me things."

Foxx noticed his cocky deflection but didn't let it dissuade her curiosity. "But were the mandrills regular mandrills or were they some extra large, super hostile, hybrid with some other creature?"

He considered her question. "They were normal, I think. They looked normal, at least. No extra limbs or anything. But as I said earlier, I've never known mandrills to act that way, so ruthlessly when completely unprovoked."

Iris finished her drawing and wrote *Mutated Mandrill (… possibly)* at the top of the page. Then she jotted down some details about the things she witnessed and their abnormalities. "So what is causing the creatures to change? Why are they going against the grain of their original design?" She made air quotes with her fingers around the last two words.

Asher looked over her shoulder at the journal, and she angled it so he could see it better. He seemed impressed by her drawing abilities and amused by her notes. "I don't know. But I do know it will continue getting worse unless something happens to alter the current path."

"How do we alter it?" Iris asked.

Shrugging, Asher returned his attention to the fire. "I'm not sure."

Foxxglove sensed him holding something back and was about to push him further when Iris said, "Well, that's enough philosophical talk right before bedtime, don't you think?" She frowned at him. "Thanks a lot, Asher. Now I'll never get to sleep."

"Hey, we are in this together now. We protected each other today, and we'll keep doing that as long as we have to, all right?" He locked eyes with both of them individually, and they nodded, though Foxx couldn't help feeling overwhelmed by his transparent assumption that they would be sticking together long-term. His instantaneous attachment felt so bizarre, as if they were reunited long-lost friends who happened to forget ever knowing each other.

Exactly how long did he expect them to be *in this together*? Until they reached the waterfall? Until they found Celestelvyra? Forever? In a way, his adamance unnerved her, but she also couldn't deny the way her foolish heart trembled with anticipation of what might come next.

"Good. Now I'm going to sleep." Asher strode over to the palm leaves and laid down several feet from where Foxx had made her bed.

Iris moved to Foxx's other side, laying down right next to her. "Love you," she told her sister.

"You were very brave today." Foxx rolled onto her side to face her. "And I love you, too."

Overhearing their interaction, Asher smiled to himself, and within a few minutes they all drifted off to dreamland.

CHAPTER 9

TREE OF KNOWING

The trio rose early and departed David and Runa's around sunrise. The previous evening, they'd asked if the couple had a map of Metsa Sateen or if they'd ever heard of a waterfall in Sadella with a giant tree at the top. The couple didn't have a map, but David knew of a tree-topped waterfall he'd visited as a child. He couldn't recall its name but remembered following a river running north to get there, which they hoped might prove useful.

With that in mind, they hit the trails walking at a northern angle toward the rising sun. They traveled as before, hiking during the day for as long as their legs would carry them, then finding a place to camp just before nightfall.

Unlike the vast, open lands they'd grown accustomed to, each trail in the jungle compelled them to travel in whatever direction it pleased. When they came to a divided path, they had to choose which side of the split to take. Sometimes the decision was obvious. Other times, not so much.

As the days progressed, Foxx began to grow more suspicious of Asher's integrity. She got the feeling he constantly knew which direction they should travel and suspected when he asked for their opinion, he only played at uncertainty. He seemed wholly acquainted with the jungle's topography, as if naturally familiar with how the trail twisted and turned, though he claimed never to have traveled their particular pathway before. She speculated it might be his fantastic tracking ability enabling him to interpret the path ahead and prepare for what came next, but her intuition warned otherwise.

At one point, they found a metropolis of at least twenty beehives towering above them in the canopy. Asher reacted with amazement, but his expressions felt artificial, as if he'd already known it existed, and it didn't actually surprise him at all.

Foxx thought it possible he'd witnessed so many wonderful things on his travels that a city of beehives didn't impress him, but then why pretend to be so utterly fascinated? Why fake his excitement? Why fake anything at all?

A similar feeling of mistrust arose when they came to a downed bridge spanning a stream too deep to cross on foot. Though Asher expressed worry over how they might get to the other side, he soon led them to a pathway of rocks crossing a thinner stretch of the stream not far off the trail.

Things of this nature continued to occur, and the sensation of constant deception began to wear on her, chiseling away at whatever fragment of a bond had grown between them. Previous doubts and suspicions returned in full force, and the wall she'd allowed to slowly crumble rose again. All along, the plan had been to keep him at a distance. His kindness and charm had sucked her in, but too many signs pointed to him being a liar. Hiding—practically everything—and maybe even playing them for fools.

Her inner chant became *arms length*, and she clung to it with fervor.

A week after departing David and Runa's it began to storm. For three full days the sky rampaged with peels of thunder, shocks of lightning, and destructive winds, leaving them little opportunity to interact. The trail became muddy, and the near constant torrent made travel too dangerous to press on. After the second day, they remained in a shelter beneath the roots of two conjoined trees, deciding to endure there until the storm passed.

Though trapped in a tight space together, the tempest made it almost impossible to hold a conversation, so they kept to themselves and did their best to rest until it passed.

On the fourth day, the storm ceased and the rain returned to its usual pitter-patter as it drizzled through the canopy. Rising early, they continued on, eager to make up for lost time. They hiked all through the morning and didn't stop to eat until long after highsun. Just off the trail, they found a small clearing cut in half by the trunk of a felled tree. Much of the bark had crumbled away, leaving a smooth surface for them to rest comfortably.

Asher harvested fruit to eat with the mixed nuts left over from Kesken Ala. They'd eaten through the cheese and most of the dried fruit and only had a handful of jerky left. That night when they built a fire, they would heat up the last of the mandrill meat Runa gave them, so unless they came upon a shop or crossed paths with a merchant, they would soon be hunting for their meals.

Asher handed each of them a round fruit with goldenrod skin and spikes all over it.

Iris examined it eagerly before asking, "What is it?"

"It's a pitahaya. Also known as yellow dragon fruit. It's sweet, almost like a kiwi. Have you ever had kiwi?"

"No we haven't." Distain seeped into Foxx's tone. So far, her plan to maintain distance hadn't been very successful. Asher remained persistent for her attention, forcing her to resort to direct incivility.

Facing her, Asher smiled. "Well, that is a tragedy in itself, love, because kiwis are delicious." Foxx turned the fruit over in her hand. White hair hung in a curtain between them, concealing her scar and irritated expression. His kindness continued, despite her rudeness. "Do you want me to show you how to eat it?"

Foxx peeked at him through the wall of her hair. His stuck out at all angles, stiff and unwashed. He'd changed his shirt from one with buttons to a tunic with a split down his chest and a thin rope strung back and forth between holes on either side. The lighter linen, cream instead of mossy green, offered a significant contrast against his tanned skin, especially where the sleeves cut across his biceps.

Foxx had been struggling to ignore the enticing visual since the moment he put it on. "I think I can figure it out myself." If her distant tone upset him, she didn't glance his way again to find out.

Iris glowered at her and tapped Asher's shoulder. "You can show me, Asher."

The lighthearted smile erased by Foxx's ill-mannered words returned as Asher spun to Iris, who sat on his opposite side, and asked for a knife. She handed back the fruit and one of the throwing knives strapped across her torso.

Mimicking the motions as he spoke, he explained, "You can peel the skin off and cut up the fruit inside." He sliced the knife through the thick skin, demonstrating how it could be peeled away. "Or, the easiest way in my opinion is to cut the whole thing in half and scoop it out with a spoon." He cut it down the middle and handed her one of the halves.

Auburn eyes sparkled as she inspected the strange flesh inside. Pale gray, the flesh was littered with tiny, black seeds. Her enthusiasm faltered and her nose scrunched up in distrust. "It kind of looks like... there are bugs in it."

Asher laughed. "I promise it doesn't taste like bugs." Holding up his index finger, he cut off what he knew would be her next sentence. "And yes, I *do* know what bugs taste like."

Iris squirmed. "Gross!"

Foxx remained silent throughout the entire interaction, slicing her pitahaya in half and spooning out the center, like she'd overheard Asher instruct.

As Asher distracted himself combing his bag for a spoon, Iris eyed her sister with scrutinizing eyebrows. Foxxglove's brows moved in the opposite direction, high up her forehead in innocence, as if she had no idea why her sister might be scolding her.

Asher handed Iris a spoon. "Trust me. You're going to love it."

Foxx rolled her eyes and mumbled something incoherent.

Iris glared at her. "What is wrong with you?"

"Nothing," Foxx snapped back.

"Clearly." Iris blew hair away from her face in frustration.

Asher stayed mute, feeling marginally frightened sitting between two quarreling sisters, especially ones with a plethora of weapons at their disposal and the skills to use them. He cleared his throat and rose from his seat. "I'll be right back."

As he hastened out of sight, Iris pushed her fist into her hip. "Seriously, what is going on? I thought we liked Asher now."

"We do."

"Then I ask yet again, why are you being so mean to him?"

Foxx stared at the half-eaten fruit in her hands. "I'm not trying to be. He's just so pushy. I'm attempting to keep my distance, but he won't take the hint."

Iris' accusations faded into apprehension. "Why?"

"Because as time goes on, things keep happening that make me question his true motives. I don't trust him. I want to. I mean, I *really* want to." She sighed, finally meeting Iris' gaze. "But I don't. I know he's hiding something big—something important—and I'm terrified of what it might be."

Iris had also been wondering what could be so bad that he refused to be honest with them about it. Though they'd known him just under three weeks, their constant and pleasant interactions left her feeling a significant friendship blossoming between them. So why wouldn't he open up about whatever he kept hidden? The only plausible explanation was that he suspected they might run if they found out the truth.

Though in his defense, they had yet to reveal their secret to him, either.

Iris observed her sister, and the expression on her face had her words ringing true. Foxx really *did* wish she could trust Asher without a shadow of a doubt. Maybe more than she'd ever wanted to trust anyone.

Still, Iris couldn't help but wonder if the reasons behind her resistance had more to do with her own fears than Asher's secrecy. "Are you positive a lack of trust is the real issue here?"

"What else would it be?" Foxx crinkled her brow.

Iris kept her suspicions to herself and stood, keeping her dragon fruit in her hand as she shouldered her pack. "We know he isn't telling us everything, but he's been good to us, Foxx. Maybe he isn't always sincere, but can't you see the genuineness in him, too? Maybe we should trust that whatever he's hiding, he has a good reason for it. Or, if you feel that strongly about it, we can go our separate ways. Nothing says we have to stay with him all the way to Lacuna Kaput. But if we do decide to stay, I don't think it's fair of you to keep treating him like this. It hurts his feelings when you snap at him."

"I'm not trying to snap at him. If he wasn't so pushy and over-bearing, then I wouldn't have to—"

"Are you ladies ready to move on?" Asher reappeared in the clearing, picking up his pack and taking a drink of his water.

Foxx said, "Fine," just as Iris said, "Sure!"

Asher looked from one to the other and back again. "All right, let's hit the road."

C

Several hours later, they stopped by a crystal-clear stream to fill their water sleeves. The day had grown hot and muggy without the rain to cool them, a fact Foxx gleefully threw in Iris' face since she always griped about the rain. Iris responded by sticking out her tongue.

Little had been said aside from that since they stopped for luncheon. Asher had attempted to start a dialogue multiple times before giving up, deciding that walking in silence was better than direct rejection.

The stream had an unexpected chill to it. Water cascaded in charming pathways, tumbling over tree branches and trickling through rocks as it carved its descent. Allowing one of the small falls to pour into her cupped palms, Iris splashed water in her face. "What I wouldn't give for a bath."

"Actually, that's not a bad idea. The stream should be safe to rinse off in. It won't be as dangerous as a river at least, and who knows when we might come across another one this size." Asher knelt at the stream's edge, scooping water directly into his mouth before pouring handfuls in his face and down the back of his neck. Foxx already had her boots off and was dipping her feet in the current downstream.

"Oh, yeah. That's happening." Iris rose to her feet and loosed her pack from her shoulders. "We can take turns. I'm going first."

Asher stood, shaking beads of water from his hair. He slid a hand over his head, pushing damp locks from his face. "Check yourself before you get dressed. Make sure there aren't any weird stream creatures on you."

Iris paused in the middle of removing her torso sheath. "Is that something I should be concerned about?"

"It's a clean stream, but it's still the jungle. We'll hang out by the trail and make sure no one bothers you." Without waiting for Foxx, Asher veered back toward the trail and disappeared from sight.

Iris stood with her hands on her hips, squinting impatiently at Foxx, who pretended not to notice until Iris obnoxiously cleared her throat.

"Can't I just stay?" Foxx whined from her comfortable spot in the grass. "It's not like I haven't seen you bare before."

"No, you cannot. I would like a few minutes to myself. Go stand with Asher and be nice." She shooed her sister away with her hands.

Foxx grumbled and stepped from the water. "I'm leaving my boots and bag here."

"Fine."

"Fine!" Foxx growled and made her way back to the trail. When she emerged from the brush, she saw Asher reclined against a tree with his arms crossed over his chest. He grinned at her, and she rolled her eyes, crossing her own arms. Despite their similar stance, she didn't feel nearly as casual or relaxed as he appeared.

"Everything all right?"

"Everything's fine." Foxx turned away from him, facing east and staring down the trail. It narrowed up ahead, overgrown with foliage.

After a minute or so, Asher asked, "What did you think of the pitahaya?"

Without looking his way, she contemplated the narrowness of the trail, lifted roots, leaves and vines hanging above the path—pretty much anything within eyesight to distract her attention. "It was fine." He reiterated her monotone words under his breath, and her head snapped to him, brows knitting together. "What did you say?"

"Nothing."

She sighed, turning away again.

Then he said, "I don't understand what happened."

Foxx rotated her whole body to face him without relaxing her arms. "What do you mean?"

He paused, debating internally how much to push. "I mean, are we really back to this? I thought we were…" His words reflected his dejection as he left his sentence open-ended and dragged his gaze away. "Never mind."

The smile she loathed was replaced with a heartbreaking frown as he retreated into his thoughts, and she suddenly realized she hated the frown even more than his arrogant grin. She took a step toward him, her feet moving of their own volition. Detecting the movement, his eyes shifted back to hers, struggling to convey all the things he couldn't speak.

She decided to provide him with a little transparency. Maybe then he would be willing to open up about all the things he kept concealed. Or at the very least, maybe they could meet in the middle on some common ground. "Look, I…"

The moment she reached for that transparency, anxiety and insecurities swallowed up her words. She didn't know how to articulate that she needed to protect herself. And her sister. How could she explain that the mortifying intensity she felt for him shook her to her core? That she feared letting him in only to have her suspicions confirmed.

Long ago, she'd learned to be sparing with trust, and she couldn't help but worry that her brewing feelings would cloud her judgment if she let her guard down. In many ways, they already had.

In her head, she repeated the words over and over: *Arms length, arms length, arms length.*

"It's fine, Foxx. You don't need to say anything. I understand completely." Though his tone did not indicate he understood anything at all.

"Fine."

Another silent minute passed. Foxx suspected Iris was taking her time, intentionally forcing Foxx into an uncomfortable situation.

Unhitching from the tree, Asher took a step toward her. "You know what?" Fire returned to his voice and hopelessness drained from his eyes, replaced with an alarming determination that weakened her knees. "It's actually not fine. I want to know. What have I done? Why are you so hot and cold with me?"

"I'm not hot and cold." Foxx attempted to ignore the electric currents sizzling in the shrinking space between them, vibrating her fingertips and scattering goosebumps up her arms.

"Yes, you are." He took another step closer. Her skin grew hot in his nearness, though her fingertips became painfully cold. "I've been nothing but kind and helpful and respectful to both you and your sister. Haven't I proven I can be trusted?"

"You lie to us every single day, Asher." Foxx refused to allow his closeness to make her recoil, or worse, surrender to her own longings. Though with him standing so close, she found herself having a difficult time focusing on anything past the smell of his warmed skin: woodsy, but not like the trees around them. Something sweeter. A scent she recognized but couldn't place.

"We know essentially nothing about you. You keep it all hidden and out of reach. We don't know where you're from or why you're in Metsa Sateen. How you just happened to run into us en route to Celestelvyra of all places. We don't know if you have siblings, parents, friends, a wife, children." As she realized the length of the list of mysteries, her voice grew progressively angrier. "How did you make a living before your search began? How do you know so much about so many things? What are your hobbies? I don't even know how old you are!"

Again, he seemed to argue with himself, as if tugged in two directions. Finally, patient words spoke low in the space between them. "You haven't exactly been honest with me either, love." His hand lifted from his side, pushing her hair behind her ear and exposing the jagged scar carved into her face. Her breath hitched as she averted her eyes, unable to accomplish much else as his fingers grazed the outer cuff of her ear, the length of her jaw.

"I understand you know little about my past, but can't my present be enough for now? I wish you would stop pulling away from me. I wish I understood what you're so afraid of. Every time it seems like you're drawing closer, you switch directions and run."

His hand dropped to her hip and his fingertips rested gently against the fabric of her tunic.

"I'm afraid you aren't what you appear to be." The blood pulsing in Foxx's ears drowned out the ambiance of the forest. "I'm afraid the things you hide must be awful, because otherwise, why wouldn't you just tell us?"

"Someday I'll tell you everything, love." His fingers crawled the top hem of her pants, slowly creeping around her back as though he intended to pull her against him. "But for now, I'll answer one of your many questions." With his arrogant grin securely back in place, he said, "I'm twenty-eight." Fingers tickling the fabric at the small of her back sent new ripples of electric heat radiating from the point of contact.

She wondered if he could feel the charged energy coursing between them, threatening to shatter her from the inside out. He whispered her name, and she nearly crumbled to the ground. Her gaze became entrapped by the gold flecks dancing within his irises. No words came to her. Oxygen eluded her.

Iris materialized from the bushes, her hair hanging free of the pony and dripping wet. "Who's next?"

Foxx and Asher split apart like an explosion.

Iris paused mid-step and looked back and forth between them. "What's going on here?"

The cheekiness in her tone made Foxx want to smack her. "I'm next." She darted off into the trees before Iris could say anything else.

Iris eyed Asher, still wearing her cheeky smile. "What did you do?" He chuckled and shrugged, but his grin was answer enough.

C

Foxx didn't stop until she reached the stream. When she arrived at the water's edge, she released the breath she'd been holding, intertwined her fingers together on top of her head for maximum lung expansion, and sucked in several mouthfuls of air.

What was she doing? What in the world had she been thinking?

Hadn't she just decided to keep her distance?

"Utter failure," she mumbled to herself, sighing as she began removing each article of clothing until she stood completely bare. Gazing out at the surrounding forest, she checked for peeping eyes, feeling nervous in her vulnerability. She picked up her bow and set it within reach along the bank.

The water felt like ice in contrast to her sultry skin, but her body soon acclimated to the shift in temperature. She situated herself on a flat rock within the stream. The current flowed around her, caressing the skin of her lower half. The surface licked her stomach above her navel as it swirled past in spiraling ripples.

She drew water up her body, letting it drizzle down her neck and shoulders. Leaning back, she allowed her head to fall behind her so the current could soak her hair. She thought it possible nothing had ever felt as good as that ordinary stream washing away the tension harassing her sore muscles. Immediately following that thought, her mind offered an alternative memory to disprove it, and she recalled the feel of Asher's fingers at her side. Flushing hot, she dunked her face below the surface, washing the recollection away in the cold water.

When she remerged, she saw a pale blue lepenna perched on a rock on the shore. The winged rabbit observed her curiously, sniffing the air and flicking its thin tail around the base of the rock. Feathered wings faded to white at the tips, just like its long ears, and tiny antlers extended from the top of its head.

Foxx leaned closer to get a better look at the creature she'd only ever read about. According to her mother, they were native to the Metsa, though a similar but larger breed could also be found in

Savanni. The rabbit tilted its head, and Foxx smiled. "Hello." Then the lepenna shot into the air and disappeared in the trees. "Well it was nice meeting you, too," she called after it with a sigh.

After several minutes, she pulled herself from the stream and stood in the mossy grass along the shore. Shaking her body, she let the air dry her—as much as humid, muggy air could dry a person. Then she slipped back into her clothes and rejoined Iris and Asher on the trail.

Her movements in Asher's peripherals drew his eyes, and his smile widened at the sight of her, sending her heart aflutter. "I suppose it's my turn now." He stepped too close as he walked past, and Foxx managed little more than a quick nod as he disappeared into the trees at her back.

Iris crossed her arms, eyes lit with accusation. "So, anything you want to tell me?" She lifted a brow.

"No." Foxx fidgeted with the bow hanging over her shoulder.

"When I arrived, it looked like he was about to kiss you!" Iris grabbed Foxx by the shoulders and shook her enthusiastically.

Foxx shushed her, waving her hands in the air. "Seriously, do you have to be so loud?"

"Sometimes."

"He will hear you!"

Iris attempted to contain her squeal. "So he *did* almost kiss you."

"No! He didn't almost—" Foxx lowered her voice as if to prevent the forest from hearing the secret emotions her words might divulge. "—kiss me."

"Sure looked like it from where I was standing."

"I wish I had something to throw at you."

Iris wrapped an arm around her sister's shoulder and squeezed. "I love you, too, Foxxglove."

C

Over the next three days, the trio covered a lot of ground. Bathing in the stream had rejuvenated their spirits and energized them to press forward, even more eager now to find the waterfall and the next clue.

Since entering Sateen, they hadn't seen a single soldier. This encouraged Iris, but Foxx couldn't get past her worry at why they weren't being chased. It had been three weeks since they crossed over from Kesken Ala. With the King's Legion posting their pictures up all over town and harassing citizens in the early hours of the morning, surely they hadn't given up their pursuit when the sisters fled to the jungle. So where could they be?

Foxx didn't know much about the politics of the Five Kingdoms, but she knew the Legion had jurisdiction throughout all seven territories regardless of which royal family ruled there.

Metsa Sateen being one of the larger territories, she thought it possible the soldiers had taken a different route at some point. Read the tracks wrong and veered south when they should have veered north, or something similar.

Iris pressured her to stop fretting about it and focus on the task at hand, insisting if they ran into soldiers, they would deal with it then.

They currently traveled in a denser section of the jungle. The air smelled almost salty in its dampness, and the shade from the heavy trees above left them feeling cool in the light mist. Iris had her hair down from its usual tail on top of her head and was running her fingers through long, dark locks as they walked.

They stopped for a spell to rehydrate and make a plan for the evening. The plan would be the same as every other night, but Asher always liked to announce when the time came to start scoping out a place to camp.

They stood in a triangle, Foxx and Asher swigging water while Iris stretched her back, twisting from side to side before pulling one knee at a time to her chest.

"Where did you get that white streak in your hair?" Asher asked, sparking conversation. Iris ran her fingers over it.

Foxx said, "It's been there since she first grew hair. She was born totally bald." Iris looked shocked, her hands flying up to either side of her head. "But when her hair started growing in, there was a solid white patch amongst the black."

"Interesting." Asher reached out to pinch the streak. "You know, it's almost like she has a bit of you with her at all times." He motioned to Foxx's hair, which matched the streak in Iris' perfectly.

"I never thought about it like that!" Iris exclaimed.

Asher looked up through a break in the canopy. "It's getting dark. We should make camp soon. Keep your eyes peeled for a spot." The sisters shared a small smile but didn't comment on his predictability.

Asher and Foxx began walking side by side on the widened path. Iris remained stationary a minute longer, flipping her hair upside down and shaking it out before pulling it into a pony. Swishing it back and forth as it draped to the ground, she pulled her fingers through the tacky strands, trying to work the knots free.

Before straightening, she spotted a soft light glowing from somewhere deep in the darkening forest. Squinting as she stood, she tossed her hair over her head, ruining the effort she'd put into detangling. She stepped to the edge of the trail to get a better view through the dense trees and called out to Foxxglove and Asher, requesting they come back and check it out.

"What could that be?" Foxx wondered aloud as the three of them stood on the fringes of the trail, peering out into the swelling darkness.

"Want to go find out?" A hint of adventure permeated Asher's voice.

"It's getting pretty dark," Foxx said, ever the adult. The moon was nearly new as the month of Susi slid into London and would offer little light once twilight ebbed from the sky.

"We want to camp off trail anyway," Iris pointed out.

Foxx shrugged. "It's probably someone's house, right?"

"You two can wait here if you want, but I'm going to check it out." Asher stepped off the trail, drawn toward the light. After a shared look of hesitancy, the girls followed him.

The luminescence began small, a tiny glowing lantern off in the distance. As they drew closer, they realized the light originated from something bigger than a house lantern.

"It doesn't look like firelight." Asher pushed his way through thick, off-trail vegetation. "It's white. Maybe even blue?"

"What could create that color of light besides the moon?" Iris' boots crunched through foliage he'd already stamped down.

As they stepped from a thicket of trees into a bright clearing, the source of the light became immediately clear. In the heart of the glade stood a magnificent weeping willow radiating a velvety, cerulean aura. Its sturdy trunk sprouted asymmetrically from the earth and grew thinner as it rose, though at no point could it be labeled frail or flimsy. It was massive. From the boughs branching off the main stalk, thousands of thin shoots grew, drooping like a cascade of falling rain. The dense crown shot threadlike branches covered in rows of long, narrow leaves toward the ground. The boughs swayed as if propelled by the wind, though the air in the glade was entirely still.

Foxx's mouth fell open in amazement, but all she managed to get out was a whispered, "Wow."

"I've heard of this place." Asher's tone became soft and reverent. "The Tree of Knowing. It's said it can show you your life: past, present, and future."

Iris advanced on the willow, letting her pack fall to the grass. "How does it work?"

"It has something to do with the weeping branches, but I wouldn't get too close." Asher reached for her arm and missed, and she continued on, ignoring him as if in a trance. "Iris, I've heard of people driven mad by the things the willow manifests. Stay back."

Iris didn't listen, mesmerized by the intense evocation as the summoning tree invaded her senses. She moved toward it, one small step after another until standing beneath the swaying branches. A feeling of unimaginable peace bloomed in her heart. She looked up into the dome where tiny creatures glided in loops and spirals. The green light shining from them made it hard to perceive their exact shape, but as they flitted past, intrigued by the visitor, Iris caught a few glimpses of iridescent wings.

Then the tree's leaves fluttered, their vibrations humming like a thousand butterflies all flapping at once. A familiar voice whispered her name in the wind. Her mother's?

Holding up her hand, she grazed the leaves with the back of her arm, introducing herself. The whips twisted tenderly around it, embracing her, saying hello. They wove their way through her fingers and up her arm. Several more drifted toward her, grazing her shoulder, entwining her hair, and wrapping around her other arm as she lifted it to greet them.

Her lids fell closed as the tree formed a stream of vivid images inside her mind: Iris as a child picking hibiscus in the garden; dancing on her mother's toes in their tiny kitchen; Foxx combing her hair with her favorite brush; running into her father's arms as he walked through their front door in his Legion uniform; building tall sandcastles with Foxx on the beach; splashing in the crystal blue waves; her mother singing her to sleep; the seashell necklace she'd given her for her 12th birthday.

Iris sucked in a breath as sadness crept into the memories. The whips hugged her tighter, washing her in calming peace. Even as more traumatic memories surfaced, they didn't swallow her in misery: her mother crying, raving, throwing things; glass shattering; Foxx squeezing her tight in the dark; her father screaming; chasing her mother as she dragged Foxx into the sea; her mother's chalk white face, vomit on the bathroom floor as Foxx pushed her out of the room; her father's promise to return soon.

A tear ran down her cheek, and she felt an arm around her waist, but the visions kept coming. Faster and faster they floated through her mind like a slideshow of pictures from her whole life: two niedas on the beach; soldiers destroying their home; traveling Alunda; the kind fisherman who fed them when they were starving; Maeve in Savanni; the building in the Wilds, the dark corridor; the men they met in the desert; Mr. Magpie laughing; Seth hugging her; running from soldiers; Asher's smile; Foxxglove's blushing cheeks; laughter, fire, blood, skinned mandrills in the barn; a lovely stream of crystal clear water.

A gathering of children; an abandoned building; crossing blades with Foxx; a raindrop carved into an old desk; a city glistening in the treetops; enchanting flowers; anger, fear, fighting; plummeting off a cliff into a bewitching lagoon; mountains; a gorgeous valley; a land covered in white.

Then, a city on fire; people screaming and running frantically through the streets; dead bodies strewn across the cobblestone; a beast flying through the air; a hooded figure at the center of the blaze; a woman who could be none other than the Queen of Arkaemor, her countenance filled with fury; Foxx on the ground with blood spilling down her face; the younger man from the desert pulling her away from Foxx's limp form.

Iris' eyes snapped open as she yanked her arms from the branches. They remained gentle, letting her pull away with ease. Not a single leaf broke from the vine despite her anxious tugging. The peace she'd felt when the tree held her left the moment it released. Foxx hugged her. Asher stood next to them, concern painted across his features.

Turning to embrace her sister, her head fell onto Foxx's shoulder as sobs wracked her whole body. All the overwhelming sadness and fear she'd experienced momentarily consumed her. Foxx squeezed her tight. Asher put his hand on her back, his eyes lifting to the retreating tree spirits, now floating high up in the boughs.

When Iris' weeping settled, she pulled away from her sister, appearing more vulnerable than ever before.

"What did you see?"

Iris wiped the tears from her cheeks and pressed the heels of her palms into her eyes, wishing to scrub the images from her brain. She drew in a deep breath, held it, and released. "I saw our past: Mother, Father, us as children. Snapshots from our whole life. I saw Seth and Mr. Magpie and the men from the desert and you." She glanced at Asher. "And the mandrills and so many things I didn't understand. A city on fire. The Queen."

She chose not to mention her sister bleeding on the ground or Declan, so aloof and cold when they'd met, looking the epitome of concern as he dragged her away from her fallen sister.

Facing Asher, she asked, "Are the things I saw only possibilities or are they set in stone?"

Asher shrugged. "The lore isn't clear, so I honestly don't know. You are brave for confronting it, Iris. I'm afraid to."

Foxx cleared her throat. "I think we've had enough emotional stimuli for one night. Asher, do you think it's safe to make camp here by the light of the tree?"

"I'll leave you two to talk while I get things set up." He lifted Foxx's bag from her shoulders before crossing the clearing and leaving them alone.

Iris put her hands on her head, interlacing her fingers. Foxxglove pushed her sister's white streak behind her ear and wiped a rogue tear from her cheek. "Are you all right? You don't have to talk about it if you don't want to."

"I'm okay. I just need to breathe." She inhaled a breath and exhaled slowly. "It was… beautiful. But also intense and so bizarre. The future things were scary and too vague to truly understand. I imagine that's how you feel about the vision you had in the Wilds. As though you know something bad is about to happen but have no idea how to go about preventing it."

Foxx thought that must have been how their mother often felt. Did her insanity spawn from living in constant fear of a fragmented future? Foxx brushed those speculations aside, not having the energy to delve into more thoughts of visions and mothers. "If you want to talk more about it, I will listen." She glanced over Iris' shoulder to where Asher worked. He had their beds already made up and didn't bother building a fire.

The space was so still, unbelievably silent in comparison to the rest of the jungle, as if not a single living creature roamed anywhere near the glowing glade. Not even the chirping and titters of night-time insects reached their ears.

Foxx wrapped her arm around Iris' waist, and together they joined Asher at the campsite. With few exchanged words, the three laid down and quickly drifted to sleep, lulled by the rustling sound of kissing leaves.

CHAPTER 10

ATARAXIA

Over the next week, things settled back into what had become their normal routine. Iris needed as many days for her bubbly self to return. Foxx could sense she hadn't completely recovered from all she'd encountered at the Tree of Knowing, but Iris insisted she was fine, and Foxx knew better than to push it.

After much deliberation, Foxx acknowledged the senselessness of remaining hostile toward their male companion. Civil unity not only made things more comfortable but safer for everyone.

By the first quarter of London, they'd spent an entire month together. One month since he'd heroically saved them from the nieda. Her suspicions about the truths he kept hidden hadn't vanished, but the more time they spent together, the more she found herself trusting him. She couldn't help it. Even within the tangles of his web of mystery, she sensed his reasons were pure of heart.

She did worry about the relationship building between him and her younger sister. Not out of jealousy at their closeness, but with concern for how Iris would handle it if Foxx's original suspicions proved accurate and Asher really did intend to betray them.

Even still, as they journeyed alongside him, it became impossible not to share their lives. They described what growing up in Alunda had been like and told stories about their experiences traversing the territories.

Asher remained vague about the particulars of his childhood

and never answered directly when they asked for specifics. Nevertheless, he did share many exciting and entertaining tales of his own adventures.

Many of the hilarious anecdotes he recounted included a friend named Lavi. Lavi was a man he seemed to look up to, and Asher spoke of him so often, Foxx couldn't help but question whether or not he might be Asher's *only* friend. As was usually the case, when she attempted to delve deeper into the subject, he diverted the conversation.

Asher continued to help them better develop their hunting and tracking skills, quizzing them as clues became visible from the trail. They sparred in their down time, both hand-to-hand and with blades. Asher, of course, proved to be an excellent swordsman, and Foxxglove wondered with mild irritation if there was anything he didn't excel at.

The current path caked their boots in thick, brown muck. Most of the trails in the rainforest had been formed of compact dirt that resisted water, even during times of hard rain. Sometimes it had a light, grassy layer that collected the constant precipitation, so it felt squishy beneath their feet but not marshy.

This path, however, was one of sludge. Every step came with the added effort of yanking a suctioned boot from its grasp. Though the sky wouldn't begin to darken for several hours, exhaustion had already begun creeping in. Thick clouds above let minimal sunlight through the canopy, a fact that contributed greatly to their persistent fatigue.

Eventually, the trail widened so they could walk next to each other. The nearness made it easier to remain in conversation and combat tiredness.

"Do you think it's strange we haven't come upon the river yet?" Iris practically dragged her boots as she walked.

Foxxglove's legs felt equally heavy, and her lungs already gasped for breath despite the early hour. "We've seen a few streams. Surely some of them must lead to the river."

Asher walked with Foxx at his left and the forest at his right. He'd already started looking for a spot to camp, thinking the girls wouldn't mind taking the rest of the day off. "The trail hasn't followed any long enough for us to find out. Though I'm hoping we're able to follow the trail most of the way. I don't fancy walking along the river. I'm slightly terrified of what might find us there."

A shiver tiptoed up their spines. Asher never seemed afraid of anything, so to hear him express *terror* was concerning.

Iris said, "Rossnetta told us it was only a short way off the trail. So one of these paths should lead us to the waterfall whether we find the river or not."

"Yes, I like that plan better." Asher's expression relaxed. "Then we don't have to worry about being eaten by horrendous river monsters or getting bitten by poisonous sea serpents."

"Or having our flesh gnawed off by piranhas," Iris added.

"Or sucked to death by leeches." Asher's tongue fell from his mouth in disgust.

"Or being gobbled up by an irate crocodile."

Foxxglove terminated their distressing banter by blurting, "Okay, so avoiding the river then?"

"Definitely avoiding the river," Asher agreed.

Walking on Foxx's opposite side, Iris noticed a set of stone steps rising up the embankment. Six in all, each had been created by three flat stones pressed into the ground. A dirt path began at the top of the staircase, weaving deeper into the forest. Next to the steps, a sign with sunshine yellow lettering read *Ataraxia Mission*. In smaller letters, *Orphan Shelter* had been written beneath it in tangerine.

Iris pointed to the sign. "What's this? An orphan shelter?"

Foxx stopped next to her. "That's what it says. I didn't know there were any orphan shelters in Metsa Sateen. I wonder how long it's been here." Bending to get a closer look, she ran fingers over chipping paint.

"Should we check it out?" Iris asked.

Asher shrugged noncommittally, appearing distracted by something on the other side of the trail.

Foxx said, "They may not welcome strangers."

"Then they can ask us to leave, right?" Iris walked up two steps and turned back to them. "Please? Let's at least creep up and take a peek."

Foxx looked at Asher, who shrugged again. "Words, please?" She furrowed her brow. "What do you think?"

He looked at the path disappearing into the jungle, then at the sign. "I think you're right. They probably don't like strangers."

Iris took another defiant step. "I'm going to check it out." Without awaiting their reply, she cleared the steps to the path and strode out of sight.

Asher and Foxx shared a sigh, both knowing the futility of trying to change Iris' mind. "How about you two go check it out, and I'll go on ahead to see if I can find us somewhere to stay tonight. I'm ready to call it a day, and I can see you two dragging your feet as well. We can pick up the trail again in the morning."

Foxx felt a spark of panic. "You want to split up?"

The dazzling smile revealing his dimpled cheeks sent a different kind of electricity through her. Taking a step in her direction, he said, "Not for long, love. If you get finished before I'm back, walk the trail. I won't be far." His hand fidgeted at his side, his fingers flexing wide before squeezing into a fist as he restrained himself from touching her. Then he walked away, leaving her alone on the path.

Standing frozen for a moment, her eyes remained locked on the spot where he'd stepped from sight. After inhaling a breath to calm treacherous nerves, she ascended the stairs in search of Iris.

The path leading away from the top step continued for 50 *sylis*, roughly 300 feet, at a slight incline. Iris came into view as the walkway leveled out. She hid outside the front entrance of a gated compound. Though the front gate was open, fences spread out between the trees in both directions. A wooden sign reading *Ataraxia Mission* hung from the archway above the entrance. Iris stood behind the wall on the left, peeking her head out to peer through the opening.

Foxx stopped behind her. "What did you find out?"

Iris jumped and scowled, prompting Foxx to chuckle at her accidental scare. "There seems to be some kind of market over there." Iris pointed to a row of wagons and tables set up beneath fabric-strung canopies. A smorgasbord of produce, fabrics, and other items littered the tables. Then she pointed to the back of the property. "And over there, they have a bunch of tents set up, see?" Foxx followed her direction and saw tents, bamboo huts, hammocks strung between trees, and an area of wooden tables scattered in a disorganized array.

They saw a few adults and several older kids who didn't look much younger than Iris, and children ran about everywhere. The whole compound bustled with energy. Some worked the market while others relaxed by the campground. They sat together at tables chatting and laughing and chased each other around the grassy, open area in the center.

"Are these all orphans?" Foxx stood in awe at the sight.

"Isn't it incredible? They seem so happy! And look: there's a market, so I bet they do welcome strangers. It probably helps fund the shelter."

"I think you're right." Foxx glanced back the way they'd come, wondering if they should inform Asher of their discoveries. "Let's go refill our food supply and see what else they have available. What do you think?"

Iris' eyes nearly burst with enjoyment. "Yes!" She stepped out into the entrance and paused under the sign. Foxx joined her.

They were spotted immediately. One of the little boys playing in the middle of the yard stopped mid-run. Another slammed into him from behind. The first boy yelled, "Miss Charlotte! There's peoples here!"

The other, younger boy called out, "Miss Charlotte! There's peoples!" followed by a chorus of other children bouncing around excitedly, yelling Miss Charlotte's name.

The first boy ran over to them, stopping abruptly and causing the smaller boy following him to again barrel into his back, nearly knocking both of them over. "Whatcha doing here? You heres to shop the market?"

"You heres to adopt us?" the smaller boy called over his shoulder.

The first boy elbowed him in the stomach, inciting a groan of pain as he scolded him with Katutaan words they didn't understand.

"I's just aksin', Chaisai!" the younger boy whined.

"Stop askin' so many questions!" Both boys wore little more than matching shorts above dirty, bare feet.

A young girl approached and pushed the boys out of the way, causing them to trip over each other and stumble to the ground. The girl curtsied, pulling the hem of her tattered dress out on either side. "Pleasure to meet you, misses. I'm Ah-Luiah. This is Chaisai and his little brother, Tanawat." Bronze hair hung in a loose braid over her shoulder.

"I's Tanawat," the littlest boy repeated, fumbling with his brother as they tried in unison to stand up, only to find themselves falling again. "I's four years old!" Then he whispered to the other boy, "I's told them I's four years old!"

Chaisai replied back through his teeth in dramatized annoyance.

"I hear-d you, Tana! I's right here." He mumbled again in the language of Sateen, and Tanawat bickered back.

Ah-Luiah waited for the boys to stop squabbling before saying, "Miss Charlotte is on her way."

Iris dipped her head. "Nice to meet you Ah-Luiah. And you as well, Chaisai and Tanawat. I'm Iris, and this is my sister Foxx." Several other children drew nearer without directly approaching them, wanting to get a closer look at the newcomers.

Ah-Luiah curtsied again as Chaisai and Tanawat regained their footing and dusted off their shorts. Chaisai nudged Ah-Luiah's hip with his shoulder. "I was talkin' to thee stranger ladies, Luiah. Let me talk to 'em." He dragged out the last word in a whine, thin eyes squinting as his olive cheeks puckered.

Ah-Luiah eyed him quizzically. "You can talk to them, Chaisai. They are standing right in front of you."

He crossed his arms and looked away from her defiantly. Tanawat mimicked his brother, harrumphing and turning his face in solidarity. Ah-Luiah rolled her eyes and whispered to the girls behind her hand, "They're always like this." Iris and Foxx chuckled.

Then a woman emerged from one of the huts across the yard, followed by a small band of children. More kids latched onto the group, as pollen gathers against a bumble's legs, and by the time she reached them, a huge cluster congregated around her.

The woman's kind smile accentuated pleasant and peaceful features. "Welcome." She placed her palms together and bowed her head. Her voice sounded as tranquil as her smile indicated it might be. "Welcome to the Ataraxia Mission. My name is Charlotte, and I'm the housemother."

Foxx introduced herself and her sister. "Your children have given us such a warm welcome."

Charlotte eyed Chaisai and Tanawat suspiciously, clearly knowing their persnickety nature. Their eyes moved all around, obviously looking everywhere possible except at Miss Charlotte. She smiled, before asking the girls, "Have you come to shop the market?" A loose dress of flowery designs fell to the tops of her bare feet, and wavy hair with ribbons and beads strung through at random rippled down her back.

Iris wondered if the children had woven the decorations in for her. "Yes, if that's all right with you. Our supply has run fairly dry, and we would like to restock for our journey."

The woman dipped her head and gestured toward the market. "Ah-Luiah will show you the way."

Chaisai whined, "But Miss Charlotte, I—" Charlotte held up her finger to silence him, but he continued indignantly. "I sawd them first!"

"Chaisai, is that how we speak to one another?" Charlotte's smile radiated patience. He continued to argue in Katutaan, and she stopped him again. "Arkaen, please, Chaisai. You shouldn't speak in a language those around you cannot understand."

He dropped his chin in shame. "Sorry, Miss Charlotte.

"*Arikau*, Chai. Thank you. Now, I'm sure if you and Tanawat can behave, Ah-Luiah will allow you to assist her in showing Iris and Foxx around."

Both boys looked to Ah-Luiah expectantly. The young girl put her fingers under her chin, as if inspecting them. After a drawn out examination, she said, "I think they will be good, Miss Charlotte." Charlotte nodded to Ah-Luiah before making her way back to the camping area. Some of the children followed her. Others hovered around the interesting newcomers.

As they walked toward the market with Ah-Luiah leading the way, Chaisai latched onto Iris' hand. Tanawat then grabbed Foxx's, and several other kids encircled them, holding their free hands or the backs of their packs. Anything to stick close by.

The kids chattered so much the girls could barely keep up, but they tried to answer every individual question thrown at them.

When they reached the market, Ah-Luiah turned around and cleared her throat. The group grew quiet. "Okay everyone, it is time to return to what you were doing. Chaisai, Tanawat, and I will show Iris and Foxx around the market." An eruption of groans echoed from the group. "It will be too cluttered with all of you hanging about. Now, off you go." She shooed the crowd with the backs of her hands and they steadily dispersed, heads drooping, toes dragging. "Very good. Okay, Foxx, Iris, we can start on this end. We have nonperishables here and perishables down that way. How does that sound?"

"Sounds great, Ah-Luiah, thank you." Iris walked toward the first set of tables, Chaisai never letting go of her hand. Foxx and Tanawat followed.

Ah-Luiah clasped her hands behind her back and continued. "This first table has blankets, towels, and all things fabric made.

There are even some clothes to choose from." Iris and Foxx also saw cloth bags, scarves and headbands, hats, socks, and much more, all crafted of beautifully dyed fabric or woven from naturally colored rope.

A young boy with slanted eyes and black hair down his back stood behind the table. Ah-Luiah introduced him and explained they could ask him questions since it was his shift to work the table. Each table now had a child standing behind it, available to assist and happy to have customers.

Foxx picked up a hammock and showed her sister. "What do you think of this? I bet it's more comfortable than sleeping on the ground."

Iris lifted a section of it away from Foxx's hands, spreading it out between them. It displayed abstract designs in clover and hickory. "It might be too heavy to add to our packs, don't you think? Though I agree it would be nice not sleeping on the ground."

Foxx put the hammock back on the table. "Maybe next time."

Ah-Luiah said, "Oh, I should have mentioned, most of what you see in the market is handmade, grown, or harvested by the children who live here, and all the proceeds help fund the Ataraxia Mission."

"Look ats that bag there." Chaisai tugged on Iris' hand and pointed to a bag on the table. "It's pretty and sturdy. I could drag Tanawat 'round in it."

"Hey!" Tanawat cried.

Iris picked up the cloth bag, made of bright wine and flaxen woven fabrics, and found it big enough to hold about six large grapefruit. "I love this, Chaisai! Thank you for pointing it out." His cheeks brightened.

Foxx grabbed three pairs of socks, encouraging Iris to do the same.

"Socks!" Chaisai exclaimed, his shyness instantly washed away. "I never wears socks but theys look comfy."

"I wears socks on my hands sometimes." Tanawat held his hand out in front of his face and examined it.

Iris and Foxx shared a glance, trying to hold back their amusement. "I've never tried that," Foxx said as seriously as she could manage.

Tanawat's eyes bulged with disbelief. "You should!" Chaisai shook his head as though embarrassed by his brother's antics.

At the next table, Iris found a strap for their old water sleeve, as the one currently on it had begun wearing out since they'd entered the jungle. Foxx picked up a new quiver crafted of leather and covered in beautiful sage fabric. It had two straps, one for her shoulder and the other for around her waist to keep it steady, and two pockets on the outside with gold, leafy designs.

Noticing her inspection of the quiver, Chaisai asked, "You shoot that bow on you shoulder?"

"Why would she have it if she didn't know how to shoot it?" Ah-Luiah asked.

"Maybe shes jus' likes it." Tanawat shrugged.

"I do shoot it, yes." Foxx tried not to chuckle at their ever-present adorableness.

"Yous any good?" Chaisai inquired suspiciously.

"Don't ask things like that, Chai!" Ah-Luiah scolded.

"I's jus' askin'!"

Tanawat stood up for his brother. "Yeah, Ah-Lue-ee-ah, he's jus' aksin'!"

Ah-Luiah rolled her eyes again, sighing.

When they reached the pottery table, Foxx and Iris explained it would be hard to keep pottery nice while traveling. The girl standing behind the table showed them several pieces anyway, very excited about her wares. They spent a few minutes admiring the artfully sculpted pottery before moving on to the last table before the food. A sign hung from it reading *Odds and Ends*.

"This is my fave-rit table." Chaisai let go of Iris' fingers and clung to the edge of the table.

Tanawat let go of Foxx's hand and stood next to his brother. "Mine too!"

"There's always fun stuff here." Chaisai picked up a beaded necklace.

"Yeah, always fun stuff here," Tanawat repeated.

"Stop copying me, Tana!"

"Sor-ry," Tanawat scuttled back to Foxx's side and clutched her hand.

Iris bought a bookmark made of dried leaves, and Foxx found a set of pencils she thought Asher might like. It came with a pouch matching the leather-bound book he always wrote in.

When they moved to the food tables, or *perishables* as Ah-Luiah had called them, they picked out some more yucca roots—having enjoyed the ones they bought in Kesken Ala—curly-topped mushrooms, dried plantains, fiddleheads, coconut meat, and python jerky —something they were eager to try since the grocer told them it was his favorite.

Once they finished shopping, Ah-Luiah introduced them to Hann, an older woman who tallied up their purchases and gave them a price. Feeling the cost way too low, the girls threw in a few extra *metts* and one of their few remaining *faeru*. If they'd had any *terras*, they would have gladly given one of those instead, but *terras* were made of gold and not easy to come by through trade and simple jobs.

After stuffing their items into their packs, Iris asked, "So what's the deal with this place, Ah-Luiah?"

Ah-Luiah led the group over to the tables across the yard. Several other kids who'd been waiting on the fringes of the market for the girls to finish shopping joined them along the way. Iris and Foxx sat across from each other with their hand-holding tagalongs next to them. Ah-Luiah sat facing them on the end of the table with her feet on the seat next to Tanawat. The other children filled in around them.

"The Ataraxia Mission is a place for orphans." Ah-Luiah spoke so professionally it seemed as if she were reading the description from a book. "We can stay here, learn to work and make things, sell the things we make to earn money to support the mission, learn about the forest and what is safe to eat, and learn to farm and harvest. We provide a market for travelers and locals. We take food out to the elderly and needy nearby. In fact, in the past few years, some people have moved to this area to have access to our services."

"And we're a family!" Tanawat squealed with glee.

Ah-Luiah nodded. "Tana is right, Ataraxia is a place to find a new family when you've lost your own. It's a fairly new operation, but I suspect it will last generations." Foxx and Iris' hearts swelled with love for these children. Iris felt tears springing to her eyes and she tried to force them away. How had they not known such a place existed? If they had, maybe they wouldn't have spent the last six years alone.

"Are you all from Metsa Sateen?" Their diverse ethnicities made Foxx think they probably weren't, but if not, how had they ended up at this particular shelter in the middle of the Metsa? They'd seen orphan homes before and even considered approaching them a few times, but they'd always seemed so… not like a home. Not like this.

"We are!" Chaisai and Tanawat shouted together in answer, which came as no surprise to either sister since they were a perfect depiction of the people of the forest—hair black as night and eyes more narrow than Foxx's.

Ah-Luiah said, "I'm not. I'm from Reginaterra. There are kids here from all over."

Iris rode her sister's wavelength without realizing it. "But how did you all get here?"

Ah-Luiah cleared her throat, seeming proud to have the information requested. She flattened her dress against her thighs with her palms. "Actually, I myself, like many others, was brought here by Prince Alexander."

"And the Wacky King!" Chaisai exclaimed.

"The *Mad* King," Ah-Luiah corrected. "And he's the Konungr of Cordillera. You shouldn't call him the Mad King. It's disrespectful." Chaisai mimicked her words with annoyed lips.

Foxx and Iris looked shocked. "Royals brought you here? I didn't think they cared about such things."

Chaisai cried in the Prince's defense. "Prince Alexander cares a *lot!*"

"And hes comes ta visit us sometimes!" Tanawat added.

"You know, Iris and I are orphans, too." Foxx's declaration caused a number of bulging eyes among the group.

"You are?" Several of them shrieked.

Iris glared at her. They still searched for their father, so they couldn't really call themselves orphans yet.

"Well, technically, we aren't sure about our father. When we were young, just 12 and 14, our mother died, and our father left." Foxx realized it didn't feel as difficult admitting this truth out loud as it had in the past. Something about knowing the kids would understand and could relate to being a child who lost a parent made it easier to speak. "We're traveling now in search of him."

"Wow," Chaisai whispered.

"How'd you su-vive not at the mission?" Tanawat asked in obvious awe.

"We took care of each other." Foxx smiled at her sister. "Like you and Chaisai take care of each other, Tana."

His face lit up. "Oh gee, Chaisai always takes care o' me."

"Tha's right." Chaisai puffed out his bare chest. "'Cause I's the big bro-ver."

"I know exactly what you mean, Chaisai." Foxx winked at Iris.

Ah-Luiah asked, "So you're searching for your father? All by yourselves?"

"Well, we have another friend with us now, but we were by ourselves for many years before that." Iris thought of all the time they'd spent together and how Foxx had always taken care of her, even before their mother died and father left.

"Where's you friend now?" Chaisai fiddled with a crack in the table.

"He went ahead to find shelter for the night." Foxx realized then how long he'd been gone.

"You can stay here!" Tanawat shouted.

"Tana!" Ah-Luiah looked between Foxx and Iris, embarrassed. "Miss Charlotte doesn't like strangers here overnight."

"That is totally understandable," Iris assured her.

"Iris is right, and I'm sure our friend will find us somewhere safe. He's really good at that."

"Sorry," Ah-Luiah said.

"Don't be! I'm so glad we got to meet you all!" Iris hugged Chaisai around the shoulders.

"Wills you come see us?" Tanawat asked.

"He means later," Chaisai explained. "Will you come sees us later?"

Foxx and Iris shared a look. "I would love to come back, but I don't want to make any promises I'm not sure I can keep. We hope to travel back this way eventually, and if we do, we'll definitely return to see you all."

Tanawat climbed up on his knees and leaned across the table to whisper to Chaisai behind his hand, though his whisper was loud enough for all to hear. "Sees? They's might be back."

"I hear-d them, Tana."

"It will be getting dark soon though, so we should probably get going." Foxx stood and looked up at the sky, visible through the break in the trees. Though it was still a few hours until nighttime, the wind had picked up, carrying in thick, gray clouds that indicated an incoming storm.

"We will walk you out." Ah-Luiah hopped down from the table.

The boys slid off the bench, grabbing Iris and Foxx's hands

again. A few more kids joined them, too, while others stayed behind at the table or ran back to the camping area.

Ah-Luiah turned to face them when they reached the entrance. "I'm glad to have met you Iris, Foxx." She curtsied to each of them.

"It was a pleasure to meet you all, as well." Foxx bowed back.

Iris said, "It was wonderful! We will try to come back to visit."

"We'lls be here!"

Chaisai's words sent a shot of pain through Iris' chest. After many more hugs and merry farewells, Iris and Foxx exited through the gate. The children continued to wave at them until they walked out of sight.

Foxx and Iris followed the dirt path back to the steps and discovered Asher sitting on the fourth one down. Iris called his name, and he looked up from his leather book.

"Why didn't you come up?" Foxx asked.

He tapped the book in his lap with his pencil. "I had a few things I wanted to write down quick. I was going to come find you when I finished if you didn't get here first."

"You're not wearing your pack," Iris noticed. "Does that mean you found us a place to camp?"

He smiled proudly. "I did. It isn't far. Are you ready to go?"

"Ready!" Iris skipped past him on the steps.

He stood when Foxx reached him, tugging down the bottom hem of his freshly changed tunic. "What did you find up there?"

"A bunch of orphans, as the sign suggests." Foxx tried to keep her voice casual and her eyes focused on his face rather than the contours revealed by the snugness of his switched attire. She'd noticed before that his hunter green shirt hugged him tighter than his others, and she couldn't decide whether she preferred it to the looser but lighter one that contrasted his skin.

"Orphans, huh? How were they?" His emerald irises glistened despite the sunless sky as Foxx's lips broke into a smile.

"They were magnificent."

Asher nodded before descending the remaining stairs. Then he turned back and said, "Good."

CHAPTER 11

OF THE MORROW

After walking only fifteen minutes, they rounded a bend, and Asher spread his arms as if presenting a glorious treasure. "Ta-da!"

Rising from beneath the overgrown foliage stood a massive structure. Iris crowed with amazement. "What is that?" As they moved closer, the building began to take shape. Fashioned of aged, stone bricks, vaulted ceilings gave the single story building extra height. Parts of it had eroded away with time and constant rain, leaving cracks and holes throughout. Vines of ivy scaled the walls in every direction, climbing from the ground all the way to the roof. With a jolt, it occurred to Iris, "It has a roof! Actual shelter from the rain!" She jumped up and down, clapping her hands.

Foxx scrutinized the property, again feeling the same familiarity she'd felt gazing at the building buried in the desert. She tried to coax the memory to surface with clarity. Instead, she chased it around, missing it with each grasp: an image foggy and just out of reach.

Stopping at the foot of the mossy steps, Iris shook Asher's shoulders from behind. "Do you think it's safe?"

He nodded, pleased to have triggered her giddiness. "Watch for critters. Make a lot of noise when you enter to scare them off, just in case."

Clapping again, she toed the first step before hurrying up to the building, crossing the threshold, and disappearing from sight.

Hysterical shrieks echoed through the jungle, startling birds from a nearby tree.

Asher laughed. "Spot on. Exactly like that."

"You would think she'd never seen an old building before." Foxxglove moved to follow her and spotted something carved into the first step. Crouching, she peeled away dark moss to reveal lettering hidden beneath. *"Monastery of the Morrow,"* she read. Seeing the words again sent her curiosity reeling. First on the painting of Lacuna Kaput, and now here. Her head swiveled to Asher. "Have you heard of this?" Asher looked from her to the words, then up to the building, stalling. "Tell me. Please."

"Yes, I've heard of it." He offered no further information as he started up the stairs.

To his back, she called, "Care to share any of it?" He disappeared through the doorway without reply.

Huffing, Foxx took in the full scope of the structure, trying to see through the ruins and envision what it used to be. She rubbed her fingers over the rough words, tracing each letter, and wondered how long it had been since they'd been etched into the stone.

At last she stood, her mind spinning with questions, not only about the mysterious and desolate building, but about the strange, intriguing, and frustrating man who seemed to know so much and yet explained so little.

Inside, she found Iris digging through her pack. Asher had vanished. The entrance hall was bigger than she'd imagined from outside. Broken furniture lay spewed about the room. An azure rug covered a fair portion of the floor, tattered with age. Viridian vines had forced their way up through cracks in the stone. Cut into the outer walls, two windows faced east and west. The western wall also contained two doorways, each leading to a smaller room. Three pathways extended out into the rest of the premises. Unlit torches hung in sconces on every wall, and Foxx wondered if they could still be lit or if moisture had rendered them useless.

Seeing Foxx at the center of the room, Iris pointed back one of the hallways and announced through teeth clutching an article of clothing, "He went that way. I'm going to change into dry clothes. Finally! Dry. Clothes!" She bolted into one of the open rooms.

Foxx moved deeper into the entrance hall, stepping cautiously over debris. She squinted down each of the three corridors. Fairly certain Iris had pointed to the center passage, she decided to take the one on the right.

Despite the shadowed hall, she could see a faint light shining in the distance. Walking past two darkened doorways, she stepped into a dim room at the end. A single window let in light above her head.

Floor to ceiling bookshelves lined three of the four walls like a library. Rows of spines stared at her from their homes among the shelves. At her feet, broken covers and pages littered the floor, all saturated from the moisture of the jungle. As she stepped through the rubble, her boots disturbed long unruffled mildew, sending the smell of wet parchment into the air.

Making her way to the back wall, she saw a row of books looking less moldy and disheveled than the rest. One by one, she lifted them from the shelf, examining the covers and flipping through stiff pages. A book with a soft cover of maroon caught her eye. Pulling it from between two others, she opened it, letting the pages fall where they may. In the dreary light, fading by the moment as storm clouds darkened from dust to slate, Foxx couldn't make out the words printed on its pages. She placed it back on its shelf, thinking she might return to it later.

A desk sat at the center of the room cluttered with stacks of parchment. A vase lay fallen next to an abstract patch of ink. Through the disarray, Foxxglove thought she spotted something on the desk itself and began brushing its contents onto the floor. When she'd cleared away the mess, she stumbled back. A symbol had been carved into the desk. Not the skull they'd seen in the Grim Wilds, but the outline of a raindrop. She traced the symbol with her finger, unsure what to think of it. Even more questions flooded her thoughts.

It looked too similar not to be connected. Did that mean the buildings were related? Could the building they discovered in the Wilds have been another Monastery of the Morrow? How many were there, and what had been their purpose before falling into such drastic states of disrepair?

At the sound of her name, Foxx pulled herself from the room, vowing to return later and decipher its mysteries. When she got back to the entrance hall, she found her sister hanging clothing from Mr. Magpie's rope, now stretched between two torches along the wall.

Asher had returned from wherever he'd ventured off to and busied himself making a fire in the hearth against the eastern wall. Though much of it had withered away, the chimney seemed intact, and he'd lined the outer edge with broken bricks to help contain the fire.

"Are you going to change, Foxx?" Iris hung her last article of clothing from the rope. "I left some space for you on the clothesline. You too, Asher."

Thanking her, Foxx collected her pack and headed off to the doorless room Iris used to change. Asher stayed by the fire, already dryer from the heat of its blaze.

☾

With the darkening clouds came a harsh storm. Lightning scattered throughout the room as it broke through fractures in the walls. The sky exploded in loud cracks that shook the building. Their fire whipped in the wind, though the trees and the structure of the Monastery did a fair job of blocking most of the larger gusts.

The trio sat in front of the hearth eating dinner, feeling relaxed and safe in the confines of a shelter during the storm.

Foxx scarfed a rambutan, spitting the pit into the fire. "Gosh, I love the fruit of the jungle. I thought Alunda had delicious fruit, but Sateen definitely has it beat."

Iris nibbled on figs Asher picked earlier in the day. Figs grew abundantly in Alunda, and Foxx had always thought them one of her favorite fruits. It pleased them both to find them plentiful in the rainforest, too. After biting into the plum-purple skin to expose magenta flesh inside, Iris wiped dripping syrup from the corner of her lips. "It's lucky we found this place when we did. This storm is fierce."

"Yes, very lucky." Asher split his own rambutan with his knife and squeezed the outer shell to pop the white fruit into his mouth. "It's a bit tattered, but it's better than being out there." He pushed another fruit from its spiky shell.

"I like it." Iris admired the room around them.

"Me too. Maybe we could stay here for a few days. What do you think?" Foxx directed the question at Asher, but her eyes shifted to Iris who cried, "Really? I love that idea! Can we please? I want to be dry and rest my feet, just for a couple of days. Pretty please?" Iris batted her lashes at Asher, begging irresistibly.

He pretended to mull it over before admitting, "I already set a few traps around the perimeter. Maybe we'll catch something tasty to cook up for breakfast." He winked at Iris and turned to Foxxglove with hints of anxiety peeking through his guise of arrogance.

Foxx smiled. "Okay, but only for a few days. A constant fire in one place is sure to draw unwanted attention."

Iris squealed and hugged Foxx around the shoulders, shaking her back and forth as she danced around. Standing, she ran over to Asher, hugging him awkwardly from above and wrapping her arms around his head.

He tapped her arm affectionately. "I think there's a fairly empty room back that hallway with your name on it." He pointed to the corridor on the eastern wall.

Impenetrable delight radiated from her. "My own room?" Another shriek. "We are never leaving this place." She picked up her pack along with Mr. Magpie's lantern and skipped back the hall.

"Just a few days," Foxxglove yelled after her. Receiving a hollered, unintelligible reply, she and Asher shared a laugh.

Outside, the storm raged as if the Monastery sat beneath a streaming waterfall. The white noise of pouring water vibrated throughout the room. Foxx watched as flashes of lightning revealed obscure mysteries in the shadows. Tiny streams of water drizzled through hollows in the ceiling and trickled down the walls.

The building was bruised and broken, but it remained strong despite the tempest raging outside.

Her thoughts drifted to herself and her sister and the similarities they shared with their temporary sanctuary. Riddled with holes that sometimes let the storms leak in. Filled with scattered debris, fragmented rubble, and shadowy hallways, yet standing firm in the midst of the jungle.

Now alone with Asher in the amber light of the fire, Foxx found the gumption to press him about the conversation he'd run from earlier. "So... you were clearly avoiding my questions before." Drawn by the sound of her voice breaking through the droning noise of the storm, his eyes slid to hers before quickly returning to the hearth. "Will you please tell me what you know about the Monastery of the Morrow? I can't help but feel like it's connected to us somehow. Maybe your perspective could shed some light on it for me."

Asher stayed quiet for a long time. So long, in fact, that Foxx thought he may be trying to pretend he hadn't heard her, though the pensive expression on his face told otherwise. After much deliberation, he sighed. "The Monastery of the Morrow was a group of scholars and teachers who studied the Before, the Deviation, and the After." He paused, weighing her reaction. When she revealed none, he continued. "They believed in a higher power named Elohim, a Creator of a world superior to the world we know now. Students would come here to learn what the Monastery viewed as genuine history."

"What happened to them?"

Asher leaned back on the palms of his hands, his countenance serious. "The Monastery believed that millennia ago during a time known as the Before, some decided they no longer liked the idea of serving the Creator and would prefer to rule instead. In an effort to accomplish this feat, they abandoned their Creator-given mission and spread cruelty across the lands. According to the Monastery, the Deviation brought about a great battle that eventually led to the separation of Arkaemor and Celestelvyra, and that since then, most evidence of the Creator and the Sacred Realm has been eradicated. Celestelvyra was taught as a fairytale rather than a real place. The creation of Arkaemor became a mystery, a story that varies with each culture and people group."

"Like that we began as tiny sea creatures and eventually emerged from the Suola Meri on the shell of a giant turtle?"

Asher chuckled. "Exactly. When the scholars of the Monastery of the Morrow began teaching that the Creator lived and was the True Ruler of this world despite the efforts of the betrayer—they were silenced."

Tilting her head, Foxx studied him, curious about the way he viewed the world and in constant awe of how much he knew about so many things. "Do you believe like the Monastery of the Morrow?" She watched him closely, wondering if he would answer honestly or if she would even be able to tell if he didn't.

He returned to his upright position and scanned the room, seeming apprehensive. Then he glanced down at the tattoo on his wrist and rubbed his thumb across the tinted skin. "I am leery to admit my beliefs, even in the confines of these walls, even in this roaring storm. What the Monastery believed is grounds for treason."

The word *treason* struck a nerve. Treason is what her father had been accused of.

Her mind's eye returned to the letters carved in ancient stone. Gazing into the firelight, she mulled over his words and again tried to imagine what the building had looked like before it stood in shambles. At a time when it was filled with teachers and students rebelliously seeking truth. "So how do you know about such things if they are so treacherous and secret? And don't say it's because you're handsome. Give me a real answer."

He looked at her, amused. "You think I'm handsome?" Foxx returned his cheeky grin with comical disapproval. Asher ran a hand down the back of his head and smoothed his dimples into submission. "History intrigues me, I suppose. I believe it's essential to understand and acknowledge where we have been so we can better discern where we ought to be going. We should never be so blind to the truth that we become unteachable or unwilling and unable to see fact from fiction."

"Are there others?"

"Others with views like them? Definitely. Though some of the world believe the Monastery of the Morrow and the Realm of Celestelvyra to be a myth—a fairytale to entertain children or a warning against possible insurgents—there are many who believe the hidden truths laced within these stories."

Pulling her eyes from the fire, she said, "I meant are there other Monasteries?" Though his response generated even more questions.

"Oh, yes. A long time ago there was one in every territory except Reginaterra. Six in all, or so the legends claim."

"Does this have something to do with the animals?"

Asher's expression turned serious again. "Everything is always connected, love. You must never forget that."

Foxxglove stared out the window at the downpour, trying to wrap her head around everything he'd revealed. An entirely new world had opened up before her. She felt as if she stood at a door, peeking through the keyhole, dying to step inside.

She'd heard of the After—the place people go when they die—but the Before and the Deviation were foreign terms, and the idea of a higher power was something she'd never really considered. Her mother had told them stories of a magical Creator, but Foxx hadn't thought them any more factual than the other fairytales she told them about mermaids and dragons, warrior princesses and boys who could fly.

Despite her curiosity of all the newly discovered unknowns, knowledge of a greater force at work had an unfamiliar feeling of peace sweeping through her. It warmed her insides all the way up to the pinks of her cheeks.

"Is that a blush I see, Lady Foxxglove?"

Her eyes flashed to his as her hands flew to conceal her face, inadvertently making the truth of her blush obvious.

"What could you possibly have been thinking about to cause that splash of color?" he taunted, his serious demeanor fading to make way for his usual charm.

She pressed her lips tightly, a hopeless attempt to halt her blossoming smile. "You can't even tell what color my cheeks are in this light. You're just trying to tease me." She kept her palms on either side of her face and pulled her knees up under her chin.

"You make it too easy, love." His eyes sparkled in the fire's vibrations, somehow more alive in the night, awake and buzzing like the jungle around them. "So. Are you going to tell me?"

Wrapping her arms around her legs, Foxx pulled them tighter to her chest. "I guess at the moment I'm feeling… safe." Once spoken aloud, she realized how absurd it sounded.

"Safe?" He chuckled. "In this dreadful jungle? Filled with niedas and a number of other ferocious monsters?"

Giggling shyly, she put her head down. "I know. It sounds crazy." She thought not only of the monsters but of the crimson-clad soldiers searching for them and wondered when, if ever, would be the right time to share that truth with him. How long did he need to prove his honesty and good nature before she trusted him with their secret?

Foxx stammered as she tried to explain her thoughts. "It's peaceful though, the way you talk about these things. Higher beings and plans for the world. I'm not sure I believe them, but I can feel something in me wanting to."

"I know what you mean."

An animal howled in the distance drawing Foxx's gaze back to the window, but he didn't pull his eyes from her. He examined the soft curve of her lips and her dark eyelashes.

His attention caught on her scar, traveling the entirety of it in a way she hadn't previously allowed him to. A clean slice from top to bottom, it had healed like a cavern with layers of darker scaring through its center that lightened as it expanded out toward the olive skin of her cheeks. He wondered why it hadn't been stitched closed and how painful and dangerous it must have been for her when it first happened.

If the wounds of her heart could be seen, he thought they might look very similar to the rugged scar. What kind of stories lay within the dark caverns of her soul? What kind of horrors had she seen, and what agonies had transformed her? And yet, by some unfathomable miracle, she found it in herself to experience joy in the rain.

After another long moment of thoughts he shouldn't allow himself to have, he cleared his throat. "How did you end up here, Foxx?"

Surprised, she turned to him, tilting her head. "We want to find Celestelvyra, like we told you."

Asher shook his head. "Two young women traveling alone and searching for some whisper of a fable?" A sharp wind blew through the window, pushing her hair forward to frame her face. "No, there's more to the story than just sanguine dreamers hoping to find a magical city."

Foxx stayed silent for a while, wondering if her desire to let him in could be trusted or if the rhythm his voice played in tune with the murmurs of her own heart clouded her judgment. Was his interest superficial—a way to gain information to somehow use against them? Or did he truly wish to see her? "Why are you fishing for information?"

His lips turned up at the corners. "I'm not fishing. I'm trying to understand. The more I get to know you, the more I can't help but wonder, isn't there anyone, anywhere, missing you?"

Foxx watched the fire's flames dance with the wind. "Our mother used to tell us stories about the realm of Celestelvyra. She believed it was more than an old fable."

When she paused, Asher coaxed her forward. "Believed?"

"Yes. Past tense. She begged our father to take us there, to travel to every corner of this world until we found it so we could leave this cursed place. To hear you talk about the world being cursed..." She cut her sentence short, unable to confront what it meant for another person to believe the same things her mother spent her final years ranting about.

"Anyway, she had visions. I guess." Stumbling over the words, she realized she'd never said them out loud to a single soul. Even when discussing it with Iris, they tiptoed around the topic. Memories of her mother's illness had her wondering again if they might be a glimpse into her own future. "She saw a place that sparkled, where *truth is revealed,* she used to say. She would rave about how a wicked king and queen had cursed the lands and thought if we could find Celestelvyra, we would find the answers we needed to set everything straight." Foxx laughed without humor. "It's possible she was out of her mind, deranged."

Asher didn't speak for a long time. The playful confidence she'd gotten used to had faded again, making the room feel somber. At last, he said, "Let's hope she was right." Feeling insecure in his detachment, Foxxglove remained quiet. Then again, as if his severity had never existed, his mood changed, and the hard lines on his face softened. "Thank you for sharing that with me."

Foxx released a breath. "I've never talked to anyone about this before. Our mother, I mean. Iris knows some of it, though I think many of her memories have been filtered to remember the joy over the heartache."

"And you?"

Foxx didn't answer immediately as she tried to pull the truth from the depths of her heart. "My memories are jaded. I know they've made me cynical. Iris says *pessimistic.*"

"I don't think you're cynical," he said. She shot him a look of disbelief. "Okay, maybe a little cynical." He grinned, drawing a small smile to her lips, too.

"I envy Iris' memories with our mother. I wish I could look back on them the way she does. Especially now that she's gone."

Asher's expression was unreadable, and Foxx realized he had no idea what had happened to their mother or how tragic her death had truly been.

"I suppose I should explain: when I was thirteen—almost fourteen—and Iris was twelve, our mother—" Foxx choked on the words. She inhaled a breath and ran her hands down her face. "I'm sorry."

"You don't have to talk about it if you don't want to."

Foxx shook her head. "I do want to. I've never said it. Never spoken the words, but I need to. Our mother killed herself." She heard the sharp inhale of Asher's breath. "I found her on the bathroom floor. Iris tried to run in, but I pushed her out and closed the door. I'm not sure how much she saw. We've never talked about it."

Shock crept over his face as the realization settled. "You were the one who found her," he reiterated, barely audible. She didn't look at him, but he found himself unable to drag his attention from her troubled expression. "You were so young."

"I don't even know how I knew to come inside. Perhaps it was the work of your mysterious Creator. I was out walking on the beach. A storm had arrived suddenly, and I'd gone out to stroll through the rain. Then I felt something. I don't know how to explain it. A pull, I guess, in the pit of my stomach. So I ran back inside, and there she was, chalky white and covered in her own vomit. Our father wasn't home." Anger toward her father had her stoic strength returning. Her back straightened at the reminder of his betrayal, and the walls around her heart began erecting themselves again, brick by painful brick.

"He worked for the King's Legion in some special unit and was always gone. I took care of Iris. I took care of our mother. And when I discovered her on the bathroom floor, I cleaned her up and got her into bed. I made it look as if she'd died in her sleep." A single tear slid down her cheek. Even a stone-cold heart surrounded by walls can't prevent every tear from falling. She wiped it away with the back of her hand.

Asher placed a hand on hers where it rested at her side. Liquid fire shot up her arm into her chest. "Sometimes we hide the scary things to protect the people we love." His eyes bore into hers. Even as she tried to pull away, she felt snared in his understanding—seen as she never had been before. "But you don't have to hide your tears from me, Foxxglove. They aren't a weakness but a reflection of your human heart."

Taken aback by his words, she sucked in a breath. "Our mother used to tell me that. *Tears are a reflection of your human heart.*"

Asher smiled, freeing her from the heat of his touch and the potency of his gaze. "Perhaps even through her illness, she had wisdom." Pulling both hands up into her lap, she focussed her attention on them as her breathing settled. "What about your father?" he asked, not yet ready for the conversation to fizzle out. "Where did he end up in all of this?"

"When my father came home that day and saw her, I think something broke in him. He decided he needed to find Celestelvyra for her. He left the following day, promising a quick return." Foxx lifted her eyes, looking at him through heavy lashes. "That was more than six years ago. I guess he went a little mad, too."

A slow nod had his eyes pensively searching the air. He leaned back on his hands and stared into the distance. "I think I'm starting to see the whole picture."

They sat in silence for a long while, both lost in their own thoughts. Eventually, Foxx yawned. "I need to sleep." Standing, she pulled her bedroll and pillow from her bag and returned to her previous resting spot. "Is it all right if I sleep here by the fire?"

His lips curled into that heartwarming smile. "You can sleep wherever you like, love."

Spreading out her roll, she laid down and curled her knees into her chest. The jarring storm outside had melted into a calm trickle, and without the breeze pushing its way through the cracks and windows, the air around her felt heavy.

Or maybe her world felt heavy, weighed down with so many pressures and responsibilities. Still, her confessions to Asher left her feeling as if someone else stood next to her, helping carry the load. "Will you stay here with me?" Her eyes had already fallen closed.

He didn't answer right away, but she thought she could hear the smile in his voice as he said, "It would be my honor, Foxx. Merry night."

C

Foxxglove stirred awake and rolled onto her back. From her position on the floor, she could see the drizzle through the western window. Outside, an orchestra of droplets pitter-pattered against the roof and splattered the foliage, harmonizing alongside the birds singing praises to the morning sun.

"Merry morning." Asher's voice startled her into sitting up.

"Oh! Merry morning, Asher." Her cheeks warmed as memories surfaced of the night's conversation and the personal things she'd shared. The daylight shattered the unguarded and intimate atmosphere provided by darkness, and she couldn't help but question whether it had all been a dream. After shaking away a sleepy fog, she looked his way to find him in the same position he'd been in the night before and writing in his leather-bound book.

"What are you writing?" She stretched her arms high above her head. Her movements felt awkward as she grasped for the ease she'd felt with him by the light of the fire. She couldn't figure out what to do with her hands as they fidgeted from the floor to her lap, fingered the seam of her bedroll, and then flew to her hair to straighten any bedhead strays.

Asher closed the book and tucked it into his bag. "Nothing of consequence."

"Oh, that reminds me." She stood to retrieve the pencil case she bought in Ataraxia and handed it to him. "I got this for you yesterday."

He accepted the gift with an expression of surprise and unfolded the pouch to find three sharp pencils inside. His face gave away little emotion, and as his silence dragged on, she began to feel a sickening tug in her stomach. Had it not been appropriate to offer him a gift?

"I don't know what to say," he confessed.

"You don't have to say anything. I don't even know why—"

"It's amazing," he interrupted, at last turning to face her. His beaming smile instantly extinguished her worries. "It's perfect. Thank you for thinking of me. It's been quite a long time since—" He looked back at the gift in his hands. "Well, anyway. Thank you."

"It wasn't a big deal." She now felt shy by his immense gratitude and frustrated by her capricious emotions.

"It is." Pulling his book back out of his bag, he held it up next to the pencil case. "They match." The words poured from his lips in the most adorable way, with unshakeable glee. "Thank you, Foxx."

Iris' footsteps sounded in the hall. "Merry morning, you two." She entered the room looking more rested than she had in many moons. "What's for breakfast?"

"Yucca and mushrooms." Asher slipped his leather book and new pencil pouch into his bag and set his skillet over the fire to heat it up. "Why don't you come help me?"

Agreeing, Iris sat down on the floor next to him, closer than Foxx would have dared. "Sounds delicious!" He handed her a root of yucca and a knife while he got to work on the mushrooms.

Foxx's thoughts continued to rotate in an unending cycle, replaying the night before, as well as his extreme reaction to the pencils and all the other significant moments they'd shared together. In all the romance novels she'd read, nothing had ever described the nauseatingly magnificent feeling bubbling inside her, nor did they prepare her for terror and thrill in the same breath.

Once everything was chopped and cooking in the pan, Foxx dragged herself from her musings and asked Iris, "How did you sleep?"

"Wonderfully." Iris hugged herself amid a relaxing breath. "I don't ever want to leave here."

"We have to leave eventually." Though Foxx very thoroughly understood her sister's love for their temporary home. For half a minute, she let herself imagine what it might truly be like for the three of them to stay there forever. "We have a plan."

"I know, I know. I know we have to go, but I don't want to."

Foxx glanced at Asher, surprised he hadn't commented further. His lips curved, but his eyes looked solemn, a drastic change from minutes ago, and she wondered what troubled him.

Their breakfast cooked quickly, and Asher divided it among them. Iris dug in, expressing deep sounds of enjoyment after her first bite. "So good," she complimented through a mouthful. "What's the plan for today?"

Foxx shrugged in response, enjoying her breakfast as well, though not quite as dramatically as Iris. Asher said nothing as he set his plate on the floor beside him. Foxx said his name. "Anything you want to accomplish today?"

He didn't meet her eyes as he announced, "I actually have something I need to take care of today." The girls exchanged a jolt of surprise. "I'm going to head out in a minute. You ladies should check the traps to see if we'll be eating fresh meat tonight." He emanated total nonchalance, but Foxx couldn't help sense it might be forced, especially since he seemed adamant not to meet her gaze.

"You're leaving?" She tried to restrain the echo in the words emerging from the chasm suddenly opening in her stomach.

"For a little while. I'll be back before the waxing moon rises. Barely long enough for you to miss me desperately." More teasing bled through his tone, but he still wouldn't meet her eyes. She knew he must feel her looking his way, but he persistently ignored the pull.

Iris kept quiet, setting her plate of roots and mushrooms in front of her lap. Her head swiveled back and forth between them.

Asher stood. He picked up his bag and slung it over his shoulder. Then he grabbed his rifle. Foxx willed herself not to unveil her panic as she watched him meticulously packing up his belongings. "Check the traps, and stay safe." When he moved to the doorway, his eyes finally latched onto Foxx's. He held her gaze for an excruciating moment before turning to the open door. "Don't have too much fun without me."

"No promises," Iris called after him. He waved a sign of recognition without turning back around, and then he was gone, leaving them and his untouched breakfast behind.

CHAPTER 12

SEEKING A STONE

Foxx and Iris finished checking the traps before highsun and made their way back to the Monastery, carrying a single souvenir. Neither knew the name of the furry rodent, but it seemed meaty enough to provide protein for the day.

"It must be native to the jungle," Iris said, pulling Foxx out of her head and into the present. She'd been silent most of the morning, lost in thoughts she feared admitting out loud.

"Huh?"

"The rodent." Iris tried to rein in her exasperation at her sister's melancholic fog. "Since neither of us knows what it is, it's probably native to Metsa Sateen, don't you think?" Foxx nodded blandly, and Iris rolled her eyes. "Maybe Asher will know what it is."

The intentional trigger caused a visible pulse through Foxx's body, the only indication she'd heard her sister's words.

They walked on in silence for several minutes until Iris blurted, "Are we going to talk about it or are you going to be miserable all day?"

Foxx stopped short. "I'm not miserable."

"No? Asher leaving abruptly with no clue as to where he was heading didn't bother you at all?" Iris examined Foxx's reserved expression.

"Did it bother you?" Foxx asked.

"Not really. I'm sure he'll be back by the time the moon rises, as promised."

"So am I."

"Well, okay then. Moving onward."

"Onward." Foxx fell into step with her sister.

They were nearly back to the Monastery when Iris bubbled with sudden excitement. "Do you want to spar? It's been days since we've had much cause to use our weapons. Though I don't relish the idea of crossing blades in this rain." Her face traveled skyward as if to glimpse the clouds, but the dense canopy hid them from view.

"It's important to train under a myriad of conditions so you're prepared no matter what scenario you find yourself in." Foxxglove felt a little pep return to her step at the idea of combat, knowing it had the potential to be an adequate distraction. As the Monastery came into view, they quickened their pace, eager for the chance to expend some energy. After hanging the dead rodent from a broken torch stand, they went inside to grab their weapons.

Foxx pulled a long dagger from the sheath attached to the outside of her pack. Already armed, Iris bounced impatiently on the balls of her feet. They traveled a little ways up the trail to a clearing they'd discovered while investigating Asher's traps.

When they reached the open glade, they squared off. Foxx held the handle of a single knife guarding her face. The blade, exactly one foot long, stretched out from the bottom of her grip, and she'd curled her other hand into a fist.

Iris held Thorn and Bloom in their regular positions, forming a protective X in front of her upper body.

Both women crouched wide and low, their stances primal, their bodies ready to unleash pent up emotions. Foxxglove side-stepped, one foot crossing over the other, and Iris mimicked her. Moving in a circle, each getting acclimated with the surroundings in their peripherals without breaking eye contact, the sister's waged war.

Iris struck first, springing forward with her dagger outstretched. Foxx moved her head to dodge the attack as Iris swung Bloom, aiming to slice beneath her arm. Foxx's blade caught the shortsword at its hilt and redirected the blow to send Iris past her. Regaining her footing and crouching low, Iris wiped rainwater from her face as they began circling again.

Foxx shifted sideways, stepping up on a rock and thrusting her dagger downward. Iris caught the strike with both blades, but Foxx quickly spun to the left, getting behind her and striking again. Iris nimbly spun the opposite direction and blocked a second time. Standing back to back, opposing one another even in their breathing, each waited for the other to make the next move.

Foxx spun left again and Iris mirrored her. Another clash.

Iris charged with three quick jabs: dagger-sword-dagger. Foxx kept her blade centered, parrying every blow. She spun toward her sister, gaining momentum, and swung her blade in a wide arc aiming for Iris' face. Iris caught it with her shortsword, hooking the hilts and twisting her sister's arm until she'd trapped it against her chest. Then she rammed her dagger in from the right, stopping before it pierced Foxx's ribcage. Iris smiled, pleased with herself.

"You've been practicing," Foxx said between breaths. Separating, each sister stepped back a few paces.

"Asher taught me a few things." Iris shrugged a shoulder at Foxx's narrowed eyes.

A troop of tiny, tan monkeys gathered in the trees around the edge of the clearing. They watched the girls fight, bouncing with delirium and hanging upside-down by their tails with finesse.

Foxx lunged forward again. Swiping her sword back and forth rapidly, she hoped to catch Iris off guard. Iris deflected or dodged each blow until Foxx trapped her shortsword, spinning her blade in a circle and stunning Iris as Bloom flew from her hand. Iris grinned and threw Thorn into the ground next to the felled sword. Raising her fists, she adjusted her hips, centering her gravity. Foxx dropped her blade and lifted her hands into a fighting stance.

The ball of Iris' foot dug into the earth, propelling her forward and closing the gap between them faster than Foxx expected. Foxx shifted her body sideways, barely avoiding her attack. She pivoted on her heel and thrust her fist into her sister's ribcage. Iris released a yowl of pain. Rebounding from the backlash, she swung again, but Foxx ducked and dropped to the ground, rolling away.

"That hurt." Iris pouted and rubbed her side.

"You have to learn to not leave your center open."

The sound of a breaking stick alerted the girls to a visitor at the back of the clearing. In sync, Iris and Foxx scoped out the treeline.

Golden spheres reflected among the shadows in the tall ferns. The creature crept closer without breaking the line where the ferns ended and the clearing began.

Frightened, several of the monkeys fled.

Iris opened her mouth to say Foxx's name, but she shushed her. Foxx signaled that Iris should retrieve her weapons and step to the left, internally cursing herself for not bringing her bow. Both women crouched and lifted their blades from the grass.

The glowing eyes seemed to wobble back and forth as the creature prepared to pounce. Sensing the predator, a bird flew from the tree behind them, and the brief distraction gave the animal an opening. It jumped into the clearing with teeth bared and lunged at Iris. Coming to a halt in front of her, it snapped its jaws in a warning.

Foxx recognized the dimeti from the stories their mother used to tell them. *The scariest feline you could ever come across,* she'd said. A mohawk of white informed them the feline was male.

It leapt for Iris, swiping at her with one of its monstrous paws. Dodging the attack, she swung Bloom and missed her target by an inch.

The remaining monkeys whooped and shrieked; some watched with trepidation while others joined the battle, hurling fruit gleaned from the trees at the tiger-like creature disrupting their entertainment.

Foxx attacked it from behind, but its scorpion-like tail hurled toward her, nearly stabbing her chest. She thrashed at it again and managed to hit it, only to find her sword glancing back as if she'd struck stone. The beast roared, showing off the long, indigo fur around its neck and chest that gave the impression of massive muscle.

Iris shifted to the side, and the dimeti circled in between them. It slashed its tail at Iris, who caught it within the X of her blades. The spike at the end almost grazed her nose, and as it squirmed within her grasp, a droplet of lime-colored liquid dripped from the tip.

Unable to break free, the dimeti called up its next line of defense. While it fought off Foxx's attacks with its front paws, six, thin tentacles flipped up from where they'd been curled around its tail. They tangled in Iris' blades, and she squeezed with all her might as she yanked the swords back. The tail came away with two slices on either side, and the end of a tentacle dropped to the ground, continuing to flail in the grass.

It roared again and whipped around, its tail swaying in the background as the remaining tentacles moved freely near the spike like seaweed swaying in water.

Foxx lunged, thrusting her blade deep into the side of its body. It howled as she ripped the blade free, and its tail smacked her shoulder, knocking her backward. Accepting defeat, the creature fled the clearing, yowling as it disappeared into the trees.

Iris and Foxx met at the center of the glade, weapons drawn, eyeing the treeline. "Do you think he's gone?"

After a few moments, Foxx let her blade drop to her side and straightened. "I think we scared him off." Her free hand massaged her sore tailbone. Then she slid her blade against the wet grass, cleaning away the blood.

Iris sheathed her blades and threw an arm over her sister's shoulders. "I think I'm done sparring for the day." Foxxglove agreed wholeheartedly. Iris looked up and waved at their monkey audience. "Thanks for your support!"

The monkeys chattered happily in response, doing flips on the tree branches and hanging upside-down.

C

Iris skinned the rodent from Asher's trap before cleaning her blades.

Foxx reignited the fire, adding another log to the still hot coals. Pouring water onto a rag, she wiped the remaining blood from her dagger before reattaching it to her pack. She ran her fingers along the bow hanging on the wall and said aloud, "I promise I won't leave you behind next time."

When Iris returned with the rodent, Foxx began the process of cooking it over the fire. As the smell of roasting meat filled the room, Iris broke the silence. "Do you think Asher will actually come back?"

Foxx sucked in a breath, slowly surveying the room to verify what she already knew: he'd taken all of his things with him when he left. "We already talked about this."

"I know. I was thinking about how weird he was this morning."

"He was. But I really don't know." Foxx let the dancing flames hypnotize her as the words spilled out. "I want to think he will. I would like to trust that he is the person he seems to be and that the bonds we've forged over the past month can't so easily be abandoned." She twisted open the lid of the water bag and took a drag from it.

After lunch, they spent the afternoon relaxing. Foxx read her book on the front steps until the rain started again. Iris sharpened all of her blades.

As the day grew darker, they sat once more by the fire, eating together and reminiscing about their trip so far; laughing over all the crazy things they had been through and remembering all the interesting people they had met. They talked of the men in the Grim Wilds, avoiding the topic of Foxxglove's vision, and about the crazy mandrill attack, as well as their chattering audience of monkeys.

They decided to revisit the Ataraxia Mission before leaving the Monastery, though neither suggested the idea of Asher going with them this time. Iris admitted how deeply she missed Seth. Discovering the kids at the orphan shelter had summoned him to the forefront of her thoughts.

They talked until weariness overtook them and Iris grew tired of fending off the fire's smoky fumes. They wished each other a merry night, and Iris padded back to her bedroom. Foxxglove reclaimed her spot by the fire. As she drifted off to sleep, her last thoughts were about Asher, and how he had not returned.

C

Seven days passed. One whole week and Asher had yet to find his way back to them.

The day after he left, Foxxglove had shown Iris the carving on the desk in the library. They spent days exploring the Monastery, finding more tunnels and passageways than they'd realized existed within the ruined structure.

They found a kitchen that was no longer operational. At some point it had a working pipe system that supplied the scholars with fresh water. The pipes had since corroded, but it looked as though they would catch rainwater and store it until the levers over the water basins were activated, allowing the water to pass through.

Bedrooms with empty, wooden bed frames were scattered throughout. Each had two beds, two small dressers, and one desk placed in front of an open window. Upon examining the drawers, they found old robes, bits of parchment with faded writing, feathered quills, incense, and unopened bottles of ink.

Stairs at the end of a hallway led them down into a basement storage area containing folded piles of fabric bedding that smelled of mildew and mothballs. From there they found another room with crates of scrolls and other remnants of an existence long past, likely lost down there for hundreds of years. Iris had attempted to unroll one of the scrolls, but it crumbled to pieces, so they left the others alone.

After scouring every nook and cranny, they stopped searching for the stone matching the carved raindrop in the library. Foxx had been sure it would have a twin, equivalent in shape and size to the skull and acacia stones they already had, but if a matching stone did exist, they hadn't found it in the building.

They took time to spar and reset Asher's traps several times during their weeklong stay. One clear night when the rain ceased, they climbed to the top of the Monastery and spent hours watching the resplendent moon make its journey across the sky through a sparse section of canopy.

They walked the path to the Ataraxia Mission twice to visit the kids. Chaisai and Tanawat, with Ah-Luiah's help, had made beaded bracelets for each of them. When they'd realized their mutual love for reading, Ah-Luiah gave Foxxglove a copy of her favorite book, *The Enchanter of Celestelvyra*. After spending so many hours at the Mission, Iris and Foxx knew they would be visiting the children again in the future.

Something had shifted in their hearts over the past few months: they'd begun letting people enter the inner workings of their two-person existence in a way they never had before. In a matter of days, they'd come to love those kids so deeply they could burst, and never seeing them again was no longer an option.

They decided to spend one more day at the Monastery before moving on. It seemed ages had passed since they'd stayed in one place for so long. Now with the Legion hunting them, it was even more important to keep moving. Iris suspected Foxx had taken the risk of extending their stay in the hopes that Asher would return, but it was too dangerous to linger any longer.

The day before their scheduled departure, Foxx and Iris remained close to the Monastery. When the sun next rose, they would pack up and say a bittersweet farewell to their sanctuary in the jungle.

They disabled all the traps and packed most of their belongings. Then they spent the rest of the day relaxing. After luncheon, Iris went to sit in a sunny patch she'd discovered a few days prior. A hole in the canopy allowed the afternoon sun to pass through and warm the grass.

Foxx pulled her nearly finished novel from her bag and carried it outside. She'd packed the book with the soft, red cover from the library, as well as the book she'd gotten from Ah-Luiah, and she was determined to finish her current read so she could leave it behind.

Settling down on a step in the middle of the staircase leading up to the Monastery, Foxx opened her book to the page marked with a dried foxglove bell. The pressed flower was a gift she'd once received from Iris, and she hadn't used another bookmark since. Lifting it from the page, she twirled it around between her thumb and index fingers, examining the flower her mother had named her after. Iris flowers were known for their beauty and sweet perfume. Foxgloves were known for the lethal poisons they created.

More than once she'd wondered if her mother had known, even before they were born, who her daughters would be. Could she have somehow predicted Foxx's rough and cold demeanor compared to her sister's glowing, radiant warmth?

Footsteps sounded on the trail. Foxx scanned the open page of her book, attempting to find her place before Iris appeared, hoping it would look as though she'd been reading and not sitting there brooding. In her frantic repositioning, she dropped the foxglove, and when she bent forward to pick it up, an unexpected voice startled her.

"You know, those things can be pretty deadly. You really should be more careful."

Bewilderment had her dropping the flower again as she tilted her head toward the voice.

Limping to the steps, he leaned his rifle against the stone knee wall before kneeling in front of her. He reached to recover the fallen flower, picked it up, and placed it on the open book in her hands. "Hello, love." His grin barely masked the worst of his exhaustion. "Did you miss me?"

Foxx momentarily lost her ability to draw breath.

Asher sat with a grunt, one step down from hers, and bits of stone crumbled onto the next step as he situated his back against the wall. His bag tumbled from his shoulder and hit the ground next to him with a thud.

Foxx scrutinized the new additions to his face, seeing dried blood above his brow. Swollen skin around his opposite eye bloomed the dark hue of an eggplant, and it wasn't the only bruising she could see. A split cut through his bottom lip. His clothes were sliced and stained with blood.

Seeing her examine his injuries, he offered an explanation. "I had a little dispute with a fig tree. It insisted I offended its neighbor by removing the figs from its branches. I tried to explain that I was so hungry and, after all, fruit is meant to be eaten, but it was unsatisfied with my response. Who knew fig trees could be so violent?" Clearing his throat, he shifted his weight so he could stretch out his injured leg.

Barely hearing his words, her heart raced through a plethora of feelings all at once: happiness at his return, confused about why he'd stayed away for so long, and concerned by the obvious beating he'd taken. After much deliberation, she settled on anger. Who did he think he was, strolling back like everything was perfectly normal? Making jokes about figs and *smiling*. Her cheeks flushed crimson in a fury.

Witnessing the final resolve in her expression, the charming smile fell from his face, replaced with a shadow of fear. "I can see now is not the time to joke. Though I did bring some of the pilfered figs along as evidence if you would like to see them." His lips curled up on one side, imploring her to return his smile, to play along.

"Where have you been? You said you would be back the day you left. It's been seven days. And you bring back *figs*?"

Asher allowed her to pour out her wrath without interruption.

She hadn't let herself feel it. He left, and she'd forced herself to be fine. She was always fine, had to be fine, had to take care of Iris. At the sight of him now, rage consumed her. Him with his arrogant smile and his mocking words.

She hadn't realized she'd risen to her feet. "Answer me. You've clearly been through an ordeal, so if you have a valid excuse for staying away, then I want to hear it. The *truth*, Asher." Her teeth bit into her lip with too much pressure as she awaited his response.

His gaze slid back and forth between her eyes, but his lips remained unmoving. A minute passed and still, he said nothing.

Iris appeared around the corner of the building after running toward the sound of her sister's distress. "Foxx? What's wro—" Her voice caught in her throat as the sight of him stopped her in her tracks.

Asher lifted his hand in a gentle salute. "Hello, Iris."

Her mouth remained open in shock as she gaped back and forth between them.

"Ask. Him." Foxxglove stomped into the Monastery and out of sight.

Asher took a long breath, dragging his hand down his face. His rough palm scraped tender skin, and he winced, remembering his injuries.

Iris stepped toward him, glancing back at the door her sister had disappeared through. "Wow, she's really mad."

"It's to be expected," he admitted, feigning calmness. A labored sigh revealed a hidden injury beneath his shirt and he winced, lifting his hand to grasp it.

Iris sat down on the top step and examined his wounds as Foxx had. "Where were you?"

His fingers moved to his brow, resting there with his elbow propped on his knee. "I was…" The sentence faded away. Beginning again, he said, "I didn't plan to be gone this long."

Iris nodded. "I should go talk to her."

Asher accepted that without looking up.

Iris found Foxx in the room she'd claimed as her bedroom, sitting on the floor with her back to the wall and her head resting against it. Sliding into the spot next to her, she said, "This is my room, you know." Foxx didn't respond as she stared up at the splintering ceiling. "We should at least hear him out."

Foxx turned her head without detaching it from the wall. "He left us." The anger had dissipated, no longer marring the panes of her face or the tone in her voice. All that remained was the sad sound of trauma wounds being prodded, scratched, ripped open. "The last night he was here, we talked about…" Her chin dropped to her chest at the end of her exhaled breath. "I told him things. Then he woke up the next day and abandoned us." She could sense herself overreacting, but the grief felt so deeply rooted inside her heart that she couldn't combat it with logic and reason.

Their mother abandoned them. Their father abandoned them. Since then, they'd kept all others at a distance to avoid ever feeling this way again. They needed no one but each other.

Iris placed her hand on Foxx's arm. "I know it hurts. It's totally reasonable for you to feel this way, but after the worst has passed, you should give him a chance to explain. I don't know what kept him away, but he did come back. After you hear what he has to say, you can decide how you want to proceed, and I will support whatever decision you make." Fixing her with a tender expression, she asked, "Okay?"

"I think I would like to be alone for a while if that's all right with you."

With exaggerated and playful sarcasm, Iris said, "I suppose I can let you borrow my room." She wrapped her arms around her sister and squeezed, affirmed aloud how much she loved her, and left to give her the space she needed.

C

Sometime later, as the moon made its entrance into the sky, Foxx emerged from Iris' bedroom. Creeping down the hall, she paused in the doorway to the main room. Iris and Asher sat by the fire. Whatever Iris said pulled a full belly laugh from him, causing him to rock backward with his hand on his chest. Despite herself, the sound of his laughter made Foxx feel cozy, like being wrapped in a warm blanket.

As she stepped into the room, the merriment stopped.

Both turned to her, and Iris broke into a smile. "There she is." She patted the floor next to her. Asher turned back to the fire and ran his hand over his head.

Foxx approached, sitting on the floor beside her sister who hugged her with one arm.

"I'm glad you finally decided to exit my room. I'm exhausted." Iris yawned, and Foxx couldn't tell if it was forced or not. She kissed her sister's cheek and stood. "See you guys in the morning!" Then she stepped around Foxx and pranced off to her room, taking her effortless ease along with her.

As Foxx and Asher sat together in the quiet of the Monastery, the sound of raindrops battering the roof seemed to overtake them, daring them not to drown in the silence as it dragged on between them.

At long last, words came to her, and she whispered, "Thank you." Startled, he turned from the fire to gawk at her. "For coming back, I mean."

The corners of his mouth turned up, giving way to his adorable dimples, and confusion transformed into happiness and relief. "Thank you for having me."

"Oh, I'm still undecided about that," she jested, almost flirting. Rising to her feet, she crossed the room to her bag. Asher watched her maneuvering among the shadows.

When she returned, she knelt down in front of him and leaned forward to examine his face. "We should stitch these." His eyes expressed his surprise at her unexpected closeness, but he made no comment as she lifted a finger to touch the skin near one of the deeper gashes on his forehead. "This one at least." Sitting back on her heels, she opened her aid pouch and fingered through it.

Asher was speechless, and she couldn't help but feel a mild triumph for rendering him so. She pulled out the needle and thread, and scanned his person. He'd changed his clothes, making most of his injuries no longer visible. "Are there others?"

"More bruising than anything else." He lifted his shirt to reveal the plum and indigo patches on his ribs.

Foxx winced at the sight before leaning in to inspect the cuts. "These should be fine with a little cura. We can wrap your ribs so they heal faster. Why were you limping?"

"I already wrapped my knee." He let his shirt drop.

Foxx waved the needle in the fire before threading the hole. She could feel his gaze on her, so acutely tuned to her movements, but she ignored him and focused on her task.

Situating herself closer, she rose to her knees so she had a better vantage to work. "I am interested in having one of the figs if you still have any left." The words didn't emerge as casually as she'd hoped, but he didn't seem to mind.

His face brightened as he reached into his bag and pulled out two purple figs. "Iris was mad at me for not letting her have more than one, but I told her you were the big sister and big sisters get two." Foxx chuckled at that, imagining Iris whining about the unfairness of the situation and reprimanding him for not bringing back an even amount.

Asher set the figs on a stone brick next to them and closed his eyes as Foxx pinched his skin together. "She also forgave me much quicker, and I needed to make sure I held on to my leverage."

Foxx pulled the thread through and tied it off. "She has always been more forgiving than I am."

Asher hummed as if he knew it to be true. Rather than his

presumption irritating her, she felt pleased with how well they were getting to know each other. It felt good to be known. Her knife sliced through the thread, and she proceeded to the next stitch.

"Exactly why I saved two for you." He winced as the needle punctured tender skin. "You see, I am very intuitive, and I knew you would need extra persuading."

After cutting the next stitch, she accused, "You are so full of yourself." Asher laughed, and she shook her head. "You think you're already forgiven, don't you?"

He looked up at her through hooded eyes and that shamelessly delicious grin. "Aren't I?"

Foxx sighed, unable to suppress her smile but attempting to hide the blush on her cheeks as she pulled the third stitch through. "I will keep you posted." Another burst of laughter poured from him as she tucked the needle and thread back into her pouch and pulled out the curavenum, using her finger to spread it across the stitches.

"Thank you, Foxxglove," he said, compelling her blush to deepen.

Again sitting back on her heels, she looked at him. "You're welcome."

Foxx returned her aid kit to her bag. Then she reclaimed her spot by the fire, pulling her legs against her chest and resting her chin on her knees. They sat there for a long time in comfortable silence. Occasionally, their line of vision would cross and coax a smile.

Eventually, Foxx laid down on her bedroll and watched him watching the flames, wondering what he might be thinking about but too afraid to ask. Instead, she observed the muscles of his arms, the way the firelight danced across his skin, and the scruffiness of his jaw, clearly unshaved since before he'd left. As the lids of her eyes became too heavy to hold open any longer, she mustered the courage to say, "Promise you will be here when I wake up?"

A chuckle rumbled his chest. "I promise, love."

C

The next morning, they sat on the front steps of the Monastery enjoying the lack of rain and discussing how to move forward. When they told him their intentions, Asher seemed delighted to still be included in the plans and didn't argue with the idea of leaving the Monastery right away.

He hadn't volunteered information about where he'd run off to, and they didn't press him for it.

To Iris' utter disgust, Foxxglove had given Asher more of their curavenum. Their jar was almost empty, and Foxx asked them to remind her to acquire more when they found a town.

Iris despised the salve and avoided it like a plague. It smelled absolutely atrocious, but it worked miracles. She wished they'd been able to acquire some when Foxx received the gash still visible on her face after so many years.

"I will not be able to walk behind you while you wear that repugnant smell." Iris' thumb and forefinger pinched her nostrils.

"I guess you'll have to lead the way for a while then."

Iris lit with excitement. "Yes! I love that idea."

"You wouldn't mind me hanging out in the back of the line with you, would you Foxx?" Asher nudged her with his elbow.

Her cheeks flushed and goosebumps rose across her arms, but she kept her expression neutral. "Or maybe I'll stay up front with Iris and leave you in the back to stink all on your own."

He pretended to stab himself in the heart, holding the hilt of an invisible sword and thrusting it into his chest. "Lady, you wound me! I'm absolutely gutted!"

Both girls laughed, and Iris pretended to whack him repeatedly over the head with an invisible mallet, then jumped away when the smell again hit her nostrils. Gagging and holding her nose, she said, "You smell repulsive!"

"She would probably be nicer to you if you'd given her two figs, you know," Foxx said.

Iris' eyes widened as she remembered his infraction. "That's right, *friend!* You'll remember this next time." She crossed her arms and stared at him with raised brows.

Asher glared at Foxx for reminding her of his transgression before lifting his hands to Iris in surrender. "Okay, okay, I promise to find you more figs." Iris grinned, looking pleased to have won the battle. Then he added, "I will find you more figs *if* you persuade your sister to walk with me in the back while you take the lead. I'm injured, remember?" He gestured to his knee which still refused to hold the entirety of his weight without struggle. "I may need extra help as the day goes on. Plus, I get very lonely when I am stuck all alone at the end of the line." His tone matched his countenance, overly dramatic and intentionally ridiculous.

Foxx said, "It's barely a *line* with only three people anyway. We will still only be a few feet from each other no matter what."

Iris shook her head. "Ummm… no. I need him to stay *way* in the back until that hideous smell fades."

Asher donned his most precious pouting face.

Then they all fell into a fit of laughter.

CHAPTER 13

PETRICHOR

As Foxxglove, Iris, and Asher continued their journey through the forest of Sateen, they encountered other travelers, a few houses, and a merchant selling wares along the trail. From the merchant, they bought a loaf of bread and two arrows to replace the ones Foxx lost to the mandrills.

They also happened upon a compact village of seven huts all gathered together in a hollow, but Foxx thought it had an ominous feel to it, so they didn't move closer to check it out.

The moon rose and fell another fifteen times, dwindling more and more with each passing day until Storm's new moon took its place in the sky. A few hours before sundown on the day following the new moon, they came to a lifted root cutting through the trail. It rose waist-high on the southern side and plummeted as it crossed the walkway, allowing a small alcove to climb over.

When Iris stepped up on the root, Asher stopped her with her name. He examined the tree before slipping out of sight behind its trunk.

Foxx and Iris eyed the direction he'd gone, wondering what he could be doing. Foxx shrugged and leaned against the sturdy root, thankful for the reprieve, and Iris crouched to inspect where the root met the ground.

With most trees, the majority of the root system stays invisible beneath the dirt. However, many of the kapok trees they'd seen throughout the Metsa sat elevated atop triangular roots with sharp ridges and sides sloping down until they melted flush with the earth. This particular tree stood aloft on its tiptoes, presumably in an attempt to run its finger-like branches through the clouds above. Its trunk seemed composed of a family of thinner trees all growing into each other.

The sound of three horn blasts had Iris squealing in fright and Foxx nearly tumbling from her resting place. Asher reemerged from the foliage, giddy with energy. They stared at him in alarm. He'd just announced their location to the entire jungle, and for some reason, he looked ecstatic about it.

"What's happening?" Iris asked.

He held up a finger, instructing her to wait as he lifted his chin to the treetops. Following his gaze, they saw a square object towering above them and drawing nearer. Asher crossed his arms, pleased with himself, and motioned for the girls to step out of the way.

Iris squinted. "It looks like a huge basket." Moments later, woven strips of bark held together with vines and rope touched down in front of them. The area inside looked big enough to hold four or five people at most, and the outer rim rose to their stomachs. Ropes extended from the basket's roof, held up by poles at each of the four corners, and stretched far up into the trees.

Asher pulled open a small door on the side facing them. "Your carriage, my ladies." Holding a hand out, he bowed like a gentleman.

"Where will it take us?" Foxx asked.

"Why don't you step aboard and find out?" Wiggling his hand, he encouraged her to take it and helped her balance as she stepped precariously into the vessel.

Iris joined her inside, followed by Asher, who closed the door behind him. Tugging three times on a rope hanging outside the lift, Asher said, "You might want to hold on." The basket began to rise, abruptly hoisted away from the ground. Both women grabbed a corner pole for stability as it lifted them into the treetops.

Foxx leaned over the edge to peer down at the shrinking ground while Iris clutched her pack to ensure she didn't fall. "Seriously, where are we going?" Foxx couldn't hide the thrill of adventure shining through her tone.

The question required no answer as they emerged through a lower layer of branches to discover a city suspended in the trees. When the basket came to a halt, Asher stepped out and held open the door. A platform crafted of solid teak led to a railing opposite the lift where they stopped to take in the view.

"This is…" Foxx's mouth hung open, waiting for words to materialize.

"Spectacular!" Iris finished for her, just as awestruck.

"Breathtaking." Deep contemplation and a hint of confusion spread across Foxx's features.

Asher noticed the alteration and stepped up next to her. "What's wrong? Don't tell me you're afraid of heights." His breath skimmed her neck as he spoke close to her ear, causing her to shiver and side-step away from him.

Since his disappearance at the Monastery, Asher had refrained from pushing too hard against the boundaries she endeavored to hold in place. But his dripping charm never ceased and seemed to grow with each setting sun. A friendship had blossomed alongside flourishing trust, and she found herself accepting the bond knotting between them more every day.

"No." Foxx feigned overconfidence as she shook away the mushy feelings clouding her senses. "I'm not afraid of anything."

"I believe that. So what's your face doing?" He motioned with his hand to her head, unwittingly scrunching up his own features in the process.

She rested her chin on her fingers. "It's fascinating to me how many things I've recognized on this journey, as if our mother somehow painted every place we would end up."

"You think Mother painted this?" Iris asked.

"How else could I know it? Both Monasteries were familiar to me, and now this, as if I've seen it before."

"*Both* monasteries?" Asher asked.

Foxx nodded "The painting we found of Lacuna Kaput was signed as a gift to the Monastery of the Morrow. At the time, we had no idea what that meant, but after you said there was one in each territory, I realized the building we discovered in Vallemortis was probably the Monastery of the Wilds."

"That's why you were so intrigued when you saw the words written on the steps."

Iris gestured to the treetop city. "I don't remember this one, though. Perhaps I didn't see all of her work."

Foxx nodded. "Our mother painted so many things, but in all

three instances, I felt as if I'd seen them before, even though there was obviously no way I could have. They all sparked a memory."

"That's very interesting." Asher scratched his chin.

Before he could say more, a woman stepped onto the platform to greet them. *"Selaa. Baikchaku."* She bowed to Asher, her palms pressed together in front of her head, and then to the girls. Robes hung in pale green layers all the way to her sandaled toes, and she'd wound her hair into a tight bun on top of her head. She spoke a sentence in the language of Katutaan, and Asher shook his head in answer. *"Hai,* yes. Welcome to the City of Petrichor. I am Pearl."

Asher leaned in and spoke to her in secretive tones the girls couldn't hear. Pearl nodded in understanding. Then he handed her a small pouch, which she slid into the pocket of her robes.

"Wonderful! If you would follow me right this way, please, I will take you to your lodgings." She bowed again, and this time Asher returned her bow, thanking her as they followed her onto a bridge extending from the left of the platform.

Buildings made from a mixture of teak and bamboo hung between and around the trees of Petrichor. Thin roads of covered bridges connected the buildings together like the spindles of a giant spider web hovering high above the forest floor.

Lanterns dangled in long rows from rope strung throughout the whole city, making the thatched roofs dance with starlight as the breeze pushed the lanterns from side to side. More driädi like those they'd seen at the Tree of Knowing flitted amongst the lanterns, their pale green light a contrast next to the orange flames.

Unique in design, each treehouse had been molded to fit the contours of its nesting tree. Some couldn't have contained more than one or two rooms; others rose two and three stories tall, climbing high up into the emergent layer of the rainforest.

Residents lounged on porches encircling their houses. Other buildings displayed signs above the doors to indicate a business within, rather than a home.

Porches and walkways had planters of fruit trees and berry bushes. Moss covered portions of every structure, making it seem as if each wooden building bloomed with bright patches of green. Vines of ivy, mandevilla, and vincas twisted their way around guardrails, lamp posts, and anything else they could cling to. Pastel wisteria dripped from the rooftops and underneath bridges in breathtaking bundles, separated only by groupings of string of pearls, trailing jade, baby tears, and hanging ferns.

An interesting building with vibrant paintings propped up all around its porch and hanging on its outer walls caught Iris' attention. She leaned over the railing, squinting and trying to read the sign above the shop's door.

Then horror struck her. In a panic, she grabbed her sister's arm, yanking her backward and ducking to the ground behind the bridge's bamboo banister.

Foxx was pulled down alongside her. "What's going on?" Her irritation reflected in her tone. She'd been bewitched by the magical city and did not appreciate being interrupted.

Iris held her hand to Foxx's ear and whispered, "Legion."

Foxxglove's expression fell, replicating her sister's horror. Peeking over the railing, she scanned the direction Iris had pointed. Standing near the artwork, a member of the King's Legion talked to the shopkeeper with a piece of parchment in his hand. Crouching again, she sat next to Iris with her back to the banister.

"Um, ladies?" Asher's voice drew them back to focus and they realized simultaneously how ridiculous they must look. Iris pulled her pack around and dug inside for their hat. She placed it on Foxx's head and tucked her white hair into it. Then both women rose with awkward expressions. "Are you ready now?" Asher asked, ever calm in their absurdity.

"Yes! Sorry about that. It was… my hair. It needed…"

"A hat!" Iris finished, motioning to the hat now adorning Foxx's head.

Asher glanced across the gap at the soldier. "Had an issue with the King's Legion recently?" His obvious suspicion transformed into playful banter.

"Well, you know what a troublemaker our girl Foxx is." Iris nudged her sister, trying to diminish all traces of fear and lingering awkwardness.

"Yes, I do." He grinned slyly at Foxx, eliciting a new blush from her already inflamed cheeks.

Pearl didn't seem troubled at all by their strange behavior. "Very good." She dropped her chin to Asher and continued on her way. The building she led them to sat wide around three separate trees and rose three stories tall. An olive sign with gold script read: *Passiflora Inn.*

Crafted of pale wood, each level of the inn bore elaborate balconies decorated with fancifully carved balustrades and sparkling lanterns. As they drew closer, the bridge widened into a large terrace with raised gardens bursting with flowers and creeping ivy.

The lobby displayed tropical greenery and blossoms in large pots, giving the impression that the jungle had followed them inside. At the center of the room, a reception desk wrapped in bamboo was painted with abstract flowers, textures, and designs. Vases on top held living versions of the flowers, with multiple layers of petals surrounding rows of lavender spikes.

Pearl led them to the desk and introduced Octavia. Then she bowed to each of them before dismissing herself. The receptionist checked them in. With hair dark like Pearl's, Octavia's locks hung in thick waves. A pointy and petite nose next to a tiny birthmark on her cheek fit beautifully on her heart-shaped face.

The girls glanced at each other when Asher gave her a false name, though they didn't question it. Octavia pulled a wooden leaf from beneath the desk and handed it to Asher. Then she directed them to a hallway off to her right and wished them a merry stay.

Following the hall to a set of stairs, they ascended to the second level. A sign directed them to go left for rooms 200-205. When they turned, the outer wall disappeared as the hallway became one of the open balconies they'd glimpsed from the bridge below. A delicately carved banister rose to their waist on the left and the room doors lined the wall on the right. They passed rooms 205 and 204 before stopping in front of 203.

Illuminated with crystal lanterns and a wide open window opposite the door, the room held a dresser against the side wall and two beds with an end table in between. To their left, a door led to a personal bathroom.

"Beds!" Iris bolted into the room. "Real beds!"

The low dresser displayed mini candles and a vase of the same exotic flowers from the reception desk. Next to the vase sat a sweating pitcher of water with citrus slices floating on the surface, three glasses, and a bamboo platter of sweet treats.

Iris looked at the plate, picked out a soft cake topped with azalea sugar cream, and tasted it. A satisfied moan spilled from her lips as she stuffed the rest of the treat into her mouth.

Foxxglove pushed open the door leading to the bathroom. It had an actual toilet, a sink, and a tub all squeezed into the tiny space. She wondered how they had plumbing this far off the ground but worried questioning it out loud might make the magical illusion disappear.

Iris had already made her home on the bed closest to the open window, her feet still planted on the floor as if she'd only meant to sit down but had fallen back in delirious comfort. Asher set his pack on the floor between the other bed and the wall, and let his weight settle into the soft mattress. Throwing his hands behind his head, he laid back against the pillows. His boots thudded to the floor as he propped his feet on the silky sheets and crossed his ankles.

Foxx stood between the beds. "There's a bathroom!"

"And beds!" Iris reiterated.

"And pillows." Asher's eyes had already closed.

Foxx laid down next to her sister, who had scooted up to put her head on a pillow after seeing Asher's comfort. She said his name, but he didn't respond. His chest rose and fell in the slow rhythm of blissful unconsciousness. Looking at Iris, she motioned to him and both women giggled quietly.

"I guess he was sleepy." Iris stood to pour herself a glass of water and grab another sweet. When she returned, she handed Foxx the drink to taste. "This place is phenomenal."

After a moment of gazing around the room, Foxx said, "I'm going for a bath."

Iris allowed her head to fall to the side. "You do that. I'm going to take a nap." Rolling over, she pulled her knees up to her chest and let her lids fall closed.

Foxx smiled, loving the serenity she saw in Iris' features. Pulling fresh clothes and the novel she had gotten from Ah-Luiah from her pack, she headed to the bathroom. Inside she found a small box of firesticks next to an oil lamp on the edge of the sink adorned in a mosaic lampshade. When she scratched the stick on the side of the box and lit the wick, a plethora of colors danced against the walls in tempo with the flickering flame.

A jar sat on the rim of the tub, and Foxx uncorked it to breathe in the floral scent. Drizzling some of the fuchsia liquid into the basin, she turned on the water and let it fill and bubble as she got undressed.

Stepping into the warm water felt like a dream. The scent of rose petals flooded the room as she situated herself into a comfortable position and turned off the faucet. Taking a deep, calming breath, she let the water relax her sore muscles. Then she picked up her book and sat there for a long while in a perfect bubble of peace.

C

When they woke the next day, Foxxglove gathered everyone's well-traveled clothing and filled the tub with water. Adding more of the delicious smelling rose oil, she began washing one garment at a time, fully submerging each item, then shaking it around a bit before letting it marinate in the fragrant water.

While sorting through the clothes, she came across the shirt Asher had been wearing the day he returned to the Monastery. It was stained with blood and littered with slices.

It'd been over a week since he stopped putting cura on his wounds. When she'd caught a glimpse of his torso a few days back, she saw that the gashes had faded into thin scars, and the bruising was in its final stages of yellow and lime.

The laceration on his neck from that fateful nieda, still healing on the day they'd met, remained maroon. A healer in Kesken Ala had lathered it with cura, so the scar didn't look nearly as dark as Foxx's, but its coloring made her wonder if scars from nieda venom ever truly disappeared.

Dipping the shirt beneath the water, she scrubbed at the bloodstain. The deep red only faded marginally, and with the slits in the fabric as well, she decided to trash it and buy him a new one if he complained.

Next on the pile were the pants he'd been wearing that same day, also stained in blood. When she lifted them from the floor, something fell from one of the pockets. After dropping the pants in the water, she dried her hands and picked up the worn square of parchment, holding it in her outstretched palm.

Knowing it may be private, she considered whether or not she should open it. They all had their secrets. Didn't he deserve to hold on to his, as she did?

Examining the edges up close, she noticed familiar lettering in the fold. No longer caring for his privacy, she unfolded the parchment, already knowing what it would reveal. Seeing a reflection of her own face staring back at her, she read the word *Wanted* written in bold letters across the top.

Her stomach instantly knotted. Her heart slammed against its cage.

Question after question swarmed through her brain until her vision went cloudy. Gripping the parchment tight in her hand, she fell to her side on the floor, nearly convulsing.

Iris and Asher appeared in the doorway, but she couldn't see them panicking. Iris yelled her name.

"What's happening to her?" Asher dropped to the floor and scooped her up with one hand under her knees and another beneath her head. He carried her to his bed as her body continued to shudder.

The vision rocked through her, disabling all limb control.

The sound of her own groaning and crying echoed in her ears, but she couldn't make it stop. Couldn't still the blood coursing through her veins. Burning through her like fire. Slicing her bones like sharp ice.

A massive building stood tall but damaged. Moons decorated the ground at her feet. The vision of the broken building melted into inky blackness before instantly reigniting as consuming fire roared around her, so close she could feel it melting her skin. The ground quaked as buildings crumbled. Screams of agony made her cover her ears to block out the devastating sounds.

Then in an instant, all of the horrific noises disappeared, and she saw Asher sitting next to her. Night turned to day, and he looked at her, his face creased with concern. Their hands were clasped together on her lap. His lips separated, but before she could hear his words, darkness, again, swallowed her.

As lucidity began resurfacing, her eyelids cracked open, and she shot into a sitting position. As before, her head seemed filled with stones. Asher knelt next to her, and her sister stood over his shoulder, their expressions painted with distress.

Her breathing felt ragged, as if all the air had been sucked from the room. Her limbs tingled, and her fingertips were ice cold; so bitter they burned like sunlit sand. Trying to speak, she sputtered between breaths, "Can't… breathe." More unsuccessful gulps for air followed the words. Was her heart supposed to hurt like this?

Suddenly, she felt light as a floating feather, only to feel hard ground at her back moments later. Fresh air filled her nostrils, still having no access to her lungs. Pressure on her cheeks had her eyelids fluttering open, though she hadn't realized she'd closed them. Emerald eyes stared back at her. The murmuring of unintelligible whispers reached her ears.

Gasping again, her lungs opened, letting a small amount of oxygen in. Mild relief, but not enough. Not nearly enough.

"Foxx, you have to calm down. You have to breathe."

Her eyes widened as she realized Asher was yelling at her. She didn't know why or what she'd done to prompt it, but she really needed a deep breath. Another small puff of air slipped into collapsing lungs, and she wished her heart would explode already so it would be over. So it would stop hurting.

Lifted again, her arms hung loose at her sides.

Cold water pelted her face and the shock had her sucking in a huge gasp of air. Pulled from the water, she again heard Asher's voice. "Come on, love. Come back to me."

Inhaling another long breath, she released it slowly, feeling on the fringes of calm. Her fingers and hands remained numb, but her chest had begun to settle. Coming to grips with her surroundings, she discovered she now lay on the balcony outside their room with her body practically limp in Asher's arms. Letting her head fall into his shoulder, Foxx breathed a pitiful, "I'm sorry."

"Let's get her back inside." Iris's words reached her from high above as the world turned pitch black.

C

When Foxx opened her eyes again, she saw their room. Rain pelted the leaves outside the window. Asher knelt on the floor next to her, and Iris sat on the other bed behind him.

She inhaled deeply, feeling her restless muscles relax as she, at last, exhaled a full breath. A bead of sweat tickled her forehead.

"Hello there," Asher cooed, and Foxx loved seeing that smile spread across his cheeks. When had she started loving that? "You scared the hell out of us, love." Her eyes caught his through eyelids suddenly too heavy to hold open, and she matched his smile.

Iris asked, "What did you see?"

Foxx laid mostly unresponsive. A pained expression formed between her temples as her eyes fluttered back open for less than a second before closing again.

Asher furrowed his brow. "What do you mean what did she see? What did she see when?" Iris didn't know if she should share this secret with him, though she knew they would need some kind of explanation for what happened. Asher glared at her, waiting for an answer. "Iris, tell me." He glanced back at Foxx, whose eyes remained closed, then again at Iris, saying her name. Anger she hadn't heard from him before seeped into his voice as he barked for her to explain.

Though she didn't much appreciate being told what to do, she knew he deserved an answer. "She has visions. I think, at least. She had one before when we were in the Wilds, and it looked very similar to this."

Asher's eyes turned down with sorrow. "Like your mother."

Iris hadn't realized Foxx revealed the truth about their mother's sickness. She never talked to anyone about it. Ever. Her expression told him what her words wouldn't.

Asher looked back at Foxx and pushed a piece of hair away from her forehead with all the gentleness of a mother caressing an infant's soft cheeks. Foxx stirred again, her eyes finding his. Iris repeated her question, but Foxx didn't pull her focus from Asher's radiating concern. Instead, she slipped the crumpled parchment into his palm. "I saw you." Then her lids fell as she passed again into oblivion.

CHAPTER 14

TELLING TRUTHS

For breakfast, the staff delivered hot meat with boiled eggs and more delicious sweets to their door, but even the sweets couldn't tempt Iris' anxious stomach. She sat on her bed staring at her sister, willing her to wake up. Asher sat on the end of the bed, looking down at the wrinkled parchment in his hands.

Iris didn't know what Foxx meant about seeing him in her vision. Her tone had sounded more despairing than fearful, but Iris hadn't yet mustered the courage to ask what Foxx shoved into his palm before passing out.

As if hearing her thoughts, Asher turned and stretched out his hand, uncovering the parchment inside.

After taking it and unfolding it, she blanched. "You knew? For how long?"

It took him almost a full minute to answer. His eyes traveled to the floor, then to Foxx before landing back on Iris, filled with shame. "Since before the nieda."

Iris' breath caught in her throat, her silence saying enough.

Asher stood and began pacing from one end of the room to the other. On his second time through, he stopped in front of the bathroom door and noticed the dirty clothing left in a stack on the floor and floating in the tub. "I am going to finish cleaning these." He looked at Iris.

She didn't know what to say, though she suspected he needed to busy his hands. She struggled with the stillness that had settled over the room as well. "Are you really here to hurt us? Did you plan on turning us in?"

Grief wrinkled his features. "No. I swear it, Iris. Not for one single moment." He gave no further explanation before disappearing into the bathroom and closing the door behind him.

C

By the time Foxx awoke, the room had grown dark. Only a single lantern remained lit on the table between the beds. It took her a moment to realize she'd passed out in Asher's bed instead of the one she'd shared with Iris the night before. Across the space between the two, she saw her sister curled up in a ball under the blankets. She felt a spark of joy at her peacefully slumbering sister until she realized what being in Asher's bed might mean. Warily, she turned to find him reclined next to her, wide awake and staring at the ceiling. His journal lay open on his chest, but he wasn't engaging it.

The fact that neither of them were under the blankets was a mild comfort.

"Do you ever sleep?" she asked.

He turned to her in surprise, but his tone expressed relief. "You're awake. You slept all day."

"I can see that." Foxx motioned to the darkness surrounding them.

"How are you feeling?" His quiet words did nothing to mask the pain in his voice as he rotated his head back to the ceiling.

"Somehow, I'm still tired." She rolled onto her side and adjusted the pillow under her cheek, pulling her knees to her stomach as she studied his face.

"Nightmares tend to have that effect." After a long moment, he spoke again to the space above. "I know you have no reason to believe me, but I hope you do. I was never going to turn you in, Foxx."

"I know."

Asher looked at her. "What do you mean, *you know*?"

Foxx tucked hair that had fallen into her face behind her ear. "Well, I guess I shouldn't say I *know*. It's just a feeling. I assume Iris explained? About the visions, I mean." He confirmed she had with a swift nod. "Like my mother."

Uncharacteristically uncomfortable, his eyes shifted from hers.

"This one was horrible. Different from last time. Everything was burning. So much screaming." She repressed a shudder. "Then the images shifted to a calmer scene, and you were sitting next to me." She left out the part about the hand holding. "I don't exactly know how to explain it, but I felt safe."

His expression lightened, and relief filled her as she watched the corners of his lips curl and the tight rhythm of his chest settle. He dropped his book to the floor and turned to face her, shifting his weight so he laid on his side. The bed was barely wide enough for two people, and his proximity in the dark sent shivers through her nerves.

"Are you okay?" he asked.

She dropped her chin, unable to speak.

He ran his thumb down the length of her scar. Warmth flooded her system, and her hand flew up to cover his without her permission. Again she wished she could figure out how to name his scent. Woodsy, sweet, maybe a hint of citrus? Fresh, like the rain.

He pulled his hand away, freeing her lungs to breathe on their own. "Where did you get this?"

The damage sullying her once pretty face was not something she liked to talk about. Nervously, she admitted, "It was a nieda." She allowed the familiar, ambient sounds of the jungle outside the window to calm her. "Iris and I were alone. This was after our parents…" She paused and took a long breath. "We were walking along the beach, close enough that the incoming tide slid across our toes. Two attacked us, not as big as the one here in the forest, but to two little girls, they might as well have been giants.

"They'd burrowed in the sand, and we didn't see them until one of them seized Iris' ankle and yanked her backward. It dragged her along the shore faster than I thought I could run, but I managed to catch up. I grabbed her arm and pulled her as hard as I could. She was screaming my name and kicking at the monster. Eventually, I don't know if she kicked in the right place or if it became tired of pulling, but it released her. It stumbled backward, giving us a moment to escape, but when we turned away, another stood right behind us, even bigger than the first. We both screamed, frozen in place. The second nieda picked me up and slammed me to the ground. Iris began throwing conch shells at the first, yelling at it to go away. The larger one climbed on top of me." Foxx flexed her fingers to relieve the tension, noticing they felt cold again. She wondered, not for the first time, how her entire body could feel sweaty, yet her fingertips burned like ice. "It was going to bite me, but Iris cracked it across the face with one of the shells before it could latch on. As it staggered away in response to the blow, one of its fangs sliced my cheek."

"How did you get away?"

Foxx shrugged a shoulder. "To this day, I don't know. All I could see was blood. There was so much blood. The poison hit me instantly, or maybe it was the shock and pain of such a deep wound, and I passed out. The next thing I knew, Iris' face was above mine, tears streaming down her cheeks as she screamed for help, but no one came. When I was able to stand, Iris helped me to my feet, and I saw both niedas dead in the sand. I was so woozy from the poison, Iris practically dragged me back home. We didn't want anyone to know we were living alone, so Iris did her best to fix me up. It's amazing it didn't get infected. I was sick for a few days with a bad fever, but eventually my body healed. Aside from the scar, obviously."

"You never asked Iris what happened after you passed out?"

Foxx shook her head. "She must have been so brave. I didn't want to make her relive it unless she offered the information willingly, but she never has."

"Wow." Asher gazed into the dark room, picturing the scene. "It's a miracle you both survived, and astounding you were able to fight that nieda in the jungle without freezing in terror."

An expression of shame shadowed her face. "But I *did* freeze. If you hadn't come along when you did, I know we would both be dead."

Smiling at the idea of being viewed as their savior, he rolled onto his back, crossing his feet at his ankles. "Or Iris would have destroyed it with her mysterious nieda-defeating skills. And, hey, we match." He pulled his shirt collar down to lay bare his own nieda scar.

She smiled shyly at that. They sat in the stillness for a while, lost in their own thoughts as they watched the lantern light the room in constant motion. Asher's hand absentmindedly slid into his pocket and pulled something out. His fingers twisted it in lazy circles.

Foxx noticed the motion, but the object remained hidden in the shadows of her silhouette. "What is that you're holding?" Asher froze, grasping tight to another secret about to be exposed. Sitting up on her elbows, she pressed, "Asher? And before you answer, please remember we agreed not to lie to each other."

"You mean like how you withheld the fact you and your sister are being hunted by the King's Legion, with no regard for the danger you put me in by traveling with you?" An unfamiliar irritation bled through his words. "I'm essentially harboring fugitives. That's treason and punishable by death, if you didn't know."

"You knew the entire time and didn't mention it," she snapped back. "And really, we didn't exactly lie about it."

"Is that what we're going with?"

Foxx huffed a frustrated breath. "You can't really be mad about the danger we put you in if you knew and chose to accept it from the start."

"I'm not mad." His indignation seemed to fizzle out, though his brow remained pinched tight as he handed over the object.

Foxx held it up into the light. The pink stone, transparent like a crystal, had been cut into a flake of snow. Though she'd never seen actual snow, she was familiar with its design—six identical spokes spreading out from a centerpoint. Her intake of breath revealed her shock. "Asher. Why do you have this?"

He sat up, all traces of anger vanished. "Do you know what it is?"

She grabbed her bag from the floor and pulled out the acacia tree and the skull, laying them in her palms next to the snowflake. "We don't know what they are, but we have these. One is from Savanni and the other from the Grim Wilds."

Each of the three stones had been cut from a different rock into a different shape, but they were analogous in style and size as if part of a matching set.

His face lit up at the sight and he reached into his bag, unable to contain the swells of excitement as he pulled out a fourth. It was cut from an orangey-brown stone into the shape of a forward-facing crown with seven holes across the head and seven spikes across the top. "It's amber. The snowflake is pink tourmaline. I found these in their represented territories: the crown from Reginaterra and the flake from Crystavium. Each territory has a key required to unlock the door that leads to the Sacred Realm of Celestelvyra."

He placed the crown on her palm next to the other three and eyed her expectantly, clearly nervous as to what her reaction would be.

Foxxglove's mind swam with questions. "So you've been traveling around unearthing these keys?"

"Don't you see? We have four of the seven already. Metsa Sateen should have one, though I searched the Monastery and couldn't find it, and Cordillera and Alunda will have the others. Once we have all seven, we'll be able to open the door."

She considered this, trying to fit it into the knowledge she already had. Then a thought struck her. "If you were trying to find the key for each territory, how did you end up in Metsa Sateen without the center three?"

This question startled him, as he realized that, yet again, he'd given away more information than he'd meant to. "What?" he asked, feigning confusion as he scrambled for an explanation.

"If you traveled all the way from Reginaterra, you would have passed through Savanni, Alunda, and the Grim Wilds before you entered Metsa Sateen, so why don't you have those keys also?"

Asher raked a hand through his hair. "Well, you have two of those." She eyed him skeptically. "I couldn't find them so I moved on to Metsa Sateen. Most of the Monasteries are hidden, no longer marked on maps, unless you have access to extremely old maps. Since I had a fairly good idea of where the Monastery in Sateen was located, I made my way there first."

"We searched the Monastery while you were gone." A swirl of pain filled her gut at the memory. "We think it will be shaped like a raindrop. There was a desk in the library with a raindrop carved into it. We saw something similar in the Wilds, a desk with a skull carving matching the shape of the stone."

Asher remained silent, thinking over what she'd shared.

Foxx let her brain wander, too, ruminating on all they had discussed. It seemed an unlikely coincidence he'd run into them in Metsa Sateen without first finding the stones in Savanni, Alunda, and the Grim Wilds. Though he had a point in that she held two of the three, he didn't seem the type to give up so easily and move on. She also wondered how he'd managed to find the keys from the two territories in the far west. Had he started his quest there? Could

Reginaterra or Crystavium be his homeland, or had he started there for another reason?

"You really didn't know they were keys?" Asher asked, interrupting her thoughts. Not realizing she'd stood up while clutching the stones in both hands, she shook her head. "Then why do you have them? How did you know to search for them?"

"A woman in Savanni gave us the first one. She told us it was our destiny to find our father and Celestelvyra. I told you about the map that led us to the old building in the desert. We found the skull behind my mother's painting, and it matched the carving on the table, as well as the size and style of the stone from Maeve." Foxx looked down at the stones in her palms. "So many things seem connected, even more than I realized before. Why would my mother have gifted the Monastery such a painting? Both buildings we saw must have been destroyed hundreds of years ago, so what would have been the point anyway? It's not like she could have known them. And why was the stone stored behind it? How did it get there? I still have so many questions, but now that I know for sure the stones have a purpose, I feel even more confident we're on the right track. Maybe we will find the rainforest stone when we reach Lacuna Kaput. Though I have no idea how we're supposed to find a stone in the middle of a lagoon."

"The stones are the only way into Celestelvyra. Even if it means diving the entirety of the lagoon, we have to find them."

Her hands fell to her sides, causing her shoulders to slump. "So if what you say is true, and these really are the only way to get there, that means my father has spent six years searching for Celestelvyra and because he doesn't have these, there is no way he made it?" She felt a deep sadness creeping into her voice.

He heard it, too. Standing, he walked around the bed and sat down in front of her with a knee on either side of her legs. "Foxx, I don't know about your father. I don't know what he knew or where he is now, but I do know that with these stones, we can enter Celestelvyra." He touched her hands. "And we can fix everything."

Not knowing how to grasp all of this new information, Foxx's emotions whirled in every direction. Pain for a father most certainly lost, hope for a future of fulfilled destinies, confusion about her feelings for the man sitting in front of her, and the tingling sensation his touch triggered up her spine. She sighed and captured his gaze with a serious expression. "What are you really hoping to find in Celestelvyra, Asher?"

He seemed to mull over whether or not he should tell her the whole truth. "Can I trust you, Foxxglove Belamour?" He took the stones from her and placed them on the bed before sliding his fingers into her hands and staring up at her with more intimacy than he ever had before.

She hadn't realized how close she stood to him, with her legs between his knees and his head in line with her heart. She wondered if he could hear it speeding up.

"And are you sure you want to know? Knowing could put you in danger, and you will not be able to unhear it once I tell you. Once the words are out, they're out forever." He sat patiently, waiting while she thought over his questions.

Could Asher trust her? It seemed a peculiar concept, since from the moment they'd met, she'd questioned whether or not they were able to trust *him*. He kept so many secrets, and she knew he held many things back from her even now. But she had her own secrets. Not only from him, but from Iris as well. Maybe everyone had secrets they hid from the world.

Looking into his eyes, she searched for answers, for truth. Then she said, "You can trust me. And Iris, too." She knew they wouldn't be able to keep this secret from her sister once it was let loose. Still he waited, watching her, trying to decipher her thoughts. "I want to know. I want to understand why my father left, why my mother went crazy, and what it all has to do with us. You said everything is connected, and I believe that now more than ever. I *need* to know the truth."

He waited longer still, ablaze with the most serious expression as he gave her one last chance to change her mind. Then he said, "I don't have all the answers, but for my part at least, there is something in Celestelvyra I need to find. Something that will allow me to destroy Queen Sirena Aldrich. The prophets say the world will be made new in wake of the dark queen's destruction. That a new king will rise—one who walks with the Creator and sets the world right."

A shockwave rippled through her, but she tried to keep her expression serene. "By *destroy*, you mean...?"

Asher looked past her to where Iris slept. Foxx followed his gaze. Then he exhaled, and the sound drew her eyes back to him as he said, "Yes, Foxxglove, I mean to kill her."

C

Queen Sirena sat at her vanity observing herself in the looking glass. Thin, golden brows arched high above starless eyes: sharp, striking, and rimmed in charcoal.

Astell, her lady's maid, stood behind her tying off a loose braid with a red ribbon. It began as two braids woven away from her temples and coming together at the nape of her neck before trailing down to the small of her back. She pinned two enormous amaryllis blooms behind the Queen's left ear and placed an elaborate diadem onto her head. Rods of gold twisted around a ruby, wrapping it in a nest of jagged tangles.

"All finished, Your Majesty." Astell slid the wide braid over her shoulder and adjusted the ringlets framing her face.

Next to the vanity in a golden cage stood a magnificent drakin-ferno. His falcon-like beak was the color of the sunrise after a night of battle. An artistic mixture of scales and feathers sprouted from the top of his crown to the tip of his long, serpentine tail. He wore a pair of membranous wings like those of a dragon, and sharp ears to match. Sirena ran her hand down one of the bars of his cage, admiring the ombre of his coloring: mustard-seed yellow into blazing, fire red.

"Thank you, Astell, it's lovely." The Queen's kind words lacked emotion.

Astell picked up the brush and unused pins, returning them to a drawer in the armoire. Then she clasped her hands together behind her back and viewed Sirena in the looking glass. "Is there anything else you need, my lady?"

Sirena shook her head, turning away from the cage and meeting Astell's eyes in her reflection. She flitted her hand in the air as if to shoo her away. Astell bowed and left the room.

In front of her lay the parchment of the Belamour family. The Queen ran her fingers along the image of Foxxglove's face, feeling equal parts hatred and remorse as she stared at the familiar countenance. Her fingers crawled to the jeweled stiletto laying next to the parchment. Rubies decorated the hilt of the golden blade.

Then she plunged the tip of the blade into the center of

Foxxglove's likeness. The drake at her side coughed a plume of smoke in response to the disruption. "Calm, Kaen," she seethed. He shifted in his cage, adjusting himself, and stilled.

A Watchman rushed into the room after hearing the thud of a knife penetrating wood. A quick examination of the scene gave no evidence of danger, so he stopped where he'd landed and stood at attention. "Is everything all right, Your Majesty?"

When Sirena let go of the knife, it remained there. Again she came face to face with her own reflection. "Does it look like I am all right, Renegard?"

Fearfully, he considered which answer would be safest.

The Queen's expression shifted from annoyance to rage. She spun on him. "The answer is *no*, Renegard. Half of the royal Legion is out searching for this bastard and his little brats, and they still haven't managed to catch them."

"I am sure they are doing their best, Your Majesty." He swallowed, wishing to suck the words back in as if he hadn't spoken them. Indignation filled her features as daggers formed behind dark pupils. "I just mean that, I am sure they will find them soon, Your Majesty."

"It has been six years since that traitor stole from me." She sighed, trying to calm her loathing so she didn't accidentally kill her favorite Watchman. Renegard was one of the few sentries Sirena felt she could fully trust. He was strong and attractive and definitely had his uses. Plus, it would be too much trouble to replace him.

"Yes, my Queen, but you have never before tried with such force. The King's Legion will track them down and retrieve what was taken. Commander Kayvan is—"

The Queen scowled and stood abruptly, grumbling the commander's name under her breath. Her fury reignited. "That fool! Why my idiot husband named him commander of his Legion I will never understand."

She drew closer to her Watchman, eyeing him seductively as she circled him. He held his breath, doing his best not to move while she ran a finger across the width of his shoulders. When she faced him again, she dragged her finger up his throat to the tip of his chin. Then she spun away and perched on the edge of her bed, the centerpiece of the room and, in her opinion, the most extravagant bed in the entire Five Kingdoms. Though she didn't share her sleeping quarters with the King, the bed was wide enough to hold at least four people comfortably–a number she knew for a fact to be true.

Wrought iron made up the frame. Talon-like curls decorated the edges of the bed, and the headboard was crafted to look like the wings of a dragon. Sharp scales lined the poles holding up a maroon canopy, and a matching duvet bore gold-lace designs.

"It is a shame you are so good to me, Renegard. Otherwise, you may have had a chance to hold Hector's position." Again she said his name with disgust.

The soldier held her gaze. "I would be anything my Queen wished me to be."

"As you have proven, my dear." She slid her palms sensually across the duvet. "The King's Legion is surely missing a wonderful addition to its ranks, but I'm too unwilling to part with you."

"I am at your command, my Queen." His eyes drifted from hers, tracing the swooping neckline of her dress.

All at once bored with his unwavering devotion, she rose from the bed and sauntered back to her vanity. "You may go, Renegard."

"Yes, my Queen." He bowed and returned to his post outside her chambers.

Sirena stared once again at Foxx's face, running a finger down the ragged scar marring her jaw. Catching her own eyes in the looking glass, she smiled. "The *King's* Legion, indeed."

C

Iris took the news about murdering Her Royal Majesty far better than Foxx expected. The three of them sat on Asher's bed as Asher and Foxx shared the details from their discussion the night before.

"The Queen is super evil. That's why Mother so desperately wanted to run away to Celestelvyra." Iris had the tray of sweets she'd ordered with her luncheon sitting in her lap. The sweet in her hand had a silver, ribbed wrapper around the bottom half. She peeled it off one rib at a time before popping the lavender-iced chocolate into her mouth.

When Foxx said nothing in reply, Iris rolled her eyes and said, "I know, I know. Mother was crazy, but based on everything we have seen so far, aren't you starting to believe her? Savage, mutated monsters? Rabid monkeys?" Iris' mouth was stuffed full of sugar and cake as she spoke. "Sounds like a curse to me. And this isn't the first time we've heard complaints about the Queen of Arkaemor. Remember that couple at the teashop in Aeonian?"

Foxx had not anticipated her sister's sensible view on the subject. They'd grown up in a world of monsters. There was nothing to suggest this wasn't the way it had always been, aside from Asher's word. And their mother's.

But Iris had always been more trusting and willing to believe fanciful tales.

Foxx sighed. "I agree there is more wrong with the world than I originally thought. And yes, I see the connections between the things Mother used to say and the reality around us, but how do we know it's actually the Queen's fault?"

Asher looked up from his journal, setting one of his gifted pencils in the centerfold. "Do you have other ideas on what could have caused all of it?"

Foxx met his look with questioning eyes. "No, I guess not, but just because I can't come up with a logical answer doesn't mean there isn't one."

"There is a logical answer. Queen Sirena cursed the world and has been ruling it for millennia, immortal and unopposed." The fire in his voice didn't often arise, but flames could practically be seen in his irises when he spoke of the Queen. "She does whatever she wants to whomever she wants, and she never receives any justice for her crimes." He looked down at the book in his lap, trying to alleviate his frustration. "You just have to trust me." His eyes lifted to Foxx's, and the new emotions she found within them melted her heart. "Don't you trust me?"

Iris interrupted, saving Foxx from responding. "So Asher, you think killing her will return everything to the way it was originally meant to be?"

Asher pulled his gaze from Foxx and set his book on the bed. "Not immediately, but it will start the process of returning the world to what the Creator always intended."

"You mentioned the rising of a king who walks with the Creator," Foxx said.

"Yes. The Great King. I'm not sure who he is, but I imagine Elohim will make him known eventually. For all we know he could already be out in the world somewhere striving for this very goal."

Iris placed the empty tray of sweets next to her and hopped off the bed to pace as she pelted him with more questions. "So you think there is something in Celestelvyra that will help you get rid of the Queen?"

"It is the only thing that will kill her, to my knowledge. The Queen is resilient, immortal, and protected."

"Protected by what?" Iris asked.

Asher slid to the edge of the bed and put his feet on the floor. "Her magic, first of all. The entire King's Legion. And I can't say for sure, but history tells us other immortals lived a long time ago. I suppose it's possible some might still stand at her side."

"Like King Pollux?" Iris asked. Asher shrugged.

"Is the thing you need to find in Celestelvyra some kind of magic?" Foxx asked.

"Ancient magic. Gifted to us by the Creator Himself."

"The Creator—" Foxx began, but Iris cut her off, her hands waving through the air as she reiterated the information Asher had provided and plotted out a plan.

"So we find the last three keys, then we find a doorway to Celestelvyra."

"Correct. There was thought to be an entrance in every Monastery at one point, but actually finding one might be tricky. I searched the Monastery here in Sateen, but I didn't find anything. Maybe a door will present itself somewhere else, but there aren't a lot of Monasteries left standing."

Iris nodded and continued. "Once a doorway is found, we can use the keys. Hopefully then we will figure out exactly what this magical object is." She stopped pacing. "Wait, do we know what the object is?"

"Actually, it isn't an object, per se, but pure water with magical properties from a fountain residing there. According to the stories, Pyhä-ki is the only thing that can kill an immortal."

"Okay, so scoop up some magic water, travel to Inaravale, and use it against the Queen." Iris lifted her fist into the air in victory, letting herself get swept away by the proposed quest, full of sorcery and monsters, hidden realms and enchanted fountains. "World. Saved."

"*I* will travel to Inaravale and kill the Queen," he corrected. "*You* will both stay in the protected realm until it's safe." He picked up his book and slid it into his bag as if the conversation were over.

Iris stared at him, mouth agape. "Absolutely not!"

"We are in this together now," Foxxglove agreed. "You're the one who said so, remember? We protect each other. If she is protected, then you need protection, too."

"No, this is different." His tone grew serious, not with anger but unyielding. "This isn't some stroll through rough wilderness. The Queen is more fierce than anything you will find in the wild. It's going to be incredibly dangerous."

"Yes, it is." Foxx reached over and bravely squeezed his hand, looking him square in the eye. "That is exactly why we're not going to let you go alone.

CHAPTER 15

FALLING FOR RAIN

After their discussion over luncheon, Asher went to bathe, leaving Iris and Foxx alone to talk. When he'd finished washing the clothing in the tub the night before, he'd hung them on the rotating clothesline outside the window. An overhang extended from the roof, providing cover from the falling rain.

Unclipping each item, the sisters folded the clothes before laying them out on the bed in separate piles. "This line is a nice set up, isn't it?" Iris asked.

"It is."

Noticing Foxx's distraction, Iris nudged her shoulder. "So what do you really think about all this? Are you feeling okay with everything?"

"I'm nervous, especially since I know we still don't have all of the information, but I'm more willing to trust than I was before." She pulled a shirt from the line and held it up to determine who it belonged to.

"I can tell." Iris caught the shirt Foxx tossed to her. "You never told me about your vision. What did you see?"

Foxx squeezed her eyes shut as the memories resurfaced. "Oh, it was horrible, Iris. I saw a building, huge and destroyed. It could have been another Monastery, but I don't know for sure. Moons decorated the ground at my feet. Then everything was on fire. It felt so real. I swear I could feel its heat."

"Were you in a city?"

"Yes. How did you know?"

"The Tree of Knowing." Iris shivered at the memory. "It showed me a burning city with people running and screaming. There was a beast in the sky."

"I remember you mentioning a city on fire. I didn't see anything in the sky except billowing smoke reflecting the firelight."

"What do you think it means?" Iris asked.

"I don't know." Foxx stared out the window in thought. Her mind drifted again to the chaotic scene of citizens caked in soot and buildings crumbling to the ground. "It's troubling though. It seems the path we walk is leading us to that city. Something awful happens there. And we'll be right at the center of it."

☾

Once they'd completed their chore, they returned everything to their packs. Iris left out a fresh set of clothing so she could bathe when Asher finished with the tub.

They planned to head out into the city as darkness fell. With soldiers in town, they didn't want to risk being seen in the daylight. Pearl had dropped by that morning to see how they were fairing, and Asher had requested some clothing to help them blend in with the rest of the civilians. She happily obliged, agreeing to gather some items and return with them before dinner.

When Asher exited the bathroom, his hair still dripped with water. He scrubbed the top of his head before joining Foxx by the window and clipping his towel to the clothesline.

Iris announced her departure and disappeared into the bathroom.

Leaning against the frame of the window, Foxx stared out into the rain. Asher hovered near her, his palms sweaty. A connection had formed between them in the dim light of a single lantern, as it often did by a fire. His tightly clutched secrets had come undone, and he worried speaking now might unravel the bond that had stitched them together the previous night.

"I'm fine," she said.

He grinned. "I wasn't going to ask."

"You wanted to." She turned to look at him as a slight smile curved her lips.

He ran his hand down the back of his head. "I was trying to

devise a charming way to thank you for not abandoning me after finding the, uh, thing. In my pocket."

"Yet." She meant to sound serious so he recognized the thin ice he walked, but her heart wasn't in it, and it emerged like a tease instead. "Thank you for finishing up the laundry." Her eyes again found the jungle.

"No problem." He rested against the opposite side of the frame, looking out at the forest with her. The Passiflora Inn sat at the far end of the city with nothing beyond it but trees. "Are you excited to explore Petrichor?"

"I am."

"It should be fun. Maybe when we return this evening…" He paused, searching for the words, or perhaps the bravery to say them. "Maybe we can talk more."

She glanced over, trying to catch his eye, but he continued staring out the open window. "Talk more about what?"

A long minute passed before he answered, "Just… more."

Foxx wondered if he meant to imply he might reveal more of the truths he'd yet to divulge. "I would like that."

A knock at the door unveiled a smiling Pearl. She wore a magenta robe similar to the one she'd worn before, except this robe's pattern displayed flowering birds-of-paradise. After handing Foxx a stack of colorful fabrics, she bowed and disappeared down the hall.

Iris exited the bathroom as Foxx closed the door. "From Pearl?" She gestured toward the clothing in her hand. Foxx nodded. Asher moved to the bed and reclined his back against the pillows to write in his book.

The girls pulled the colorful robes over their clothing. Foxx wore plum with lavender accents. Even though the skirt of the robe fell all the way to the floor and the sleeves belled out to cover her hands, the thin fabric felt breathable enough to provide comfort in the humid forest.

Iris helped pull the dark purple sash across her middle to hold it all together and tied it around the back. Her robes were an opposite yet mirror image of Foxx's: sunshine yellow with dark honey accents.

After helping her sister tie the matching sash, Foxx noticed her own robes came with an extra scarf. She surveyed her outfit, trying to see if she'd missed something. "Where does this go?"

Iris scrutinized her, circling her person. "Oh, Pearl, you brilliant beauty!" She wrapped it in a cocoon around Foxx's head, hiding her radiant hair. Tucking in escaped strays, she adjusted it to look like an elegant fashion piece rather than a cunning disguise.

Iris twisted her long hair around itself until it lay in a high, tight bun, similar to how Pearl wore hers. Taking a flower from the vase on the dresser, she tucked it into her hair tie.

Both women turned to Asher, seeking approval. When they caught his attention, his face brightened. He stood, walking around the bed with his chin propped on his hand in jovial appraisal. Twisting his finger in the air, he motioned for them to spin. "I suppose these will do."

"Asher!" Iris squealed. "What do you really think?"

He laughed. "You really are two divine flowers in an enchanted wood." His eyes lingered on Foxx a little too long. "Absolutely gorgeous."

Her cheeks reddened, and Iris donned a pert smile. "That's enough, you two."

Foxx smacked her sister's arm with the back of her hand, shushing her and provoking another laugh from her companions.

Iris started toward the door. "Let's get going! I want to see all that this mysterious city in the canopy has to show us."

"Wait." Foxx stopped Iris before her hand touched the doorknob and lifted her blade belt from the bed. "We better take these, just in case." Iris agreed and attached her weapons low on her hips, tucking them as discreetly as she could beneath her sash. The scabbards hung at her sides, subtly hidden by the folds in her robes.

Foxx rustled through her bag for the miniature dagger she kept but rarely used for anything other than cutting up food. Opening the robe to expose her leg, she propped her foot up on the bed and tied the knife around the top of her knee-high boot with a handkerchief. When she caught Asher's perusing eyes, she flushed again and quickly hid bare legs beneath her robes. Then she slid her bow and quiver over her shoulder, and Asher did the same with his rifle.

Fully armed, they stepped from their room and out onto the balcony, feeling more at ease in their costumes. Pausing by the railing, they absorbed the atmosphere of the captivating city.

Asher locked the door. "Keep watch for soldiers. The disguises should fool them at a distance, but if they see you up close, it may not be enough."

They followed the balcony to the stairs and down into the lobby. With a wave from the receptionist, they were out the door to explore the heart of Petrichor.

C

They strolled effortlessly through the city, following the pathway of bridges wherever it desired to lead them. They planned to hit a few shops and resupply, knowing they would be departing the treetop metropolis at the break of dawn, but they had agreed to save that for the night's end. They wanted to experience the city and decided to wander for a while with no destination in mind.

The bridges and shops were filled with patrons. Many smiled in greeting as they walked by. It was a welcome change from the restful walkways they'd witnessed upon arriving. Most of the ladies wore robes similar to theirs, crafted in all different colors and variations. Many of the men wore more simplistic attire: flowing pants and long tunics hanging to mid thigh.

Rows of lanterns stretched between trees, casting radiant light through the city as the ropes swayed in the breeze. Vines of passiflora climbed up and around the trunks and bridges.

Tan-furred monkeys roamed the city. They walked the railings and hung from the tops of buildings. As the trio strolled past, several held out their hands as if begging for food. Lepennas hopped across rooftops and drifted through the air on feathered wings, and brightly colored birds speckled the lantern ropes, blessing those who lived below with their beautiful tunes.

Asher and Iris each bought an ale from a pub serving refreshments through a window. Foxx opted for a fruity drink smelling of sweet and sour pineapple and embellished with a bamboo straw. Then they meandered the city's labyrinth of bridges and chatted while sipping their delicious drinks.

As the unseen sky turned from twilight to dusk, the rain descended in heavier spells. It thundered against the rooftops. Though the monkeys ran for cover, the driädi were undeterred. When one flew near, Foxx lifted a hand, and it landed on her finger. She'd never seen one up close, nor had she expected the creature within the glow to wear the shape of a furry human with a tail like a fox and tiny horns atop its head.

Hiding up in the rafters of the bridges, tinaeras protected their wings from the escalating rainfall. Iris stopped at the corner of a bridge and looked up at one. It turned to face her, staring down at her with big, black eyes. Pastel fur covered its body and legs, and feathered antennae stuck out from its head.

"I didn't know they got this big," she said. "The ones we have in Alunda are a little bigger than a coconut. These guys are almost twice that."

Asher and Foxx had joined her examination. "Tinaeras: the giant moths of the jungle. I once saw one twice as big as this one."

After another minute observing the creature, they continued on. Eventually, they found their way back to the outdoor pub. Each purchased another drink before continuing to mosey aimlessly, enjoying the sound of the harsh rain, the foggy view of the lanterns, and each other's effortless company.

Iris bubbled, humming and spinning in front of them as they walked. She held her robe off the ground with one hand while the other hung in the air, draped over an invisible partner's neck. "Foxxglove, isn't my companion the most handsome dancer you've ever seen?"

Foxx giggled but didn't otherwise respond to her sister's question, fearing she might admit something foolish if she did. Her cheeks were flushed red as poppy flowers from her fruity drink.

Amused by their joy but anxious to return to the room and discuss more of the things he kept tucked out of reach, Asher suggested, "We should probably find a supply shop before it gets too late and everything closes. Then we can head back to the room. We want to leave tomorrow with the rising sun."

Iris stopped in her tracks, her hand still in the air. "Aww, but this place is so magical. I'm not ready to say merry night yet!"

Foxx glanced at Asher, tucking her head into her shoulders. "Just a little longer?"

They came to a large deck in front of a restaurant called *The Bengal Bistro*, according to the handsomely illustrated marquee. Neither the awning in front of *The Bengal Bistro* nor the roofs of the attached bridges stretched out enough to cover the deck, leaving it open to the rainfall.

At its center stood a tall pole with a covered lantern atop it, much bigger than the ones hanging from the ropes and bridges around them. Like the crystal shade in their bathroom at the inn, the lamp held a globe of rainbow glass. The fire's light shone through the globe, dispersing in the raindrops and creating a myriad of hues reflecting in all directions.

The trio stopped under the bridge and stared out at the spectacle. "What is this used for?" Iris asked.

"There is a restaurant there." Asher pointed across the promenade. "They probably bring tables out here when it's not raining so guests can have dinner under the trees. Or perhaps the space is used as a dance floor for parties and weddings."

Foxx's face was alight, entranced by the orchestra of pigments coloring the rain. Before either of them could stop her, she fled the dry safety of the bridge and sprinted out into the downpour. Each drop felt like freedom. She stopped within the barrier of the prismatic light and watched the colors reflect off her wet skin. A melody of water and light waltzed across her cheeks, and she smiled more brilliantly than she had in as long as she could remember.

In the distance, a voice called out. Her name perhaps. She was enjoying the moment too greatly to respond. Hearing the call again and recognizing Asher's voice, she withdrew from the embrace she shared with the clouds to peer at him.

"What are you doing?" He held his hands around his mouth to amplify his voice. Iris giggled and continued her dance under the roof of the bridge, peacefully ignoring them both.

"What are *you* doing?" Foxx called back. Even through the blurry shower, she could see the amusement forming around Asher's eyes.

"I'm staying dry," he said.

"I'm… not doing that!"

He laughed and crossed his arms. "I can see that." He didn't bother calling out over the rain.

Then, before she could change her mind, Foxx stood in front of him. As if her limbs no longer obeyed her will, she grabbed his hand and leaned into him, her lips brushing his ear as she breathed, "Join me."

Not giving him the chance to deny her, she dragged him from the shelter and into the downpour. Pulling him along, she danced back to the lamppost, following the steps the rain taught her. The raindrops pounded the wooden platform to create a musical rhythm that only she knew how to follow. Catching sight of Asher's smile, her heart jolted in her stomach as if suddenly falling. "Isn't it stunning?" She slowed her dance to catch her breath.

Taking a step closer, Asher brought her movements to an abrupt halt. His eyes found hers, paralyzing her with their intensity, and his fingers crawled behind her neck as he ran his thumb up the bone of her jaw. His other hand slid around her waist, pulling her taut against him, locking her body within the confines of his arms.

Her lungs broke or disappeared or died, refusing to take in air. Her heart pumped so hard she thought it might actually explode. With a familiarity that hadn't existed before that moment, her hand lifted to his side and grabbed his shirt as if holding on for dear life.

The mixture of the rainfall and the vehemence of his touch sent currents throughout her body. Her eyelids fell closed as she breathed in the scent of him, woodsy and sweet and smelling of fresh rain. He moved his thumb to the top of the scar above her brow and traced it all the way down to her chin. Her breath caught in her throat, and her mouth parted as his thumb brushed across the plumpness of her bottom lip. "*You* are stunning, love."

Her eyes fluttered open again to find his devouring her. Swallowing her up. Drowning, drowning, drowning. Not from the harsh rain but from the weight of the emotion in his gaze, as if his eyes could admit in a single look all the things he hadn't said aloud. The crinkles at their corners matched the smile on his lips.

The hand at her waist eased further around the small of her back, pulling her closer and sending tremors up her spine. With his thumb under her chin, he lifted her face upward.

Iris' voice reached their ears, laced with shock and terror, and the moment shattered like glass. "Foxxglove! Look out!"

They followed the direction of her outstretched hand and instantly sobered as they discovered a band of soldiers dressed in royal red heading in their direction.

Time slowed and accelerated in tandem. Asher grabbed Foxx's hand and wrenched her forward, yanking her arm so hard she felt it may rip free of its socket. As they raced toward Iris, their boots pummeled the deck, throwing arced sprays of water in all directions.

Iris was ahead of them, her previous tranquility evaporated. Fighting the layers of her robe, she scrunched it into a bundle in her left hand, allowing her legs freedom to run.

Foxx noticed Iris' brilliance, but she wouldn't be able to use her weapon with a single hand. Instead, she slid her fingers behind her back and slipped the knot of her sash free, pulling it from around her waist and letting it fall to the deck behind her. Her robe separated, enabling her to run without hindrance as the sides flapped behind her like a cape in the wind.

Glancing over her shoulder, she counted five Legion soldiers, but like those who chased them in Kesken Ala, not a single shot was fired. This confirmed her suspicion that they were to be captured alive.

Turning back around, her eyes shifted to Asher's fearful, yet determined, expression. Iris remained several paces ahead, leading the way.

They needed to return to the Passiflora Inn for their belongings. They wouldn't survive the wild without them. Unless they escaped now and returned for them later? The city was a network of bridges. Perhaps they would be able to lose the Legion in the maze of Petrichor and vanish into the jungle below. Should they split up? Stick together?

A storm of possibilities hammered Foxx's thoughts as the raindrops pelted the roofs above, drowning out all noise but the thudding of their boots.

The citizens of the city soon became aware of the chase developing. Many paused their evening festivities to observe the unfolding events. The trio did their best to avoid a collision, and luckily, no one stepped into their path to assist in their capture.

Asher glimpsed the pursuing Legion and realized their numbers had grown, not with more red soldiers but with Petrichorian Patrolmen hoping to help apprehend the criminals invading their city. "Don't look now, but there's more."

Foxx ignored his warning and glanced over her shoulder to see the proof of his words.

Iris did the same. "Why aren't they shooting at us?"

"I doubt they'll risk harming a civilian," Asher yelled back. "And they must be under orders not to kill you, otherwise they might have already tried."

"What if we attack first?" Foxx asked. "Will they fire on us then?"

Asher didn't have an answer, but she'd already dropped her bow into her hand and nocked an arrow. She needed to slow the soldiers down and give them a fighting chance to get away.

Foxx pulled the string and rotated her body in perfect synchrony, releasing the arrow so it struck one of the soldiers in the thigh. He tripped and dropped to the ground, holding tight to his leg. His fall caused a second soldier to stumble, but barely. The rest parted around the felled man without hindrance.

A second arrow plunged through a shoulder. The soldier's body spun with the force of the blow, and he hit the man running next to him in the face with his flailing arm. Both men toppled to the ground. An intersecting bridge brought three more Patrolmen into the pack, replacing the three she'd taken down.

"This is pointless." Foxx slung her bow back up over her shoulder, no longer willing to forfeit her arrows. "More Patrolman. We need a plan."

Asher again grabbed Foxx's hand and pulled her forward, encouraging her to run faster. They passed the outdoor pub and the grocer that had all the supplies they would need to restock before trudging back out into the forest, but he couldn't worry about that now.

Throwing another glance over his shoulder, his brain raced to generate a plan. The man Foxx shot in the shoulder had ripped the arrow free and rejoined the hunt with blood dripping down the arm of his uniform.

Up ahead, Asher saw the road splitting in two directions. One led to the Inn and the other would usher them deeper into the city. Asher called Foxx's name and her eyes shifted to him. She'd also seen the split and knew what he would say. Shaking her head, she shouted, "No! We need to stick together!" But her heart wasn't in it, a truth made visible in her conceding eyes.

"We can't. If we split up, they will too. I'm pretty sure General Wraith will follow me. I can lead him away."

Foxx eyed him strangely, wondering what kind of trouble he might have been in to be familiar with the Legion's general.

Before she could question it, Asher said, "Just trust me! He will follow me. You and Iris make your way toward the inn and grab our things. Then meet me at the entrance to the city."

"I don't understand!" The rain seemed to have picked up, making it harder for Foxx to hear him. Or perhaps it was her heartbeat pulsing against the drum of her ear.

At last they reached the split. Iris had already followed his orders and veered left. The soldiers gained ground but were still far enough away to give them a few moments to speak.

Through ragged breaths, he pulled her close, willing her to hear him. To listen. "Foxx, you have to trust me. Splitting up their pack is the best option. Take down the few who follow you. Do whatever you have to do to get away, do you understand? They don't deserve your decency. When it's safe, retrieve our belongings from the Inn, and meet me at the entrance."

Foxx glowered at the soldiers drawing closer with every passing second. There wasn't time to protest. She focused on his eyes, trying to read the message in the golden flecks dancing around within the green as they attempted to convey every promise he wished to make her. Every word he didn't have time to say.

He pulled her into his chest, pressing his lips to her temple as he vowed, "Foxxglove, I *will* find you." It was the only commitment he had time for. Then he pushed her backward so hard she stumbled, and yelled, "*Run!*"

Foxx obeyed, sprinting after her sister without looking back. Iris was already a bridge ahead, but Foxx ran fast and gained ground quickly despite her burning eyes and lack of oxygen. Her throat felt swollen, as if her heart had lodged itself within it.

The next bridge intersected a landing with a circular building belonging to a shoemaker. A man stood in the doorway and watched the spectacle unravel. The sisters darted around the building and onto the next bridge to find the towering Inn within their sights.

Foxx tried to halt the torment creeping in. She couldn't allow herself to be distracted. *Calm in the storm*, she coached herself, but her emotions continued to overwhelm her. What if Asher didn't find them? What if he was captured, and it was all their fault?

Out of control emotions promote out of control mistakes.

Her mother's words, but she'd stamped them on her heart long ago. She needed to pull herself together, but the thought of losing Asher made her stomach feel like rot and her legs weighed down by sandbags.

The emerald of his eyes slipped into her mind, and his promise played on repeat inside her head: *I will find you.*

Glancing over her shoulder, Foxx saw a soldier catching up. She spun and released an arrow, taking him down. Rotating forward again, she tripped over a person sitting in the center of the bridge. Foxx tumbled to the ground, rolling and landing on her feet in a crouch next to an elderly woman draped in heavy layers.

The wrinkles in her face revealed her age, and the smell of liquor permeating her skin gave explanation for her sitting in the middle of the walkway. The woman looked at Foxx in horror.

"I'm sorry! I didn't see you. Are you all right?" Foxx's eyes flashed past the woman at the pursuing soldiers.

The woman's eyes grew wider, and she reached for Foxx's robe, drawing her attention as she clutched the extra fabric around her arm with feeble fingers. The crone's voice was scratchy and weak as she shouted, "The Great King. The King! The Seer marks his way. But she will destroy them all! Watch out, take heed, take heart! The Great King will surely rise, and she will surely fall!"

Hands slid under Foxx's arms, dragging her to her feet and out of the woman's grasp.

"What are you doing?" Iris cried. "We need to run!"

The hag called out after them, "Take heed, take heart! The Seer will fall!" Her words faded into the rain and the pulse in Foxx's ears as she ran as fast as her feet would take her. She turned around again and let two more arrows fly. The first hit its mark, dropping him to the ground. The second missed, dodged by the other soldier in pursuit.

Iris spun and charged the man, catching him off guard as she cracked him in the temple with the hilt of her blade. He dropped on impact, and she hoped it wasn't a fatal blow as she raced back to Foxx.

They saw no other soldiers in pursuit. Perhaps Asher had been right in that they would follow him instead. But why, when it was the Belamour sisters they seemed so desperate to find?

One more bridge to go. As they rounded the next building, a hand grabbed Foxx's arm and yanked her sideways. For the briefest moment she felt a swell of relief that Asher had found his way back to her already, but the foolish thought vanished as quickly as it had come. Before she could react to the assailant, she was spun into a man's chest. Her bow slipped from her grasp and clattered to the ground, and her quiver pressed hard into her spine by the chest at her back.

The man stretched his hand over her mouth to silence her before she could scream and whispered into her ear, "You would not believe how hard it has been to get you girls alone."

Momentarily consumed by deja vu, she realized why the scene felt familiar. She'd felt it before—in her vision in the desert. Gripped from behind, a hand across her mouth, the vision played itself out in her head in time with her present.

Iris whimpered next to her. Foxx found her sister to her left, arms locked together at the wrists by a man's hand. He held a knife to her throat with his other. It took only a moment to recognize him as one of the two men they'd met in the Wilds. Declan's stoney eyes gazed back at her from over Iris' shoulder.

She could feel Orion's hair unbound and dripping onto her neck. "We've been looking for you ladies." He spun her around by her shoulders, removing his hand from her mouth and grabbing her wrists. "Now, you are going to do as I say, or my friend here is going to slice your pretty sister's throat. Do you understand?"

Glimpsing Iris' pleading eyes, her chest heaved as she tried to collect herself. Thoughts of the Legion's chase faded. Concerns for Asher's whereabouts dissipated on the breeze.

No longer distracted, she knew only the present moment. The threat to her sister's life. The knife at her throat. The smell of Orion's sweat still lingering in her nose. Though her heart raced, her breathing became steady and her eyes narrowed. A frigid feeling coiled in her chest, a cold-blooded darkness she couldn't quell. All of her senses grew attentive and sharp, taking in everything they could about Orion, Declan, and her peripherals.

Then she leveled Orion with a glare and gave a single nod.

"Good. That will make this infinitely easier." Orion stepped closer to her. She felt his breath on her skin. "Here is what's going to happen: You're going to bend down and pick up your bow." He removed her quiver as he spoke. Foxx realized Declan had already taken Iris' belt of blades. "Then we're going to walk straight out of this city without alerting anyone there's an issue, are you following me?" She confirmed her compliance with a shift of her chin. "Once we're safely out of Petrichor, you're going to lead us to your traitorous father."

Though this last statement surprised her, she didn't expose her confusion. She glanced at her wrists, waiting for him to release them. Inspecting him from top to bottom, she saw the pistol at his hip, a drop of sweat beside his eye, and his dirty clothing and disheveled hair. He let go of her hands and took a step back. She rubbed her wrists, taking her time obeying, and surveyed her surroundings as she tried to come up with a plan. Iris stood motionless behind Declan's knife. Declan remained stone-faced. Foxx could get no read off of him. On the fringe of her vision, she could see the brightly lit Passiflora Inn. "We need to go back to the Inn and get our things."

"So we can run into your boyfriend? Not going to happen. Now pick up your bow."

"He isn't going that way." Her insistence was calm but defiant. "He sent us to retrieve our things so he could lead the soldiers away. We won't survive the jungle without our supplies."

Orion grabbed her wrist again, drawing her close. His breath smelled faintly of ale. "You are not in charge here, Foxxglove Belamour. Pick. Up. Your. Bow." He spun her so she faced the weapon and released her with a shove.

A soldier in red, black, and dark gray rounded the building in a hurry, his eyes ballooning when he saw them stopped in front of him. Before his lips could part in surprise, Orion pulled his pistol and shot the soldier between the eyes. Iris cried out as he slumped to the ground in a heap.

Foxx, outwardly unaffected by his hasty act of violence, stood a moment longer in rebellion, trying to waste time and hoping a plan might materialize. She peered back at him without turning around. "You do not frighten me, Orion."

"Maybe not." His grin was repugnant as he waved his pistol at Declan and Iris. "But he should."

She glared at him before scrutinizing Declan, still failing to find anything informative about him. He held the knife to her sister's throat, his face void of emotion.

Bending down to where her bow had fallen, Foxx paused, her mind racing. They needed a distraction. Her head rotated up to her sister as she reached for the bow. Iris—clever, amazing Iris— wiggled her knee, her eyes wide in a silent message.

As she grabbed the bow, Foxx slid her other hand into her robe, now pooled around her on the ground, and retrieved the dagger she'd tied to her boot. Releasing the bow, she spun on her knee and plunged the knife into Orion's thigh with both hands.

"You bitch!" He backhanded her across the face, and she fell to the ground. She retrieved her weapon and attempted to scramble away, but he grabbed her hair through the scarf and yanked her to her feet, growling in her ear. "That was not very smart, Foxxglove. This is your one and only second chance." He drew her closer. "Another trick like that and I will kill your sister myself. I only need one of you to take me to your father." Orion shoved her forward, releasing her hair. Her knees and palms hit the ground hard, and her loosened scarf fell in front of her face. "Now move."

Orion signaled to Declan, and Iris fell away from him as Foxx began moving forward. Orion followed her. Declan pushed Iris between the shoulder blades, cuing her to move. They walked back across the bridge, with Orion directing Foxx where to go.

Foxx's mind scrambled as she clung to the notion of an escape plan. She heeded some of the locals but couldn't bring herself to endanger them, fearing Orion might be even more brutal with anyone who tried to help. She scanned her surroundings, silently begging Asher to appear, and even searched for a soldier, thinking she and Iris may fare better in Reginaterra than traveling with kidnapping criminals. But she saw neither. All she could do was hope Asher's mysterious higher power would have him somehow arrive at the city gates at the same time they did.

Lost in her own thoughts and unfamiliar with the layout of the city, Foxx noticed too late that they'd arrived at a different exit. A smaller basket than the one they'd ridden up awaited them on the platform. She hadn't known more than one way in and out of the city existed, hadn't realized she needed to be watching the paths they took.

Orion and Declan were abducting them through a back exit. Asher wouldn't be meeting them there. He would have no idea what happened to them. She considered fighting back again. She considered running, but she felt certain Orion might truly shoot one of them in the back if they tried.

They entered the basket upon his command. As the lift lowered them away from the city, Foxx watched it disappear from sight and tried her best not to let misery consume her as all hope seemed lost.

Part Two

Staggering Divergence

Two can manage most things,
but it takes more than a pair to steer ships as grand as these.

~An ancient proverb, circa 1190
Author Unknown

CHAPTER 16

DISCOVERY OF BIRDS

"Let. Us. GO!" Iris hurled herself toward Orion's back. He strolled ahead of her on the trail with such abominable nonchalance, she was finding it impossible to suppress her outrage. Her bound fists waved in the air, begging for the chance to pummel his face. From behind, Declan slid an arm around her stomach and scooped her up, lifting her off the ground and spinning her away from his partner. She bucked and thrashed to squirm free of his grasp.

"This is not how you get those hands untied." His forearm held her in place and when she felt his warm breath against the back of her neck, she snapped her head to whip him with her ponytail.

"I don't care. His smug face is so *punchable!*"

Orion had ceased his stroll to look back at them, watching with amusement as Declan wrangled their snared beast. Iris leaned around Declan's side to spit at him, but he stood far enough away to remain unscathed. Grinning devilishly, he blew her a kiss before resuming his walk toward Foxxglove, who stood several paces ahead of them on the trail, examining the map with unbound hands.

Iris growled and lunged again, but still failed to break free of Declan's hold. "Just one good punch, come ON!"

Declan massaged his temples with his free hand. "You have to calm down."

Iris turned her head to scowl at him and found his face next to hers. New waves of indignation coursed down each vertebrae of her spine. Still, she tried to settle, willing her fiery rage to fade to embers with an exhale. She attempted to cross her arms, only to find them still attached at the wrist. Stomping her foot, she blew the white strand of hair away from her face in one sharp breath.

Declan asked, "Have you finished now? Are you going to control your temper?" She huffed, but he released her, sidestepping so he stood at her shoulder. He wore a similar getup to the one he'd worn the day they'd met in the Grim Wilds: pants tucked inside his boots and a plain short-sleeved shirt. The long tuft of tawny hair hanging in his face slid sideways with his tilting head. "Throwing tantrums is not going to get him to free your wrists."

His placation angered her more than his tendency to wrap his arm around her waist to prevent her from attacking Orion. He had the power to set her free, yet chose to keep her restrained like an animal.

Declan's gaze slid up the trail to Orion and Foxx, and Iris jumped at the opportunity in his distraction, punching him across the jaw with all her might.

He swore, spitting blood, and off she shot, sprinting west down the trail. She held no fantasies of completing the journey back to Petrichor with tied wrists and zero supplies, but it didn't matter. Her momentary freedom and her tenacity to fight back were victory enough.

Catching up faster than she'd hoped, Declan grabbed her again with both arms. She kicked and screamed, trying to draw attention from anyone who might be close by. He clamped her mouth shut with his fingers and growled her name in the most commanding voice she'd ever heard it spoken. "Iris, that's *enough!*"

At last, she yielded to his authority and stilled but for the harsh rise and fall of her chest as she caught her breath. Declan released her mouth and the muscles in his arms slackened, but he didn't unhitch himself from her torso. "Now you've had your fun. Are you going to play nice?"

She huffed again, refusing to respond.

Letting her go, Declan rubbed the back of his neck with both hands, ignoring the flames in her glare. "You know what, Iris? Fine. Keep your chains if that suits you. It means little to me." A growl gurgled in her throat, and he inhaled another steadying breath. "But you have to walk with me or he's going to make me drag you. So will you walk for me? Please? I would really rather not have to carry you over my shoulder the rest of the way, and I'm certain you don't want that either."

Her hip jutted out, and she tilted her head. Then she began moving forward without uttering a word.

"Maybe you should get her a leash." Orion cracked a smile. Iris' scream was primal.

They'd already been trudging through the jungle for nearly a week without their packs or any sightings of Asher. Though they didn't progress forward over the first few days as quickly as the men had hoped, they were already a fair distance from Petrichor and growing closer to the Cordilleran border with each passing hour. At night, Orion made sure they camped deep in the forest away from the trail, hoping to avoid detection from the soldiers combing the Metsa for them.

Deciding the girls' Petrichorian robes were too outlandish to blend into the trees, Orion tossed them after leaving the city, though he did force Foxx to keep her hair covered by the scarf. Beneath her robes, Iris had worn the breathable pants they'd purchased in Kesken Ala. Foxx had changed into shorts before they ventured into Petrichor and paid for it now with thorn-scratched legs.

On their first night together, Orion had grilled them about their father. Foxx told him about the very loose trail they followed, leaving out the parts regarding the Monastery of the Morrow, the stone keys, and Celestelvyra. After hearing her story, Orion agreed that finding the waterfall might lead them to the next clue.

For the first three days, Orion and Declan kept both women restrained. They fought hard, cursing the men, refusing to walk, and yelling at the top of their lungs. After luncheon on the fourth day, they released Foxx from her restraints and muzzled Iris with a shirt tied around her mouth.

Orion's words had dripped with condescension as he explained, "When you can behave like your sister, we'll release your wrists. It will be easier on all of us if I can trust you to obey." Iris had snarled through her gag.

The men hadn't returned their weapons, a fact Foxx found irritating but understandable. Orion carried Foxx's quiver in his knapsack, the arrows sticking out over his shoulder, and her bow tied to the outside. He wore Iris' blade belt around his waist, and Foxx thought he might be deliberately vexing her.

So far, they hadn't run into any predators, but Foxx knew they would eventually. She hoped to convince Orion to return her bow before they encountered anything too vicious, and with this in mind, she'd agreed to compliance.

Having the opposite notion, Iris continued fighting the men every step of the way.

Assisting with the map also allowed Foxx to slow their pace. She couldn't believe Asher hadn't found them yet and feared he may have passed by them in the night. Though knowing his tracking abilities, she doubted it. If he'd been caught by the Legion, he could be seriously hurt, or worse. He'd told her the punishment for concealing fugitives, but she couldn't waste energy obsessing over those possibilities.

Having an actual map of Metsa Sateen was the sole bright spot of their situation. Foxx stopped to examine it. Orion halted next to her and grabbed the edge so the map stretched between them.

"I think we have less than a week until we reach Lacuna Kaput. When we find the river, we'll know we're close. It should run us right into the falls." She traced their current path with her finger.

"Fantastic planning, Foxxglove." Orion called back to Declan. "Should reach the falls in a few days. Keep your ears open for running water." Declan lifted a hand in response.

Iris returned Orion's announcement with a murderous scowl.

Foxx let Orion take the map and return it to his knapsack. The movement sent a pained cringe into his features, and she couldn't help but feel a spark of triumph. After leaving Petrichor, he'd put curavenum on the wound and tied cloth around his thigh. The knife injury healed quickly, a slight limp and occasional winces the only indications the attack had occurred. Though it didn't have the effect she'd been hoping for, it pleased her to see it hadn't been totally fruitless.

Another growl drew Foxx's eyes back to where Declan argued with her sister. She wondered, not for the first time, which of them was handling the situation correctly. Should she be helping these men or fighting them like Iris?

It would be near impossible to break free if restrained, and she reasoned the opportunity to escape would be more prevalent if the men trusted them not to attempt it. She understood Iris' response but felt, at least in this situation, obedience was the more likely road to freedom.

Orion followed her gaze and chuckled. "She's feisty, huh?"

"When she isn't getting her way, yes, she can be."

"She *spit* at me!" His tone rang with disgust and disbelief, but something in his expression told her he might also be impressed.

"You could free her, you know. I'm sure she would be helpful and civil if allowed to move of her own volition." Foxx glanced back at Iris again to see her barking expletives at Declan. "Probably."

His brows lifted in response to Iris' outrage. "So she can slit my throat while I sleep? No, thank you."

"She could do that anyway, honestly. It's not like you tie her to a tree." The moment these words emerged, Foxx realized she shouldn't have given him the idea.

Orion pulled his tie free and shook out hair darker than the fancy chocolate they'd once splurged on when visiting the royal city of Aeonian. Iris had gotten a piece with raspberry filling, and Foxx, a slab of nutty bark with a drizzle of cream. "We both want the same thing here. You're being cooperative, so why can't she? As soon as she proves she can be trusted, I'll unbind her."

Foxx scoffed, thinking him so arrogant she considered slitting his throat in his sleep herself. "You kidnapped us and now hold us prisoner, yet you demand trust and respect as if you've earned it. You're the criminals in this scenario. Why should we have to prove our integrity to you?"

"Because I'm in charge, and you are not. If she wants to be released from her chains, that's what she'll have to do." He combed his hair with his fingers, letting it hang loose over his shoulders.

"I'm not loyal to you, Orion. Yet I stand here free of chains." She looked down at herself with hands extended as proof of her claim.

Orion grinned. "You're smart though. You realize we're on the same path. Maybe you don't agree with my methods, but you're willing to bend for the bigger picture. You aren't my prisoner and neither is she. When she learns to behave, she will be freed, as you have been."

Unable to comprehend his ignorant self-importance, she spat, "You ripped us from a city against our will. From our belongings and our friend. My sister's wrists are cuffed, as were mine two days ago. Of course we're your prisoners, Orion. Even free of bound wrists, if I try to escape, you'll stop me. Tell me, what exactly is your definition of the word *prisoner*?"

Orion's brows pinched together in contemplation, his expression growing angrier with each passing second as he considered her words. He yanked Iris' dagger from his belt. "You're right, Foxx. But nothing is going to stop me from completing my mission. Not you." He pointed a finger at her over Thorn's hilt. "Or her." Then he turned toward Iris and Declan and stomped back the trail.

"Wait!" Foxx grabbed for him but missed. He moved swiftly, holding the blade with wrathful determination. She hastened after him, wishing she had a weapon; wishing he wasn't twice her size; wishing she could be strong enough to take him.

Alerted by Foxx's cry, Declan looked up and saw his comrade coming at them with the knife and a cross expression. He seemed to consider moving in front of Iris to block her from the attack, but restrained himself. Foxx thought his features matched her own, and she cried his name, imploring him to step in and stop Orion's madness.

Iris saw Orion and for one second, fear consumed her, but fury quickly devoured it. He grabbed one of her wrists, yanking her toward him. Her glare could have set him on fire. Then he did what none of them expected and sliced the blade between her hands, cutting her ties. He held on to her wrist too tightly for a moment longer, his eyes locking on to hers, taking in her anger and accepting it. "However, I agree. Trust is earned." He looked at Foxx, as his words had been meant for her. After a long moment of silent communication that she didn't understand, he walked away from them and continued down the trail.

Foxx sighed, her eyes filled with relief as she took in her sister's equally confused expression.

Iris squeezed her wrists, rubbing away the lingering tingle from the absent ties. Both women glanced at Declan but saw little to betray his thoughts. His expression returned to a picture of calm. Shrugging, he held out his hand, signaling them to lead on.

C

They stopped to camp at sunset. Orion seemed leery of sleeping now that Iris was unrestrained. When she gave him attitude about the food he'd provided for dinner, he threatened to tie her to a tree so he could sleep soundly.

In a moment of privacy, Iris and Foxx discussed escaping while the men slept, though since they slept in shifts, it would be a tricky feat. Fleeing one would be easier than fleeing both, but with the men's knowledge of their destination and their lack of supplies, they knew they'd never get far enough away that Orion and Declan wouldn't catch up.

Every stride carried them one step farther from Petrichor where their bags had been abandoned. With no weapons, no food, and nothing to start a fire in the damp jungle, their captors catching up would be the least of their worries. Iris suggested stealing the mens' packs if they did manage to escape, and Foxx filed it away as a possibility.

The following day, the group stopped for a late luncheon. The sky hadn't precipitated more than a mist since they departed Petrichor, as if the clouds knew Foxx couldn't enjoy their showered blessings in her captivity.

Foxx sat on a felled tree where thin, half-moon mushrooms filled the ridges in the bark. She unwrapped a piece of bread that ended up feeling dryer in her mouth than it seemed in her fingers. It crumbled into a sandy texture as it touched her tongue, making it hard to swallow. Surveying the area, she scouted for fruit growing nearby.

After receiving a lecture from Orion about not wandering off, Iris left the men on the trail to join her sister. Snagging a low-hanging orange as she passed beneath the tree's branches, she peeled back a section of the rind and held the fruit to her nose, inhaling its citrus scent.

Standing with Declan in quiet discussion, Orion saw her smelling the fruit and called, "Hey, you can't just eat anything you find in the jungle. It could be poisonous."

"It's not." She took a bite of the orange, staring at him obnoxiously. Declan said her name like a parent warning a child not to open the lid of a cookie jar, and she rolled her eyes. "Our friend taught us which fruits were safe to eat, so you don't need to worry. I'm not an idiot." Orion eyed her as if that were debatable and returned his attention to Declan.

Immediately solemn at the mention of Asher, Foxx regarded the bread in her hands with a heavy chest. Every passing day chipped away at her hope of being reunited. Every passing day fueled her rising fury. It knotted in her chest, growing harder and more rigid every second. She'd fought the bitterness in her heart all her life. Now it spread throughout her whole being like a fungus. Like poison infecting her veins, or invasive kudzu, stretching its tendrils without care until everything in its path is consumed.

Iris sat down at her side and handed her the half eaten fruit. "Hungry?"

Foxx took it in exchange for the bread. "You could try to be more amiable."

"You could try to be *less* amiable." When she saw her sister's face, Iris nudged her shoulder and whispered, "I'm sorry I brought him up. He will find us. He promised."

Hearing footsteps on the trail, Foxxglove sat up straighter and held her breath. The others heard them too, and everyone froze in anticipation.

Iris suddenly worried what the men might do if Asher appeared, and dread superseded her hope. It would be three against two, but all three men had firearms and neither Foxx nor Iris had their weapons. Orion was a little bigger than Asher, naturally built with a wider frame, but they hadn't seen any proof of his fighting abilities, so it was difficult to say how well he could handle himself in combat.

As the thuds of boots on dirt drew closer, they realized the travelers were heading toward Petrichor, not away from it. Iris and Foxx sighed in unison. Sharing a glance, they both felt the same painful relief in knowing it wouldn't be Asher arriving to save them.

A man and a woman came into view. Declan popped a sliver of jerky into his mouth and lifted a hand in casual greeting. Orion kept his eyes on Iris and Foxx, waiting to see if they would alert the strangers to their plight. In warning, his hand rested on the pistol at his hip.

The couple met them with joyful waves. "Merry luncheon," the woman said to the girls. The man nodded to Declan before observing Orion strangely. Iris mirrored the woman's words and tone, and in less than a minute, the couple hiked out of sight.

Orion met Iris' sour gaze. If she didn't know him to be vile and inhuman, she might think his expression one of gratitude. Returning her attention to her sister, she found Foxx's mixed feelings matching her own and wondered where in the world Asher could be. She scanned the trees, thinking it possible he hid nearby, waiting for his chance to strike, though she knew it was more likely he'd assumed them captured by the Legion and had hit the trail heading west toward Reginaterra.

Iris thought Foxx must be riding the same wave because another long exhale arose from deep in her chest, releasing as water breaks against the shore.

"I'll be right back." Foxx stood and hastened up the trail out of sight.

Witnessing her flight, Orion lifted his finger to interrupt Declan and met Iris by the tree. Noticing his approach, she began cleaning the dirt from her fingernails and pretending he didn't exist.

"Where's she going?" He gestured in the direction Foxx had ventured.

Iris regarded him as if he were the biggest imbecile she'd ever encountered. "She's upset, obviously." She returned her attention to her cuticles. "Don't worry though, she won't run. She'd sooner sacrifice herself to ensure my escape than leave me behind with the likes of you." In her peripherals, she saw genuine confusion.

"Upset? Why?"

Iris blinked. "You're seriously asking that question?" He looked at her with a furrowed brow, and she thought he couldn't possibly be as idiotic as he seemed. "Maybe because you kidnapped us? You think because she's docile and compliant that her pain has magically evaporated?"

He nodded slowly—realizing his stupidity, she hoped. "She seemed fine."

"Yeah, she's good at that." Though she wasn't entirely sure why, since she didn't wish to converse with him at all let alone explain the inner workings of her sister's suffering, Iris yielded some of her ground. "She's mostly upset because when you took us, we left someone behind, and she's grieving because she misses him."

Orion stared up the trail with interest. "He was her lover?"

Iris hadn't imagined any derivative of the word *love* would be in his vocabulary. "He was her... someone. It was unspoken, but there was definitely something there. Something special." She watched his countenance fluctuate as his thoughts sifted through the revealed information. The skin above his nose creased as he pursed his lips, and his jaw clenched in contemplation.

Memories sparked of the kindness he'd conveyed when they'd first met in the desert. He'd helped them, asking nothing in return. Offered them shelter and protection when she'd felt lost and alone. His natural charm, handsome smile, and eyes as blue as the Suola Meri had sent delighted shivers throughout her whole body.

Having spent the past six days with Orion, she'd assumed the past version of him to be a counterfeit. An act with the sole purpose of weaseling his way into their good graces. Maybe he was still doing that, though she couldn't help thinking his expression looked sincere.

Then he said, "Perhaps the fact that it was left unspoken is part of her pain. Fear he may never know how she truly feels."

Iris gawked at him and kicked herself for her lapse in anger. Every fragment of pleasantness vanished. "As if you would know anything about a woman's feelings."

Orion continued to stare after Foxx, unaffected by Iris' hostility and lost somewhere in the catacomb of his own memories. At last, he pulled his eyes from the trail. "And do you have a *someone*, Iris Belamour?"

Appalled, she grimaced, refusing to be swayed by his moment of gentle refinement. The weight of her fury returned. "That is absolutely none of your business, Orion." She stood with the intention of storming away, but he caught her arm, the previous glint of his humanity evaporated.

He squeezed too tightly as he snarled through clenched teeth. "This had better not be a trick. You cannot escape me, and it is foolish to try."

Iris yanked her arm free of his grasp. "You're the foolish one. Foolish and foul and vile. I promise you, Orion, when I do escape, you will be on the ground bleeding out in the mud and watching as I stroll away from you with zero remorse."

Turning on her heel, she took a step away only to find herself yanked back again, this time with a wide hand clutching the back of her neck. He pulled her against his body and the warmth of him made her skin crawl. "Do not ever threaten me again, Iris, do you hear me? When we find your father, I mean to set you and your sister free. *Don't* make me change my mind." He let go of her with too much force, and she fell, burning her knees on the ground.

Glaring up at him from all fours, she spit at his feet. In response, he kicked the ground, spewing dirt in her face. She looked at Declan and saw him watching the altercation without emotion. "Enjoying the view, Declan?" She squinted her eyes to combat the painful dirt particles. "Too much of a coward to stand up for a woman unarmed and half his size?"

Declan flinched, but said nothing.

"Don't expect Declan to save you. We've been through far too much to betray each other."

Iris stood, rubbing her neck where his hand had assaulted her muscles before wiping the grime from her clothing and consoling her skinned knees. A hole split the fabric where she'd hit the ground. Enraged by his savage behavior, she stomped back to the trail and stood in line several paces in front of Declan, waiting for them to be ready to move on. Orion watched her go, balling his fingers into tight fists as his temper momentarily consumed him.

Then Foxx returned, out of breath as if she'd been running. Her face was blotchy with sadness, but her eyes sparkled. "Come!" She waved for them to follow. "You must see this!"

Orion's features morphed from rage to curiosity. When Foxx disappeared again, he looked back at Iris. "Part of your tricks?" She glowered in return.

After sharing a glance with his companion, Orion jogged after Foxx. Iris peered over her shoulder, but Declan only offered her a meager shrug. Sighing, she ran after the others, eager to see what her sister had discovered. Declan trailed slowly behind, seemingly uninterested.

When they rounded the bend, the riot of color rendered Orion and Iris speechless. Gawking, they took in the magnificent assemblage of birds gathered in the trees above, bedecked in every hue imaginable.

Performing like the symphony of a grand orchestra, hundreds of birds chirped and sang and hopped from branch to branch in harmonious glee. They soared across the rift in the trees created by the trail, playing together; chasing and battling each other as they barrel-rolled through the air.

"Wow." Orion said. The captivating harmony of the chattering birds was so tumultuous, they had to raise their voices above the roar to hear each other.

"It's sensational!" Iris linked her arm with Foxx's. "Isn't it, Foxx?"

Foxx nodded, sadness erased and jubilation she hadn't felt in days reignited. The discovery of birds altered the mood of the entire group. Even Declan's controlled detachment appeared slightly moved by the spectacle.

Iris and Foxx strolled through the tunnel of birds with their faces to the trees. After a few minutes, Foxx unlatched herself from her sister and walked ahead, seeking solitude to take it all in.

Orion approached Iris from behind with borderline friendliness, as if the interaction mere minutes ago hadn't happened. "That's a blue and gold macaw," he murmured over her shoulder. She flinched, not having realized his face lingered so close. He pointed past her to a bird with lapis lazuli feathers covering it from crown to tail and bleeding into the tops of its wings. The underside of its wings, belly, and legs were an impressive shade of goldenrod.

The macaw swooped in front of them, having noticed the human invaders and curious to get a closer look. Other birds did the same, flying in a wide arc only a few feet from their heads. Some flew in groups of four or five, diving in synchronized twists and twirls as if dancing on parade. Shafts of light cut through the understory like a spotlight, casting the birds in a bright illumination as they passed through.

Orion hovered behind Iris, leaning in over her shoulder. Her mind flashed to Thorn and Bloom hanging at his waist, thinking she could use his casual closeness to her advantage. In seconds, she could pull Thorn from its scabbard and attack.

Another macaw flew over them from behind, causing them both to duck their heads. "Look! That's a scarlet macaw. The scarlet's body is red, but they share the gold and blue feathers of the other. Plus a few green ones."

Iris watched him watching the birds. His eyes, the color of deep oceans and sparkling sapphires, gleamed with passion, and she couldn't fathom how this could be the same man who'd handled her so roughly minutes ago. "They're so graceful. Thank you for sharing that with me, Orion." The kindness in her words, made more prominent by her soft expression, startled him. She would have sworn he even looked embarrassed. Or sick. He straightened, his face flattened into nonchalance as he took a step away from her.

After the peculiar interaction, Iris caught Declan observing Orion with curiosity. When their eyes met, Declan returned his gaze to the treetops. Iris noticed him smiling a few times and mocked him playfully for it. Her jest didn't stir him, and he relaxed his freckled face into an expression of boredom. A purple blotch bloomed high on his cheekbone where she'd punched him, sparking a twinge of regret in the pit of her stomach despite feeling justified for her actions.

Swallowing fragments of guilt, Iris moved several paces forward and placed herself more evenly between Foxx and the men. Continuing their saunter through the parroted canopy, the bright hues of the birds peppering the trees outmatched that of the green foliage. Dozens sat in wide rows across low hanging branches, stacked right up against each other in broad pops of color. Iris decided birdsong was her new favorite sound.

Less than three minutes after Orion had recoiled and Iris moved ahead, it became apparent he couldn't maintain his stubborn aloofness for long. Suddenly at her side again, he returned with full-on enthusiasm. He spewed all kinds of detailed information about the macaws; knowing their species, their temperaments, and how big they grew.

Iris watched him again. Mystifying her, he prattled on with an unceasing smile. His eyes lit up as he combed hair away from his face. His square jaw was freshly shaven, and a slightly crooked nose gave evidence to fighting in his past, which didn't surprise her based on everything she'd witnessed so far.

She glanced at Declan over her shoulder, again trying to determine his opinion of his friend's behavior, but he kept his emotions in a steel cage. Returning her attention to Orion, she found him looking at her, grinning expectantly. "How do you know so much about these birds?"

Again he raked a hand through his hair, his eyes shifting to his feet. "There's an island in Alunda." He cleared his throat, his eyes sliding back to hers as he casually mentioned her homeland. "A man moved there from the Metsa a few decades ago. I guess when he left, he couldn't bear to part with the beautiful creatures, so he took several along with him. Over time, they bred, and new birds were born. The island is full of them."

"We grew up in Alunda, but I've never heard of this island of parrots. How did you happen across such a place?"

Orion chuckled and turned his gaze back to the canopy. "I have a good friend who captains a ship that sails the Suola Meri. She took me there once." His eyes glazed over, lost in the memory.

"You have friends?" Iris asked in mock surprise. Well—actual surprise, if she were being honest.

Orion looked back at Declan who continued watching the trees. "Not many." He chuckled again to himself.

Now within earshot of the conversation, Foxx felt equally

shocked by his knowledge and openness, and she, too, wondered how the brutal and vicious man they had come to know over the past week could transform into the humane nature lover standing in his place.

Too soon, they passed through the melodious atrium and the jungle settled into its normal tuneful rhythms. It began to drizzle, and Foxx looked pleased. The birds and the rain had lifted her spirits, allowing her to move past her sadness and fears, and refocus on finding their father.

Orion had advanced to the head of the pack and seemed to be walking with extra pep in his step. Foxx found his current mood troubling. Declan remained a puzzle as well. Where Orion was fiery, passionate, and clearly full of erratic and unbalanced emotions, Declan was bland, unimpressed, and restrained.

Regardless of what strange kindness they may exhibit on occasion, both Foxx and Iris knew they couldn't allow themselves to trust either of the men. Their intentions for their father were undoubtedly nefarious in nature, otherwise a kidnapping wouldn't have been deemed necessary.

They would need to ferret out a way of escape eventually, whether Asher located them or not.

Foxx peered back at Iris and wondered how she must be feeling about everything. Iris smiled and mouthed *love you*. Foxx returned her sentiment and rotated front, hoping they would have privacy to talk again soon.

CHAPTER 17

ONCOMING STORM

Nearly two weeks had come and gone since Foxx and Iris were spirited away from Petrichor. They felt almost certain now that Asher was traveling toward Reginaterra, tracking the soldiers he assumed had captured them.

Life with Declan and Orion continued on with frustration and uncertainty. Five days ago, Orion grabbed Iris by the neck and shoved her to the dirt, only to morph into an entirely different person minutes later beneath the canopy of birds.

This, it seemed, was his usual pattern. He fluctuated between anger and kindness, irritation and joy. Iris excelled at pushing his buttons, and Foxx wondered more than once if her sister was intentionally striving to get them killed or if she just couldn't help herself.

Except for a few rare occasions when someone managed to entice a small smile to his lips, Declan remained cold as mountain stone. He spent the majority of his time lingering close to Iris, endeavoring to contain the near constant quarrels she stirred up with Orion.

As highsun approached on the twelfth day, Orion stalled in his tracks and halted the others with a raised hand. "Do you hear that?"

The trail had grown wide enough for Foxx and Iris to hike next to each other. Declan trailed at the back, keeping his distance. Foxx wondered if he was purposely giving them privacy or if he just happened to be dragging his feet a little slower than the rest of them.

At Orion's direction, they listened carefully, trying to hear a whisper above the perpetual and rumbustious tunes of the forest.

After a long moment, Iris' face lit with excitement. "Water!" She darted off the trail, weaving effortlessly through the foliage. With renewed energy, the others chased after her, racing through the undergrowth. Iris emerged from the line of trees and heard the splash of water beneath her boots. She immediately remembered Asher mentioning the potential for aquatic monsters and sprang backward to escape the soggy river, crashing directly into Orion. They tumbled in reverse until he sat on the turf with her in his lap. Declan and Foxx crossed the treeline and witnessed their accidental indecency with a gasp. Iris swung around and slugged Orion in the shoulder before scrambling off him.

Orion massaged his bicep. "Quite the right hook you have, Iris."

Declan's eyebrow disappeared beneath his bangs. "You're not kidding."

Foxx stifled a chuckle.

"Well, stop running so close to me, then!" Iris brushed her palms over her clothing, purging any remnants of him that might be stuck to her. She pulled the tie holding up her hair from its home and let her locks cascade down her back.

Orion remained in the mud where he'd fallen. "You bounded into me!"

Foxx and Declan loitered at the fringes of the trees, sharing a look of obvious entertainment. Foxx realized she hadn't seen Declan smile with his teeth until that moment and decided he looked handsome when his expression softened. His boyish face bore a splattering of freckles, and his gray eyes sat charmingly a little too close together. Returning her attention to Iris and Orion, she teased, "So you found the river?"

"Seems they found more than the river," Declan quipped, crossing his arms and grinning at them with feigned suspicion. A surprised laugh burst from Foxx's lips, and she covered her mouth.

Iris stuck her tongue out at both of them. "Declan, if you're going to start making jokes and having opinions all of a sudden, they better be nice, or I'll happily ensure your left eye matches your right."

Orion frowned. "Oh, Declan has *loads* of opinions. Trust me."

"Could have fooled me," Iris mumbled under her breath. Her eyes slid back to Declan to find his face returned to normal but for a minute upturn of his lips.

Orion rose from the soil and kneaded his sore tailbone before brushing the mud from his pants, which mostly resulted in smearing rather than removing. Recovering himself, he reiterated Foxx's words. "So we found the river! The Elysian River to be precise. We should be able to follow this all the way to the top of the waterfall."

Iris silently mimicked his words with vexation, moving her lips as she flipped her head upside-down and drew her hair back into a ponytail.

The gap between them and the opposing shore measured about 60 *sylis*. Encumbered with trees and other plants, the northern coast of the river mirrored the forest behind them. The current ran rapidly, crashing against rocks protruding the surface and generating foaming ripples. The midday sunshine reflected off the water creating blinding flashes of white.

Foxx said, "Let's hike along the edge of the river until it starts to get dark. If we still haven't arrived at the falls by then, we can make camp and continue on tomorrow."

"Sounds like a plan to me." Orion turned from the turbulent river, pressing gravel into sodden sand beneath his feet. The others followed, and the sound of boots crunching stones blended with the burbling waterway.

They trekked along the riverbank, only cutting back through the treeline a few times when the current punctured the shore or the vegetation and boulders became too tricky to maneuver. They hiked for several hours, monitoring the sun as it slipped beneath the overstory. As the sky above faded to a dull gray, the sun disappeared and the moon took its place. Freckles of stars pierced their way into the illumination of twilight.

Stopping when they happened upon a pasture carved into the forest's edge and sizable enough to hold the four of them plus a fire, they made camp for the night. As Foxx constructed a fire, Declan vanished into the trees in pursuit of dinner. Iris found respite on the earth next to Foxx and helped prepare the kindling. Orion stood preoccupied on the riverbank observing the waves cresting over a mass of rocks.

When Declan returned, a huge bird dangled over his shoulder.

Iris speculated it might be a turkey, but she was feeling antisocial and didn't fancy asking. Even she and Foxx remained voiceless as they sat by the crackling flames.

Declan maintained his silence as he plucked his quarry's feathers, removed its entrails, and chopped off its head. Orion rejoined the campsite as Declan hoisted the bird above the fire.

The four of them encircled the blaze, attuned to its pops and cracks as their dinner roasted. Declan twisted the bird to ensure an even bake. Eventually, the smell of cooking meat wafted into their nostrils and the aroma triggered a ravenous growl in Iris' stomach. Foxx met her eyes and smiled before returning her attention to preening her cuticles. Iris shredded blades of grass into pieces, allowing them to flutter one by one to the soil.

Growing weary of the silence, Orion said, "Well, aren't we a lively bunch?"

"It's been a long day, Ri." Declan sounded on the verge of irritation, though Orion hadn't behaved notably annoying in quite a while.

Orion ignored him. "If we get up early, we should reach Lacuna Kaput before luncheon."

"Are we safe so close to the water's edge?" Iris stopped tearing apart the grass and leaned back on her hands.

Declan mumbled, "Are we safe anywhere in this jungle?" at the same time Orion asked, "Why wouldn't we be?"

Iris replied to Declan first, then Orion. "That's a fair point, Declan. And our friend was lacking on the details, but he made it sound like the rivers of the rainforest contained some not so fun creatures."

"Your friend?" Orion's eyes shifted to Foxx. She prodded the fire, appearing impervious.

Iris redrew his attention and motioned toward the river. "Yes, our friend. I'm wondering if there might be anything in there that would potentially make its way out here while we're sleeping." The suffocating fumes of the fire gravitated in her direction, and the smoke burned her eyes and nose. She covered her face to let the smog pass and whined, "Is it just me or do I attract smoke like flames attract moths?"

Foxx chuckled and waved her hands to help blow it away. "You do have a certain allure the smoke seems drawn to."

Declan said, "The smoke is hot and seeks a temperature similar to its own. If the air around you is cooler than your body, it will naturally be drawn toward you. Also, the air flow will be affected by movement. If I'm moving while cooking, Foxx is stoking the fire, and Orion is fidgeting, it will respond by flowing away from us and gravitating toward your stillness."

Foxx lifted a brow. "So what you're saying is that Iris is full of hot air and should be pulling her weight rather than sitting lazily by the fire while we do all the work?"

Declan opened his mouth to respond before freezing mid-word when he realized the trap he'd set for himself. Iris put her hands on her hips as she waited for him to proceed. His jaw snapped shut, and he busied himself with the bird.

"Or you have excessively bad luck." Orion pulled his hair up into a bun at the back of his head.

Declan changed the subject. "As far as water monsters are concerned, we should be fine."

"Declan here barely sleeps, so chances are, even if something were to come up out of the water, we would have plenty of warning before anything disastrous happened."

Foxx found this comment strange and wondered if the men had stopped sleeping in shifts.

After several minutes of silence, Orion severed it again. He folded his legs beneath him and cleared his throat. "When I was a little boy, about six I think, I fell into the river by our house. It was wider than this one with a much stronger current."

"Oh, is it story time? I love story time." Iris wrapped her arms around folded legs and rested her chin on her knees. Orion scrutinized her, trying to determine whether or not she spoke in earnest. When he didn't continue, she prompted, "What territory did you grow up in?"

"I grew up in Reginaterra, same as Declan. Though Dec was a city boy, born and raised in the extravagant Inaravale." He elevated his hands. "I grew up in a cabin in the woods on the outskirts of a village called Sylva."

Iris analyzed the two men, attempting to match their contrasting upbringings with their present characters. She hadn't visualized Declan as a spoiled city kid. Though she hadn't spent much time surmising anything about his past at all. Instantly overcome with curiosity, she wondered what circumstances might have led them down the path of kidnapping criminals.

Orion interrupted her musings and proceeded with his story. "I fell in the river, and my father stood on the edge watching as I kicked and screamed. I could barely swim at the time, and the current was rough. I remember feeling things in the water wrap around my legs. It was terrifying. It took me nearly an hour to reach the shallows, and by the time I did, I was half a mile from home."

"Why didn't he help you?" Iris asked.

"I asked him that very question when I finally made it to the shore behind our home. I was soaked, exhausted, and covered in mud. He answered saying he wanted to see if I could swim." Orion shrugged as if it didn't matter, but concealed anguish darkened his eyes. "But hey, turns out I could. I suppose he thought his beloved Creator would save me whether he helped or not. He certainly felt that way about my mother."

Orion's hostility toward Asher's Creator startled Foxx. His feelings seemed to contrast Asher's entirely, and again she wished she could remember all the things her mother had taught her about the being some credited with creating the universe. Since she'd never realized Him to be an actual living creature, she hadn't paid enough attention to the details. Now she couldn't help wondering why her mother had been so cryptic about so many things.

Iris said, "That's horrible. Your father is the person who's supposed to protect you. Not abandon you." Orion looked at her, but she didn't return his gaze as she watched the flames dance and spark.

Declan surprised everyone by responding, "Yours didn't."

Iris met his eyes across the fire and held them intently. "That doesn't make my statement untrue."

"All baby birds get pushed from their nests." Orion sat up straighter and dusted off the front of his pants, brushing away old memories and building tension. "They either learn to fly or they don't. Besides, my father got what was coming to him in the end."

"We've all suffered our traumas." Declan began cutting chunks of meat from the bird and setting them aside on a plate. Iris sighed, wondering if she would ever understand all the tribulations of these men.

Or if she even wanted to.

C

As the sun ascended the following morning, the company cleared camp and resumed their walk. The river produced a broad break in the tree-filled jungle allowing them to see the sky above. Shafts of sunlight shot through ashy clouds that bloated close to bursting, ready to release a downpour. They hoped to find the falls before the storm struck, but it didn't look promising as the sky grew darker by the minute.

Shortly after they abandoned their campsite, they emerged from a cove of trees to find the river splitting. A shard of jungle sliced through it, coercing the current to travel one side or the other.

Frustrated, Orion retrieved his map in hopes of decoding which path they ought to take. Foxx joined him on the riverbank to offer assistance.

Iris raised her gaze to the darkening clouds. The sun had completely disappeared from view, but she recalled where it had risen earlier in the day. "It has to be this way right? The sun rises in the east. We need to go northeast." When Orion and Foxx didn't respond, she looked to Declan for confirmation. He shrugged and turned his face to the clouds in his typical state of aloofness. Iris rolled her eyes and walked over to where Foxx and Orion studied the map. "Don't you think?"

"Yes, I think it's that way, but Orion isn't convinced."

"I want to make sure we don't end up hiking in the wrong direction." They stood quietly for a long minute, absorbing the area surrounding them. The air grew dense and heavy, more proof of the coming storm. Humid wind blew in gusts as opposing temperature pressures collided. As if sounding the alarm, birds and other animal calls eclipsed the acoustics of the roaring river and wind.

Iris crossed her arms, her attitude swelling. "Well, I think we voted and you lost. So we should go this way."

"Exactly," Foxx said.

"We should find shelter." Declan's words bore a hint of uncharacteristic concern. "We can agree on a path once the storm has passed."

"We've traveled during storms before." Foxx looked up, lifting a hand to guard her eyes from the wind.

"We need to keep moving forward," Orion agreed.

"No. We need to find shelter." Without waiting for their acceptance or permission, Declan trekked off into the jungle.

Indignantly, Orion rolled up the map and slipped it back into his pack. "Okay. I guess we're finding shelter."

☽

Declan found a formation of rocks nearby and ushered everyone inside. He constructed a door from an animal hide, stacking heavy rocks on top of it to hold the barricade in place. Climbing inside, he retrieved a small lantern from his pack and set it ablaze. The cave was too shallow to stand, but spacious enough to sit comfortably without being on top of each other.

"Well found." Orion rested a hand on Declan's shoulder. "Now, why was it so important for us to find shelter? We've certainly traveled through enough storms."

"You'll thank me in a minute." As if on cue, an ear-splitting crack erupted from the sky, causing all but Declan's hands to fly to their ears. A thundering rumble shook the structure, prompting a light dusting of dirt and tiny stones to fall on their heads. Declan observed Orion with raised brows.

"All right, brother. I was wrong. Thanks."

Iris and Foxx stared at him, jaws hanging.

Another blast shuddered throughout the cave as rain began to pour. Trickles and drips spilled down on them through the cracks. The tempest fought Declan's provisional door open and extinguished his lantern more than once. It was too loud to engage in conversation so they sat together in silence, listening to the wild storm. Lightning lit the world outside, followed by another loud crack that sent sharp vibrations into the earth.

"That one was close." Foxx braced herself with palms flat on the floor.

Moments later the eerie screech of a leaning tree reached their ears. It creaked in the high winds, straining to remain upright, until at last succumbing to the pressure and crashing to the ground. Iris and Foxx yelped as the crown of the tree landed atop their shelter and shifted some of the rocks.

"This is insane!" Iris yelled.

Foxx and Orion agreed. Declan adjusted the door as another bolt of lightning struck. A second tree cracked and collapsed, again landing on top of them. Then a third.

"What is going on?" Iris covered her head with her arms. "I thought lightning didn't strike the same spot twice?"

The rocks above shifted more, becoming unstable. Orion yelled Declan's name. Replying to the question he hadn't asked, Declan said, "We have to run." He looked at both girls and saw terror in their eyes. "Are you ready?"

They nodded, unsure of what he planned to do but trusting him, at least in that moment, to lead them to safety.

Declan ripped the hide from the entrance, letting it fall to the mud. "Let's go!" He climbed out the door before bending down and offering a hand to Iris, who let him help her to her feet. Foxx came next, then Orion. The wind and rain flowed with such violent gusts it seemed the entire forest might collapse. Another tree fell, prompting them to duck and cover their heads as more branches enveloped them.

"We need to get away from the trees," Orion yelled.

Iris said, "We're in the middle of the jungle! There are trees everywhere!"

"We can't go to the river. The lightning could kill us." Foxx's hair had come undone, and she attempted to use the scarf as a shield over her head.

"These trees are going to kill us," Orion shouted.

"Our best bet is the trail. It will be easier to move freely." Declan ran, and the others followed, climbing through the felled trees in the direction of the trail. The cave crumbled behind them as a solid trunk landed on top of it, provoking another scream from Iris. Orion grabbed her arm, dragging her forward.

Declan paused in front of a huge tree laying on its side and blocking their path. He looked down the length of the trunk and then up over it, trying to decide which way to go.

Foxx stopped at his side. "We go over?"

He nodded and helped hoist her up. When she reached its summit, another tree toppled in front of her and knocked her backward. Declan caught her as the wind swallowed her screams. When she didn't immediately leap from his arms, he glanced down to find her eyes open, fogged over, and staring blankly up at the sky.

"What's happening?" He turned to Iris for an explanation. If he couldn't feel Foxx's heart beating against his chest, he would have thought her dead.

"Oh no, Foxx, not now!" Iris ran to her sister, tapping her cheeks and trying to drag her from the vision devouring her senses, but she remained unresponsive. Iris closed Foxx's eyelids to shield them from the pelting rain. "We have to carry her!"

Another tree crashed behind them, shocking them into action. Declan heaved Foxx up over his shoulder. "Go!" He pointed down the trunk. Iris obeyed, doing her best to avoid felled branches as she went.

C

Foxx's neck craned backward as an invisible fist yanked her up by the front of her shirt. Dark clouds swirled around her, heavy with rainwater. She shivered, somehow freezing in the humidity. Peals of thunder rattled bones and muscles beneath icy skin.

Straightening where she floated in the dense atmosphere, Foxx looked around. The surrounding jungle as far as she could see appeared entirely untouched by the storm. Somehow, the squall had struck her and her comrades with pinpoint accuracy. She'd never seen a storm behave this way, and realized something must be attacking them… or someone.

A woman's voice cackled in a piercingly painful echo that forced her to cover her ears. *That's right, Foxxglove. I think you're beginning to understand the gravity of the situation.*

Foxx plummeted from the sky. Her stomach made a home where her heart had vacated, and she screamed. Moments later, she noticed the ground hadn't gotten any closer. Torpedoing wind continued to whip through her hair and burn her skin. Crystals of ice scratched her body like the thorns of a bramble bush.

The voice spoke again, even more malicious than before. *I see you. He isn't the only one with access to your thoughts.*

Scanning the sky, Foxx searched for the owner of the voice, to no avail.

This time, the voice hissed directly into her ear. *I see you, Foxxglove Belamour. And I'm coming for you.*

Then she plunged toward the ground, her body slamming like a stone into the hard earth below.

C

Iris burst through the treeline onto the trail, fighting the tunneling currents of wind. Declan emerged carrying Foxx, followed by Orion, who yelled for them to keep going as he took the lead. Trees continued to fall, their roots lifting from the dirt to trip them, but they pressed forward, making every attempt to outrun the storm.

Foxx began coughing atop Declan's shoulder. Blood spilled onto his shirt, dripping from her ears and staining her lips. He called Iris' name, and she turned to see her sister moving in his arms. She and Orion pivoted and ran back to them. Foxx coughed up more blood. It slid from her nose, painting her chin in crimson.

Her eyes opened into slits, no longer looking foggy. They lifted to the sky, and just like that, the rain ceased even quicker than it had come. The atmosphere brightened above them, and the thunder and lightning faded, not as a storm moving on, but as one that had never existed. The assaulting trees grew still.

Declan lowered Foxx to the ground, leaning her against lifted roots. Iris dropped next to her, calling her name. Before she could respond, Foxx's eyes fell closed again.

New images flashed before her: an intricately decorated double-door depicting a moon like Asher's tattoo and symbols that disappeared too quickly for her to decipher. Both doors swung open of their own accord, and she traveled through them as if floating on air. Beyond them stood an exquisite garden, blossoming with flowers and greenery.

Then, the most magnificent creature she'd ever laid eyes on appeared before her. With fur as white as her own hair and huge spiral horns, she thought it must be a ram, though she'd never realized rams could be so extraordinary. The creature's dark eyes bore into her own, leaving her feeling exposed and vulnerable. As if the ram saw into her heart. Into her very soul.

A warm breeze blew past her face, caressing her skin, and she heard a male's gentle voice say, *I can see you, too.* With a flash of the ram's eyes, the scene vanished.

Foxx's eyes opened to find Iris in her face, looking worried. A glance up saw Orion and Declan standing over her. Her chest heaved, failing to consume enough oxygen. Her heart raced, sending numbing tingles to fingertips that burned like ice.

Iris said her name again. "Slow deep breaths. Let the air fill your lungs." She wiped away another drop of blood as it fell from her sister's nose. "Are you all right?"

Orion put a hand on his head. *"Is she all right?* What the hell just happened?"

Iris whipped around to glare at him. Declan looked equally disturbed, though he didn't share Orion's anger. "She's going to need to lay down for a while," she said, ignoring Orion completely.

"Oh, we don't have time for this. The day has barely begun, and we're almost there."

Declan said Orion's name with authority, drawing his attention away from the women. "Walk the trail and find us a clearing." Orion eyed him with disdain, but Declan kept his pensive gaze on Foxx. Moments later, and to Iris' absolute disbelief, Orion obeyed and turned to trudge the trail, mumbling to himself as he went.

Declan crouched on Foxx's opposite side and slid the bag of water from his shoulder. "Could she use a drink?" Iris nodded and accepted the bag, unscrewing the cap. Holding it to Foxx's lips, she encouraged her to take a sip.

"Is this the same thing that happened before we found you in the Wilds?"

Iris hesitated as she watched Foxx's chest rise and fall in short breaths. She reattached the cap and handed it back to him before scanning the wreckage around them. Trunks and branches littered the trail as though a tornado had cut through the land. "No, I don't think it was the same." Her eyes lifted to the sky.

"It felt like we were under attack." Declan followed her gaze to the cloudless expanse above. "The storm stopped when she woke up."

Wiping more blood from below Foxx's ears, Iris exhaled a heavy sigh. "I don't know what to say."

"Let me carry her. We'll walk the trail until we find Orion. Then we can let her rest." Declan scooped Foxx into his arms and motioned for Iris to lead the way.

Iris shook her head. "No way. You go first. I'm not letting her out of my sight."

"I'm not going to hurt her, Iris."

Though he sounded sincere, she shook her head again. He'd already hurt them. She couldn't trust him not to remove a very clear obstacle in whatever ridiculous plan he and Orion had concocted. "Just go. I'll follow you."

The emotion on his face drained, and his stony demeanor

returned as he started down the path with Iris shadowing close
behind.

C

Foxx slept through luncheon and into the afternoon. Iris sat next to
her, cross-legged in the slick grass and ignoring the men across the
clearing. They looked deep in a heated discussion, speaking too
quietly for her to overhear more than a few contorted exclamations.
When Foxx finally awoke, she sat up, blinking away exhaustion.

"Hey." Iris pushed her sister's hair out of her face. It lay loose
now, free of the Petrichorian wrap lost to the storm. "How are you
feeling?"

Foxx squinted up at the sunny streaks splintering the canopy.
Her eyes felt raw and scratchy as if polluted with saltwater and
sand. "I'm tired."

"I believe you. Have some water." After unscrewing the cap, she
handed over Declan's waterskin, and Foxx consumed the liquid
with gratitude.

Declan noticed Foxx waking and looked their way. His face
conveyed a puzzling expression of anger mingled with concern.
Orion followed his line of vision, his storm-disheveled hair pulled
up into a bun. A macaw flew across the clearing between them and
perched on a nearby tree, drawing both Iris and Orion's attention.
From his lesson, she could name it a scarlet macaw. She'd seen
countless colorful birds since entering Metsa Sateen. Asher had
named toucans, lovebirds, hawks, cockatoos, and hornbills, and
though he'd pointed out the colorful macaws on numerous occasions, he hadn't listed their distinct species as Orion had.

Over the past week, Iris had seen dozens of scarlet, blue and
gold, and great green macaws, among others, and she wasn't sure if
having a name for the rainbow-feathered parrots made her more
aware of them or if their current location in the rainforest had a
larger population. Either way, each one stood as a reminder of
Orion's shocking kindness, and she still wasn't sure what to do
with it.

Pulling their eyes from the bird, their gazes met, but he was too
far away for her to decipher his expression.

Foxx saw Iris watching the men, and embarrassment blossomed
on her cheeks. "Are they mad?"

"Hard to say. You don't have to tell them anything you don't want to. They can't force you to talk."

"They might try." Foxx returned the water sleeve and crossed her legs underneath her, sitting upright. She wondered what kind of explanation the men had created to understand what happened. Would they blame her? Think she had somehow been in control of the storm and used it to attack them? Surely they must know she wouldn't have put Iris at risk.

"I'll protect you," Iris promised, a hint of wrath creeping into her tone.

"I'm supposed to protect you." Foxx's lips upturned with happiness despite their circumstances.

"We protect each other." Iris booped her big sister on the nose with her pointer finger. "Do you want to tell me about it?"

Foxx sucked in a breath as the memories resurfaced. "I don't think it was a vision."

"I thought as much. So what was it?"

Foxx looked down at her hands, watching her fingers fidget nervously. "It was a message. From the Queen." Her skin felt hot and cold all at once as she remembered the wicked voice that had rattled her body and drawn blood from her ears.

Iris' back straightened. "What? What was the message?" Glancing over at the men, she saw Declan take a step toward them, sensing their distress. A look from her stopped him in his tracks and melted any trace of emotion from his countenance. He rotated to face Orion but continued to watch them from the corner of his eye.

"I didn't see her. Not that it matters since I have no idea what she looks like, but it was definitely her. The storm, all of it. She said my name. She said, *I see you, and I'm coming for you.*" A shiver rattled up her spine from her core.

"But how do you know it was the Queen? Did she tell you?"

"No. I don't know how to explain it, but I'm sure it was her. I was up there in the sky among the clouds. I saw the forest for miles in every direction, and there wasn't a single storm cloud but the ones above us. Then she threw me to the ground, and when my body crashed into the earth, I blacked out again. I remember opening my eyes for a few moments, but something took me back under. I was in a garden and there was this white ram. I swear he was the most magnificent thing I've ever laid eyes on." Her thoughts drifted at the memory.

Iris wrapped her arms around her sister's shoulders and rubbed her hand down her back. "I'm so sorry, Foxxglove."

Foxx yawned. "I'm very tired. Am I allowed to sleep more or do they want to get moving?"

"It doesn't matter if they do. Get some more rest. I'll go talk to them."

When Declan glimpsed Iris moving toward them, they met her at the center of the clearing.

Orion asked, "Is she all right?"

"She will be." She glanced over her shoulder at her already slumbering sister.

"She has visions or something similar, doesn't she?"

Iris' startled eyes widened, and she crossed her arms. "How could you possibly guess something like that?"

Orion folded his arms to match her stance. "My father used to talk of such things. As did yours. Your mother had them, too."

Iris blanched. "And what exactly do you know about my mother?" Orion held her unfriendly gaze without response. "Who are you, Orion? Why won't you tell us?" Her emotion was clear in her tone and the sheen in her eyes. She looked back and forth between them, waiting for answers.

"What does she need?" Orion glanced past her to Foxx.

Iris crossed her fingers on top of her head and took a breath. "She needs sleep. We should probably make camp and start fresh in the morning." Again she looked between them, concerned what their reactions might be. Declan gave no indication of his opinion, but instead stood next to his friend, still as a statue.

Orion sighed. "Let her rest." His fingers bridged the space between them and squeezed her upper arm. Iris' mouth fell open at his comforting gesture. Without another word, he strode between her and Declan and began gathering rocks to construct a ring for a fire.

Closing her mouth, she glanced awkwardly at the ground and brushed away the warmth left behind by Orion's touch. Her eyes glanced his way, then to her fingers—anywhere but to Declan, whose examination made her shiver with all kinds of weird energy. Despite spending nearly two weeks with them, she couldn't comprehend the dynamic between the two men.

When she felt brave enough to meet Declan's gaze, she found his gray eyes disclosing nothing. Cold as the stone color that made them. She scoffed for seemingly no reason and turned away from him, deciding to make herself useful by helping Orion with the fire.

Declan crossed the clearing to grab something from his bag before walking toward Foxx. Iris noticed his movements and watched cautiously from a distance. Then she remembered Orion saying they only needed one of the sisters for the journey, and she wondered if she'd turned out to be the least difficult sister after all.

Her hand reached for Bloom's hilt only to remember Orion still had her blades. Declan bent next to Foxx, and Iris began to rush toward him. She stopped abruptly as she saw him lifting Foxx's head and placing a rolled blanket beneath it.

Declan looked back to see Iris' anxious expression. Then he strode off into the jungle and out of sight.

CHAPTER 18

INTO THE LAGOON

The next morning, everyone woke feeling refreshed and determined to find Lacuna Kaput. Knowing they must be very close, they decided not to stop until they discovered it. According to the map, their current route ran parallel with the river, so they opted to remain on the trail and keep their ears open for the sound of water rather than facing the perils of the river's banks.

It was around luncheon when Orion spun to face the others, excitement alight in his eyes. "I think I hear it."

Everyone listened closely. Birds sang whimsically in the misting rain, making it hard to hear, but after a moment, Iris exclaimed, "Me too!" Her boot lifted as if she meant to run, but Orion reached for her arm. She glanced at his fingers and regarded him with curiosity.

"Don't go running off this time, Iris." He eyed her seriously, and she pouted, deflating. "We go together." The moment her expression revealed her acceptance, his lips broke into a cheeky grin, and he bolted past her, fleeing into the trees and cackling with victory.

Iris' mouth fell open. "Did he just…?"

Foxx laughed. "He definitely did."

Fire kindled in Iris' eyes as she darted after him, yelling accusations of deceit into his dust.

Turning to Declan, Foxx found his countenance indifferent, as always, and sighed before following her sister and Orion down the trail they carved through the foliage.

Orion had nearly breached the treeline when Iris shot past him, blasting him in the shoulder and throwing him off balance. He hollered her name through frustrated laughter and picked up speed. When he reached the edge of the trees, he found Iris standing awestruck on the ledge of a cliff. Stopping next to her, he nudged her shoulder. "You beat me."

Iris grinned. "You cheated. You deserved it."

Moments later, Foxx stepped up to the edge and stared in amazement at the spectacle. The girls had not known it was possible for something to be more enchanting than the city of Petrichor, but there they stood, gaping in wonder at the most glorious natural masterpiece they'd ever laid eyes on.

"Lacuna Kaput," Foxxglove said, her voice full of reverence. She inhaled a deep breath of air that smelled like the ocean on a crisp, cool day.

The painting they found in the desert had been created from their exact location. Despite their mother's talent, her artistry could not touch the magnificence before them. Even Declan, who had at last joined them on the cliff, stopped short, stunned by the sight.

Across the cavern on the opposing cliff stood a towering kapok tree. Luscious leaves and exotic branches stretched out in all directions. The tree loomed above the jungle, staking its claim as the tallest and most majestic tree in the land. Curving tendrils of roots dripped over the edge into the dazzling, teal lagoon far below. Waterfalls poured over the cliff from the river at its back, falling throughout the roots and cascading in shimmering streams that fed the pool. The sound of the water hitting the pool reminded them of waves crashing against the beaches in Alunda and filled each of them with their own distinct sense of nostalgia.

Beaming like a child holding sweets, Orion dropped his knapsack and Iris' blade belt to the ground and began scaling down into the cavity. Iris considered retrieving her weapons as they lay perfectly available to her, but after a glance at Declan, she decided against it. Instead, she and Foxx followed Orion.

The vegetation and flowers growing around the lagoon were the largest and most vivid they'd seen in the whole forest, as if the water feeding them produced a magical fertilizer, encouraging them to grow bigger and brighter than naturally possible. Passiflora, orchids the size of plates, and huge bromeliads burst with color throughout the cavern. Pink lilies rested on pads floating around the edges of the water.

They climbed around the inner edge of the cavern, headed for the massive roots of the kapok tree. They traversed thin ledges, climbed rocky paths, and fought through foliage.

Reaching the tree first, Orion climbed up through the tangle of roots, making his way to the base of the trunk. When he felt pleased with the height of his ascent, he mounted a wide stone jutting out over the pool. Scooting carefully toward the edge, he leaned his head out and looked down the falls. Then he raised his arms and released a wild scream that echoed throughout the cavern—not of terror, but of release. Empowered and free.

Iris stopped on a root a *syli* under him, with Foxx close behind her. When they heard his shout, they looked up in alarm, but the pleasure on his face forced them into fits of laughter. Iris cupped a hand around her mouth and howled like a wolf worshiping the moon. Foxx joined her ballad.

Orion again stepped closer to the edge and slid his shirt over his head. Iris found herself drawn to his toned chest and arms, the sharp ridges of his stomach, and felt an instant flush of shame at her attraction to her captor. Before she could drag her gaze away, his eyes caught hers.

Grinning, he whipped his shirt at her, and she caught it with her face. Pulling his hair free of its bun, he shook out black locks and howled at the sky before swan-diving toward the lagoon. Foxx covered her mouth, her eyes widening in disbelief. After a colossal splash, they waited in suspense for him to reemerge. Though Declan did not seem concerned, Iris scanned the pool for what felt like way too long for someone to hold their breath.

At last, Orion's face burst through the surface of the water. He flipped his long hair away from his eyes and yowled with delight. Iris seriously wondered if he might have lost his mind. Foxx still held a hand to her mouth. Turning to Iris, she found her lost in a frenzy of laughter and couldn't help but laugh along.

Then Iris considered the ledge Orion had jumped from. She peered down into the lagoon and back up to the base of the tree, trying to work out the distance in her head.

Foxx realized her intention and warned, "Don't you dare!"

Iris ignored her and followed Orion's footpath up the roots. When she stepped out onto the ledge and looked over the cliff, she felt a rush of nerves and fear in the pit of her stomach. Though not normally afraid of heights, it was extremely high. As she peered down at the lagoon, a thought sparked in her memory. She'd seen the view before, only for a brief second, when she'd been at the Tree of Knowing. In the vision, she'd been falling toward the water. That alone stood as proof she had to take the leap, didn't it?

She decided a running jump was her best chance at quelling her panic, and she stepped back a few paces. After a deep breath, she charged, slapped her palms together above her head, and dove. As she plummeted through the air, she thought she'd never felt so free. Her life, filled with abandonment and monsters and constant travel through rough terrain and hunting for their food and running from soldiers and being kidnapped by strangers and every other thing that threatened to tear her down; everything she fought against; the constant battle to smile, to stay positive, to stay happy, to stay safe, to find the sunshine—it vanished for that long moment while she spread her wings and flew.

She hit the water and found it deeper than expected. Spinning, she swam upward until breaking the surface into the open air.

Orion floated next to her, grinning like an absolute fool. "That was thrilling, wasn't it?" he asked, his eyes bluer than the dark depths of the lagoon.

She nodded breathlessly, combing her hair away from her face and smiling from ear to ear. Foxx's waves drew her attention. Then she looked at the ledge they'd jumped from with swelling pride. It seemed significantly higher from below than it had from above. Her eyes shifted back to Foxx to find her still waving, but the look on her face revealed frantic warning rather than excitement at Iris' success. She reached for Orion's shoulder, alerting him to her sister's anxiety. They followed her gestures to the foaming water at the base of the falls, but before they had a chance to react, something painful latched onto Iris' ankle and dragged her under.

Foxx screamed her name, her voice shrill and echoing throughout the canyon. She jolted into action before realizing with dread and a newfound hatred for Orion that she did not have her bow. Her eyes shot to Declan up on the cliff who had just noticed the commotion.

Understanding immediately what she needed, he grabbed her bow and quiver from Orion's pile of belongings and began climbing down to them.

Foxx moved in his direction.

Orion dove in search of Iris.

When Foxxglove and Declan converged, he passed her the weapons, and she nocked an arrow.

Declan aimed his pistol at the water. "We can't fire until we can see her."

Foxx called Orion's name. "Where is she?"

He didn't respond before diving again. Already having pulled his knife from his boot, he held it in his right hand as he swam, frantically scouring the depths for a sign of her. Though mostly clear from above, dark cavities and tunnels filled the deep lagoon. Water pouring from the falls stirred up the pool, making it difficult to see anything beneath the surface.

Finally, he caught a flash of white. He pushed himself forward until Iris' body came into view. Her eyes bulged from lack of oxygen and terror. A bumpy tentacle had wrapped itself around her waist and down one of her thighs. Blood clouded the water surrounding her. She fought the beast, kicking and punching with all the ferocity of someone fighting off death, but the tentacle didn't budge.

Orion swam up for a gulp of air. "She's here!" He dove again, slid an arm around her waist, and pulled. The pressure released a silent scream, spawning a cloud of bubbles from her mouth. Excruciating pain flashed across her countenance as the water darkened. He motioned for her to wrap her arms around his shoulders, and she did. Then he stabbed the tentacle, and though the blade barely pierced its tough hide, it recoiled and released her, allowing Orion to drag her toward the light above. When her face shattered the surface, she lost herself in unrestrained sputters and coughs as water forced its way from her lungs. Orion held her tight as he hauled her to the stone foundation below Foxx and Declan. Foxx dropped down to help him heave her to the shore. Blood spilled everywhere, coating her wet skin and clothes.

"Where is it?" Declan's eyes combed the water. Orion focused on Iris, supporting her back as she coughed violently. Blood drenched his hands and the ground surrounding her. "Rion!" shouted Declan, demanding his focus.

Orion turned, his body still in the water.

From under the falls, a thick appendage slithered like a serpent out of the lagoon. Grabbing one of the kapok roots for support, the creature drew itself higher. More limbs appeared and fastened to the roots pouring from the great tree until five tentacles held the creature suspended above the water. The tentacles were coal-colored and covered in evergreen bumps like barnacles on a ship's hull. The undersides throbbed with slits that separated as the creature moved, exposing long rows of teeth. Seeming to hang upside-down, its elongated body had even larger lumps, like massive, crusty tumors. It balanced above the water, bobbing back and forth.

Iris' coughing subsided, but the bleeding continued. Foxx helped her sit up, only because she refused to remain on her back.

Orion had yet to pull himself from the water. He gaped in horror, his eyes following the elegant sway of the monster.

Iris felt off balance, rattled by the experience and woozy from pain and blood loss, but when she saw Orion floating on the edge of the lagoon, her awareness crisped into focus. She screamed for him to get out. Foxx lifted her bow. A bullet shot from Declan's pistol sent echoes into the cavity at the exact moment Foxx released her arrow. In response, the monster dropped back into the water with a hulking splash.

"Is it dead?" Declan and Foxx scanned the surface. His gun stayed raised in preparation, and she'd already nocked another arrow.

Iris yelled Orion's name again, and he spun to her. "Will you get out of the water, you idiot!"

He nodded and flattened his palms on the shore to lift himself out. A tentacle breached the surface and twisted around his torso. His eyes met Iris' for a brief, terrified moment as the monster yanked him into the deep.

Iris shot to her feet. Fresh blood spilled from her wounds as she moved, but adrenaline dragged her through the drowsiness. Foxx yelled for her to stop, but Iris ignored her. When she reached the wall, she began the trek back up the root system.

More than a *syli* up the roots, Declan appeared at her side, having already been a level above the shore. "Be careful," he called over the roaring falls as he found his footing and followed her.

Instead of climbing all the way to the tree's base, Iris changed course and shimmied horizontally through the web of roots, weaving around the streams of water. The agony across her stomach became almost unbearable, but she pressed on. Creeping out around a wide cluster of roots, she hooked both heels into apertures along the wall to steady herself. Standing above where the beast had originally surfaced, she grabbed hold of a root tendril with one hand and leaned out over the edge, watching and waiting.

Orion was hauled up out of the water as the beast began scaling the falls. Blood-curdling screams had the creature dunking him back under the surface and drawing him up moments later. When his wailing didn't subside, it tried again, and again, slamming his body into the water.

Eventually, Orion stopped screaming.

Foxx shot a second arrow into the monster's body, though it barely penetrated its tough skin. The creature thrashed in a rage, shaking the tree. Iris tipped back against the wall, grasping for purchase as it rocked her foundation. She scoured the roots around her, trying to formulate a plan as another shudder shook the tree. Declan had his gun clutched in his right hand as he clung to the roots, but his vantage left little opportunity for a quality shot.

As the beast climbed higher, a tentacle slithered up through the roots a mere foot to Iris' right. She let go with one hand and leaned out over the falls to examine it as it drew closer. Another wave of anguish coursed through her as she stretched her stomach. Declan called her name, but she paid no heed to his warnings. She fought to focus despite the fuzziness clouding her mind, as if her brain were swimming around in a pit of sludge.

At last, a potential chink in the creature's armor revealed itself. She saw a small, fleshy hole between two rows of eyes. It seemed to fluctuate, growing and shrinking as if sucking in air. Reaching for the dagger that no longer rested on her hip, she glared down at Orion's limp body dangling awkwardly in the air.

Then the beast spotted her. It froze for a moment, scrutinizing its prey. All at once, every one of its beady eyes stared up at her. It crept closer without haste, taunting to provoke a deeper fear. The tree shook. Iris readjusted her grip so she wouldn't fall. Bending her knees, she anchored her heels into divots in the wall and leaned out over the lagoon. "Declan! I need a weapon!"

Without missing a beat, he tossed his pistol. She caught it midair and gripped it tightly with both hands, aiming straight down between her boots. The monster lingered below her, less than a *syli* away. Its tentacles encompassed her on all sides. Dirt and broken twigs tumbled onto her head and shoulders.

Iris blocked out the looming peril and allowed herself one steadying breath as she aimed at the circle of soft flesh. She squeezed the trigger, and the result was instantaneous. The monster released Orion and he plummeted. The entire cavern seemed to quiver as the creature crashed into the lagoon. Then the surface stilled except for the ripples produced by the falls.

Declan dove from the wall to rescue Orion.

Iris leaned back against the dirt and roots, trying to catch her breath. Her head spun, but she was cognizant enough to know she needed to get to a safer location. Her legs wobbled as if she'd downed one too many ales, but she quickly and carefully climbed across the root system, hoping to make it to flat ground before losing consciousness.

Foxx stared into the pool, an arrow still slung in her bow, waiting for Declan and Orion to reemerge.

Iris reached the ledge as her knees gave out, forcing her to tumble forward. Leaning drowsily against the cavern wall, she mumbled her sister's name and passed out.

C

Iris awoke in the dark to the sound of a crackling fire. Above her, leaves rustled in the trees, the firelight prancing about them as they swayed. Through patches of branches she could see the Storm moon three days past full.

The scent of cooked fish wafted her way. Then she caught a familiar whiff of something foul, but in her drowsy state, she couldn't place it. She sniffed the air and attempted to sit up, wrestling against the fuzziness in her brain as her neck fought to support her head. Pain burned her stomach and down her thigh, causing her to cry out.

Foxx heard and rushed over. "Hey, hey, slow down." She pushed her backward and propped her up on her cushion. "You were cut pretty deeply and lost a lot of blood. Declan stitched you up." Iris looked puzzled by Foxx's worried expression. "Then he put some… cura on it." Iris' face scrunched with revulsion, and Foxx continued swiftly, trying to get all of her encouraging words out before her sister could rage. "Wasn't that so nice of him? His stitch-work was excellent. Hopefully it will heal quickly and with barely a scar. But until then you need to rest."

Iris scowled, groaning with disgust. "That's the smell! Nasty, mutant spider juices. Gross!" Foxx shrugged, trying to hide her smile, as this reaction was more or less what she'd expected. Iris heard a chuckle beside her and rotated her head to find Orion horizontal at her side, looking even worse than she felt. Patches of black and purple spotted his exposed skin.

"You are ridiculous."

She scoffed again, more dramatically. "I am not ridiculous. I just don't appreciate waking up smelling like three-day old, sun-roasted vomit."

"You smell more like five-day old vomit to me."

Iris wished she had the energy and pain tolerance to smack him.

Foxx cut in before Iris could retort. "Well, appreciate waking up *alive*. Declan really saved you." She looked sharply at Orion and added, "Both of you." Orion groaned, hating the idea of needing a rescue.

Iris glanced at Declan sitting by the fire lost in his thoughts. She hadn't known he could stitch a wound, and it again occurred to her that she didn't know much about him at all.

Not having realized Foxx walked away, it surprised Iris to find her sister returning to hand each of them a bowl of food.

Foxx tucked the white streak of hair behind Iris' ear. "I'm glad you're okay. You were very brave. It was really stupid though, climbing back up that tree. You could have died. So, what did we learn?"

Iris furrowed her brow. "Don't swim in monster infested lagoons?"

"How about, *don't scale giant trees when covered in lacerations?*"

"That's a good one, too."

"Especially to save this jerk of all people." Foxx gestured to Orion, who looked taken aback, apparently not having realized Iris' role in his saving. Foxx touched a kiss to her sister's forehead. "I am going to clean up. You should try to eat. I placed a water skin between you. Make sure you *share*." She pointed meaningfully at both of them, the way a mother would threaten siblings. Then she returned to Declan and the fire.

Iris snatched the bag before Orion could reach for it. The swift movement pulled on her stitches, and she grimaced in pain.

Orion smirked. "That's what you get for being greedy."

She rolled her eyes and took a swig. Once she started drinking, she found it difficult to stop. She hadn't noticed how thirsty she'd become until the taste touched her tongue. After setting it down between them, she scooted up into a position closer to sitting, maneuvering slowly so as to not alert Foxx.

As she began picking through her bowl of food, she noticed Orion observing her in her peripherals. "Did you want something?"

Pulling his stare away, he investigated his own food. "No."

They ate together in silence for several minutes, though she continued to feel his eyes slide to her. Irritated, but assuming he didn't plan to stop, she decided to extinguish the awkwardness by making pleasant conversation. "So. You look like garbage."

This pulled a surprised laugh from him that led to an immediate groan as waves of soreness pulsed through his body. "Thank you. I feel like garbage, as well." He attempted to sit up at her level, but the pain was too great, and he gave up, resolving to stay laying until it was absolutely necessary for him to move.

Iris ignored him as she thought over all of the things that had happened since departing Petrichor. She'd been a feral prisoner, with her wrists in cuffs, wild and fighting and threatening to murder Orion even after he'd released her. Recalling his violent hands on her, grabbing her arms and neck, filled her with fresh vexation.

Then she thought of the birds, of his kindness and enthusiasm; the story about his father; his understanding of Foxx's needs after the storm. And the waterfall—the joy on his face before he jumped, followed by his concern when trying to rescue her from the giant cephalopod.

It didn't make sense he'd worked so hard to save her. As he so blatantly pointed out before, he only needed one of them to find their father. He could have let her die, freed himself from the most challenging of the two sisters.

In the two weeks they'd been together, his personality swung like a pendulum from one extreme to the other. Maximum levels of harsh and kind, malicious and thoughtful, angry and happy. On one hand, it seemed impossible to think his motivations for rescuing her had been the result of human decency. But on the other…

She also considered why she'd been so determined to save *him*. She'd risked her life, climbed up the side of the cavern, injured and spilling blood everywhere. Surely with him gone, they could have easily escaped Declan. He may even have let them go willingly, not often seeming to care what was going on one way or another. Iris sighed.

"You are now thinking about how much you regret saving me."

Orion spoke low, as though he didn't want her to hear his observation.

She looked at him, having forgotten his presence and concerned she'd been speaking her thoughts out loud. "No, I—"

"It's all right. I deserve it. I know I do."

"Well. That's true."

This prompted another laugh. Then he said, a little too seriously, "Even still. Thank you, Iris."

She remained quiet, not sure she wanted to accept his gratitude. A long, uncomfortable moment passed before she said, "Killing the monster saved all of us. Don't think I did it for you." A lie, she knew. Declan and Foxx could have handled the creature. It was Declan's own gun she'd used to kill it. There had been no real reason for her to jeopardize her safety scaling the tree.

Orion didn't respond, and she thought she might have offended him or hurt his feelings, but she didn't much care.

They sat for a while, staring into the dark jungle in front of them. Foxx and Declan discussed something too quiet for them to hear. Watching her sister interact with him filled her with admiration. Foxxglove had the uncanny ability to be pleasant with her enemies. She was smart and controlled enough to know when to keep the peace and when to fight back. She knew how to bide her time, waiting for the perfect moment. In some situations, tactical maneuvering ensured survival. They needed to be clever and adaptable.

Iris' was often filled with joyful energy, unwavering love, and kindness. But she could also be reactive, uncooperative, and argumentative. No matter what she felt, she wore her heart on her sleeve.

Foxx kept hers in a steel trap.

At least, she used to. Since their journey into the Grim Wilds began, Iris couldn't help but notice her hesitant willingness to let others in. She thought of the people they'd left behind in Kesken Ala and the Ataraxia Mission. And of course, there was Asher. Iris smiled with pride as she realized that something along this fated road was softening her sister's heart, allowing it to open and shaping it into a different creature than it had ever been before. And even, quite possibly, setting her free.

She lifted her face to the sky above, and Orion followed her gaze. With a humorless chuckle, he said, "The Storm moon. Ironic, don't you think?"

"In more ways than one." Iris took another bite of fish. It'd been quite some time since they'd eaten seafood, and she loved it. After washing the bite down with a swig from the water bag, she passed it to Orion without reattaching the cap and ignored the strange look he gave her in response to the gesture.

When she set it back between them, he asked, "Why did you do it, Iris?"

She waited to reply, mulling over the answer. Setting her bowl down beside her, she returned to her supine position. The trees above continued bouncing in shades of persimmon and cedar, reflecting the firelight. "Honestly, part of me wishes I hadn't." Without turning to him, she watched his reaction from the corner of her eye. He tilted his head, as if in understanding, but said nothing. After a while, more truth forced itself from her lips, and she admitted, "I guess... in the heat of the moment, something in me saw something in you worth saving."

CHAPTER 19

LACUNA KAPUT

Shortly after sunrise, Declan ventured from camp in search of breakfast while Foxxglove foraged nearby. It didn't take her long to gather four plump oranges, two perfectly ripe avocados, and a handful of figs.

Discovering the fig tree had been bittersweet, immediately throwing her into thoughts of Asher. She wondered if he might be thinking of her as often as she thought of him, or if he'd ever find his way back to them, as promised.

When she returned to camp, Iris stirred awake. Kneeling next to her, she set down the bag of fruit. "How did you sleep?"

Iris yawned, and Foxx helped her sit up. Once situated against the trunk of a tree, she answered, "Not terrible. But you know: the pain, the rain." Iris shrugged, accepting her poor slumber as an inevitability.

"I know. We need to find a better shelter."

"We need to find the rainforest key and hopefully Asher along with it so we can move on." Iris winced as she attempted to shift into a more agreeable position. "If there is really one in each territory, there will be one in Cordillera, too."

Foxxglove peeked at Orion, breathing a sigh of relief in response to the steady rise and fall of his chest. "You're right. Declan and I will search the falls today. I still have no idea how I'm supposed to find a single stone in that huge cavern, though." Iris shook her head, thinking the key could be anywhere. One tiny rock in a big pile of rocks.

Foxx pulled one of each fruit from the bag. "I found us some breakfast. Are you hungry?" Iris swiped the fig. Foxx tucked the avocado back into the bag and began cutting into the tough skin of the orange with her fingernails. As she worked on tearing rind from pith, her thoughts drifted, and a melody began to hum from her chest. Iris listened to the familiar tune, letting the song sweep her away to a time when their mother was happy and singing. Then a thought struck her, and she sat up in a rush, swearing as pain burned across her stomach.

Startled from peaceful meditations, Foxx asked, "What is it? What's wrong?"

"Foxxglove, you remarkable genius!" Iris wrapped her arms around her sister and groaned at the abrupt reminder of her injuries. Her hand pressed against the wound, and her face puckered.

"What are you talking about?" Foxx tried to coax Iris back into a resting position, but Iris teemed with too much excitement.

"The song, Foxx! The song you were humming." She attempted to keep her voice down so as not to wake Orion, but her elation overrode her desire for secrecy.

"It was one Mother used to sing to us. I haven't been able to get the tune out of my head for days. I'm not sure what triggered it."

Iris put a hand on either of Foxx's shoulders. "The lyrics, Foxx. The lyrics. I can't believe we didn't realize this before!" Foxx looked puzzled as she tried to remember. The words of the song lingered just out of reach, hiding on the fringes of her memories.

Iris went on. "Each verse is about a territory, right? *Continuous rain in the Metsa Sateen. Water cleanses, brings life that's luscious and green. At Lacuna Kaput they took shelter at last, when at Imber—*

"*The temple was ripped from their grasp.* Oh my goodness, Iris. The temple was ripped from their grasp."

"So they took shelter at Lacuna Kaput. They took shelter here! How is it possible we didn't recognize these names before? The whole song is about the Monastery of the Morrow!" Gears turned behind Iris' eyes as she tried to discern how they could have so blindly forgotten. She had the lyrics written in her journal and must have flipped past them thirty times since their journey began.

Foxx shuffled through similar thoughts. "I don't know. It seems so obvious now. Even when we first saw the painting and Asher talked about the Monastery of the Morrow, the names didn't sound familiar to me at all." Like a lifted veil, the memories snapped crisply into place. "Something kept us from remembering."

"Maybe it's an enchantment? That could be why the Monastery is hidden from so many and why much of the world believes it to be a fairytale."

"If the Queen destroyed the temple and the scholars had to flee, the stone wouldn't have been left at the Monastery. It was important. They would have kept it with them."

Iris nodded along enthusiastically. "It has to be here. Somewhere they would have been able to stay together: like a shelter or a hideout. You can find it, Foxx. It won't be a stone lost at the bottom of the lagoon. It'll have been kept safe." She leaned over, grimacing yet again as she wrapped her arms around Foxx.

The ruckus woke Orion just as Declan reentered the campsite carrying the carcass of a small wild boar. "What's so exciting?" Declan asked.

"Merely the bonds of sisterly love," Iris answered. Foxx stood and walked over to help him with the boar.

"Well, it's annoying." Orion rubbed his eyes.

"You're annoying." Shifting to face away from him, Iris called to her sister. "Is it entirely necessary I lay this close to him?"

Orion exhaled an exaggerated sigh.

"Safety in numbers. If Declan and I are going to search the waterfall, it will be better for you two to be together."

Iris and Orion groaned in unison.

Declan stifled a laugh.

☾

After a fruit and pork breakfast, Declan and Foxx departed the camp and headed up the thin trail to the summit across from the waterfall. They toed the edge of the cliff, peeking down into the lagoon. Foxx felt sick, unwittingly picturing the lagoon monster yanking her sister under the water and slamming Orion into its surface over and over again. Her hand lifted to her stomach.

Declan noticed the movement. "Are you going to be okay?" She affirmed with a stiff nod. "Well, that's super reassuring. Here." He handed her a knife from a sheath around his waist. He'd reclaimed her bow after the attack, knowing Orion would not allow her to keep it.

She'd been disappointed, but hadn't resisted. "Are you sure Orion would be all right with you giving me that?"

He held the handle closer to her. "Orion isn't here, and after yesterday, I don't want to be down there with someone who can't watch my back. Return it to me before we go back to camp?"

Accepting the weapon, she held it tightly in her fist. She looked over the edge once more and examined the water below, paying special attention to the base of the falls where the creature had plummeted. "She definitely killed it, right?"

Declan joined her observation. "Almost definitely. Though there might be more than one." Foxx's eyes shot to him. He shrugged before striding past her and beginning his descent. "Any idea what we are looking for?"

"Not really, no." She followed him down the steep wall, keeping the knife in hand except when she needed more than her fingertips to climb. On those occasions she held it between her teeth. Streams of light cracked through the canopy above in wide shafts, making the lagoon's teal water sparkle. "Maybe we should split up? Cover more ground?"

"I would rather stick together in case we aren't alone down here."

Foxxglove nodded. She didn't really want to split up anyway.

When they reached the first landing, still at least three *sylis* above the base of the lagoon, they stopped. Each swallowed a drink from the water bag as they surveyed the surrounding area. Mud at their feet coated the bottom of their boots as it hadn't done the day before. Foxx lifted her foot to glimpse the tread beneath and scowled, knowing climbing would be far trickier with muddy shoes. Declan noticed her grimace and chuckled, drawing her eyes to him.

"What?" she asked, startled by his jovial expression.

He shook his head and took another swig before reattaching the cap. "So. A clue to lead us forward." Declan clipped the water to his pack and scratched the scruff on his chin. Foxx continued scanning the cavern, lost in her own thoughts. "Did your father come here when he was looking for Celestelvyra? Is that the trail we're following?"

Foxxglove sighed. "We already told you, Declan. We really don't know where my father is. We found his map. It led us to a building in the desert. The only notable thing we found there was a painting of our mother's depicting these falls." Though she did wonder if their father had found the painting and followed it to Lacuna Kaput as they had. If so, how had he known where to go from there? "It's possible he came here and was eaten by the horrifying, tentacle creature, and this is all a hopeless dead end."

"I doubt he would have let the lagoon monster best him. He was a little tougher than that if memory serves."

Taken aback by his admission, it occurred to her for the first time that Declan and Orion might have known her father better than she did herself. Based on the knowledge they seemed to possess, she'd suspected they might have been soldiers in the King's Legion, as he had been, though she'd never confirmed this suspicion. "Was he? I wouldn't know."

Foxx's obvious scorn toward her father surprised Declan. Though, after thinking it through, he realized the girls were young when he'd abandoned them. Maybe the men in his unit weren't the only lives crushed by Sawyer's misdeeds.

In light of that, he couldn't help but feel curious about why she seemed so intent on finding Sawyer while harboring such contempt. Certainly not for the same reasons they were, and not a childish hope to be reunited with her father, either, though he suspected that may be Iris' main goal. Foxx seemed less sentimental. Declan's curiosity got the better of him, and he asked.

Foxx replied with a bitter whip. "I don't want to talk about this. You haven't given us your reasons, and I don't feel the need to reveal mine. Let's just try to find the clue so we can move on." He obliged without argument and eyed their surroundings again. "*At Lacuna Kaput they took shelter at last,*" she said.

Her mumbled words sparked his attention. "What's that?"

"It's a song my mother used to sing." She repeated the important part. "A shelter. Where would someone find shelter here?"

"Maybe a cave? I didn't notice any yesterday, but it could be well hidden."

"Let's climb down to the water."

Declan found his footing and began climbing backward down the side of the cliff. Foxx followed his path. When his feet hit the ground, he held out his hands to help her the rest of the way, but she rejected his assistance and maneuvered around him.

The shore of the lagoon encircled the water in a horseshoe, beginning on one side of the waterfall and ending on the other. Despite the rain, a large patch of blood stained the ground where Iris had lain. Though both obviously noticed it, neither acknowledged its presence. From the bottom, they could see all of the cavern walls. They rotated, taking in the entire scope of the area, but if any crevices, openings, or pathways leading to a hidden shelter existed, they remained concealed.

Foxx looked up, blocking a shard of sunlight with her hand. "It could be up in the tree? Or behind it?" She caught sight of an eclipse of tinaeras huddled together in a dark crevice beneath one of the cliffs. Smiling, she almost pointed it out to Declan, though quickly decided against it.

"Maybe. Let's finish down here and then climb up the other side." They combed the grounds, scouting behind large rocks, outshoots in the walls, and under big leafy plants, but found no passages.

Foxxglove approached the waterfall's edge, leery eyes penetrating the water. For such a huge beast to have lived there, she thought the lagoon must be incredibly deep. Movement in her peripherals caught her eye, and she jumped back, pulling her blade. On a small ledge outside the reach of the water, a tiny face appeared, no bigger than her thumb. Foxx squinted to get a closer look, trying to see through its yellow glow. The creature tipped its head at her before creeping out further, revealing more of itself. Wings flapped slowly at its back, similar to those of the driädi.

When its full body came into view, Foxx's lips broke into an intrigued smile. "Hello. I haven't seen a creature like you before. Though I imagine you must be some form of henki. Am I right?" It had the upper body of a woman with long hair covering its chest and shoulders. Its lower half had four legs, like a horse or a goat. Hearing a soft tinkle, Foxx turned so her ear leaned closer to the creature.

Another appeared, zipping past the first and heading straight for Foxx. It flew around her head and circled back to face her. Then it landed next to the first and seemed to quarrel with it, though Foxx couldn't hear any words. The first pointed at the waterfall with an arm no bigger than a blade of grass. Then the second fluttered away in exasperation.

"What are you looking at?" Declan asked.

Foxx kept her eyes on the creature, worried if she looked away it might vanish. "Um… Honestly? A tiny person with wings and the body of a horse."

Declan started walking toward her from the opposite side of the lagoon. "Don't let it out of your sight. It's a pixū, and it might know how to find what we're looking for."

Foxx smiled again at the pixū, and it bowed in return. "We're looking for a cave or somewhere people might have lived. Is there anything like that around here?"

Another tinkle reached Foxx's ear. The creature's wings began to flap faster as is rose into the air. Then it flew past her and disappeared behind the waterfall. Leaning against the stone, Foxx peeked behind the falls to see where the pixū had fluttered off to. That close to the pool, the water fell away from the tangle of roots, allowing space wide enough to climb through. "I think it's behind the waterfall." She glanced over her shoulder to see Declan halfway to her.

"Wait for me," he called back.

Slipping her blade into the strap on her boot, she latched onto the wall and placed her foot precariously on a ledge of rocks. She shifted her body sideways, shimmying behind the delicate tendrils that thinned as they grew closer to the water. A constant mist dampened her back, but the flowing stream didn't touch her.

Looking down, she saw bubbling water below. No solid ground would catch her if she fell, only a pond infested with monsters and the deadly suction of the falls. Inhaling a breath and determined not to stumble, she pressed forward.

Declan called her name, and his muffled voice echoed through the cavity between water and stone. When she looked back at him, a smile filled her cheeks. She read the words *be careful* on his lips and nodded. Grasping a sturdy root, Declan placed his feet where she had and began making his way toward her.

Foxxglove kept moving until her hand gripped a corner. She leaned sideways and found the wall turning inward, away from the flowing water. Excitement coursed through her as she anchored herself more securely in the roots above, pulled away from the wall, and stepped onto flat ground. To her utter delight, a tunnel stretched away from her into the dark.

She shouted Declan's name, her body a bundle of nerves and exhilaration. Then she looked around for the pixū. Though it seemed to have disappeared, she thanked it and hoped it would hear.

Declan reached the tunnel soon after she did. "Good find, Foxx, but please wait for me before putting yourself in mortal danger. Iris will have my head if I let anything happen to you in her absence."

Foxx felt giddy and revealed this by giggling at his joke. Though after taking in his serious expression, she thought he might not actually be joking. "The pixū led me here. She pointed at it and then flew beneath the falls to show me the way. Are pixūs a species of henki?"

"Yes. They're smart creatures and generally trustworthy in my experience." Declan gazed blindly into the dark corridor. "Where do you think this leads?"

"To the next clue." Though she'd thought it before, she now believed more than ever that her mother hadn't led them astray. Her insane visions, incessant stories and ramblings about the world, and all of the things about her that had driven Foxx mad, had been set in place to lead them to Celestelvyra. She thought that—just maybe— her mother wasn't the crazy woman she'd believed her to be.

Maybe she was magnificent. A magnificent artist who saw through the veil between fiction and reality and glimpsed truths about the world hidden from most. Who believed fairytales were real; full of secrets and dreams and destinies.

And Asher was the same.

Foxx took a step toward the darkness, pausing when Declan touched her arm. "Foxx, wait. We don't know what's back there. We should go back for a torch."

"But we found it, Declan. We can't let fear of the unknown stop us now. We have to find out where it leads." She knew it wasn't logical, but she truly worried if they left, they may not be able to find their way back.

Things had finally begun to fall together, connecting in ways she'd hadn't imagined possible. Hope like she'd never felt before bloomed inside of her, and she wasn't ready to let it go. If, by some cruel twist of fate, this turned out to be a dream or a hallucination, she wasn't yet ready to open her eyes.

"I know, and I agree. I am just suggesting we proceed with caution and take a light source into the dark tunnel. What if that lagoon monster also lives in caves?"

Foxx considered this possibility before saying, "Let's go a little farther and see if it's even a cave. It could end right here." Without waiting, she stepped forward into the black, halting suddenly as something lit up the ground at her feet.

Declan bent to examine it. "It's a mushroom."

"A glowing mushroom." Another tinkle sounded, and Foxx looked around. "Did you hear that?"

He nodded. "Some stories tell of henki that are known for playing tricks on humans."

Foxx leaned over to get a closer look at the mushroom. It rested against the tunnel wall and shined with delphinium blue light. Straightening, she said, "I think we can trust her. Another appeared and didn't seem pleased to find her helping me." She took another step forward, and two more mushrooms brightened next to the first, forming a row along the cave wall. "They're lighting the way, Declan."

Ignoring his warning to use caution, Foxx followed the mushrooms lighting her path, feeling certain in her gut they would lead her where she needed to go. She rounded a bend with Declan close behind her, and more mushrooms sparked to life on the opposite side of the passage wall. They continued on deep into the tunnel, guided by the bright rows of blue on either side of them. As the air grew colder, Foxx knew they must be pretty far underground, but she felt no fear at whatever mysteries lay ahead.

Suddenly halting their progression, the mushrooms rose up from the floor. They turned in at a right angle, and both sides met in the middle, framing a doorway in light. Stepping beneath the fluorescent archway, Foxx and Declan found themselves in an underground chamber. More mushrooms blazed to life all over the room, no longer following the command of their footsteps. Scattered throughout, sharp clusters of amethyst, lapis, and jade jutted out from the stone floor, radiating with luminance. Many rose from the ground even higher than Foxx's waist.

Aside from the obviously enchanted crystals and fungi, the chamber itself looked as one would expect an underground cave to look. Stalactites hung from the ceiling like icicles, dripping water that created puddles and divots into the floor. Trickling water could be heard throughout the damp hollow as the river above provided life to the leafy foliage emerging through fissures in the rocks.

"What is this place?" Declan asked.

"I have no idea." Foxxglove approached one of the purple crystals and touched it. It brightened, as if sensing her presence. "It's like the cave is alive. Like it knows we're here, don't you think?"

"Magic?"

Foxx met his gaze and lifted a shoulder, but goosebumps prickled her skin, both from the chill of the underground cavern and the idea that they stood encompassed in sorcery. "It has to be, doesn't it?"

Declan said, "If that's true, then the question is, what does it plan to do with us now that we're here?"

Then they heard the grinding sound of stone against stone, drawing their attention to the wall across from the room's entrance. A flat slab slid into existence from within the wall. Half a *syli* above the ground and a foot thick, it looked like a shelf or table. Giant crystal clusters sprouted from the floor right before their eyes and mushrooms climbed the edges, framing it as they had the doorway and surrounding the shelf in glowing light.

Foxx and Declan shared a hesitant glance before stepping closer. Atop the platform sat a stone chest. Just over half a foot wide, the rectangular box was topped with a domed lid. Silver embellishments, tarnished with moisture and time, decorated its corners and edges with intricate curls. A once beautifully scripted *M* had been engraved into the top, now barely visible from the years of dust coating its surface.

"Seriously, Foxx, what is this place? You don't seem at all surprised by the obvious sorcery at work here. So what aren't you telling me?" An unfamiliar tremble of anxiety slipped into his tone, barely distinguishable. Foxx thought if they'd been above in the boisterous forest, she wouldn't have noticed it, but in the silent stasis of the preserved cave deep in the earth, every quiver was detectable.

Light erupted from the wall above the stone slab, attracting her attention before she could respond to his question. As though painted by the steady hand of an artist, a line began as a single dot and ended as the outline of a crescent moon stretching tall above their heads. Lacy designs emerged from within both tips, materializing one curved stroke at a time until entirely filled in.

Stanzas of four lines each shimmered into existence, beginning to the left of the moon and proceeding first to the moon's center and then to its right. In each designated position, three verses appeared.

"It's a poem. A song." Foxx's eyes trailed the familiar words as bumps swept across her shoulders and down her arms.

Arkaemor is a world of mystery and wonder,
Seven realms, with each their own treasure to plunder.
One never forgets lavish stories of old,
But can we remember a history untold?

Reginaterra is where the Queen made her home,
A luxurious castle built on flesh and on bone.
Unhappy in life, so the world they remade,
Giving little regard to the price that was paid.

Captured souls in a prison of sinners condemned,
In the depths of the earth vile Strayed apprehend.
Snared in the wasteland of Crystavium,
A Monastery tainted; corrupt and succumbed.

Norsukylä's haven was razed, set ablaze,
In Savanni, where lions and elephants graze.
Chronicles in ashes furnish memoirs rewritten,
Consumed by the wrath of an adversary unbidden.

The sea ebbs and flows with the wind's gentle breeze,
Much like life that transitions between trials and ease.
Alunda's temple was lost, felled deep below waves,
Did the scholars escape? Or sink down to their graves?

Out in the desert where the Wilds are Grim,
Vallemortis redeems when all hope has grown slim.
By an oasis once thriving in the depths of the land,
An old fortress stands lost and covered in sand.

Continuous rain in the Metsa Sateen
Water cleanses, brings life that's luscious and green
At Lacuna Kaput they took shelter at last
When at Imber, the temple was ripped from their grasp.

Oh, great Cordillera! Oh, grand Jericho!
Home of the Monastery of the Morrow!

Just in time for them to read the poem to completion, a tenth verse sparked to life beneath the moon.

"This is a song my mother used to sing to us." Foxx's unsettled emotions clouded her eyes. It seemed impossible that she and her sister hadn't put such an obvious puzzle together, and even more impossible that her mother had long ago given them all the answers they needed.

Finding that poem written on the wall beneath Lacuna Kaput solidified any doubt she'd been harboring about the words Maeve had spoken in Savanni and the destiny she'd claimed was meant for them. It also verified everything Asher had taught them about the world. Each territory had a Monastery that was destroyed, and each would come together to unlock the doorway to Celestelvyra and bring about the start of a new world—a world of freedom, peace, and joy.

Declan backed away from the wall. "This is about the Monastery of the Morrow," he said, his nervous tremors now easily perceptible. His eyes darted about the room, and his hand came to rest against his pistol. Lowering his voice to a near whisper, he demanded, "Foxx, what the hell are we doing here? Do you know the danger we're in being in this room?"

Foxx ignored him and took two steps toward the stone table. With care, she unhooked the silver latch and lifted the lid of the chest, already certain of what she would find. Inside sat a silver cloth wrapped around and tucked under an object that could fit in her palm. Foxx pulled the object from its abode and peeled the cloth away, only to find a plain, round stone encased within it.

Disappointment plagued her as a wave of sickening vibrations spread from her chest to her stomach. She examined the rock with pinched brows, letting it rest in the palm of her hand. It was nothing spectacular. Just a smooth gray stone, roughly the shape of a flattened egg, and clearly lifted from the floor at her feet. She ran her thumb across its surface, wondering for a moment if the true key wasn't hidden by some kind of magic—an enchanted disguise.

Then she noticed a scribble of charred wood on the stone's flattest side. Holding it to her nose, she sniffed the blackened smudge. "Ash," she whispered to herself, suddenly feeling an entirely new wave of erratic energy. She'd felt so sure he was on his way to Reginaterra, following the Legion's trail. But here lay almost indisputable proof of her error.

Declan said her name again, begging for an explanation.

"Someone else got to it first." She held the stone out in front of him. When he grabbed for it, she pulled it out of reach. "But it's fine. I know what to do now." Pointing to the words on the wall, she puzzled over the plan out loud. "The next step is in Cordillera—in Jericho, if the song is correct."

Declan grabbed her arm with stifled aggression, no longer able to be ignored. "Foxxglove, you need to tell me what's going on. The truth." His grip loosened on her arm as he peered deep into her eyes for a long breath. "I know it doesn't feel like it, but you can trust me."

She studied him curiously, finding a fracture in his stony shell. Then she pulled her arm from his grasp and backed away. "You're wrong. I can't trust you." A breeze forced its way down the tunnel from the waterfall above, sending another chill across her shoulders and down her spine. As her heartbeat quickened, the tips of her fingers grew ice cold.

"You can." He took another step forward, worried their voices would reverberate down the tunnel if they spoke too loudly.

Unafraid of being exposed in a cave deep in the ground at the center of a jungle, Foxx put more space between them, backing up at an angle and placing herself between Declan and the exit. "Regardless of what I think of you, I cannot trust Orion." She examined the stone in her hand once more, rolling it over in her fingers to make sure she hadn't overlooked another clue. Then she dropped it to the floor, and the crack of stone bouncing off solid ground sent a cacophony of echoes throughout the chamber. Before Declan realized what was happening, she'd pulled the dagger from her boot and gripped it defensively. "And you are with him." She planted her feet beneath her shoulders.

Declan lifted his palms as if approaching a frightened animal. "Foxx, just listen." He took a step closer, though she couldn't tell if this showed his lack of fear or if he angled to remove the blade from her grasp. She took another step back. "I know about the Monastery of the Morrow. I know what they believed and what they wanted to do. This nursery rhyme is more than a song. It was written by a prophet in Savanni, long before the Monasteries were destroyed." His eyes glanced back at the words on the wall. He took another step closer and this time she didn't back away. *"They rose once before and they'll rise yet again.* Foxx, whatever you and Iris are involved with, I want in."

"You can't be serious. How can you even ask that of me after everything you've done?" She scrutinized him. He said her name again, thick with anxiety, unveiling more emotion than she'd witnessed from him before.

He'd kidnapped them. Held a knife to Iris' throat. Followed along with everything Orion had done without stepping in, even when it seemed like he wanted to. Foxx's mind reeled with possibilities of his intentions. If he and Orion had been soldiers in the King's Legion, as she suspected, they could be working for the Queen even now, hunting her father so they could turn him over to her. They could be planning on turning her and Iris over, too, though if that was the case, they probably would have let the Legion take them in Petrichor.

Instead, they'd captured them for their own purposes. So perhaps they weren't working for the Queen, but what then? And why all the secrecy? Like with Asher, she couldn't understand the purpose for so many secrets. Wouldn't it be easier to tell her and Iris what was really going on? Wouldn't it be more efficient if everyone knew the whole story?

And why now, after everything, was Declan trying to sway her to trust him?

Maybe he thought earning her trust would ensure success in their schemes. She supposed they could have been playing them all along: a good guy and a bad guy, dividing to conquer. Her eyes turned again to the words on the wall. Words that had given people hope of a better life for longer than Foxx had realized. Maybe, however impossible it seemed, Declan grasped for that hope, too.

Letting the knife loosen in her grip, she yielded, "I can't tell you everything. I definitely don't trust Orion, despite the kindness he sometimes reveals, and I don't know if I can trust you." She studied him again, willing her gut to lead her to the correct choice.

"Tell me how I can prove it to you." His sincerity appeared unquestionable, reminding her of Asher's desperate pleas for trust. But she felt no loyalty to Declan after seeing him hold a knife to her sister's throat, and she certainly wasn't struggling with confusing feelings like she had with Asher. She had no reason to risk trusting him more than any prisoner trusts its captor, but if he could help get them where they needed to go, then perhaps it was her only option.

"Iris and I need to get to Jericho. That's the next step in our journey. I'll be honest though, regardless of whether or not you deserve it, I really have no idea if this will lead to our father or if it's a different path entirely. I don't fully understand everything that's happening. Our friend taught us about the world and the Monastery and..." Her words trailed off before she could say *the Queen*.

"Then let's head to Jericho."

Foxx wondered about this new personality, so different from the cold and stony man he'd been over the past two weeks. Much like with Orion, she couldn't decipher which version of him was authentic. Both were obviously lost, adrift in the whirlwind of misguided fates, but could it be possible their fates had transformed them along with their circumstances, disfiguring them into remnants of their true selves?

Just as her own circumstances had disfigured her.

Perhaps the fragments of goodness peeking through were scraps left behind, evidence of the men they would have been if destiny's blight hadn't intervened.

"Why are you doing this?" She lowered the dagger from its defensive position and let it come to rest at her side. Declan opened his mouth to answer, but she cut him off to specify, "I mean both of you. Why are you searching for my father? What was so important that abduction seemed like a good option? Who are you really, Declan?"

Declan considered his answer, trying to decide what to reveal. In the end, he didn't answer at all. "Orion will come around. Until then, we need to get away from here. Away from Lacuna Kaput and out of Metsa Sateen. Anything could be watching us."

Foxx thought his wording peculiar, as he hadn't said any*one*. "Were you in the King's Legion with my father?"

A flash of surprise darkened his eyes. Reluctantly, he answered, "Yes."

"Are you still in the Legion?"

Declan paused for a moment before shaking his head. "No, we aren't."

Foxx hummed in thought. "Iris and Orion won't be ready to travel yet. They need a few days at the very least."

He crossed one arm over his chest and let the other rest on his wrist as he scratched behind his ear. "One more day for them to rest up, and then we need to move on. You don't realize how quickly they can get to us if they know where we are, and I worry us being here might have triggered some kind of alarm or something."

She didn't question who he meant by *they* as she recalled the words of the Queen, hearing them as acutely as she had when Her Majesty first spoke them. Her voice had been like the sharp edge of a razor blade, like a hissing cobra waiting to strike. The memory of her vicious timbre felt like a thousand bugs skittering across her skin.

I see you. I'm coming for you.

But she hadn't come for her yet. Foxx wondered what she might be waiting for.

Accepting his previous statement without words, she turned toward the exit. Declan took hold of her hand, and she spun back to face him. Searching his eyes, she found herself unafraid. She hadn't even instinctually lifted her blade at his touch.

"I promise that you and Iris can trust me. I know a promise from me means little right now. I know I've done nothing to prove it." He let go of her hand, appearing suddenly embarrassed as his eyes scanned the floor. Crinkling his brow with determination, he returned her gaze. "But the truth is, I care about her. Iris, I mean. There's something about her that I can't seem to—" He shook his head. "Anyway, I didn't expect it, and it definitely wasn't part of the plan, but it is what it is. And I don't wish to see you hurt either, Foxx. I never wished to see either of you hurt. This was a fool's mission from day one, and I'll deny ever saying this, but neither of us really knew what we were getting into."

Despite his previous transgressions, Foxx thought his declaration felt true. That didn't mean she trusted him, but... it was something. "I believe you, but none of that proves you'll choose us over Orion if put in the position to do so. I have to protect Iris above everything else."

He nodded, agreeing or simply understanding, she wasn't sure. Then he said, "I know it sounds impossible, because he has been utterly atrocious, but Orion isn't a bad man. I think... I hope... you'll come to trust him, too."

Foxx's brows rose high on her forehead. Shaking her head with disbelief, she said, "Sorry, Declan. I really wish that were true."

Chapter 20

Crossing Over

When Foxx and Declan returned to camp, Iris was seated upright on her bedroll. She laughed so hard her hand clutched her stomach as the tightening of muscles disturbed her injury. Orion's face contorted in irritation, suppressing the amusement made evident in the upturn of his lips.

Iris noticed their approach and turned to face them. "Did you find anything?" Her words drew Orion's eyes to Declan, and Foxx noticed a moment of silent communication pass between them.

"We think we know where to head next." Foxx and Declan took turns explaining what they'd discovered, leaving out almost everything except the image of the moon on the wall which led them to believe they should head to the City of the Moon. Despite what Declan claimed, Foxx didn't feel comfortable sharing the parts of the plan involving the Monastery of the Morrow with Orion. Declan agreed to withhold the information, mainly for fear of discussing it again so close to the lagoon.

Orion seemed content with the new plan, regardless of the flimsy evidence.

Iris opened her mouth to inquire further, not so easily swayed by the vague clues, but after reading Foxx's expression, she kept her thoughts to herself until they could talk freely.

It was raining again, stronger than it had in days. Foxx moved closer to Iris and Orion, sheltering herself beneath the thicker canopy. "I think we should stay in the forest a while longer. You both need some time to let the curavenum heal your wounds. It's pointless for us to move forward only to end up carrying you through the mountains because your gashes get ripped open or infected."

"Not necessary." Orion's eyes, like his tone, sharpened. "We don't need to put it off any longer now that we have a destination. Our wounds will be fine. We leave immediately." He pulled himself into an upright position with excessive effort and began sliding his feet into damp boots with determination. As he tightened the laces, his face revealed a grimace.

Iris winced as she watched his movements. "Maybe another day or two wouldn't hurt."

Orion lifted his hands to the sky, growing more aggressive. "I am sick of this rain! I'm ready to taste the cool air of the mountains. We've wasted enough time already, so, injuries or not, it's time to cross the border and continue on."

Foxx pushed a fist into her hip. "You're not the only one with wounds, Orion. My sister is recovering, too, and if you recall, she is the only reason you're alive right now to give your opinion. I think you owe her another day to heal."

"I don't owe either of you anything," he spat back, struggling with a knot in the saturated laces like a bear caught in a trap.

Declan suspected Orion would hate the idea of waiting once they discovered their next objective, as his determination to press forward had been the fuel that drove them all these years. However, a glance at Declan had Foxx suspecting he may not have anticipated this level of hostility. His eyes found hers.

Noticing their exchange, Orion's anger swelled. "I'm not waiting. I've waited long enough."

Iris stared at him, the outer corners of her eyes turned down in sadness. Foxx wondered what might have transpired between them for his behavior to produce such a severe expression of what looked like disappointment.

As quickly as it arrived, Iris' sadness dissolved into a wrathful ire. "You've already been waiting six years. Surely one more day of rest is an acceptable ask." Orion opened his mouth to respond, but she put a finger to his lips, halting whatever nonsense he'd been about to spew. The action stunned him into silence. "Even if we leave today, we'll be moving slowly. We definitely won't be getting to my father any faster if our wounds get infected, assuming we even make it to him at all. I know you refuse to listen to anything we say, but as we've attempted to make explicitly clear, we don't know where he is. Maybe he's in Jericho, and we'll find him when we get there. Maybe he's across the world. Regardless, putting this absolutely *enjoyable* adventure off for another day or two can't possibly make a significant difference since we're stumbling around in the wilderness, hoping for the best anyway!"

Iris dropped her finger as he growled, "Lies!" He leaned closer, and the physical agony of the movement was clear on his face. "All lies! You mean to deceive us, like your treacherous father!"

"Rion!" Declan yelled, indignation so blatant in his tone that both Iris and Foxx's mouths fell open. Orion didn't turn his glower from Iris as Declan leveled himself from outrage to stern. "That's enough. There's no reason for you to speak to her that way. She saved your life, though I honestly have no clue why with the way either of us have treated them. Have you even considered that leaving you to die would have allowed them to escape?"

Orion's gaze finally met his friend's, his expression like the snarl of a provoked wolf bearing its teeth. In truth, he hadn't *stopped* considering this, and he had yet to discern what could have possibly driven her to choose his salvation over her own freedom.

"I'm making an executive decision." Declan's voice returned to its unemotional articulation. "If one of you hurts yourself more, it will be me carrying you up the mountain pass. We're staying in the jungle until I decide you're both well enough to travel, be it one day or fifteen. If that is not acceptable to you, you may leave whenever you damn well please." Then he turned from them and stalked off.

After they watched him go, Iris gave her attention to Foxx. "Well, that settles it then."

Orion remained motionless and quiet as he sat with one boot on and the other laying on its side next to him. His snarl dulled, and he seemed so disheartened, Iris almost felt bad for him despite his belligerence.

Gingerly rolling onto her hands and knees, she pushed herself to her feet. Her whole body felt sore and tired, and her wounds burned like hot cinders as the movements tugged at her stitches. Finally vertical, she felt off balance and put her hands out to steady herself. The movement drew Orion's attention, and their eyes met, though he said nothing and quickly returned his gaze to his boots.

When she saw Iris rising, Foxx paused her tidying and watched from a distance to make sure she didn't need help. Iris seemed fine on her own, so Foxx continued putting the dishes back into Declan's bag. She found it strange he so casually left it lying around. Everything they would need to survive without the men was in her hands.

Another glance at Iris limping toward the hollow path where Declan had fled revealed the reason he had no concern for leaving it.

Iris ambled along the grassy trail until reaching a break in the trees. Pulling her eyes from the ground, she saw Declan sitting with his feet dangling over the edge and staring at the massive tree towering over Lacuna Kaput.

Hobbling over, she sat down next to him with more effort than she allowed her face to divulge. The cavern felt peaceful again, as it had when they arrived. Though she wasn't about to dive back into the deceptively tranquil water, she felt glad the experience hadn't shattered its beauty. Turning from the lagoon to look at Declan, she found his face steady. No longer revealing anger. No longer revealing anything.

She tapped the side of his forehead as if knocking on a door. "Are you alive in there?"

A startled smile turned up one side of his lips. "Sorry. Yes. Hello Iris."

Returning her eyes to the tree, she leaned back on her hands. "Want to tell me about it?"

He glanced at her without rotating his head, trying to comprehend her easy demeanor despite... everything. After a long moment, he sighed. "He was not always like this. And it's frustrating."

Iris nodded, believing him. She tried to imagine a younger Orion; a carefree Orion with his whole life ahead of him. Closing her eyes, she could see him standing barefoot in the sand on an island full of birds. Having fallen prey to his passionate and charming disposition more than once, it was easy to picture a version of him who existed like that all the time.

"He has become obsessed. Obsessed with your father. Obsessed with revenge." He picked up a pebble and tossed it into the water below, creating an echoing splash. Ripples spread out from where the stone punctured the surface, and Iris leaned forward to glimpse the circles before they faded. "As is often the case with obsession, he doesn't see the damage it's causing. He's lost his sense of justice. He thinks he's setting things right and getting what he's owed."

"What exactly did my father do to you? Neither of you actually explained the reason for all this." Memories of her father were few and far between, but the ones she did have were pleasant. She knew he worked for the King's Legion and always imagined him to be a respectable man who did what he thought was right. Maybe his perceptions of *right* had been skewed, like Orion's. Or maybe he wasn't the man she'd thought him to be. He had abandoned them, after all.

She watched lines of thought crease Declan's forehead as he considered what details to share. A wave of golden hair tumbled down one side of his face, and he lifted his fingers to twist the tip. A coarse beard covered his cheeks, and though Orion shaved almost daily, she'd only seen Declan shave once since leaving Petrichor. She decided she liked his face better rugged and scruffy.

Declan sent another pebble plummeting toward the water, sending vibrations across the surface. "Your father was the lieutenant of a special unit called the Reko Raptors. The day Sawyer deserted, he tricked us into helping him steal something from one of the royal vaults in northern Reginaterra, outside the royal city. At the time, we thought retrieving it was an order from the sovereigns, though the whole mission felt strange even while it happened. We probably should have questioned it then, but we trusted him.

"It wasn't until he disappeared without a trace and we were being summoned in irons to the Hall of Sunsets that any of us figured out something was wrong. We tried to explain our ignorance, but it didn't matter. Queen Sirena was furious. We were all convicted of treason, and the unit was disbanded."

"What did he steal?"

"It was some kind of vial, glass and empty by the looks of it. It must have been really important because we were given an opportunity to clear our names."

"Return the stolen item," Iris guessed.

He nodded. "If we could find Sawyer and return what he stole, we would be cleared of all charges. Of course, we all tried to find him at first, the sting of betrayal fueling our motives like kindling fuels a fire. But eventually, as far as I know at least, the others gave up and went into hiding."

Iris couldn't imagine what her father could have taken to make him not only abandon his children but risk the livelihoods of his team. "Why aren't you obsessed with clearing your name like Orion is? Don't you want to be free from a life of running and hiding?"

"Of course I do. Trust me. The cost of his deception was greater for me than simply living a life on the run. I haven't spoken to my brother Johnathan in six years."

The nugget of honesty about himself filled her with curiosity. What all had he lost when her father betrayed them? His home, his position, his right to live freely. Now a brother as well. What else had he been forced to leave behind?

"But." He paused, dragging his hand down his face. "Well, if I'm honest, I really respected your father. I want to believe that he had a reason for what he did. I was furious at first, don't get me wrong. But mainly I came along to watch out for Orion. He can be intense, and he doesn't always make the best decisions."

"Clearly." She lifted a sarcastic brow. "Why do you care about him so much? Why stay with him all this time if you think he's crazy?"

His demeanor lightened as his outer shell fissured. "I didn't say crazy."

"Um. He kidnapped two girls who honestly might have helped him willingly if he'd explained the situation." Iris picked up a rock of her own to toss down to the water. The simple thrust of her arm made the slice across her stomach burn.

"You would have helped hand your father over to the Queen?" He met her gaze directly for the first time since she'd arrived. Up close, she noticed a splash of green bleeding in from the outer rim of his irises. Not a bold emerald like Asher's, but softer, like the fuzzy lamb's ears her mother used to plant in their garden or the pale lichen that grows rampant on trees.

She pulled her eyes from his and looked at the waterfall. "No, perhaps not."

"I did suggest we try to talk to you first, thinking maybe we could convince your father to return what he stole in exchange for his freedom. Maybe even tell the Queen he attacked us and we had to kill him, as a way to keep him safe. Orion didn't want to risk it. In his head, he'd already presented the option of traveling together when we first met in the Wilds, and you didn't go for it."

Iris gaped. "He gave us zero indication that your journey had anything to do with us personally! Of course we were weirded out by two strange men requesting we travel together after just meeting them. There are some real creeps out there, you know?"

Immediately drawn to the memory of agreeing to travel with Asher after knowing him less than an hour, she wondered what had prompted her to trust him so quickly. Even Foxx, who'd resisted closeness with him at every turn, had allowed them to stick together.

"I know, I know. Sometimes he doesn't hear logic."

"Still, it would have been nice to have Asher with us, too. If you'd invited us rather than spiriting us away, we could have all traveled together." Though in truth, she couldn't picture Asher and Orion getting along, even though she was fairly certain Asher could get along with pretty much anyone.

His face distorted into an expression she didn't understand. "Asher? Who's Asher?"

"The man we were traveling with before you took us. You must have seen him. I assume you were the ones who alerted the guards to our location with the intention of getting us away from him." Her tone and crossed arms implied she had no doubt about it.

"Oh, that." Embarrassment made his boyish face even more endearing. "You figured that out, huh?"

Iris' angry facade turned playful. "I put it together, yeah." Pulling her hair free from its tie, she began running her fingers through it, realizing she hadn't done so since nearly being eaten by a lagoon monster. "Anyway, he was a huge help to us, and we miss him."

"Asher, huh? Not a very common name."

"I guess not." She pursed her lips as his aura of contemplation returned and conversation stalled. "You're a little broody, aren't you?"

Declan choked on a laugh. "Sometimes." He shook his head, smiling in such a relaxed way that Iris couldn't help but stare at the unfamiliar expression.

The rain had slowed, but with fewer trees hanging over the lagoon, she felt exposed to the sky. Wiping water from her cheeks, she wrung out her hair before continuing to detangle it.

Declan watched her from the corner of his eye. "You know, it was a bit of a fluke that we even found you. When we drew close to Kesken Ala, it was swarming with soldiers, so we traveled south and crossed into Sateen by another path. We tried to head north from there hoping to run into you, but weeks passed, and I was beginning to think we would never see you again. Then by some miracle, we happened to be coming up the trail as the Petrichorian lift carried the three of you up into the trees. It almost felt like destiny or fate or whatever you want to call it. We didn't realize you were traveling with someone else, though. Even when we saw Foxx standing with him in the rain, we assumed you'd met on your way up and reunited while staying in the city."

"Maybe it *was* more destiny than fluke." Iris sifted back through her memories. "I actually knew we would see you again."

"What do you mean?"

"There's this tree west of here. It's called the Tree of Knowing."

He nodded. "I've heard of it."

"Well, it showed me some of my memories, as well as glimpses of the future that made little sense. It wasn't a great experience if I'm honest, but in the scenes of the future, I saw you."

Twisting the tip of his bangs, he asked, "What did you see?"

Again she noticed the flash of green in his gray eyes. His expression became curious and expectant, as though she were about to offer answers to questions he hadn't known he'd been asking. "We were in a city, definitely outside the jungle, and it was on fire."

"Jericho?"

Iris shrugged. "I can't be sure. I've never been there. But Foxx was injured on the ground, and you were pulling on my hand. Pulling me away from her." Declan grew even more pensive. "I don't think you were trying to hurt me," she added, though her reassurance didn't alter his expression.

They sat quietly for another few minutes, thinking over all they'd discussed. Then Declan sat up straighter. "To answer your question, I stay with Orion and endure the *crazy*," he made quotation marks with his fingers as he spoke the last word, "because, despite everything, he's my brother. We've known each other a long time and have made it through countless trials at each other's side. I know he hasn't displayed the best of himself to either of you, but he truly is a good man. I owe him my life." Smile faltering, he shifted where he sat, sliding a few inches away from her as if to put more space between them.

Though she noticed the distance he'd created, she didn't speak on it. "He saved your life?"

"In more ways than one." He turned to look her square in the face. "Thank you for saving him, Iris. Most people would have made their escape. In fact, you probably should have, but I'm really glad you didn't."

She lifted a shoulder. "Too bad for you, though. If you'd been quicker than me, you could have been the one to save him. Then your life debt would be paid." She bumped his shoulder with her own. "Next time maybe you'll move faster than the bleeding girl and make the shot yourself."

He chuckled. "It was worth an extension of my servitude to see you catch my pistol and shoot that monster in the head like a badass."

Her brows flew up, and her eyes widened. "Was that a joke, Declan? Rolled up in a compliment as well? I'm stunned, truly." Her mouth hung open, but a smile played at her lips. "You are full of surprises today, aren't you?"

He grinned, looking down at his hands shyly. He didn't know what else he'd done to surprise her, but his mind immediately—and foolishly—swarmed with a list of things he might sacrifice in order to find out.

Iris laughed. "I like it when you're talking. You should do it more often."

"I'll try to work on that." He stood unexpectedly and held out his hands, offering to help her up. "We should get back."

As they strolled next to each other following the trail toward camp, Declan kept pace with her steps. The path was small, forcing them to walk so close their elbows bumped more than once.

Iris cleared her throat, drawing him from his thoughts. "So I was thinking, Foxx is pretty sure we're close to the border. What if we head to Cordillera today and try to get there before moonrise?" Watching his mouth open as if about to disagree, she quickly contin- ued. "Hear me out. If she's reading the map correctly, we should hit mountains within a few hours at most. We could camp out in a cave along the trail for a few days and give Orion and I the chance to really heal up before we move further into the territory. That would get us out of this rain and keep us better hidden than we are now."

The lighthearted playfulness she'd recently discovered in him vanished completely, and his composed and serious expression returned. "Let me think about it."

"Well, hurry up and decide because if we're going to do it, we should head out right away."

He agreed but said nothing more until they arrived back at the campsite to find Foxxglove and Orion bickering. Orion had moved to a spot in front of the firepit, clearly trying to prove he was well enough to get around and didn't need more rest. The scowl on his face and the palm flat on his stomach told a different story.

When he saw them, he shot a glare at Declan. "Where have you two been?"

Iris noticed his silent reprimand and glowered, her eyes sharp like spears. "We were trying to figure out the easiest way to toss you back into the lagoon."

Orion groaned. "Don't you start, too. I have had enough from your sister."

Foxx rolled her eyes but made no comment.

Stopping next to the fire and shoving a hand into his pocket, Declan said, "Iris had an idea. I think we should consider it, but we have to act now if we're going to."

"What's the idea, Iris?" Orion asked.

"We leave now," she answered. Foxx frowned, and Orion brightened. Iris quickly explained the plan she'd suggested to Declan before confirming with Foxx, "You said we're close, right? I think Orion and I can tough it out so we can get to a safer location."

Declan added, "Once we cross the barrier, I can scout ahead and find us something. I actually already have a place in mind."

Orion turned to Foxxglove, lifting his eyebrows as if seeking her opinion.

Foxx's eyes flitted from his to Declan's before landing again on Iris. At last, she yielded with a shrug. "All right."

Orion rejoiced, excited at the compromise in the works. "Let's get packed and hit the road. We're going to need to move fairly quickly if we want to accomplish all of this before sundown."

Iris clapped, then grimaced as the passionate movement sent a shot of pain through her body.

Declan lifted a single brow and teased, "Yeah, you're going to do fantastic."

C

Within the hour, they'd packed the campsite and started off toward the mountainous territory of Cordillera. Fearing the King's Legion would be patrolling where the paths met the barrier, they hiked off-trail. The vegetation was dense, thorny, and slick with relentless rain, making it difficult to see and strenuous to walk. Even with injuries less severe than Orion's, Iris struggled to climb over leafy bushes or duck beneath low hanging branches. Orion had not voiced a single speck of his affliction since they began but wore a permanent frown as though his jaws had been wired shut.

Declan had completely resorted back to his serious silence, and Iris already missed his pleasant smiles and gentle humor. Walking between him and Orion in the dreary rain had become quite a miserable experience.

Up ahead, Foxx put her fist in the air to stop them before turning to show her finger in front of her lips. She pointed off to their left, prompting them to incline their ears and listen over the rain. Voices ahead told them they must be near the barrier.

Declan moved to the front of the line and directed them away. After walking north for several minutes, they cut east and saw light pouring through an archway of trees. The striking change in scenery became obvious as they drew closer. On the other side of the translucent barrier, they could see blue skies, bright sunshine, and very little green. A burst of silent joy ricocheted throughout the group.

"I love this part," Foxx whispered.

Declan stepped aside. "After you, then."

Beaming, she stretched her hand through the barrier, feeling the warmth of the sun and the cool breeze gliding through her wet fingers. Glancing back to share a quick smile with her sister, Foxx stepped through the wall dividing the territories. Momentary suffocation preceded the tangible barrier stretching around her body. It slid across every exposed skin cell, and when her face crossed over, bitter Cordilleran air rushed to fill her lungs.

The others found her standing on the edge of a cliff surveying a picturesque valley of rolling hills. Tributaries flowed from the mountains, uniting with a river that cut the valley in half. As the terrain rose toward the ranges, tapered evergreens dotted the landscape. The slope soon became thick with a layer of conifers that thinned out again near the mountain peaks.

Iris joined Foxx on the cliffside and shivered. "It's chillier than I expected." The sun warmed their skin, but the frigid wind caused bumps to crawl up their arms and legs. Iris' shirt stopped above her navel, and though she wore pants, they weren't suitable for frosty temperatures.

Foxx's boots came to her knees and her tunic covered her stomach, but her arms and thighs were bare. "I didn't expect us to be so high up in the mountains already. I thought the barrier would drop us at the bottom of the range, not in the middle."

"We'll be okay. Especially once we're able to dry off." The breeze had already dried their skin, but water saturated their hair and clothing.

"I think we're in the clear," Declan said. Foxx and Iris spun away from the view to face him and Orion. "I can't see any soldiers from here, but we need to find shelter soon. It will get colder as the sun goes down." He held his jacket over Iris' shoulders, allowing her to slide her arms into the sleeves. She drew the front together, blocking the wind with gratitude. Then he offered Foxx a short sleeved shirt. "It's not much, but it might help a little." She thanked him and slipped the extra layer over her tunic.

Orion pulled his jacket from his bag and seemed to consider keeping it for himself before offering it to Foxx instead. She eyed him with shock and mild suspicion as he extended it between them. "I'll gladly keep it if you don't want it," he said.

Iris smiled as Foxx accepted the jacket and thanked Orion for his kindness. He mumbled something dismissive and turned his attention to Declan.

"Stay with them and head this way." Declan pointed northeast up a road leading deeper into the mountains. "I'll hike ahead and make sure the shelter is clear. Then I'll come back for you. Stay on the path."

"We should be safe for a while. No one will expect us to cross the border without being spotted." Orion put his hand on Declan's shoulder in a gesture of trust and companionship. Iris thought of how Declan had called them brothers, but Foxx was reminded of her prediction that if it came down to it, they would stick together, regardless of the effect it had on her and her sister. "Be careful, my friend, and keep your eyes open."

"You, too." Declan disappeared down the trail without a second glance at either of the girls.

After watching him go, Orion turned to Foxx and Iris and quirked a cheeky grin. "Are you ladies ready to traverse the wondrous mountains of Cordillera?" Iris rolled her eyes, scoffing at his newly chipper demeanor and feeling dizzy from his mood swings.

Foxx observed, "I think I like him better when he's mean and angry versus this overly cheerful, smiling man." She looped her arm through Iris' and pulled her close, soaking in her warmth. The men's jackets helped combat the chill, but the sun continued to descend and the temperature already felt several degrees lower. "Let's get moving. We'll be warming ourselves by a fire soon enough."

Iris held out the crook of her arm to Orion. Astonished by the gesture, he stared at it blankly. "It will be warmer if we stick together." She wiggled her elbow.

He continued to stare for a few seconds before carefully shimmying his pack from his shoulders and kneeling to rifle through it. After untying the bow strapped to the outside and retrieving the quiver from within, he presented them to Foxx. Her jaw dropped, and she swiped the weapons before he could change his mind. His fingers wrapped around the hilt of her blade, though he seemed to reconsider the moment he began handing it to her. It hung in the air between them as phantom pains cut through his thigh. With a faint wince, he shifted his weight from the leg she'd stabbed and her eyes were drawn to the movement.

"You deserved it," she said.

Dropping his chin, he relinquished the blade. Slipping the bag back over his shoulders, he turned to Iris and removed her blade belt from his waist. "Please don't murder me in my sleep."

She laughed outright, taking it from him and wrapping it around her waist. "No promises."

Foxx pulled her empty bowstring and aimed it toward the mountain, flexing her arms. Her muscles remembered the stretch, and elation filled her to the brim.

Iris unsheathed both Thorn and Bloom and took a step away from them. Ignoring the stinging across her stomach, she crouched into a fighting stance and sliced the air a few times with a grin. "I feel complete again." She kissed both hilts before returning them home. Then she held out her elbows. Foxx and Orion accepted an arm as she pledged, "I will try very, very hard not to murder you in your sleep."

Orion laughed and squeezed her closer to his side. "I'd really appreciate that."

CHAPTER 21

DELUSIONS IN THE DARK

Foxxglove, Iris, and Orion huddled together as they walked the road that hugged the outside of the mountain framing the vast valley below. Biting wind tunneled around them, forced into their path by the contour of the mountain wall.

Despite the bitter wind blowing in their faces, they couldn't take their eyes off the magnificent sunset casting colors across the valley. Chartreuse, magenta, and cerulean blended perfectly with ocher, violet, and periwinkle, and Foxx thought she'd never seen a more beautiful skyline.

As the sun finally set and the world around them dimmed, they began to wonder at the reason for Declan's delay. They heard wolves howling in the distance and knew wild canines weren't the only dangerous creatures lurking in the mountains. Foxx felt a little more secure with her returned weapons, but with Iris and Orion injured, it would be on her to defend them should trouble arise.

Soon, the Storm moon began its ascent, and though it provided ample light into the valley below as it waned into its third quarter, it failed to offer much illumination for them to navigate by.

Compared to the constant noises of Metsa Sateen, the ominous silence of the mountain territory set Foxx's nerves on edge. Aside from the wolves, the only sounds they'd heard in close to an hour were their chattering teeth and the occasional chirping of crickets. It felt jarring after spending so long in a territory that never sleeps.

Footsteps on the road up ahead sent tendrils of fear down their spines. Foxx let go of her sister's arm and nocked an arrow, aiming into the darkness before them. Iris and Orion pressed themselves against the wall, huddling close and invisible in the shadows. They waited, silent and alert as the steps drew closer.

Declan appeared, and when he saw Foxx's arrow aimed his way, he threw up his hands. "Don't shoot! It's me!"

Relief flooded Foxx so profoundly she thought she might collapse. "Declan, you have no idea how good it is to see you." She let her bow drop to her side as she recovered her breath.

Orion and Iris unhitched from the wall and stepped into view, arms still linked.

Declan separated them, sliding his hand between them and lifting Orion's arm up over his shoulder. "Foxxglove, help your sister. I found the cave. It isn't far, but we should move quickly."

"Thank you, brother." Orion sounded almost delirious in his pained exhaustion.

Iris let herself lean on her sister as Declan and Orion took the lead, fighting the wind as they went.

C

The cave was well hidden in the shadows of a mountain. A boulder positioned next to the entrance made it nearly invisible from the path. Dull moonbeams peeked through the mouth, cutting into the shadows cloaking the outer edges of the cavity. The floor sloped downward into a hollow chamber where several arches along the outer wall led to passages of darkness. Stalactites hung like icicles from the ceiling, formed from melting snow high up in the range, and stalagmites shot from the floor like sharp cones that glistened in the moonlight.

"This is perfect." Foxx and Iris made their way down the slope, avoiding small pools of water and divots in the ground. The edge of the light showed a circle of rocks on the left side of the chamber, indicating the cave had been used by other travelers of the mountain pass.

After helping Iris find a seat against one of the flat stones perfectly positioned around the pit for lounging by the fire, Foxx hastened to gather kindling so they could light up the room and get warm.

"There's less wind, which is nice." Iris pulled her knees to her chest within Declan's jacket and wrapped her arms around them to trap her body heat. A light breeze flowing into the space from the tunnels sent a chill down her spine, but it was still better than outside.

Orion leaned on Declan's shoulder as they ambled down the slope from the entrance. When they reached the firepit, they stopped across the ring from Iris. Orion released him and waved his hand, shooing him as if to say *I've got it*. Without a word, Declan joined Foxxglove's mission to start a fire. Orion wobbled around the back of the ring and precariously lowered himself to the ground next to Iris. He scooted right up against her so their shoulders touched. Whether he craved her warmth or her presence, she didn't know, but she was so numb from the cold she decided not to care.

He unclenched his jaw to whisper, "I must admit, that walk was far more difficult than I anticipated."

Iris chuckled. "Don't let Declan or Foxx hear you say that." She shivered, tightening the jacket around her. "It was made worse by the bone-chilling cold. I'm still freezing. I wish I had dry clothes to change into." Orion hung his head, his cheeks flushing with shame she couldn't see in the shadows of the cave.

Within minutes, Foxx and Declan had a fire lit before them.

Declan handed out bowls of dried venison and wild tomatoes. "That's nearly the last of our supply. We'll need to hunt tomorrow."

Foxx sat down next to Iris and popped a juicy, cherry tomato into her mouth. "I'll go. I'm delighted to have my bow back more than you can even imagine."

Declan tore off a chunk of jerky with his teeth. "No one should leave the cave alone. I'll go with you." Foxx grinned and thanked him, thrilled at the idea of exploring the mountains and reuniting with her bow in the wild.

When they'd emptied their bowls, Foxx cleaned up, and Declan set blankets on the ground between the fire and the cave wall for her and Iris to share. He and Orion would layer up their clothing until they made it into a town to purchase more supplies.

Declan dug through their bags and pulled out dry clothing for them all to change into, handing two tunics to Foxx. "Do you and your sister want to sleep in these? We can let the clothes you have on dry overnight."

She accepted the garments and helped Iris stand. On the other side of the cave, they removed their wet clothing and pulled on the dry tunics. Iris put Declan's damp jacket back over her shoulders. Foxx helped her change out the bandages around her thigh and stomach, adding a fresh layer of cura before tying new dressings over the wounds.

When they returned to the fire, the men had already changed. Both averted their eyes to avoid looking at the girls' bare legs. Foxx laid their clothing out to dry, hanging it over the rocks surrounding the pit. Iris sat back down and handed Orion the jacket Foxx had been wearing. With effort, he slid his arms into it, thankful to have it back.

Declan handed Iris a blanket to cover her legs. Curling them against her chest as she had before, she cocooned herself within it to prevent air from seeping in. "Thank you, Declan. I think I'm finally starting to get warm."

Declan offered a small smile in reply. Then with a nod to Foxx, he laid down facing the wall.

After making sure Iris had everything she needed and could make it to their bed when she was ready, Foxx wished her sister a merry night. She didn't intentionally exclude Orion, but she didn't make a point to speak directly to him either.

When the fire began to die out, Orion leaned forward to add more wood to the flames. Then he scooted in close again so they sat shoulder to shoulder. Iris leaned into him ever so slightly, unable to prevent herself from soaking up his warmth. They sat for a while, with little more than the crackling fire and whistling breeze breaking through the silence.

After soft, shallow breathing indicated Declan and Foxxglove had fallen asleep, Orion whispered Iris' name. She turned to look at him, but he didn't pull his troubled gaze from the dancing flames. "I'm sorry for the way I've handled things. Sometimes I get…"

When he couldn't seem to find a word to finish his sentence, she offered, "Insane?"

"A little."

She lifted a brow. "Just a little?"

"A lot. Very insane. The most insane."

Iris chuckled, pushing closer to him without really thinking about it. He didn't seem to mind. Cool air found a chink in her armor and sent a quiver up her spine. She adjusted her blanket to remedy the leak. "I shouldn't have complained about the rainy jungle. I think I prefer it to this bitter chill."

Quieter than before, he said, "I don't understand why you're so nice when I continue to treat you poorly."

Iris hummed thoughtfully. "I'm not sure either." She felt him tense in response to her honest reply. "I guess I try to see the good in people." His face looked so sad she couldn't stand it, even though she knew he deserved every shred of remorse he felt. "Also, fighting is *exhausting*." She nudged him, trying to ease his mood. The corners of his lips lifted, but not much.

Whether she liked it or not, she couldn't deny that she saw good in both men. Orion especially seemed so lost. She suspected the reason for his unpredictable behavior stemmed from his inability to decide how to act, think, and feel about the situation he'd gotten himself into.

It reminded her of a fairytale her mother used to tell them about the White Princess and the Hunter. In the story, the Hunter had been tasked with capturing and killing the Princess for the Evil Queen. Instead, he fell in love with her. She'd seen the goodness in him even after he tried to murder her, and he fought with himself about which path to take. Should he hold tight to his mission or follow his heart and keep the Princess safe, even if it meant putting himself at risk?

In the end, he decided to present the Queen with the heart of an animal, claiming it belonged to the White Princess. When the Queen discovered his treachery, his plan fell to pieces, and he ended up fighting alongside the Princess, eventually sending the Queen to her grave.

Perhaps Orion and Declan would do the same—forgo their mission to help fight back against the evil Queen—even if it meant not getting their revenge or their freedom. In the short time they'd spent together, she'd seen both men soften. Maybe planning an abduction only sounded like an achievable plan until they spent time with the actual humans they'd taken.

Iris and Orion watched the fire for a long time, listening to it pop and sizzle as the wind continued to whistle through the tunnels. Orion glanced over at Foxx and Declan, and Iris wondered if he was about to speak.

Moments later, his voice dripped with chagrin. "Declan said it was a bad idea. He tried to talk me out of it, but I didn't want to listen."

Iris nodded. "I know. He told me."

"He did? He talked to you about us?"

"He told me why you're searching for my father. Not all the details, only that he stole something, and his unit was left behind to take the blame." Iris paused, and Orion sighed. "I'm sorry that happened to you. I guess Foxx and I weren't the only ones hurt by my father's transgression. Until we saw the King's Legion hanging our pictures in Kesken Ala, we honestly had no idea his leaving us was anything more complicated than him running from the loss of our mother."

Orion furrowed his brow, digesting that information. Somewhere along the line when wrath had devoured decency, he'd forgotten what happened to their mother. He considered asking her what she knew about it but felt too vulnerable in the discussion already to delve deeper into the topic of mothers. His was gone, too, though her tragic story was a little different than Amaryllis'. Changing the subject, he said, "Declan likes you."

Iris noticed his solemn tone and couldn't comprehend what reasons might lay behind it. "I like him, too. He's kind. Aside from that whole kidnapping thing, of course."

Orion shook his head. "That's on me. I sometimes take advantage of our friendship without meaning to."

Iris readjusted herself inside the jacket before sticking her palms out to the fire. "Whether he agreed or not, he was a willing participant. He held a knife to my throat." Her gut churned at the memory as she considered the man she'd come to know—strangely aloof in the desert, aggressive with a knife to her throat, inconceivably calm while she fought against him, curiously concerned when she was hurt, jovial and humorous when they were alone.

Anxiously tugging her hand at the center of a burning city.

"Try not to hold it against him. I see the ease between the two of you. He tries to mask it, in solidarity to me I would guess, but he feels comfortable around you." His brows lifted with his broad shoulders. "We've been alone for so long, comfort and ease in the presence of others is not a luxury either of us have experienced in quite a while. I'm surprised he opened up to you at all, especially after such a short time." With another heavy sigh, he added, "It seems you have that effect on people."

Iris remained still as she watched the fire, not knowing what else to say and needing time to make sense of the information he'd shared.

After a minute of silence, Orion changed the subject again. "Maybe we can explore the tunnels tomorrow while they hunt."

"That sounds exciting." Realizing she'd spoken too loudly, she lowered her voice. "But we really should rest more. It's kind of the whole reason we're here." Pulling her arms from the jacket sleeves, she slipped both hands around her sides and hugged herself in a cocoon of heat. Orion watched from the corner of his eye before holding his own hands out to warm his palms. Iris chuckled as he wrapped them around himself and visibly basked in their warmth. "Smart, right?"

He nodded, and his eyes fell closed as he soaked it in. "We don't have to go far." He pushed his shoulder into hers as if coercing her to agree.

"Let's see how we feel tomorrow. I think it's time for sleep." Standing carefully, she tried not to disturb her wounds as well as keep the heat trapped inside her jacket. "Merry night, Rion." Her left side felt cooler separated from his body, causing another shiver to scuttle up her spine. He smiled at her casual use of his name. Then she stepped over him and laid down next to her sister, pulling the blanket over herself and snuggling in close.

C

As the sun rose, a panel of light crept across the floor from the mouth of the cave. Declan and Foxx awoke first and began the preparations for their hunt. Declan loaded his pistol and tucked it into his belt holster. Foxx ran her fingers over the fletching at the end of each arrow, straightening them before slinging her quiver over her shoulder and strapping it around the front of her chest. Her dagger had already been re-tied to her boot.

Iris stirred and sat up, wiping sleepy sand from her lashes. "Are you guys leaving?"

Foxx knelt next to her. "We won't be long. Are you going to be okay with him?" Her eyes shifted to Orion. "Keep your blades near you."

"I can handle him." Iris stripped off Declan's jacket and handed it to her. "You'll need this more than I will."

Foxx kissed her cheek before moving to join Declan at the exit. Iris called a merry farewell to him, prompting him to lift an arm in a halfhearted wave before stepping out into the sunlight.

Sighing at his aloofness, Iris wondered if he might start shifting back and forth between two personalities as well. Or perhaps she and Orion had been wrong and their effortless connection above the falls had meant little more than Declan mourning his past choices and the disgraceful behavior of his friend. Perhaps he'd needed someone to confide in and she'd been there, but it didn't signify anything deeper than that.

Iris changed into dry clothing, thankful for the fabric covering her legs. Her wounds felt better after a decent night's sleep, so she mulled around the cave and the grounds outside gathering more twigs for the fire. After piling them by the pit, she found Declan's container of cura sitting on the rock she'd been leaning against the night before, as if he'd set it out for her. Grumbling something about stupid men under her breath, she removed the bandages around her stomach.

Declan's stitches looked exquisite, and she felt certain that if she continued applying the salve, they would heal with minimal scarring. With that in mind, she unscrewed the lid and stifled her urge to vomit. Her obnoxious noise of disgust roused Orion from his slumber, and he rolled away from the wall, shielding his face from the light bleeding into the room with his hand.

"Are you okay over there?"

"This. Salve. Is. Disgusting!"

He laughed and sat up, turning to lean against the wall and groaning as he forced rested wounds into motion. "It's pretty bad, yeah, but it works miracles." His eyes scanned her exposed stomach. "Your gashes look nearly closed already."

Iris opened the lid again, having resealed it for fear of losing the contents of her stomach, and held it away from her nose. "I am starting to wonder if it's worth this horrid smell." She dipped her fingers and began rubbing it in between and around her stitches, trying not to gag. Though she had to admit, the longer it sat open, the more she got used to the odor filling the room.

"It's definitely worth it. We'll be able to remove the stitches in half the time. Maybe even less. Bring some over here, will you?"

Iris finished with her torso wounds and left them uncovered to breathe. She wished she'd had the forethought to check the wounds on her thigh before changing into her pants, but decided to wait until she had more privacy to deal with them. Carrying the curavenum over, she knelt next to him. "Do you want some help? At least around your back?"

Her offer bewildered him, but he tried not to let it show. Attempting smoldering charm, he said, "Are you asking if I would like an attractive woman rubbing nasty ointment all over me?"

Iris's cheeks flushed crimson in response to his suggestive statement along with the fervency in his night-sky eyes. Laughing awkwardly, she moved to stand up. "If you don't want my help—"

Orion reached for her arm, gently, not forcefully as he had in the past. "Iris, will you please help me apply this grotesque salve?" His face became an exaggeration of helplessness. "I'm not sure I can manage without you."

She chuckled again, feeling more relaxed with his blatant satire. "All right, lean forward."

He obeyed, raising his arm over his head and lifting his shirt. The entire bottom half of his torso was wrapped in gauze. Untucking the end, she unraveled it, gently peeling it away from tacky skin. A sharp intake of breath escaped her when she saw the terrible thrashes laced across his back.

"It isn't as bad as it looks," he said. "It's mostly bruising at this point."

She had no idea how he could possibly know that since he couldn't see the horror before her. The skin on his back was almost entirely covered in shades of sick green bleeding into yellow that surrounded patches of indigo and violet. Gashes cut through the bruises in varying levels of severity. They looked far worse than hers, as if the monster had lost its grip when slamming him into the water over and over and had needed to keep readjusting.

It had been less than forty-eight hours since the cura had first been applied, and though Orion was correct in saying it worked miracles, even the amazingly effective curavenum couldn't heal wounds this bad in that short a time.

"I don't actually understand how you're even walking. Or sitting. Or laying. This looks seriously awful, Orion." She watched his ego swell and told him to knock his smug grin from his face before she did it for him. Twisting the lid off the cura, she set it next to her, doing her best to ignore the smell. She dipped two fingers into the tin and covered their tips with greasy ointment.

Their eyes met for a moment over his shoulder and she gulped down a ragged breath. The lacerations had shocked and distracted her at first, but now she felt overwhelmed with nervousness at the thought of putting her hands on a man's bare skin. She'd never touched a man like this before. At least not while bubbles erupted in her stomach. She'd had no problem touching Asher, but something about being within the aura of Orion's intensity had her hand quivering and stalled midair. Her gaze traveled the length of his back, taking in the sight of his toned muscles and the inflating of his thick bicep as he held his shirt above his shoulder.

"You won't hurt me," he said.

"It's cold." She sucked in a breath with her bottom lip between her teeth. He flinched when her fingertips first brushed his skin, but soon relaxed as she covered each and every one of his wounds. When she finished with the minor cuts, her fingers traced the deepest gash, stretching from the center of his back around his ribs and ending above his navel. "Sit back."

He let his shirt fall, though the fabric stuck to the ointment and refused to lay right until she tugged it down. Leaning back, he lifted the front of the shirt out of her way. The cuts on his stomach looked even worse than those on his back. He winced as her delicate fingers glided over them, though he found himself unable to cease studying her expressions with profound concentration.

Iris continued to worry her lip as she struggled to resist meeting his gaze. Despite her efforts to ignore him, her temperature rose as he responded to her touch, shifting and squirming and not pulling his eyes from her for a single second. "This is not any easier with you staring at me like that."

A mischievous smile twisted his cheeks. "I wasn't trying to make it easy."

She replaced the lid and cleared her throat, feigning nonchalance. "All finished." Standing, she kept her eyes to the floor as she returned the cura to where she'd found it. "Do you need help rewrapping?"

Orion tugged his shirt down and rose to his feet. "This will be enough for now. I'll wash the wrap in a bit. I'm sure they'll know of a nearby water source when they return."

Iris nodded and busied herself folding the shirt she'd worn to bed, seeking distance to let the blood dissipate from her cheeks. Everything about Orion was intense. His kindness, his anger, his motivation, his frustration.

And his utterly potent stare.

He thanked her by name, strolling toward her as his eyes tracked her every movement.

"Not a problem." She moved past him to stoke the fire pit. The coals remained warm from the night before, glowing with hot embers. Adding some kindling beneath two thicker logs, she bent down and blew on the shining cinders, watching as they sparked to life.

Sensing her discomfort, Orion remained where he'd stopped across the cave. "Did you want to explore the tunnels?"

Iris didn't answer immediately, still feeling overwhelmed by whatever had just passed between them and frustrated with her undeniable attraction to him. She and Foxx had agreed not to trust him. He'd proven himself untrustworthy on more than one occasion. Even if their presence had prompted some inner battle against circumstantial wickedness, he was dangerous and way too charming. Despite what she'd told Foxx before they left, being alone with him was scary. Just not for the reasons Foxx had implied.

"Come on," he pressed. She turned to find his expression playful. "Don't you want to go on an adventure with me?" His smile expressed arrogance and overconfidence, but she sensed hopeful vulnerability, too.

At last, she surrendered. "Only if you wipe that cheesy look off of your face."

Instead, his grin widened, his lips splitting open to reveal teeth. He ambled over to his knapsack and pulled out a wooden stick with a blackened end. After letting the tip catch in the flames, he handed it to her. She tried to ignore the tingle spreading up her hand as their fingers touched.

"Lead the way." He gestured toward one of the tunnels.

"You only have one?"

"Declan has the other in his bag, but don't worry. I'll hold your hand if you get scared."

Scowling, she marched off ahead of him, entering the tunnel directly across the room from the cave's entrance. Orion's chuckles echoed all around her as he hurried to catch up.

The tunnel was remarkably dark—darker than the jungle at night on the new moon. The flame from her torch lit a small circumference around them before being swallowed by the thick black. The ground was fairly even, gently sloping up or down at times, but not littered with scattered debris for them to trip over. Iris ran her hand along the wall, letting its rugged texture scuff her palm. Water dripped down the walls from stalactites lining the edges of the ceiling, creating pocket puddles in the floor.

The deeper they went into the cave, the colder and darker it got. With the blackness came a silence so loud, Iris thought she could hear their heartbeats thumping in their chambers. In an effort to ease her growing fright, she decided to talk. "You don't think anything lives down here, do you?"

"It's hard to say. I haven't seen any remnants of life so far, but that's not necessarily a guarantee."

"The fire pit was already built in the main room, so someone must have stayed here before. Maybe even lived here?"

"Nomads traversing the mountains. And soldiers."

At times, the tunnel walls drew closer together and allowed more light to reflect from the torch held between them. "We should have thought to bring weapons," Iris said.

"I think we'll be fine."

The tunnel curved at a sharp angle and took them down a steeper path, though not so steep as to be worrisome. There had been no cross tunnels yet, so for now, only a single path would lead them out with no possibility of getting lost.

Still, Iris' discomfort in the eerie and soundless absence of light increased. "How old are you?"

Orion chuckled as it registered that her ramblings divulged a growing unease. "I'll be thirty soon. How old are you?"

"Eighteen. I was only twelve when he left us. Foxx was almost fourteen. My father, I mean." When he didn't respond to this statement, she made an attempt at changing the subject. "You and Declan have been traveling together for a long time, huh?"

His eyes narrowed, though she wasn't looking at him. "Yeah, about six years."

By now, she should have ceased asking questions. She hadn't known herself to be afraid of the dark. She'd spent countless hours peering out into the night beyond the firelight without worry, but Orion's growing frustration and the suffocating shadows began to overwhelm her.

"What did you do before that?" she asked, again meaning to change the subject but finding herself right back where she'd started.

"Didn't Declan already tell you all this?" His voice elevated with irritation, and he forced a calming breath. "Declan and I were soldiers in an elite unit working directly under King Pollux. We carried out special missions, things that needed to be handled secretly and swiftly."

"Did you enjoy working under the King? What's he—"

Orion stopped abruptly, rotating his whole body to face her. Iris moved the torch to avoid burning him. Illumination from the flames exposed his clenched jaw and the sharp crease between his brow. "Listen, this is not something I care to talk about, all right?" His voice became harsh, jarringly direct, and filled with its former malice.

Iris suddenly felt stupid for allowing herself to travel into the tunnel with him. He'd shown how vicious he could be and had revealed his brutality. The bright pops of kindness and playful flirting didn't matter. No amount of affection could quell the hostility and hatred hiding underneath, biding its time, waiting to breach the surface.

Naturally, rather than trying to calm the beast as Foxxglove would have, her anger superseded her fright. "I am just trying to understand you, Orion. Gosh, you're infuriating! I swear I can't keep up with you. Half the time, you seem sincere and decent, and I actually almost enjoy your company. The rest of the time I am desperately trying to comprehend what turns you into this." She waved her hand around at his current state. "This irate and hideous monster. I am not my father. Whatever he did to you has nothing to do with me or Foxx. It's unfair and, frankly, idiotic for you to treat us the way you feel he deserves to be treated." Her literal growl resounded through the tunnels as her outrage continued to swell. Tears pricked her eyes. "As I have already explained, I was twelve when he left us. *Twelve*, Orion. Foxx was not even fourteen. We were children. I barely knew my father. In fact, you undoubtedly spent more time with him than I ever did."

He reached for her arm, the corners of his eyes turned down with regret. "Iris, I—"

"No! I am not finished, Orion." She yanked her arm from his grasp as guilt permeated his features, but she didn't care. She couldn't take it anymore. "You can take my weapons. You can bind my wrists and treat me like your prisoner. You can punish me however you see fit. But no matter what you do to me, I still won't be *him*."

All the wrath seething within her from the moment they left Petrichor boiled over, erupting in a red-hot rage. She glared into his eyes with such a blazing fire, he thought he might ignite where he stood. He stared back at her as the silence dragged on, having no words to respond.

Then, without thinking it through, he grabbed both sides of her face and pressed his lips to hers. The magma inside of her melted into him, and his arm slid around her back, pulling her against him. She dropped the torch and threw both arms around his neck, her entire body vibrating with unfamiliar sensations. Her fingers tangled in his long hair as she kissed him back with all the fiery passion burning through her.

He pushed her backward until they hit the tunnel wall as his tongue slid between her lips. Calloused hands caressed her waist, somehow taking gentle care not to touch her wounds. They slid down her thighs, her hips, drawing her closer.

She slid her hands over his shoulders, roamed the curves of his arms and down his sides, gripping his shirt and drawing him nearer with every touch. He flinched as her less experienced hands grazed his injuries, but it didn't slow him down. Lips trailed her neck, finding the soft pocket above her collarbone before meandering up to the flesh beneath her ear.

Somewhere in the back of his mind, he thought he heard the torch sizzle. Returning his mouth to hers, he forced his passion to fade into tenderness. Whispering her name into her ear pulled a soft hum from her lips, and he chuckled. "I think the torch went out."

Her eyelids rippled open into smothering darkness. Even his face, just inches from her own, was invisible. Her heart skipped and her body flushed with fear. She squeezed the sides of his shirt, allowing herself time to adjust to the spooky blindness. Trying not to obsess over the fact that they had no way of relighting the torch and would be traveling back the tunnel devoid of sight, she took a deep breath. "Well. That was… unexpected."

Realizing he still had her pinned to the wall, Orion tried to take a step away, but she held tight to his shirt, not wanting to lose her tether. He could feel her shaking beneath his hands. "I'm sorry, Iris," he whispered, as people often feel the need to do when enveloped in shadows. Again, his remorse was clear in his tone. "I shouldn't have done that. I don't know what I was thinking."

"You regret it?" Her voice cracked with insecurity. He didn't answer immediately, and she worried he truly did. She hadn't thought she'd done it wrong, though she had nothing to compare it to.

"I regret upsetting you more than I already have. And ironically, I regret… taking without distinct permission."

A sharp laugh burst from her lips. "I'm not mad. It's just that… well, it's never happened before, so it surprised me, and now with the torch… I'm mildly freaking out." She willed her breathing to remain controlled but felt herself very quickly losing her grip.

Orion stayed quiet again, and she tried to find the glint of his eyes. "What do you mean it's never happened before?" When she didn't answer, his hand lifted to brush her cheek as understanding took hold. Warmth pooled beneath his fingers, and he wished more than anything he was able to see her. "Iris Belamour, have you never been kissed?"

"Shut up." She turned her head from his hand.

Orion leaned into her, resting his nose against her cheek. In response, she rotated until their noses were side by side. Her chest felt light and heavy all at once, as if half of it was so weighed down she could hardly breathe and the other half fought to lift her into the sky.

His lips touched hers, barely a flutter, and her entire face caught fire. It burned down her throat and into her stomach, fizzling out at the tips of her toes. With senses heightened in her blindness, the touch of his skin against hers sent continuous and turbulent tingles throughout her body. His breath caressed her cheek, and the elevated rise and fall of his chest indicated his own nervousness, but he didn't back away, and she didn't want him to.

Still, she cleared her throat, nowhere near catching her breath but desperately needing to be free of the tunnel. "Should we try to find the torch?"

Their faces lingered close enough that she could feel his nodding response even if she couldn't see it. His hand found hers. "Don't be afraid. I'm right here." He spoke to her as if to a delicate flower. A puffy, white dandelion he might scatter to the wind.

Together, they crouched and began reaching around for the felled torch. It didn't take long for Iris to grab something the shape and size of their lost light source, but when she went to lift it, it wouldn't budge. She tried to confirm its texture, only to realize it didn't feel like wood at all, but scratchy, like coarse hair cut short and frayed at the ends.

A hole opened in her stomach as she removed her hand from the object and backed away, gripping tightly to Orion's fingers.

"What's wrong?" Feeling her panic, he strained to see. "Iris?"

"Orion, I don't think we're alone." She felt prodding at her side, a wiggling like fingers grasping for purchase. She shrieked and scrambled away.

Something wrapped around Orion's ankle, and he yanked free, hurling himself in what he hoped was the direction of the tunnel's exit. Tightening his hold on her hand, he said, "Iris, listen to me." As they backed away, they could hear the mystery creature drawing closer, its familiar chitter rattling their bones. "We're going to stand up and turn around. Do not let go of my hand."

She nodded, knowing he couldn't see her but unable to speak through the crushing lump in her throat. Standing, she followed his movements.

"Keep your hand on the wall so you have something to follow." Orion turned, punched the creature as hard as he could, and screamed, "Run!"

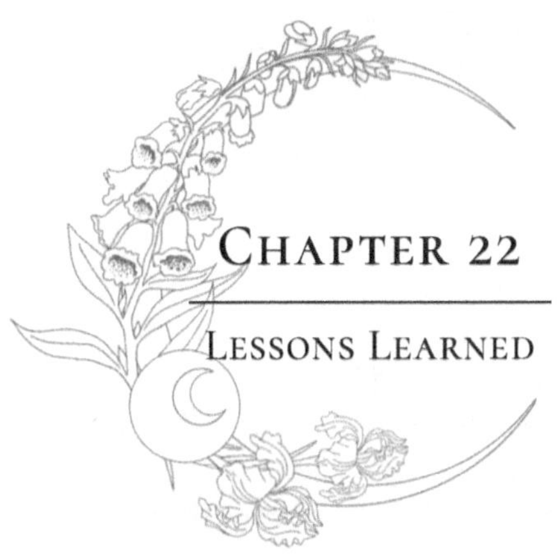

CHAPTER 22

LESSONS LEARNED

Hidden in the midst of the conifers, Foxxglove and Declan stalked their prey. From ten or so *sylis* up the slope, they watched an immense tryka grazing in the grass. Outmatching them in height, the beast stood proud on four muscular legs, and a colossal rack of antlers crowned its head. More antlers grew from its spine down its neck, and a full tail swept the ground.

Declan signaled for her to follow him as he crept closer.

Foxx already had an arrow nocked in her bow. As she passed through the branches of a fir tree, ducking to avoid a collision, she inhaled a breath to calm her heart and caught a familiar scent on the breeze: sweet and woodsy, with a hint of citrus.

Joy and despair washed over her in equal measure as she identified the smell she'd been unable to place. The comforting, heartwrenching scent she detected when Asher stood a little too close… was evergreen.

Though she'd never seen an evergreen before crossing into Cordillera, her mother had worn an oil that smelled just like it. *A gift from a king*, she remembered her jesting, making quite a dramatic presentation of dabbing a drop of the oil on each wrist and pressing them together. Then she would take Foxx's tiny hands in her own and allow a single dot for both wrists to share.

Foxx's stomach flipped, triggered by memories of her mother's loss and Asher's prolonged absence. A new determination filled her, and she resolved to find him again. No matter what she had to do, no matter how long it took, they would be reunited.

"You good?" Declan's voice jarred her from her thoughts, and she glanced his way, nodding. He motioned with his hand to a boulder within range of the tryka. When they reached it, Foxx angled her bow around the edge and drew back the arrow.

"Careful," Declan instructed.

She dismissed him and pursed her lips. As she was about to release, she felt a tremor beneath her boots that had her turning around to see another tryka galloping toward them from higher up the hill. Foxx and Declan dropped into a crouch as the beast vaulted over them, clearing the boulder with ease and heading straight for their quarry. Spooked, the first tryka fled.

The earth continued to rattle, and the two hunters turned to find a dozen more charging their way.

"Get back!" Declan yelled, and they separated, running in opposite directions. Foxx pressed herself within the branches of another fir and was again consumed by their scent. Forcing herself to focus, she found Declan amongst the trees and met his gaze with a nod. As the rumble dwindled, she darted after the last of the herd. Glancing sideways, she saw Declan keeping pace with her.

Sprinting until the shot became clear, she skidded to a stop and let the arrow fly. It struck the hindmost tryka below its shoulder blade, and the beast tumbled to the ground. Relief and victory filled her. She wiped sweat from her brow, pleased with their teamwork and the exhilarating pursuit.

Declan jogged to the felled creature and checked for signs of life. After a slice across the animal's throat, he called, "It's dead. We should clean it here and leave what we don't use for other animals to pick through."

Foxx made her way to him at a slow trot. "Lovely imagery, Declan."

His lips curled as he rifled through his bag, pulling out their water, several knives of different sizes, a few square sections of fabric, and some rope. "Have you done this before?"

She put a hand on her hip. "How do you think my sister and I survived in the wild this long?"

Grinning fully, he handed her a knife.

C

Iris had no memory of the sharp curves of the tunnel's passage on their way in, but as they sprinted back, the constant zig-zags made traveling blind an arduous task. They bounded through the dark, hearing nothing but the scuffs of their boots against stone and the high pitched shrieks of the monster trailing them.

Running faster because of her smaller stature and finesse, Iris dragged Orion behind her, refusing to let go of his hand.

The bulbous monster reached for them, scratching the backs of their arms and clawing at their clothing and hair, but they stayed far enough ahead to elude its grasp.

Both could feel their stitches ripping holes in their skin, but they pushed through the pain. After what felt like far too long, they saw a light up ahead and knew it must be the sun shining in through the cave mouth. A spark of energy pushed Orion forward so he sprinted alongside her. The hole of light brightened, growing bigger until the archway materialized, signifying the end of the tunnel and the entrance to the main room where they would find their weapons. As they crossed the threshold, Iris' boot caught on a crack in the ground and she fell, losing Orion's hand in the momentum.

He skidded to a stop and turned to find her on her stomach clambering forward and screaming as the nieda latched onto her calf and dragged her backward. Her body had almost disappeared into shadow when Foxx and Declan entered the cave, beckoned there by the sound of her screams. Orion froze in terror. Declan shouted his name and ran for the tunnel. Foxxglove pulled her bowstring and struck the nieda at close range. She nocked a second arrow and shot it again. After a momentary wobble, the beast fell forward, dead, and trapped Iris underneath it.

Foxx yelled her name and ran for her.

Declan was already skidding to his knees at her side. "I've got you." He slid his hands below the nieda to lift it off of her. "Rion, help me!"

Snapped from his paralysis, Orion hastened to help Declan lift the weight of the monster.

Foxx hooked her hands beneath Iris' arms and dragged her free. Iris moaned and rolled onto her back as Foxx dropped to her knees, giving her a soft place to rest her head. "Are you all right?" She pushed hair from her face and checked her injuries.

Iris groaned again in response, out of breath, exhausted, and bleeding through torn stitches. The men left the beast and hurried back to them.

"I'm fine, I'm all right," Iris insisted, though every movement produced a wince. She lifted her head to get a better view of her stomach, but the clenching of her abdomen sent new waves of agony through her.

Declan knelt and pressed cloth over the open wound, soaking up the blood. Holding his hand over it to apply pressure, he promised, "You'll be alright. I can fix this." He forced a smile as he fought to contain unpleasant emotions. "We'll have to get your leg cleaned up, too." He gestured to her calf where the nieda had ripped through her leggings. Iris grimaced, not having felt her new leg injury until he brought it to her attention. Declan's angry gaze shifted to Orion. "What were you doing? Why were you just standing there?"

Orion didn't respond, and Iris looked up at him. Haunted eyes stared back at her. His lips parted, caught on words refusing to surface.

Declan replaced the bloody cloth with a fresh one. He smiled again for her benefit, but he couldn't hide his fury.

Orion felt a pang of jealousy as he watched Declan caring for her, though he immediately realized the true reason for his anger and balled his fingers into fists. He couldn't even begin to comprehend the foolishness of what he'd done. As if their mission wasn't complicated enough. As if stealing Sawyer's daughters from Petrichor wasn't the worst idea to begin with, now he'd dug himself deeper by stealing the youngest daughter's first kiss.

He should have known that would be the case before heedlessly shoving her against the wall. She'd been living in the wild since she was twelve. That didn't exactly leave a lot of opportunity for romantic experience. She'd been a child. She was *still* a child.

But he hadn't known; hadn't realized; hadn't thought it through.

And because he was an absolutely inconceivable idiot, he hadn't been able to help himself.

"Are you okay, Rion?" Iris' voice sent a shiver through him, and his gaze latched on to her auburn eyes, taking in the soft curve of her pained smile.

"Fantastic." His tone had gone bitter, like the wind they'd fought on the mountain pass. At his heartless demeanor, the color drained from Iris' face, but he said nothing further to her. Instead, he began to interrogate Declan about the hunt.

Ignoring him for the moment, Declan laid Iris' hand on her stomach in place of his own. Then he glared at Orion before standing and waving him toward the mouth of the cave. The moment they walked out of sight, their raised voices resounded back into the cavern.

Foxx ignored the men and focused on Iris. "Maybe this time we can go a full week without you being attacked by a savage beast. What do you think?"

Iris chuckled, flinching again as the pain deepened with her tensed stomach. Declan shouted something louder, and though she couldn't hear his exact words, she cringed at their increasingly aggressive tones. Suddenly, her adrenaline dissipated, and she felt like bursting into tears. "I'm sorry. I'm so sorry."

Foxxglove looked taken aback. "Sorry for what?"

Iris gestured to herself. "This mess. Now they're fighting, and my stitches will take longer to heal and—"

"Stop it." Foxx put a finger to her sister's lips. "Let Declan worry about Orion. Your stitches don't look bad. Dirty from the ground mostly, and either way, I'm sure Declan can fix those, too."

Despite Foxx's words, Iris knew the entire situation could have been prevented if she'd answered Orion's invitation differently from the very beginning. Her face flushed, and she smothered memories of her momentous first kiss by scrutinizing the dead nieda laying at the entrance to the tunnel. "Not nearly as big as the last one. Almost half the size, I think. When I get my journal back, remind me to add a note about the niedas of Cordillera having dark gray hair with black accents, okay?"

Foxx looked at her scoldingly and helped push her into a seated position. Iris shooed Foxx's mothering as she pulled herself to her feet and shuffled toward the fire pit, craving its warmth. The running and anxiety had spiked her internal temperature, but as she calmed down, sweat left her feeling cold.

Since Iris insisted she could manage on her own, Foxx promised a quick return and headed outside to see the men. When she arrived, Orion appeared to be reprimanding Declan, though she couldn't wrap her mind around how after what they'd witnessed. Their conversation ceased as she approached. Declan attempted to mask his irritation before asking if Iris was all right.

"She should probably have those stitches fixed, if she will even let you do it. She was being stubborn about me helping her, but she made it to the fire okay by herself."

"See?" Orion growled. "She is perfectly fine, as I said. Now, can we get back to this?" He gestured to the tryka meat, antlers, and hide before them. Declan rubbed his temples.

Foxxglove crossed her arms, cocking her hip out to the side and meeting Orion's aggression with equal measures of hostility. "You should have your stitches redone, too, Orion. You're bleeding all over yourself, if you hadn't noticed, and it's disgusting. Also, there is a revolting carcass in our shelter now. Please remove it as soon as possible. Thirdly, whatever issue you two are having, knock it off. We have a job to do. The sooner we find my father, the sooner we never have to see you again."

She looked pointedly at Declan. Then her eyes snapped back to Orion before she turned on her heel and disappeared into the cave.

Iris remained where she'd left her, poking the fire with a stick and coaxing the embers to reignite.

Joining her on the ground, Foxx removed Declan's jacket and passed it back to her sister, who laid it across her lap. "I really do not like Orion."

Iris flushed again, but Foxx didn't notice. She was too busy stewing. "Yeah, he's all over the place. I'm finding it hard to keep up."

Foxx nodded. "I'm really trying to make the best of this situation since we're stuck for the time being, but he makes it very difficult."

Iris removed her tie from her hair. Without direction, Foxx shifted onto her knees and ran her fingers through it, combing it out for her. Iris let her eyes fall closed, enjoying the comfort of someone else's fingers massaging her scalp. Lowering her voice to a decibel only Foxx could hear, she asked, "Do you think we should try to escape? They don't guard us like they did before. They don't sleep in shifts anymore, either."

Foxx leaned closer. "Without our belongings, it's going to be very hard. We don't have any money to resupply and would most certainly die before making it through the mountains. We could try to steal one of their packs, but even still." She thought it over, letting her head fall from side to side. "If I felt like we were in real danger, we would risk it. Since we aren't at that point yet, I think we should hold off."

"They're going to buy us clothing when we reach the city. Maybe before that, depending on what we come across along the road." Iris tucked her hands under Declan's jacket, warming her fingertips behind her knees. "We can try to find an opportunity to flee once we're more equipped to handle cold weather."

At the idea of branching out on their own, unexpected sadness struck Iris' heart. Her mind drifted to her experience with Orion in the tunnel: his husky voice in the dark when he'd realized it was her first time; his final, tender kiss–far more intimate than the ones that had come before it.

Sickness crept into her stomach as the memory of how unfriendly he'd been afterwards chased away the recollection of their embrace. Each time she thought his heart was softening, he proved her wrong, and she didn't understand why she kept allowing herself to fall for it. Embarrassment drew more blush to her cheeks.

Then she thought of Declan: his protective anger, their relaxed conversation on the cliffs at Lacuna Kaput, and all the instances where she'd discovered a crack in his stoic exterior. A small smile curled her lips, and she felt even more ashamed by the progression of her musings.

As if reading her thoughts, Foxx said, "We might be able to trust Declan." She'd begun braiding Iris' hair, starting above her forehead and weaving it down the back at an angle so it laid over her shoulder. Though Iris usually let her white streak hang free, Foxx included it, creating a beautiful contrast as it criss-crossed through the black braid.

Iris agreed with a nod and sighed. "I wish Asher would find us."

Tying off the braid, Foxx sat back down so she could see her sister's face. "He left us a message beneath the falls. I haven't had a chance to tell you."

Iris' eyes lit up. "What was the message?"

"A clue that he'd been there and retrieved the rainforest stone." Noise from outside had both women glancing toward the cave mouth. "I am almost certain we'll find him in Jericho. But until then, all we can do is what we've always done: save ourselves."

Iris lifted her hand to her sister's scar, running her finger up and down the length of it. "We save each other," she corrected. "We could try to make it back to Petrichor to retrieve our things."

Foxx shook her head, and Iris' hand fell away. "No. That's too far in the opposite direction. We need to keep moving forward."

Iris understood and agreed, though she still didn't like the idea of their belongings being lost forever, especially since those items included the only remnants she had left of her mother: the stories that filled the pages of her journal and the necklace she'd received for her twelfth birthday. The last gift her mother had ever given her.

Iris was only four when Foxx first pulled her into the kitchen cabinet to hide from their mother's first chaotic tantrum. After that, Amaryllis had long stretches of lucidity, her fits few and far between. It took a few years for them to become more frequent than not.

By the time Iris was about to turn twelve, Amaryllis' mental state had grown thoroughly unpredictable. With each passing day, more and more of her crumbled away as she tumbled into insanity, but Iris remembered perfectly how crystal clear her mother had been on her twelfth birthday. She'd made her a necklace from a mixture of shells collected on the beach behind their home and her personal collection of Ranta's famous pearls. The centerpiece was a clamshell carved from a navy and white stone that resembled ocean waves. As her mother lifted her hair and placed it around her neck, she'd instructed Iris to always keep it with her so she would never forget where she came from.

The following morning, Amaryllis had left them alone, as she had many times throughout their lives. She never stayed away too long, and she never told them where she went. They would imagine her off having wild adventures, sailing with pirates across the Suola Meri, hunting for exotic treasure, and gleaning more amazing stories to share with them.

She always returned from her trips happier, as though the absence had recharged her. Toward the end, they began looking forward to the days she would leave, knowing she would be herself again when she returned, if only for a short while.

The last time she came back, less than a week after gifting Iris the seashell necklace, she did not return healthier or happier. It was mere days before Foxxglove found her on the bathroom floor.

"I need to make more arrows," Foxx said, interrupting Iris' forlorn train of thought. "I collected some sticks that should work, but they need to sit near the fire for a while before I can clean and shape them."

"I'll help." Iris shook away the buzz of tension building inside her bones at the reminiscence of her mother.

Foxx got up and pulled a few stones away from the fire ring, spreading them out and making the pit wider. Then she used the poker and scraped out some coals, keeping them close enough to the fire to stay hot, but not so near that the sticks she placed over them would ignite. She retrieved her sticks and laid them longways, balancing them above the coals.

The men returned carrying the sacks of tryka meat. After dragging the dead nieda deeper into the cave and out of sight for the moment, they joined Foxx and Iris by the fire. Orion busied himself by putting some of the meat on to cook. Foxx asked if he wanted help, and he grumbled something inarticulate in answer.

Declan sat next to Iris with his med-kit in hand. He flipped open the lid and pulled out the supplies he would need to perform more stitches.

Iris gulped before breaking the silence, hoping to distract herself from what he was about to do. "Shouldn't we be worried more niedas will come through the tunnels and attack us while we sleep?" She watched his fingers, unable to pull her eyes from the needle.

Declan responded without looking at her, his attention focused on his hands as he cleaned the needle in the fire. "I'm more concerned about this delicious smelling meat bringing in animals from outside. As long as we have the fire lit, the niedas will keep their distance. They're afraid of the light."

Iris' anxiety continued to increase as she pictured the sharp needle dragging string through her skin. She gagged when he began threading the hole, prompting him to glance at her with a smile tugging at his lips.

Foxx said, "Afraid of light? We've been attacked by niedas in the daylight numerous times."

"True, but the mountains of Cordillera are swarming with cave niedas. Their eyes are so accustomed to the darkness, even the moon is bright enough to deter most from vacating their mountain hideaways."

"I doubt Iris and Orion were exploring the tunnels in the pitch dark."

"I would like to circle back to the phrase *the mountains of Cordillera are swarming with cave niedas*," Iris said.

Declan nodded in agreement with Foxx's statement. "It is strange you guys were attacked. Didn't you take your torch with you?" He directed the question at Orion, who refused to meet his gaze but instead looked pointedly at Iris.

"We did have a torch." Orion returned his attention to flipping the meat.

"I dropped it in a puddle," Iris admitted, leaving out the details as to how or why she might have managed to do so. "We were attacked pretty quickly after it went out. Which is super freaky now that I think about it. It must have been lurking nearby." Her gaze drifted to the side in thought, only to fall right in line with Orion's. Again her cheeks caught fire.

Declan noticed the variation in color and tilted his head. Then he tied off the end of the string. "Okay, let's do this." When he held up the needle to show Iris it was ready, she cringed but slid herself forward without complaint and leaned back on her elbows to give him a flat space to work.

After shifting closer, he handed her a rolled piece of cloth to bite down on. He cleaned the open wound with water before using a dropper from a tiny glass bottle to apply liquid along the tear. Iris reached for Foxx's hand and clenched her jaw as it burned and fizzed.

Declan cooed calming words. "You're okay. I want to make sure it's clean." She mumbled a noise of agreement, but when he dropped more into the opening, she groaned and let her head fall back so she couldn't watch. He dabbed the skin around the wound, drying it off. Then his cold fingers grazed the side of her stomach, sending a shiver through her that covered her in goosebumps. He pinched the skin on either side of the opening. "Ready?" She grunted through the fabric. With all the tenderness of a practiced nurse, he guided the needle through her skin. Her whole body tensed as she forced herself to remain motionless. "Try to relax." She took a steadying breath, willing her muscles to loosen. Tying a knot, he cut the excess string, and she felt a slight release in pressure. "That's one. Only three more to go." She groaned again, and he chuckled.

"Don't you dare laugh at me!" she spit through the cloth as he pinched her skin in preparation for another stitch. Her aggression made him laugh harder, and she growled. Her toes curled as she fought to remain stationary. "Fabulous bedside manner, Declan."

Foxx lost her grip on her own suppressed laughter.

Declan made quick work of it and soon had all four stitches

completed. He dropped a little more of the painful liquid across them, cleansing any lingering germs and blood before blotting it dry. Twisting the lid from the cura, he said, "It's your favorite part." His smile widened as he remembered her distress the first time she woke up smelling of dead spider juices.

Her head flew up, and her eyes shot daggers at him. Dropping the cloth from her mouth, she said, "I thought you were the nice one." He grinned and leaned forward to apply the salve. The tips of his fingers grazed her skin as he dabbed the wound. More goose-bumps rose across her stomach, and she didn't miss the reddening of his freckled cheeks when he noticed her reaction to his touch. She watched him, thinking he was taking an awfully long time and might be intentionally letting his fingers skim the sensitive skin of her stomach.

When he finished, he replaced the lid and packed up his med-kit. Standing, he left the fire to return everything to his bag. Then he exited the cave without saying a word.

CHAPTER 23

THE ROYALS

Storm's third quarter waned to a crescent as Iris' wounds healed enough to remove the stitches. Declan coached Foxxglove how to extract them rather than doing it himself, reasoning that she should learn the correct way to pull them out. Iris hadn't been looking forward to feeling his fingers against her skin and was relieved when Foxx permitted his instruction.

Orion's stitches needed a few more days, but his bruises looked better, with very few dark patches remaining amongst the pale green. Despite his pain lessening, he hadn't relinquished his contemptuous demeanor.

Iris decided she liked his constant attitude better than the ups and downs. It made it easier to avoid him and offered little room for confusion.

After a week in the cave, they packed up and departed.

Jericho sat on the northern edge of Cordillera, high in the Lunalakota Mountains, and the road that brought them to the cave would carry them all the way to the royal city. Unlike the frequently vacant trails of Sateen, the path to Jericho would be heavily traveled. They hoped the King's Legion still lingered around the border but had no way of knowing for sure. If not, Foxx and Iris' pictures might be plastered in every establishment along the way. Even still, hiking off the road and out of sight wouldn't be an option.

Only the journey itself outweighed their fears of encountering the Legion. The uphill hike brought with it strong winds, freezing temperatures, and eventually—snowdrifts. Foxx made pants for herself and Iris from the tryka hide, but they wouldn't be enough when the snow became constant.

Though the early hours of the morning remained crisp, warmth blessed the travelers as the sun ascended into the sky. They remained quiet for much of the day, only speaking when they came across something interesting or needed to stop for a break.

A few hours into the journey, a rumble at their feet startled the girls into stopping with their hands braced at their sides. Declan noticed their fearful expressions with amusement. "Don't worry about that. It's normal for the region."

Iris gaped. "Vibrating ground is normal?" Orion didn't pause but chose to walk several paces ahead and ignore them completely.

Declan lifted his eyes to the mountain peaks. "It comes from the hyvä mon, a race of stone giants dwelling high in the mountains."

Foxx's face matched her sister's. "*Giants*?"

He chuckled. "Yes, giants. Despite their size, they're generally docile creatures that keep to themselves."

As they continued on, Iris scoured the mountain ridges, searching for signs of the allegedly gentle hyvä mon. An hour past noon, she removed Declan's jacket and tied it around her waist, allowing sunbeams to heat her skin. "You seem pretty familiar with Cordillera, but Orion said you were from Reginaterra. Have you spent a lot of time here?"

Declan walked at her side. "Our missions for King Pollux brought us to Jericho more than once. When he or Sirena needed to communicate with the Kirkavalls on matters unfit to utter by letter, they usually sent the Raptors."

"The Kirkavalls," Iris repeated. "I've heard the name."

Foxx said, "The Konungr and Dróttning of Cordillera. Like the other royals of Arkaemor, they rule beneath Sirena and Pollux, right?"

"That's a tricky question." Declan had strapped the antlers cut from the tryka to the back of his pack, causing it to hang off balance. After shifting the straps so it settled comfortably between his shoulder blades, he explained, "Pollux and Sirena Aldrich are the High King and Queen to all of Arkaemor. The other royals don't rule beneath them so to speak, but they don't oppose them either.

"By the year 2000, Arkaemor was divided into Seven Kingdoms, with sovereigns ruling from each of the seven territories. The

Aldrichs kept the Kingdoms in line, and history claims the world experienced a long period of peace. When the Monastery of the Morrow rose against the Aldrichs many centuries later, some of the sovereigns joined them. This is why we now only have Five Kingdoms, despite there being seven territories. Four if you don't count the Grim Wilds."

Foxxglove rattled off, "Sirena and Pollux rule Reginaterra and Crystavium. The Valentinos are the sovereigns of both Savanni and Alunda. The Grim Wilds has no ruler, and Metsa Sateen and Cordillera have their own sovereigns. The Raja in Sateen, I believe, and as you said, the Kirkavalls in Cordillera."

"Raja is correct for Metsa Sateen. Raja Decha Narong. There are other monarchs throughout the lands that govern smaller nations, but none with as much power as those who rule the Kingdoms."

Iris drew her eyes from the valley, where the river now seemed a mere stream from her vantage. "How do you know so much about this, Foxx?"

"Mother," Foxx replied. Amaryllis had been keen on teaching Foxx about the monarchs of Arkaemor. She found them fascinating, and when Foxx grew old enough to inquire more deeply, her mother had delighted in sharing her knowledge of the people who ruled the unique territories of the world.

Disgruntled, Iris wondered why their mother had never taught her about these things. "So why doesn't the Grim Wilds have a monarch?"

Declan looked at the sky. "It's been named *terra nullius*, which means unclaimed land, though I'm not entirely sure why. Some kind of agreement between the royals who lived long ago, I guess. The last king who ruled there lost himself to sil ōnni. He had no heir when he died, and the Aldrichs never replaced him, so the royal city eventually fell to ruin."

Iris quirked a brow. "Sil ōnni?"

"It's a drug. Addictive and lethal." Orion's voice surprised them, as he'd been silent for the better part of two hours.

Declan nodded. "There are a few small nations left in the Wilds, but without help from a sovereign, much of the territory has faded into small towns and tribes. Its major export is still salt, a necessary resource everywhere, but the territory provides little else to the world at this point."

"Olives," Orion added. "Grapes, too. So wine."

"Yes, true. Maybe someone will step in one day and bring prosperity back to the territory, but until then, it remains unruled. To answer your first question Foxx, as long as all other sovereigns rule in compliance with the King and Queen of Arkaemor, they rule freely."

"That doesn't sound very *free* to me." Iris startled when Orion shushed her. Then he glanced at Declan with an expression of rebuke. Iris ignored him. "So what message did you communicate to the Konungr and Dróttning when you last visited Jericho?"

"Last time Orion and I were in Cordillera as soldiers, we were sent with a message of reproof concerning the Jerichonian Guard. The King and Queen of Arkaemor have set regulations to limit how big the other Kingdoms' forces can grow, how much money can be spent on artillery, and the like. At the time, they thought Konungr Vali was getting a little overeager in building up his Guard."

"And how did the Konungr receive that message?" Iris looked thrilled to hear his answer.

"About as well as you might expect a king to respond to a reprimand," Declan said. Orion hummed in agreement.

Iris chuckled and looked sideways at Declan. Resuming their journey seemed to have revived him from the despondence he'd shown in the cave. She'd missed his easy smiles and lighthearted demeanor. "You're doing that talking thing again."

A smile broke across his lips. "I can stop if you like."

"Yes, you definitely should," Orion said.

"Please don't." Iris glared at the back of Orion's head. Then she returned her gaze to the valley, observing the tops of the trees a layer below and inhaling the piney breeze. "I wonder if we'll get to see the Konungr while we're in Jericho."

"Let's hope we don't." Orion lifted his hands behind his head, stretching his shoulders as he walked.

"Strictly speaking, Orion isn't allowed to return to Jericho." Declan raised a brow, and Iris eyed him with curiosity. "Since you've spent some time with him, I'm certain you can discern why."

Orion grumbled. "Very nice."

Iris covered her mouth, and Foxx glanced back at them with a smirk. "I guess since we're all fugitives, we should be avoiding royals as a general rule."

Declan tilted his head as he weighed his answer. "Actually, aside from Orion, Konungr Vali Kirkavall would likely delight in pulling one over on Sirena. If he finds out she's hunting you, he might lock you up in his palace and throw away the key. But he's a bit of a wild card, so it's probably better not to risk it."

"The Mad King." Foxx echoed the nickname the kids in Ataraxia had used to describe the male sovereign of Cordillera.

"Since I'm part of this foursome, we will be avoiding the Kirkavalls at all costs," Orion said.

A bird with a wide wingspan flew in an arc toward the valley. Sprigs of longer feathers sprouted from the top of its head and the bottom of its tail, and its beak curved sharply toward the ground. Iris pointed at the bird, and Declan named the creature an ignälis.

Foxx paused on the cliffside, and the others stopped next to her. "I didn't know ignäli were real."

Declan said, "Only in Cordillera, to my knowledge."

"Do they really burst into flames?" Iris asked. "The red and orange feathers are as vibrant as fire."

Declan shrugged. "So legend says, but I've never seen it happen in real life."

"I have," Orion said. "Just once. A new one was immediately reborn in the ashes."

Iris hugged herself to combat the chill. "That sounds incredible." After watching it soar out of sight, Orion continued on, and the others soon followed.

They traveled for another quarter of an hour before Foxx broke the silence. "Have either of you heard the name Wraith before?"

Declan pulled his attention from the valley to look at her. "Dagon Wraith? He's the Legion general."

"He's a jerk," Orion said.

Foxx chuckled. "Is there anyone you actually *do* like?"

Orion seemed to think it over. "Maybe Declan. Sometimes. Though less and less as time progresses." Declan barked a laugh and pushed his friend's shoulder. Orion looked back at him with a friendly grin, though the moment his eyes met Iris', his smile vanished, and he returned his gaze forward.

"Where did you hear that name?" Iris asked Foxx.

"Asher said it when we were being chased through Petrichor. He said if we split up, General Wraith would chase him instead of us."

"That's odd." Iris furrowed her brow.

"Asher?" Orion cast a glance back at Declan, who answered the question in his expression.

"The man they were traveling with before us."

Iris scratched her chin. "Now you've both gotten weird when you heard that name. Do you know him? Was he a soldier?"

"If he knew Dagon, then it's possible," Declan said.

"Is it possible he would have known him if he wasn't a soldier?" Iris asked.

Orion's shoulders lifted. "Maybe. If he was a criminal."

"He didn't seem like a soldier." Foxx's tone made the word *soldier* sound like an insult. She glanced at Orion, and Iris told her to be nice. Taking a moment to consider Orion's suggestion, she thought Asher didn't seem much like a criminal either. Though, as he currently sought a magical potion to murder the Queen of the whole world, perhaps he was.

Declan adjusted the antlers again, and when Orion heard the movement, he slid his own bag from his shoulders and offered to switch. Declan sighed relief when the lighter bag fell into place against his back. "Dagon is pretty well known. Commander Hector Kayvan as well. The ruthless leaders of the King's Legion."

Iris shivered and decided it was time to change the subject. "What is Jericho like?"

Seeming pleased with the divergence, Declan brightened. "Jericho is like most cities. A lot of people, a lot of places to shop and explore, and brimming with rich history. The Monastery of the Morrow built the framework for the city almost two thousand years ago. The sovereigns of Cordillera ruled from Villa Montis before it was erected, but Jericho has been the royal city ever since."

Foxx noticed him lowering his voice as he spoke of the Monastery of the Morrow and wondered if it was safe to discuss the history as long as your position regarding it remained neutral. "We stayed at the Monastery in Metsa Sateen. What was left of it anyway."

"There is a ruined Monastery in almost every territory of Arkaemor. Reginaterra never had one that I know of, and the one in Crystavium was converted into a prison known as the Ashgate Fortress. The rest sit in ruins, if not completely demolished. Even the first one, the one we might get to see in Jericho, is a remnant. The Immortal Queen wrecked them all."

Foxx flinched at the mention of the Queen's proclivity for devastation.

Declan sighed. "It's definitely a tragic chapter of Arkaemor's history and unfortunately, not common knowledge to most. Many believe the stories of the Monastery to be fictional. Especially in Reginaterra."

Iris touched her heart. "When was the Monastery of the Morrow destroyed? Was it all at once or did it happen over a period of time?"

Declan's brow scrunched in thought. "3081, I think?" Orion confirmed his guess with a nod. "And it happened all at once. All in one single night, so the stories claim."

"Almost a thousand years ago." Iris unhooked the water sleeve from the bag on Declan's back without permission, though he smiled and paused his step to let her.

"Yes. 948 years."

Orion said, "The same night as the comet, legends say."

"Arella's Comet?" Iris asked, and he nodded.

Foxx looked back at her sister. "Like from the poem? But which comet would it have been in 3081?"

Iris quoted what she could remember, and Foxx joined in.

Year of woe, year of weep,
Year of hope, the bad ones reap.
Year of trials, and one of snow,
Year of knowing, then watch it grow.
Year of rest and year of sorrow,
Of victory followed by the morrow.
Then came the lost, then came the found,
And quakes that rocked and shook the ground.
Year of dragons, year of tears,
Brought with them a year of fears.
Year of sleep and one of old,
Then marks the year all mysteries unfold.

Iris smiled at her sister, feeling waves of nostalgia as thoughts of her mother emerged.

Foxx said, "Year of tears, I think."

Orion cast a glance over his shoulder. "The next one is coming soon. Just a couple years off now."

"Then marks the year all mysteries unfold." Foxx scratched her cheek before adjusting her bow. "I sure hope it doesn't take years

for all the mysteries to unfold." Orion chuckled, and she looked at him in surprise.

Iris asked, "So what does that have to do with the Monastery of the Morrow? Or was it a coincidence they were destroyed on the same night as a comet that only passes by every 237 years?"

"I don't often believe in coincidence," Declan said. "I imagine it must be significant, though I've never heard anything that confirmed this suspicion. Nor am I familiar with the poem you recited. So, who can say for sure?"

"The Monastery of the Morrow was a flock of fanatics." Orion busied himself with kicking a stone along the trail. "History doesn't care that they're gone."

"They weren't fanatics. They were faith teachers, historical scribes, and healers."

"Religious, extremist teachers, scribes, and healers, you mean."

"No, actually, I don't." Declan returned his attention to the girls, whose eyes had grown wide in the heat of their argument. "Anyway: You asked about Jericho. It's called the City of the Moon."

Iris looked at her wrist, remembering Asher's tattoo. "I've seen the symbol for the city, but I don't know why it's a moon."

"The view of the night sky from the city is said to surpass any sight in all of Arkaemor, but the main reason for the focus is attributed to the Monastery of the Morrow. The Monastery believed in a higher power, a Creator of all things."

"We have heard of Elohim." Foxx kept her voice low, as he did.

"One of His common characteristics is that He is a Light in the darkness, as the moon is a light in our darkness. At night when the sun slumbers below the horizon, the moon shines bright to guide our steps. Even with the Monastery gone, the city celebrates the moon and its connection to Elohim. You'll see what I mean when we arrive."

"Never took you for a religious zealot, Declan." In Orion's irritation, he struck the stone he'd been kicking too forcefully and propelled it over the ledge of the cliff. Clattering echoed through the mountains as the stone tumbled toward the valley.

"I never took you for a bigot, Ri," Declan shot back.

"That's enough you two." Foxxglove heard her mother's voice in her own tone. Then a feeling of discomfort washed over her, and she placed a hand against the wall for balance. Her head shivered with energy and her vision blurred, forcing her eyes closed. A single image materialized within her mind's eye: a man she didn't recognize adorned in gray and white fur. He had hair like pale smoke, but he was young, not much older than Orion, she guessed. And frightfully handsome.

A hand on her shoulder had her head clearing as quickly as it had fogged. The tips of her fingers felt painfully cold and she flexed them to improve circulation. Yearning for gloves, she blew hot air against her palms. "Sorry. I felt a little lightheaded."

Iris eyed her with scrutiny, wishing they could speak freely. "Do you want some water?"

Still feeling pressure on either side of her skull, Foxx nodded and squinted her eyes against the sun. Declan passed Foxx the water, and she took a few sips before returning the bag and rubbing her temples with her thumbs.

"If you're finished with whatever that was, can we move forward?" Orion's request received a glower from Iris.

Foxx pushed away from the wall. "Yes, we can. Just a little aftershock from before, I think."

Iris didn't look convinced. "It's been almost two weeks. Isn't it strange to be having residual effects now?"

"I don't really know what's strange and what's normal." The image of the man resurfaced, and Foxx wondered who he could be. There'd been no time to glean any contextual clues past his striking face.

The group began walking again. The only sounds to break the silence were their shuffling boots, birds chirping in the trees below them, and the whir of the breeze as it blew across the mountain ridges. When they stopped for an afternoon snack of dried tryka and greens they'd picked along the road, Iris and Foxx hung tired feet over the ledge of the path and stared down at the valley. The sun shone from high above, warming their skin to combat the wind.

Declan and Orion stood several paces away, speaking in hushed tones. Iris noticed Foxx glancing at them over her shoulder and asked, "What do you think they're talking about?"

Foxx watched a few seconds longer, but Declan felt her eyes on him, and after meeting her gaze, both men strode back to join them. "Is everything okay?"

"Everything is fine." Declan moved away from Orion and sat down on Iris' other side, hanging his legs over the ledge like they did. After taking a swig from his waterskin, he offered it to Iris.

When she finished, she passed it to Foxx. "Do you really think the King and Queen are immortal like they claim?"

Declan popped a sliver of jerky into his mouth. "Sirena was supposedly here at the beginning of creation, if you believe what the Monastery professes. I'm not sure anyone really knows exactly how old she is. I've heard conflicting opinions about Pollux. Some say he's immortal like the Queen. Others say the Queen's enchantments keep him alive and that he is otherwise entirely human."

Foxx thought of how Asher had mentioned the presence of other immortals in history, though he hadn't known if any still existed. If they did, she wondered exactly how many immortal beings they might be dealing with when the time came to fight.

Iris said, "I don't think I would want to live forever. It seems like such a very long time. Though maybe with a partner by your side, it wouldn't be so bad. Do you think they still love each other after all these years?"

Orion made a noise of irritation, drawing all of their eyes to him. He turned to look down at the valley, standing on the edge next to Foxx. For a brief moment, she considered pushing him off.

Declan thought it over before lowering his voice and answering, "If I'm honest, it's hard for me to believe the Queen is capable of love, but I suppose it's possible. Did you know they have children? A prince and a princess."

Iris swallowed another chunk of jerky. "The kids in Ataraxia mentioned a prince, but they didn't say which territory he belonged to. Since they said he visited the orphanage with the Konungr, I assumed he was the Prince of Cordillera."

Foxx shook her head. "They were talking about Prince Alexander. And remember, Ah-Luiah said he brought her from Reginaterra. Cordillera doesn't have any heirs that I know of. At least, they didn't when Mother taught me about them."

"What is Ataraxia?" Declan asked.

Iris brightened. "It's an orphan shelter in Metsa Sateen. I guess some of the kids were brought there by Prince Alexander and the Konungr." Declan looked thoughtful, but before he could comment, she added, "Hang on. If Alexander is the Prince of Reginaterra, how could he and the Konungr of Cordillera even know each other? At least enough to be affiliated with some random orphan shelter in the middle of Metsa Sateen. There's an entire world between them."

Foxx said, "I was wondering the same thing. Though the kids

didn't necessarily say the Prince and the Konungr came at the same time, did they?" Iris shrugged, unsure.

"For all of the Royal families to rule cooperatively, it makes sense they're acquainted, right?" Declan looked down at his lap and brushed his hands against his thighs. "Alexander's sister—"

"Princess Avaline," Foxx interrupted, and Declan nodded.

Iris glared at her sister. "You have failed as my teacher." Foxx choked on a surprised laugh and a few drops of the water she'd just swigged trickled down her chin. Iris shook her head with disappointment before looking back at Declan. "Are they immortal, too? How old are they?"

"As far as I know, the Queen, and possibly the King, are the only immortal beings. The heirs are quite young, and their story goes like this: the King always wanted children, but the Queen thought she was barren. They tried for years and years with no results. Then a few decades ago, Crown Prince Alexander Aldrich was born, and Princess Avaline came several years later."

Iris asked, "So Alexander is the heir to Pollux and Sirena's Thrones? What are they like?"

Foxx hadn't considered the heirs when she and Asher discussed killing the Queen. Would the Prince be as cruel as his mother? Could they get him on board with the plan to get rid of her? The reminder of this knowledge added an entirely new layer to everything they were planning. Perhaps Asher already knew the temperament of the heirs and was counting on them to take over once the Queen was gone. Could Alexander be the Great King prophecies claimed would walk with the Creator?

Answering Iris' question as well as Foxx's internal musings, Orion snarked, "Prince Alexander is a selfish, arrogant prat. Always getting into trouble. Throwing wild parties, wandering day-drunk throughout the castle, and hitting on everything that walks. Certainly not the man you want as heir to the Thrones. And Lady Avaline is…"

"Careful," Declan warned. Iris' expression matched her sister's confusion. Orion opened his mouth to go on, and the girls eagerly awaited what he would reveal, but he seemed to think better of it and remained silent.

Iris moved past Orion's descriptions of the royal children and asked, "But if the Queen is immortal, she doesn't need an heir, does she?"

"Not unless something kills her." Foxxglove handed the water sleeve back to Declan.

Orion said, "Nothing can kill the Queen. She's a witch who's lived forever. She cannot be killed."

Declan's voice returned to its former whisper. "I don't know if I agree with that. Everything has a weakness. Whether or not someone can find her weakness is a different story."

Speaking under his breath, Orion eyed their surroundings as if scouting for spies up in the mountain cliffs. "We shouldn't be talking about this out in the open."

"I will agree with you there."

"Let's talk about something different then," Iris suggested.

"Let's not talk at all," Orion said.

The skin between Iris' brows creased, and her lips puckered like she'd eaten something sour. Declan nudged her arm with his elbow and winked, instantly dissolving her anger with a rush of delight. She'd never seen Declan wink before.

He rose to his feet and offered a hand to help her stand. Foxx was already vertical and brushing dirt from her clothing.

"Onward?" Iris' eyes flitted amongst them.

With unanimous agreement, the foursome continued on, working their way higher and higher into the Lunalakota mountains.

CHAPTER 24

PEREGRINE MANOR

Four days had come and gone since they'd abandoned the cave. The path at their feet twisted and turned as it rose in elevation along the mountain's edge, and Iris and Foxx enjoyed the steady incline. Many years of travel had made their legs strong, but they could feel new muscles developing, and the burn felt oddly pleasant.

The atmosphere grew increasingly bitter with each passing sunset. The physical hike helped ward off the chill during the day, but the nights became frosty, and the thinner air had the girls' temples throbbing.

Clouds draped over the mountain peaks, shrouding them in a near constant fog. Eventually, dirt and rocks became the travelers only companions. When they looked out over the cliffs, the cerulean, clover, and pine colors of the gorge blended together into a murky mixture that reminded Iris of her mother's dirty paintbrush water.

On the afternoon of the fifth day, Iris and Foxx started dragging their feet. "Do we have any idea how much longer until we reach Jericho?"

"Another day or two at most," Declan said. Iris groaned.

Orion gestured up the trail. "There's an inn near here. If memory serves, it shouldn't be much further. Hopefully we'll all be sleeping in beds tonight."

"That would be lovely," Iris said.

"Whoa." Foxxglove pointed as milky specks began drifting down from above. A flake landed on her cheek, and she flinched. When her hand rose to touch it, it had already melted against her skin. "This must be snow."

"You've never seen snow before?" Orion asked.

Iris snarked before her sister could respond. "No, we have not. We grew up on the beach, remember?" Orion made his usual unintelligible grunt, but she ignored him. Lifting a hand to the sky, she let the flakes kiss her palm.

"It's so pretty." Foxx opened her mouth and stuck out her tongue to catch the flakes.

Orion watched Iris' joyous energy as she mimicked her sister, closing her eyes and lifting her face to the falling snow. It collected on her long eyelashes, making them sparkle. Feeling his gaze, she dropped her chin, and their eye contact startled him from his fascination.

Clearing his throat, he said, "We better get moving. We may be able to get some warmer clothes before the snow gets too dense."

Not long after the snow began to fall, they came across a cobalt sign with formal, gray lettering. The words *Peregrine Manor* had been painted above an arrow that pointed down a road branching off from the trail. Orion gestured them forward, and Iris took the lead, climbing the path to its highest point where it leveled out into a wide plateau. Neighboring peaks rose high on all sides, surrounding twenty or so log cabins. The tallest stood centered against the back wall, and the others stretched out on either side in a crescent.

"Welcome to Peregrine. We'll be staying in the Manor." Orion indicated the most impressive structure before pointing to another building off to the right. "That's the shop where we can get you ladies some new clothes and whatever else we need."

"It's adorable!" Iris exclaimed.

Icicles dripped in silvery spikes and a smoking chimney jutted out from every snow-covered rooftop. Despite there being little to no vegetation along the road for days, plants grew all across the plateau. Scattered patches of jade grass sprouted up through the snow. Gardens grew in front of the cabins, and potted plants lined walkways and porches.

Iris caught a glimpse of something fluttering near one of the potted spruces and pointed it out. "Is that a henki?" Its white glow made it difficult to discern its shape, but it reminded her of the driädi they'd seen in Metsa Sateen. Alunda had a few species of henki, too, so the creature was not unfamiliar to her, though she'd never seen one that glowed white.

Declan nodded. "An orädi, the henki of the mountains. Like the driädi you saw in Petrichor."

Foxx leaned to the side, tracking the creature as it sprinkled light into a nearby shrub. "Alunda has kuki and nyädi, too. I never realized so many different kinds existed. Declan and I saw a pixū at Lacuna Kaput, Iris. It looked like a flying woman with a horse's body."

"I'm bummed I missed it!"

Orion said, "People from Cordillera often call the orädi mischief makers or crag tricksters, because they can be destructive."

"They don't look destructive. That one seems to be helping the evergreens grow, like the kuki help the flowers." As the words left Iris' lips, a crash up the walkway drew their attention. A potted fern had toppled from a knee wall and shattered. They heard the familiar tinkle of the henki, but with a hint of mischievousness, as if it might be giggling.

Orion folded his arms. "See? They can't help themselves."

"Sounds familiar," Iris mumbled. Orion's eyes snapped to her, but her attention remained on the first orädi they'd seen. It darted toward the felled pot, seeming to scold the other as it went.

The road morphed into a mosaic path that encircled a well made of dark stone cemented together by gray adhesive. Two towers rose up either side, and a rod stretched between them to hold a rope and bucket. Foxx ran her fingers along the painted designs as she admired the structure's craftsmanship.

Iris soon tugged Foxx from the well to observe the Manor. Constructed of dark cherry wood, the Manor stood as a striking contrast against the snow. Gardens of winter jasmine and juniper bushes carved into cones lined the perimeter, and ivy grew up the walls around midnight-blue shutters.

A knocker shaped like a hawk hung from the center of the door, its shine faded by time and weather. Climbing the steps, Orion led them into the foyer. A staircase greeted them, wide and grand, and to their right a door led to *Peregrine Pub*. They could hear chatter and laughter from within as the dinner crowd enjoyed their meals.

The foyer stretched to their left, where they saw a coat rack, a bookshelf, and a reception desk in front of a woman who greeted them as they entered. Thick hair the color of burgundy berries hung in waves over one shoulder. Her dress covered her arms all the way past her wrists and dipped low in the front, exposing a busty chest.

Orion approached the woman with a coy grin. "We would like a room for the night, please." His tone had Iris' stomach twinging with jealousy. Shame washed over her, quickly transforming into disgust toward both him and herself.

"Our rooms are designed for singles and couples." The woman placed her elbows on the desk in a way that revealed more cleavage. "Will that be satisfactory, sir?" Her words sounded sweet like straw-berries, but her distasteful gaze raked over Foxx from head to toe before sliding to Iris. Then her lips curved into a smirk.

Orion rested his elbow on the desk, leaning closer and putting his chin in his hand. "Two rooms then." The woman wrote down his name and the room numbers before handing him two keys, each with a blue ribbon tied around the silver.

The staircase, framed in matte black banisters, tapered as it rose to the second floor. They turned right at the top of the landing and followed the hallway until the numbers on the keys matched those on the doors.

Orion stopped in front of door twelve, and Foxx held out her hand. "Oh, no you don't. You think I'm going to let you girls share a room so you can escape like thieves in the night?" He unlocked the door and shoved it open.

"You were the thief in the night, if you remember, Orion." Foxx's hip jutted to the side as she glanced at Declan, who'd crossed the hall to the door with a scripted eleven.

"Exactly why I know not to trust you now." Orion handed Declan the second key and said Iris' name, motioning for her to enter the room.

Iris' mouth dropped open. "You have got to be kidding me. Why do you get to decide which room I sleep in?"

"Because I don't trust Declan to be as rough on you as he may need to be should you try anything shifty." He looked at Declan, who seemed to be studying the gray swirls on the carpet, before tapping the open door. "Inside. Now."

Iris stomped past him, but paused in the doorway. "Keep in mind, you returned my weapons. It may have been safer for you to let me sleep where I pleased."

Orion cracked a smile and nudged her the rest of the way into the room. Then he turned to Declan and pointed at Foxx. "Keep an eye on this one."

"You don't have to resort back to this, Orion. People respond much better when you aren't being an ass." Declan disappeared into the room, and after a satisfied huff, Foxx joined him.

C

Asher pulled his hood over his head as he approached the iron gates of Jericho. Hoping to remain shrouded from soldiers patrolling the city, he'd ventured into a tiny, picturesque town the day before and bought a cloak from a shop called Peregrine Purchases. On top of the Jerichonian Guard, soldiers of the King's Legion also patrolled the royal city, so stealth was imperative if he hoped to avoid detection.

Flakes drifted soundlessly from the sky, coating everything in a layer of white, like icing on a cake. He tried to catch a glimpse of the gate Guard, but the blur of snowflakes obstructed his view, making it impossible to discern whether or not he knew him.

Decked in Jerichonian regimentals, the Guard wore light grays, dark purples, and a silver crescent across his breast. His hand moved to the hilt at his waist as Asher drew closer. "What is your business in Jericho?"

"I seek an audience with the Morrow." Knowing what these words would mean to the soldier, Asher hoped they would garner trust without him having to reveal his identity.

The Guard lowered his head. "Then enter, and go in peace. The Morrow will greet you."

Asher bowed as the soldier sidestepped to allow him passage through the gate and onto a charming terrace with a fountain at its center. A mosaic of the moon's phases surrounded the fountain, partially hidden beneath a gauzy layer of snow, and atop it stood a sculpted bighorn ram, encircled by a crescent moon.

A woman perched on the fountain's edge was holding a basket of long-stemmed roses. She wore a hat and gloves to match her fur-lined boots. "A rose for the gentleman? A single *mett* for the beautiful flower of Jericho." Violet roses were the Konungr's favorite, and his wife knew the trick to keep them blooming all year long, undeterred by the low temperatures.

"How about two *metts*, and you answer a question as well?"

The woman agreed, handing him a flower and accepting both coins. "Ask."

"I'm looking for an inn that won't ask too many questions. One where a person could remain inconspicuous if they decided there was a need for it."

The woman inspected him, her head tipping to the side as she considered his question. "All the inns in Jericho are lovely, but I should think the White Luna would suit your purposes." She pointed across the entrance plaza and down a street leading away from the front gate. "It usually has rooms available, and the owner, Gabriel, is a good man, always willing to help someone in need."

Asher bowed. "Thank you very much, miss. Go in peace."

"Go in peace," she echoed, bowing in return.

He tucked the flower in a loop on his pack, tugged his hood forward, and strode toward the White Luna Inn.

C

Iris observed the decor of the room with approval. A bed centered against the wall had been draped in fur pelts and woven blankets. To her right, a dresser held a circular looking glass, and directly across from the door, a triangular stack of logs embellished a fireplace. Next to the hearth, a table held a kettle, a glass jar of tea sachets, and two stone mugs, each with a shiny glaze around the brims.

She squealed, dashing to the table and holding the jar to her nose. "Tea! It smells like Rossnetta's. Let's make a fire." She spun to face the room, and her excitement vanished.

"Who's Rossnetta?" Orion began discarding his layers on the floor next to the side of the bed he'd obviously claimed—the one closest to the door. Iris failed to drag her eyes from the lower half of his stomach, briefly unveiled as he pulled off his shirts. When he noticed her staring, he smiled.

"Your wounds are looking better," she said, thinking it seemed a suitable explanation for her attention.

"I had an excellent nurse."

She turned back to the table. "Yes, Declan was clearly well trained."

A low chuckle reverberated through his chest as he closed the space between them and lifted the jar to his nose. "It smells good. Like peppermint." Iris made a noise of agreement and continued fidgeting with the top brim of one of the mugs. After replacing the lid with a *clink*, he turned to face her. He hadn't been within a few feet of her since their moment in the tunnel unless absolutely necessary. He'd kept a miserable distance with no explanation as to what had triggered his detachment.

In the span of a single day, he'd gone from returning her weapons to sharing body heat, producing somersaulting butterflies in her stomach, to kissing her with a fierce passion she thought only existed in the sappy novels her sister liked to read—to glacial unfriendliness. A wall of hatred, annoyance, and fury.

She would never admit to him how often she thought of their kiss or how many times she'd dreamed of him as he slept so close to her, yet so far away. She would take to her grave how much his treatment pained her and would forever deny how greatly she desired his playful and alluring charm.

Orion said her name, breaking through rapid thoughts she shouldn't be allowing herself to have. His husky tone drew her eyes, and as if by magic, the man she yearned for lingered on the fringes of his gaze. The mysterious enigma who'd taught her about the birds.

"What?" She'd hoped for more vexation in her tone but seemed unable to produce it. His proximity, after so many days of frigidity, had her heart racing, and the privacy of the closed door left her feeling vulnerable. She waited for him to speak, her eyes moving back and forth between his as she tried to understand what transpired within their depths. When he didn't answer, she asked, "Will you say something? Please, Orion."

Though his expression overflowed with longing and regret, he answered, "I can't."

"Why? I don't understand, but I want to. And you want to tell me. I can see it in your eyes, so why won't you? Just tell me what's going on." Memories of her fingers caressing his battered skin drew pink to her cheeks. Even now, she could feel his hands on her in the dark, his lips colliding with her own, and his shift into tenderness when he'd realized what he'd taken. Her heart fluttered in its cage. "Talk to me. Let me help you. Whatever it is, we can figure it out together." Her fingers grazed his arm, but he flinched away as if startled from a dream. Two steps backward put more sobering space between them.

"There is no *we*." His tone had gone as cold as the still-falling snow.

Iris crossed her arms, creating a barrier between her own heart and his. "Fine, then." Orion stomped from the room and closed the door. Iris growled at the empty space he left behind.

When she knocked on Foxx and Declan's door, her sister answered and noticed her distress. Rather than commenting on it, Foxx said, "Declan is going to take us to the shop. Are you ready to head there now?"

"Definitely."

At the bottom of the staircase, they found Orion inclined over the reception desk flirting with the woman in the black dress. Inconceivable rage stopped Iris in her tracks. The woman noticed her pause, and her expression revealed the kind of cruelty only a beautiful woman can inflict with a single look. Orion followed her gaze, his eyes landing on Iris for less than a second before he said something to the woman that drew her attention back to him.

For a short, insane moment, Iris considered marching over and punching him square in the nose. Or possibly punching the woman in the nose. Or maybe wrapping her arms around his neck and reminding him of the passion they'd shared within the darkness of the tunnel.

Orion bent closer to the woman and whispered something in her ear.

At that, Iris tossed away all potential plans and followed Foxx and Declan out into the cold, allowing the frigid temperature to stifle the fire erupting in her veins.

Flakes continued to fall in crystalline sheets, coating everything it touched in a layer of white. Their boots crushed prints into the snow with each step, and both girls thought they'd never felt a similar sensation. Even walking in sand felt nothing like the *shush* of trampling snow.

They followed the invisible path toward the shop Orion had pointed out. As they passed by the well, an orädi zipped in front of them on its way to the Manor. They tracked its path and saw three more, each fluttering near a potted plant and dressing it in a white glow.

Declan answered the question in Foxx and Iris' expressions.

"They're protecting the plants so the snow doesn't harm them. The light will fade when the snow ceases to fall. If the flurries continue, it will be quite a sight after the sun goes down."

A sign reading *Peregrine Purchases*, twin to the one on the mountain pass, hung over the door. A bell chimed above their heads when they entered. Foxx and Iris shared a mournful glance as the sound invoked memories of the Briar Tavern. Nearly three moons had come and gone since they'd fled Kesken Ala, but not a single day passed without thoughts of their friends.

Declan carried the tryka antlers to the merchant behind the counter, hoping to barter a trade. Iris and Foxx headed to the clothing racks and grabbed wool pants, tunics with long sleeves, and fur lined jackets with hoods. They found a bag to carry all of their items, as well as woven gloves, hats, scarves, socks, and a water skin.

After working out a bargain with the clerk, Declan gathered dried berries, nuts, meat, and a few canned items. When they finished, the girls met him at the checkout counter and placed their items next to his food. A display on the counter held tiny, leather pouches with a steel rod and a shard of flint. Foxx snatched one and added it to the pile. When Declan looked at her, she shrugged and pretended to focus her attention elsewhere.

"They're with me," Declan told the clerk, who then added their attire to his total.

Aside from their jackets, which they pulled on right away, Foxx and Iris shoved their belongings into the new pack, planning to organize it better when they returned to the Manor.

As they trudged back through the snow, Declan asked, "Are you girls hungry?"

"I could definitely eat something hot," Iris answered, and Foxx agreed.

"We should put our stuff in the rooms and have dinner in the pub."

"Only if Orion doesn't have to join us." Iris stuck her finger down her throat in a mocking gag. When they reentered the Manor, Orion no longer ogled the receptionist, but that didn't stop the woman from leering at Iris as they passed by.

In room eleven, Foxxglove dumped their bag on the bed, and the girls dug through the pile of clothes, selecting the items they wished to change into. Turning to Declan, who sat distracted on the bed, gazing into the unlit fireplace, Iris cleared her throat.

Declan startled and looked at them over his shoulder. Taking in the new clothing in their hands and the expectation on their faces, he stood abruptly. "You want to get changed."

They nodded, grinning as his cheeks blushed, and Declan hastened out the door.

CHAPTER 25

THE GREAT ESCAPE

Still feeling the urge to bathe, but pleased to finally have clean and dry clothing, the girls locked the door to room eleven and ventured downstairs to locate Declan in the pub.

To Iris' dismay, they found him at a table with four chairs, but only two were vacant. "So much for not dining with Orion."

Foxxglove smiled and nudged her shoulder. "Try to be nice. Isn't that what you're always telling me?"

"He makes it impossible."

"You are in control of you. You can't control how he behaves, but you can control how you respond."

Iris glanced sideways at her. "Maybe *you* can." Foxx chuckled, snagged her arm, and pulled her forward.

When they approached the table, Orion greeted them with unexpected excitement. "There they are!" Declan offered Iris a look of apology, and Orion stood, stumbling as he pushed his chair away with the backs of his knees. "Sit, sit." He motioned to the chairs across from them.

"Had a little too much already, Orion?" Foxxglove sat down opposite him. Pointing at her, he winked playfully as he plopped back into his seat.

Iris sat across from Declan, who said, "We ordered food and drinks for the table. I hope that's all right. I knew you were hungry and wouldn't want to wait."

"It's fine, Declan, thank you." The glass in front of Foxx had a frosty finish around the bottom and dark umber liquid inside. She and Iris clinked in cheers and took a swig. The drink instantly burned their throats.

Iris made a whooping sound followed closely by a cough. "That's rough."

"It is a bit rough," Foxx agreed, already feeling tendrils of the potent spirits tickling her brain.

"But effective." Declan took a sip from his glass.

A young man wearing a navy apron approached them with a bowl of greens and fresh vegetables. "Welcome ladies. I hope you're enjoying your drinks. The rest of your food is on its way, but I have your salad ready." He added a stack of bowls and forks to the table.

Iris smiled, her mouth salivating as the sight of food triggered her hunger. "This looks delicious. Thank you so much!" The man bowed to her and left the table. Sitting up in her seat to better examine the contents of the bowl, she noticed Orion staring at her with an irritated expression. Furrowing her brow, she snarked, "What is your issue now?"

Orion straightened his back and took a bowl from the stack, filling it with crisp salad greens. "No issue, Iris, I was just admiring your ability to flirt with every man you meet."

Iris' mouth dropped open, but Declan spoke before she could respond. "Don't start, Orion."

"I'm just saying, you flirt with me, you flirt with Dec, now the waiter. It's a little pathetic don't you think?"

Iris' face flushed a boiling shade of red. It took every drop of restraint to stay planted in her chair and not leap across the table. "I'm not flirting, Orion. It's called being nice, but it makes perfect sense that you would be unfamiliar with the behavior since you're not nice to *anyone*."

Orion opened his mouth to strike back, but Declan swore under his breath, and it drew his attention. "Seriously, Ri. Please stop."

"Can't we enjoy a nice meal together? This salad looks amazing." Foxx piled some greens into a bowl and offered it to Iris.

"And another thing." Iris ignored the bowl and took a long swig of her drink before setting it down too hard on the table. Declan met her eyes, and she saw his silent request to leave it alone, but she didn't want to. She was sick of Orion treating her like a dirty toy he didn't want to play with anymore. "What gives you the right to speak to me about flirting after you were so shameless with that busty receptionist? Talk about pathetic."

"Jealous, were you?" Orion taunted.

"Jealous you might treat someone else like garbage instead of me? No way. Maybe I should tell her you're a kidnapper. See how she feels about you then."

"Iris—"

Cutting Declan's sentence short, the waiter returned carrying two steaming plates. He seemed to notice the tension, but his smile remained firmly in place as he set the browned potatoes, smelling of delicious herbs, at the center of the table. Next to it, he set a plate piled with carrots sliced into thin strips. "We're only waiting on the meat now. Can I get you anything else at the moment?"

A lengthy silence followed. Iris and Orion glared at each other with nearly tangible bolts of rage erupting in the space between them. Declan observed Iris with reproach.

Foxx finally responded to the patient waiter. "I think we're all right for now, thank you." He nodded before rushing away, and Foxx tapped the table with her fork. "All right everyone, that's enough. We're stuck together for now, so can we please find ourselves stuck peacefully?" She stared at each of them individually until they acknowledged her and accepted her instruction. Orion was the last and most stubborn of the group, but he begrudgingly agreed to play nice. "Good. Now let's eat."

As Orion's anger dwindled, his tipsy cheerfulness returned. More than once, he caught Iris' eyes across the table. Each time, his friendly smile made her heart tick. He didn't say a single word to her throughout the entire meal and instead spent much of the time interacting with Foxx, while Iris and Declan talked amongst themselves.

Declan's alcohol consumption made it far easier for Iris to crack his outer shell, and she was having a little too much fun poking at it. She wondered if the fissures she'd been making would remain permanent this time, and even continue to grow. The moment she had the thought, she realized its irrelevance. The cracks would seal themselves back up the moment she and Foxx left. They had clothing and supplies now. Foxx had been exceptionally cordial with the men all evening, as if doing her best to keep any possible suspicions at bay, so Iris suspected the time for escape drew near.

Despite all odds, the foursome had fallen into a working routine. They'd figured out how to get along—for the most part. Iris wondered if they should stay with Declan and Orion, but knew deep down they could never truly be a team while being controlled. Orion, at least, would never see them as equal partners.

After their plates had been cleared, the girls said they wanted to bathe and departed the table. Declan and Orion remained in the pub, promising to head up shortly, and Foxx couldn't fathom the mens' trust in them. She and Iris could escape right that moment, and they wouldn't know until returning to their empty rooms.

When they reached the second floor, Foxx glimpsed a maid at the end of the hall and told Iris she could bathe first. Iris scurried off to the washroom, and Foxx strode the length of the hall, looking over her shoulder to make sure Orion and Declan hadn't followed them.

Noticing her approach, the maid ceased dusting and turned to face her with a kind smile. "Yes, ma'am, how may I help you?"

Foxx glanced back at the staircase again before answering in a near whisper. "I'm sorry to bother you, but do you happen to know how far we are from Jericho?"

"It's less than a day's journey on foot, ma'am. A long day with the heavy snow."

"Wow, that close?"

The maid nodded. "Yes, ma'am. Follow the mountain pass from here, and you'll run right into it." Foxx's gaze drifted as she calculated possibilities. "Is there anything else I can do for you, ma'am?"

"Will you please keep this conversation between us?"

"Of course." Bowing, she returned to her dusting.

Foxx hastened back to her room and got to work. With one eye on the door and ears listening for footsteps, she rummaged through Declan's pack. Pilfering some dried berries and nuts, she shoved them into the bottom of their new bag and refastened his buckles. She returned to her side of the bed as a knock sounded at the door. Scrambling to close her own pack, she dropped it at her feet and plopped onto the bed.

Declan paused inside the doorway and looked from her to the bag. She tried to smooth her pursed lips into a nonchalant smile, but knew she hadn't fooled him for a second. Her mind tore through her options as she waited for him to make a move. Her knife lay within reach, but Iris was likely already naked and in the bath. She didn't think she could injure him badly enough to give them time to escape, especially knowing Orion might be right behind him. She could stab him in the chest or slice his throat and sneak away. As long as he didn't scream, Orion may not know what she'd done until after they'd fled. But she'd never killed a human before, and despite everything, she didn't think she could live with herself if she did.

Declan stepped the rest of the way into the room and closed the door without a word. Foxx picked at her fingernails. When he reached his side of the bed, his eyes found his bag, and he stared at it for a long moment. Then he said, "The food here was great, wasn't it?"

Foxx nearly fell off the bed as his voice shattered the silence. When she realized what he'd said, she managed to choke out a hum of agreement.

Kicking off his boots, he laid down on his back, not bothering to get under the covers as he slid his hands behind his head and turned to look at her. "Did you get a bath yet?"

Letting out a breath, Foxx stumbled over her answer. "No, Iris is in there now. I was about to go give her a towel." She stood up. "I didn't see her carrying one."

"Orion is still downstairs." He latched onto her gaze, staring into her eyes as if reading every intention before simply saying, "Enjoy your bath." She spun and took a step in the direction of the door, but before she could take another, he spoke her name, and her heart lodged in her throat. "Maybe take your new water sleeve, and fill it up while you're in there. Then you have it if you need it."

Grabbing the empty bag, Foxx left the room without another word and hurried down the hall to the washroom. She knocked and entered, finding her sister sitting in the tub.

"Oh, thank goodness!" Iris exclaimed. "I forgot a towel." Foxx held it between them and faced away so she could dry off. When she whispered her name, Iris heard the tension in her voice and paused drying. "What is it?"

"I talked to the maid, and she said Jericho is close. Only a day's journey. We're leaving tonight after the men are asleep."

Iris stepped from the tub, wrapped the towel around her body, and touched Foxx's shoulder so she would face her again. "Are you sure?"

Foxx tucked a strand of hair behind Iris' ear. Neither had taken the time to trim their locks since their journey into the Wilds began. It hung all the way to her hips now. "Yes, I already packed our bag. I took a few things from Declan's, and I brought our waterskin so I could fill it up. Orion is still downstairs, but Declan is in bed."

"Okay. It's not going to be great traveling on no sleep."

"I know, but this may be our only real chance to escape. Once we're in the city, it will be easier to remain hidden. We can find a place to stay and sleep for as long as we need to." Foxx sensed Iris' hesitancy and knew more than lack of sleep fed her resistance. Still, she would not miss the opportunity. "Go back to your room, and go to bed. Get an hour or two if you can. I'll knock when it's time to go. Be ready."

C

When Iris returned to her room, she was grateful to find it empty. She didn't have the heart to face either of the men she'd grown to care about despite her efforts to hate them. In another life, under different circumstances, perhaps they could have been friends.

She wondered if Foxx had second thoughts, too, but knew her sister didn't often grow attached the way she did. From the beginning, Foxx's kindness had been a ploy to woo the men into passivity as she waited and prepared for this very moment. She'd gained their trust with the sole intention of making her escape.

Foxx was careful and smart, predominantly ruled by her head, and calculating. Iris lived by her heart, and her heart wanted to heal the brokenness inside Orion and tear down every single one of Declan's walls so she could find out exactly who he kept hidden behind them. They'd both revealed hints of their true natures, but what kind of bond might it take to see them in that light all the time: as they saw each other?

Knowing she needed to get to sleep, Iris towel dried her hair and left it hanging free of its pony, hoping it would dry completely before they ventured into the cold. She didn't have much to carry since Foxx had their bag, but she did find a small pouch in one of the dresser drawers and stuffed it with some of the tea sachets by the fireplace.

Climbing into bed, she snuggled beneath the layers, endeavoring to soak up enough warmth to carry her all the way to Jericho. As her eyes fell closed, a knock sounded at the door. She waited a moment, assuming Orion would come stumbling in without her needing to answer. When the door remained still, she dragged herself from the pelts and opened it to find Declan staring back at her.

The hallway had grown darker since the maids dimmed the lanterns, and Declan spoke in a hushed tone, as if the low light inspired a quiet voice. "Hello, Iris."

"Hi Declan." She leaned against the frame with her arms crossed over her chest. He seemed nervous and a little confused, making her feel confused as well. "Can I help you with something?"

"No, no. I just…" He shifted his weight from one foot to the other. His gaze dropped to his stockinged feet before rising again as he regained his courage. "I wanted you to know how sorry I am."

She furrowed her brow. "What are you sorry for?" Declan looked at her as if it were obvious, and she lowered her voice. "Oh, right. That whole kidnapping thing." She chuckled as a smile spread across his lips. "Well, I guess I forgive you. I think you've more than made up for it."

"Good." He examined her face, seeming to memorize every curve and crevasse. "I didn't mean to bother you. It's been a long day, and I'm sure you're tired, but I wanted to say it now, in case I didn't get to later."

"It would have been an equally acceptable apology in the morning," she jested, though her stomach felt sick with the deception. By the pained expression he attempted to conceal, she wondered if he suspected what they planned to do. "But still, I appreciate you saying it now." He nodded and shifted like he was about to walk away, but she said his name. Already she could sense his walls returning, her blatant lie sending him scurrying back behind his fortifications.

"Thank you. For helping me, I mean. With Orion mostly, but with other things as well. I know the situation is…" Her words faded, and memories from the Tree of Knowing resurfaced. She glanced at his hand, as if confirming its existence would prove the Tree's prediction. "I know the situation is difficult, but I'm really enjoying getting to know you."

Another smile tugged at his lips. "I'm enjoying getting to know you, too, Iris." He scrutinized her again, exhaling a slow breath. "I like your hair when it's down." Straightening, he continued awkwardly, "I mean, I always like it, but it's very nice when it's down like this."

A blush blossomed on her cheeks, and she fidgeted her fingers against her ribs, willing herself not to shy away from his serious gaze. "Thank you, Declan."

His fingers twisted the end of her white streak, and her blush flared deeper. "Merry night, Iris Belamour." Then he turned, stepped across the hall, and disappeared into his room without looking back.

C

Orion returned sometime later. Iris had been sleeping lightly, but the door's latch clicking into place roused her. He lumbered across the room and carelessly plopped his weight down on the bed.

Facing the fireplace, she remained still, pretending to sleep through his blundering. He wriggled atop the bed, and her body went rigid as his fingers slid over her waist. Her mind flew to her weapons, feet from her. Drunk as he seemed, she could easily take him out if he intended to try something dishonorable.

Then he pushed her waist, shaking her back and forth and saying her name. "Iris, are you awake?"

An annoyed sigh slipped through her lips. "I am now." She turned, pulling back the covers to see him better. He lay next to her with his torso propped up on his elbow. His eyes shined like glass in the lantern light. "What do you want?"

He smiled and didn't remove his hand from where it had slid from her waist to her stomach as she'd turned to him. His breath filled her nostrils, smelling of the sweet liquor they drank over dinner, and she scrunched up her nose.

"I will do better." He hiccuped, stumbling over his words. The hand on her stomach moved from side to side absentmindedly, and it made her shiver for many conflicting reasons. "Tomorrow, I mean. From now until… I'll try. I'll be better."

Iris blinked in disbelief. Now he would do better? Now that she planned to leave? "I don't have any idea what that means, Orion, nor do I care. Please shut up, and let me sleep." She rolled away from him, her heart hammering.

He nodded, understanding her reaction and knowing he

deserved it. He slid his arm from her hip and let his head fall to the pillow, passing out before removing his boots.

Iris listened as his breathing transformed into snoring. It hadn't been her intention to be so mean, but drunken promises couldn't be trusted. The moment the issues within him resurfaced, he would go right back to being awful, as had been the case every other time his kindness peeked through.

And regardless, they were leaving. So it didn't matter anyway.

She whispered his name several times with no response before sitting up and nudging him. He didn't budge.

When she picked up her weapons, the buckle sent clattering echoes through the whole room. Iris froze, and her eyes shot to Orion, but he didn't stir. Sighing relief, she picked up her jacket and boots and crept to the door. A shaft of light cut the room in half. Turning back, she wondered if this would be the last time she ever laid eyes on him. The Tree of Knowing had revealed Declan in her future but offered no guarantee Orion would be with him.

Her heart ached for him, and as she watched his body rise and fall in slumbering breaths, she wished she had more time to figure him out. More time to help him heal from whatever had broken him so thoroughly.

When she stepped out into the hall, she saw the maid Foxx had spoken to making her way up the staircase. She smiled at Iris before turning the opposite way down the hall.

Iris sat on the carpet to pull on her boots, knowing if she attempted to do it while standing, she would not succeed in doing it quietly. Then she stood and strapped her weapons belt to her waist as the door to Foxx and Declan's room opened. Freezing, her eyes bulged until she saw a flash of white hair.

Foxx backed out of the room and startled when she found Iris standing behind her. "Oh! You're already awake." Iris reached for the bag in Foxx's hand, but Foxx stopped her. "Let's go downstairs first."

When they reached the top of the steps, a low whistle drew their attention, and they turned to see the maid waving them toward her. With cautious curiosity, they followed her to an empty room. Holding the door open, she said, "You can get dressed in here."

"Why are you helping us?" For a moment, Foxx wondered if it might be some kind of trick to lock them in the room so she could alert the men of their attempted escape.

"I can tell when women are not happy in their company. I was once in a situation of pretending as well. A stranger helped me, as I am helping you. Now hurry in here before anyone else sees you. When you are ready to leave, I will show you to the side door."

Inside the room, they layered up for the cold. As Iris slid her arms through her final coat, Foxx noticed an unfamiliar pouch at the bottom of the bag. Drawing Iris' attention, she pulled it out and showed it to her. "Is this yours?" When Iris shook her head, Foxx dumped the pouch on the bed, and both girls gasped as coins tumbled out into a pile. Several *faeru* shined amongst *aeses* and *metts*, and a little digging revealed two *terras*.

Iris' eyes grew wide. "Foxxglove, did you steal money from them?" She looked warily at the maid, but saw no judgment.

"Of course not!" Foxx lifted her hands in innocence. "I'll admit, I did think about it, but I decided against it, I swear."

"Declan? Did he know we were leaving? He came to see me."

Foxx thought of the strange way he'd reacted when returning from dinner and realized he must have added the coins to their bag after she left for the washroom. "Maybe he did."

Iris felt a twinge of regret at the undeniable proof. Declan had known they planned to escape and had helped them. His nervous behavior in her doorway had been a concealed farewell. "Maybe we shouldn't go." Iris looked back and forth between the money and her sister's puzzled expression.

At last, Foxx handed the woman a *faeru* for helping them and returned the rest to the pouch. "Declan made his choice. If he knew we planned to leave, he could have chosen to come with us."

"He wouldn't leave Orion. They're family. Just like I wouldn't leave you."

Foxx nodded. "Exactly."

"If you are ready, we should hurry," the maid said.

Foxx buckled the bag shut and swung it over her shoulders before pulling up her hood. Iris shouldered the water skin, and both girls slipped on their gloves.

When they stepped outside, the snow came up to their ankles. An untouched layer covered the entire plateau, but flakes had ceased falling from the sky. Potted evergreens glowed with dimming light as the magic of the orädi faded, and the new moon of Ammil offered little illumination to move by. Still, the snow lit the world in a way they'd never experienced, seeming to reflect the light of the stars and paint everything in a dusky gray. It could be nearly dawn with how bright everything appeared, or even a stormy day.

When the maid closed the door, Foxx and Iris were entirely alone. Iris gestured for Foxx to lead on, and they trudged across the silent plateau, following the road to the mountain pass that would lead them all the way to Jericho.

CHAPTER 26

BIRDS OF PREY

Pollux's office remained one of the few places in Castle Solís where the King could enjoy time to himself. His staff didn't often bother him behind that oak door, except on occasions of emergencies or when the time came for his afternoon tea. Pollux found sanctuary seated at his desk with his quills and stacks of correspondence. He liked the smell of sealing wax the moment it reached its melting point, as well as the scent of fresh parchment.

There was no end to the paperwork of a king. Pollux spent most of his days sorting through requests, answering letters, and settling disputes. Not only did he consider it a king's responsibility to address matters personally, but it gave him something to do in the privacy of his office and allowed him a smidgen of control in a life he had very little control over.

As he sipped his afternoon tea, promptly provided each day at two hours past highsun, he read over a letter from the governor of Falcon's Quarry regarding a lost export of gazelle meat. The Savanni governor promised a new order would be shipped out to replace it but suggested the King send soldiers to determine what happened to the missing transport. According to him, criminal activity against the Thrones seemed likely.

The transport had been on its way to Tunturia, in Crystavium, and since Tunturia was the main supplier of provisions to the Ashgate Fortress, the looting came as no surprise. The prison had been converted from one of the old Monastery's, making it a common target for rebels who thought themselves revolutionaries.

In his return letter, King Pollux assured the governor he would contact the Warden to let him know the delivery would be behind schedule and send troops to inspect the situation.

When he finished sealing the letter with his royal insignia, a knock sounded at the door. He looked up to see Hector stepping into the office.

"May I interrupt you for a moment, Your Majesty?"

The King placed the letter in a basket of outgoing mail and waved him forward. Then he twisted his signet ring back onto his finger and folded his hands together on the desk. "You have news for me? Not stopping here instead of the Hall to avoid our magnificent Queen, I trust?"

As that was precisely the reason he'd come to the King's office and not the Hall of Sunsets where he knew the Queen to be, Hector felt momentarily nauseous. When he saw the upturn of Pollux's lips, he registered the King's jest and released a breath. "Of course not, sire. I was heading to the Hall of Sunsets to speak with both of you when your courtier happened past me and told me you were in your private quarters."

Hector cast a glance over his shoulder, worried the Queen might somehow overhear and detect the lie, and stepped to the side so he could see the door in his peripherals.

The King chuckled. "I understand. Do tell me your news. I shall relay it to the Queen myself if I deem it necessary."

"Yes, Your Majesty. I have further reports of the Belamour sisters." Hector paused, restraining the fidgeting fingers at his back. "And also, possibly, of Prince Alexander, if you would like to hear it."

Pollux leaned forward. "Go on, Hector. Start with my son. And keep your voice low, if you please."

Another knock had the door opening without invitation. Her Majesty the Queen strode in wearing a jasper gown that hugged her hips. Gold cording laced up the spine of her bodice, pulling the fabric tight around her ribs and effectively exhibiting her chest. She stopped in the middle of the room, looking like a centerpiece of dramatic artistry; macabre and sinister in a way that makes onlookers give a wide berth, but so tantalizing they find themselves unable to glance away. Her hand perched delicately on the curve of her hip and her chin lifted enough for her eyes to look down on anyone she spoke to. "Commander, I hear you have news for us."

Hector cursed the courtier he'd spoken to, knowing the man must have run promptly to the Queen.

Now leaning with his elbows on the desk, King Pollux massaged his temples. "Welcome, my dear. I told Hector we should summon you before discussing anything."

"I am certain you did, my darling." Sirena dipped her chin to her husband before returning her attention to Hector. "Well? Out with it."

Hector cleared his throat and forced his eyes from her bewitching physique. "The Belamour sisters are on their way to Jericho." He paused, intrigued by the twitch in her jaw provoked by the name of her rival city. "They were seen last evening dining at Peregrine Manor with two men. I believe they will be entering Jericho any time now, if they haven't already."

The King's eyes brightened. "What men?"

"Based on the description, I suspect Orion O'Connell and Silas Declanaire. Though I'm only speculating."

The Queen's face flushed with anger. "And why exactly would O'Connell and Declanaire be with the Belamour sisters?"

"If I had to guess, I would say they're helping them find Sawyer, though the sisters may not know the mens' true motives. The original order for the Reko Raptors was to turn him and the Artifact over in exchange for their freedom, was it not?"

The Queen began pacing in the cramped room, fury radiating off of her in ripples.

"You say they're on their way to Jericho?" the King asked.

Sirena said, "And we know they stayed at the Monastery in Metsa Sateen. They must know about the keys. I had hoped—oh, but of course they would know."

The King rose to his feet, his wife's name on his lips. "It's significantly more likely they're hoping to receive aid from the Konungr."

"Which isn't much better. With Valerian on their side…" She let the sentence fall away, not wishing to speak misfortune into existence.

Pollux circled his desk to stand in front of her. "The soldiers never knew about the keys. Not even the Raptors. Very few alive today know these truths, and even less believe."

"*She* knew. Amaryllis knew." The Queen cursed her own foolish heart for past alliances. "If she spoke to them—to Foxxglove—of the Morrow, then it's entirely possible that is exactly what they plan to do."

"We have no way of knowing what she told them. They were so young when she passed."

"But of course she would have told them, Pollux! They have been conspiring against me from the very beginning!" In a low voice, she growled, "She never truly left him. A small part of her always clung to what they had, and even after her death, their bond thwarts my every turn."

Pollux grazed her cheek, pulling her scattered eyes back to his. "All will be well, my love. We will find a way to endure, as we always have." Sirena unshackled a breath, and Pollux smiled.

"I'm sorry, Your Majesties, but I'm feeling a little lost." Hector's voice startled the sovereigns, as if they'd forgotten his presence in the room. "What keys are you referring to?"

"Commander." Sirena met Hector where he stood, stopping so close her sugary perfume had his head swimming. She cradled one of his hands in her own with an expression so sincere, he nearly dropped to his knees in reverence.

His throat swelled with confused emotions. "Your Majesty?"

"We need you, Hector. More than ever before." Sirena lifted a hand away to reveal a set of circular pins in his palm.

Hector's eyes bulged at the sight. "These are…"

Pollux tried to interrupt, but Sirena cut him off.

"No, Pollux. This is our only choice. We are running out of time and options."

"You wish for me to reestablish the Reko Raptors?" Hector asked, unable to comprehend the reason for such an extreme maneuver. Sirena had hated the Raptors. Their power outside the authority of the King's Legion made them difficult to control. He couldn't fathom what would prompt her desire to reform them. Especially since the nature of their disbandment had obvious ties to the current situation. He tilted his hand, and torchlight danced across the owl emblems.

A log toppled in the fireplace, breaking the silence and making Hector flinch. Sirena put her hand back on top of his. Helplessness bled into her features in a way Hector had never witnessed, and he wondered if he might be having some kind of bizarre hallucination.

"Yes. That is exactly what I wish for you to do."

"But the Rap—"

"Then call them whatever you like, Pollux!" Sirena's head snapped to her husband. "Call them the Hummingbirds for all I care! Or don't call them anything at all. We need them. The Legion has failed us, and if the Belamours are already in Jericho, we can't afford to send an army to the city and risk all out war with the Mad King."

"What could be so important to risk any of this?" Hector asked.

Sirena returned her fearful gaze to him. "You must take your most trusted soldiers to Jericho and retrieve them immediately. You may appoint a lieutenant if you wish, but you are to remain with them until the mission is complete. We cannot allow this to continue. Speak to no one but the unit you take with you."

Giving up his argument, Pollux shook his head. "It would be to your benefit to remain unseen by the Konungr's Guard."

"There is no way to enter Jericho but through the front gate," Hector said.

The Queen nodded, her eyes drifting in calculation. "Then so be it. The Belamours must be captured. They cannot be allowed to leave the city except in your custody."

Hector couldn't unravel the motives beneath her desperation, but in that moment, he felt so overcome with veneration, he thought he might willingly do anything she asked. In her vulnerability she seemed almost human, and despite past discrepancies, he felt privileged to obey her—as privileged as the day he joined the Legion with every intention of honorably serving his sovereigns and the citizens of Arkaemor. He dropped to one knee and bowed his head so it touched the back of her hand. "Yes, Your Majesty. I will see it done. I will gather a team and leave right away."

She pulled him back to his feet. "You know the way. Take only those you can trust. You will travel through the barrier and arrive in Jericho by the next moonrise. Waste no time. If you do not find them before it's too late, we are certain to lose everything."

Hector saw gloss pooling above her lower lashes, and it rattled him. Her fright and torment shook the foundations of everything he knew to be true about the Immortal Queen of Arkaemor. She was steadfast, wicked, and strong. Unmoved, unchanging, and impervious to all forms of suffering.

Or so he'd thought.

Only once in all of his years serving had he seen her erratic with tears. She'd burst into the castle in a bundle of raw agony after Amaryllis Belamour had been discovered dead. But those tears had been of loss and mourning, not defeat and fear. Not like this.

Hector pressed a kiss to her knuckles. "You have my word, Your Majesty. I will not let you down." Then he bowed to the distressed King and hastened from the room.

C

After summoning five of his most trusted soldiers to the warroom, Hector made his way there to suit up and await their arrival. It had been centuries since an actual war gathered people to the chamber, but Hector liked to use it on occasion for meetings amongst the High Legion. An oversized table displaying a complete map of Arkaemor took up the majority of the room's space. He pulled out a stool but decided against sitting and pushed it back under the table. Clasping his hands together, he exhaled a breath.

The first of his team to arrive was Jax Blackmoor. A captain in the King's High Legion, Jax was the man Hector trusted most in the world. He strode into the room with a rifle strapped to his back and a pistol at his hip. In addition to the standard King's Legion uniform, a layer of chainmail lined the inside of his shirt, and plates of black armor rested on top. The bendable armor had been crafted of palm-sized metal plates resembling reptilian scales. It was sturdy and effective but also light and maneuverable.

When Jax crossed the threshold, he approached Hector with a salute before pulling him into a hug. "Good to see you, Commander. It's been a long time."

Hector kept his hand on Jax's shoulder. "You've been keeping busy in Crystavium."

"Rebels are causing quite a bit of trouble for us at the moment, yes. Your timing was impeccable. I returned to the city with the new moon. Though I'm to leave for Tunturia again in the morning."

"If you join my team, you won't be returning to Crystavium for a while."

"I'm sure they won't be pleased to hear you've summoned me away, but I'll never complain about a reprieve from Ashgate. What is the mission, Hector? And why so secretive?"

Hector clapped Jax on the back and turned his eyes to the table, his hand falling to the pocket carrying the Raptor pins. "Wait until the others arrive, and I'll explain it to everyone at once."

Though he hadn't heard anyone else enter, Jax felt a tap on his shoulder. He turned, but saw no one. Then a fist connected with his jaw, and he swore. Regaining his balance, he pulled his pistol.

"Getting a little slow, eh Jax?" A woman stood at the muzzle of his gun, smirking. "Or is your excuse that Marie kept you out too late and you're simply over tired?"

Jax tilted his head, confused by her remark given that he currently held a gun to her forehead. Then he felt pressure at his side and looked down to find the tip of a dagger pressed beneath his ribcage.

"Shall we test who's faster?" Raven Nightshade winked and slipped the dagger back into one of the many scabbards on her person. Like Jax, she wore High Legion battle gear, to include her usual fingerless gloves. Though she didn't have a proper title naming her High Legion, Raven had a unique skill set allowing her access to certain perks afforded to those above her station.

Jax released the bullet from its chamber and put the weapon back in its holster. "Always great to see you, Raven." After running his hand across his sore jaw, he slid it back over dark hair.

"Commander." Raven dipped her chin.

Hector returned the gesture before glancing at Jax. "Marie?"

Jax grinned.

Raven crossed her arms. "No point remembering the name, Hector. You know it will be someone new next week anyway."

"Next week I'll likely be back in Crystavium, and Marie will be all but forgotten." Jax glanced at Hector. "You know how hard it is to resist those Tunturia girls."

Shoving him, Raven demanded, "What exactly are you implying?" Jax zipped his lips.

Hector laughed but changed the subject. "Raven has been hard at work in the dens. A few cropped up in the city over the past few months."

"Sil ōnni hit Inaravale, too?" Jax asked. "I guess no city is safe, but I'd have thought it less likely in the royal regions given the prosperity here. Though I suppose we have low-income districts like anywhere else."

Raven nodded. "Not even the Queen herself can stop sil ōnni. It's ruthless. And don't think the higher class immune. I traced one of the dens back to a banker in the royal district living blocks from the castle and high as a kite. Addiction ends in the slums, but it starts where the money is."

Jax scratched the scruff of his beard. "I'm surprised to hear you're working in the drug dens given your history with sil. Has it been hard to deal with? I'd think your expertise could be better used elsewhere."

"Taking care of my father gave me the perfect experience for the job."

Jax furrowed his brow. "That doesn't mean it's easy. I'm sure our commander would send you elsewhere if it's too much."

Hector looked between them. He hadn't considered how being around people in the throes of addiction might affect her, only that she had the appropriate skills to hunt out the dens. "Raven, I—"

"It's fine, Hector. I don't mind. Jax is just being overprotective." She narrowed her eyes at Jax for opening his big mouth.

Wyatt and Marshal Hearne arrived next, stepping into the room with matching bows and quivers. Hector had recruited and trained the brothers years ago and considered them two of the best archers the Legion had to offer.

A large and burly man named Dominic Ives entered last and closed the door behind him. He and Hector had joined the Legion around the same time, and despite the drastic differences in their personalities, they'd gotten along from the moment they met. His weapon of choice was a rocket-launching bazooka, but he generally only carried a short-barreled shotgun, several hand grenades, and a hatchet.

Hector's hand slid into his pocket as he gathered everyone around the table. "I want to thank all of you for coming under such mysterious conditions. I've selected you to assist me, should you choose to accept, on a mission for the King and Queen. I'm sure you've all heard of the special operations unit known as the Reko Raptors." As the pins spilled from Hector's hand and clattered against the table, an intrigued energy spread through the room like a bolt of electricity. The group leaned in to get a closer look, though no one reached to pick one up.

"If you didn't know, the Raptors were a group of soldiers who worked directly under the King and Queen. After the betrayal of their lieutenant, the sovereigns no longer wanted any special units working independent of the Legion and the outcome was the disbandment of the Reko Raptors. However, the current situation is a desperate one, and the Queen has instructed me to put together a new team. My most trusted team. Unfortunately for all of you, there is no time to think it over. You must decide right now: are you in or are you out?"

Silence fell over the room as everyone waited for someone else to speak first.

Then Raven asked, "With what the name Reko Raptor now implies and everything these pins represent, what would inspire the King and Queen to go down this road again?"

"Something serious." Wyatt pulled his fingers over the fletching of his arrows.

"The Queen suggested we could call you the Hummingbirds, if you prefer." Hector chuckled as Raven's mouth dropped open.

"She did not."

Hector picked up a pin, flipping it through his fingers as his eyes tracked the movement. It depicted a great horned owl encircled in a ring with wings outstretched. Then he tapped it against the table. "I think we should try to remember what these pins *used* to represent. Their purpose from the beginning was to serve the citizens of Arkaemor to the highest standards, regardless of the cost and regardless of the danger to themselves. They were warriors, trusted and revered."

"And you're picking us to fill these roles?" As the youngest of the group, Marshal had a hard time imagining what living up to those standards might look like. Not only that, he wondered what it would take for a new band of Raptors to change the stigma of the past.

Hector clasped his wrist with his opposite hand. "I was instructed to recruit the best."

Jax offered a lazy salute above thick brows. "Well, you know I'm in, Commander."

"Hell, yeah." Raven lifted a shoulder. "Definitely in." The others agreed.

Hector grabbed the golden pin. "Jax, I name you Lieutenant Blackmoor, of the Reko Raptors. Sawyer left this behind when he defected. I now entrust it to you." Jax grinned as Hector pinned the emblem to his chest. Hector encouraged the others to grab one of the remaining pins, each displaying the same horned owl, but crafted in burnished bronze.

"Though the previous Raptors didn't work under the Legion commander, the Queen has instructed me to stay with you until the mission is complete. I'm honestly not sure what happens after. Perhaps the unit will be disbanded once again. Perhaps our sovereigns will be pleased with your work and wish for the group to continue on. Either way, as long as you're Raptors you take your orders directly from Lieutenant Blackmoor or myself. Aside from that, no other soldier, regardless of rank, can stand above you."

"Wraith is not going to be happy about this." Raven smirked as Marshal and Wyatt nudged each other with delight, causing their blond ringlets to jiggle.

"Dagon Wraith has no say here," Hector said. "Our mission is to enter Jericho and recover two women—"

"Women? What's the royal majesties want wit' two women? Ain't we got enough of 'em here?" Dominic's Reginaterran accent was brash and untidy. Though Hector and Jax also spoke with the common intonation of the territory, they'd been raised in the city around the higher class, so their cadences were faint.

Raven scolded, "If you shut your big mouth, Dom, I am positive Hector is about to share that with us."

"Two specific women, Dom: Foxxglove and Iris Belamour. Daughters of Sawyer Belamour, the previous lieutenant of the Reko Raptors." As Hector spoke the familiar names, the faces of the company lit with understanding. "The Queen thinks they have discovered something harmful to her and to Arkaemor, and she wants them recovered as soon as possible."

"Mucking things up, jus' like they dad and mum." Dominic pressed his fist into the surface of the table.

"So it would seem," Hector agreed.

"They're in Jericho?" Wyatt scratched behind his ear. "Is that going to be an issue for us given Reginaterra's unstable political relations with the royals of Cordillera?"

"Not if we don't get caught," Raven remarked.

Scuffing his jaw, Jax said, "The Konungr is crafty. It may prove difficult to remain under his radar for long."

"I would prefer to avoid confrontation with the Konungr and his Guard, but since we'll be walking through the front gate, he'll likely be alerted immediately." Hector looked down at the map, his eyes lingering on the symbol indicating the city of Jericho. "Our best bet will be to get in and out as quickly as possible and try to remain out of sight while conducting our search. I don't know all the details or why the Queen so desperately wants these women found, but they're on their way to Jericho right now, and it is our job to find them."

"Sounds like as good a plan as any," Wyatt said.

"There's something else." Hector lifted his eyes from the map to look at them. "There's a chance we might find them traveling with two ex-soldiers. Ex-Raptors, actually. Orion O'Connell and Silas Declanaire."

Raven sucked in a sharp breath as fury ignited her features. "Silas, huh?" She cracked her knuckles against her palm. The brothers met eyes again, entertained by the tiny, yet fierce, warrior next to them. Wyatt pushed her shoulder playfully, knocking her free of her stewing.

"We don't know the intentions of O'Connell and Declanaire. They may be aiding the women hoping to betray them and turn Sawyer over to the King and Queen. Or they may have other motives. Until we know for sure, we treat them as targets alongside Foxxglove and Iris."

"The plan is to retrieve the targets and bring them safely back to Inaravale, correct?" Jax asked.

"That is correct."

Dominic propped a hand on his hatchet. "And how do you s'pose we get ourselves all the way to Jericho before these girls move on?"

Hector shared a glance with Jax and Raven. "The way we do that, Dom, is by letting you and the Hearne brothers in on one of the world's best kept secrets."

☾

Queen Sirena stormed into her bedroom and closed the door in Renegard's face. Marching to her vanity, she stared at herself in the looking glass before slamming her palms on the vanity's surface, scattering jars of makeup.

Renegard knocked and spoke to her through the door, but she ignored him.

Kaen shifted his wings and squawked. Smoke blew from his beak, a common tell he felt stressed or uncomfortable.

"Hush, Kaen." Sirena stroked the drakinferno's cage before flipping the hook on the door and pulling it open. The dragon stomped wildly. "That's right, my baby. It's time for you to go on a little trip." She held her arm near the cage and the drakinferno stepped toward it, pulling his wings tightly around himself to better fit through the door. Clutching her arm, he tried not to hurt his mistress with his sharp talons. She escorted him to the window, stroking his back as he stretched his wings out wide. Sirena closed her eyes and drew him closer, touching her forehead to the dragon's own. His eyelids dropped closed as he took in the images she showed him. "Fly to Jericho and watch for the sisters."

The drakinferno caressed his mistress's cheek in answer. After another squawk, he shifted his feet against her arm, readying to take off. The Queen opened the window pane and held her arm out into the cool air as Kaen pushed off into the sky.

C

After their discussion in the warroom, Hector provided High Legion armor to Dominic and the Hearne brothers, and each of the five Raptors pinned an owl to their chest.

The closest barrier took three hours to reach on horseback. As they traveled, Hector explained how to jump the barriers with very simple instructions: focus on the desired destination, and the barrier will handle the rest.

A man who owned a farmhouse on the outskirts of Reginaterra stabled their horses. Like his father before him, he had manned the royal stables on the western barrier for much of his life. Hector liked the man because he took exceptional care of the horses. Better even —in his opinion—than the Legion stables in Inaravale.

Wyatt, Marshal, and Dominic couldn't conceal their amazement at the outer barrier. Rather than the transparent walls separating the territories, the wall around the outer edge was black as tar and shimmered like starlight, even in the darkness of the night. It rippled in constant motion, as the disturbed surface of a lake reflects a galaxy sky.

Hector explained that most people aren't aware the outer barriers exist, despite them surrounding the entirety of Arkaemor, because of an enchantment that subconsciously forces onlookers to shy away from it.

"Freaky," Marshal and Wyatt exclaimed in unison. Wyatt added,

"I can feel it. Like my stomach wants me to choose between vomiting and looking away."

Hector crossed through the black wall first, stepping out on the other side high in the Lunalakota Mountains of Cordillera. Raven followed him through, leaving Jax behind to help the first timers make their maiden voyage after explaining with very scant evidence that it was obviously his turn.

The Hearne brothers crossed after Raven, stepping out onto the mountain ridge moments later. Dominic followed, laughing from deep in his stomach, and Jax came through last, taking a deep breath of mountain air to combat the strain of such a long transport.

"That was awesome." Wyatt inhaled and exhaled as his eyes explored the scenery. He turned back to face the wall, now even more visible in the brightness of Cordillera. "Took my breath away though. I wasn't expecting that."

"The longer the distance, the more time without oxygen," Hector said.

"Why doesn't everyone know how to do that?" Marshal put his hands on his head to give his lungs maximum access to the cool air.

Raven said, "Imagine the chaos if the whole world could travel so far with such ease. Imagine that knowledge in the hands of criminals."

Hector nodded. "Only the High Legion and a few trusted others are privy to the ability. And the royals, of course."

Jax adjusted his rifle and pulled on a pair of gloves. "Some of the rebels know, too, and we deal with a lot of annoying complications because of it."

Dominic clapped Hector hard on the back. "You're full'a tricks, ain't ya, Commander?"

"What's this?" Jax knelt to examine the ground at the foot of the barrier. Raven lit a small torch and handed it to him.

Crouching at Jax's side, Hector touched the dark grass lining the wall. "The earth is turning black." He looked at his hand to see if the perplexing color left a residue on his fingers.

Jax ripped off a piece of the charcoal grass and stood up, handing it to Raven who drew it close.

"Is it charred?" She checked her own fingers to find them clean. Then she held it to her nose and took a whiff. "It doesn't smell burned, but even the snow seems to be avoiding it."

Wyatt pressed his boot across the clear line between the

blackened ground and the fresh snow, causing the snow that touched the mysterious earth to melt away instantly. "It didn't look like this on the other side, did it?" Jax shook his head, and Hector shrugged, unsure how to comprehend the phenomenon.

Marshal shivered and hugged himself. "It's cold here! We should have prepared better for snow."

Wyatt said, "Some of us *did* prepare for snow. And *some* of us refused to listen to others' advice regarding the temperature of snow." Marshal smacked his brother's head. Wyatt responded by punching him in the stomach.

"Enough." Hector stood and faced the city. The starry night lit the snow covered path and reflected the distant peaks of the mountains. "We have to hoof it, but we can be there before sunrise. Lieutenant?"

"Raptors, move out." Following Jax, the team started down the trail toward the City of the Moon.

C

Thick snow made the mountain path difficult to travel. Foxx and Iris found it impossible to hold a conversation between ragged breaths, so for the most part, they journeyed in the eerie silence of Cordillera with nothing but the swishing of boots crushing snow to accompany them.

Even with their added layers and the rigorous hike inflaming their muscles, their bodies felt numb. If they hadn't waited for Declan to supply them with proper attire, they felt certain they would have frozen to death.

When the sun began to rise, they stopped for a break to scarf some food and admire the sky's exquisite palette of morning colors.

Iris swallowed a swig of water, her thoughts elsewhere. The men would be waking soon, if they hadn't already. "Do you think Declan will try to slow them down?"

Foxx shoved some dried fruit into her mouth and swallowed before answering. "I honestly don't know. I would like to think so, but we also know how relentless Orion can be. He will definitely be pushing to find us as soon as possible." She washed the fruit down with some water and handed the bag back to Iris.

"You really hate him, don't you?"

"Who? Orion? No, I wouldn't say I hate him. He's very broken, and it seems like a big part of the blame rests on our father. I don't trust him, nor do I like the way he treated us—especially you—but I also think I might understand him." Knowing her sister's heart, Foxx added, "That doesn't mean I hope we see him again."

Iris studied the snow at her feet. "So what's the plan once we get to Jericho?"

"Find somewhere to sleep. Visit the Monastery. Hopefully we'll understand how to proceed from there, like we did at Lacuna Kaput."

"And we have to find Asher, right? He has the other keys. Maybe even the keys we had from Savanni and the Wilds."

Foxx's stomach twisted when Iris said his name. From the moment they'd fled Peregrine Manor, she hadn't ceased obsessing over how they might find Asher within the walls of such a huge city. "We won't get to Celestelvyra without him." It was her turn to carry the pack, so she pulled it from Iris' shoulders and slid it onto her own. "Ready?"

They pressed on, hiking the remainder of the day. Eventually, the sun slipped below the mountains and the sky darkened with barely a sliver of a rising moon to light their way. Frost had crept so profoundly into their bones they thought they may never thaw. Their lethargy felt so overbearing, they had no idea how they managed to remain on two feet. After a few hours of hiking in the dark, the moon reached its peak, and the road turned north. Before them, at the top of the hill, they at last saw the walls surrounding the great city of Jericho.

CHAPTER 27

CITY OF THE MOON

The mountain pass led Foxx and Iris to the city's entrance, where a soldier in military garb stood sentinel by an iron gate. Rather than the royal reds they were used to seeing, he wore a uniform of light gray and plum. A silver moon stitched to his chest filled Foxx with hope.

"It is very late. What are such young ladies doing traveling to our city at this hour?"

Fighting her languor, Foxx answered, "We're looking for our friend. He was heading this way and may have arrived within the past few days."

The Guard tilted his head. "Many travelers come and go from these gates."

"Then may we enter? As you've said, it's late, and we're exhausted."

After eyeing their weapons and cold-chapped faces, he bowed and stepped aside. "Go in peace, young travelers."

Dipping their heads in return, Foxx and Iris passed through the gate. A dusting of snow overlayed the ground at their feet, a stark contrast to the amount piling outside the city walls, but neither girl had the energy to overanalyze the peculiarity. They entered a plaza with a fountain carved into a bighorn ram at its center. Foxx observed the ram in sleepy amazement. In her mind's eye, she saw the magnificent creature who'd spoken to her after the Queen's storm.

Deciding it safest to avoid an inn right inside the entrance, they crossed the square and followed a road leading away from the gate in search of a more inconspicuous location. They ambled on jelly-filled legs for two blocks until seeing a sign for the White Luna Inn.

"I like the sound of that." Iris' voice emerged thick with fatigue, as though her jaw felt too cold and tired to open properly.

"Let's see if they have a room available."

Crossing the threshold, they found a man asleep in a chair behind a desk. Foxx pulled back her hood and cleared her throat, prompting the man to jump to his feet. "I'm so sorry, ladies! Will you be needing a room?"

Foxx nodded. "If you have a vacancy, that would be lovely. We've traveled a long way and are in desperate need of sleep."

"I imagine so." The man looked down at a notebook on the desk. "Might I have your name?" Iris and Foxx shared a tired glance, unable to decide in their weariness whether or not they should lie. Noticing their silent communication, he offered, "Or perhaps we can discuss names after you've had some sleep?" He retrieved a key from under the counter and handed it over. "Up the stairs, second room on the left."

They thanked him and dragged their feet up the narrow staircase. Once in the room, they removed their boots and coats and collapsed into bed.

C

Hector and his company entered the city as the sun began to rise.

The man guarding the gate had not been happy about granting more Legion soldiers entry, but he stepped aside after threatening to inform the Konungr of their presence.

Hector walked through first, followed by Jax, who nodded to the scowling Guard. Raven waggled her fingers, and Marshal scrunched his features into a humorous expression. Wyatt shoved him past the Guard and dipped his head in silent apology for his brother's antics. Dominic walked by with both hands resting on his stomach, his wavy orange locks flopping as his chest quaked with laughter.

Hector chose an unremarkable tavern on the outskirts of the entrance plaza. As they passed the fountain, Raven stopped to admire it until Dominic nudged her forward.

When they reached the front door of their chosen establishment, Hector halted them. "It's still early. We're going to head in here and try to get a few hours of rest before we begin our search." He looked pointedly at the Hearne brothers and Dominic. "*No* hanging out in the pub. Get yourselves some sleep, and I will wake you soon."

☽

As the city began to awaken, Asher roused from a restless sleep. He'd spent the entire previous day lingering near the entrance plaza watching the gate and willing Foxx and Iris to arrive. He wanted to reconnect with them before exploring the Monastery, but his efforts had been fruitless.

In Petrichor, Pearl told him she had seen the girls being escorted from the city by two men, though she'd insisted they weren't dressed like the King's Legion.

He'd left a message for them at Lacuna Kaput after retrieving the rainforest stone but had no way of knowing if they'd made it to the waterfall or found the hidden tunnel behind it. He had no idea who had taken them or where they would have gone. They'd been separated for an entire month. For all he knew, they could be traveling in the opposite direction.

He believed the Creator worked in His own ways, and that if they were meant to be reunited, they would be. He tried to have faith in Elohim's plans and allow that peace to wash over him, but they'd come so far on this journey, and it wouldn't feel right completing it without them. On top of that, the idea of never seeing them again felt inconceivable, especially after how long he'd spent searching.

Still, as much as he wanted to wait, hoping against hope they would appear, he couldn't keep putting his mission on hold while the world fell to pieces. He felt Elohim's tug on his heart and knew what he needed to do. With that in mind, he headed downstairs, tipped his hood to Gabriel, and strode out into the city.

The Monastery in Jericho stood like a castle against the northwestern wall. Not only was it the first and most famous of all the Monasteries, it was also the largest and most grand. The people of Jericho fought hard to keep the building in one piece despite Sirena's attempts to destroy it.

Asher already had an idea of where the key might have been

kept. According to the records, a hidden staircase led to a basement treasury. Though most of the valuables kept there had likely been looted, he thought the key would have been effectively hidden.

Signs all over the building warned trespassers to keep out, but he walked past them. Ducking through the door hanging by a single hinge, he climbed over the debris and entered the most ancient Monastery of the Morrow.

C

Hector sat on the edge of his bed, staring out the window at the square below. It had ceased snowing for the moment, and the plaza had filled with the luncheon rush. He needed to wake the others so they could begin their search, but he hadn't been able to drag himself from his ruminations. His body felt heavy, and the thought of rising to his feet felt almost daunting.

Raven stirred from sleep in the bed opposite his and rolled onto her side. Blinking away sleepy sand, she observed him, and his position mystified her. Hector's posture was habitually flawless. In all the years she'd known him, she'd rarely seen him slouch.

He sighed, and his shoulders drooped deeper, as if dragged down by weights.

She pulled the blanket back and slid her legs off the side of the bed. "Did you get any sleep?" Hector didn't turn from the window, but his lips pressed into a fine line.

They hadn't brought a change of clothes. Hector had hoped the mission would be short and sweet, and he had encouraged them to pack light. Raven pulled on her boots and tied her hair back into its usual braid, allowing the shorter strands framing her face to fall away as she wove it down to her tailbone. "What are you thinking about?"

Hector almost answered, *Johnathan.* "I'm trying to figure out how this can all go smoothly. If the women are with O'Connell and Declan, things could get tricky." Her brow creased at the mention of Silas's name, and though he didn't look her way, he sensed her reaction. "Is that going to be an issue for you?" He knew he should have asked about it before leaving Inaravale, but he'd feared her answer.

She scowled at his lack of faith in her loyalty. "No, of course not."

At last, he turned to her, and his dark gaze sent a shiver down her spine. "I need to know you're with me on this."

"I'm with you." She willed him to read the truth in her eyes. She had no intention of betraying him for Silas. Silas left. *He* betrayed *them*. Betrayed her. "Silas will not be an issue."

"So if I order you to take him down, if it comes to that, you will follow orders?" Hector scrutinized her expression. He wanted to believe her, but he knew her history with Declan far exceeded his own. He struggled to guess how he would handle it if removing Declan from the situation became the only option. Could he truly take out Ryder's son? After everything?

He hoped he wouldn't have to find out.

"I will follow you, Commander. To my death, if necessary." Swallowing hard, Raven added, "Or to his." Hector turned back to the window, and she studied his profile, attempting to decipher every thought and worry. "We don't know for sure it's them, do we? Silas and Orion?"

Hector exhaled. "I would bet a month's wages on it. But no, it's not a fact. Just instinct."

"It makes sense." She sat down next to him, and their shoulders touched.

Hector continued to watch the people moving about the square, counting the crimson and violet uniforms. Not many reds to be seen, but he knew personally the number of troops he had stationed in Jericho. What concerned him was the amount of Jerichonian Guard uniforms he'd noticed. Konungr Vali forever refused to play by the rules.

"So what's the plan? You can't expect them to come willingly." Raven pushed her shoulder against his, trying to draw him from his brooding. He shook his head in reply. "And we aren't supposed to make a scene or alert the Jerichonians of our presence. Are we arresting them?"

"We're doing whatever it takes. The Queen demands to see them in Inaravale, so we will get them there however we need to, even if it means hogtying the four of them, tossing them over our shoulders, and dragging them home." He took another breath and let it out slowly, unhappy with the plan and not relishing the idea of arresting soldiers—even ex-soldiers.

He also wasn't looking forward to seeing the look in Johnathan's eyes if this resulted in him hauling his brother into the Hall of

Sunsets. Again. Or having to face Raven, for that matter. Hector knew of her and Declan's history. The secrets he kept from her regarding his part in the situation ate at him every time the subject arose. He'd never intended for it to become a secret, but each time the words made their way to the tip of his tongue, he hadn't been able to release them. Now, he kicked himself for bringing her along. It had been a foolish mistake.

But he'd wanted her at his side.

So he hadn't allowed himself to face the truth. Now it stared him in the face, and he didn't know what to expect. So many possible outcomes, and not many ended with her still at his side when the dust settled.

"I'm sorry I never considered how working with addicts would affect you."

She put her hand on his thigh. "Hector, stop. It's fine. I'm a criminal from the slums. There were far worse paths in my future than sniffing out drug dens for the Legion."

Looking down at her hand, he considered taking it in his but decided against it. "Still, I should have discussed it with you."

"Forget about it. We need to focus on the job and leave the past in the past." Raven stood and began strapping on her weapons. "I have to be honest: it kind of feels like we don't have a concrete plan." When she finished and he still hadn't responded, she said, "I'll go wake the boys."

Hector said her name, his voice rough with torment. Raven crossed the room in three steps and stood above his shoulder. "There's something I haven't told the others." He looked down at his hands, then his hickory eyes slid to hers. "I don't think I'm going to, but I also don't want to be the only person on the team who knows."

"The Reko Raptors are starting off with secrets?" She ran the back of her knuckles down the edge of his goatee, trying to soothe away the stress lines. "I don't think that bodes well for the future of the team, do you?"

"You're right." He leaned his cheek ever so slightly into her hand. "I know you are, but I don't know how they'll respond or how it will affect the mission. It isn't that I don't trust their loyalties, I just think it's safer to keep it between you and me for now." She dipped her head in agreement, encouraging him to continue and promising trust with her expression.

Hector sighed, feeling the tension heavy on his shoulders. Then he divulged his crucial concern. "I have long suspected Alexander might be with them."

C

Orion settled into a volatile rage the morning he and Declan awoke to find Foxx and Iris missing. His hangover had been blatant in the spidery veins tarnishing the whites of his eyes and in the shadows below them. By the time he and Declan checked out of the Manor, he'd snapped at the receptionist and almost got into a fist fight with someone who bumped into him on the stairs.

Declan had tried to settle him, reminding him that they knew the girls' destination, but none of his calm logic had cut through Orion's ire.

He'd been furious with himself. He'd drowned his misery, and in doing so, stifled his ability to remain alert. Iris and Foxx had fled, and with good reason. He'd have done the same.

Declan didn't bother attempting conversation as they hiked, and Orion's face never lost a smidgen of its ferocity. The following day, they entered the City of the Moon after luncheon. Snow had begun to fall, but the city streets were all but clear aside from the flakes falling around them, as if some sorcery kept the snow from accumulating within the walls.

They picked a tavern on the edge of the entrance plaza. Having already dodged a few Legion soldiers on the way in, they wanted the option of a quick exit.

After placing their things in the room, Declan suggested grabbing a late luncheon before venturing out into the city in search of the girls. The luncheon crowd had fizzled out in the pub, but the woman behind the bar pressured them to sit at one of the outdoor tables.

"The snow is barely falling, and the sun is shining bright! I'll bring your food out when it's ready."

Orion agreed without hesitation, liking the idea of keeping an eye out for Foxx and Iris while they ate.

C

Iris woke to find they'd slept through most of the day. Foxxglove snoozed soundly in the other bed.

Though smaller even than the one they'd shared in Kesken Ala, their room at the White Luna Inn suited them fine. The beds had plenty of blankets and pillows, the curtains were thick enough to block out some of the cold, and the lantern she'd lit upon waking had been crafted of a stone pot that helped warm the room.

Pulling back the curtains, Iris thought it must be late afternoon or early evening. Her stomach growled, confirming this speculation. Still, she let her head fall back against the pillow and watched the sun drift toward the tops of the buildings.

Eventually, Foxx shifted in her sleep and yawned. Facing her sister, she smiled. "You're awake. What time is it?"

"Around dinner, I think."

Foxx sat up too quickly and felt her head rush. "We slept through the whole day? What will the innkeeper think?"

"That we're weary travelers who got here very late in the night? He seemed nice enough. I'm sure as long as we pay him, it'll be fine."

Foxx dropped her feet to the floor and stretched her neck. "You're right, sorry. I'm still asleep. And starving." She held her hand above the hot stone. "It's like a miniature furnace. I've never seen a lantern that provides more heat than a mere candle's flame."

"We've never been somewhere cold enough to require such a lantern." Iris grabbed the nuts from their bag and tossed them over. "We should get ready to head out into the city. Maybe we can grab some dinner before checking out the Monastery. What do you think?"

Foxx fought sleepiness as she munched on her snack. "That sounds like a good plan. I want to bathe, too. Maybe when we return this evening." Standing, she stretched her back and legs, trying to awaken her muscles before tugging on her boots. Iris did the same. They layered up and left their pack behind, stuffing their pockets with a few possible necessities. After Iris slung the water-skin over her shoulder, they descended the steps to find the same man sitting behind the desk.

In response to their footfalls, he pulled his eyes from the pages of his book. "Merry evening, ladies. I was wondering when I would see you." He stood to greet them properly, extending a hand. "Name's Gabriel. Are you enjoying the room?"

Iris nodded. "Yes, it's perfect."

He looked down at his notebook. "Will you be staying long?"

"We aren't exactly sure. We want to take in some of the city while we're here. Maybe even visit the ruins of the Monastery." Foxx studied him, gauging his reaction.

He smiled through a salt and pepper beard. "Yes, the Monastery of the Morrow is a very popular tourist attraction." Looking back at his notebook, he tapped his pen against the parchment. "Room two, was it? What names shall I be writing down for you?"

Foxx handed him a few *metts*. "Just our initials would be good, if you don't mind. F.I.B. And let us know what more we owe you. Should we pay daily?"

Gabriel wrote *Ammil 4, F.I.B.* next to the bold number two. "This is plenty for now. We'll square up when you check out. Anything else I can help you ladies with?"

Foxx and Iris shared a glance. "Actually, yes. Do you think you could point us in the direction of the Monastery?"

"I can do you one better. I can draw you a map."

C

"So your plan is to sit here and hope they happen to pass by?" Orion and Declan had finished their hot chicken sandwiches some time ago but had remained at their table on the outskirts of the square. The sun had already begun to set, painting the sky in hints of red.

"That's the idea." Declan nursed his mug of coffee, enjoying its nutty flavor, like chestnuts roasted over a fire. He'd always liked the coffee in Jericho, and with not sleeping for an entire day, he was grateful for the energy.

"But we've been here since early afternoon. Now the sun is beginning to set. Don't you think we would have better luck searching the city?"

They watched the citizens roaming the plaza. Patrons crowded the outdoor tables, sharing meals together despite the light snowfall that couldn't decide whether it wanted to continue or not. A group of older women stood by the fountain, chattering like hens. Some people carried bags of groceries, likely on their way home to make dinner, while others milled into one of the many taverns.

"Don't you remember learning that if you're lost, you're to stay in one place until someone finds you?" Declan asked. Orion growled something indiscernible under his breath, and Declan hid his smile behind another sip. "Listen, the only way in and out of the city is through that gate right there. Jericho is huge, and they could be anywhere, but they won't stay here forever. Eventually, they'll need to exit through that gate, and when they do, we'll be right here waiting for them."

"If you say so." Orion swigged his coffee as Declan's eyes drifted back to the plaza.

A woman sat on the edge of the fountain selling roses from a basket. To her left, children played Ring Around the Rosebush. They danced in a circle with clasped hands as they sang, and when the song ended, they fell to the ground in fits of laughter, only to get back up and do it all over again. Other children chased the orädi tending the plants in the containers lining the square. Two mountain henki seemed to be running interference while others quickly sprinkled the plants with magic.

"They're cute, huh? The kids. Rambunctious, though. Did you ever want kids?"

Declan's back straightened. "I never really thought about it. I've been in the Legion since I was old enough to join. You know I had someone before. Maybe if—well, maybe if things were different, but it is what it is." His eyes glazed over, staring at nothing.

"Not falling in love is always the safest option. I personally have never been in love and am all the better for it."

Declan glanced at him with a smirk. "Better for it? I'm not sure about that."

"Hey, watch it, friend."

"I also don't believe you've never been in love." Declan scratched his chin. "What about Camille?"

Orion slapped the table, unable to contain his laughter at the absurdity of the thought. "Definitely not! Maybe for like… one minute. But no. You know what Camille means to me. It was never about that." After a moment, he added, "She saved me."

"I know." Declan smiled as he sifted through his own memories of Camille. "Teagan always had a thing for you."

"What? No!" Orion laughed harder, throwing his head back, and Declan joined him.

"Camille said you were nice to her though, even when you were a jerk to everyone else. That has to mean something—a peek into that big heart of yours." Declan nudged Orion's shoulder. "And you were friendly enough every time I saw you together."

Orion rolled his eyes. "Tea is shy. I didn't want her to feel lonely. That's all it was. And shut up."

Declan lifted his hands. "Fine, fine. What about before that?"

Orion shrugged, shaking away thoughts of Lacy Robinson. Time spent with her seemed like a lifetime ago—someone else's lifetime. Some experiences change the core of a person so thoroughly, not even a remnant of who they were before survives. The boy who knew Lacy was a stranger to him now. A fleeting memory of dreams forgotten. "No. There's nothing."

Several minutes passed as they watched the citizens move about, the indecisive snowflakes in no way discouraging their evening plans. Then Declan asked, "What about Iris?"

Orion choked. "What about her?" He wiped spilled coffee from his chin.

"You felt something for her. Your general bad temper and crabbiness gave it away."

"I am always bad tempered and crabby."

"Not *always.*"

Irritation bubbled over. "What's it to you anyway? Why are we even talking about this?"

Declan shook his head and rested his elbows on the table. "Point proven." Orion growled again and crossed his arms. "You behave like such a child sometimes, Ri." He looked past the fountain and glimpsed a familiar flash of black hair. Leaning to the side, he tried to verify his suspicions. When his gaze met hers, he realized she wasn't who he'd expected, and his chest tightened.

Orion said, "So what about you? Do you ever think about going back to—"

"Raven."

"Yeah—"

"No, Orion. It's Raven." Declan stared at her, and Raven responded with a roguish smile.

"What?" Orion set down his mug and searched the square like a dog on high alert.

Declan traced the area again, combing through each face until he saw another soldier in black gear. Then another. Raven alone seemed to notice them, unless the others hid their awareness. His eyes shifted back to where she'd stood, but she'd since vanished.

"Something's happening. Raven is here. And Jax Blackmoor. They're armored in High Legion battle gear."

Orion swore and stood up. "What are they doing here? Are they looking for us? Or the girls?"

"I hear you've been hanging out with the wrong crowd, O'Connell." Raven's blade lay flat on his shoulder, motivating him to return to his seat. He froze stiff but for the bending of his knees as he became reacquainted with his chair. She looked at Declan and dipped her chin. "Silas." Declan breathed her name with discontent. "That's it? Six years and you can't even say the word *hello*?" Her tone sounded playful, her mouth curled into a pleasant smile, but her eyes were malevolent.

"Based on the knife you're holding to my friend's throat, I can only assume your intentions are unfriendly. What are you doing here, Raven?" He kept his voice cold, and for a brief moment, her smile shifted to a sneer, but she regained control and composed her features into indifference. Then Declan noticed the great horned owl pinned to her shoulder, and his stomach performed another flip. "Raptors?"

"What?" Orion tilted his head, trying to get a view of Raven's gear without cutting his neck on her blade. From the corner of his eye, he saw the familiar bronze pin. "No way."

"Is Hector here too? I saw Jax lingering like a creep across the square."

"I am here to collect your young ladies. The Queen is dying to meet them. Do tell me where they are so I can be on my way." Raven took a step closer, her blade sliding along Orion's shoulder.

Panic coursed through Declan, but he kept his face a picture of calm. "What ladies?" He looked around as though it should be obvious that no ladies accompanied them.

"Don't play dumb, Silas. It doesn't look good on you."

"It looks good on you," he shot back with a grin.

Raven leaned across Orion to stab her blade into the wooden table, rattling their mugs. "Where. Are. They?"

Declan locked onto her gaze, and her eyes flared. Then he leaned back in his chair, crossing his arms. "I have no idea what you're talking about."

Raven opened her mouth to protest again, but Orion cut in. "Oh, come off it, Raven. Clearly there are no females with us. They gave us the slip in Peregrine Manor. We're in Jericho looking for them, same as you."

"You must have some idea where they've scurried off to."

"If we knew, we'd have them right now. We wouldn't be sitting here in the snow, wasting the day away, now would we?"

"Perhaps." She tugged her blade from the table and sat down in the available chair. Her eyes never left Declan. She scrutinized his appearance, comparing it to the many memories she had of him all those years ago. "Did you miss me, sweetie?"

"Not very often," he admitted, his nonchalance shattered for a brief instant as his gaze found the ground. He hadn't *not* missed her. During his first years on the run, she'd been one half of the arrow on the compass drawing him home.

Raven rolled her eyes, not wanting to reveal—not even wanting to think about it long enough to decide—how his answer truly made her feel. "So here's the deal. I'm looking for Foxxglove and Iris Belamour. Help me find them, and I'll persuade Hector to let you walk free. We'll take them back to Castle Solís, and you can continue to do whatever it is you do with your miserable, traitor lives."

"We aren't going to help you capture two perfectly innocent women so you can turn them over to the Queen." Declan leaned forward with his elbows on the table, all previous nostalgia erased by her declaration.

"We couldn't even if we wanted to since, as we have already explained, we don't know where they are." Orion finished the last swig of his drink.

Raven relented, blowing her bangs away from her face in a way that reminded Declan of Iris. "Hector is not going to be pleased with these results." She tapped her fingers on the table.

Orion leaned toward her. "Then tell Hector for me, next time he wants information, he should come himself and not send his little slumrat to do his dirty work for him."

CHAPTER 28

DRAGON'S BREATH

After a quick meal at a nearby café, Iris and Foxx made their way to the Monastery with Gabriel's map. The brick roads bustled with citizens, and they passed a few soldiers in red, but they were concealed enough in their cold-weather gear to remain unspotted. Since they hadn't seen their pictures posted up anywhere, they wondered if the Legion stationed in the city even knew to be looking for them.

According to the map, the Monastery stood against the back wall on the northwestern side. A fortress far bigger than the one they stayed at in the Metsa, Jericho's Monastery of the Morrow was three stories tall with spires shooting up from the corners of pyramid-shaped rooftops. Though much of it looked disheveled, it was easy to imagine how magnificent the architecture must have been in its prime.

They could see painted windows on every floor, including a circular one above the entrance. A *syli* in diameter, the glass was laced with intentional holes and spirals, a glorious representation of the full moon. A courtyard similar to the one in the entrance plaza lay at the building's base. In lieu of the fountain, another full moon sat at the center of the same circle of phases.

As they took it all in, Foxx realized she'd seen the courtyard before. A wave of worry flushed over her, and she touched her sister's arm. "Iris, this is definitely the city that burns."

Without pulling her eyes from the Monastery, Iris nodded. "I've been thinking the same thing. Do you think we should try and warn them? Tell someone?"

"Who would we tell? Who would believe us?"

Iris shrugged. "Maybe the Konungr?"

"So we should march up to the Jerichonian Palace and ask to speak with him? I doubt he's taking meetings with random commoners. We aren't even citizens of Cordillera. Plus, we have no proof. He'll likely think we're mad."

"Declan said he might help if he knew Sirena hunted us."

Foxx shook her head. "No, Iris, Declan said he might lock us up and throw away the key."

They approached the entrance, ignoring the signs strewn about the outer walls telling them to *keep out*, and ducked under the crooked door. Stepping over a pile of rubble, they avoided the lifted edges of an old rug and stood at the room's center.

The smell of dust and mildew consumed their senses as they surveyed the piles of debris throughout the room. Every surface was coated in a layer of grime—a telltale sign of untouched age. Iris dragged a finger through the dust atop a small table. It only had three of its four legs and tilted under the pressure of her touch.

Moth-eaten fabric hung from the windows, and in every available crevice, ghostly cobwebs drooped and swayed with spooky elegance. They admired the window above the door from the inside, garnished in more gossamer-like webs.

Two staircases lead to a second floor landing in front of them, one on the left and one on the right. Under the landing stood a set of double doors, and to their right were three doorways to choose from. The two doors on the left side of the room had long ago caved in.

Iris felt overwhelmed by the enormity of the structure. Shadows stretched across the floor as the sun continued to set. Very soon, the building would be draped in darkness. "Where do we even begin?"

"Should we split up?" Foxxglove crossed the room and pulled two torches from sconces on the wall. With the flint and steel she'd gotten at Peregrine Purchases, she lit one and handed it to Iris before lighting the other for herself. "Be careful. I don't know how stable this place is."

"I'm thinking *not very* by the looks of it."

Foxx pulled her sister in for a one-armed hug and kissed her forehead. "If anything starts to go wrong, meet back here. Or if it gets too dark, we can come back tomorrow in the daylight."

Iris agreed and toed the stairs toward the second floor landing.

Foxx disappeared through one of the doorways on the right side of the room. Guided by the radiance of her torch, she wandered empty halls and dug through trashed rooms. In nearly an hour, she hadn't come upon anything that seemed a likely hiding place for the Cordilleran key.

As she scoured the once extravagant Monastery, she wondered if Asher had already come to retrieve it. Perhaps they should be looking for him instead, but in a city as immense as Jericho, she had no idea where to begin, if not the one place they knew he would also visit.

The furthest room at the end of the hall opened up into a massive library. Its sheer size more than quadrupled the one she'd discovered at the Monastery of Sateen. Not only did shelves of books line the walls, but freestanding shelves stood in long rows at the center of the room. Foxx thought she'd never seen so many books in one place.

As if a whirlwind had blown through, books and torn pages lay scattered about, cluttering the shelves, floors, and other surfaces with parchment long forgotten and poetic words from years past.

Striding over and around the piles, Foxx searched the library. She progressed through an aisle near the center of the room until she arrived in a spacious area with a wooden desk at its center. Like the one in the jungle, it was peppered with books, papers, and writing supplies. Shoving the items to the floor without regard, she looked for a carving on its surface, but found little more than scuffed wood. She sighed in frustration but didn't abandon her quest.

Walking along the outer walls, her fingers slid over the rows of remaining spines. Lifting her torch, she did her best to scan every inch of the room. She didn't know how, but something deep in her felt certain the key would be in the library.

A skylight had been cut into the ceiling, but with the vanishing sun, it didn't provide much light to search by. She combed every shelf, moved every book, and hunted high and low for any possible indication of where a secret key might be hidden.

Stepping back to the table at the center, she held out her torch and rotated in a circle. Her mother had taught her the importance of taking in the whole picture and how it often made clear that which was unclear.

Once again, her mother's words rang true. High atop a bookshelf on the far side of the room, she saw a crescent moon carved into the wall. It couldn't have been bigger than the palm of her hand, but she knew it was the sign she'd been hunting for. Approaching the bookcase, she began the task of removing all the books from its shelves.

Her mother had read them countless stories where the characters had searched for hidden doorways. There was always a handle, a button, a key. Pull on a lantern, slide a book from a shelf, push a random object, lift a lever.

Her fingers slid across the shelves and traced every vertical wall holding them in place until they brushed a strange seam in the wood—a ridge she hadn't felt anywhere else. After prodding its edge, she realized she could pull it toward her like a lever.

A clank rang throughout the room like the gears of a clock. She stepped away from the wall, holding the torch in front of her. The entire bookshelf slid forward before swinging open like a hinged door and revealing a dark passageway behind it.

C

"What does she want with them?"

Raven swiped Declan's mug from the table and downed the last of it before responding. "How should I know? I'm just a soldier doing what I'm told. You know how that is, Silas." With a devilish smirk, she amended, "Oh wait, I guess you don't."

"You have no idea what you're talking about, Raven." Declan knew it wasn't her fault. He'd kept her in the dark and left without a word. He shouldn't expect her to understand. Still, he couldn't help wondering whether she'd ever truly known him at all if she'd so easily fallen prey to rumors slandering his character.

Leaning against the back of the chair and crossing one leg over the other, Raven said, "Then explain it to me."

"No," Orion and Declan said in unison, provoking a scowl.

Declan kept his focus on her but continued to scan the square in his peripherals. Jax lurked about somewhere out of sight, and Hector likely lingered nearby, too. He wondered who else might have made the team.

The formation of a new kettle of Raptors was shocking news. His mind wandered to the prophecy promising the downfall of the Queen, and the conversation he'd had with Foxx when they discovered it. He wished he'd convinced her then to divulge more of her plans. Or that he'd pressed for information at Peregrine Manor when he realized they planned to make their escape. He could have bribed her with freedom in exchange for the truth. Instead, he let them enter the city unprotected, where birds of prey stalked the streets, hoping to swoop in and capture them for their wicked master.

He'd helped them flee the boiling pot only to be thrown into a raging fire.

"Where is Hector?" Orion sounded calmer than Declan imagined he felt. "Is he going to make an appearance or is he letting his cronies do the work for him while he hides in the shadows?"

"I'm here." Hector appeared behind Orion.

Raven and Declan looked up at him. Orion harrumphed and lifted his coffee to his lips, putting it down in a huff when he remembered he'd already emptied it.

"Did you get anything out of them?" Hector directed the question at Raven. Her gaze was drawn to his blond hair, now wet from the melting snow. Rather than its usual smooth, high and tight, it clumped together in tiny spikes. Noticing her stare, he ran his hand over his head, breaking her concentration.

"No, sir. They claim to have no idea where the Belamour sisters could be." Her words came out thick with sarcasm as she eyed both men in disbelief.

Declan ignored her remark. He'd determined not to engage her, not even to look at her. She was out of her depth whether she realized it or not, making her opinion of the situation irrelevant. "What are you going to do with them?"

"That is no business to a traitor." Hector didn't bother looking at him as he brushed snow from his shoulders.

"You know all about being a traitor, don't you, Commander Kayvan?" Orion's words dripped with venom, spitting Hector's title as though it tasted sour on his tongue.

Unsure what to make of Orion's accusation, Raven's dark eyes flashed to Hector.

Declan noticed her surprise, which confirmed what he'd already suspected: she didn't have a clue. "Let it go, Ri. He's not worth it."

Hector chuckled, shaking his head as he removed his gloves and tucked them into the pocket of his pants. "I saw your brother the other day in the Hall of Sunsets, Declan. He seems to be doing well for himself. At least one of Ryder's sons is making him proud."

Declan shot to his feet like a rocket blasting into the sky. His chair clambered to the ground behind him as he met Hector chest to chest. "What did you say to me, you dirty bastard?" Rage coursed through him, heating his blood so sweat beaded on his forehead. Hector kept his feet planted as he leveled his contender with a stone-cold glare.

People around them curiously observed the altercation. Raven was shocked by Declan's ballistic response. She'd never seen him react so ferociously to anything. More in the know than Raven, Orion wasn't surprised, though both had jumped to their feet.

Hector's eyes flickered to Raven for less than a second, but the expression on her face left him feeling sick to his stomach. He knew he shouldn't have provoked Declan. It'd been a cruel waste of time and absolutely unnecessary. He had no reason to feel animosity toward him to begin with.

Clearing his throat, he refocused. "We're here to complete a mission. Stay out of our way, and we'll stay out of yours. Don't make me drag you both back to Inaravale in chains as well."

Orion scoffed. "I'd like to see you try."

"Is that your plan for Iris and Foxx?" Declan asked.

"The Belamours will have the option to come willingly."

Orion slid a hand between the men. "Cool it," he breathed, his instruction mellow and unstirred. He pressed against Declan's chest, encouraging him to step away. "This is not the time, nor the place. Remember what's important."

Declan's nostrils flared as he pulled his wrathful stare from Hector to look at his friend. Orion's expression of understanding allowed him to release a breath. Taking two steps back, he relinquished his anger and held his hands up to indicate a ceasefire.

Raven's eyes darted among the men as she tried to read between the lines of what she'd heard.

Declan put his hands on top of his head, trying to decide their next course of action. His gaze flashed to Orion to find him already looking his way. Orion wasn't often the one calming *him* down, though he could think of a few times when his friend's wisdom had pulled him from the ledge. Declan wondered now about the change in his demeanor. When he'd stopped him from assaulting Hector's smug, pretentious face, he'd looked as if he'd just realized what truly mattered himself and was ready to fight for it.

If the Queen had reinstated the Raptors to track down Foxx and Iris, the roots in the situation must be deeper than they originally realized. It seemed impossible now that turning Sawyer in would result in a peaceful pardon. Perhaps the time for that had long passed. Perhaps it had been a ploy all along; another manipulation.

In that moment, they agreed on the need to protect the girls, and their minds raced with possibilities of where they might find them.

"What is going on?" Raven looked to Declan first, but he only met her gaze for a second. Turning from him to face her commander, she said, "Hector?"

Then, a clamor of horrified screams ricocheted throughout the plaza.

C

Foxxglove descended the spiral staircase into darkness. Her torchlight flickered against the walls, so narrow they brushed her shoulders as she walked. Remnants of spiderwebs adorned the ceiling, some sagging so low she had to duck to avoid them.

The stairs seemed to continue downward for a very long time, and the passageway smelled of mud and mold, worse than it had throughout the rest of the Monastery. The air grew colder with each passing step, and even standing so close to the fire of her torch, she felt the tightness in her jaw chattering her teeth. She tucked her scarf more securely around her neck and tugged on her hat, making sure it covered both ears.

When the stairs ended, a short hall led to a room. She progressed forward with caution, unsure what she might find. The room was cramped and damp, with walls made of dirt and stone. A table stood at its center, and to Foxxglove's delight, a shape had been carved into its surface—a circle with a small crescent moon inside, and an exact replica of Asher's tattoo.

"This is it," she said to the shadows fighting for purchase in her torchlight.

Suddenly, a thunderous rumble shattered the stillness, followed by a second reverberation that shuddered the building. Scanning the room, she willed the key to reveal itself, mentally summoning it in the hopes it might magically appear. She searched the walls, looking for a crack or anything that might indicate a hidden location.

Dust and dirt fluttered down from the ceiling as the distant noises above grew more tumultuous. A massive quake had her grabbing the table to steady herself, and she dropped her torch.

With a final glance about the room, she abandoned her search, swiped the torch from the floor, and fled back up the stairs in search of Iris.

C

Declan's calculations melted into panic. "What's happening?" The rumbles of collapsing buildings synchronized with screams of terror. The ground trembled beneath their feet, and the plaza erupted into chaos. Mass hysteria had the citizens scrambling about, crashing into each other and fighting to free themselves from oncoming doom. Many ran toward the entrance gate, fleeing the city. Others raced deeper into Jericho, heading home, searching for loved ones, or trying to find shelter. The origin of the bedlam had yet to be discovered, but the sounds of crumbling bricks and shouts of anguish continued to escalate.

Previous calm vanished, Orion closed the gap between himself and Hector in one long stride. "What did you do, Kayvan?"

Hector ignored him, his eyes anxiously sweeping the clouds rolling in with unnatural speed. Peels of thunder and lightning brought the expanse to life as flames and smoke sprang up across the city. Raven said Hector's name again, following his gaze and trying to discern what he searched for.

All at once, the soldiers saw the source of the attack rising from the east. Amongst the gathering clouds, the garnet scales of a dragon shimmered against the setting sun barely visible on the horizon. Plumes of fire poured from its mouth, setting the city ablaze as it climbed high above the rooftops. With a roar, it changed directions and plummeted downward, smashing its enormous body into the structures below.

There was no clear path to avoid the onslaught, so citizens ran amok.

Hector yelled Raven's name over the pandemonium. "We have to go!" Without a second glance at Declan and Orion, they darted off down an alleyway. The second they disappeared from sight, a burning building the next block over toppled into its neighbor. That building crumbled, filling the alley they'd just traveled.

Declan shouted Raven's name, but Orion grabbed his arm. "Declan, we need to move."

Despite the pain in his chest over the potential loss of Raven and Hector, Declan agreed. Another tremor rocked the ground, and he braced himself. "What's the plan?"

"There's the exit." Orion pointed to the gate. "The city is lost, let's go." He made to bolt, but Declan grabbed him and spun him back.

"No! I am not leaving without Iris and Foxx." Declan searched Orion for the man who'd surfaced in his eyes moments ago. The people around them continued to scatter as the dragon careened atop the city. The woman selling flowers by the fountain knelt to gather the contents of her overturned basket. When the dragon circled back to the plaza, it hurtled toward the sculpted masterpiece and crushed the woman beneath it.

The screams were endless. People couldn't decide whether they should take shelter in the buildings or flee to the streets. The shattering of glass windows became a constant hum alongside the crackling fire consuming everything in its path.

Soldiers, both Legion and Jerichonian, helped herd people into groups, trying to get them to safety, but even they seemed unsure of what to do. Some had weapons raised and attempted taking the monster down.

Orion grabbed Declan by his shirt and pulled him close, dragging his eyes away from the mayhem. "You are not listening to me, Declan. That beast belongs to *her*. Which can only mean she's *here*. We need to leave Jericho. Right now."

"Belongs to who?"

Orion shook him again. "He belongs to the Queen!"

☾

Foxxglove crashed into Iris in the entrance hall. After squeezing her tight, she put her hands on either side of her face and inspected her for injuries.

"Foxx, I'm fine." Iris swatted her away with fluttering hands. "I'm all right! What's going on out there?"

They rushed to the exit and escaped beneath the door. Dark clouds covered the city, and the sounds of screams and turmoil reached their ears. Blazes of fire towered above the rooftops as far as they could see, sending smoke billowing into the expanse.

"It's happening," Iris said between shallow breaths. "We're too late."

Frozen in place, the sisters watched the dragon rotate in the air and soar in their direction. They hastened away from the Monastery, racing across the courtyard as fast as their feet would carry them.

The beast roared and swooped low, forcing them to the ground with their hands shielding their heads. Nearby citizens did the same, frantically crawling away. People in the cross streets outside the courtyard turned to watch the dragon plummet toward the building. Like a cannonball fired into the hull of a rival ship, it torpedoed into the heart of the fortress. The building crumbled like a sandcastle pulverized by the tide. A plume of dust and disintegrated rock blasted out from the bottom as the top floors collapsed, covering those nearby in a coating of grime. The beast returned to the air, spraying fiery breath into the heap of rubble for good measure.

Foxx's hand found Iris' back, trying to rub away her cough. Their lungs burned. "The monster you saw was a *dragon*? An actual dragon!"

"I told you!" Iris covered her head to block another outburst of dust and hugged her waterskin to her chest.

Foxx pulled her closer as the air filled with soot and ash that smothered their lungs. "You didn't say it was a dragon!"

"Does it matter?"

They lifted their eyes to observe the reptile. The gold of its head blended down its neck into burnt orange. The orange faded to crimson and then to the hardy maroon of a blooming chrysanthemum. Its vibrant body rivaled the sky in its backdrop where scarlet and mustard danced against nightmarish clouds, making the scene devastating and spectacular in tandem.

"Iris, we need to run." Foxx dragged her sister to her feet, but with the threat of the dragon gone for the moment, Iris couldn't wrench her eyes from the Monastery. Those around them reawakened, fleeing to the streets and seeking shelter. Iris stumbled as Foxx yanked at her arm. Then together, they sprinted away from the flaming ruin of the first and grandest Monastery of the Morrow.

Hector and his Raptors met at their rendezvous point, a heather-bricked well a block from the entrance plaza. Panicked citizens whirled around them as dragonfire spread throughout the city, littering the streets with trampled bodies and unfortunate souls crushed by rubble.

"What in the *hell* is going on?" Dominic tossed his hatchet back and forth between his hands with anxious energy.

They shuddered as another blast rocked the city. Hector balanced himself with a hand on the well. "The Queen must have changed her plans." Bolts holding the sign identifying the storefront to their left gave way and the timbers toppled to the ground. Jax grabbed Raven's arm, hauling her out of the way and shielding her from the brick dust that followed.

Steady on two feet, she asked, "That beast belongs to the Queen?"

Hector nodded. "Yes. He's her pet drakinferno, Kaen."

Dominic gaped. "Where does she keep it?"

"Will you put that away before you hurt someone!" Raven touched the axe as it landed in the hand next to her. Dominic grinned and obliged.

Hector kept his eyes to the sky. "He isn't always that large." His reply only served to confuse them more, but no one asked followup questions. Hector had only seen Kaen in his dragon form a few times, each occurrence bringing with it mass hysteria and destruction. He never expected Sirena to use the beast against one of the royal cities, though. Certainly not Jericho. Did she intend to flatten the city, as he'd seen her flatten others? Was she taking a stand against Valerian Kirkavall at last?

Jax clapped his hands to refocus everyone. "What is the new plan?"

"The sisters are still the mission. I'm not sure what drove Sirena to attack now, but I will say, I've never seen her as desperate as she seemed when she gave me this assignment."

"Desperate?" Dominic croaked. "Bleedin' bird's gone mad!"

Raven tried to meet Hector's gaze, but it alternated between scouring the sky and staring right through her, focused on whatever thoughts rolled through his head like a sandstorm in the Wilds. Jarring him from his introspection, she asked, "She sent us here so she could burn the city down around us? Are you sure this wasn't a trap?"

"It wasn't a trap." Hector shook his head to dispel racing thoughts. "She just doesn't know what she's doing. Split into pairs and search the city. I don't want the sisters harmed. Find them and protect them. Meet at the front gate when the commotion dies down. Wyatt and Marshal. Raven with Dom. Jax, you're with me."

"What about Silas and O'Connell?" Raven asked.

For the first time since regrouping, he locked eyes with her, willing her to obey. "Leave them. They are not a priority." Then he ordered the rest of the team to, "Move out," and the three pairs scattered in different directions.

C

Declan and Orion stood flush against a wall in an alley outside of the fountain terrace. "If we find Iris and Foxx, we can all escape together." Another bang rocked the city, and they winced. Then a group of civilians blackened with soot ran past, pinning them flatter to the bricks.

Orion shielded his face as a burst of smoke and debris ballooned past the alley's entrance. "Once we're outside Jericho, we can come up with a new plan. If we run deeper into the city, we risk not making it back out, but right now, we're at the exit." Declan said his name, but paused, unable to argue with Orion's logic. No one was safe in a city with collapsing buildings and a raging dragon.

Orion wiped sweat from his brow. "We can leave now and come back for them when everything calms down. I'm not saying abandon them, but we need to get to safety now and find them later. You were the one who pointed out the enormity of the city and how unlikely it was that we would find them. Imagine trying to track them down in this mayhem."

Declan growled in frustration. "If we wait outside the city, Hector and his team might find her before we do. There's likely five or six Raptors and only two of us."

"Her?" Orion's brow creased into a glare. A squad of Guards crossed the intersection, and they pressed themselves even more flush with the wall.

"Them," Declan corrected himself. "Hector and his team might find *them*."

Orion peeked his head around the corner of the alley, pretending to scan the area as he hid his expression. The Guards who'd just ran by halted a few blocks away. Each wrapped cloth soaked in wax around their arrows' tips before lighting the bundles with the fire of a nearby building. As the dragon swooped low, they lifted their bows and released.

Orion watched anxiously with hope in his heart, but their efforts were fruitless. Angered by the attack, the dragon descended and set the squad on fire. The sounds of screaming soldiers turned his stomach, but he couldn't look away as they fought to extinguish the flames.

Returning his attention to Declan, Orion breathed deeply, forcing his eyes closed as if he could erase the images from his mind. A woman and child hastened past them down the alley. Blood drenched their clothing and tears streaked soot-coated cheeks. When they reached the cross street, the woman scooped the child into her arms and disappeared from sight.

Declan said, "We have to find Foxx and Iris before the Raptors get their hands on them. If they turn them over to Sirena, we'll never see either of them again."

"Well, it was your stupid idea not to look for them in the first place!"

"I know, I know." Declan pounded the brick at his back and cursed as he willed a functional plan to surface.

After a long moment, Orion swore his surrender. "Let's split up. Find the girls and get them to the gate. If we don't find them, we'll meet in the square when everything settles." He pushed away from the wall and pointed around the corner. "I'll head this way."

Declan met him where he stood and threw a thumb over his shoulder. "I'll take the alley through there and scope out the east side."

"Lay low. Avoid all soldiers." He added special emphasis on the word *all* before putting his hand on his friend's shoulder. "And Declan? Don't be a hero."

CHAPTER 29

CONVERSING WITH QUEENS

Reaching the end of an alley, Foxx and Iris searched the street for something familiar. After running from the Monastery, they'd lost their way in the madness and didn't know how to get back to the inn. When they rounded the next corner, Foxx looked up to see three men in Jerichonian Guard uniforms standing high on a flat rooftop. Moments later, a trebuchet released a ball of fire at the dragon. It soared through the air, but before hitting its mark, the dragon's tail batted it back at them. It crashed into the rooftop and exploded, demolishing the trebuchet and the building next door.

Foxx pulled her eyes from the scene, not wishing to see proof of the soldiers' fate. The dragon roared, relishing in its victory.

The screams of the city were tragic and unending. Tears streamed down Iris' cheeks as the evidence of bloodshed and ruination assaulted their senses. They found destruction around every corner, and the smell of blood, smoke, and broiled flesh thrashed their nostrils.

Iris' hand kept flying to her mouth as though holding back vomit. Foxx dragged her along, ducking and weaving them through piles of debris and frantic civilians. Felled buildings blocked many streets, making the labyrinth of the city significantly more complex to maneuver.

Even more than her violated senses, Foxx's mind harassed her with worries, questions, and possible outcomes. When they reached the end of a street, the dragon swooped low above them, causing them to crouch and tremble, hearts pounding in their ears. Another explosion sounded to their right, making their ears ring, and both girls flattened themselves against the nearest wall. Foxx fought to remain focused on the task at hand, repeating the same words over and over in an attempt to block out all others: *inn, belongings, escape, avoid death by dragon.*

The road they traveled led them to the square at the entrance to the city—a blessing, since they could almost definitely find their way back to the White Luna from there. Too open in its enormity to provide shelter, the plaza was nearly empty of people. Foxx and Iris stuck to the edges of the buildings for cover. The dragon flew above them, and they dropped again into a crouch. Staying there for a long moment to catch their breath, they waited for the beast to move on.

"It's okay, Iris. Rest a minute. We're going to be fine." Foxx scoured the plaza, taking in the toppled tables and demolished fountain. Corpses lay strewn about, disfigured and brutalized by felled bricks and fleeing hordes. It'd been easier to bypass the dead as they raced through the city, but now at a standstill, she couldn't pry her eyes from them. Many were children, too small to keep up or be seen in a frenzied crowd. Foxx choked down bile and hoped Iris wouldn't notice.

At the center of the square next to the fountain, a spiraling tornado touched down from the sky. Foxx rose from her crouch, lifting a hand to contain her hair and shield her eyes as wind stirred up dust and debris. Squinting at the absurd weather, she thought she could see something at the tornado's center. As the whirlwind slowed, the figure of a woman materialized. At first, she looked nearly transparent, like a mirrored reflection in stagnant water, but there was no questioning her identity.

Foxx and Iris plugged their ears as a piercing ring preceded a menacing voice. Though the woman at the center of the cyclone stood several *sylis* away, both heard her voice clearly.

People of Jericho! I am Queen Sirena Aldrich, Supreme Ruler of Arkaemor.

Foxxglove dropped to a knee and clutched her ears, reacting as if spikes penetrated the drums. Iris grabbed her, trying to comprehend her agony.

I come to you tonight with a request. I must apologize for the way the evening has transpired, but this is a matter of grave importance affecting every single one of us. There are some amongst you this night who wish to destroy the extraordinary world we inhabit. Arkaemor is old and unique and takes care of us all. She is our refuge, our home. But these two women seek to destroy this Kingdom we hold so dear.

Iris looked up to find her and Foxx's faces, big as buildings, shimmering in the sky above the city.

Foxx sobbed. Blood dripped from beneath the hands covering her ears. Iris scanned the area to see if anyone else responded like her sister, but the few in sight looked more fearful than pained. She said her name, and Foxx met her eyes. Through blood soaked lips, stained with the crimson dripping from her nose, she mouthed, "It's so *loud.*"

My drakinferno is angry, as am I. As, I am sure, are you.

Foxx's other knee hit the ground. Her ability to contain the consuming torture ceased as she released a brutal, gut-wrenching wail. Lightning flashed in the clouds above as if responding to her anguish, crackling fiercely and illuminating the sky.

Sirena turned to them as she spoke, an evil smile revealing her lack of surprise at their close proximity. *I assure you, Jericho, Kaen will stop burning this fair city the moment these women are brought to me. So find them. Find them and bring them to your Queen in the entrance plaza, and all will be restored!*

Foxx's screams died with Sirena's words. Her forehead slumped to the ground. Tears and blood drenched her hands, her hair, and the bricks below.

The dragon blew a wide arc of fire in the air and returned to its mission of destroying the city. Sirena remained at the center of her whirlwind, observing them with barbaric glee.

With eyes on the Queen as she stood, Iris tried to scrutinize the situation like Foxx would. She wondered why the dragon continued to attack if Sirena could clearly see them. Why didn't she scoop them up and carry them away?

What was she waiting for?

Long moments passed as the turmoil pressed on. The Queen remained stationary. Watchful. Waiting. Allowing her dragon to continue its destruction.

Iris felt a tug against her leg and turned to find her sister in the process of standing. Helping her up, Iris held Foxx's arms until she stood steady. "Foxxglove, I need you to focus. I don't know what to do."

Foxx's strength recovered much faster than it had the last time Sirena meddled in her head. A memory of the white ram standing in the garden flashed into her mind, and she smiled. A bizarre—yet somehow familiar—power vibrated throughout her entire nervous system. It sparked within every cell of her being from her head to her toes, making her feel lighter than air.

She exhaled a breath, and a flash of lightning shattered the sky. Ashen snow began to fall.

Balling her fists at her sides, Foxx locked eyes with the Queen. Another feeling consumed her, not as familiar as the first, but not a stranger either. Her heart tingled as she stared at Sirena. Dauntless hostility blending with vengeful wrath had her veins feeling hot like a raging fire. The tips of her fingers burned like ice. Anger filled her close to bursting, and her lips curled into a cruel smirk she'd never worn before.

Inside her mind she thought the words, *I see you, Sirena.*

A new image appeared in her thoughts: a city by the sea, shrouded in sinister darkness. Then she blinked, and it vanished from her memory.

The Queen's smile broadened, her lips splitting open to reveal teeth. Foxx had expected astonishment, but Sirena's expression was ripe with approval and pride.

Foxx didn't know how or why the silent communication had succeeded, be it the Queen's doing or her own, but she felt the tendrils of her mind span the distance between them as she reached out again. *You've done quite enough damage for one day. Take me, and leave my sister and this city alone.*

The Queen's fists rose to her hips. *No.*

This time, the voice didn't pierce like razors. The pain in her head was gone, replaced with bitter, icy-hot fury. *Yes! You don't need both of us. You seek revenge on a dead man, but it is futile. If you kill us both, there will be no one left to mourn us, and your revenge will be a failure.*

Sirena snickered. *What a clever, clever girl you are Foxxglove Belamour. If only you knew the whole story.*

No matter how long she lived, Foxx would never forget the voice of Sirena Aldrich: like poison that tastes sugary sweet on your tongue, or the tickle of a thousand spider's legs moments before all their fangs puncture your skin. She brushed away the shiver creeping across her shoulders. *Tell me, then. Explain it to me so I can understand.*

Sirena tapped her lips. *Your boldness has me curious, woman with hair like snow. I hadn't expected it, though perhaps I should have. I do like your idea of a bargain, but suppose I don't take you and kill you. Suppose you join me instead.*

Foxx stepped back in shock. *Join you in what?*

Sirena's keen gaze seemed to take in Foxx's entire being. *There is more darkness in you than there ever was in her. I can feel it from here. It spills from you like a boiling pot about to overflow. Join me, Foxxglove. Imagine all we could accomplish together. We could rule the world.*

Foxx felt sick. The previous enmity consuming her recoiled, shying away from the spotlight Sirena shined upon it. "I don't understand," she said out loud.

"What?" Iris asked, drawing Foxx's attention.

She cleared puzzled thoughts with the shake of her head. *I won't join you, Sirena, but I will come with you, as your prisoner, if you promise to leave Jericho in peace.*

How quickly your fire dies. Perhaps you are more like Amaryllis than I imagined.

Heart in her throat, Foxx sucked in a breath. *You knew my mother?*

Sirena grinned. *So ignorant, aren't you? I thought she would have prepared you better for the destiny that awaits. Though, perhaps that will work in my favor. I can mold you into whatever I wish for you to be. Come, Foxxglove. Great power is within your reach. Come, and I will teach you everything she failed to.*

Her mind reeling with questions, Foxx took a step toward the Queen as a calloused hand wrapped around her arm. Startled, she turned to find Declan standing behind her.

"Where do you think you're going?" His shoulders fell with relief, but his eyes were wide.

"Declan!" Iris wrapped her arms around him and squeezed.

He allowed one arm to slide around her back but kept his other hand on Foxx's arm, refusing to break her stare. "Foxxglove, you can't. You don't know her. She'll kill you on the spot."

A company of Jerichonian soldiers suddenly surrounded the square. Most carried bows, though a few held firearms, and all had their sights fixed on Sirena. Following closely behind them, hundreds of tiny lights appeared, swallowing the Queen like a swarm of bees. Sirena flailed, swatting at the illuminated insects in a fury. Then she lifted her hands and thrust them toward the ground as she spoke a word none of them recognized. In an instant, the creatures froze mid-air. Then they plummeted like a burst of rain. Their lights flickered out, until not a single glimmer remained.

Foxx drew her eyes from the new arrivals and gestured to the felled creatures. "If it ends all this then it's worth it. A single life for hundreds. For thousands!" Her expression, though swollen with tears, was unwavering. She looked ferocious: splattered with crimson, white hair mussed and stained like carved flesh, and a dark scar marring her face next to black, narrow eyes.

"Foxx, no!" Iris grabbed her hand.

Foxx ignored her. "This will work, Declan. You take Iris and run. I know you'll take care of her. I'll turn myself in and convince her you'll both stop searching for Celestelvyra." She registered with a jolt that she hadn't previously exposed the Sacred Realm as part of their plan.

The spark of fear in Declan's eyes confirmed it. He glanced at the Queen. "It will never work. The Immortal Queen has struck down anyone who has ever stood against her. She won't be satiated until she's crushed us all."

"She will!" Foxx said, floored to realize Declan still thought he had a fraction of control over her decisions. "Sirena singled me out when she carried me into the clouds. She didn't take Iris or you or Orion—just me. She said my name and told me she could see me; that she was coming for me." Declan hadn't known what had happened during the storm, but it didn't matter. Whether Foxx understood why or not, Sirena wanted her. "She's still talking to me. Right now, I can hear her in my head, and she can hear me. She asked me to come with her."

"Now?" Iris asked.

"Not at this exact moment, but..." Foxx faced the Queen and thought, *Do we have a deal or not? If I agree to come with you, will you leave the city?*

The Queen smiled again, tilting her head to the side as if thinking it over. Foxx wondered if she could hear their conversation or if the connection ended in her mind. How deeply could Sirena dig around within it? Could she see through her eyes or hear what her ears could hear? Glimpse the whispers of her darkest fears and deepest longings or observe the spectrum of her dreams?

Seeing the Queen's response, Declan and Iris gaped.

"I told you. We can hear each other. I have no idea why, but I asked her to take only me and leave the city alone. She seems to be considering it." Foxx took Iris' hands. "I love you, Iris. You have to let me do this. Then you have to stop everything we've been doing and let it be over. Run and hide and never look back."

Tears continued to slide down Iris' cheeks. "But what about Father? What about everything Mother taught us?"

Foxx realized now that their mother hadn't taught them nearly enough, but she didn't say so. "It's over, Iris. I'm ending it right here."

A soldier from the outer circle stepped alone into the square. He held his weapon in the air, indicating he didn't plan to use it. Sirena turned from Foxx to look at the man, watching to see what he might do. All within range of the cyclone could hear his voice in the wind. "Your Majesty, please stop this." Kneeling, he set his weapon on the ground and lifted his hands in surrender. "We humbly beg of you to call off your drakinferno. Please, Your Majesty. What is it that you want from us? Surely the Konungr would meet your needs if you simply asked."

Sirena cackled. "That fool of a king was never able to meet my needs." Black lightning shot from her fingertips and struck the soldier in the chest. Electricity pulsed throughout his body until he crumbled to the ground.

Wincing and shielding her eyes, Foxx looked at Declan. "Don't you see? I'm the only one who can stop this. I don't want to see any more lives lost to save mine. Please, try to understand."

"What about Asher?" Iris asked.

Foxx sucked in a breath. She'd hoped Iris wouldn't bring him up, though it was foolish to imagine she would leave such a crucial factor out of the equation. He would never stop fighting to fulfill his destiny, and if Sirena took Foxx, she feared he might never stop searching for her. He'd promised to find her, and deep in her heart she knew he would go to the ends of the world to keep that promise. "Asher will choose his own path." Foxx grabbed her sister's shoulders. "Run and hide, Iris. Promise me."

Iris didn't have words. She shook her head, unsure herself if she was truly denying Foxx's wishes or simply refusing to accept what needed to be done. More soldiers poured into the square. Birds lined the wall around the entrance and what remained of nearby rooftops. The white lights of the orädi lingered amongst the soldiers, and rumbles like footsteps drew attention to the outer wall where stone faces peeked up over the parapets. Foxx and Iris remembered Declan telling them about the hyvä mon, the *generally docile* rock monsters living in the mountains, and thought they didn't look very docile right now.

Foxx met the Queen's gaze. *Do we have a deal, Sirena?*

Sirena straightened her dress and rolled her shoulders. *While that does sound utterly delightful, dear Foxxglove, nothing is ever that simple, is it? I fear you are too weak to be what I need you to be. Darkness within or not, I now see that your heart is like hers. Frail. And disappointing.*

A hooded figure approached from Sirena's right, again drawing her attention away from Foxx.

"Who is that?" Iris pointed at the person striding toward the Queen. "Didn't they see what happened to the last soldier?"

"I don't think it's another soldier," Declan said. The figure stopped before the Queen, keeping its back to them. The robes adorning the person swayed in the wind, but the hood remained intact.

"It isn't Orion, is it?" Foxx asked.

"It isn't Orion." Declan scrutinized the figure, gleaning what he could from the minute details he could see. Orion had wider shoulders, though the physique did look masculine.

A man covered in soot and wet with snow rushed out from around the building behind them and nearly clambered into Foxx. He halted, his face flushed with fear as he opened his mouth to apologize. Then his eyes widened in recognition. "It's you! You're the ones she wants!" He grabbed Iris' arm and tried to pull her away from them en route to the Queen.

Declan yanked him backward and knocked him out, and the man crumbled to the ground, his nose dripping blood on the bricks.

C

Raven and Dominic hurried through the streets, staying close to the plaza in case their quarry tried to flee the city gates. The other teams had scattered out into the depths of Jericho.

Soon after their search began, the Queen appeared in a whirlwind. Crouching behind one of the planters lining the square, they spied through the plants what followed.

"Mad! Didn't I say?" Dominic whispered, bumping Raven's shoulder until she shushed him. "But look at her!"

Leveling him with a glare, she opened her mouth to scold him when the Queen's voice began to play in their ears, announcing *Arkaemor's most wanted* to the whole city.

"What do we do now?" Angst replaced Raven's annoyance. Then she noticed the Queen's attention to their right and followed her gaze to find Silas standing next to two women on the outskirts. His hand clutched the arm of the woman with white hair, keeping her restrained, it seemed. The other clung to his waist like a scared child. "I knew it!"

Dominic's freckled face scrunched into a scowl as her elbow jarred his ribs.

Then Jerichonian Guardsmen filled the plaza, circling the Queen in a wide berth. Soon after, they watched a swarm of lunae-lumen and a soldier approach the Queen. She immediately slaughtered both. Dominic grimaced and looked away, but Raven couldn't pull her eyes from the scene.

"If Sirena can see the Belamour sisters right now, why is her dragon still destroying the city?"

Shrugging, though not putting much thought into her words, Dominic pointed a stubby finger at the Queen's location. "Who's 'at?" Raven looked at the cloaked figure. Though the person faced them, a hood hid their profile. Finally tracking with Raven's previous observation, Dominic exclaimed, "Is'at Declan? Hey, them's the girls we're looking for!"

"Shut. Up!" Raven mouthed. She scanned the plaza, wondering where Orion might be. A heavy man ran out from behind a building near Declan and the female fugitives. Moments later, Declan clocked him in the nose, and he dropped.

Raven and Dominic winced, then grinned, impressed.

☾

Jax called Hector's name when he found a clear route for them to pass through. Debris and collapsed buildings cluttered the streets, making it tricky to search for their targets. Only minutes ago, they'd fled a city block in time to avoid being flattened by Jericho's enormous clock tower as it collapsed, taking out at least ten other buildings along with it. Jax was not the only Reko Raptor beginning to lose hope in their search, but he pressed on, trusting his commander's orders.

Hector met up with Jax and followed him down the alley. They reached the end of the buildings and were about to turn left onto another marginally clear street when Hector glimpsed a woman seated on the ground against a wall. She sat utterly still, covered in soot and blood. Though not the first corpse they'd come across, this particular body had a little girl kneeling next to it. She cried as she gripped the woman's dress and touched her face, calling out for her mother and trying fervently to wake her.

Jax jogged past the scene but halted when he noticed his commander's hesitation.

Hector regarded Jax, then the child, feeling frozen to the ground as if ice had formed around his boots. Jax repeated his name as a question, and Hector held up a finger, signaling for him to wait. He knew they had a mission to fulfill. Every second brought with it countless deaths all over the city. They didn't have time to stop and help everyone.

It wasn't their city. It wasn't their job.

They belonged to the King's Legion, not the Jerichonian Guard. Their only duty was to their Queen, to retrieve the Belamours and return home.

The little girl's sobs escalated with each breath. Another young girl's face appeared in Hector's thoughts. Just as young. Just as scared.

And just as dead as this one was sure to be if someone didn't intervene.

Mobility returning alongside his integrity, Hector dropped to a knee. "Hello." His soft voice prompted her to rotate toward him, and her sorrowful expression broke his heart into pieces.

She looked five or six at most. Despite the grime coating them, the woman and young girl's kinship couldn't be denied. Both had thin, wispy hair the shade of sun-bleached brown and nearly identical facial features, with the exception of the child's chubby cheeks.

"Mister. Mommy won't wake up. Can you help me wake her up?" She reached for him, tugging on his sleeve with blood-soaked fingers.

"I don't think I can." Hector pressed two fingers against the woman's neck, feeling for a pulse.

The girl whimpered as more tears dripped from her lashes. "But why not?"

Hector glanced at Jax, who had taken a step closer to them.

"Sir, what are we doing? The Belamours?"

Hector thought for a moment, ignoring the question. He looked at the little girl: motherless, lost, and maybe even completely alone. "Where is the rest of your family?"

She dropped her chin and shook her head, her eyes shifting again to her mother's body.

At that, a decision solidified somewhere deep in his bones. He tapped the bottom of her chin, entreating her to meet his eyes. "I'm going to need you to trust me. Do you think you can do that?" She nodded and wiped tears from her cheeks, leaving them smeared red. "My name is Hector." He held his hand out to see if she would shake it.

The girl played nervously with her fingers, swaying back and forth on her feet as she considered his offered hand. At last, she wrapped tiny fingers around two of his own. "Hello, Hector. My name is Annie."

"It's a pleasure to meet you, Annie. This is Jax." He looked at his comrade, and the girl followed his gaze. When she met Jax's eyes, she recoiled closer to Hector, grasping one hand to the black gear covering his bicep. Jax attempted a smile, but it didn't seem to help. "He's nice, I promise. He only looks scary." Hector smiled, and she brightened as she offered Jax a cautious wave. "I'm going to find somewhere safe for you, all right, Annie?"

Annie lifted her hands trustingly. Hector scooped her up in his arms, situated her on his hip, and continued down the passageway.

C

As the man dropped like a tossed sack of flour, Iris' mouth fell open in the shape of an O. Without a word, Declan refocused his attention on the Queen and the hooded figure, as though knocking out a complete stranger was a perfectly normal thing to do.

In response to the new arrival, the wind roared more aggressively than before. Foxx's hair, now pink and sticky with stained blood, lifted into the air, blowing chaotically in the gusts. The blood across her face and neck had already dried and begun peeling off in flakes.

When the person standing before the Queen spoke, they could hear it like a soft reflection floating on the wind. "Mother, this has to stop."

Even from a distance, they could see the Queen roll her eyes with crystal clear accuracy.

"Did he say mother?" Iris asked. Foxx had already stepped forward, but Declan wrapped his hand around her arm again, warning her to stay put.

The man continued. "Leave the Belamours alone, and I will come home with you."

"Alexander." Sirena shook her head, her voice flippant. Black eyes scrutinized him with stifled fury. "It's been a long time. Not getting yourself into trouble, I hope."

"I—"

"What are you doing here, Alexander? Why are you in Jericho?" Despite the rage in Sirena's tone, Foxx detected no trace of surprise. She'd expected her son to confront her in the city, and Foxx wondered if she might have visions of the future, too. "Visiting your precious Konungr? You two aren't consorting with those girls, I trust."

Alexander's voice remained peaceful in contrast to Sirena's venom. "You know what I'm doing here." Foxx tilted her head so her dominant ear faced the scene, thinking the voice dancing in the wind sounded familiar.

"You seek to dismantle us. To tear apart Arkaemor piece by piece until there is nothing left." One hand rested gracefully against her hip and the other lifted to adjust her hair, somehow securely in place despite the wind. Kaen appeared in the air above them, gliding in a gentle circle as he awaited his next orders. "Don't you care about your father and I? What about your sister? Have you forgotten about Avaline? She surely hasn't forgotten about you. It destroyed her when you left, did you know? That child still isn't right in the head because you abandoned her."

The Prince felt slugged in the gut. "You're the reason Avaline is what she is, Mother. Your corruption bred despair and guilt and agony until there was nothing left. She was gone long before I fled." The Queen's face grew redder with each passing word. "I seek to put things right in Arkaemor. That's why I'm here."

"Things *are* right. You seek my Thrones. My power. You always have. Let's not pretend you're on some noble mission to save the world."

"Mother, that's not t—"

"Enough!" A gust of wind erupted from her body, blowing the hood from his head to reveal shaggy, chestnut hair.

Foxx gasped as every drop of oxygen forced its way from her lungs. She took another step forward, but Declan's hand tightened. He said her name in warning.

"Is that Asher?" Iris shouted.

The Prince's body flinched as if he'd heard his name, but he didn't turn to them. Declan spoke near Iris' ear, though his voice carried faintly on the wind. "That is the Crown Prince, Alexander *Asher* Aldrich, heir to the Thrones of Arkaemor."

Foxx shook her head, her heart a torrent of sparring emotions. "No…"

Queen Sirena's smirk turned toward them, confirming Declan's suspicion that if they could hear Alexander and the Queen, then Alexander and the Queen could hear them.

Iris spoke the questions Foxx couldn't set free. "How can he be? That's the man we were traveling with before you found us in Petrichor."

"That may be true. But he's also, most certainly, Prince Alexander."

Asher's true name left Foxx's lips in a whisper. His head rotated toward it, a look of torment staining his features. Her heart broke in two as warring reactions fought for purchase. She'd missed him so much; had longed for the moment they might be reunited. She'd indulged in daydreams about what his lips might have felt like against hers as they danced beneath the canopy, showered by frolicking rainbows of light and rain.

But if he truly was the Prince of Arkaemor—Sirena Aldrich's son —then he'd deceived them from the very moment they'd met. He'd lied to them about everything.

Queen Sirena did not miss their exchange and wheeled on Foxx with a vicious grin. *He is charming, isn't he? Do you love him, Foxxglove? My beautifully troubled Prince? It seems to me your little speech about revenge may be less true than you would have me believe.*

Another tear slid down Foxx's cheek. Her eyes leveled on Asher's, unable to look away. His expression showed his shame and misery, and she didn't know what to think or how to feel. All that registered was the devouring ache in her chest.

I think he might love you, Foxxglove. Look at him. Can't you tell?

After dragging her attention from Asher's gaze, Foxx spat back, out loud for all to hear, "If he is really your spawn, then I have been devastatingly fooled."

Sirena's eyes widened, expressing surprise for the first time since entering the city. She looked to her son and then back at Foxx. Asher tried to get her attention, knowing Foxx's words must have been a response to private provocation. *Oh, how devilish of him,* the Queen crowed, keeping her applause between Foxx and herself. *You had no idea.*

"Sirena!" Asher's voice cut into their conversation, and Sirena smiled at him.

"Hush, Alexander. Mummy is busy. You gave up your crown when you abandoned your family. You no longer have a say in the affairs of this world."

"I had to, Mother. You know I had to." Asher almost looked sad, and it occurred to Iris how hard it must have been for him to leave his family when he set out on his quest. If he really was the Prince, then he'd given up everything. A whole life.

Foxx's face had gone cold.

"You've taken this too far," Asher said.

"No! *I* say when it is too far. Not you. And not that deplorable Konungr!"

Declan and the girls could feel the shift in the air as Sirena screamed at her son. The whirlwind grew stronger and more dense. Chairs, tables, and all other manner of things lifted off the ground. Most of the soldiers on the outskirts ducked for cover, unable to hold their aim steady in the turbulent weather.

Asher focused on the Queen, no longer allowing his eyes to linger on Foxx. "Look at you, Mother. You're so consumed with fear that you're burning a city to the ground. Does this make you feel powerful?" He lifted his hands at his sides. "What in the world have you become?"

"I remain who I have always been. Those women you care so much for mean to destroy me and everything I hold dear. Just like their rotten parents."

"You hold nothing dear but your own selfish greed," Asher said with a coldness neither of the girls recognized.

A furious and unfamiliar voice bellowed from somewhere outside the square, vibrating the already trembling plaza. "SI-RE-NA!" Peals of thunder preceded bolts of lightning in the clouds. One broke free, striking the dragon and producing an agonized whine. It flapped its wings, attempting to reclaim its balance on the wind. Sirena's head whipped toward the sound of her name before rising to look at Kaen. Then she released a deafening scream from the pit of her stomach.

The man's voice echoed around them, loud and fierce and unrelenting. It boomed like the worsening storm, a roar of merciless thunder. "You are not welcome here. Be GONE!"

The winds surrounding the Queen spun out of control. Asher threw his hand up to block his face as he backed away. Sirena's feet lifted from the ground, her magic pulling her into the air. "I will allow you this round, Alexander. You seem to have made an intriguing mess of things on your own, and I'm curious to witness how it will all turn out for you. However, you will stop searching for Celestelvyra. You *will* stop fighting against me. If you disobey, if this continues, I will destroy every single one of you. I will never stop hunting until each of you is torn to shreds." The Queen's eyes left the Prince in search of the man who'd ordered her to leave.

He shouted her name in a final warning.

The buildings continued to quake as she rose higher. Declan tried to pull Foxx and Iris away from the edge of the terrace, but Foxx wouldn't budge.

Asher's eyes met those of the man who'd triggered Sirena's retreat. The man called out, but Asher ignored him, turning on his heel and sprinting toward Foxx. Four Jerichonian soldiers appeared at his sides, guarding him from flying debris.

The building next to Iris, Foxx, and Declan began to crumble. Bricks rained down like enormous hail. Declan and Iris jumped out of the way, but Foxx was locked on Asher, trapped in her head, her thoughts, her memories. As he ran at her, flanked by armed soldiers with the Queen's turmoil in his backdrop, a serious and commanding expression on his face, he really did look like a prince.

Before he reached her, a brick from the building at her back cracked her across the head. Her body dropped, her knees slamming to the ground like stones against concrete, and she landed on her side, unconscious.

Iris screamed as she took in an exact replica of the vision the Tree of Knowing had revealed to her.

Declan wrapped an arm around her stomach and pulled her backward as more rubble crashed around them. "Iris! Alexander will get her. We have to get out of here!"

When Asher and his Guard reached them, two soldiers dropped to uncover Foxx. Asher hoisted her body into his arms and looked at Declan. "Lead the way." To the Guards at his back, he yelled, "Protect them."

Declan yanked Iris' forward, pulling her hand until she followed him without hesitation. They fled the square with Asher carrying Foxx at their heels and Jerichonian soldiers guarding them on both sides.

The Queen floated high above the entrance plaza with her drak-inferno circling around her. Vibrations rippled outward from the square in waves, demolishing the surrounding block like an earthquake. Fissures sliced through the brick streets, and the few surviving glass windows shattered into shrapnel. Only the outer wall remained intact, held in place by the might of the city and the strength of the hyvä mon.

Then, as if it had all been a horrible nightmare, Queen Sirena let fly one more blaring shriek, and she and her dragon disappeared in a puff of smoke.

The city grew still.

The ground ceased shaking.

All fell silent but for the wails of the people left behind in ruin.

Part Three

RIGHTEOUS UPRISING

When you are broken, cry out to Me.
Find comfort in My fortress, your secret place.
Do not be dismayed, even when all hope seems lost.
I am here. I am with you. I know the way.
I have already walked the path.
Put one foot in front of the other, My child,
Go in peace as the sands shifts beneath your feet.

~*An excerpt from Jumalan Sana.*
Found in the Poems and Songs transcribed by Kafki the Navi

Chapter 30

A City In Ashes

It had been three days since Storm shed its coat for the new moon of Ammil to take its place. The feather hanging in the sky offered the faintest light on Jericho in wake of its ruination. Little could be heard but the shuffling of people wandering about, lost, without home or destination, and the tragic cries of lament.

Declan held tight to Iris' hand even after they found an empty alley for Asher to lay Foxxglove down and check her injuries. She hadn't woken, despite him sprinting with her in his arms.

A soldier bent next to him and looked her over. "How can we help, Your Highness? The hospital was hit, but we might be able to find a clear path to the palace."

Asher shook his head. "It's too far, Jorunn, and there's no telling how long it would take us to maneuver through the debris." He looked up at the soldier, then to the others. "You four need to make your way deeper into the city. There will be lots of citizens requiring your assistance."

"Leave you, Your Highness?" Another soldier knelt on Asher's opposite side.

Jorunn looked between the Prince and Foxx. "She is the one the Queen was after, yes? As well as the other?" Asher nodded and glanced at Iris. "Then perhaps they should be taken to the Konungr right away, sire."

"No. I'll handle it from here. Vali will have plenty to deal with already."

"But, Your—"

"Red," Jorunn scolded, silencing the second soldier. Red rose to stand with the others.

Asher said, "Sirena won't come back tonight. We'll find somewhere safe to stay until things settle. I'll regroup with Vali in the morning."

"Yes, Your Highness." Jorunn stood and gestured for the other soldiers to get moving. Before leaving the alley, he looked back at them. "Be careful, Prince Alexander."

"You as well, my friend." Asher returned his attention to Foxx. He wiped her cheeks, adjusted her clothing so it lay comfortably, and tucked stray hairs behind her ears so they didn't tickle her face. He inspected her arms, her hands, and her legs for unseen injury, oblivious to the two people standing behind him, watching his every move.

"Is she going to be okay?" The Tree of Knowing hadn't revealed the outcome of Foxx's wounds, nor had it indicated what Iris was to do about the man standing next to her, grasping her hand. She said Asher's name and, with resistance, he pulled his gaze from Foxx and stood. When he held out his arms, Iris released Declan and ran to him, burying her face in his shoulder as her sobs broke free. He clutched her tighter, sliding his hand up and down her spine and murmuring calming words in her ear.

When she settled, she pulled back without letting go and looked him in the eyes. "Alexander?" The evidence was overwhelming. He'd just commanded soldiers—and they'd obeyed him. "*Prince* Alexander?"

"Surprise?" His head shrank into his shoulders, but his lips curled into that playfully boyish grin she'd missed so much. If she had the energy, she might have slugged him, but instead, she rested her forehead on his shoulder and allowed her breathing to return to normal.

Asher looked past her to where Declan stood with his hands in his pockets. "Thank you for taking care of them."

Considering the circumstances, Declan hadn't the slightest clue how to respond. He also didn't know what to think about Iris embracing the Prince so intimately. He'd thought Foxx was the one in love with the man they'd left in Petrichor, but now he wasn't sure. After a long moment, he bowed. "Of course, Your Highness."

Asher winced. "Please, no title or formalities are necessary." Iris punched his ribcage with the minute strength she had left. He pulled back from her again and chuckled. "You must be tired. I know you want to hit me harder than that."

Laughing weakly, she stepped away from him and returned her hand to Declan's.

"To be fair, I'm not technically the Prince anymore. I forfeited the title when I ran away. I'm little more than a traitor now, as I think was pretty obvious in the plaza."

"There's always an excuse for your secrets." Iris tried to determine whether the sting of his betrayal outweighed her joy at being reunited. Asher shrugged and crouched next to Foxx, caressing her cheek again and encouraging her to wake up.

Hearing footsteps from the direction of the square, Declan aimed his pistol at the mouth of the alley. Raven and Dominic appeared in a rush, but at the sight of his weapon, they froze and threw their hands in the air.

"Don't shoot!" Hair fell from Raven's braid in a fraying mess, and both she and Dominic wore a heavy layer of brick dust and soot.

Declan didn't lower his weapon as he acknowledged both of them by name. "Why are you following us? If you think you're going to take them from me now, you're severely mistaken."

Raven and Dominic shared a look.

"You know them?" Iris scanned the newcomers from head to toe, thinking they seemed a peculiar duo. The woman was tiny, with oval eyes and pale skin. The man towered over her, his width nearly three times her size.

Asher stood again and turned to face them. When Raven and Dominic saw him, both Legion soldiers dropped to one knee, heads bowed. "Stand up, stand up." Asher waved his hands, already annoyed by the customary practices after less than five minutes of his title being unveiled. They obeyed, and when he extended a hand, Raven furrowed her brow. "It's Asher. Pleased to meet you both."

Declan's pistol remained level, hovering between their heads. "This is Raven Nightshade and Dominic Ives. They're here with Hector's crew, the Reko Raptors, if you can believe it." Both Asher and Iris' eyebrows flew up. "They were searching for the girls. Their mission was to find them and turn them over to the Queen."

Raven shot arrows at him with dark pupils.

"Is that so?" Asher's gaze shifted between them. "And now?"

Dominic threw his hands in the air. "Well, it's all gone to bloomin' hell now, asn't it?" Raven scowled at her partner, reprimanding him for swearing in front of the Prince.

Asher chuckled. "Yes, I suppose it has."

Declan directed Asher's question at Raven and waited for her response as he watched her calculating eyes take in the scene. She looked at Foxx, bloody on the ground, Iris' hand clasped within his own, and Prince Alexander standing in unity with them.

"I think I am beginning to understand," she said.

Asher glanced at Declan before saying, "I think we're safe from Sirena for the night. Right now we need to get a handle on the situation, and then we can come up with a new plan. Whether that plan involves you or not can be decided later. At the moment, I want to get Foxx somewhere safe and see what's happening throughout the city. There will be people lost, injured, and needing our help. Can I count on all of you, at least for tonight, to follow me in this task?" His request came out so commanding and princely that Iris thought it might be impossible for anyone to refuse him.

Dominic laughed and pulled at his ginger beard with chubby fingers. "Wonder what Hector's gonna say about this."

Raven took longer to respond. The gears behind her eyes turned as she processed the situation. Then she said, "At least for tonight."

"Don't think I won't raise my weapon against you just as easily tomorrow if you try to carry out your previous mission." Declan looked only at Raven. She held his gaze, scrutinizing his expression alongside his harsh words.

Another thumping of footfalls sounded from around the corner, and Wyatt and Marshal skidded to a halt at the mouth of the alley. "Hey! We've been looking everywhere for you."

"Is that Prince Alexander?" Marshal asked.

Iris blurted out a single laugh, and Asher forced an awkward smile. "Maybe we need to get you a sign to hold," she suggested. "Or a nametag."

Wyatt bowed. "Hi, Your Highness. Sorry for our lack of respect, but you guys *have* to come see this."

"See what?" Raven asked.

"Is she alive?" Marshal pointed at Foxx.

Iris and Asher exclaimed, "Yes!"

"Then bring her along, and follow us!"

Asher exchanged another look with Declan. He knew of the old Reko Raptors, but since Declan seemed to know the current soldiers personally, he deferred to his judgment. Eventually, Declan shrugged, thinking they didn't have a better course of action at the moment.

Asher lifted Foxx into his arms.

Marshal, tactless and excited, followed by Wyatt who smacked his head and told him to calm down, exited the alley the way they'd come. Dominic dipped his head to the Prince and strolled after them. Raven briefly inspected Declan, Iris, and their attached hands before turning and hurrying to catch up with Dominic. Asher carried Foxx, with Iris and Declan trailing him.

Wyatt called back to the company, "If you see anyone along the way, invite 'em to come with us, all right?"

Raven and Dominic shared a skeptical glance. "Wyatt, what's going on? Where are you taking us?"

"You'll see, you'll see!" Marshal said.

As they followed the Hearne brothers, they observed the depths of the city's destruction. While some buildings remained in decent shape, many had been obliterated. Piles of bricks and debris littered every walkway. Furniture, potted plants, produce from outdoor markets, and wood planks from porches lay scattered about, blocking the paths.

The streetlamps hadn't been lit before the commotion began, so the company traveled in an eerie darkness, brightened at times by remnants of the dragon's breath. Snow began to fall, but rather than the crisp white it had been before the attack, it fell in shades of gray. The smell of smoke and char filled their nostrils without reprieve.

Citizens moved about the city, searching for family and friends, clearing walkways to their homes and businesses, helping the injured, and checking bodies for life. Hands and legs protruded from piles of rubble. Declan paused a few times to check the pulses of bodies lying along their path.

Iris could barely handle the tragedy around every corner and instead turned her eyes to the sky. Smoke reflecting the amber flames darkened the expanse, but the stratosphere remained visible amongst ashen smog. Painted in wisps of aster, magenta, and chartreuse, the sky twinkled with a million stars.

Then light at their backs drew their attention, and Iris and Declan turned to see a swarm of bright insects flying toward them.

They lit the area like a torch, covering everything in bursts of white. "What are they?" Iris lifted a hand as the insects surrounded their company on all sides. Most stayed at waist level, lighting the ground at their feet. Others swirled around their heads, or scattered to search nearby buildings, returning to the humans before they passed on.

"Lunae-lumen. Or more commonly, moonflies." Declan smiled at Iris' fascination. "These are the same flies that attacked the Queen."

"They're lighting our way," she said, and Declan nodded. Hearing a scuffle behind her, Iris whipped around to find a young boy hiding behind a pile of felled bricks. Stopping, she encouraged Declan to go on without her, but he didn't. Stepping toward the boy, she extended a hand. "You can come out. It's safe now." The boy didn't move, his head perfectly still over the top of the pile. Clumps of flaxen hair looked singed, as if he'd barely escaped a fire. "Are you alone?"

Several of the lunae-lumen noticed Iris and Declan's separation from the group and zipped back to them. Cautiously, the boy stood, revealing charred clothing and sooty skin. Four moonflies left Iris to examine the boy. He didn't cower in their presence, and she thought he must be familiar with the strange, luminescent insects. "Come on. You can come with us." A second boy popped his head above the pile in a jolt, and Iris' smile widened. "You can both come."

The boys stepped out around the debris and moved closer. The oldest, a boy maybe eleven or twelve years old, took her hand first. A single lunae-lumen circled their combined hands before dashing back to the younger boy and flying around his head. The older of the two glanced back at him and confirmed he would be safe. After a nudge from the moonflies, the little boy ran to them and took Iris' other hand.

Together, they spun and caught up with the rest of the group. Declan let them pass before falling into step behind them.

As they continued on, other citizens joined. Some they invited, but many were simply drawn to the crowd, needing company to combat their loneliness and desperation in the midst of tragedy. Those leading the group attempted to travel streets with maneuverable debris, though sometimes climbing or shifting the rubble became unavoidable. Soon, they reached the end of a road that opened up into a wide courtyard, and the lunae-lumen scattered. It only took Iris moments to realize they stood at the foot of the Monastery of the Morrow.

Torches illuminated the courtyard with blazing firelight, revealing the citizens who'd congregated there. On the left, they saw people with broken bones, cuts and bruises, and horrible burns. Those well enough to be helpful tended to the injured or ran about the place with buckets of water or bandages or food.

Iris saw a large cypress at the back of the courtyard with a group of children gathered beneath its weeping branches. Some held each other, some wept, while others giggled and played. Iris pointed the children out to the boys holding her hands, and the youngest hugged her around the waist before they walked on to join their friends.

At the center of it all stood a man handing out orders like a gentle commander: making sure everyone was taken care of, sending people out on supply runs, and issuing scouts to round up more citizens in need. Dominic let free a deep belly laugh that Hector heard from across the yard.

When he saw them, he moved to greet them. "I am glad you guys are here. We could really use the help."

Raven's mouth fell open as she spoke his name.

Hector offered a small smile. When he saw the Prince, his back straightened out of habit. Then he noticed the desperation on Asher's face and the woman in his arms. "Is she badly injured?"

"Hit by falling bricks."

"Take her over there." Hector gestured to a woman across the yard using a rag to clean ash from an elderly man's face. He put a hand on Asher's shoulder, holding his gaze for a long moment. So many thoughts bubbled to the surface of things he wished to say, but instead, he promised, "Maia will take care of her." Asher thanked him by name and hurried away.

Marshal and Wyatt grinned at each other, but when Hector lifted his eyebrows at them, they scurried off to make themselves useful.

Raven still looked shocked, her lips hanging open as she scrutinized her commander. She said his name again, and he turned his attention to her. "You did all this? In an hour?"

Hector sighed. "A lot of people are making it happen, and there's still far more to do. Jax is running around somewhere. Some of our soldiers and some of the Jerichonian Guard, too. Plus several citizens who managed to make it through the attack unharmed." Raven shook her head, words failing her.

Hector extended a hand to Declan, who stared at it for a moment as if debating whether or not it might be a trick or trap. So much history stretched between them; so many broken things. Both men remembered simultaneously their dispute earlier in the day and Hector's spiteful comment about Declan's brother.

Still, after catching a glimpse of Iris' encouraging smile, Declan accepted the handshake. "Okay, Commander, what can we do to help?"

C

When the commander of the Jerichonian Guard learned of the people congregating at the Monastery, he arrived to investigate. Though astonished to find an enemy commander at the helm, Abram Havlar greeted Hector like an old friend.

With Abram came General Eero Asger, Captain Solvi Brenna, and all the troops they could gather. They worked all through the night, their numbers growing as darkness dwindled into the fringes of dawn.

As the rising sun unveiled the full weight of the city's devastation, the commanders at last began to feel some semblance of organization. Assembling the able-bodied men and women, they divided into teams.

The first task was to gather blankets to keep people warm and shield the courtyard from the snow. Fabric and pelts were stitched together into a canopy that spanned the yard.

As that undertaking began, the injured became the next priority. Jericho's hospital had been ravaged by the onslaught, but many private practices throughout the city had survived. They provided medical supplies and took in some of the more severely wounded. Even still, people continued to die as the day went on, succumbing to their burns and injuries.

Other teams began clearing debris from the streets. Eero formed a group to round up the wounded and the lost. Marshal and Wyatt joined him, while Jax and Raven organized another team to spread out and recover the fallen. Gabriel, of the White Luna Inn, helped guide them, making sure not a single street would be left unsearched.

Dominic partnered with Solvi Brenna in building stone-lined pits outside the wall. While he rallied helpers from within the city, Solvi headed outside to recruit hyvä mon lingering nearby. She'd always found the creatures fascinating and, even as a little girl, had faced the giants without fear. Though they couldn't communicate through speech, she knew she could convince them to help.

Iris and Declan stayed at the Monastery with Hector and Abram. The injured filled more than half the courtyard and spilled out into the connecting streets, and more arrived with each passing hour. Declan helped Maia and the other healers, while Iris jumped back and forth between checking on the children and running errands.

Orion had yet to surface, and Iris and Declan worried his body might eventually turn up with the lost. As the hours progressed, both attempted to push thoughts of him from their minds and focus on their current duties.

Asher spent most of his time at Foxx's bedside. Maia and Declan both examined her and found her injuries minor but for the knot on her head. Asher wondered if the head wound could truly be the cause of her continued sleep, or if it had more to do with her broken heart.

Pushing hair from her face, he dabbed her cheeks with a damp cloth and spoke softly to her. "Please wake up, Foxx." He hadn't been able to dispel the memory of her expression in the plaza from his mind: so much rage and sorrow. He leaned closer and squeezed his eyes shut, restraining tears. "I know you're angry, and I'm sorry. I'm sorry for so many things. But I need you to wake up. I can't go through this again. I can't. Please don't make me, love." Holding her hand in both of his, he leaned to kiss the back of it.

Declan's voice broke through his grief. "Are you talking about Lady Avaline?" His hands absentmindedly rinsed soot and blood from a soiled rag as the Prince turned to him. Upon seeing Asher's unconcealed emotions, Declan fumbled for words. "It's just... I heard she's in pretty bad shape."

Without responding, Asher turned back to Foxx, worried talking about his sister on top of everything else might completely tear him in two.

C

Several hours past sunrise, an envoy arrived at the entrance to the Monastery. Soldiers on stocky, Cordilleran steeds surrounded a vuokara-drawn carriage embellished in violet and silver.

Some of the soldiers dismounted as Commander Havlar approached to greet them.

Hector had been across the yard trying to convince Maia to get some rest. When he saw the envoy, he gave up his argument and moved to join the commander. Three steps later, he hesitated, the weight of recent decisions hanging heavy on his shoulders. For a brief moment, he questioned everything. Should he flee? Return to the Queen and plead insanity? Could he even make it to the city gates before they caught him?

On the other side of the yard, he saw Raven and Jax in deep discussion and wondered if they, too, questioned his sanity. When they noticed the carriage, they scanned the area in search of him. With a nod from Jax, Hector understood that they were ready to fight or flee—to faithfully obey whatever he asked.

He nodded back and casually lifted a hand, letting them know he would handle it. When he stopped at the commander's side, Abram's eyes slid to him and matched his concern. Others working in the courtyard began to notice the new arrivals and paused their tasks to watch.

The soldier leading the envoy stopped in front of Abram and folded his hands behind his back. His uniform, like the others with him, bore the same colors as the Guard, but fur lined their collars and cuffs, and silvery moons had been embroidered down each arm in phased order.

"Viggo, I apologize for not returning as expected." Abram gestured to the courtyard. "As you can see, we have been quite busy."

"I *can* see, Commander." Viggo bowed to Abram and offered a brief nod to Hector. A brown braid hung below each ear, and several more followed the arc of his head, weaving toward a bun in the back. Like most Jerichonian men, he wore a thick beard, though not nearly as long as Abram's. "You owe me no apology, of course. His Majesty was merely concerned and insisted on finding you."

The door to the carriage opened and a man stepped out, though all but his legs remained hidden behind the door as he turned back to the cabin. A woman joined him, and both walked out around the open door, leaving one of the Guards to shut it behind them.

The man ran a hand along one of the vuokara's single horns as they walked past, then approached Viggo, Abram, and Hector with his wife on his arm. The soldiers bowed in unison as he raked a hand through his hair, which he kept short and parted down one side. Despite its pale gray hue, he looked young for a king, hardly older than Hector himself.

Abram lifted a hand in presentation. "Commander Kayvan, I believe you have met our sovereigns, Konungr Vali and Dróttning Ingrid Kirkavall."

Hector dipped his head. "It's an honor to see you again, Your Majesty."

Without more than a cursory glance at Hector, the King looked at Abram and scratched his clean-shaven chin. "So glad to have found you, Commander. You had us all worried when you didn't return with a report. Imagine my surprise as I arrived to find you consorting with the enemy." He looked pointedly at Hector with feigned kindness. "Commander Kayvan, please explain to me in great and intricate detail why I shouldn't have you arrested right this moment for heinous crimes against Jericho. How is it that you happened to be in my city when it was attacked?"

Hector's tongue caught in his throat, but Abram responded for him. "Commander Kayvan has come to our aid, Your Majesty. Working ceaselessly through the night."

"Work that would be unneeded had his queen not endeavored to convert my city to rubble."

"He should be detained for questioning. Surely he knew of this attack. We cannot trust him." Dróttning Ingrid's accent was classic Cordilleran, scattered with pinched and rolled Rs, and rounded and emphasized Oos. Her teeth touched her lower lip when she spoke the letter W, making it sound like a V.

Much like his appearance, the Konungr's accent was entirely different from his citizens. His words rolled gracefully from his tongue like a fine wine. "I must say, I am inclined to agree with my brilliant wife, Kayvan."

"I had no idea what Queen Sirena was planning. She sent us here to retrieve two women she's been hunting them for quite some time, but our plan was to take them and go without disturbance. I'm not sure what inspired this attack, but I am attempting to make amends."

"You thought yourself so bold as to come and abduct two

women from *my* city?" Vali pulled at his sleeves without breaking eye contact, casually adjusting the crescent cufflinks at his wrists.

"They're not citizens of Cordillera. They're nomads, and fugitives."

Vali tilted his head as if in confusion. "Once someone steps through the barrier, they are under my protection. You have no jurisdiction here, Commander. Certainly not in the royal city."

Losing himself in a moment of irritation, Hector said, "I am commander of the King's Legion. I have jurisdiction everywhere." Abram's eyes widened next to him, as did Viggo's.

The Konungr remained unmoved but for the upturning of his lips. "Is that so?" he purred, like a cat toying with a mouse before slaughtering it. "And tell me, Kayvan. The women you were hunting, did they happen to be the faces we saw in the sky?"

Hector swallowed hard, and Vali's eyes lit with a sudden fire. "Arrest him." Two of his Royal Guards clutched Hector's wrists behind his back before he had time to react. As they moved to drag him away, Vali lifted a hand to halt them. "The Belamour sisters, is that correct? And where are they now?"

Hector didn't fight the men holding him steady. "They are here. One was injured in the attack, and the other has been helping us through the night, but you need not worry. They have nothing to fear from me or my team."

"Says the man about to be clapped in irons." Ingrid adjusted the fur stole draped across her shoulders. The head of a wolf empty of its skull rested over her heart.

Hector didn't respond immediately, never taking his eyes off Vali's intense stare. He fumbled for time, trying to figure out how he could get himself out of this mess. Raven and Jax remained in position across the yard. He could feel their eyes on him, though he didn't dare look and make their presence known. How would they respond if the sovereigns really did put him in chains? Would they attack or stand back to let things play out?

"Konungr Vali, Dróttning Ingrid." Hector cleared his throat as a bead of sweat formed on his forehead. Vali let his chin drop, signaling he was free to speak. "I have lived a life full of mistakes. Many things that can never be redeemed. I can't change that, and honestly, I wouldn't even if I could. The man I have been is not the man I wish to be, but every single moment of that life has led me right here, to a night of lamenting citizens and the constant smell of burning flesh I fear may never leave my nose. Everything I have done has led me to this morning, this city, standing before you right now."

Vali's lips curled in amusement.

Hector didn't know whether to take it as a positive sign or mockery, but he pressed on. "If you wish to arrest me, then so be it. I am an adversary in your city. A commander behind enemy lines. Were I in your position not long ago, I may have ordered myself beheaded on the spot. I will comply with whatever you deem just, Your Majesties." Hector forced his shoulders to relax.

Vali's eyes flickered with surprise, his lips pressing into a straight line. Abram stepped forward and opened his mouth to speak, but Vali silenced him with a finger in the air. He scrutinized Hector as if trying to read the depths of his soul. After a long moment, his gaze surveyed the courtyard, finally taking in the scene in the background of their conversation.

He observed the injured on the far left, the supplies being gathered, and the people working together in unison, both Jerichonian and Legion. His vision slid right, to the children huddled beneath a tree. Some were just waking. Others seemed like they'd been playing for hours. A woman sat with them, and he thought she might be one of the women he'd seen in the sky, though he'd been fairly distracted when their faces had been on display. He watched for a moment as she spoke to them, moving her hands about with excited energy as if telling them a story. The children seemed enthralled by her enthusiasm.

"It seems you have been tireless in your efforts, Hector." Vali returned his attention to the soldiers in front of him.

"I don't know about tireless. At the moment, I believe I could sleep for a week and not feel rested. I'm not entirely certain I wouldn't enjoy the reprieve of a cell, if it is your will to see me in one."

"Changing sides can have that effect on a man." Vali adjusted the cuffs of his sleeves again. His eyes followed the work of his hands before flashing back to Hector as he added, "I should know." He snapped his fingers. "You may release him, Elijah, Sten."

Hector rubbed his wrists, thinking over the Konungr's words. He didn't know much of Vali's history or what he meant about changing sides, though his outlandish personality and often unconventional antics were well known throughout the territories. When

Hector had personally come in contact with him, he'd always found him to be audacious and unyielding, never truly obeying Sirena's instructions and constantly toeing the lines drawn for him.

Yet the Queen rarely punished him as she did others who defied her. Hector had always been curious about their relationship. Why, even to her utter annoyance, had she allowed him to get away with so many things? Why tolerate such blatant disregard for her wishes?

When she spoke of him in the King's office, she'd sounded fearful of his probable involvement, yet hours later she'd laid waste to his city.

So did Sirena have a soft spot for the Mad King? Did she hate him? Or did she fear him?

Hector wondered now if it wasn't perhaps a touch of all three.

CHAPTER 31

CREMATORIUM

"You have much to prove, Commander." Ingrid's voice broke Hector's stare. Then something caught her eye, and she left her husband's side. Alerted by her escape, three members of the Royal Guard hurried after her.

Ingrid held up the fabric of her plum dress as she walked, revealing boots with silver buttons that matched the embroidery on her belt. Stopping several feet from where Foxxglove lay, she said, "Prince Alexander?"

Asher looked up to find the Queen of Cordillera standing before him. His heart tightened as he rose to greet her. "Dróttning Ingrid."

"You have grown." She smiled as she inspected him from head to toe.

Relieved by her pleasantries, he leaned in for a hug. He should have expected her kindness, despite what his mother had done to their city. Aside from Avaline, Vali and Ingrid were more his family than his own blood. "I'm twenty-eight years old, Ingrid. I don't grow anymore."

Ingrid pinched his bicep, testing the muscles. "No? I believe your moons on the run have strengthened you. Perhaps in more ways than one?"

"Living in the wilderness will do that."

Hazel eyes, lined in deep purple, flashed in the sunlight. "Indeed. You should not have stayed away so long, Alexander. Vali has been worried about you."

Asher scratched the back of his head. "I know, I should have checked in or sent word. I'm sorry."

Ingrid glanced behind him, eyeing the woman with the white hair. "It seems we have much to catch up on. Walk with me?" She extended the crook of her elbow, requesting him to escort her. "You look very tired, Alexander."

"You look good enough for the both of us, Ingrid." Asher took in her timeless beauty. She stood with her head high, elegant and confident without a hint of arrogance. A blonde braid arched over her head and smaller braids lay in rows from her temples, hanging free down her back atop loose hair. Though the Konungr almost never wore a crown, a thin silver circlet tapered to a point between her eyebrows, embellished with a crescent moon.

"Still the shameless Prince we know and love, I see."

"Some things never change." He chuckled. "However, if you don't mind, I've been going by Asher. "

"Asher? Hmm. It seems some things *do* change." She eyed him with intrigue. "We heard of your departure from Castle Solís many moons ago. Why did you not come to us, Alexander?" Putting her hand to plum-stained lips, she amended, "I mean Asher."

"I've only been in the city a few days. I would have come to the palace, but I wanted to be discreet in case my mother had spies here." Both looked to where the Konungr, Viggo, and both commanders watched them circle the courtyard.

"I am not sure we can trust Hector. He has worked for the Aldrich's far too long. Although, here I stand arm in arm with the son of the woman who destroyed my city."

At that, Asher tugged on her arm to halt their steps and turned to face her. "Ingrid, I am so sorry for what my mother did to Jericho."

She shook her head. "All that comes and goes and rises and falls happens by the will of Elohim's grand design. Even if we do not always understand."

"You're right. And truthfully, He is the reason I'm here to begin with. I'm working to correct things."

Suddenly very curious, a familiar spark returned to her eyes. "How do you plan to do it?"

"Don't be nosy, Ingrid." Linking arms again, they continued their stroll. "I have my schemes. I need Foxxglove to heal, and then we'll be on our way. All will be explained in time."

"She is the woman you were sitting vigil with just now?" The Dróttning glanced back at the area of wounded citizens. Asher nodded, and she could feel the sadness spilling off of him. "Amaryllis' daughter, Foxxglove Belamour. We saw her and her sister in the sky. Will she be all right?"

Asher shrugged. "She hit her head, but I really don't know. In truth, I worry she may be hiding in her subconscious so as not to face me." His cheeks blushed, shocking Ingrid so her mouth fell open.

"Alexander! What have you done to this girl?"

Eyes down in shame, he said, "She didn't know I was the Prince until she found me talking to my mother in the entrance plaza."

Ingrid frowned. "She should be proud of your title. And so should you, *Asher*."

"Even with a mother like mine?" he asked, truly seeking an answer somewhere in the caverns of his chest.

Ingrid's tone was almost scolding. "Sirena is no reflection on you, my friend. She never has been, and she never could be. Anyone who knows your heart can see that."

A small smile returned. "That means a lot, Ingrid. Thank you."

With a kiss to his cheek, the Dróttning returned to her husband's side as Vali extended a hand.

"My darling, Ingrid. You seem to have picked up a stray. Alexander, we heard you left the castle. I wish you had come right to us."

"I know, and I'm sorry, but I had other plans. Things I needed to take care of." Asher looked at Hector and nodded in greeting.

"I understand, of course." Vali's eyes drifted sideways, again finding the woman entertaining the children beneath the tree. "So you found them. After all this time. The daughters of Amaryllis Belamour."

"That's Iris, the youngest. Foxxglove was injured."

"Is she all right?"

Asher cast a glance over his shoulder. "I think she will be."

Vali peeked around him, trying to get a look, but nurses crowded his line of sight, tending to her now that Asher had left her side. "We saw them in the sky. Foxxglove was the one with hair as white as snow? What a strange color for one so young." Ingrid slipped her arm through the Konungr's and nudged his shoulder. Nodding, Vali looked at the men standing behind him. "I'd like a Guard on each of them, please. I fear some of our civilians may not be as friendly as others. Keep your distance. They need not worry without proper reason." Elijah and Sten bowed and left.

"Do you really think that's necessary?" Asher asked.

Vali shrugged. "It can't hurt." His expression shifted into one of deep reflection as he murmured, "Foxxglove Belamour, hmm? The woman with white hair. And Amaryllis' daughter, at that."

"You're being weird." Asher lifted a brow, though he'd long ago grown accustomed to his friend's idiosyncrasies.

Vali chuckled and wet his lips. "Well, I am pleased you have found them at last, Alexander."

Wanting to change the subject, as thoughts of Foxx were draining him by the moment, Asher turned to Hector. "Thank you for everything you're doing here. This is truly amazing, and I'm so grateful to you."

Hector stuttered a reply. "Thank you, Your Highness."

"I'm sorry I haven't been more helpful. I was hoping to be there when Foxx woke up. I hadn't expected it to take this long, though." He looked back again, his shoulders curling forward.

"Take all the time you need. We will have no shortage of work for the foreseeable future." Pausing, one hand rubbed the opposite wrist. "However, I would like to discuss some things with you whenever you have a chance. Tomorrow or the day after perhaps, when the time comes to make plans moving forward."

"We will make that happen." To Vali and Ingrid, Asher said, "Thank you for allowing me refuge in your city. Again." Ingrid's eyes lit with an inner glow as Vali's grin widened. "I would like to return to her if there's nothing else requiring my attention."

"Of course, Alexander," Vali said.

"He wishes to be called Asher now," Ingrid told him.

"Asher, then. Let's talk soon. For now, go in peace." As Asher walked off, Vali and Ingrid returned their regard to Hector. "Let us allow the dust to settle. We will prepare the palace to hold as many as we can manage. So many homes have been destroyed, and people will need places to stay. Abram and I will talk of sending the Guard around to see the full extent of the damage and figure out how we can provide enough food and shelter until things can be rebuilt. I know there are many sectors of the city nearly untouched. We will make use of them as we require."

Abram tugged at his beard. "Strange the Queen did not attack the palace, Konungr Vali, is it not? I doubt that was accidental. Could it be some kind of message?"

"Perhaps she felt that foregoing a full assault on my home would allow the artificial peace between us to remain intact. Unfortunately for her, she was very, very wrong."

C

Around highsun, Iris gathered some of the older children to hand out luncheon to those hard at work. A market near the Monastery provided them each a basket filled with fruit, vegetables, bread, and cheese, as well as a clay vessel to hold water. They went to the Monastery first, and after everyone there had their fill, they began their trek into the city. She put them into teams of three, instructing them not to wander farther than a few blocks and not to worry if they couldn't find everyone. "People will come for food when they get hungry. Stick together and stay safe."

The teams spread out. Other surviving establishments provided what they could, refilling their baskets as needed. After nearly two hours, the kids were ready to return to the courtyard. Iris and two of the oldest boys agreed to finish up.

As they crossed through the entrance plaza on their way to feed those working outside the wall, Iris glanced back over her shoulder and noticed a Jerichonian soldier following them. Before she could question it, James said, "The square is totally destroyed."

Iris drew her eyes from the soldier to survey the area. "This is where the Queen attacked. I was standing right over there when it happened." James and Oliver gaped at her.

They exited the iron gate, nodding to the Guard as they passed through, and followed the wall to the far edge of the city. The moment they rounded the corner, Iris realized how unprepared she'd been to face what lay beyond the wall.

First, they saw three giants carrying rocks up the hill. The ground trembled as they walked. Then they saw the stone-lined pits; long rectangles of land surrounded by a row of rocks. Corpses were stacked within the confines of the mass graves. Further examination of the piles revealed that many of the bodies arrived incomplete. Some were missing limbs. Others had been burned or mutilated so thoroughly, neither age nor gender could be determined.

Acid bubbled up Iris' esophagus, and she forced it back down, covering her mouth with her hand. She choked out the names of the boys helping her, and when they didn't respond, she turned to find them frozen in place, eyes wide. "Leave those baskets there and head back inside."

Jolted awake, the boys looked at her. Oliver almost objected, but James hushed him. They put the baskets on the ground against the wall and left Iris alone.

Raven and Jax walked past her, each dragging one side of a travois. Pulling up next to one of the piles, they added more bodies to the carnage. Both noticed her standing lost in the tragedy of what she saw, and Jax motioned from her to Raven. Raven glared at him and shook her head, but Jax raised a brow. *Why me?* she mouthed. Jax's responding expression indicated he thought her question dumb.

Raven looked back at Iris, and a smidgen of pity materialized in her gut. With a sigh, she shooed Jax away and walked up behind her. When she touched her shoulder, Iris leapt from her skin. Dropping her basket, she whipped around with Thorn pointed in Raven's face. Raven threw up her hands. "Whoa, whoa! Cool it, lady."

Iris surveyed Raven's person and realized—though heavily armed—she didn't hold a weapon. Disarming with a breath of relief, she slipped her dagger back into its scabbard. "Sorry. I was just…"

"I know." Raven crossed her arms and stepped forward as Iris turned back to face the corpses. "You shouldn't stare at them. Trust me when I tell you—nightmares."

"I know all about nightmares," Iris said, powerless to look away. She hugged herself, her hands sliding up and down the sleeves of her jacket. "Any idea how many there are so far?"

"A few thousand at least. We think there were about 30,000 people in the city when she attacked. The bodies might be 1 in 10, but it's hard to know for sure right now. Destroyed land mass is even higher."

"A few thousand? That's…" Iris pushed the heel of her palms into the pocket of each eye, trying to force away the images and the tears accompanying them. Whispered words burned as they crawled up her throat. "This is all our fault."

"No, it's not." Raven wondered if she should console her by

petting her arm or something, but she decided against it. She had never been great at putting people at ease, though Jax hadn't been wrong about her being better suited between the two of them. If Wyatt was around, they would have made him do it.

Iris breathed away her tears. "She was looking for us. For me and my sister."

"Well, that's true," Raven agreed. Iris looked her in the eyes, and Raven did the thing she least expected: she smiled. "What I meant was, even if she was looking for you, she's the one who chose to attack. She sent us here to capture you and then didn't give us any time to complete the mission. I don't know why she did what she did, but whatever her reasons, it was because of her. Not because of you."

Another tear slid down Iris' cheek as she consumed Raven's arguments, so contradictory to the guilt plaguing her since the moment the Queen said their names. Unsure how to respond to such clear and rational points, Iris looked the soldier over. She hadn't removed the black gear covering her uniform, as though still prepared for battle. Iris' eyes lingered on the bronze owl pinned to Raven's shoulder, and she wondered what it represented. It looked familiar, but she couldn't place it in her memories.

Then she remembered Declan naming them Reko Raptors, and she realized her father had worn a pin identical to it.

"It's the symbol of the Raptors," Raven said.

"My father had one. But gold." Iris' gaze lifted from the pin to meet Raven's.

"Jax has the gold one. It's for the lieutenant." After bending to gather the spilled contents of Iris' basket, Raven handed it to her and retrieved the ones the boys had left behind. "Let me help you. Come on." Without waiting for Iris to respond, she began walking toward Dominic.

Upon seeing them, the burly man bellowed, "Oh, yes! At long last. A proper excuse for a break! These bleedin' rocks are a real backbreaker." One of the hyvä mon grunted, and Dominic pointed a finger at it. "I don't wana hear it from you, ya great ol' beast. Back ta work, eh?" He trudged toward Raven and Iris, limbs weary. Raven passed him the vessel of water, and he took a long draw from it before calling to Solvi and the rest of the crew, telling them it was time for luncheon.

"There's more to bring out. I couldn't carry it all." Iris extended a hand into the space between them. "I'm Iris Belamour, by the way. We haven't officially met."

He shook her hand with a jolly laugh. "Dominic Ives, at your service."

"Can they talk?" Iris gestured to the hyvä mon plodding away from them.

"Nah, just grumble a little."

"They understand." Solvi took the water from Dominic.

"Solvi here whispers to em, an' they obey."

"Since I was a girl, I have visited them. They are kind creatures."

Iris liked Solvi's thick accent. Though she'd met people from Cordillera before, none had the heavy accents of those she'd encountered in the city. She loved to listen to the people of Jericho talk, especially the children. "They didn't frighten you as a child? They're so big!"

Solvi shook her head.

When the empty water jar made its way back to Raven, she said, "I'll help you grab more. We'll be back in a flash, Dom." He tipped a nonexistent hat to them, and Raven turned toward the city gates, with Iris following after her.

They walked in silence for a while, neither knowing what to say to the other. Raven hadn't hidden her evaluation of Iris and Declan's combined hands the night before, and Iris wondered if an affection for him was the reason Raven decided to show her kindness. Thoughts of Declan made her stomach swirl. He'd released her hand when they reached the Monastery the night before and hadn't touched her again since. On top of that, they still hadn't found Orion.

She cleared her head of thoughts of the men, only to be met with the images of the dead forever burned into her mind's eye. The smell of melting skin still lingered in her nostrils, and they hadn't yet begun burning the corpses.

Raven's voice graciously invaded her thoughts. "It's not an easy thing to get used to."

"What?" Iris tried to shake away pictures of charred and broken children as they crossed through the city gates. Without her permission, images of Seth and the children of Ataraxia flashed into her mind; each a different variation of mangled; each dead simply for knowing her. She squeezed her eyes closed, willing the imaginings to disperse.

"All the bloodshed. It's not easy to get used to."

"I don't know what kind of person could ever get used to seeing that."

Iris hadn't intended it as a dig at Raven's character, though Raven took it as one. Rather than biting back, she said, "Well, I generally handle it with an ever present chip on my shoulder and a gut full of whiskey."

Iris laughed unexpectedly, and Raven looked pleased by her accomplishment, though she couldn't imagine why Iris' joy mattered or brought her even the slightest pleasure.

All the pubs and markets in the square had been flattened by the shockwave of the Queen's ascension, but a grocery three streets over remained in decent shape and had goods to salvage. The owner and his two employees had been digging through the rubble to gather anything they could save and leaving it in a pile to be distributed. Iris led Raven there first, thanking Ivan again as they piled as much as they could fit in two of the three baskets.

Iris left one behind in case Oliver and James came back and needed it, and she and Raven headed for the water well. "So, what's your deal, Raven?"

Raven narrowed her eyes, instinctively defensive. "Meaning?" Drawing water with the new bucket Iris and her helpers had reattached, she filled the clay vessel.

When Iris turned and strode toward the entrance, her eyes were drawn to the remnants of Foxx's spilled blood, and she shivered. "You were sent to Jericho to capture me, and now you're helping me carry food baskets. It's a little strange, don't you think?"

"I guess," Raven said, not having put much thought into it until Iris brought it to light. "Would you prefer I arrest you or something?"

"I'm wondering how it's possible your whole team switched sides with such ease."

"You!" An aggressive voice had them spinning around to see a man stomping toward them. "You're her, aren't you? You're one of them." He stopped in front of Iris with tense shoulders and clenched fists. Right away, she noticed the red rims around his eyes, bloodshot with sorrow. "Are you pleased with yourself? Well? Are you?" He lifted his hands and looked around at the demolished plaza.

Iris was speechless, her lips parting for words that wouldn't emerge. She wanted to help, to comfort him, but she knew he wouldn't be interested in any kind of comfort she could offer.

Raven stepped forward and put a hand between them. "Watch it, buddy. We don't want any trouble."

The man looked her over and snarled. "And who are you? Legion scum. You're as guilty as she is. Get out of Jericho. Flee like your Queen! You are not welcome here."

Raven's hand rose to her hip. "If you have an issue, take it up with your King. Harassing people in the street isn't the way to handle your grievances."

"Why, you—"

"Enough." A soldier grabbed the man by the back of his collar and yanked him away. "I won't see you speak to either of these women again, do you understand? By order of the Konungr."

The man gaped at the soldier and squirmed to break free of his grasp.

"You're with Vali's personal Guard." Raven looked around, searching for evidence of the sovereigns nearby. "What are you doing all the way out here?"

"How can you tell?" Iris scoped his person for clues until Raven pointed out the moons embroidered on his sleeves.

"Fancier uniforms."

"I'm following orders." The soldier shoved the man so he stumbled. "Spread the word. Iris and Foxxglove Belamour are not to be harmed. Punishment for the disobedient will be severe." As the man scrambled away, muttering as he went, the soldier bowed to the women. "My name is Elijah. It's nice to officially meet you, Iris Belamour and Raven Nightshade."

Iris tilted her head. "You've been following me."

"As I said, orders. The Konungr worried some of the citizens might be hostile, so he sent me to protect you. One of my comrades is watching over your sister."

Raven leaned back, her eyes on Iris. "One sovereign seeks your death, the other your protection. Who are you really, Iris Belamour?"

Iris' gaze fixated on the basket in her hands. "I wish I knew."

"I'll keep my distance, but know you can call on me if needed. Go in peace." Elijah bowed again, but didn't walk away.

Raven motioned with her head for Iris to follow and started for the gate. "This doesn't prove it's your fault. People are hurt and angry. They need someone to blame, and your faces lit up the sky. But the Queen is still the one in the wrong here. I was in the square when it all went down. She saw you, and still Kaen attacked."

"That beast has a name?"

"It's her pet, apparently. Anyway, it's not about switching sides but about following our commander. He led us here to capture you, we followed. He told us to help the city, we obeyed. If he tells us to turn on you, we'll do that, too." She glanced back at Elijah, who'd begun following them again, and hoped that last option wouldn't come to pass.

Iris hummed, appreciating Raven's honesty, even if it was mildly concerning. "So all of this is just about being a soldier and doing what you're told?"

Raven thought for a moment. When Hector defected, she should have deferred to the next person in charge, which would have been Jax. If he also followed Hector, she supposed the next person in line was the King of Arkaemor. Or possibly Dagon Wraith. Instead, she'd remained under Hector's command, despite his rebellion. So perhaps it wasn't as simple as following orders after all.

She didn't know Hector's motives, but she suspected they might have something to do with the continuously growing piles of innocents outside the city walls. He was good at following orders, too, but as she'd watched him over the years, she'd noticed it often pained him when those orders were awful and immoral. Perhaps this had been the final straw.

Raven hadn't often had the luxury of worrying morals. A criminal turned soldier, she'd once thought joining the King's Legion would correct the wrongs of her past. As it turned out, being a soldier under Pollux and Sirena Aldrich often required far worse actions than the theft of her youth.

When Hector asked her to join the new unit, she hadn't even questioned it. She'd considered what the Queen might do to the women once captured, but it didn't stop her following him. Regretfully, she thought she would probably do anything Hector asked of her.

They passed Victor guarding the gate, and Iris addressed him by name. Raven had yet to answer her question. "It seems pretty stupid to traumatize yourself lugging around dead bodies to follow orders. I don't think I could be a soldier."

"I think you already are," Raven said.

Iris turned to look at her, her ponytail whipping around her shoulder, but Raven kept her gaze straight forward. "I believe in what I'm fighting for. Whether I understand the full extent of it or not, I'm standing up against evil people who do horrible, evil things. That's different than following blindly."

Raven shrugged. "Iris Belamour against the world, huh?"

"If that's what it takes." Iris ground her teeth. "You know, you're going to have to pick a side eventually, Raven. Your superiors stand on opposing sides, so you can't blame your choice on someone else's orders. It will be up to you to choose a path."

Before Raven could respond, Dominic and his group met them halfway between the front gate and the crematorium, hoping to down some food away from all the butchery. Some sat on the ground, but others feared if they let themselves rest, they may not be able to get back up. The entire city seemed to exist under the cloudy haze of exhaustion.

"What'sa plan for sleepin' tonight?" Dominic asked.

"One of the groups is out collecting blankets and bedding for us to camp out until things are more organized. The palace is opening its doors, but it can only fit so many, and for now those spots are reserved for civilians. Most of the places left standing will be filled with civilians as well." Raven took a carrot from one of the baskets and bit into it.

"The barracks?"

"You'll have to talk to Hector about that. I haven't had a chance to pull him aside, but I imagine he won't be asking to bunk with the Guard. Certainly not so soon after the attack."

Dominic nodded. "In the snow it is, eh? Seems fitting I s'pose."

Iris fought to avert her eyes from the graves. She pressed against her fingers to stretch them, and then cracked her knuckles one finger at a time. "Let things settle a little. You guys have been fundamental in everything that's happening here. Especially Hector. I can't imagine you'll be sleeping in the snow too long."

"You don't know Hector," Raven said, and Dominic grinned. "There are quite a few more buildings in good condition than we originally thought. Some parts of the city are nearly untouched. Others are obliterated. Like the hospital, for instance, which was gruesome." Obliging his silent request, she tossed Dominic a carrot.

Solvi said, "Today we build graves. Tomorrow we map out what can be salvaged and what needs to be rebuilt."

Jax and a few others passed by dragging another load of bodies. Two vuokaras followed them, pulling their own travois of corpses. On his way back through, Jax stopped to stand with them, leaving the others to go on ahead. "It feels never-ending." He sighed and wiped sweat from his brow.

"I'm done and ready to help again." Raven kept her eyes on the vuokaras as they walked back toward the city. She'd never cared for the mountain goats, with their furry ankles and the single horn sticking out from their foreheads. Though she had to admit, their ability to haul immense loads did come in handy.

"Let me stand here for a minute." Jax lifted his face to the sky and put his hands on top of his head. The sun shone brightly, but the air felt bitter, especially with sweat and blood soaking his clothes.

"When did you get that?" Raven poked the black bird on Jax's arm.

He twisted to look at the tattoo on the back of his bicep. "Few months ago."

"It looks like a raven."

Jax grinned. "Might be. The ship is for Hector, steady on the stormy sea. I put the bird next to it." He waved his arm in her face as proof, and she shoved it away, wrinkling her nose.

"There's something wrong with you."

"You love me."

Raven gagged. "I tolerate you. I can't believe you got a raven tattoo. What a freak."

Iris said, "I can help, too. Lugging the bodies, I mean. I'm finished with food distribution." Jax and Dominic's jaws slackened.

Raven said, "No. You're needed back at the Monastery."

Iris glared at her and crossed her arms. "Are you implying I'm not capable of doing what you're doing? I'll have you know, my sister and I have lived in the wilderness for more than six years. I may not have special training or gear like you, but I'm strong and plenty capable of dragging a body."

"I'm implying your talents are better used elsewhere," Raven snapped, matching her tone. Though she didn't know why she was provoking her since she hadn't intended her comment as an insult anyway.

"What do you know about my talents?" Iris shot back, mirroring her scowl.

After a long moment, Raven exhaled and shook her head. "I can see why he likes you." Turning toward the city gates, she walked away. Bushy brows rose up Jax's forehead, then he shrugged before following her without comment.

Dominic clapped Iris on the back with a hearty laugh. "Well, Iris Belamour. Seems you got more fire in your belly than 'at bleedin' dragon."

CHAPTER 32

FORGIVE AND REGRET

Declan nursed a mug of warm water as he leaned against a wall outside the Monastery courtyard. The mug was crafted from a goat horn. A flat bottom replaced the sharp point and a dark liquid had been poured over it, sealing the crack and looking as if it defied gravity by dripping from the bottom.

Every muscle in his body felt sore. The hike to Jericho had been long and hard, and he hadn't slept since leaving Peregrine Manor. Letting his head rest against the wall, he closed his eyes. If he could sleep for a few minutes, it might refuel him enough to survive the remainder of the day. Moments later, a shadow blocked his sunlight and his eyes flew open in alarm, his hand grasping the stock of his pistol.

Asher stood above him, offering a sandwich wrapped in brown paper. "You look beat. Room for me on that wall?"

Declan sat up straighter, still getting used to the idea of Asher being a normal person rather than the Crown Prince of Arkaemor. As one of the Raptors, Declan had spent a fair amount of time at Castle Solís and crossed paths with the Prince more than once. He'd always thought Alexander to be an arrogant troublemaker, like Orion had described him: breaking the rules, drinking from the flask he kept in his jacket pocket, flirting with every woman he saw regardless of age, beauty, or rank. He'd never seen this version of Prince Alexander; a man who sat by Foxx's bed in agony and teared up over thoughts of his sister. Accepting the sandwich, Declan gestured to the open spot next to him.

Asher sat down, unwrapped his own luncheon, and took a giant bite. In response to Declan's stiff demeanor, he said, "Relax, mate, seriously. You don't have to be so formal. I won't scold you for insubordination or anything." He took another bite and spoke with his mouth full of bread and meat. "I walked away from my title, and you're no longer a soldier, yeah? So perhaps we can meet each other where we are and start fresh. What do you say?" He extended a hand, his charming smile enticing Declan to accept.

Relaxing at last, Declan unwrapped the sandwich and took a bite. "Okay. Asher it is then."

"Thank you. It's been quite a while since I've spent time around people who know my identity, and I have to say, I don't fancy the lot of you gawking at me." As if to prove his point, two nurses walked past on their way back to the courtyard and giggled before scurrying off.

Declan laughed. "You're not what I expected. Not what you seemed, I should say."

"I've never been what anyone expected me to be. Seems I'm never doing any of it right, you know? Prince, brother, son, outlaw." He grinned cheekily. "Certainly didn't do any of it right with Foxx." His demeanor shifted, becoming more solemn and regretful, so Declan didn't respond.

They sat in silence while they ate the rest of their luncheon. As Asher crinkled up his empty wrapper, he said, "Hey, I'm sorry about before."

"I shouldn't have been eavesdropping on such a private moment. I shouldn't have spoken her name or inserted myself at all. I'm sorry."

"It's fine." A minute passed before Asher admitted, "You were correct, though. I was thinking of Avaline."

"How is she?"

Asher sighed and ran a hand over the top of his head. "A ghost of herself—a shadow. She hardly speaks. Her eyes look right through you. Often she sleeps all through the day. Countless times I've found myself sitting in her room, endlessly checking to make sure she's still breathing. If she wakes, she spends the day in bed or staring out her window. Sometimes she ambles around the castle with no destination in mind until someone discovers her and escorts her back to her room." Asher shook his head, dispelling the memories as he stared blankly at the ground. "But none of it makes a lick of difference. My sister locked herself somewhere deep within her heart, and she refuses to come out. I didn't want to leave her, but..." He paused, realizing he didn't know how much Declan knew about Foxx and Iris' plans. "I just had to."

Declan hadn't thought the Prince would understand anything about suffering. Even with Sirena for a mother, nothing ever seemed to phase him, as if he stood above it all. "I haven't talked to my brother in six years. I've seen him a few times from a distance, but he lives in Inaravale, and I tend to avoid the royal city. I miss him."

"He was young when you left?" Asher asked.

"Fifteen."

"Avaline is eighteen now. Actually her birthday was last week." His countenance darkened as if he'd only then realized he'd missed it.

"Dang." Declan felt for the first time in a while how much time had passed. Last time he'd seen Princess Avaline, she was a little girl moseying around the castle grounds. Her eyes had glistened with life and adventure, and she interacted with every person who crossed her path, no matter who they were. He'd had several random and pleasant conversations with the young Princess when he'd frequented the castle.

At that moment, Declan understood the relationship between Iris and Asher. He'd found himself slightly jealous watching them interact and wondered if Iris wished Asher had chosen her instead of Foxx. Knowing the Prince's history, it wasn't outside the realm of possibilities to think he'd been seeking attention from them both.

He realized now that Iris reminded Asher of Avaline. They had the same fire, the same spunk, all wrapped up in a heart of gold.

"Well, well, well..." Iris' voice sparked light into their depressing conversation. "What are you two up to?"

"Just talking." Declan lifted his shoulders, straightening them from the hunch they'd slid into.

"Talking about what?" Iris plopped cross-legged on the ground. Her high pony hung crooked and messy on top of her head, and her clothes looked damp with sweat and blackened with soot, like everyone else's.

"None of your business." Asher grinned.

"Fine." Iris rolled her eyes in faux annoyance. "Well, I didn't think I could see anything more devastating or horrific than the remains of this city and all of these injured people, but I have just been proven wrong."

Asher drew his head back. "You didn't go outside."

"Except that, yes, I did." Iris sighed and leaned back on her hands.

"Nightmares guaranteed for the foreseeable future." He handed her his horn of water.

Declan sat forward, drawn in by her distress. "Are you all right?"

After taking a few sips, she returned Asher's mug. "I'll be fine. I didn't expect there to be… so many. Raven thinks they're numbered in the thousands."

Shifting in his seat, Declan asked, "You talked to Raven? Was she nice to you?"

"No, in fact, she was not." Then she cocked her head to the side, pulling her ponytail in front of her shoulder and twisting it around one finger. "Well, yes, actually." More pensive contemplation preceded a sigh. "I'm not sure, to be honest with you."

"Sounds about right."

"Who's Raven?" Asher asked.

Declan answered, "One of the new Raptors," at the same time Iris said, "Declan's ex-girlfriend."

Declan gawked at her. "What did she say to you?"

"Nothing really. It was just a guess. Thank you for confirming."

"Blimey." Asher took a sip from his mug to hide his chuckle.

Leaning back against the wall and crossing his arms, Declan blew out a breath. "That was unkind."

"But humorous," Iris countered. "Asher, you met her right after the Queen's attack. Anyway, how is Foxx?"

Asher's eyes fell into shadow as if drawn over by a curtain. "She hasn't woken."

Iris reached for his hand, holding on to it until he looked at her. "She's strong. She's going to be all right." Giving his hand a squeeze, she released. "Is there a Guard watching over her?"

"Vali assigned them." Asher looked past her to where Elijah stood across the street.

Iris and Declan followed his gaze. "I'm grateful. A man confronted me near the entrance, and Elijah stepped in to get rid of him."

"I'd hoped Vali was being overprotective, but I guess not."

Straightening again, Declan asked, "What did the man do? Did he hurt you?"

"He told me it was all my fault and that I wasn't welcome here. Raven got between us first, but Elijah ordered him away." Hearing Raven's voice, Iris turned to see her and Jax walking toward them. Jax said something too far away for them to hear and laughed when Raven punched him in the arm. "You know, I had thought Hector, but now I'm wondering about the two of them."

Declan leaned to see who Iris meant. "Raven and Jax? I don't think so."

"You never know."

Declan lifted his chin as the soldiers passed by. "Jax has a new woman in his bed every week. At least he used to. Raven needs someone kind and attentive. She's had a really rough life, and she needs a man who will chase her if she runs. Someone steady."

Iris lifted a brow. "Speaking from experience?"

Blushing, Declan cleared his throat. "You should be more careful walking around on your own."

Iris smiled at Elijah over her shoulder. "Well, now I'm not alone. I am worried about Foxx though. She's not exactly in a state to defend herself."

"The soldiers watching you are from Vali's personal Guard. She'll be fine." Asher looked back toward the Monastery. "There will be a burning ceremony tonight. Even if they haven't finished recovering everyone."

"It's looking pretty horrendous, and I definitely won't be attending." Iris shivered. "Besides, I'm exhausted and ready for sleep."

Declan nodded. "Me too. I haven't slept since we left Peregrine."

"No!" Asher and Iris cried in unison.

"You must be bone-tired! You lot should go find somewhere quiet to lay down. We have plenty of help here."

Iris noticed Asher's accent more prevalent now, as if he no longer felt the need to suppress it. His secret was out, and as adorable as she found the variation, it stung to know he'd kept even the intonation of his speech hidden from them along with everything else. "There is still so much to do," she said, but her heart wasn't in it. She put her elbow on her knee, resting her head in her hand.

"I think we can survive without you for a few hours. Not longer though. The city might well collapse without you here holding it up." Asher winked at her and stood, offering his hands to help her up.

She accepted the gesture and let him pull her to her feet. "That's not funny, considering this whole thing was our fault to begin with."

Asher grabbed the top of her arms, squaring her body with his. Sounding like the Prince she now knew him to be, he said, "Stop it. I refuse to let you carry the weight of this situation. There is so much you don't know, things I plan to share with you as soon as Foxx wakes. Until then, I need you to trust me. Sirena may have come here looking for you, but the entirety of what's happening is so much bigger and absolutely, positively, irrevocably *not* your fault. Do you understand me, Iris Belamour?"

Iris gulped as a tear slid down her cheek. "Yes, Prince Alexander. I understand you."

His stern expression melted into a smile. "Don't you start, too."

Chuckling through a chest tight with emotions, she leaned into him, finding solace in the protection of his arms. Then she turned to Declan, still watching them from his seat on the ground, and extended a hand. "You coming?"

He stood and wished Asher luck with Foxx. Then he and Iris left the busy courtyard in search of a place to rest.

C

As the sky grew dim, the city faded into stillness. Those who wished to witness the burning ceremony gathered outside the walls. Those who didn't took the coming darkness as a much needed reprieve.

Inns and taverns opened their doors to anyone they could hold, and the palace had begun allowing people inside at sunset. Rooms in three separate wings were made up for citizens to sleep in, as well as two of the palace ballrooms. Bedding lined the walls of numerous hallways, and a special ballroom and several members of staff had been devoted to the unclaimed children previously congregating in the courtyard beneath the tree.

Raven entered the yard to find Hector looking exhausted and wondered when he'd last stopped to rest. She thought back to the previous morning when she'd woken to him staring out the window. At the time, she hadn't understood the burdens weighing on him. She now suspected he must have been battling with rivaling loyalties since the moment they left Inaravale—maybe longer than that.

When he finished speaking to one of the nurses, Raven approached him, donning her biggest smile. "Merry evening, Commander."

His face brightened at the sound of her voice, a fact that pleased her deep in the hollows of her heart. In an unexpected turn of events, Hector's arms slid around her waist as he pulled her against his chest. After a moment of bewilderment passed, her arms encircled his shoulders and she hugged him back.

With the exception of one very late night so many moons ago, Hector never hugged her. Now he held tight, inhaling her as if she were the only source of air to his lungs.

Raven pulled back without letting go and searched his eyes. "How are you?"

One of his hands released her waist to push a strand of hair from her eye, and she shuddered as his fingers grazed the skin of her temple. "Tired." His other hand lingered on her hip, his fingers curling around the fabric of her uniform. Based on his wobbling, she suspected it remained in place for balance rather than a desire for comfort.

Hector had always kept himself at an unreachable distance. The ease between them was often effortless, like they were on the same page, sharing thoughts, working seamlessly together without discussion, but he'd never indicated a longing for anything deeper than that. His intimacy with her in that moment transcended his usual detachment as he absentmindedly rubbed his thumb back and forth across the owl pinned to her uniform. He traced the wings and the circle surrounding it, studying it with a vacant expression. "We should have a meeting. Discuss what we're doing."

"I think it's pretty obvious what we're doing, Hector."

The side of his mouth lifted ever so slightly, but his eyes remained transfixed on the pin.

Touching his hand to pivot his attention, she said, "And I told you already, I'm with you."

He met her eyes, his expression instantly alert and serious. "This is different, Raven. This is—"

"I know. I know what it is." Gaining courage from his familiarity, she lifted his hand from the pin and drew it to her lips, whispering a kiss on the back of his knuckles.

He watched her intently until she let it drop to his side. "I can't believe Vali didn't arrest me. I thought it was the end of everything when I saw him enter the courtyard."

"And yet you approached him willingly?"

"Should I have run? What good would that have done? Maybe part of me knew it was the least of what I deserved." His eyes faded again into nothingness.

Raven changed the subject, unable to bear seeing her stoic commander full of doom and gloom. "Are you going to watch the ceremony?"

"No. I don't know anyone who died, and I loathe the smell of burning flesh." His hands traced her upper arms, sliding from top to bottom and back again.

Thinking he must be delirious from fatigue, Raven decided not to think too much of his casual touch. She had always strived to be whatever Hector needed her to be, to give him anything and everything he required. If he needed comfort tonight, then she would give it without hesitation, and if he only needed his soldier tomorrow, then she would be that, too. "I don't think you'll be escaping it within the walls, but I understand." His fingers slid all the way down her arms until they landed in her hands. She tugged at him, imploring him to follow her. "Let's go find somewhere to sleep."

"I can't sleep." His eyes drifted around the courtyard, scanning everyone in sight. It was emptier than it had been all day but still brimming with things that needed taken care of.

"Yes, you can. Not only that, you need to. Come on." She pulled on his hand again and, begrudgingly, he followed her to an empty spot against the Monastery beneath the weeping cypress. Along the way, she grabbed a pair of blankets off of the available pile. Spreading one out on the ground, she kept hold of the other and gestured for him to lay down. He did so without complaint.

She attempted to remain neutral, as if this was the most ordinary thing they'd ever done together. Hector stared at her with sleepy eyes, watching her every movement as she sat next to him and pulled her braid free with her fingers. When she finished, she laid down on her side with her back facing him and drew the second blanket over them.

Hector rolled toward her and wrapped his arm over her waist,

434

pulling her up against his chest. Cocooned in warmth beneath the blanket, Raven scooted closer, soaking in his heat to combat the cold of the night, and within minutes, sleep took them both.

C

After Declan and Iris left him, Asher went to check on Foxxglove. He stayed with her until the sky began to darken, whispering pleas to the Creator that she would awaken soon.

Though knowing he should get some sleep, he decided to go to the burning ceremony outside the wall. Exiting the city gates, he found an immense crowd waiting for the cremation to begin. Moon-flies surrounded them in a wide crescent, cocooning them in light.

Jerichonian Guards stood at the front of the congregation holding torches between the mounds of bodies and the civilians. Lunae-lumen surrounded the graves on all sides, blanketing them in their white light.

Abram spoke prayers over the dead, and Asher wondered if they were the old prayers written down centuries ago by the Monastery of the Morrow or if new words had been written for the occasion.

The Konungr and Dróttning sat in chairs up front but off to the side, easily seen by their people without drawing attention from the ceremony. Hand in hand, their eyes remained fixed on the commander as he spoke the poetic words.

An atmosphere of hopeless devastation hung heavily in the air as archers standing behind the crowd drew back fiery arrows and released. In unison, the crowd lifted their heads to watch the arrows flying above them like stars shooting across the sky. The pyres of corpses and dried timber ignited on contact, scattering the lunae-lumen and spraying flickering embers into the darkness as flames consumed the mass graves.

When the fires began, so did the wailing. The cries of mothers and fathers, husbands and wives, and devastated children calling out in mourning over the lost was unbearable. Asher didn't endure it for very long. When he returned to his room at the White Luna, he kicked off his boots, laid down on the bed, and passed out.

C

Hector woke as the sun peeked over the walls surrounding the city. His shoulder felt numb where it lay flattened into stone, but he kept his arm draped over Raven's side for a while longer, holding her against him as he considered the day ahead.

With most of the deceased removed from the city and things growing fairly stable, it was time for his team to choose a path. The city officials would soon be making plans on how to respond to Sirena's attack, and Hector knew they wouldn't tolerate any active Legion within the walls. Lines were about to be drawn, and the Reko Raptors needed to pick a side.

Hector already knew what he needed to do. Only one path stretched toward redemption. Though no actions could truly vindicate him, it was a start. His thoughts drifted to Declan and his father, but he shook away the memories, knowing he would be reliving them soon enough.

Pulling Raven closer, he nuzzled her hair, getting lost in the waves left behind by her braid. She smelled earthy and clean, despite the events of the past few days.

The movement stirred her and she startled, forgetting where she was. She touched the arm around her waist, then with an exhale, she relaxed into him. Intertwining their fingers, she pulled their hands against her chest and kissed the back of his knuckles as she'd done the night before. "Merry morning," she whispered, nervous and mystified by his closeness. Before sleep had taken her, she'd wondered what waking up next to him would feel like or if he would even be there when the sun rose.

But here he was, smiling against the back of her neck and sending goosebumps down her spine with the tip of his nose. In spite of her efforts, she failed to tame the swirling in her stomach and the fluttering in her chest as he, without any warning or discussion, held her.

Memories of the night they'd spent together lingered at the fringes of her mind, stirring more spirals throughout her nervous system. How many times had she revisited that night? Longing to feel his skin against her own; the strength of his corded muscles; the loveliness of whispered words revealing the desires of his heart.

The most magical of nights had slid into the most extraordinary dawn. The dark sky lightened from navy into a palette of pastels, and they'd watched as the approaching sun swallowed the stars. Then they'd fallen asleep wrapped in each other's arms.

When the sun crested the horizon, time had ceased its standstill and life continued on as though their intimate encounter had been little more than a dream. He'd never spoken of it, and so neither had she.

Hector had always regretted leaving before she woke, but it never seemed the correct moment to apologize. Drawing light to that night would force other questions into existence—questions he hadn't been ready to answer.

There was so much she didn't know, and when she found out the truth, he suspected she would run from him. If he'd let himself get close to her first, losing her might have broken his heart in ways he could never mend.

It was risky even now, allowing this closeness between them, but he'd been so weary, siphoned dry, and she'd been there, willingly laying next to him, soft and cozy and comfortable in his arms. If this was his last chance to enjoy the feel of her body against his, it was worth what he might lose.

"Merry morning." The warm breath of his reply sent another shiver through her. He tried to remain stationary, but he couldn't seem to contain his lips as they pressed a flurry of kisses against her neck, nor could he deny loving the way her body responded to the feeling. Brief thoughts of what it might be like to wake up next to her every day danced through his mind without consent.

"How long have you been awake?" She rubbed drowsiness from her eyes with her free hand.

"Not long." To his dismay, he felt her pull away, releasing his hand so she could roll to face him. Seeming to regret it immediately, if only for the chill the separation of their bodies fostered, she pressed her lower half against him, entangling their legs.

Raven inspected his face, noting the lines formed overnight and the dark pockets under his eyes. "You have the look of a man who's been stuck in his own head far too long. Are you sure you slept at all?"

He smiled, thinking her adorable for caring, but not saying so. "I slept well, actually. Though I have also been spending quite a lot of time in my own head."

"Care to share the burden?" She slid her hand across his ribs and around his back.

"I'm afraid to." The weight in this admission was clear in his eyes, even as his lips continued to widen in response to her touch.

Raven hummed, mildly distracted by his early morning form. She couldn't remember ever seeing him with rumpled clothing and a shadow of hair yet to be shaven. His eyes were glossy, either by emotion or the remnants of sleep. "Maybe I can help."

"Maybe you'll leave me." He'd meant to say *hate me* or *be angry with me*, but his truth broke free. He could handle hate and anger. He didn't know what he would do if she left his side. His eyes shifted from hers to stare up at the pale sunlight peeking through the canopy of fabrics. Others around them had begun to stir, and several people had already returned to the Monastery from whatever hidden nook they'd found to sleep in the night before.

"I don't think so."

With a sigh, he said, "I was thinking about the meeting I need to have with the Raptors."

"That makes sense. Are you worried I'll return to Inaravale? I already told you, I'm with you, whatever you decide."

He nodded, pausing for a long moment before adding, "And, I was thinking about Declan."

Untangling her legs from his, she pushed herself onto her elbows. The cold he felt at the loss of her body's heat seemed representative of the expanse about to form between them. "Why were you thinking about Silas?"

Hector sighed again and sat up, crossing his legs and leaning his back against the wall. Raven readjusted so she sat comfortably across from him, pulling the blanket they'd been sharing up around her shoulders

He knew she couldn't fully understand his decision to stay in Jericho if he didn't tell her the entire story. It wouldn't be fair for her to make such a trade—Inaravale for Jericho; the King and Queen for a defecting commander—if she didn't know the truth.

He just didn't know where to begin, and he told her so.

"How about the beginning?" she suggested, as if it were that simple.

His chest felt hollow, his mouth dry. He wet his lips, and once he started, the words spilled from him like water bursting free of a dam. "Many years ago, Dec—Silas'—father, Ryder Declanaire, was my friend and mentor. My father and I didn't have the best relationship, and when I met Ryder, he took me under his wing. Taught me things, trained me up. He had two boys at home, but his duties often kept him away. At times I've wondered if I reminded him of Silas, though I can't know for sure.

"About ten years ago, the King and Queen grew concerned about the rebel compound on the outskirts of Norsukylä. Their numbers were growing exponentially, and they were becoming organized and even influential. So Pollux sent a small band of soldiers to handle the situation. It was the kind of operation the Reko Raptors usually took care of, but at the time, they were in deep with something else and couldn't add it to their plate.

"The Queen asked for Ryder specifically, instructing him to put together a team and get it done. He was an honorable and exceptional soldier, known by many for his model behavior and irreproachable skill. He may have even made commander one day, if he'd survived long enough to do so."

Raven's thin brow pinched together as she realized she was about to learn the truth of Silas' father's death. He'd never been open to discussing it in detail, only sharing that he'd died, and Silas had joined the Legion to care for his younger brother, Johnathan.

"The plan was to go in and shut down the compound. Let flee those who wished to and arrest those who stood their ground. There was always a chance the group would fight back, but we hoped it would be dealt with quietly and cleanly.

"Whether by the Queen's intention or simply by misinformation, we walked into that underground compound and found not only rebel fighters but women and children, as well—families. The compound wasn't only a military base housing rebels—but a home. When they saw us enter with guns raised, everyone in the building froze, eyes locked on us.

"Ryder signaled for us to hold, unsure how to proceed. All of the smaller rebel groups we'd encountered had been able-bodied men and women. Fighters. Renegades. There had never been children or elderly people in the encampments before. We were at a stand still; us watching them, them watching us.

"A man in the crowd moved, stumbling into a little girl standing in front of him, and she fell forward. The energy of the room was so high, and I don't even know how it happened, but... I flinched." Hector paused. He hadn't spoken the next part out loud since those first few days when he'd tried to tell his side of the story. It'd been ten years, and the image of what he'd done still made his stomach foul with bile.

"I flinched," he repeated, swallowing saliva as he tried to get the words out. "And shot the girl between the eyes before her knees hit the ground. She couldn't have been older than seven."

Raven sucked in a breath, and Hector stopped again, scrutinizing her face, trying to read what she must think of him, but her expression revealed nothing.

"Someone screamed. Then the room erupted in gunfire and fury. I couldn't breathe, I didn't fire another bullet. I ran straight out of that compound and left my team behind, seeking the breath in my lungs the fresh air would provide. I vomited instead. The image of the bullet piercing the girl's forehead replayed itself over and over inside my mind. Sometimes it still does. I was outside but moments, trying to temper my thoughts. Trying to breathe. Panic consumed me. I could hear the stream of bullets inside, but my feet wouldn't budge.

"We didn't see the gunpowder, at least I didn't. I'll never know if anyone else did, but regardless, they must have had barrels of it. The next thing I knew, a shockwave blasted me from the building. I landed several feet away on my stomach and covered my head. The aftershocks kept coming."

Raven lifted her hand to her mouth.

"Nearly everyone died. Maybe a few rebels escaped out the back before the explosions began but most of them, the kids, the families, and my team: gone, devoured by the earth within the collapsed compound." Tears burned his eyes as he relived the memory.

"I tried to explain it to the King and Queen, but I was so shell-shocked the words wouldn't come out. Then I realized Pollux was congratulating me for taking down the rebel forces. The King was shaking my hand. They called my team *tragic collateral damage* and said it was to be expected when fighting rebels. I tried to argue, to explain that it was all my fault, but they wouldn't listen.

"Ryder died, and I was left behind—a hero. The King began promoting me up the ranks faster than any soldier before me, and less than three years later, at the absurdly underqualified age of 26, I became the youngest commander in the history of Arkaemor." Hector cleared his throat for no other reason than that he needed a moment before going on.

"As you may already know, Ryder's wife died shortly after. Of grief, some thought. Silas was sixteen, Johnathan was twelve. Silas joined the Legion the day he turned seventeen, hoping to provide for his younger brother. He made himself a new life within the Legion, he found you, and I think, despite his circumstances, he was some version of happy."

A smile upturned one side of her lips as she thought of the man she'd known Silas to be. He *had* been happy.

Without meeting her eyes, Hector went on. "Until that business with Sawyer Belamour, when he became unjustly labeled a traitor." Emotion choked his voice as he fought to hold back the words he knew would change everything.

"Unjustly?" The word caught in her throat as she repeated it.

Hector's heart pounded, and his stomach churned. He desired more than anything for the chance to end the conversation right there. "I wish you would tell me what you're thinking."

"I will tell you when you've finished."

Already Hector felt the terrifying—though not unexpected—bitterness seeping into her words. He tried to glean what he could from her expression and wondered if he'd already pushed her too far. He thought back on the circumstances that transpired after Ryder's death.

When Declan joined the Legion, he'd avoided Hector, only acknowledging him long enough to eye him with disdain. His hate was justifiable, and it didn't prevent Hector from watching over his mentor's son from a distance. He'd even suggested Sawyer make him a Raptor.

Hector hadn't known Raven existed until he'd seen them together. She'd been another soldier among many. When Declan was forced from the Kingdom, Hector watched closely as Raven's confused pain morphed into resentment. To this day, he wondered if a small part of him had made taking care of her his duty. It wasn't long before she became the person he trusted over anyone, save Jax.

He never expected it to progress the way it had, never imagined his feelings for her might become more than protective penance for his crimes. Looking back over his life, he saw many things he could never have predicted.

Running his palms down his face, he blew out a breath and pressed on. "Unjustly, yes. The Raptors had no idea what Sawyer was doing. They were innocent. The Queen knew it, too, but she wanted to give them the motivation to hunt him down so she could get the Artifact back. Part of her always hated the idea of the Reko Raptors and the freedom they had. She couldn't control them like she could the Legion, which made them too great of a liability, regardless of their usefulness. She hoped naming them all traitors would kill two birds with one stone, but then Belamour vanished and, as far as I know, hasn't been seen since."

He paused again, wishing to postpone the next admission, if only for a few seconds. "The truth is, Raven, I'm the one who turned them in. It became immediately clear Sawyer was the only betrayer, and I reported it that way to the Queen, but she wasn't about to let the others walk free. So I did what I was told. I dragged them into the Hall of Sunsets as equal partners and let her bestow her wrath.

"At the time, I thought… I don't know what I thought. I was so caught up in my status as commander. I'd only held the position a few months, and I was so young; way too young to be the commander of the whole Legion. I'm still too young." He shrugged, fiddling his fingers in his lap. "But I clung to that power, to pleasing the sovereigns in any way I could, to hiding the truth about how I'd gotten there to begin with, and honestly Raven, I lost myself." His eyes lifted to hers.

Raven took her time making sense of his words. Her gaze drifted from him, scanning the courtyard and seeing it now for what it was —penance. A cry for redemption.

When Silas left the Legion, he'd left her behind with it. No farewell, no explanation. She'd convinced herself he wasn't the man she'd thought him to be. She'd allowed hatred to stifle the pain that arose whenever she thought of him. But she'd been wrong all along. She'd spent six years hating him for nothing. He'd been out in the wilderness running, surviving, and totally innocent. His entire world had been uprooted on the whim of an insane lieutenant, a barbaric queen, and a cowardly and selfish commander.

The reasons for Silas' fury in the entrance plaza crisped into focus. She remembered Hector's cruel mention of Johnathan and their father, and grimaced with disgust. "So not only did you kill Silas' father, you took him away from his brother, and me, and forced him into exile knowing his innocence?" Hector nodded. "If you knew Silas, did you know who I was when you approached me that day?" Once prideful memories of the esteemed commander of the King's Legion singling her out among so many made her sick. "Was befriending me some kind of twisted atonement for what you'd done? Or did you just feel the need to steal everything that belonged to him?"

Hector didn't have words, but his shame was clear in the sheen in his eyes.

"So Silas isn't a traitor at all?"

Hector shook his head.

"He was innocent. And you, in fact, are the actual traitor? Not to the Thrones maybe, but to humanity and morality in general?"

His eyes fell away from her, no longer able to bear the disappointment and revulsion in her expression. "Yes, I am."

Then Raven did exactly what he'd expected her to do, exactly what he'd known would be the outcome the moment he set his secret free. She stood, letting the blanket they'd shared fall from her shoulders, and walked away without saying another word.

CHAPTER 33

WHERE WE STAND

As the morning sun cut through the window, revealing the constant flow of dust twinkling about the room, Iris woke with a yawn and a stretch. She'd been grateful when Gabriel said they could keep their room at the White Luna until they no longer needed it, and she appreciated it even more now that she'd gotten a solid night of sleep.

Declan, ever the light sleeper, heard the rustling of her movements. Looking across the space between the two beds with groggy eyes and heavy lashes, he murmured, "Hey." His hair hung in a wave over his eyes, and with the soot washed away and the shaft of sun shining in through the window, the pale brown looked flaxen.

Iris had fallen promptly into bed when they entered the room the night before, but he'd wanted to bathe first. Though she had known, it surprised her to see him so clean. He'd trimmed his beard, making the freckles across his cheeks more visible. As he smiled at her, his irises pranced as if permeated by wisps of smoke.

It had made sense to bring him with her to the inn. Foxx's bed lay empty, and Jericho didn't exactly have room to spare. They'd spent nearly a month sleeping near each other when traveling, so it hadn't occurred to her what waking up with him in the room might feel like. Now, alone in the light of day, her nerves had her heart thudding a little too quickly.

Defying anxious energy, she slid her feet to the floor and sat up.

Declan did the same, matching her movements so they sat knee to knee. "How did you sleep?" He pushed floppy hair from his eyes and rubbed the back of his neck.

"Like a bear in hibernation. You?" Her sleepy gaze was drawn to his fresh attire, namely, the off-white shirt hugging his torso.

"I slept all right." Noticing her roaming eyes, he smiled. Then the room fell into silence, and Iris looked out the window. Declan began pulling on his boots. "How would you like to start the day?"

Iris considered his question as she watched the street. Gabriel was talking to a member of the Guard. Elijah stood across the road, inconspicuously tucked against an alley. She thought about the coming day and what it might bring before glancing back at Declan still tying his boots. She and Foxx always started the day discussing the plan. When they traveled with Asher, it had been fairly standard to figure it out over breakfast.

It felt unfamiliar coming from Declan. When they'd traveled with him and Orion, she hadn't had much say in what their plans would be.

Though she couldn't place the exact moment it happened, the dynamics between them had changed, and she no longer knew the rules. She certainly wasn't his captive anymore, but then what were they to each other? Friends? Something more? Her thoughts drifted to the night he'd arrived at her door with a covert farewell, and her heart fluttered.

"I would like to bathe. Then I guess we should head back to the Monastery to check on Foxx and find out what Asher is doing. Maybe someone there will know the next step in helping the city. Or maybe Asher will have a suggestion regarding..." When she paused, their eyes met again.

He grinned, lifting a single brow so it disappeared beneath his hair. "Regarding... whatever you three were up to before Orion and I got in the way? Something involving the Monastery of the Morrow? And Celestelvyra?"

His speculations hung in the air between them, undisputed but unanswered. She moved to stand up at the same time he did, and they ended up face to face. Though a small crevice of empty air remained between them, the fissure filled with heat.

Declan ran a finger down her arm, causing an eruption of goosebumps to trail behind it. Another flurry shimmied up the back of her neck. "I promised your sister I would prove I could be trusted." When his fingers reached her hand, he latched on, weaving them between hers. "I think I have kept that promise since the moment I made it. Haven't I?"

"I guess that depends when you made it." She smiled playfully, a futile attempt to lighten the weight of his tone and the sweatiness of her palm against his.

His smile widened. "I made it when I was with her under the waterfall."

Iris pretended to think about it, tapping her chin with a finger.

He drew out her name and snatched up her other hand as she dropped it to her side. "I need you to let me be a part of it."

She tilted her head, studying his smoky eyes. "Why is it so important to you?"

"How am I supposed to protect you if I don't know what's going on?"

"Maybe I'm protecting you."

Leaning closer, he whispered in her ear, "Don't." A wave of warmth washed over her. Then he released her and laid back down on the bed. With his hands behind his head, his eyes fell closed.

Iris found the bathing room down the hall. It consisted of a standard sized tub with a spigot. A stove with a large cauldron had been provided to warm the undoubtedly freezing mountain water, but she had neither time nor inclination to deal with such an undertaking and decided a quick, cold bath would do.

Filling the tub halfway, she climbed inside and allowed her feet time to get used to the temperature. Pain from the frosty water began in her toes and worked its way up her legs until her muscles settled somewhere between aching and numb. Lowering herself into the basin, her breath hitched as the surface of the water touched her stomach.

She examined the evidence of the lagoon monster's attack, finding her wounds healed to scars, and remembered Declan stitching them up for her after the incident with the cave nieda. Thoughts of the cave brought other memories to the surface, and her stomach felt sick.

A bar of soap sat atop the outer edge of the tub. Scrubbing it into her rag, she washed her body in the piney scent. She thought of what passed between her and Declan back in the room, and the memory warmed her ice-cold cheeks. Then her thoughts drifted to Foxxglove, still asleep even though no one seemed to understand why.

Dunking her head under the water, she allowed her hair to absorb the wetness before massaging soap into it. She wondered what new horrors she might see in the coming days. Her mind flashed to the corpses piled up outside the wall, and she squeezed her eyes closed. It was only then that she noticed the tears spilling down her cheeks.

So much had happened in just over a day—destruction and trauma dispersed in staggering capacities. Unbearable truths had been declared. She permitted her tears to fall.

After rinsing her hair, she allowed the water to drain out around her until she sat in an empty basin with her arms wrapped around her knees, shivering. When she found her composure, she wiped the tears from her cheeks and stepped out of the tub. Drying off with an available towel and pulling on fresh clothes, she turned the faucet back on so she could wash the soot and sweat from the clothing she'd worn the day before.

Cracking open the door to her room, she peeked inside. Declan lay where she'd left him, his eyelids lifting at the sound of the door. Keeping her head down, she felt his eyes following her as she moved about the room. She hung the washed clothing and wet towel from the wall and began pulling fingers through damp hair. She wanted it to dry a little more before tying it up but also needed something to occupy her hands. Sitting down on the bed, she tugged wool socks onto her feet before looking up to find Declan sitting across from her.

"Have you been crying?"

She shook her head without words, for fear if she spoke, more tears would feel privileged to fall.

Seeing through her lie, he knelt in front of her. "What's wrong?" He cupped her cheek and wiped away a newly fallen tear with his thumb. "Iris?"

"I was... thinking about everything that's happened and feeling..."

"Overwhelmed?"

His smile was so beautiful it made her want to cry even more for reasons she couldn't understand. "Yes, I guess."

"A lot has happened over the last few days." Another tear escaped, and he caught it on its journey down.

After a steadying breath, she looked into his eyes. The green ring bleeding into the gray was visible again in the rays of sun pouring into the room. "You're different."

He furrowed his brow. "What do you mean?"

His other hand sat on the bed, resting next to her thigh. Reaching for it, she said, "I didn't expect you to be this way. So..." She thought of how he'd been those first few days. Annoyed and burdened by her savage and constant fighting, yet refusing to leave her to her own devices. Dragging her away from Orion so she couldn't make things worse for herself. Trying to keep her logical and calm. Perhaps he wasn't so different after all.

"So warm. You were cold before. Shutting me out. Guarded." She thought of the conversation they'd had above Lacuna Kaput, the first time she'd seen cracks in his chilly armor. There had been hints of fractures before that, but when they sat together above the falls, he'd opened up to her—like she was an actual person and not his captive. Like she might be his friend.

"I hope I haven't become too transparent." His smile shifted into a fox-like grin.

"No, certainly not. It's only that I thought you were this impenetrable shell. I kind of made it my goal to pierce it as often as I could." She pinched her lips between her teeth.

"You've succeeded with abundance," he remarked wryly.

Chuckling, she straightened her shoulders. "And now you're..."

"Now I'm what?" He leaned closer.

The vehement spark in his eyes took her breath away. She inhaled through her nose, longing for oxygen, and was met with the masculine scent of his skin. He smelled of leaves floating on a gentle breeze; of smoky sage, freshly lit.

His body lingered intimately near hers, and despite her racing heart and the newness of his close proximity, there was a level of comfort that felt eternal, as if it had always been and always would be. "I think I like you."

His eyes widened a fraction and the corners of his lips curled so the spray of freckles frolicked across his cheeks. Someday, she would take the time to truly examine them; to connect the dots and discover the mysterious stories they portrayed.

Rather than focusing on his eyes, packed with mysteries of their own, she lifted her hand to the lock of hair hanging down his face, running her fingers through it and twisting its pointed tip as he did in moments of deep contemplation.

Declan had dropped his hand from her cheek and pressed his fingers into the side of her thigh, sliding them back and forth, as if they fought to grab on and drag her closer, but his dwindling willpower held them back.

The hand fidgeting with his hair dropped to his chest, coming to rest over his heart. At that, he removed his fingers from hers and slid both hands up her thighs, encircling her backside and pulling her to the edge of the bed.

Unhurriedly, he inclined forward and brushed his lips against hers. Soft and gentle, like the first raindrop that warns of a coming downpour. Like the tiniest sip of hot tea, when its temperature is still uncertain. In defiance of his subtle, feather-like caress, sparks shot down her throat and into her chest before radiating all the way out to her fingertips. Then he backed away ever so slightly, awaiting her response.

Their very short history had been tangled and messy, but his sincerity was enough to erase every single one of her uncertainties. She leaned into him, cuddling up in the circle of his arms and wrapping her own around his neck to pull his mouth nearer. His lips tasted like mint. His tongue, like buds of clove.

His hands glided up her sides like a potter shaping pliable clay with his mindful touch. Then his arms were around her, and he lifted her with ease. Her legs slid around his waist with such natural finesse, it was as if they'd done it a thousand times before. He stepped in reverse until the backs of his knees hit the bed behind them. Their kisses continued as he sat down and situated her onto his lap.

He touched his mouth to her cheeks, her chin, her forehead. "I think I could kiss you all day," he murmured, sending more goosebumps out from where his breath caressed her skin.

Iris giggled and guided his lips back to her own. "I think I would let you."

C

After Raven left, Hector rose from the makeshift bed they'd shared and folded the blankets. Placing them back on the pile, he saw Jax enter the courtyard with a woman on his arm. She whispered something in Jax's ear and planted a kiss on his cheek before hurrying off.

"Morning, Commander." Jax's eyes roamed the yard, looking for anything new that may have appeared in the night. When Hector didn't reply, Jax looked at him. "Want to find some coffee?"

"Yes, let's."

Turning, Jax fell into step next to him. "Raven and I found a place yesterday a few blocks from the palace."

Hector nodded distractedly in response.

They walked Thornby Road for several blocks without speaking. Thornby was the most direct route from the Monastery to the palace. Hector had wondered how the Konungr's carriage managed to make it all the way to them the previous day, but he now saw that Vali must have had the road emptied before making the trip. Very little debris lingered along the edges.

"Are you worried about talking to the team?"

"A bit." Hector's attention caught on an elderly woman cheerfully watering the plants and potted pines decorating her porch. A glowing orädi peeked its head around the corner of her house and shot sprinkles of light into the pots from afar.

"Is it something else then?" Jax asked.

Hector looked at his friend, then clapped him on the shoulder. "Thanks for caring, Lieutenant."

Jax stopped in front of the café and held the door open for Hector to walk through first. "Whatever it is, coffee makes everything better." After receiving their hot beverages, they stood outside, letting their mugs rest on a brick wall until cool enough to drink. "Busy day ahead of us, huh? Did you get any sleep at least?"

"Yeah, I did. You obviously didn't though."

Jax shrugged. "I slept pretty well after."

Hector chuckled and shook his head. "You should be ashamed of yourself."

Laughing, Jax tested the temperature of his coffee. "Where did you end up?"

"In the yard, under the tree." Hector lifted a hand in greeting to a pair of soldiers walking by, one in purple and one in red.

With obvious insinuation, Jax asked, "Alone?" Hector's silent avoidance had Jax laughing again. "Well, it's about damn time."

"Oh, shut up." Hector sipped his coffee and swore when it burned his tongue. The foul word drew the eyes of a woman exiting the café holding hands with a little boy no older than six. Hector offered an apologetic glance and scuffed his jaw. His teeth ground together, then Jax's serious tone drew his eyes.

"Hey, Commander? Does she know?" Jax blew on his coffee, but Hector suspected it was an excuse to avert his gaze.

"Know what?"

Jax looked up the street toward the palace, though little could be seen of it from their vantage but for the tallest spires. "Does she know what happens to the people when she finds the sil ōnni dens?"

Sighing, Hector gave his attention to the brightening sky. "She knows they get sent to the farms." Jax nodded but didn't question him further. "Don't worry, Jax, I am well versed in the sheer magnitude of my sins, but I've just told her about Ryder and Declan. I think I'd like to keep the other skeletons buried a little while longer, if you don't mind."

"How did she take it?"

"I guess we'll know soon enough, won't we? Why don't you go roundup the others. We need to have a meeting."

Jax breathed in the delectable smell wafting from his mug before nodding for them to walk back. "Meet at the original rendezvous spot?"

"That's as good a place as any."

When they reached the intersection where Grove crossed Thornby, Hector split off to head in the direction of the well near the entrance plaza. He'd already rehearsed what he planned to say, but as the minutes drew closer, his anxiety increased. Arriving at the well, he attempted to sit calmly on the stone edge, but soon stood back up to pace. He observed the surrounding area. Having not been to the city's entrance since they'd met up at the start of the attack, he hadn't fully comprehended the level of its ruination.

Turning from the plaza, he looked at the ground as he paced, focusing on the conversation ahead. There was no telling what the rest of his team would think about his decision to stay in Jericho. Would they hate him? Fear him? Adore him? If nothing else, would they follow him?

He wondered if hearing his story had changed Raven's mind about staying. She said she was with him, but after he'd revealed some of his deepest, darkest secrets, she'd left him with barely a word. Had their bond been weaker than he'd imagined? Perhaps to her, it had been nothing more than a soldier's loyalty all along.

Even still, he felt no regret sharing it with her. He'd gripped it so tightly for such a long time, and being honest with someone about it had been an immense relief. Jax was the only other person who knew. He'd been at his side from the beginning and walked with him through it all.

Jax and Dominic arrived first. Moments later, Marshal and Wyatt joined them, laughing and punching each other in a fit of brotherly love and discontent.

Minutes passed and Raven still didn't show. After a quarter of an hour, Hector really began to wonder if she had already left him. She could be halfway to Inaravale if she'd departed immediately after hearing his confessions. Truthfully, he wouldn't blame her if she had.

"Did she say she would be here?" he asked Jax.

Jax shrugged. "She didn't seem pleased about it, but she agreed to come."

"I'm here." Raven rounded a corner and entered the plaza. "I said I would come, and I came." Hector could feel the heat of her anger radiating off of her from a *syli* away. Refusing to meet his eyes, she crossed her arms and looked at Jax. "Lieutenant. Can we get this moving?"

"You got somewhere else you need ta' be, lovey?" Dominic taunted, nudging her with his shoulder. She scowled at him, prompting one of his belly laughs. A soft dusting of flakes began to drift down from the clouds, dancing on the cool breeze in spirals and waves.

Hector stood tall and sturdy, taking a calming breath before he began. He brushed snow from the top of his head, then dropped his hands, clasping them together behind his back. "I called you all here to discuss what we plan to do going forward."

"Yes, yes, we all know why we are here." Dominic punched one fist into the palm of his other hand. "Get on with it, what'sa plan?"

Hector cleared his throat. "Obviously, for reasons unknown to us and entirely out of our control, our mission was interrupted. Though I'm sure Jericho appreciates your efforts, rescue and recovery was not part of the assignment. In fact, our continued presence in Jericho may be viewed as yet another Raptor rebellion."

A wave of tension reverberated through the group, but not surprise. The story of the previous Reko Raptor's treason hung heavy in the air around them. "Now that we are all together and things have begun to settle, I think it's time to draw a line in the sand and determine which side we stand on."

"What are the two sides?" Jax wondered aloud, wanting it clearly spelled out for everyone so there were no misunderstandings.

"I guess, if I had to put it as simply as possible: we either stand with the King's Legion, or we stand against them." Hector tried to read from their demeanors what they might choose. Each seemed lost in thought, furrowing their brows and looking up at the sky or down at the ground. Dominic scraped his jaw with his hand.

"I want you to know, I do understand the gravity of this decision, but I also need to make this abundantly clear: as of this moment, I am—" Hector's sentence caught in his throat. Again, his eyes scanned his team as the words stuck to his tongue like molasses, fighting to remain unspoken. "I am no longer the commander of the King's Legion." He released a weighty exhale. "And so you are under no orders from me to remain here. I wouldn't order you to, even if I could, but the time has come for the King's Legion to leave this city. The Aldrichs no longer have any say here, a fact she made sure of when she slaughtered thousands of innocents.

"The Jerichonian Guard has been whispering about the Legion's presence in their territory, and after speaking briefly with Vali, I would not be surprised if he plans on claiming Jericho as the base for a all-out revolution. I don't think they will take this tragedy sitting down. It has been viewed as an act of war, and they mean to fight back."

"Are you sure, Hector?" Uncharacteristic anxiety crept into Jax's voice. "An actual war?"

"One like our generation has never seen. One like hasn't been seen in centuries, if ever." He closed his eyes for a moment, rubbing his temples with his thumbs before continuing. "I think it's important for me to also clarify, if the Konungr and his Guard do not yet plan on organizing an uprising, I will be the one to push the issue with him and the Dróttning and make it so."

A choir of questions and surprised exclamations shattered the stillness of the empty plaza. "I know I'm not their favorite person, but I think they will support this decision, especially if it comes with the added bonus of Sirena's commander. I believe Vali hates her more than anything and would delight in such a prize. Either way, I can no longer sit by and watch the Queen's reign of terror. This attack on the city was the final stroke of the sword. Of course, I have witnessed far more of the inner workings in Castle Solís than many of you, and I understand if you don't feel like you have enough evidence to justify such severe actions. You can go back to Inaravale, tell the Queen of my betrayal, and perhaps one day we will find each other again, facing off on the field of battle."

A full minute passed, and no one spoke. "Also, someone should probably let Wraith know he's been promoted." Hector's attempted joke provoked a multitude of reactions. Marshal and Wyatt chuckled, though their eyebrows rose awkwardly high into their hairlines. Dominic swore excessively, stringing more expletives together than Hector had ever heard expressed in a single sentence. Jax wore a sour expression. Raven wore no expression, remaining speechless and unmoved.

"You don't have to decide right now, but you should decide soon. After I speak to Vali and Abram, I plan to give all of the Legion present in the city the same opportunity. You have but days to choose if you will leave Jericho in peace, unharmed, or stay with us and become a traitor to the Thrones of Arkaemor."

C

"Are you going to leave your bag in here?" Declan asked when they at last untangled themselves from each other's arms.

"Yes. You can, too, if you like." After shoving feet into her boots, Iris pulled her hair back into its high pony. "Are you ready to go?"

He nodded, and they met by the door. As she slipped her hand into his, he pulled her up against him, placing a few more kisses on already swollen lips. Then he drew his fingers through her hair. "You should leave this down." He smiled lazily, his eyes alight with unfamiliar joy and contentment. "I like it down."

Dragging the tie out of the pony, she let her locks fall free around her shoulders. "Better?"

He played with the white streak hanging in her face, then he opened the door and turned to face the hall, only to discover Asher closing a door a few rooms down. "Ale—Asher?"

"Hey! What are you two doing here?" Asher's eyes drifted to their laced fingers, their lingering closeness, and his smile widened.

Iris ignored his obvious examination and looked him over. He'd bathed, as they had. His bangs swept sideways above emerald eyes, which appeared awake and ready to take on the horrors of the day. "This is where Foxx and I have been staying since we arrived."

Asher gaped. "What? No way! What are the odds? Perhaps Elohim really has been drawing your sister and I to each other all along." Iris smiled, thinking he might be the most adorable thing in the world, and he told her to shut up before igniting with more excitement. "Oh! I've a proper surprise for you! Come here."

Slipping his key from his pocket, he opened the door to his room and stepped inside. Iris and Declan followed. Standing between two beds, Asher turned to face them holding both her and Foxx's backpacks.

Iris squealed. "My bag!" Rushing into the room, she swiped it from him and sat down on a bed, tearing through it like it was the greatest treasure she'd ever discovered. She pulled out clothing and old food and when she got to her leather-bound journal, she squeezed it tight to her chest.

Declan wondered about the book and felt another pang of regret regarding his role in the abduction. Not only had he taken them away from Asher and held them against their will, he'd left behind their only possessions.

Iris set the book down and dug in again. "Yes! It's still here!" She pulled out a necklace and held it up to show them.

Asher said her name, his eyes wide. "What is that?"

"It's my mother's necklace. It was the last thing she gave me before she… well, you know." She glanced between the men. "It was one of the things I saw at the Tree of Knowing. At the time, I didn't consider it might be more important than a cherished memory. Then I couldn't stop thinking about it after…" Her eyes shifted to Declan and back to Asher as she cleared her throat. "This is awkward. Anyway, I thought it was sadness over the loss of a gift from my mother, but then a few days ago, I realized why I couldn't get it out of my head." She stood and placed it in Asher's hand, practically bouncing with delight.

Carved into the shape of a clamshell, the blue stone had white designs resembling ocean waves. Most importantly, it was the same style and size as the other stones they'd been collecting: half an inch thick and fitting in the palm of his hand.

"Iris, is this…?" Asher's jaw went slack, his eyes fixated on the stone.

Alternatively, Declan's brow pinched, and he scratched his head. "What is it? What's going on?"

"It's the Alunda key!" Iris grabbed Asher's forearms and shook him. "It has to be, doesn't it?"

"Key?" Declan asked.

"Iris, do you know what this means? We have all seven!" Asher picked her up and spun her in a circle that barely fit inside the room. Then he reached into his own pack and laid out all seven stones on the bed: amber crown, pink tourmaline snowflake, red carnelian acacia tree, sodalite clamshell, turquoise skull, emerald raindrop, and moonstone crescent.

Iris picked up the moonstone and held it to the window. "This is gorgeous." It looked slightly opaque in that she couldn't see through the middle, though the edges had some transparency to them. It seemed to hold a smoky rainbow encased within its walls, resting in a sky of shimmering blue. She grabbed Asher's arm and held the stone next to the tattoo on his wrist. "How did you know? How did you know what it would look like?"

"It's the symbol of the first Monastery, the one here in Jericho." Asher rubbed his thumb over the tattoo.

"Hey!" Declan raised his voice, snapping his fingers. "Will someone please tell me what the hell is going on?"

Iris put the stone back on the bed and walked over to him. Taking both of his hands in her own, she said, "Sorry, Declan. I didn't mean to ignore you." She kissed him on the cheek, and he glanced past her shoulder to see Asher bubbling with enthusiasm. Despite his irritation, he found this expression an immense relief, as brothers weren't often fans of their sisters kissing their kidnappers. He wondered how much Asher knew of Declan's complicity in the abduction but was too afraid to ask.

"You said we can trust you and you're right, you have proven yourself. You wanted the truth and here it is." Iris gestured to Asher and the line of stones. "These stones are the seven keys that unlock the door to Celestelvyra."

Speechless, Declan's eyes inflated.

"The only problem is that most of the doors have been destroyed." Some of Asher's previous excitement dwindled. "I was hoping to get in through the Monastery here, but it has obviously been demolished, and I couldn't find the door in Metsa Sateen."

Iris turned back to him without releasing Declan's hands. "Actually, I think I have an idea about that, too."

"Okay, out with it." Asher collected the stones and sat down on the bed to return them to his pack.

Iris left Declan by the door and sat back down across from Asher. "I know the Wilds' Monastery is supposedly lost, but Foxx believes we found it. We followed a map of our father's to a location he'd marked in ink."

"Foxx mentioned thinking you'd been at the Wilds' Monastery when we arrived in Petrichor."

"Exactly. We can't know for sure, but it makes sense. Then I was thinking about something else the Tree of Knowing showed me. I can't get it out of my head. When Foxx and I were in the building in the Grim Wilds, there was this hallway." She paused and closed her eyes, picturing the dark corridor. "I felt so drawn to it, like I couldn't look away, but Foxx hardly seemed to see it at all."

Asher sat forward with his elbows on his knees. Iris glanced at Declan, attempting to include him in the conversation, but he looked strained. Her eyes questioned his panicked demeanor, and he responded with a quick shake of his head.

Relaxing her furrowed brow, Iris went on. "I know it doesn't seem like a lot to go on, but it felt like there was something keeping her from seeing the importance of the door. I, on the other hand, could barely focus on anything else. So much so that I became irritated with her for not paying attention. Then the Tree showed me the memory. Such a seemingly random event, yet of all the things in my history, it chose to remind me of that dark corridor."

"Sounds promising enough to check it out." A spark of Asher's elation returned.

Declan spoke then, his face transformed back into its usual impassive calm. "Actually, what you're describing reminds me of the black walls."

Asher clapped his hands once and pointed at him. "Spot on, mate. Sounds exactly the same."

"What are the black walls?" Iris asked.

Declan looked to Asher, who gestured for him to explain. "The black walls are the barriers outlining the entirety of Arkaemor. They're like the barriers between territories only they're black instead of transparent. What's familiar is the misdirection enchantment. The walls radiate with an aura that deceives people into avoiding them without realizing they're doing it."

Asher put his hands on his knees and rolled his shoulders. "You've traveled the wilderness for much of your life, and yet you've never heard of or seen them, right? That's because they don't want to be seen."

"It almost sounds like what happened with the poem," Iris mused. "The one about the Monasteries."

"The one on the wall beneath Lacuna Kaput?" Declan asked.

"Foxx and I grew up with our mother singing it to us, but somehow, we forgot it. Even when we saw the name Lacuna Kaput, and even when Asher spoke of the Monastery of the Morrow, it all felt like new information."

Asher said, "The Queen doesn't want the world to know the prophecy is more than a nursery rhyme. It has that effect on most who hear it. On myself, as well, until a few years ago. And it's not the only thing in written history like that. She's kept many things shielded. Buried."

"What happened a few years ago that made it all clear?" Iris leaned closer to look him in the eyes, immediately sensing secrets within them scurrying into hiding like a startled squirrel.

"Let's wait for Foxx."

She sighed with exaggeration, then wrinkled her brow. "So the corridor didn't want Foxx to see it for what it was, but why was I able to see it?"

Asher and Declan shrugged. "You believe in it more than she does. Foxx is practical. A realist. You're the dreamer. You're the one with faith and hope in your destiny."

"After you know about the black walls, their power becomes less effective. Like with the poem." Declan heard footsteps in the hall and shifted his weight to glance back at the door.

"So if you truly believed in your journey, but Foxx held on to her doubts…" Asher's lips curled into a mischievous grin. "… which we both know she has a tendency to do, it makes sense you wouldn't be as affected by the enchantment as her."

Iris tipped her head from side to side. "I guess that makes sense. Let's go check on her. Maybe she's woken up."

"We can drop these bags off in your room so you have them handy when you need them." Asher lifted them from the bed and started toward the door.

"Thank you so much for keeping them, Asher." Iris followed him out and unlocked her and Foxx's room. "And dragging them all this way!"

Tipping into a mocking bow, he said, "Not a problem at all, my lady."

C

Hector watched each Raptor mull over the possibilities. Their next decision would alter the course of their lives forever, and they had no way of knowing with certainty where each path would lead. Both carried the potential for danger and pain in one form or another.

Before anyone gave an answer, a commotion arose at the front gate. Tucked within the thick wall, neither the gate Guards nor whomever they spoke to beyond could be seen from Hector's vantage. As the voices grew louder, he moved to check it out. He traveled toward the fountain, seeking more information before approaching directly. Once in line with the gate, he saw Victor and two others in Jerichonian fatigues talking to someone on the opposite side, and when the outsider came into view, the reason for the disturbance became clear.

Dagon Wraith and a group of about thirty Legion soldiers on horseback sought entrance to the city. When Dagon saw Hector, he grinned as though he'd won an argument. "Ah, Commander. At last, a friendly face. Will you inform these *Guards* that they must allow the King's Legion entry to the city, as it belongs to a territory ruled by the King and Queen of Arkaemor?"

A Guard standing next to Victor shouted, "Cordillera belongs to the Konungr!" Dagon smiled with malicious glee.

Hector touched the Guard's shoulder and nodded him out of the way. With reluctance, the man stepped back, allowing Hector room to stand in front of the gate. Hector pulled the chains from the bars and opened both gates wide. The Jerichonian Guards eyed him with suspicion, probably wondering if this was the moment he showed his true colors.

Stalling for time, Hector looked Dagon up and down. Then his eyes slid behind him to Dagon's right-hand man, Amar, and the other soldiers sitting high on their horses. With informal and careless annoyance, he asked, "Why are you here, Wraith?"

Taken aback, the general replied, "Still hunting the Belamour women, of course. Like you, Commander Kayvan, have ordered us to do."

Hector watched as words spread like gossip through the other soldiers. He was used to people talking about him. At least now it would be for honorable reasons. Still wearing crimson and gray under High Legion battle gear, he stood tall with his chin up and his arms straight at his sides. "The orders have since changed. A runner was sent to inform you. I apologize the news did not reach your ears sooner."

"No one has informed us of any change." Dagon kept his temper in check, though Hector knew him well and could already see the blood vessel on his forehead pulsing. "Have the women been captured then?"

"The Reko Raptors have taken over the mission. Clearly our Majesties were underwhelmed with your abilities to retrieve them and decided to go a different route."

Dagon's jaw hung limp for a long moment. Blood coursed through his veins, and he squeezed his fingers into fists, but his voice remained calm as he spoke through his teeth. "I had no idea the Raptors had reformed. Who is their lieutenant?"

Hector brushed off the front of his uniform. "You are released from your current assignment. You may return to the royal city and await further orders."

"No!" Dagon snapped, his restraint faltering. "We have been hunting these women for months. I will not—"

"As Hector has already stated, our beloved King and Queen were displeased with your progress." Jax appeared behind Hector, putting his hand on his shoulder in solidarity. Then he moved it to the pistol at his hip.

Dagon said Jax's name. Hector found himself enjoying the continuous bewilderment on the general's face more than was entirely proper. "Or, Lieutenant Blackmoor, is it?" Jax dropped his chin in confirmation. Dagon whispered something to Captain Amar, who smirked. "Well Lieutenant, I was just saying to Commander Kayvan how very disappointed we are to have this mission stolen out from under us. We've put many months into it, you see." His words sounded formal, but there was an assertion of dominance beneath the surface.

As a member of the Legion, Jax ranked under General Wraith.

As lieutenant of the Raptors, he stood in a completely new bracket. So, despite the level of their rank, Jax was no longer required to take orders from him. "I understand your frustration, but unfortunately, the Queen herself ordered the reestablishment of the Raptors. I do apologize that word didn't reach you before you traveled all the way here. If you wish to contest the Queen's decision, you will have to take it up with her. For now, as I believe Hector has made explicitly clear, you are free to go." His fingers leisurely tapped the grip of his pistol.

Dagon took an angry step forward and was met with the tip of a broadsword at his throat.

"I believe I heard the commander say it's time for you and your men to leave this place." Raven stood in a half crouch in front of Hector, her sword aimed high so if she struck straight, the blade would pierce his throat and slide into his brain. She twisted the sword so its tip broke the skin. Stepping back, Dagon wiped away blood with a gloved finger. Raven held her stance, challenging him to press forward again.

Hector heard the pull of bowstrings behind him and knew Marshal and Wyatt must be there readying to release. Then he felt Dominic on the flank opposite Jax.

"Let's not make this harder for everyone." Dominic wiggled a grenade in one hand with his finger through the pin and gripped a rugged hatchet in the other.

Dagon took another two steps back, and Hector wondered what they must look like standing at the Jerichonian city gate, weapons at the ready, waiting for him to make a move. He hoped every single Raptor pin was visible.

Jax raised his pistol. "Last chance to walk away, General."

Dagon looked at each of them in astonishment. "All of you then?" The team held their position as he spit at the ground. "The Raptors always were a big bunch of traitors. The Queen was foolish to reinstate them. We'll leave for now, but don't think we won't be back."

Hector pushed the gates closed as Dagon turned to walk away. Before the general mounted his horse, Hector called, "Be sure to give my condolences to the Queen."

CHAPTER 34

INTRIGUING PROPOSALS

When the Reko Raptors returned to the Monastery, they found Commander Havlar and General Asger at the center of the courtyard. Rather than ambushing them with the entire kettle, Hector thought he and Jax should confront them alone.

Jax sent Raven to fetch Prince Alexander, and it didn't take more than a few minutes for her to find him entering the courtyard with Iris and Declan.

Iris waved enthusiastically and greeted her by name. Raven forced a smile and returned her salutation, her eyes sliding to their hands before shifting up to meet Declan's.

"Raven," he said in greeting.

Facing Asher, Raven addressed him as *Prince Alexander*, prompting Iris to jest, "I'm telling you, a nametag would really help your cause."

Raven rolled her eyes. "Hector would like to see you immediately. He wishes to have a meeting about his plans for—" Her eyes flicked between the three of them, landing lastly on Declan. "— going forward." Then she bolted, moving the opposite way down Thornby Road in haste.

Iris stared after her. "She's a strange one."

"You're not wrong." Declan squeezed her hand. "Asher, should we join you at the meeting?"

"To be honest, I'm going to be there whether they like it or not."

Iris glanced toward the commanders and their seconds, her heart trilling in tandem with her hands going clammy. Having spoken briefly to Hector a few times, she thought him pleasant enough. He reminded her a great deal of how Declan had been at first: quiet, controlled, and pensive.

Jax was intimidating, having the appearance of an insurgent before actually becoming one. He looked fierce and bold and strong—like a warrior. All sharp edges and dark accents. Now, he stood free of his armor with his uniform rolled to his elbows, revealing the tattoos that covered his tanned forearms like sleeves. From a distance, it was impossible to discern what each of them depicted, but on the few times she'd glimpsed them up close, she'd noticed an abstract sun, a ship on ocean waves, the bird that Raven pointed out, as well as a few others.

Abram was older and wiser than the others, with kind eyes and a small but ever present smile. The hair braided down the back had faded to gray, flecked with strands of white and black, and the beard growing from his chin stretched to his sternum.

Iris hadn't been able to get a read on Eero Asger yet, mainly because he didn't say much. Several years Abram's junior, Eero was the opposite of him in practically every way. His brow displayed a constant furrow. His hair was lengthier than Abram's, dark umber in hue, and thick. One long cluster hung down the right side of his chest with ties running top to bottom, and the rest lay loose down his back.

Iris pulled her attention from her observations and added, "Not by choice, but Foxx and I are a part of this."

Asher nodded. "And I think if Declan is going to be sticking around, he should probably join us, too."

"Let's do it then." Declan straightened the front of his attire as if making himself more presentable.

When they reached the soldiers, Hector immediately inclined his head to Asher and greeted him with *Your Highness*. A laugh burst from Iris' lips, and she stifled it with her hand so as not to seem rude.

Asher filled his lungs with air and ran a hand over his head. "It's Asher, if you don't mind Hector. I've been using my middle name since leaving Castle Solís. Traitors can't be princes, after all."

"We're all traitors now," Declan said.

Abram cleared his throat. "Indeed. Now, Commander Kayvan,

would you please introduce your guests and then explain what you would like to discuss."

Hector passed around introductions. "We all know Alexa—Asher. The Crown Prince of Arkaemor."

Abram dipped his head. "A pleasure to meet you once again."

"Abram, you've already met my right hand man, Jax Blackmoor. And this is Silas Declanaire, of the previous Reko Raptors. He answers simply to Declan."

"Your name is *Silas Declanaire*?" Iris shrieked. "Are you kidding me?"

Declan shrugged. "I never use my full name except on official business."

Iris pointed between Asher and Declan. "You boys are going to be the death of me, I swear."

Asher chuckled and lifted Iris' hand as if presenting a princess to the royal court. "And this, Commander Havlar, is the endlessly lovely Iris Belamour." Iris curtsied in jest.

Seeming amused rather than annoyed by the antics of the young people, Abram bowed back. "A pleasure, Iris Belamour."

"I wonder if Vali should be present for this conversation." Asher suspected he already knew Hector's intentions. With the ability to jump barriers, his mother would have expected Hector to return to Inaravale right away—by the previous day at the very latest. The longer he remained absent, the more suspicious she would become of his treachery. Hector would have known that when he decided to stay.

"Yes, I think—" Clopping hooves cut Hector's sentence short. The company turned toward Thornby Road to see two horses galloping into the yard. One, a dapple gray with black spots and silver hair, held Viggo, captain of the Konungr's Royal Guard. The other, a black roan with splatters of white, carried the Konungr himself, draped in a fur-lined cape that covered the majority of the horse's backside.

They rode directly to the commanders and their guests and dismounted smoothly. Viggo took the reins of both horses and stood back a few paces from the group.

Vali approached them, appearing in no way like the king of a city recently attacked by a dragon. "What a lovely morning it is to be planning an uprising! If only we could be standing in the sunlight instead of under this ghastly ceiling. Business in the shadows is ever so troublesome." He looked up at the patchwork fabric draped above them with appraisal. "Though it was a very clever idea."

"We can move from the courtyard if you wish, Your Majesty," Abram said.

"Yes, I would. I prefer to observe intentions in the light if you don't mind." Without waiting for anyone to reply, the Konungr turned on his heel and started back toward the road. Iris and Asher shared a chuckle simultaneously with Jax and Hector sighing, and the seven of them followed Vali out into the sun.

When they stopped almost a block away from the Monastery, Vali lifted his hands to the sky. "See? Isn't this better? Now we all have a proper view of each other."

"It's much better, Vali," Asher agreed.

Vali dipped his head in appreciation. "Alexander, my friend, have you yet been made aware? Someone attacked Foxxglove last night. Or tried to, anyway. She is fine, of course, and I am taking care of it."

Asher and Iris blanched. "She's okay? What did they do?"

Iris wondered what Vali meant by *taking care of it*, but she didn't ask. She looked over her shoulder at Elijah, standing a block away. He'd been waiting for them outside the White Luna when they'd left. It felt strange being followed constantly, but she was grateful for it now more than ever.

Vali flourished a hand. "Don't let it worry you. She is guarded at all times, day and night. No harm will come to her under my protection. That is a King's Promise." Then he directed his eyes to each member of the group, acknowledging those he knew with a nod. "Now, you all know me of course, and I believe I know most of you." When he reached Declan, he wrinkled his nose as if smelling something nasty. "You look familiar, soldier. What is your name?"

"Declan." He lifted a hand. "Former Raptor."

Vali's eyes flashed with recognition. "Ah, yes. You came to scold me with that horrid fellow."

"Orion," Declan filled in for him, and Iris giggled. She hadn't taken it seriously when Orion claimed the Konungr didn't like him. She'd assumed he was being grumpy, but it seemed he may not have been far off.

"Yes, him." Vali grimaced. Then his brow lifted in Iris' direction. "And… Belamour."

Iris quirked her head, and Asher clarified, "He means your father."

"Sawyer Belamour, yes." Vali reached for Iris' fingers, gently lifting them to his lips. "You must be the enchanting Iris. I say, you are even more arresting in person than when your face was shimmering high above my city."

Iris' cheeks flushed. Shyly, she managed, "Thank you, Your Majesty."

Vali tapped the back of her hand before allowing it to fall to her side. He then turned his attention to Jax, who extended his own hand before the Konungr could make the first move.

"Jax Blackmoor, Your Majesty."

Vali accepted the handshake, gripping it tightly and seeming pleased by Jax's boldness. "Now that introductions are taken care of, Commander, I believe you called this meeting?" He folded his arms and lifted a brow. Iris smiled at Asher, a thousand questions in her eyes. Vali noticed and winked at her.

Hector began, speaking confidently. "Yes, thank you. I called the meeting because I wish to discuss my proposal for making Jericho the headquarters for a revolution against the Thrones of Arkaemor." Though most already had an inkling to Hector's intentions, his dauntless declaration had their eyes widening. "There's no sense in tiptoeing around it. I think we can all agree that what Sirena did here was irreparable. I've heard murmurs from the Guard suggesting they believe it to be an act of war, and I agree. She thinks she can reign without restraint. She always has, and I think it's time we prove otherwise."

Vali rubbed his hands together, trying to restrain them from clapping with sheer exhilaration. Several moments passed without response before he encouraged, "Excellent, Hector. Please, do go on."

Abram asked, "What do you suggest are the first steps to declaring this revolution?"

"I think we need to rid the city of anyone loyal to the King and Queen." Hector's eyes met Asher's, momentarily feeling exposed in discussing such matters with someone he had always respected as a member of the royal family. It felt like a betrayal of his trust, despite the Prince standing right there with him amongst the other would-be rebels. He dipped his chin almost imperceptibly, and Asher returned the gesture with an encouraging smile. "There are still

Legion soldiers hanging around Jericho. Most have been very helpful over the past few days, but that doesn't mean they're ready to betray the Thrones. We need to figure out where they stand and give those who wish to leave the chance to escape freely before locking the city down."

"Or we make a statement." Vali tapped the tips of his fingers together. "And send a message to Sirena in the form of their severed heads."

"He's joking," Asher said.

Vali frowned like a scolded child. "Only slightly. You are right, of course, Commander. We will certainly give any swine who wishes to flee the opportunity to do so."

Hector shared a look with Jax, who shrugged. "The next step would be to work on rebuilding the city and training anyone who wants to join the fight so we can prepare to go to war. We have some time to act. Dagon and his cavalry approached the city less than an hour ago, and my team sent them away. I think it was pretty obvious we no longer stand on the same side."

Iris recognized the name and furrowed her brow. Vali's lifted in surprise.

Jax chimed in, "Dagon knows how to jump, but he won't share that information with thirty men. They will be moving fast on horses, but it will still take them a while to travel back to Reginaterra. Though he may send someone ahead with a message to warn Sirena."

Iris suddenly felt very lost at the conversation's progression. "Explain: *knows how to jump*."

Hector had to fight his habitual secrecy to respond. "Jumping is when you cross through a barrier and exit out the other side anywhere you wish."

Iris scratched her chin. "So you're saying we could exit Cordillera through a barrier and rather than crossing into Metsa Sateen, we could choose to cross into Savanni instead? Or even Reginaterra?" She tried to keep her attention on Hector, but her eyes kept drifting to the Konungr, who beamed with mischievous energy.

"That's exactly what I am saying."

Iris looked at Asher with arms folded. "Did you know about this?" A guilty smile spread across his lips, and his head shrank into his shoulders. "You did! I submit that from this point forward, there will be no secrets amongst those involved with this revolution."

"I concur," Asher cheered.

Vali asked, "What do you propose we do regarding the Queen's immortality? While I am all for a monumental takedown, if Sirena can't be dealt with, then the loss of life that unavoidably walks hand in hand with war and rebellion will be for naught."

Hector tugged at his ear before sliding his hand around the back of his neck. "I have been thinking the same thing. Though it's my understanding that killing her will be no easy feat."

"Many have tried."

"I've heard she's impossible to kill." Jax crossed his arms, lifting his eyes to the sky as the snow began to fall in heavier clusters. He'd removed his jacket earlier. Now he glanced back at where he'd left it in the square, wishing he could slip it back on.

Eero suggested, "We could lock her away somewhere? With round the clock security."

"Won't work or we would have done it ages ago." Vali's enthusiasm seemed playful, but Iris suspected he wasn't joking. She wondered if all the kings of Arkaemor were as insane as the Mad King seemed to be. If so, she didn't think she wanted to meet the rest of them.

Hector agreed. "Her magic is too strong. I don't think there is anything in existence that would hold her forever."

"Hector's right. Killing her is the only way." If Asher's ease in discussing matricide bothered anyone, they didn't point it out.

"But we have a plan to accomplish that." Iris tapped her thighs as she rocked on the balls of her feet. Feeling Vali's eyes on her, she glanced his way and flushed.

"You do?" Jax asked with obvious disbelief.

Asher met Hector's gaze and held it for a long moment, thinking it was time they both laid their cards out on the table. "Yes, we do. There's a fountain in Celestelvyra that holds purifying water known as Pyhä-ki. Since the month of Sunset, I've been searching for the keys that unlock the Sacred Realm so that I may enter Celestelvyra, retrieve Pyhä-ki, and return to kill the Queen. After long months of hunting, and with the help of Foxx and Iris, I now hold all seven keys."

Vali's eyes widened, making him appear stunned for the first time since arriving. "And so your incessant search for Belamour's daughters has finally paid off."

Iris' head snapped to Asher.

He met her gaze with more apologies before responding. "Yes, Vali, it has."

Iris didn't have words, nor the capability to mask her surprise as she realized Foxx really had been right all along. Asher had intentionally searched for them. The Prince of Arkaemor had hunted them, like Declan and Orion. He'd been more clever at worming his way in, but the truth couldn't be denied. Declan had also mentioned the Reko Raptors were reformed to find them, and Hector, the commander of the King's Legion, a soldier ranked above all others, had traveled to Jericho for the sole purpose of helping secure them.

The Queen had demolished entire city blocks, killing thousands.

Every one of them wanted to get their hands on the Belamour sisters, and Iris had no idea what about her and Foxx could possibly warrant such measures.

Vali's voice invaded her thoughts. "I hadn't known you were seeking the keys as well, Alexander. I might have helped."

"I wasn't yet looking for the keys last we spoke. I didn't know where everything was leading me. Only since fleeing Castle Solís have I hunted the keys to Celestelvyra."

Vali nodded, though his racing thoughts became evident behind his eyes.

Jax's voice fractured the strange tension. "Celestelvyra? It's not a real place. It's a story." Hector shot him a warning glance.

Abram shook his head. "I assure you it is a very real place. The Monastery of the Morrow was able to travel back and forth between the realms whenever they pleased. Though I had come to believe many of the entrances were lost."

Asher said, "You're right, Abram, but I think there could be three remaining possibilities. If every Monastery has a door, then the ones that remain standing should, theoretically, still provide access to the In-Between. I had hoped to find one here in Jericho, but I think that's out of the question now. I explored the one in Metsa Sateen with little luck, though it's possible we could still uncover it with a team and more time. I didn't get to spend as much time at the Metsa Monastery as originally planned. However, Iris thinks she discovered the entrance to the one in the Grim Wilds, so I think our best bet is to begin there."

"Vallemortis," Vali said under his breath, still wandering in his own thoughts.

"She found a corridor in an abandoned building that seemed to have magic guarding it, much like the black walls. Her father had marked the location on a map. I think it's a good place to start at least. If she's mistaken, we can do a more thorough exploration of the jungle Monastery. We can't win without Pyhä-ki, so we need to find it, whatever it takes."

Iris tapped his arm. "You said three, but it didn't sound like you were counting the Jerichonian Monastery in that number. So where's the third?"

Asher's face darkened, as did Hector's. "The only other remaining Monastery is in Crystavium."

Hector stifled a shiver. "The Ashgate Fortress: Prison of the Strayed. So we shall endeavor to avoid that option at all costs."

Hair on the back of Iris' neck stood on end as Asher continued. "Technically, Inaravale should have a door also, though I've scoured every inch of that castle, and I've never found it."

Jax cleared his throat and shifted his weight from one foot to the other. "I'm trying to wrap my head around the idea that some magical water is going to kill the Immortal Queen." Iris wanted to scowl at him, but when their eyes met, fear stopped her short.

"If you believe her to be immortal then at least a small part of you must believe in magic as well," Abram pointed out.

"I know this will work," Asher said.

"Pyhä-ki will kill an immortal. If you truly have the keys, then you are well on your way, Alexander." Vali put a hand on Asher's shoulder.

Iris noticed for the first time since she'd discovered his true identity that he didn't flinch at Vali's use of it. The men shared a friendly smile, and she wondered how deep their bond actually went. Their comfort level seemed far beyond royal acquaintanceship. It occurred to her then how much more there must be to learn about the Crown Prince of Arkaemor.

Hector looked at Jax. "I will say, the Queen mentioned the keys. She thought Iris and her sister were looking for them because Amaryllis knew what they could be used for. Perhaps that's what played into her horrific attack."

Iris drew her head back. "My mother?"

"Isn't that how you know about them?"

"No. I know because Asher told us." Exhaling a huff, she said, "I don't understand, Asher. What does my mother have to do with this?"

Before he could answer, Vali added pensively, "Amaryllis did know of the keys and the doorway that would lead to Pyhä-ki."

Iris felt a nauseating cloud fill her chest. Tears burned her eyes, threatening to break free. She knew she looked ridiculous shedding them amongst these royals and renegades, but she could no longer restrain her swelling emotions. "Asher. What is going on?" Declan grabbed her hand and squeezed it.

Asher leaned close to her ear, seeking privacy from the others. "I promised I would explain everything to both of you, and I will. I swear it, Iris." She took a deep breath to calm her panic. Vali looked between them, watching as if preparing to contain an eruption.

Hector cleared his throat. "Asher, you're sure this magic water will work?"

"Pyhä-ki, yes."

"Then it's a plan. Asher will lead a team to Celestelvyra to retrieve Pyhä-ki. Abram and I will stay here to train and rebuild. Once you return with the poison, we will make plans to march on Inaravale."

"There is one chink in the scheme." Vali looked at Asher while tapping his lips with steepled fingers. "You will need the Artifact to carry Pyhä-ki from the Sacred Realm. And the last known person in possession of it was…"

"I have a theory about that as well," Asher interrupted, and Vali nodded.

"What's the Artifact," Iris asked.

Asher's eyes flickered to Declan before he answered. "The Artifact is the object your father stole from the Queen when he betrayed her six years ago."

CHAPTER 35

UPON WAKING

The company continued hammering out details over the next few days. Hector and Abram worked cooperatively to solidify plans, with Vali and Asher joining at times to ensure all strategies were in accordance with their expectations.

Amidst planning for war, citizens and soldiers began to rebuild. A new hospital would be erected, and homes and businesses reestablished. The training center at the barracks was opened to any and all who wished to join the fight, and soldiers both Jerichonian and Legion made themselves available to share their skills.

Asher and his team planned to leave for Celestelvyra as soon as Foxx awoke. When they returned with Pyhä-ki, the real battle plans would begin.

Though he involved himself more in the planning than he had in those first few days, Asher spent plenty of time at Foxx's side, begging the Creator's assistance in rousing her. If she was to survive, she needed to wake soon, otherwise her body would shut down from lack of nutrition. It didn't seem plausible that the complexion in her cheeks remained bright or the beating of her heart endured with such vigor. He'd managed to feed her a few drops of water, but she hadn't taken in any other nutrients. The nurses continued to comment on how bizarre her condition seemed, and Asher couldn't help but wonder if his mother had done something magical to keep her asleep.

In one of the old fairytales, a prince's kiss broke the sleeping spell cast by a wicked witch. After much debate with himself regarding whether or not it was justifiable to steal their first kiss from her lips while she slept, he tried to wake her in that manner.

If sorcery really did cause her slumber, true love's kiss hadn't broken the curse.

However, two days later, over a week since the Queen's attack, Asher, Iris, and Declan entered the courtyard to find Maia rushing their way with arms waving. "Asher! Iris! Come, she's awake! Foxxglove is awake!"

Iris erupted with excitement and raced past the men to find Foxx sitting up and sipping on a cup of water. When their eyes met, Foxx's lips broke into a huge smile. Luckily, she had the foresight to set her drink on the ground before Iris tackled her. "Foxxglove, I'm so glad you're okay! I've been so worried! Don't you ever do that to me again, do you understand?"

Foxx squeezed her sister back with all her strength, but when she glimpsed Asher running toward them over Iris' shoulder, her smile vanished. The loathing in her eyes stopped him in his tracks, and his sudden halt had Declan nearly crashing into him.

Iris sat back to look her over, ignoring the anger spilling off her in waves. Foxx's eyes had opened at last, and Iris could care for little else.

"I'm fine." Foxx took her turn examining Iris for injuries. "And it looks like you are, too. I'm sorry to have frightened you. They told me I've been out for days."

"You have been! The Queen's attack was eight days ago." Iris began fussing with her sister's hair, still pink where blood hadn't been washed clean. She pushed it off her face before straightening her shirt to make sure it lay comfortably.

Foxx shooed her away. "Oh, stop it already! Is this what it feels like when I do it to you?"

Iris laughed again. "Irritating, am I right?"

Asher kept his distance, genuinely concerned Foxx might smite him with her death stare if he got too close. Declan hovered behind him. He'd been one of the nurses looking after Foxx, but he didn't know how she would feel about him assessing her now.

Foxx made a point not to look at either of them. "What's been happening here?" As she lifted the water to take another sip, she gazed around the courtyard lit with firelight and filtered sunshine. "There are people everywhere. Are we in front of the Monastery?"

"We are, yes. They crafted a patchwork ceiling to keep the snow away as we figured things out. I'll fill you in on everything else after you've had time to rest." She tucked the blanket tighter around her sister's legs to prevent cool air from leaking in.

"I've rested enough."

"Well, at least get something to eat," Iris insisted.

Overhearing this and finally feeling like he had a purpose, Declan stepped forward. "We'll go find Foxx some food and be back soon, okay?" He directed his question to Iris, but his voice had drawn Foxx's eyes. He'd never realized how dark and intimidating they were until that very moment. They pierced him, seeming to read his every thought and intention. When she turned her eyes on Asher, Declan swore she must be picturing setting him on fire or something equally unpleasant. Tugging him free of his spot and dragging him away, Declan hoped to save his new comrade from possible incineration.

"What's up with that?" Foxx motioned to Declan's back.

Iris grew momentarily shy, but her mischievousness soon returned. "One of the things I will tell you about when I explain everything. Which is not right now because, per our agreement, you will be eating first."

Foxx rolled her eyes. "I see you haven't grown less annoying while I've been asleep."

"As if that were even possible."

Declan came back with food quicker than expected, but Asher didn't return with him. Handing her a sandwich, an apple, and another cup of water, he said, "Protein, sugar, and hydration. All the things a recovering body needs."

Foxx thanked him politely, and Iris wondered how their new dynamic might change now that she had woken. Declan certainly wouldn't fit in the room at the White Luna with both sister's needing beds. For a brief moment, she pictured Declan sharing her tiny bed while Foxx took the other, and her face flushed with warmth that her sister didn't miss.

"How are you feeling?" Declan asked, testing the waters.

"I'm sure I'll be much better when I have some food in my stomach. Thanks again, Declan." Her smile looked genuine, though her head tilted in thought.

Declan touched Iris' shoulder, requesting a moment of her time.

When they stepped out of Foxx's range, Iris stopped and faced him. "What's going on? Is Asher really upset?"

"He went back to the inn and told me he would be there when you were both ready to talk. I think he's hoping she'll miraculously be less angry once she has some food in her belly."

Iris nodded and glanced back at her sister to find her watching them.

Again Declan felt the ground shift unexpectedly beneath them. "Well, I guess I'll go talk to the Raptors and see if there are any new developments. Maybe you three should talk alone?"

"You're probably right." She noticed a shadow of disappointment in his features and realized part of him had hoped she would insist he come along. It passed quickly, and he smiled before bravely brushing a kiss across her lips. Her eyes closed, and her whole body flushed with tingly warmth. "Catch up with me later." Then with a brief squeeze of her hand, he walked away, leaving her head feeling floaty.

Foxxglove ate about half of her sandwich and a few bites of the apple. The remnants of her meal lay next to her when Iris returned. "I feel like I should be starving with how long I slept, but I can't seem to eat any more."

Iris sat down next to her. "That's all right. You shouldn't force it. We'll hold on to it, and you can eat when you're ready."

Foxx eyed her sister with suspicion and teased, "I saw that kiss." Iris' already bright cheeks blushed a beet red, and Foxx hugged her again. They sat together and talked for the next hour. Foxx nibbled at her apple, and Maia came over more than once to check her vitals. Iris caught her up on the experiences she'd had in Jericho, avoiding pretty much any topic involving Declan or Asher except what she deemed necessary.

She told her about the horrors she'd witnessed beyond the wall and the soldiers and civilians she'd gotten to know over the past few days. Gesturing toward the tree in the far corner, she shared what it had been like at the beginning when she'd spent most of her time with the children.

When Foxx's eyes glittered again with alertness, Iris asked, "Do you want to try to stand up?"

Foxx put the core of her apple next to her half eaten sandwich as Iris stood and extended both hands. "Every muscle in my body hurts," she groaned

"That's because you've been sleeping on stone for more than a week, and before that you decided to get yourself crushed by falling bricks." Iris waved a finger as if Foxx had been naughty. "So, what did we learn?"

"Don't trust random men you meet in the jungle because they might turn out to be princes with evil queen mothers."

Iris laughed. "Sounds like a fairytale to me."

Foxx smiled. "How about: don't stand still when bricks are falling around you."

"And I hope you've learned your lesson!"

Offering her arm to support some of Foxx's weight, Iris guided her sister around the courtyard. Elijah and Sten, the Guard assigned to Foxx, remained at a distance, each taking one of the two main entrances to the yard.

Foxx said, "Don't look now, but does it feel like those soldiers are watching us?"

Iris nodded. "They are. They're our protection, straight from the Konungr himself. Not everyone is happy with us, you know? With our faces being the ones in the sky."

Foxx glanced between the two soldiers. "I guess that makes sense."

"Someone tried to hurt you when you were sleeping. Konungr Vali said he was *taking care of it*, whatever that means."

Foxx drew back from her. "You met the Konungr? What's he like?"

"The kind of person who looks terrifying when using the phrase *I am taking care of it*." Iris shrugged. "He's the Mad King. Super intense. I'm sure you'll meet him at some point. Apparently he and Asher are friends."

When they reached the commanders and their seconds, Hector greeted them and extended a hand to Foxx. "Hello Iris. Nice to finally meet you, Foxxglove. I'm Hector Kayvan."

"You as well, Hector."

Iris had explained all about the Raptors' original purpose in Jericho, as well as their recently altered plans. Foxx thought shaking hands with the commander of the army they'd spent months running from should feel strange, but his pleasant smile and kind eyes put her at ease.

"How are you feeling?" Hector locked his hands behind his back.

Foxx chuckled charmingly. "Very sore."

"Understandable."

Jax said, "Don't push yourself too much. It's fine to rest until you're well."

"This is Jax." Iris gestured to him, and he lifted his chin in greeting. Then she introduced Abram and Eero.

Abram looked genuinely pleased by her awakening. "We've heard much about you, Foxxglove. I look forward to working together." Eero's only greeting was the dip of his head.

Hector's eyes caught those of the soldiers from Vali's Royal Guard watching them from a distance. One dropped his chin in recognition. "I see you're well looked after, but Jax is right, make sure you rest. We have a lot of work ahead of us, and we need you healed. I imagine Alexander must be thrilled to finally see your eyes open. Very little has dragged him from your side."

Foxx blushed, and Iris replied, "Thanks Hector. Have you seen Raven recently?"

Jax threw a thumb over his shoulder. "I sent her and Declan up the road for coffee. They shouldn't be long. Did you need something?"

"Just to say hello."

Hector and Jax shared a look of amusement. Raven had complained several times about the overly enthusiastic Belamour sister, though both men suspected she secretly liked the attention. And for whatever reason, Iris seemed to enjoy Raven's snarkiness.

"I'll let her know," Hector promised.

Iris tugged on her sister's arm. "We'll catch up with you all later."

"Nice to meet you." Foxx turned away from the soldiers, and they continued their stroll, but it wasn't long until she needed to lay down. She leaned on her sister for support as they made their way to the inn. When they arrived at the door, Iris had a moment of panic. Foxx felt her shift in temperature and perked up. "What's wrong?"

Iris turned to face her, reaching for both of her hands. "I need to tell you two things. Please don't be mad." She paused, and Foxx realized she was waiting for confirmation that she wouldn't be.

"Go on," she said, willing her face into one of understanding.

"Okay, Number one: Declan has been staying in our room." In response to her sister's horrified expression, Iris clarified, "In your bed! We've been spending time together, and it made sense. I had a free bed, and with so many sleeping in the streets, it didn't seem right to leave it empty."

Foxx worried what the second thing might be if a kidnapping fugitive sleeping in her baby sister's room was the information she chose to share first. "All right, what else?"

Iris attempted a semblance of calm, but her words spilled out in a nervous jumble. "Asher is here. But wait!" Holding her finger in the air, she stopped Foxx before she could scold her. "He's been here the whole time. His room was down the hall from ours. Isn't that crazy? Anyway, he's waiting to tell us the truth about everything. I have learned bits and pieces of things since you've been asleep, and I'm dying to know the rest of the details. I know you're tired, and you should definitely rest first, but maybe later this evening or first thing in the morning we can go talk to him? Please, can you forgive him for a little while so he can tell us everything he wants to tell us, and then you can decide if you still want to hate him or not?" She sucked in a deep breath, having not taken a single one since she began rambling.

Foxxglove sighed. "Fine. We'll hear what he has to say." Iris tried to contain her joy while Foxx looked up at the inn as though she might find his face pressed against one of the windows. "He's up there now?"

"Yes, he's waiting for us in his room. But there's no rush! We can spend some time in our room first and go see him when you're ready." Iris touched her sister's cheek, drawing her attention. "I wouldn't be pushing it, but there are people waiting on us. The war can't start until we have what we need from Celestelvyra, and he has pretty much refused to go without you. I guess you could tell him to go on and leave you behind, but don't you want to see our journey through? Everything else can be figured out later. What do you think?"

When they crossed the threshold to their room, Foxx surveyed both beds. Iris' was messy and unmade. Foxx's was tidy. She eyed her sister, who shrugged innocently, then moved to sit on Iris' bed. "I'm taking yours."

Iris accepted that, and without another word, Foxx laid down, closed her eyes, and fell fast asleep. Iris laid down on the bed Declan had slept in. It smelled like him, and she inhaled his scent with warm delight before rolling onto her back and gazing up at the ceiling. Soon, she grew restless and sat up again. Digging out her journal of memories and monsters, she remembered how grateful she felt toward Asher for trudging through not only the muggy and humid jungle but also the steep and snowy mountain pass, carrying the added weight of their bags on his shoulders.

Scooting back against the wall, she rested the book on her knees, opened it to the entry on niedas, and added the new information she'd learned in the caves. *Cave niedas are afraid of light, are much smaller than niedas from other territories—though still horrifying—and have darker hair.*

Flipping to a blank page, she began to draw the tentacled creature from Lacuna Kaput. Writing in the margins, she noted all the things she'd noticed about the creature, as well as how they'd killed it.

Sifting through her memories of that day, her thoughts lingered on the way Orion had looked at her as he tossed his shirt in her face and leapt into the lagoon, followed immediately by his horrified expression when he'd found her held captive under the water.

Her worry for him had become a constant weight she seemed unable to dispel. It had been over a week since the attack, and he still hadn't appeared. The Raptors had been with those gathering bodies and building fire pits, and to her knowledge, they all knew Orion. Surely they would have told Declan if they'd found him, and since they hadn't, it meant he was either still buried somewhere beneath uncleared rubble or he'd fled the city.

Iris wondered if they would ever see him again. He'd been nothing but trouble from the beginning—almost nothing but trouble—and there was no telling how he would handle working alongside the Jerichonian Guard and the former Legion soldiers. She thought back over the first conversation she'd been present for with the Konungr. He'd called Orion *that horrid fellow,* and she wondered if maybe it wasn't better for everyone if Orion remained out of the picture.

Shaking her head, she scattered unpleasant thoughts. Despite everything, she didn't wish him any ill will. With that in mind, she decided she would think him alive until proven otherwise. She imagined him returned to Peregrine Manor, flirting shamelessly with that busty receptionist, drunkenly walking about the well in the falling snow, and generally having a grand old time.

Wherever he'd ended up, she hoped more than anything he was happy and well.

CHAPTER 36

DRIP, DRIP, DRIP

W ater dripped continuously, one drop at a time, in an unending and maddening rhythm. It fell from a cracked pipe near the ceiling all the way down to a patch on the stone floor less than a foot away from where Orion's wrists were fastened. He didn't know how many days he'd been there, but the shriveling pit that was once his stomach and the dryness of his throat that rivaled the sandy air of the Grim Wilds suggested he wouldn't last much longer.

His arms were chained behind his back and his knees had grown numb against the cold floor. He'd lost all feeling in his legs days ago. He thought. Or maybe it hadn't been that long. Or perhaps it had been longer. Time blended together with fluid inaccuracy, and he was finding it difficult to keep track.

Not a sliver of light entered his cell, so he couldn't count the days by the sun. The only thing he knew for sure was that she'd come to him six times already. Or was it seven?

Maybe it had been ten times.

If she came once a day, that could be ten days. Perhaps she came more than once a day. Perhaps she'd only come once total and the experience had been so horrible, his subconscious had broken it up into smaller bits to make it easier to manage.

His head hung forward, weighing heavy on the muscles between his shoulder blades. It had grown too arduous to hold it upright, so he kept it down, allowing his hair to sway in blood-drenched clumps that tickled his nose. He didn't have the strength to tilt his head and flick away the menacing hair, so the unscratchable itch endured, chipping away at his sanity alongside the loathsome dripping.

Blood spilled down his cheeks, his chin, his neck, and onto his chest. Was it fresh? How long had it been since she'd been there with him? It must be fresh for how much currently poured from him, another constant tickle driving him mad.

A sudden smack across his face startled him from his unhinged reflections, and it might as well have been a brick smashing his jaw.

He wasn't alone. How had he not realized? Blood filled his mouth, but he couldn't spit it out, his tongue too dry for salivation. It spilled from his lips and joined the fountain running down his chin.

"Tell me something I can use Orion, and this will all be over."

That voice.

He recognized that voice, didn't he?

The dripping pipe distracted him. It was so loud. How could it be so loud?

Something crawled through his hair. Fingers, he realized. Then he screamed, his body arching back of its own volition as she searched his mind for answers. He'd fought against her in the beginning, but he'd since given up, allowing the walls around his memories to collapse so she could soak them all in.

He nearly fell over when she released him, but something held him upright.

A crack across his cheek whipped his head to the side.

Had she been there all along and he'd simply forgotten? When had she grown metal fists? A laugh escaped him, but he didn't know what was funny.

"You fool! Why are you protecting them?"

The voice, the voice, the voice. What was that wretched voice?

"Orion!"

His eyes shot open, feeling like skin ripping apart as the crust holding his lids together crumbled. He squinted, though it was so dark, he questioned whether or not he'd opened his eyes at all. As his vision sharpened, he saw a woman standing before him, her beauty as cruel and shocking and black as the trenches of her heart. "Your Majesty?" he choked through the blood filling his mouth.

The woman turned her head to look over her shoulder and

spoke words he couldn't comprehend. Too far away, and the dripping was so loud it drowned them out.

Suddenly, it was him who was drowning. Blood covered his head. He hadn't known a person could bleed so much and survive. It suffocated him, robbing him of breath until he thought his heart might explode.

Just as abruptly, the asphyxiation stopped, and it occurred to him that it wasn't blood at all, but water. It drenched his hair and rinsed the blood from his face, burning as it carved through the gashes cluttering his cheeks, shoulders, arms, and chest. Everywhere her knife had cut him. He coughed, and more blood marred the skin she'd made clean.

Vaguely, he remembered screaming, though he didn't seem to be doing so now. Maybe he was out of screams. Could one use up all their screams?

Something slid gently down the side of his head. He closed his eyes and leaned into the caress as his mind filled with images of Iris. He whispered her name as the hand so tenderly touching his cheek moved to his jaw and squeezed.

The Queen yanked his face to hers, digging her fingernails into either side of his jaw and creating the indents of five crescent moons. Despite her rough grip, her voice was soothing. "Yes, Orion. That is exactly who I am asking about. Your lovely Iris. Tell me what she's up to."

What was she saying? He couldn't hear her over the dripping. It was so loud. More thoughts of Iris sent warmth throughout his frigid body. She was so pretty and so sweet. Her big auburn eyes stared back at him, pleading with him to let her in.

He should have. He would have. Would he ever again have the chance? Would she visit him in his ghastly cell?

Then his thoughts drifted to Declan and Foxx. His friends.

No. He tried to shake his head before realizing it was still in a vice.

"Yes. That's right. Tell me about them. Then you will be free, Orion. This misery will end. Just tell me what you know."

His eyes closed again. Was it time to sleep yet? No way of knowing if the sun had gone down. With no sun he supposed he could choose on his own when he slept. The sun would no longer control when he drifted into dreamland. It was decided.

He felt relief in his jaw but couldn't remember why it had been hurting to begin with. Then a blow hit his face so hard he fell over. His knees were no longer under him and his arms felt yanked from their sockets.

Declan. Where was Declan? Why wasn't he helping him? Surely he hadn't succeeded in pushing him too far, pushing him away, just when he'd begun figuring things out. He just needed a little more time. He would get it right.

Declan wouldn't have left him. They'd been through too much.

A thought struck him, and it all began making sense. Maybe he found Johnathan. Of course. He was with Johnathan. That was the only explanation for why he wouldn't be there with him. Orion smiled, feeling an odd sense of peace.

"Who is Johnathan?"

That pesky voice again. What did it mean?

"Orion? Who is Johnathan?"

Why wasn't it speaking his language? Maybe it was, and he'd forgotten the words.

Drip, drip, drip.

Time for sleep now. Time for sleep.

CHAPTER 37

NOT ENEMIES

Declan stood by the water well washing his hands and face from the bucket he'd drawn. The sun had barely reached its peak, and already he felt exhausted. Another of his patients had passed into the After, her burns too great to overcome. Despite their efforts, the body count continued to rise.

On top of that, unanswered questions plagued his thoughts: Why did the Queen keep her distance? What was happening between him and Iris? Did he even belong in Jericho, or was he foolishly riding the coattails of some woman he barely knew?

He wondered if he should go find Orion. They'd stuck together all these years. Part of him didn't feel right hanging out with women and soldiers in Jericho when his friend was out there somewhere, quite possibly lost and alone.

A tap on the shoulder startled him, and he turned around. "Raven, hey. What's up?" His eyes scanned the area, scouting for something amiss.

She observed him for a moment too long as if trying to figure something out. He said her name again, and she snapped out of her examination with a simple, "Hello, Silas."

He smiled and dried his face with a rag he'd pulled from the loop on his belt. "Can I help you with something?"

"No, I..." She shook her head, feeling like an idiot for approaching him.

He arched a brow. It had only been an hour since Jax sent them on a coffee run, and they'd talked a little as they walked, but not about anything important. The look in her eyes now had him wondering what had changed. "What's going on? Are you all right?"

With a deep breath, she put her hands on her hips. "Yes, I'm fine."

"Are you sure? You look weird."

Gruffly, she retorted, "Thanks, Silas. I appreciate that."

Declan laughed. "I mean, your face—" At her scowl he amended, "I mean it's strange for you to be looking for me when we were just together. So I assumed something must have happened or that you needed something. They can't be out of coffee already."

"I talked to Hector this morning."

Declan nodded hesitantly. "Yes. I noticed you two looking chummy."

"We aren't chummy!"

He grinned and pushed his bangs out of his eyes. "Well, what do you want me to say? It seems like he's doing really good things here. Maybe he's turned over a new leaf. So, good for you."

She huffed and swore. When they'd been together an hour ago, she'd opened her mouth several times with the intention of discussing it, but no words had come. Now that she'd finally mustered the courage, he was staring at her like she might be a crazy person. "You're missing my point."

He leaned against the edge of the well and crossed his arms. "You aren't exactly being forthcoming with it."

Reactions from days past evidently lingering, the mixture of his arrogant smile and the hints of moss glistening in his eyes had her heart skipping a beat. She swore again. "You're infuriating, do you know that?"

"Me?" His head fell back with amusement.

"Yes! I'm trying to tell you I'm sorry, and you're making it so damn difficult!" She stomped her foot unwittingly.

He drew back his head and tipped it to the side. "What could you possibly have to be sorry for? I was kidding when I said you picked shoddy coffee. The kind you picked was fine. It certainly wasn't bad enough to deserve these dramatics." Switching the arms crossed over his chest, he flipped his hair again so he could see her clearly. He realized he felt as comfortable around her as he always had, and he enjoyed the way her irritation made her forehead wrinkle.

With another sigh, she looked at the ground. "I'm sorry for hating you." It felt good to admit it out loud, even if it no longer felt true. She'd wasted so many hours and so much energy thinking about him and how he'd left her without a farewell, without any explanation, without a trace.

"I literally don't understand what's happening."

"That's because you won't shut up and let me get it out," she snapped. He ran his thumb and index finger across his lips as if to zip them shut. "I talked to Hector, and he told me things. About your shared past. And about your father."

A bitter shadow spread across his face. Discussing those details was not a conversation he intended to have with anyone, let alone with Raven.

"Don't get upset. He was explaining, well confessing really, but he wanted me to understand the issues between the two of you, as well as his motivation for staying in Jericho and standing against the Queen. He thought it wouldn't be fair for me to make the decision to follow him if I didn't have the whole story."

"How honorable of him."

"So now I know the whole story, and I know he's responsible for what happened to your father, and I know you were innocent when you were named a traitor. I understand why you hate him."

Declan thought back on Hector's strange expression when Jax had told them to grab coffee. He'd thought Hector was being petty or jealous, but perhaps he was simply afraid of what they might discuss along the way or what kind of Hector-hating party they might have when forced to share space. Sighing, he felt some of his coldness dissipate, supposing he no longer had the energy to cling to old burdens. "I don't hate him. Not really, anyway."

She raised a thin brow. "Well, whatever. The truth is, I had this awful idea of you built up in my head, Silas. I felt like you abandoned me and Johnathan and betrayed your duties. You left without a word. How was I supposed to know? I only knew what I heard and…"

"You were supposed to know me." Declan held her gaze. A hint of spite returned to hide the pain he'd felt when his best friend hadn't known him better than the rumors she'd heard.

Raven felt heavy with guilt for thinking the worst of him. "You're right. That's why I am trying to apologize."

He hooked his rag back onto his belt and looked at her for a long moment. Knowing the feeling of guilt all too well, he shrugged. "Okay then. I forgive you. And for what it's worth, I am sorry I never contacted you to explain. I worried if someone found out we were communicating you might be implicated somehow. Honestly, at first it was too hard to bear. Giving up my entire life. My home, my brother, my unit… you." Her eyes flashed up to his, and she felt the sincerity of his words deep in her stomach. "Everything turned upside-down. It was easier to focus on the mission and hope if I completed it, I would be able to come home and none of it would matter anyway."

"I understand. And thank you for your apology."

He nodded, his eyes surveying the surrounding area, avoiding hers. Time stretched on within an unfamiliar bubble of awkward silence. Then Declan cleared his throat. "Don't think I didn't think about you, Raven. Don't think I didn't have countless conversations with myself and with Orion about whether or not I should find a way to get a message to you or see you somehow. It never seemed like a safe choice. For either of us."

Her cheeks flushed as he prodded the remnants of old wounds and brought to light the forever flutters of first love. "I believe you." Her hands fidgeted with the hilts of the blades strapped around her waist. "I've missed you, Silas."

"I've missed you, too, Raven." He chuckled. "You know, no one calls me Silas anymore."

"Well, I'm not going to stop. Declan isn't even your real name. And it's seriously lame by comparison." A teasing smile played at her lips, and his lifted to play along. Then she looked at the ground. "I know a lot of time has passed and things are different, but… somewhere within this mess of whatever is happening right now… do you think we could find a way to be friends again? Or at least… not enemies?"

Declan pulled her into him, tucking her head beneath his chin. After a moment of surprise, she wrapped her arms around his back and hugged him, turning her head so her cheek rested on his chest. "Not enemies sounds like a good place to start," he answered.

"Good." Stepping away, she wiped a tear before it fell and rolled her shoulders, at last disentangling the thorny vines holding her prisoner in her fury for six long years.

"Good," he concurred.

She moved to sit next to him on the edge of the well, her shoulder resting against his. Together they looked out around the courtyard. "It's pretty incredible, isn't it?"

"What is?"

"This." She lifted a hand to the happenings around them. "All of these people working together, businesses supplying food, citizens sleeping on the ground. Even the Mad King's palace opened its doors. It's kind of beautiful to see how tragedy unites everyone like this. Making them their best selves or something."

"It is pretty incredible. Iris said the same thing."

Raven sat back further so her feet dangled away from the ground. Then she lowered her voice as if others might overhear. "How insane is it that the Prince is here?"

"He isn't the Prince." Declan hadn't intended to mock Asher's insistence on claiming his false identity, though it came out that way.

She looked at him skeptically and crossed her arms. "So he says."

Declan ran his fingers through his hair. "Yeah. It's certainly interesting how things are playing out." Hector entered the courtyard and noticed them immediately. His eyes darted away, as if uncomfortable. "So if he told you everything, are you guys…?"

"What?" she asked, not taking her eyes off of Hector as he deliberately avoided looking at them.

"I mean are you angry at him? He looked terrified when he saw you just now. I don't think I've ever seen Hector terrified of anything. Not even Queen Sirena herself." They continued to observe him, watching as he talked to Commander Havlar and very clearly did his best not to glance their way.

"Of course I'm angry." She exhaled from deep in her lungs. "I feel like there's this entire chapter of my life that went all wrong, and it's completely his fault. I feel like, how can I feel any kind of goodness toward him when he stole your life from you? He stole *our* life and what it might have been. Not to mention Johnathan. And your father and mother. It's all so horrible, Silas."

"Do you love him?" Declan was surprised to feel a tingle in his own stomach at the words. It was hard to imagine Raven loving anyone but him. She'd been his first love, and he hers, and because of this, a little piece of them would always belong to each other.

His question startled her, nearly as much as it had him. Did she love Hector? "I'm… not sure. That Iris is quite a character though."

"Shut up." He nudged her shoulder with an embarrassed smile. "That situation is… also complicated."

"Oh, please. Poor Silas, fallen for the girl everyone wants to get their hands on."

He chuckled. "That's not what I mean. You know we were looking for them? Well, when we found them, they didn't exactly come willingly."

Raven's eyes widened. "What does that mean?"

"I should say, we didn't really give them a chance to come willingly." Declan tapped the top of his thighs with his fingertips.

"So you what? Abducted them?"

"At knifepoint, yeah." His shame felt no less now than it had every moment he'd thought about it since it first happened.

Raven's jaw went slack. "You're joking."

He shook his head. "I wish I was. The first week I spent with Iris Belamour, her wrists were bound, and I was trying my best to corral her into not killing Orion." She covered her mouth to hide a baffled chuckle. "And trust me, she doesn't look all that strong, but it was not an easy task. The whole thing was such a mess. She clocked me pretty good in the jaw though." His fingers rose to his cheekbone.

Raven clapped her hands once and barked a laugh. "I like her more already."

"Figured you might."

Hector crossed the yard to meet Jax, and both men looked in their direction. When Hector realized they were still watching him, he quickly averted his gaze. Jax lifted a hand in greeting, and Raven waved back.

"Where is Orion anyway? I haven't seen him around."

Declan's face hardened. "I don't know, but I'm starting to get worried. He should have shown up by now."

"I'm sure he's fine. He's a brute. He can take care of himself. So you and Orion kidnapped them and she still fell for you? What a charmer you must have been."

"It doesn't make sense to me at all actually. I didn't see it coming until it hit me like a brick. I realized I didn't want to be without her and that I would do anything to protect her. By some miracle, she seems to feel the same." Declan's fingers lifted to twist his bangs. "Actually, for a time I thought something was going on between her and Orion."

"So she fell for both of her captors? Maybe she's actually psychotic."

Declan laughed outright, and she joined him. "I don't think so. I think she has a lot of love in her heart and was forced to spend much of her life alone, with no one but her sister as a companion. It's all new to her. All these connections and feelings."

Raven stuck her finger down her throat in mock gag at his sappy words. "Then how do you know it's real? Do you think things will change if Orion comes back?"

Declan contemplated her question, not for the first time. "I don't think so. I think she was charmed by him at first."

"Because Orion is so unbelievably charming."

"He has his own sort of charm, but ultimately, the man he's become in his fight for revenge pushed her away. He was cruel to her. Maybe things would have been different if he hadn't been, but…" He shrugged.

Raven nodded, understanding. They'd all grown into people they never expected to be. Herself included. She certainly never thought a little thief from the slums of Tunturia would join the King's Legion. Then on top of that, to join with the rebels on some righteous quest to take down the sovereigns of Arkaemor? The twists and turns of life are never certain, and she supposed anyone could end up anywhere.

"Well, I like her," she said. "But don't tell her I said that."

C

When Foxxglove awoke, she found her sister lounging on the bed and drawing in her journal. "You got it back."

Iris looked over the top of her book, overjoyed to see Foxx awake again. Closing the journal around her pencil, she set it on the bed. "Yes, I did. Asher brought our bags along with him from Petrichor. Yours is here, too."

His name sent a wave of anger through Foxx, causing her to groan and cover her face with her pillow.

"How did you sleep?"

Removing the pillow, Foxx furrowed her brow. "I think I had a weird dream." She tried to draw the memory to the forefront of her mind, but it slipped away as consciousness returned. "A man—actually—remember when we were walking up the mountain pass and I got lightheaded? A picture of a man I didn't recognize flashed into my thoughts. I think I might have dreamed of him. He was in my face, like leaning over me. It was different than last time. I think he was encouraging me to wake up."

"Here?" Iris asked, and Foxx shook her head.

"No. Outside the first time, I think, but I dreamed it again just now. I don't know. It's fading, but it felt strange. I don't think I've ever received a vision while sleeping. I suppose it's possible, though. I wish I knew who he was." Foxx closed her eyes, and the man's words returned to her all at once: *Summoning sól can be an exhausting business when your body isn't used to it, but the time has come to open your eyes. Wake up and face the day. The world awaits your salvation, foxy woman. As do I.*

"Maybe it wasn't a dream at all." Iris' voice had Foxx's eyes flipping open.

She considered sharing what she'd remembered, but something held her back. "So some mysterious man watched over me while I slept?"

Iris slid to the edge of the bed to hand her sister a bag of water. "Asher watched over you while you slept."

"It wasn't him." Foxx sat up with effort and drank a generous amount. "And it wasn't either of the Guards I saw today when you told me they'd been assigned to us." Looking at the waterskin on her lap, she recognized it as one of their old ones. Then she realized what Iris had said about their bags. Had Asher really dragged them all the way from Petrichor? Through the hot jungle and up the steep and arduous mountain pass? "I guess you want to go talk to him, don't you?"

"Yes!" Iris squealed. Reeling herself in, she placed her hands in her lap. "Whenever you're ready."

Foxx rifled through her pack, pulling out clothing, her books, and her long dagger. Drawn to movement, she looked up to see Iris modeling Mr. Magpie's gifted hat and wearing a cheesy, open-mouthed grin. Foxx's shoulders shook with amusement. "Can I change my clothes first? I've been sleeping in these for days. I want to bathe as well, but I'll wait until after so as to not prolong your anticipation."

"Definitely! And thank you." She put the hat on the bed and stood up. "How about I go wait with him, let him know you are on your way and give you a few moments alone to wake up and collect your thoughts."

"Yes, please."

Iris opened the door and pointed down the hall. "He's in that room there. Number four. Come whenever you're ready." She knocked twice on Asher's door, and it swung open immediately, as if he'd been waiting anxiously for them to arrive. When he noticed Foxx's absence, his face drooped with disappointment. "Yes, that's my favorite way to be greeted when I visit someone. She's getting changed and will be over when she's done."

Asher stepped out of the way to let her pass. His belongings were scattered about the right side of the room, indicating which bed he'd claimed as his own. Iris sat down on the left bed to watch him pace by the door, proving her previous suspicion.

She wondered if Declan might take the second bed now that he couldn't stay in her room. Then they could still be close together. Though she supposed they wouldn't be staying in Jericho much longer anyway, and who knew what kind of living arrangements they would find themselves in when they returned from Celestelvyra.

After a few silent minutes, Foxx knocked on the door. Rather than rushing to open it as he had when Iris arrived, Asher froze, his face turning an unnatural shade of green. Iris laughed at him, and he turned to scowl at her.

"Open the door!" she whispered.

"Right." He ran his palms down the front of his shirt and his fingers through his hair. Then he took a deep breath and reached for the handle.

Foxx's hand hung in the air moments away from knocking. Their eyes met, and her face brightened, her lips automatically curving into a smile, only to sour an instant later as she remembered her vexation.

Asher looked her over, taking in her tired eyes, the pink of her hair, still marred with her own blood, and the cracks in her lips, dry from dehydration.

"Are you going to let me in?" she asked, failing to contain her aggravation.

Awakened from staring at her, he shifted out of the way so she could walk by. Foxx crossed the room and sat next to Iris, though rather than tucking her feet underneath her as Iris had, Foxx kept hers planted on the floor.

Asher sat across from them on the opposite bed.

The silence dragged as he tried to figure out exactly where to begin. Though he'd rehearsed his words for the past two hours, the sight of Foxx's joy melting into seething fury was jarring. The spark of happiness could be a good sign, suggesting that deep down her feelings for him hadn't changed. However, he knew how stubborn and strong willed she could be. He'd charmed his way through her walls before, but with all of her suspicions confirmed, he sensed it might be harder a second time. If she decided to continue hating him, that's exactly what she would do.

Foxx's voice interrupted his introspection. "Are you going to talk or are you just going to stare at your hands?"

Sitting forward to rest his elbows on his knees, Asher pushed hair from his eyes. "Sorry. I'm working up to it." He cleared his throat. "Okay, I figure I'll tell you the basics and if you have questions about anything, I can go deeper into the details." He waited for them to confirm this as an acceptable course of action, but when they gave no indication of their thoughts, he continued. "As you now know, though I introduced myself to you as Asher, I am—was —the Crown Prince, Alexander Aldrich."

Though Foxx had heard Declan's proclamation and the Queen's confirmation of Asher's true identity, the admittance on his lips sent a new surge of hot indignation through her veins. "Was?"

"If you're going to snap at him after every sentence, this conversation is going to take a very long time." Iris reached for her sister's hand.

Foxx scoffed, but encouraged, "Continue."

Asher nodded. "I was the Crown Prince until I nicked the first two keys and ran away. Let me start further back though. I've tried to piece together what you know already and came to the conclusion that the answer is: not a whole lot. I thought your mother and father would have been more forthcoming with you about things, and I'm not sure why they kept you so in the dark—especially your mother—but I'll do my best to cover everything I can think of. And so, I guess it makes sense for me to start at the very beginning."

CHAPTER 38

BELAMOUR

After another breath to calm the hasty beating in his chest, Asher began. "When I was a child growing up in Castle Solís, your mother was Sirena's lady's maid." Both girls gasped, but he held up a finger to prevent them from speaking. "More than a lady's maid, really. In fact, I would say they were friends and even cared for each other like sisters. I believe Sirena trusted Amaryllis in a way she trusted no one else, even the King, and shared many secrets with her.

"Because of her visions, Amaryllis was well versed in the history of Arkaemor and the inner workings of the world. That made her a powerful ally to have. I don't know whether their friendship began as a way for Sirena to keep her fingers wrapped around an important piece on the chessboard or whether she genuinely enjoyed your mother's company, but either way, their bond was apparent to all who knew them.

"When Amaryllis met your father—they met at the castle, by the way—they fell in love, and your mother decided she no longer wanted to work at Castle Solís. She wanted to have her own home with a husband and a family. An admirable ambition, and fairly typical of women who fall in love, but Sirena was not pleased.

"The King was thrilled to hear of their desired union. My father has always been a bit of a romantic. He had the commander of his Legion, the one before Hector, promote Sawyer and appoint him as a member of the Reko Raptors. This allowed him to be gifted the knowledge of barrier jumping so he could still work for the castle while living in Alunda and raising a family." Asher looked at Foxx. "Barrier jumping is when you step through one barrier and exit somewhere totally different." He watched her evaluate that information, noticing the moment she realized this was the detail she'd been missing and that it answered the question of why he didn't have the keys for the three center territories—as well as several other perplexing inconsistencies, he imagined.

Asher moved forward before she could comment. "This infuriated the Queen, but despite her persistence, the union of Amaryllis Wild and Sawyer Belamour commenced, and they departed the castle. Not long after, she had you, Foxx, and then two years later, had Iris.

"For a long while, the Queen left you all to live in peace, though her spies watched you from a distance. Sawyer did well as a Raptor and was eventually promoted to lieutenant.

"I don't know all of the details behind what happened to your father. I've been able to conclude from my exploration that he was on assignment in Jericho with his team delivering a message to the Konungr, and that when the mission was complete, they left, and Sawyer stayed behind. When he returned to Inaravale, he was different. He grew secretive and distant, even from the members of his team. I can only assume he found out the truth about Pyhä-ki."

Iris interrupted, "If you and Vali are as close as you seem, why didn't you ask him about this?"

"I did, but Vali can be… difficult. He's forthcoming about some things, but with others he says it isn't time for me to know yet, or he claims not to have the answers, but I get the sense he does. I'm not sure how he decides what to share and what not to, but either way, he was a dead end in regards to this mystery.

"He did reveal today that he was aware of Pyhä-ki, so it is possible he told your father about it. Perhaps even marked the map you say led you to the Monastery in the Wilds." He shrugged. "Anyway, Sawyer spent years in and around the castle grounds in close quarters with the King and Queen. I'm certain he was not blind to the type of ruler Sirena is. There have been many attempts on the Queen's life over the years kept out of public knowledge. He wasn't the first person to turn on her, and as you well know, he wasn't the last."

"Why would our mother have been so close with her if she truly is as awful as everyone thinks?" Iris asked.

Asher ran a hand over the top of his head. "I hate to say it, but the truth is, Sirena has her own kind of loveliness. A charisma that draws you in. When she wants to, at least.

"The object Sawyer stole from her is known as the Artifact, and it's the only thing that will transport Pyhä-ki from the Sacred Realm. Your father knew the location of all the royal vaults, including the one in northern Reginaterra where the Artifact was held. The moment he left the vaults, the Queen was alerted of his crime." He paused, his eyes flickering between them as he fumbled through the next part. "If what I've deduced is correct, she went straight to your house to confront your mother, and…"

Foxx comprehended immediately what he was leery of exposing, as if a small, stubborn part of her had known it all along. Her hand flew to her mouth, her lips breathing the word *no* with barely a sound.

"She poisoned her, then she left the house without a trace so everyone would suspect Amaryllis had killed herself. It is my understanding that, at this point in her life, suicide was not outside the realm of possibilities, so no one questioned it. And you know what happened next. Your father returned home and found her, and left you for Celestelvyra soon after. I doubt he realized he would be gone so long. I imagine he jumped the closest barrier—following the map you found of the Grim Wilds—with the intention of returning home a few days later with Pyhä-ki in hand."

Asher paused again, giving them time to digest before he continued. His stomach twisted with knots, his body sweating despite the cold room. "Do you want me to stop? I'm sorry to be drudging all this up, but it is integral to the story."

Foxx sniffed and rested her shoulder against her sister's. "It's fine, go on."

He lifted his eyes to the ceiling with a sigh. "After Amaryllis' death, my mother cried for days. I tried to comfort her, but she was so angry, shutting us all out. My sister got the worst of it, as was always the case."

"She killed her and then mourned her?" Foxx's brow pinched with tamed rage.

He nodded. "And I believe her grief was honest, despite her role in it. Perhaps not in spite of but because of. Though who can accurately decipher the heart of Sirena Aldrich?"

Iris let her head fall against Foxx's and took her hand.

"So, this is where I come into the story. When I learned what happened with your parents, something changed in me. Up to that point I'd been… let's use the word *unruly*. A spoiled prince. I didn't care about the world or the Five Kingdoms or any of it. My mother was manipulative and abusive. And she's immortal, right? So it's not like I had any hope of actually being crowned king. I avoided life, drank too much, stayed out too late, broke the castle rules and played tricks on the Watchmen. Anything to be disruptive. The only thing I truly cared about was my sister, Avaline. Her illness continued to worsen, if that's what you would even call it. I believe her reality is the direct result of Sirena's abuse. Her mind crumbled, and she locked herself away in the depths of her soul.

"When I heard what happened to the Belamour's and how the Raptors betrayed us, it didn't sit right with me. The suicide, specifically, made no sense. In all my memories of Amaryllis, she was so loving and full of life. She always paid special attention to me, singing me songs and sneaking me treats when the nannies weren't looking. My own mother was cold, unfeeling, and heartless. Amaryllis Wild, as I knew her, was one of the kindest people I'd ever known. Though years had passed, it didn't feel possible for her to have taken her own life, especially knowing she had two daughters to care for. And I didn't understand why her husband, a man trusted by the Thrones enough to be made lieutenant of the Reko Raptors, would betray us on the exact same day she died. The coincidence was unnerving.

"I began investigating the castle and learned all I could from there, which wasn't much. Then I went to your house, hoping to uncover some scrap of a clue that might help me understand. I hoped to find you there, too, but the place was torn apart, rubbish strewn about. It looked like you hadn't been there for a while. What I did find was this." Asher pulled his leather-bound book from his bag and held it out to them. Foxx let it sit on her palm as though unsure what to do with it. "Open it," he encouraged.

Exchanging another glance with Iris, she placed it in her lap and flipped open the front cover. Inside, they found a message written in their mother's hand.

Foxx looked at Asher, her expression a messy concoction of sorrow and uncertainty, joy and doubt. Iris took the book from her and flipped through the other pages. It was more like a journal than she'd expected, filled with his memories and discoveries and all the information he'd compiled about the history of Arkaemor, the Monastery of the Morrow, and the Belamours.

Asher said Foxx's name, yearning to find the perfect words to ease her pain. She shook her head and looked at her hands, not liking his hyper focus on her grief. Drawing his eyes away, he scratched his ear and ran a hand down his face. "She said I was too young, so I'm not sure when she wrote the letter or why I never received the journal from her. Perhaps she knew I would come looking for it when the time was right and, by then, I would be ready to hear it. She was always so intuitive. I realize it more and more the deeper I get into this journey.

"After leaving your house, I began visiting the remaining Monasteries and the places that held relics of those that were lost. I had grown up hearing about the ancient Morrow and all of their fantastical ideas. In the castle, it was treated as an old fable, mocked as a children's story to spark the imagination. It wasn't until I started venturing into the world that I realized there are many people who view all those stories as history rather than fiction.

"I read every book and manuscript I could get my hands on and spent years researching, interviewing, and hunting anything related to the Monastery. I didn't really know what I was looking for or why I couldn't shake it from my head. I learned about the doorways and the keys and about Pyhä-ki. I gathered all this knowledge yet had no idea what I was supposed to do with it. So I tried to let it go; to forget; to just be the Prince, even if I was a horrid example of one. I walked away from the search many times, vowing to leave it alone, but it always sucked me back in.

"One night, about six moons ago, while studying the old song, I opened my book to Amaryllis' letter and realized it was entirely possible the prophecy was written about me. Amaryllis said if I listened to the words it would all be revealed. My destiny: *A childson is needed to do the unbending, to unwind the history and bring forth all mending. To shred all to ruins, he'll forfeit his crown, To rebuild the world, it must first be torn down.*

"Everything clicked into place, and I knew what I had to do. After returning to the castle, I packed a bag and crept down to the vaults to nick the amber crown and the snowflake. On my way out, I overheard a conversation between Commander Kayvan and my parents regarding the Belamour sisters. I listened in as they discussed beginning the search to hunt you down. One of the Queen's spies informed her you'd begun searching for your father and Celestelvyra. You can imagine the Queen has been very upset with the Legion for not being able to find your father all these years, but she never gave up the hunt.

"I suspect your father is stuck in the In-Between—the place holding the gate to the Sacred Realm. Once there, the Queen's spell would have kept him from leaving without the keys. He also wouldn't have been able to enter Celestelvyra. I don't know why he would have gone without them unless your mother never shared that detail with him. Maybe she would have if he'd gotten to her in time.

"I left the castle and made my way to Savanni to find the next key. While there, a woman found me and said she had a message for me." Asher nodded when Iris perked up. "You met her, too—

Maeve. She knew I was looking for the keys and told me it was imperative that I find you and that we make the journey to Celestelvyra together. She said I needed to protect you, to do everything in my power to ensure Sirena and her Legion never got their hands on you. Maeve knew where you were heading and assured me if I could be patient, I would find you in Kesken Ala. So I followed where she led me, made my way to the closest barrier, and jumped there. Then I hung out between the town and the jungle while I waited for you to appear.

"I saw you in the Myriad Market, and I knew right away who you must be. You looked so much like my memories of your mother, Foxx. I tried to come after you, but I didn't want to scare you off, so I decided to hang back and wait for the right moment to bump into you naturally. When I woke the following morning, the town was filled with soldiers, and everyone was talking about the young women they'd been chasing, so I rushed into the jungle hoping to catch up with you.

"You must know, it was not my original intention to hide so much from you. In fact, I hadn't planned on hiding any of it. Maeve said you were looking for the keys, and with who your parents were, I thought you must know the truth about everything. I expected to find revolutionaries, two women on a mission to save the Kingdoms. When I met you, I realized you knew next to nothing about what was really going on. I didn't want to freak you out or risk scaring you away, so I gave you little bits at a time and gained your trust, hoping I could eventually be sitting here telling you the truth. I realize how manipulative it all sounds, but my intentions were pure.

"I planned on telling you everything in Petrichor. That night, when we got back to the inn. Foxx, after our talk the night before, I couldn't get it out of my head all day. I should have told you then, but I was stalling because I was so afraid you would leave me. That you would run."

At that, she looked up from her hands to find his eyes boring into hers. Entreating her to understand, to forgive. She felt sick with anger and longing and confusion.

"Remember I asked you if we could talk more when we returned to the room? Obviously, you can work out why I never got around to it that night. I've been trying to catch up to you ever since, and I promised myself I would tell you everything right away. The moment I saw you, I would let it all pour out and let the pieces fall where they may.

"Somehow I managed to pass you in the jungle. I lost your trail, and when I reached the lagoon, I realized you hadn't made it there yet. I hoped you would find the prophecy and know you needed to head to Jericho. I even bribed a pixū to wait by the falls to make sure you found your way in." He took a long, deep breath. "And the rest, well, here we are."

They sat in silence for what felt like a very long time. Neither Iris nor Foxx could muster words to respond to everything he'd revealed. At last, Asher asked, "I'm sure you will have more questions as things sink in, but is there anything else you want to know now?"

Foxx sighed and again lifted her eyes to meet his. "Where did you disappear to when we were at the Sateen Monastery?" After everything he'd shared, she thought this detail might seem inconsequential, but as it was the first time she truly felt he'd broken her trust, she needed to know why.

His chin dropped to his chest with a sigh. "Ah, yes. That. Actually, this is an answer you might already know, even if you haven't realized yet that you know it." Iris furrowed her brow and tilted her head. Foxx's expression remained cold and unmoving. "After our conversation the previous night, I was... I needed time to process things. To rethink how I was handling the situation. I considered telling you everything then but, obviously, I decided against it. I considered telling you many times while we were together. Had things gone differently when I left that day, or rather, had I come back a few hours later as originally planned, maybe I would have. But then you were so angry and hurt by my staying away so long, it didn't seem like a good time to reveal the truth behind my lies."

"If you knew everything about us already, what exactly did you need to process?" Foxx's throat felt raw, making her voice dry and scratchy as if she'd swallowed sand. "I didn't share anything with you that night you didn't already know."

He glanced at Iris before again looking pointedly at Foxx. "I guess up until our conversation, I hadn't realized the severity of the damage. Which was heartless of me. I should have known two girls who lost their parents would be at least a little broken, but you both seemed so strong. It wasn't until that night that I truly saw how deep the wounds must be."

Foxx scowled, her eyes shifting to the window. "I'm not damaged."

"We all are, love. We've all been through so much. After our conversation, I realized the thin ice I walked by not telling you everything. By both of us keeping secrets from each other. I needed some time away to think, so I went to visit Ataraxia." His face scrunched as though preparing for a smack.

Their eyes widened, and Iris said, "What? Why? You acted as though you had no interest in it when we were there."

"Ataraxia," Foxx breathed, and he knew all the clues had fallen into place.

"Oh, my goodness, of course." Iris ran both hands down her face. "Prince Alexander."

He stumbled through his explanation, his cheeks warming with embarrassment. "Yes, and Ataraxia is mine. I created it. Set it up, funded it, hired the workers, even brought several of the kids in myself. Vali helped, too, as you know. After I went to your house, after your mother… and I couldn't find you, I created the mission in her honor in her home territory. I hoped you would find your way there and that it would lead you to me. I tried to spread the word in private circles, but I couldn't let the Queen know it existed. That's why I couldn't build it in Alunda. The cities are too big and open. It needed to be somewhere hidden. Based on the state of your house when I arrived, I suspected your father hadn't taken you with him. I thought you must be out in the world alone and thought there was a chance you might be drawn to your mother's home territory. I just, I wanted you to have a place that was safe. I visited every chance I got, even during periods when I'd stopped searching for answers. Each time, I arrived hoping to find you, but you never showed up."

"We had no idea it existed," Iris said.

"I know. I figured that out when we came upon it, and you were so surprised and excited by it. I couldn't go with you because it would have completely blown my cover. The kids tend to tackle me when I arrive." A smile stretched his lips as he thought of the children. "They obviously know me as Prince Alexander. Had I gone in with you, it would have given away everything. You would have run from me."

Foxx's eyes narrowed. "You don't know that."

He shrugged, knowing there was no sense in arguing past possibilities. "When I left there, I walked back the way we'd come from, an hour or so west on the trail to check things out. I wanted to make sure we weren't being followed and that our tracks were covered. It was lucky I did because I discovered some Legion soldiers tracking us.

"I tried to get rid of them. First, I attempted to reason with them: play the Prince card, even pay them off. When they refused, I tried to knock them out, but they bested me, beat me and tied me to a tree. They spent days trying to get information out of me on your whereabouts. One afternoon, after days and hours of tearing and scratching, I was able to cut free of the ropes binding me and come back to you."

The room grew quiet. It seemed like there was so much more to say… and yet nothing left to say. Several long moments passed before Asher spoke again. "I'm sorry. All I've wanted for the past six years was to find you and protect you. I worked so hard to—"

"To deceive us," Foxx cut him off.

"To know you! To help you and earn your trust. To…"

Foxx's suppressed sob cut his sentence short and drew his eyes. Her voice trembled as she tried to put words to her feelings. "I don't know what to say, Asher. You knew all of this the entire time." In her head, she stewed over his words, reiterating the main points. "When I told you about my mother dying… you knew her? You let me cry about her abandoning us when you knew the truth? I suspected you were hiding something, but never in my wildest dreams had I imagined you could be so thoroughly deceitful. How were you able to lie with such perfection? It isn't just about *what* you kept from us but every single conversation we had where you had to pretend, to respond in ways that wouldn't expose your secrets, to act like you were so surprised and heartbroken when I told you about finding her—"

"I *was* heartbroken. I had no idea you were the one who found her. I know I had to act through some of it, but that doesn't mean that every single thing was a lie, Foxxglove."

"You feigned shock when you found out we were searching for Celestelvyra! Yet you were seeking us from the very beginning, knowing exactly where we were headed."

"Because I needed to make sure you didn't run. I needed to make sure you would trust me—"

"But you didn't trust us enough to tell us the truth!"

"I thought if you knew I was part of the royal family, you would think I was a spy. You were being hunted by the King's Legion. Why would you trust me? I figured two women growing up on their own were very unlikely to trust anyone, let alone someone from the enemy's side." He put his head in his hands, no longer able to watch them cry. "I wish I could say I would do it differently given another chance, but I don't know if that's true. All I can say is, I am so sorry to have hurt you."

Foxx ran out of words.

Iris spoke instead, straightening her back and trying to keep the tears from her voice. She said his name, and he lifted his head to look at her. "I want to say first that—I love you." Foxx sucked in a breath, her eyes sliding sideways to her sister in surprise. "I had a pretty amazing sister, but I never had a brother, and if I had any choice at all in the matter, I would pick you one hundred times. But this is a lot of information to consume. I think we're going to need a little time to sort through it."

He leaned forward. "I understand. The timing is rubbish, but we do have all of the keys now, and we really should leave soon for Celestelvyra. I assume you both still want to go along, even if you're unhappy with me. We shouldn't wait more than a few days."

"Then we will talk to you in a few days." Iris took her sister's hand, and without another glance in his direction, both women left the room.

CHAPTER 39

FAMILIAL BONDS

After their discussion with Asher, Foxx and Iris holed up in their room to reflect on the information he'd unveiled. Crushed between the bed and the boulder resting on her chest, Foxx fought to catch a full breath. Her nerves teemed with energy, and her mind raced.

Iris felt drained but knew she needed to process her feelings sooner rather than later. She pulled out her journal and took notes on everything Asher had told them.

After an hour or so, Foxx rose to her feet. "We should be over helping at the Monastery. We can't just sit here for the rest of the day. There's too much to be done." Her hand found the bed to steady herself as a dizzy spell momentarily overwhelmed her.

"You should take it easy, like Jax said." Iris sat up and gestured to Foxx's obvious need for recovery. "No one is expecting you to spring into action after being knocked out for a week. You need to rehydrate and get some more food in your system. It's fine for you to rest. I promise."

"You don't seem to be taking this as hard as I am." Foxx sat back down and let her head come to rest on her pillow.

"My relationship with Asher is different from yours. It's not that I don't feel angry. I guess I'm finding it difficult not to see it from his point of view. I understand your view, too. Knowing he was able to lie so easily contradicts everything I thought I knew about him.

Though, growing up with a mother like that, I suppose he had to learn to hide things."

"Well, he excels at it now, that's for sure." Foxx let her eyes fall closed.

"All things considered, you could have fallen in love with someone far worse." Iris stood to cover Foxx with her blanket.

"I'm not in love with him." Already on the fringes of sleep, her speech was languid.

"If you say so. I'm going to get some food. I'll bring you something back, okay?" Dressing for the cold, Iris left the room. She found Declan at the Monastery tending to the wounded. When he saw her, he excused himself and met her on the edge of the courtyard. She hadn't realized her desperate need for a hug until he'd scooped her up into his arms.

When she at last released her grip on his shoulders, he took her hand and tugged her away from the courtyard to find some privacy.

"So, how did it go?"

"It was pretty terrible. Logically, I can understand his reasons for everything, but it still hurts, and Foxx is really broken up about it. I don't know if she'll ever trust another person again." Iris shivered and attempted to block the biting chill of mountain air by wrapping her scarf tighter around her neck.

"She will." Declan pulled her closer, tucking her against his side as they followed Thornby Road toward the more intact districts of the city.

The smell of fire and cooked food wafting from the homes they passed reminded Iris of her gnawing hunger. "We should stop somewhere and get something to eat."

"Keep an eye out for a place."

They continued walking, watching the buildings go by one by one.

Growing up in Alunda, Iris was no stranger to buildings packed tightly into metropolitan blocks, streets lined with picturesque homes, and interesting and unique businesses, but she felt something special walking the streets of Jericho. The snow made everything glisten like sparkling jewels, and the constant smell of smoking fires laced with pine, cinnamon, and nutmeg made her wonder if someone weren't baking a pie on every block. Now that the smell of harsh smoke and melting flesh had subsided, the true scents of the mountain city filled the air.

They glimpsed the tall spires of the palace a few blocks away, and she wondered if they would get a chance to see the inside. Since the children had been moved there from the Monastery courtyard, she'd considered going to visit them, but something about her interactions with the Konungr gave her pause, and she hadn't wanted to go alone. With Foxx awake, perhaps they could go together. "I can't believe he's the Prince. The actual Prince. Son of that wretched queen."

"Nothing like Sirena though. Nothing like he appeared to be at all, in fact."

Birds cawed from their perches on the rooftops. Iris hadn't seen many wild animals throughout the city since the dragon attacked, but she knew vultures could smell rotting carcasses from far away. Eyeing them from below, she wondered if they'd sniffed out nearby corpses yet to be uncovered.

"What else did he tell you?"

"So many things. He knew our mother. Oh, by the way, she didn't commit suicide. The Queen killed her."

"Your mother committed suicide?" he asked, overlapping her words. Several of the vultures flapped their wings, as if shooing them on.

"We thought so, but apparently not." Up ahead, Iris noticed creatures she'd never seen before. They looked like chubby, little men, no more than a foot tall, and they seemed to be tidying up remnants of debris, smaller pieces left behind by those clearing the streets. Even in the areas with less damage, the chaos of that night could be seen throughout the whole city.

"They're the gnonttūs," Declan said. "And they like to clean, as you can see."

"*Like* to clean? Nothing *likes* to clean."

"They do. They make things pretty, tend to gardens, organize houses." Declan shrugged. "They can talk, too."

"What? No way." When they drew nearer, Iris crouched to get a better look at the tiny men. They wore pants of pelt giving the impression of thick, furry legs, and wool coats that buttoned up the front. "Hello, little man. You're so cute!"

The gnonttū stopped his work and looked up at her with a scowl. "I am not a little man!" Yanking his pointed hat from his head, he waved it at her, and she backed away in surprise. His voice was much higher than she'd expected, and the removal of his hat revealed two tiny horns above his sharp ears. "I am quite large for my kind! And I am not *cute*. You should be more respectful, *giant* lady." Then he scurried off, grumbling as he went.

Iris' eyes grew wide as she looked up at Declan.

"I said they could talk. I never said they were nice."

"I didn't mean to offend him!" Iris smiled, her mood made lighter by the strangeness of the interaction. She stood, and they continued walking, turning down a side street so as not to disrupt any more of the gnonttūs. "Let's see, what else?" The thoughts in her head were a jumbled mess, like spaghetti dumped all over the floor. "We didn't meet Asher by accident. He was looking for us and apparently has been for six years. Did you know about his sister? Also, he owns the Ataraxia Mission."

Declan pointed to a building on their left with a sign reading *Grayson's Pub*, silently asking if she wanted to stop there. Iris concurred and stepped into the warm building through the door he held open for her. A few patrons sat at the bar, but the tables were vacant.

The bartender acknowledged them with the dip of his chin as Declan led Iris to a table as far from the bar as they could be. He knew she would appreciate the privacy, and he preferred to have a view with the full scope of the room. After helping remove her coat, he pulled out her chair. "I'd heard about Princess Avaline, though I haven't seen her in years. I didn't realize how bad it had gotten until Asher talked to me about it." He hung his own coat over the back of his chair and took his seat. "I guess she barely speaks, which blows my mind because the princess I remember was so lively and outgoing."

"That's really sad." Iris' heart broke for the stranger she may never know. For a moment, she let herself consider a future where Asher might take them to meet her. Maybe they could find a way to help. "I knew the Queen wasn't great, but now I see that she's way worse than I could have imagined."

The door opened, allowing in a gust of cold air. Declan looked up to see Iris' Guard position himself in the opposite corner against the wall. He scanned the room, noticing a man and a woman at the bar glancing their way with hostile expressions. Looking back at the Guard, Declan found him already watching the couple with narrowed eyes. Exhaling a small breath, he put his elbows on the table and focused on Iris. "I think you remind Asher of Avaline."

"How do you mean?"

Declan grinned as he pictured the princess. "Lady Avaline had this spark about her, like a living flame. Everyone loved her and was drawn to her. She used to walk through the castle grounds and have a conversation with every person who passed by, spreading joy everywhere she went." His eyes flashed to hers, and his smile grew.

Iris scrunched her nose. "Yeah, that sounds *exactly* like me."

"It's the you I see," he said, causing a blush to blossom high on her cheeks.

The bartender approached the table to take their order. Iris asked him for something hot and delicious with a side of warm and sweet citrus water. Declan said he would have the same.

Then Iris tried to figure out what to tell him next. She sorted through the information and settled on, "The song about the Monastery of the Morrow is about him. At least, that's what he thinks because my mother told him so in a letter she wrote to him."

Declan tilted his head, making his bangs fall into his eyes. "What do you mean it's about him?"

The bartender returned with their drinks. Iris tried to take a swig from hers and burned her tongue, sputtering as Declan watched with amusement. After wiping her lips, she said, "The part about the childson and giving up the crown."

"Interesting."

"It is. And honestly, it feels true to me. I don't know how to explain why except that it all makes sense. It all fits in this weirdly connected way. Everything he told us about our mother and the history and his destiny. My mother was... amazing." Her eyes drifted for a moment. Then her brow furrowed. "Do you know where Orion is?"

Declan choked on the sip he'd just taken and frowned. "That's a very good question. I haven't seen him since we split up during the attack."

"I wonder if he ended up in one of the piles outside." Her words spawned an unexpected ache in her chest. "It doesn't seem like him to run off like this, does it? You two have been together for so long. Would he really disappear without a word?" She took a smaller sip of her water and let the warm sensation fill her. "We should ask around. Maybe I can draw a sketch of him."

"I think if he were still in Jericho, he would've reached out to us.

Maybe he fled the city and is laying low for now. Or maybe he actually is a pile of ash outside the wall." He watched his fingers tap the table. Orion had pressed him to leave the city. If he'd died during the attack, how would Declan ever forgive himself?

"Maybe he feels bad about everything? Like, the way he treated us, I mean, so he's hiding?"

"I don't think that would keep him away this long. In fact, I can't think of anything that would make him stay away like this apart from serious injury or death." When he pulled his attention from the table and met her gaze, she could sense his profound sadness. Orion was his best friend. His brother.

The bartender returned with two hot plates of food: turkey and gravy smothering mashed turnips. Iris asked if she could have another helping of the meal to go, and he told her it would be out shortly.

"He was getting better." Declan took a bite and let the soft meat melt on his tongue, savoring it before he swallowed. "Being around you and Foxx was changing him. Maybe it didn't seem that way with how he treated you—especially you—but trust me, I've known him for a long time. I'm not going to say he was an exceptionally upstanding man, but he wasn't the man you met. I think you helped him remember the man he used to be. The man he wanted to be."

Iris sighed. "I believe you. He tried to talk to me the night we left Peregrine Manor. He was very intoxicated, but he told me he was sorry and that he would try to do better from there on out." She thought of their conversation upon first entering the room, before the dinner and the drunkenness.

Say something, she'd begged. And he'd said, *I can't.*

She'd assured him whatever it was, they could figure it out together. And he'd insisted, *There is no we.*

His harsh words turned her stomach. They'd felt like a lie the moment he'd spoken them, but it was a lie he seemed to believe, so she'd forced herself to believe it, too. Retreating from memories she didn't wish to dwell on, she said, "I, of course, bit his head off."

"Naturally."

"It was well deserved! But I can see what you mean. I kept feeling like I was sensing good in him, like I was seeing glimpses of the man he'd been when he taught me about the birds. That's why it was so frustrating when he would go dark on me."

Declan nodded, remembering watching his friend's curious

behavior as they strolled through the parroted canopy. When he realized she'd stopped talking, he looked at her to find her staring down at her plate with pink cheeks. "What's wrong?"

Guilt and unease fluttered in her chest. "I guess I feel like I should confess something to you. About Orion."

He swallowed the bite he'd taken before responding. "If it's about the cave, it's fine. I don't need to know."

Surprise permeated her features, and she wondered if he'd known all along. Had it been that obvious? Her response came out in a rush. "It's just that I don't know what's going on between you and me—not that we have to talk about it now or anything—but clearly there is something between us. At least, that's how it feels on my end. And I don't want there to be any weirdness if he does eventually show up."

"There is definitely something between us." His reassuring smile drew a deeper red to her cheeks. "Are you worried your feelings will change if he comes back?"

"No. Not at all." Iris smiled, though in her heart, she felt the slightest tingle of undefinable pain. "I think I'm still learning how this whole relationship thing works. It's always been me and Foxx, but since our journey began these past few months, I've met so many people I care about now. People I love, even." The corner of his lips curled, and she blurted, "Not, like, *in* love! I meant like Seth, the boy from Kesken Ala, and Mr. Magpie and Rossnetta. Asher and the kids at the Ataraxia Mission. And Orion and you." Her eyes lifted to his again, and she chuckled. "And even Raven. Though I think she detests me."

Declan laughed. "She doesn't."

"I feel like for the first time in my life, I have this weird version of a family. It's not a normal family, but it's mine. And I'm not sure why, but I can't help feeling like Orion is a part of it. Which is possibly insane based on how he treated me, but I sincerely hope that wherever he is, he's all right."

"It's not insane. I understand, probably better than anyone, because he's my family, too."

They finished the remainder of their meal in comfortable silence. After the bartender removed their plates and dropped off Foxx's dinner, they left Grayson's Pub and started back toward the Monastery. Many of the street lamps had already been lit as the sun slipped below the horizon, creating a golden hue over everything in sight.

As they walked, Declan asked, "So Foxxglove is pretty mad at Asher, huh?"

"Yeah, like this crazy mixture of rage and sorrow." She wiggled her fingers as if she could demonstrate the caverns of Foxx's heart. "Like my own lack of relational experiences, Foxx has always been focused on protecting me and not letting anyone get too close. Where I longed for connection, she kept herself guarded with walls around her heart higher and thicker than the ones defending this city. Asher did everything in his power to tear those walls down. He was relentless! And I think she really let him in, let him see her, you know? Like no one before him ever had. Not even me. So to find out he'd been lying to us from the moment we met, and not only hiding his title but deceiving us in so many ways, it broke her heart. Even if his intentions were honorable or for the greater good, it hurts. Especially because she tried so hard to resist letting him in. He forced himself into her heart, then he stomped on it and ended up being everything she accused him of being from day one—a liar."

Declan said, "She's strong. Anyone who meets her can see that. She'll get past it."

"I know you're right, but the whole situation feels awful, and I don't really know where I'm supposed to be standing. Whose side am I on?" They reached the courtyard and stopped to face each other. "She's my sister, and I will always take her side, but I also understand why he did what he did, and I can see what kind of man he truly is. He spent six years searching for us. He didn't know anything about us except that we were Amaryllis' daughters, and he built an orphanage hoping to find us! That's pretty amazing. And yet..." Iris worried her lip between her teeth, biting back the opposing emotions her heart wished to reveal.

"It's heartbreaking for you, as well." He squeezed her hand. "All I can say is it's obvious how much he cares about you both. I'm sure he'll be as patient and unwavering awaiting forgiveness as he was in searching for you."

Iris held up Foxx's food. "I should get this to her before it gets cold."

"I should get back to my patients." Before letting go of her hand, he pulled her into a hug. She rested her head on his shoulder for a long moment, breathing in his sagey aroma. After kissing her on the cheek, he promised to catch up with her later.

Before Iris turned toward Grove Street to head back to the inn, she caught sight of Raven standing alone across the yard and donning her usual scowl. Walking over, she greeted her with a friendly, "Hello."

"What do you want?"

Iris thought some of the previous irritation had ebbed from Raven's tone. Putting a hand on her hip, she lifted a brow.

Raven rolled her eyes before responding with exaggerated kindness. "Hello Iris, how may I help you today?"

Iris laughed. "I wanted to check on you."

"And why would you do that?"

"I noticed some tension between you and Commander Kayvan, and I heard about the altercation at the front gate yesterday, so I wanted to see if you were all right or if you wanted to talk."

"Well, stop hearing things." Raven exhaled annoyance and focused on pushing the cuticles back on her fingernails, but Iris didn't allow her hostility to dissuade her.

"I thought it might be hard always being around men and not having any girlfriends to talk to. So I wanted to extend an invitation for girl time in case you ever needed it."

"I don't." Raven glanced up from her nails, not understanding Iris' persistence despite the attitude she constantly dished out. Looking into her tired eyes, she thought perhaps it was actually Iris who needed the girl time.

"Okay. Have a pleasant evening." Offering a quick wave, Iris turned from her. She only made it a few paces before Raven called her name, her lips moving without her permission. Iris looked back over her shoulder.

"Thank you, Iris. I'll keep the offer in mind."

Iris smiled before continuing on her way, greeting Elijah with the dip of her chin as she passed by. As she became more familiar with the city, the walk to the inn from the Monastery seemed to grow shorter. The path looked cleaner every time she walked it, and she suspected she had the gnonttūs to thank for that. She'd begun enjoying the time she spent walking from one to the other, especially when unaccompanied and able to think.

When she opened the door to their room, Foxx stirred awake and sat up in a sleepy daze. Iris set her food on the table by the beds and lit the lantern before sitting down. "Got you some food." Foxx yawned and took a drink from the water sleeve next to her as Iris uncovered the bowl, releasing a puff of steam and the meal's savory aroma. "Now, eat this, and then let's talk about Asher."

"Who? I don't think I know anyone by that name."

"You're hilarious, Foxxglove."

Foxx pulled the bowl up to her nose and breathed in the smell of warm turkey gravy. "Can't we pretend I'm having post-traumatic amnesia?"

Iris began untying her boots, pulling them off one at a time. "If you think that's the healthiest option, then certainly."

Foxx mumbled something and took a bite of the turkey, taking a deep breath through her nose as she chewed. "What do you want to talk about?"

Iris settled herself in her seat, tucking her feet beneath her knees. "I think he felt he was doing the right thing at the time and the situation got away from him. He did say he planned to tell us everything in Petrichor, and I believe him. Something shifted between us once we found out about his plans for the Queen. To me at least, it felt like we were more united, and you have to remember we weren't entirely forthcoming with him either."

Foxx took another bite before responding. "So many things make sense now. Not real things, just like: looks I noticed him making, and times I felt like he was acting strange or hiding something. Well, that's because he was."

Iris scooted backward against the wall, wrapping her arms around her knees. "It's kind of weird he's known about us our whole lives, don't you think? But it's also sweet he tried to check on us. Imagine how different things would have been if we'd met him then. I mean, he literally created an orphan shelter hoping to find us. Who does that?"

"A prince." Foxx's throat swelled with conflicting emotions, and she set what remained of her meal on the table. "I really hope I can eat the rest of that later. It's delicious."

"I had the same, and you're right. So yummy." Iris' mouth watered at the memory.

"Keep your paws off of it. It's mine." Foxx laid back on her pillow and stared up at the firelight bouncing around the ceiling.

"I don't have paws!" Iris threw a pillow at her, and Foxx caught it, tucking it against her chest. "What do you think about the letter mother wrote him? Doesn't it feel like she's still communicating with us from beyond the grave?"

Foxx covered her face with her hands and groaned. "*Mother*. Can it really be true she didn't..." She bit back the words as she considered with anger and regret how much her mother's suicide had shaped her life. A small part of her hated their mother for leaving her to care for everything on her own, and that hatred had a significant impact on the woman she'd grown up to be.

Iris laid down and pulled her knees up to her chest, tugging the blanket over herself and tucking it under her chin.

Foxx let her hands fall away from her face and busied them by stretching her muscles, pulling one knee to her chest, then the other. "I still have so many questions."

"There will be plenty of time to get answers from him. I have a few of my own."

"If I ever speak to him again, that is." Foxx's eyes drifted to the food at her side. The smell lingered in the room, and though her stomach felt full, the scent made her mouth hungry.

"You will," Iris insisted. Foxx glared at her, and she amended, "Eventually. Probably."

Ignoring her, Foxx floated away, lost deep in thoughts of everything that had happened since they'd entered Jericho. Sirena's cryptic words coiled through her consciousness, as if she were in the room speaking them again.

There is more darkness in you than there ever was in her. I can feel it from here. It spills from you like a boiling pot about to overflow. Join me, Foxxglove. Imagine all we could accomplish together. We could rule the world. Great power is within your reach. Come, and I will teach you everything she failed to.

What could she possibly have meant? Could this be a clue to the true reasons Sirena sought her so diligently? Even now she could feel the darkness the Queen had spoken of. It burned her veins and frosted her fingertips. It had grown heavier with each passing day from the moment they'd left Petrichor, despite her efforts to smother it. Since she'd woken from being knocked out during the attack, it felt nearly uncontainable, as if it had festered inside her as she slept.

Shoving those thoughts deep into her core, she said, "Now that I am done crying, I just feel angry."

"I honestly don't know what I'm feeling. That makes sense, though. Sometimes anger is easier to deal with than pain."

"Anger is always easier to deal with than pain. Pain hurts and weakens, but anger strengthens. Not often in a healthy way, but it's strength nonetheless." Rotating her head to look at Iris again, she said, "I have to say, I am not a fan of the role reversal happening here. I'm supposed to be the big sister."

"Sometimes big sisters need a big sister." Iris chuckled, and Foxx joined her. "How about we change the subject? We can talk about Asher more in the morning."

"Fine." A mischievous smile spread up Foxx's cheeks. "How about instead of agonizing over that stupid boy across the hall, you fill me in on what's happening between you and Declan?"

CHAPTER 40

REVOLUTION

The Konungr had sent word out the previous evening announcing there would be an important, citywide gathering at midday and all were encouraged to attend. By the time Abram, Hector, and their teams arrived, every square foot within a block of the entrance plaza was packed tight with Jerichonian citizens. Birds lined what remained of the rooftops and rubble and heads of the hyvä mon peeked out above the wall.

The center of the plaza had been roped off. As Abram and the others made their way through the throng, he wished he'd had the forethought to rope off a walkway. When they reached the open area, Hector, Asher, and Abram moved to stand next to the fountain. The rest of the soldiers spread out around the inside of the ropes.

Foxx, Iris, and Declan came soon after and pushed their way to the front row. Both sisters scanned the plaza, looking everywhere except where Asher stood. Declan met his eyes and offered an apologetic shrug, and Asher returned it with a gesture of understanding.

Witnessing the interaction, Hector leaned over to whisper, "Are they giving you the cold shoulder?"

Asher crossed his arms and shifted his feet, trying to achieve a more comfortable position. "They are not happy with me at the moment, no."

"What did you do?"

"Told the truth." He scratched the top of his head. "After lying to them. A lot."

"Ah, I see. I assume part of that being your royal title?" Hector motioned for Jax to move closer to a rowdier section of the crowd, hoping his presence would keep them in line.

"Among other things, yes. You heard Iris at the meeting."

Hector gestured to Raven standing inside the roped off area with her back to them. "That's me as well." She glanced over her shoulder, as if sensing them talking about her, but quickly turned back around to face the crowd.

"Think she will forgive you?"

Hector brushed snow from his hair as he considered. "Hard to say. You?"

Asher looked at the girls again, deciding. "I think Iris definitely will. In fact, she probably already has. Foxx though… Foxx is strong willed. And difficult. And stubborn."

"Raven also." Hector exhaled.

Abram leaned toward them. "My late wife was the same. The strong willed ones can be difficult at times, but when they love you, they will love you so thoroughly you won't be able to comprehend it. If they are stubborn enough to fight against you, they will be stubborn enough to fight for you." Then he winked and turned to face the fountain.

They chuckled, impressed by the heartfelt advice. Asher noticed Foxx turn to him, as if drawn by the sound of his laugh. He smiled at her, but her brows knit together, and she looked away again.

"Rough," Hector said.

"You're not kidding."

The Konungr and Dróttning were the last to arrive at the center of the plaza. The crowd parted for them as they cantered in on horseback. Viggo led the way, with two guards on either side of them and another following behind. Only the Konungr, the Dróttning, and Viggo dismounted and passed beneath the ropes.

The crowd went wild, and the royals waved as they made their way to the chairs Abram had arranged for them. When they finally turned and took their seats, Foxx got a good look at the Konungr for the first time, and all the color drained from her face. In a panic, she grabbed her sister's arm and whispered her name.

Iris tried to tug her arm from Foxx's vice-like grip. "What is it?"

Following her line of sight, she said, "That's the Konungr. Yes, he's handsome, but he's not *that* handsome, geez Foxx."

Foxx shook her head. "That's not it. I've seen him before."

"How? You've been asleep."

"That's the man I saw on the mountain pass, and then again in my dreams." Foxx stared at the Konungr, knowing with undeniable certainty he was the beautiful man she'd seen. He'd bent over her, enticing her with sweet words to wake up and face the day. "It's him, Iris. He wore gray and white fur around his shoulders, like he is now."

"So what does this mean?" Iris whispered.

Declan leaned toward them. "What's happening?"

"Foxx saw Vali in a vision."

Nodding as though this were enough information to satisfy his curiosity, he returned his attention to Abram and company.

"I don't know." Foxx couldn't take her eyes off the man. She watched with intrigue as he whispered something to his wife. The Dróttning snickered and swatted his arm playfully before lifting her hand to hide her lips as she spoke back to him. He laughed loudly at whatever she'd said, and the sound made Foxx smile.

Then, like an unexpected crack of thunder, his eyes shot to her, and her stomach found its way to the ground. Worse than that, she was fairly certain the rest of her organs had toppled with it. Her hand rose to her abdomen to check.

A flash of a memory consumed her mind's eye, a fragment of the dream. *The world awaits your salvation, foxy woman. As do I.*

Iris disintegrated the memory with a whisper in her ear. "He's looking at you."

Vali dipped his chin, and his lips curled into that same, beguiling smile. Without taking his eyes from hers, he leaned over again and said something to the Dróttning. In Foxx's peripherals, she could feel the Queen of Cordillera's gaze, but it did little to assist in detaching her eyes from his.

At last, Abram said something to Vali, and he released her from the prison of his gaze. Foxx inhaled a deep breath and glanced at Asher, who was looking back and forth between her and the Konungr.

"What's going on?" Iris asked.

Foxx turned her body from Asher to look at her sister. "I don't know. He—" Her eyes flickered back to Vali, but he remained focused on the commander stepping onto the disheveled fountain.

Iris nudged her. "Are you okay?" Foxx nodded and turned her attention to Abram, who had rotated to face the suddenly silent crowd.

Abram spoke loud, his voice echoing within the boundaries of the city walls. "Jericho! Welcome! Thank you for responding so fervently to our invitation." Civilians called out to him or clapped in response. "Many of you know me, but for those of you who do not, I am Abram Havlar, commander of the Jerichonian Guard.

"I am sure some of you may have guessed the reason for this summoning. The tragedy nine days ago will sit heavy within all of our hearts for many years to come. 3,478 civilians were murdered here in our home city. On our land. Many more were injured. Not only did you lose family and friends, but many of you also lost your homes and your businesses as well, and our grand Monastery of the Morrow was demolished beyond recognition. I am sorry to every person who lost something on that horrendous day." He took a breath, offering a moment of silence to the fallen. "But we do not plan on taking this lack of human decency and blatant disrespect sitting down. We do not plan on letting the sins of that day go unpunished. We will not remain silent any longer. Queen Sirena has pushed us too far."

A buzz of energy crackled through the crowd.

"So today, on this glorious day as the Creator's sun shines brightly upon us, Jericho stands in unity with the former commander of the King's Legion, Hector Kayvan, who has bravely decided to join our cause and stand against the King and Queen of Arkaemor."

Cheers erupted through the crowd as the hope of having their enemy switch sides and join them took shape in their hearts.

Abram raised his voice even louder. "As well as the Crown Prince, Alexander Aldrich!" The cheers became an exuberant uproar.

Asher waved, thinking with a grimace that everyone would definitely be calling him Alexander now. For a moment, Iris caught his gaze. He saw her familiar, rascally smile and realized she was making fun of him. Teasing. His heart warmed at the thought. Then he averted his eyes from the happiness in Foxx's expression and wondered if that smile would ever again be directed at him.

"And of course, we are led by our valiant sovereigns, Konungr Vali Kirkavall and his beautiful wife, Ingrid!" Wild with excitement, the citizens screamed exclamations of honor and praise for their King and Queen. Vali and Ingrid lifted a hand in a wave. Abram allowed several moments of rejoicing before he continued. "Our Konungr and Dróttning have sworn since the beginning of their reign to do what is best for our city and this Kingdom."

Foxx again returned her attention to the royals, as did everyone within range to see them, but neither Vali nor Ingrid looked back at her. Shaking her head, she thought maybe she'd only imagined the intensity that passed between them. Maybe when Vali had drawn Ingrid's attention to her, he'd whispered something along the lines of *look at this crazy woman staring at me.*

Foxx felt her cheeks flush with embarrassment. She realized that was definitely what must have happened and wondered why she'd behaved so ludicrously. Again, without her permission, her eyes glanced his way.

Vali met her gaze. Lips cracking open into a one-sided smile, he winked at her.

Flushing again, Foxx looked at the ground, feeling the need to vomit and willing herself to get it together.

Once the cheering died down, Abram's voice broke through her anxiety. "Now you have heard our plan. This is the beginning of the revolution, my friends. The revolution that will free us all. But I implore you to listen very closely. Especially those of you wearing crimson uniforms." He pointed his finger around the square with accusation. "If you choose to stay and join us, you will be defecting from the King's Legion and be considered a traitor to the Thrones of Arkaemor. If you are willing to accept this label, we are pleased to have you. If not, you have until sundown to vacate the city safely. Run back to your Queen and tell her Jericho stands! And we are preparing an uprising like the world has never seen!"

Another roar swept through the crowd. Abram thanked everyone, though his voice went unheard over the howling citizens. He stepped down from the fountain and shook Hector's hand. "It is time, my friend. Time for revolution."

C

Before the assembly began, Foxx and Iris had discussed what they wanted to do about Asher and Celestelvyra. Iris explained her theory about the Monastery in the Wilds, and Foxx agreed it was a good place to start.

Though they'd told Asher they would need a few days, they understood the importance of getting things moving, so they decided to confront him after the rally and tell him they were ready to move forward.

Upon waking that morning, Iris felt even more lighthearted and forgiving toward Asher. Foxx, however, seemed to grow angrier with each passing hour. Still, they agreed getting to Celestelvyra had to be more important than anything else. With Foxx awake and the city in a full-swing revolution, the time had come to finish their mission.

When the crowd dispersed, Declan said he wanted to get back to the people at the Monastery. Foxx and Iris ducked under the rope and waited for Asher to finish his discussion with Hector and the others. The royals had already left, and neither had returned their attention to Foxx after Vali's baffling wink.

Noticing them walking his way, Asher's face became a sheet of white. He excused himself from the others, and his hand flew up to rub the back of his head as they stopped in front of him. Foxx crossed her arms.

Iris smiled in greeting. "That speech was pretty exciting, wasn't it?"

Asher nodded. "It was, yeah. Abram has a great speaking voice."

They stood there for a long moment, waiting for someone to talk. Finally, Foxx said, "Asher, may I speak with you alone, please?"

Foxx's question surprised Iris, as cutting her out of the conversation had not been part of the plan, but she hoped good things would come of them spending time alone together.

Asher looked like his breakfast might soon make a reappearance.

"I'll see you back at the Monastery, okay?" Iris walked past Asher and sharply mouthed the words *be nice* to Foxx behind his back.

Foxx shook her head and drew her focus back to him. "So listen. I know we need to get to Celestelvyra, and you were right, I do want to go along. If you're correct about my father being in the...

what did you call it, the In-Between? If there's a chance he's alive, then I want to be there when we find him. I know we can't put it off any longer, so I am willing to leave tomorrow morning, if you are. When we return, I can take time to work through everything you told us, but I know getting to Celestelvyra has to be more important than all the things I'm feeling."

He took a step forward and lifted his hand as if to reach for her, thought better of it, and let it drop back to his side. "Foxx, I am beyond joyful you decided to come with me, and I—"

Foxx put a finger up to silence him, and his mouth snapped shut. "I'm not finished. I am willing to come with you, yes, as a team member on a mission to retrieve the item that will help us kill Sirena. But nothing more than that."

Asher felt his heart in his throat. "Foxx—"

"No, Asher. No." She held her palms up and took a step back, shaking her head. "Please don't. Please don't make it harder than it already is." She inhaled a sharp breath to keep her voice from quivering. "Please understand and accept what I'm saying. Whatever there was between us, if there even was anything real, it's over."

Her words cut him like a blade, robbing him of oxygen until he felt dizzy. He'd only just gotten her back. Even in the cold of Cordillera, his skin felt wet with sweat beneath his clothing, and a bead slid from his temple into the corner of his eye.

"We can work together as allies for the greater good right now, but once this has all come to an end, you go your way and I go mine. Is that understood?"

He took another step toward her, eyes shining with desperation. "Foxx, please. Don't—"

She shouted his name, and her harsh tone stopped him in his tracks. People standing nearby paused to see what had caused the commotion. Lowering her voice, she said, "You're not listening to me. If you can't accept my terms, then I can't go with you." Forcing herself to hold his gaze, she crossed her arms again and held her body stiff, hoping with everything inside of her that she wouldn't let him witness her falling apart. "I really want to go in case my father is there, but I need a promise from you that you won't push this. If you're not able to do that, then I'll stay behind. Iris can still go with you, and hopefully you'll be able to bring my father back to me. If not, then I guess it wasn't meant to be."

Asher waited a long minute, thinking it over. He scrutinized her swollen eyes and the trembling lip pinched tightly between her teeth and thought this couldn't be what she truly wanted. She was angry and hurt, probably more than she'd ever been in her life, but they could get past this. Couldn't they?

At last, he sighed. "Okay, love. I'm good with whatever you want."

Suddenly angry, with every sliver of sorrow stripped from her expression, she snarled, "And *don't* call me that." Turning on her heel, her white hair splayed out behind her as she stormed off.

C

Once the crowd from the revolution rally dissipated, Hector saw Raven slip beneath the rope and rush off. Catching up with her less than two blocks from the square, he fell into step next to her. Though she clearly noticed him, she didn't slow her pace or acknowledge him in any way until he asked, "Hey, can we talk?"

Raven stopped so suddenly, Hector nearly stumbled as he halted next to her. She turned to him wearing an expression of disinterest. "What about?"

Recovering himself, Hector straightened the shirt of his uniform and eyed her skeptically. "How about how angry you are with me? This cold shoulder act is nerve-racking. It's been a week."

"It's not an act. And also not my problem."

He said her name, entreating her to look at him.

"What?" She glanced his way from the peripherals of narrowed eyes.

He slid his hand toward her arm, but she pulled it from his reach. "Please don't do this. We need each other right now, don't you think?"

"I don't need you, Hector." She watched people walking past them, lost in their own excited conversations. A man in Jerichonian purple walked by and clapped Hector on the back. He smiled and lifted his chin to acknowledge him, and Raven rolled her eyes.

Returning his attention to her, he reached out again. "Well, I need you." At his touch, her eyes found his, and he thought for a moment she might give in before she huffed and said again, "That's not my problem."

He looked away from her, endeavoring to keep his temper. With a low growl under his breath, he said, "I know you're mad. What I did was awful, and I can't take it back, but I am trying to make it right." He lifted his arms wide in a sweeping gesture to the entire city. "Clearly, I'm trying. I've literally given up my entire life to sleep on the ground in the snow in this demolished city. I've given up my position and everything I've spent my whole life working for, to be here, standing up for what I know to be right."

The people walking by now gave them a wide berth, staring at them as they passed and soaking up hints of the conversation. Hector met the gaze of one of the passersby, and they immediately looked at the ground before hurrying off. "Look, if you want to punch me or something let's get it over with. Please. I would prefer that to this agonizing silence."

She responded by crossing her arms and staring at him incredulously. He threw his hands in the air again before placing them on his head. Still she said nothing. Then a hand clasped his shoulder, and he turned to see Jax standing behind him.

"Cut him some slack, Raven. You know you're going to eventually, so why drag it out?" After gleaning her outraged expression, he chuckled and walked on without awaiting a response.

Hector's shoulders slumped as his hands dropped to his sides with another heavy sigh.

Still feigning disinterest, Raven examined her stoic commander, thinking she'd never seen him so distraught in all the years she'd known him. At last, her sympathy defeated her stubborn resistance. "I'm not going to punch you."

"Well do something, won't you?" He tried to appear unruffled. His ability to remain calm and collected in every and all situations had been utter perfection until a few moments ago. "Scream at me. Tell me I'm a terrible, despicable, waste of a person and that you can never forgive me for the crimes I've committed. Tell me you hate me. Something. *Anything*. Anything but this wall of ice erected between us. I can't take it. Please, Raven."

Sighing, she let her arms relax at her sides. "I can't do that."

His eyes turned down at the corners. "None of it?" She shook her head. "So you're going to continue ignoring me." It wasn't a question but an acknowledgement of acceptance. He straightened his back. "All right. I guess I understand."

"No, you don't." She took a step toward him. "I mean, I can't tell you any of that because it isn't true."

He smiled, drawing his head back in surprise. When she noticed, she told him to knock it off, and he quickly pressed his lips back into a tight line.

She tilted her head, looking up at his handsome face with a whisper of a smile playing at her lips. "Whatever happened in your past doesn't change anything between us, and it doesn't change my opinion of you or how I—" Her dark eyes widened, and she stopped herself from finishing the sentence. "I still need some time to absorb it all. I spent years feeling a certain way toward Silas and building up this awful picture of him in my head to make sense of how he ended things between us. So now to find out the truth... I need to rewrap my head around it. It's weird that you knew his father, and someday soon, we're going to talk about the inception of this." She waved a finger between them. "I want to know why you approached me like you did. But not today."

He waited to see if she would say more, wondering why she hadn't mentioned how horrible he was. A traitor, a coward. She couldn't be avoiding him because of what he told her about Declan, could she? Had she totally missed the part about him abandoning his whole team to die? Condemning all of those children to death? When she didn't continue, he asked with a note of fearful caution, "Does the news about Declan change anything? Between you and him, I mean."

She shrugged. "It means I don't hate him anymore, I guess. Or I'm trying not to, at least. I spoke with him about it, and we are working through it."

Her lack of details made his stomach sick, but he pressed forward anyway. "So... you forgive me? You still...?"

She smacked his shoulder and muttered, "Stop being an idiot."

Unable to contain his smile, he pulled her into his chest. She gasped in surprise as he wrapped his arms around her and squeezed. "I can't help it," he whispered into her ear.

Pulling back, she grabbed the front of his jacket with both hands and rose to her tiptoes. Pressing a brief kiss to his lips, she dropped back down and said, "Try." Then she smirked and walked away, leaving him feeling lighter than air.

CHAPTER 41

WHY WE FIGHT

At sunrise, Asher knocked on the door to Foxx and Iris' room.

Iris answered wearing an overly chipper expression. "Merry morning, Asher!" She'd dressed in layers, preparing to travel in the snow and then the desert. Having spent the last week within the safety of the city walls shadowed by a soldier from a king's personal Guard, she hadn't felt the need to arm herself with her myriad of weapons. She'd carried Thorn on occasion, but now the flat sheath holding her throwing knives was strapped to her chest, and both Thorn and Bloom hung low on her hips.

Gesturing to her weapons, he replied, "You look equipped for battle."

She buttoned her jacket closed around the chest sheath. "You never know what we might come across, and it's always good to be prepared." Asher tapped the rifle slung over his shoulder in agreement. Before buttoning the final button, Iris looked down at the top of the sheath and said, "I missed them."

Asher looked past her to where Foxx stood double-checking her pack. She also wore layers, with her quiver resting against her back. "Merry morning, Foxx."

Foxx offered a nod, but didn't look in his direction. She was determined to engage him as little as possible, fearful if she began speaking, all of her wrathful thoughts would pour free without restraint. Despite her anger, she knew her rampant emotions couldn't be trusted. She had no way of knowing how she might feel once she had time to work through everything, and she didn't want to be unnecessarily hurtful.

Her mother had always told her, *Out of control emotions promote out of control mistakes.* So she would keep her emotions in check and do her best to keep her distance until the fiery rage within her chest settled.

One thing she knew for sure: she couldn't wait to get out of the city and return to the wilderness. Never before had she realized her deep love for the wild until spending time trapped behind fortified walls. Her emotions felt too vast to fit within the confines of the city borders. They needed space to burst free of their cage so she could breathe again. Living in the wild was a harder—but simpler—way of life, and she desperately longed for the sounds of the birds, the smell of the wind, and the feel of the rain.

A thought struck her without warning and took her breath away. If they succeeded, Asher would be crowned king. She saw him standing before two thrones, and herself at his side with a shimmering gold crown atop her head.

Regardless of how she ended up feeling about Asher, would she even want that kind of life? Could she ever be happy behind the safeguarded walls of a castle? With the slightest sadness, she thought perhaps it was better their relationship end before it had a chance to begin.

"I'll wait for you downstairs." Asher hurried away, contemplating how he was going to handle the trip if Foxx shut him out so thoroughly the entire time. Before he stepped out into the snow, he glanced back at the steps and spoke a silent prayer: *Give me strength, Elohim. And if You don't mind, could You soften her heart to me? Just a little?*

Iris turned to Foxx. "You have to be nicer to him."

"No, I don't."

"Oh, come on, Foxx. This is Asher." Iris moved deeper into the room, not wanting him to overhear if he'd stopped to wait for them at the bottom of the steps. "Think of everything we've been through together."

Foxx straightened and looked at her sister. "Actually, Iris, that is Prince Alexander Aldrich, whom I know next to nothing about. Plus, we only spent six weeks together. Not exactly a lifetime of memories."

Iris' expression revealed her pity. "Foxxglove—"

Foxx snapped her name, eyeing her sister with narrowed eyes. "I can't do this right now. I can't think of the time we spent together. I can't think about the things he confessed. I can't." She swallowed down the lump in her throat and took a breath to halt the emotions rising from her chest. "I need to separate myself from it until we get this done. Otherwise, I'll fall apart. Right now, the mission has to be more important."

"I know. I understand, but I hate seeing you like this. I hate seeing you both like this."

"I'm handling it the only way I know how." Foxx's fingertips felt cold, and she rubbed them together before blowing warmth into her palms.

Lifting Foxx's back off the bed, Iris helped slide it onto her shoulders. "Ready?" Then she walked out the door and shuffled down the stairs.

Foxx lingered in the doorway with her fingers draped over the knob as she gazed about the room. She wondered if she would ever return to the White Luna Inn, or if this was the last time she would see it. Her eyes slid down the hall to the door that had been Asher's room all along. Sighing, she shook her head and pulled the door closed.

They'd agreed to meet Hector in the entrance plaza before departing. When Asher, Foxx, and Iris arrived, they found Hector and Declan already deep in discussion.

"Merry morning, gentlemen," Asher said as they approached.

Hector almost bowed to him out of habit but restrained himself and shifted his stance instead. "Merry morning. Are you all ready to go?" He looked them over like a commander inspecting his troops before battle, noticing the weapons Foxx and Iris hadn't been wearing when they'd met. His eyes slid from the scabbards dangling at Iris' hips to the bow slung over Foxx's shoulder with casual interest.

Asher patted himself down as if doing a final check. "I think we have everything we need. The plan is to travel to the closest border—"

"Where you and the Raptors entered when you first arrived," Declan clarified.

"And ride it to Kesken Ala. Foxx and Iris want to check on a few people when we get there, but it's right on the barrier, and we won't be staying long."

Declan chimed in again. "It will take roughly two days to travel from Kesken Ala to the Monastery in the Grim Wilds. We think."

Iris and Hector watched intently, unable to contain their amusement as the men continued to explain in tandem. Even Foxx's eyes volleyed back and forth between them.

Asher's hands moved through the air to animate his words. "And once we get there, hopefully it's as easy as placing the keys…"

"Open the door."

"Enter Celestelvyra."

"Retrieve the death water."

"And return to Jericho with the weapon in hand." Asher turned to Declan and said, "Death water?"

Declan shrugged. "Pyhä-ki is hard to say."

Iris shook her head and placed herself between Asher and Declan, setting a hand on both their shoulders. "I don't think you guys are allowed to be friends."

Asher laughed. "I don't think you can stop it. If everything goes to plan, we hope to be back here in one week."

Hector said, "Horses would make the trip much quicker."

"True, but with the uncertainty of how this will all play out, I'd rather not have horses to worry about. If they end up stuck in the middle of the desert, they may not survive. Especially Cordilleran horses."

Respecting the Prince even more for his concern for the animals, Hector dropped his chin in approval. "We'll continue to work here on rebuilding and training. When you return, we'll regroup and make plans to move forward."

"Prince Alexander?" A woman's voice had them all turning their heads to find Dróttning Ingrid Kirkavall walking toward them with two guards flanking her and two others trailing close behind.

Even in the early hours of the morning, silver dust surrounded her eyes, and her hair had been braided into an elaborate design. A black crown sat atop her head, accentuating the onyx streaks woven throughout her blonde locks. Thick fur and a long cloak covered her shoulders, grazing the ground as she walked.

Asher stepped through their circle to greet her. "Ingrid, we weren't expecting you."

"I wanted to see you off, Alexander. Vali wished to come, but he found himself distracted this morning." She handed him a fabric bundle tied with a purple ribbon. "Some provisions for you and your companions, straight from the palace kitchens. I know you have a certain fondness for our dry-cured mutton."

He beamed at her kind gesture, accepting the gift. "I do indeed."

"I tucked some rye bread in there for you as well. Be sure to share with your lady friends." The Dróttning's eyes flitted from Asher to examine his companions. Foxx and Iris stared in awe at the casual interaction. Dipping her head, Ingrid said, "Foxxglove, Iris, it is an honor to meet you both."

"It's an honor to meet you, Your Majesty." Iris bowed in a half-curtsy.

Foxx let her chin fall to her chest. "Yes, the honor is ours." When she lifted her head, the Dróttning was intently focused on her alone, and she flushed at the memory of the silent interaction she'd shared with Ingrid's husband the previous day.

Ingrid's attention turned from the sisters to Declan, who stood on Iris' right. Studying him curiously, she said, "You were here with Sawyer."

"That's right, Your Majesty." Declan bowed formally. "It's a pleasure to see you again."

Ingrid nodded by way of greeting before turning back to Foxx and Iris. "Vali and I were so sorry to hear of your father's disappearance. We very much enjoyed the time Sawyer spent here with us. He is a good man. And your mother's murder on top of that." Ingrid shook her head at the tragedy of it all. "Amaryllis was an exceptional woman. My husband in particular was devastated by her passing."

Iris and Foxx couldn't seem to string words into coherent thoughts. They stared at the Dróttning open mouthed and bug eyed. Then they looked at Asher, but his eyes were solely on Foxx as he waited for her shock and confusion to melt into more anger directed at his world of secrets.

Pulling his gaze from hers, he drew Ingrid's attention. "It's a bit of a touchy subject, my lady."

The Dróttning's lips parted. "I am so sorry! Forgive me for overstepping. It was certainly not my intention."

When she realized Foxx wasn't going to reply, Iris said, "It's fine, Your Majesty. There was a lot of information we didn't have regarding our family history until very recently. It's been a lot to take in." It occurred to her then that Konungr Vali had been the one to confirm Amaryllis' knowledge of the keys to Celestelvyra, and she wondered how many more mysteries were left to uncover about their parents. If Vali had truly been devastated over their mother's death, what did that say about her relationship with these royals? Iris' imagination ruptured with new questions and curiosities.

Ingrid smiled sweetly. "I understand. When things have settled, we should discuss it further, if you like. I am sure Vali and I could share stories with you that would bring joy to your hearts." Lifting her hand to graze Asher's cheek, like a mother caressing the chubby cheeks of a babe, her smile broadened. "You should know ladies, this man here has been searching for you for a very long time. Alexander, I'm beyond pleased to see that you've found your way to them at long last. Thanks be to the Creator for His flawless plans and exquisite timing."

Asher's cheeks burned cherry red as he scratched the back of his head. "Thanks, Ingrid. We should return in about a week. Shall we talk more then? We can have dinner."

"Of course. Take care of these girls, and come back to us soon, Alexander. You have been away far too long, and your family is anxious for you to return home."

"I'll do my best." Lifting her hand in his own, he kissed the back of her coal-tinted glove and wished her farewell. The Dróttning tugged him forward and pressed a kiss to his cheek.

As he took a step back to speak to the whole group, he tried to avoid Foxx's eyes, knowing the entire interaction likely made her even more unsettled. He lost the battle and looked at her anyway, though she didn't seem angry. The gears in her mind spun behind her eyes, mechanically attempting to place all of the pieces where they belonged in the puzzle: the Kirkavalls, the Aldrichs, the Belamours, and the inner workings of how they all fit together.

Declan held his hand out to Hector. "Good luck with everything here."

Hector accepted the handshake, pleased there seemed to be no awkwardness between them. "You as well."

Asher said, "Thank you again, Hector, for everything you're doing. It's really remarkable."

Hector's eyes slid to the Jerichonian Queen, thinking she might disagree, but she only tilted her head and offered a polite smile. "I don't aim to be remarkable, only to make things right." Looking around the group, he met eyes with each of them. "I hope your journey will be as easy as it seems and that you will safely return to us soon. Go in peace, as the Jerichonians say."

"Go in peace," agreed Asher, and Ingrid echoed him.

With one last glance farewell, Asher stepped away from the group. Declan, Iris, and Foxx followed. The Guard at the entrance gate already had the door open for them, and he acknowledged each of them as they passed by.

Foxx was the last to reach the gate. Before she passed through the wrought iron bars, she looked back over her shoulder to find the Dróttning's eyes on her. Without really knowing why, she lifted a hand. Ingrid raised hers in return, her smile widening.

Once outside the wall, the four travelers turned back to gaze at the magnificent City of the Moon. After hearing the clang of the locking gate, they faced the trail and began their hike to the northern barrier.

The journey took most of the day, though the snow wasn't as deep as it had been on their trip to Jericho, nor was the path entirely uphill. The bottom curve of the sun touched the horizon when they finally caught a glimpse of the black walls.

Like Asher and Declan had described, Iris and Foxx felt a bizarre sense of displacement as they drew closer. They knew they needed to walk toward the glittering darkness rising up before them but felt something subconsciously urging them to turn back and go a different way, like an innate survival instinct that makes a person avoid alleys at night or untrustworthy bridges.

"It's a weird feeling," Iris said. "It isn't exactly a fear, but it's like something is trying to pull my stomach in the opposite direction."

Declan said, "I remember how it felt for me the first few times as well. The enchantment tries to force you to look away and forget you've seen it."

Asher touched the wall, placing his palm flat against it. "It definitely gets easier over time. Now I feel little more than a mild sense of dread."

With effort, Foxx kept her snide remarks about Asher's experience with the outer barriers to herself. Stopping several feet from the wall, she and Iris lifted their eyes to observe its unbelievable size. Rising all the way up into the clouds, it pulsed and danced, shimmering like a galaxy of stars, as if they stood face to face with the night sky.

"It's kind of beautiful." Iris took a few steps back to widen her view.

"It really is," Foxx concurred.

"Look at this." Declan pointed at the ground against the barrier. "The grass is black here."

Asher knelt to touch it. "It looks like it's… dying." Removing one of his gloves, he rubbed his hand through the grass and checked his fingers for residue.

"Is this not what it normally looks like?" Iris leaned over his shoulder to see the result of his experiment. Then she bent lower to touch it herself.

Asher shook his head. "I've never seen anything like it."

"Nothing to be done about it now," Declan said, and Asher stood to rejoin them.

Foxx approached the barrier and reached to touch it with the tips of her fingers. "It feels like a normal barrier, like there's a higher density to the space."

"Technically, it is a normal barrier." Asher stopped beside her. "It's the same barrier we see anywhere else. It only looks black because there's nothing behind it but darkness."

"What's in the darkness?" Iris joined their ogling line.

"No one knows." Asher eerily waved his fingers in her face.

Iris swatted him away. "Freaky."

Declan stepped up to the wall. "Let's do this. Close your eyes and picture where you want to go very clearly. Then step through. I'll go first so you have someone to greet you on the other side." He grinned at Iris and pressed a kiss to her cheek before stepping into the wall and disappearing from sight.

"*Super* freaky," Iris reiterated, touching the wall where he'd stepped through it. "He's gone!"

"He's in the Grim Wilds." Asher grinned, amused by her gawking.

"I'll go next!"

"Let me go." Foxx held out a hand, surveying the wall and then Asher with obvious distrust. "Just in case."

Iris rolled her eyes and looked at Asher. "Ever the big sister, am I right?" He chuckled and lifted a shoulder.

Foxx stroked the barrier again. With one last glance at Iris, she closed her eyes and stepped through. Like every other time she'd crossed a barrier, time seemed to slow as she lost access to oxygen. A moment of panic fluttered her heart before she broke through into the desert of the Grim Wilds.

Declan pulled her from the wall and held her arm to steady her. "You all right?"

She blinked, sucking in air with her hand on her chest. "Yes, fine. It seemed to take longer than it normally does. It stole my breath."

"You traveled a farther distance than you normally do."

Iris stepped through, and Declan left Foxx to greet her the same way. Asher was the last to press his boots into the desert sand. He materialized from the wall with all the effortless, cool energy of a man who'd done it a hundred times before—a fact that annoyed Foxx to no end.

"It will get easier," he said when he saw her scrutinizing him.

"I bet." Foxx turned from him to face the village of Kesken Ala.

Iris stepped up next to her and touched her arm. "It feels like it's been forever."

"It's been more than three months. More than four since our journey began on the western border. And a lot has happened in that time."

Iris dropped her pack and began unbuttoning her jacket. "I am dying in this heat though."

Foxx smirked. "You, the girl who loves the sun."

"I love the sun on my skin. It can't get to my skin when I'm completely covered in fabric!"

Foxx laughed and followed her sister's lead.

When each of them had shed their layers, Iris embraced the sun. "Now, isn't that so much better?"

Foxx started to say, "I still pref—" but Iris cut her off with a shush.

"Don't you dare kill my bliss by bringing up the R-word right now, or I will seriously lose it."

Asher barked a laugh, and Declan asked, "Is *rain* the R word?" Iris shot him a look of fiery death, and he actually stumbled back-ward in surprise. "That would be a yes."

Asher clapped him sympathetically on the back. "Are you all ready?"

"Let's go find Seth!" Iris bubbled with energy. They followed the barrier toward the center of town. It no longer seemed necessary to hide themselves, but Asher insisted they stick to back streets anyway. They made their way to Rossnetta's first, thinking they would say hello to her before heading to the Briar Tavern and hoping she might come with them so they could all visit together.

When they arrived at her house, Iris knocked twice and was startled to find Seth answering the door. A vast wave of emotions crossed his features in rapid succession: confusion, recognition, surprise, excitement. His eyes widened as if they might pop out of his head, and he squealed, "Iris!" Then his face contorted into absolute sorrow. He crashed into her, wrapping his arms tightly around her waist, and began sobbing. Stunned by the unexpected series of events, Iris hugged him back and tried to find out what was going on, but he wouldn't respond.

Rossnetta appeared behind him in the doorway. "Iris! Foxxglove! Oh, it is lovely to see you girls. Come in, come in. Seth, let them through, son." She waved for them all to enter, tugging on Seth's shoulders so he would give them space to pass by.

"Rossnetta, these are our friends Asher and Declan." Foxx motioned to the men behind her.

"Yes, yes, everyone inside. Any friend of yours is a friend of mine, dearies, of course."

Seth's sobs faded into whimpering tears as Iris led him to the table. Foxx sat down across from her, and Rossnetta put a pot of water on the stove for tea. Asher and Declan stood against the wall, feeling cramped in the tiny kitchen.

Iris turned Seth to face her and took both of his hands. "Seth, talk to me. Why are you so upset?" Seth shook his head, scrunching his face as he attempted to restrain fresh tears. She looked to Rossnetta for answers and found her eyes turned down with sympathy.

"Oh dearies. It's about as bad as it could be."

Foxx pulled her eyes from Seth. "What is going on, Rossnetta? What happened?"

Rossnetta leaned against the counter by her stove, resting her weight on her elbow before straightening her lichen-green scarf, decorated with jewels that matched Asher's eyes. "It was the King's Legion, child. The ones who came here looking for you the night you had to flee." Rossnetta looked down, shaking her head in despair.

Iris felt her heart tense. Foxx sat up, bracing for what followed. Her hand slid across the table, reaching for her sister's, but Iris was focused on Seth. Asher and Declan shared a look, both straightening as Foxx had.

Seth spoke through tears, the words pouring from him in bursts and sputters. "They took him. They took Mr. Magpie, Iris. They took him, and they…" A protest spilled from Iris' lips and died in the air as she looked into his eyes and saw the agonizing truth. "They came and they took him, and they… and he's…" He couldn't finish the sentence, couldn't say the words everyone in the room already knew. His head dropped forward into his hands.

"Where?" Foxx stood abruptly.

Rossnetta removed the whistling teapot from the stove and placed it on a cooling mat. "It is not a fine sight to behold, child. It's up the road a ways, on the outskirts of town." She pointed west toward the desert. "The same way you entered last time."

Foxx met Asher's eyes, then Declan's. A silent decision was made, and the three of them moved toward the door.

When they reached the porch, Asher grabbed Foxx's hand, spinning her back to face him. "Foxx, maybe Declan and I should go first."

"Why?"

Asher looked past her to Declan. "Because if the Legion intended to make a statement, it is sure to be a gruesome one."

Pulling her fingers from his, she said, "Do you think I can't handle it?"

"Of course not, lo—" Her scowl at his use of her nickname halted his sentence midword, and he bit the tip of his tongue. "I would rather save you the nightmares, if I can."

"Seth saw it." She stepped around him. "Whatever it is will be ingrained in his memory for the rest of his life. I need to see it for myself." With another glance at Declan, who shrugged, Asher surrendered. Foxx turned from them and walked west.

Inside Rossnetta's house, Iris wrapped her arms around Seth and let him cry a moment longer before assuring him, "I'll be right back, okay? I promise." Her eyes lifted to Rossnetta's, whose expression filled her with deeper dread. Like Foxx, she had to find out what horrors now resided in his mind and what the Legion had done to their friend. Seth stepped away so she could rise from the chair. "I'll be right back," she said again. Then she crossed the threshold and stepped out into the setting sun.

The road running straight through the center of town was wider than all the other roads in Kesken Ala. A few blocks east sat the Myriad Market, an outdoor street market that took full advantage of the road's wide breadth. Iris looked toward it, thinking it wasn't nearly as lively as it had been on their first visit. The extravagant colors decorating the village seemed to have lost some of their saturation, as though the whole town remained in mourning, even the festoons.

On the opposite side of the road stood the Briar Tavern. It didn't appear to be open, and Iris wondered what would become of it if Mr. Magpie wasn't there to run it. Would it ever reopen, or would it sit there as a distant memory, an empty coffin?

Iris faced west and walked down the center of the road leading out of town. She saw Foxx and the men stopped in front of a tall, thin structure that hadn't been there before. At first, she couldn't make out what it was. The setting sun blinded her as she walked toward it, but the closer she got, the clearer the image became. Her steps slowed as if something weighed down her boots, restraining her from continuing forward.

Hearing her approach, Declan spun and raced back to her, shielding her eyes and wrapping his arms around her as she tried to peer over his shoulder at the hideous display. "Don't look at it, Iris. Don't look."

She pushed past him, needing to be certain of what she saw. The undiluted truth hit her like a wave that slams a diver into the ocean floor, holding them under and whipping their limbs around in uncontrollable convulsions. It suffocates and blinds as the unruly riptide yanks them deeper into the depths.

Worse than the broken city of Jericho and more painful than the piles of corpses outside the walls waiting to be burned, the scene brought her to her knees. Declan dropped with her, not letting her go as she wailed.

Foxx heard Iris' cry and wished she could run to her, but she couldn't yet drag her eyes from the depravity. Asher placed a hand on the small of her back, but she pushed him away.

A wooden post rose from the ground high above their heads. Two thirds of the way up, another beam stretched horizontally, like a tree with only three limbs. From that tree hung the bloody, heinously beaten, rotting corpse of Mr. Magpie. His body sagged limp between arms stretched out and tied to the horizontal beam. His skin had been scorched by the blistering sun. The little clothing left on him had been shredded, and huge lacerations covered his body, as though birds and insects had been eating away at whatever wounds had been inflicted.

Foxx felt her body fold in half, and vomit sprayed from her mouth. The raucous sound ricocheted throughout the vast desert. Asher handed her a rag from his pack, and she accepted it, spitting out a raspy, "Thank you," as the bile continued to burn her throat raw. When her spasms settled, she stood up and wiped her lips with the rag. Asher had opened his water sleeve and offered it to her, another gesture she accepted with gratitude.

A giant ball of saffron glowed brightly behind the post holding Mr. Magpie. Washed in magenta, tangerine, and violet, the contrast of the beautiful sky magnified the awful scene. A shadow stretched long and thin, cutting the road right down the middle all the way to where Iris had fallen.

Seth stepped out onto the porch. From his vantage, he could see Iris and Declan on the ground, but Foxx and Asher were out of sight. Rossnetta came up behind him and put her arm around his shoulder, squeezing him firmly.

Iris continued to weep as Declan held her, whispering words of comfort in her ear.

Foxx handed Asher back his water sleeve, and their eyes met. At that, something inside her shattered, and she let her face fall into his chest. He wrapped his arms around her and held tight as her tears soaked through his shirt. "This is all our fault. Again. They did this to him because he helped us."

Asher didn't know what to say. He worried if he contradicted her statement, she might push him away. Instead, he remained silent and let her cry. When the tears began to subside, he whispered, "Come on, let's go back to Rossnetta's."

Startled, as though waking from a dream, she pushed him away and apologized under her breath. Asher didn't understand what she'd apologized for until he felt the bitterness return between them. He took a step closer, and she took another step back.

"I'm sorry. I shouldn't have—" She wouldn't meet his eyes. "Thank you." Returning her gaze to Mr. Magpie, she inhaled a deep, furious breath. Her fingers burned so severely, she looked down at them. Soft white crystals covered the tips like thimbles. Her chest heaved, her lungs fighting back against the grip of her ribcage. When she curled her fingers into fists, the ice melted away.

"You don't need to thank me, Foxx. Or apologize."

Foxx looked at him as if she'd forgotten his presence. Rubbing her fingers together, she shook her head and turned toward her sister. Without another word, she walked away from him. The space growing between them felt tangible, like the dark and dense presence of the black-walled barriers.

Foxx touched Declan's shoulder and heard him whisper, "Foxx is here. I'm going to stand up, okay?" Iris nodded, wiping snot from her nose with the back of her hand. When Declan stood, Foxx took his place.

"This is our fault," Iris cried in her ear. "Again, it's our fault. Foxx… he's…"

"I know." Foxx had ceased crying. The icy bitterness on her fingers had spread throughout her whole body, enduring in the heat of the desert. Anger and wrath permeated her entire being, swallowing her up until it was all she felt. She closed her eyes and saw a city on the beach surrounded in clouds of darkness. It felt like a memory, though she had no point of reference as to where it might be. Then she opened her eyes, and it disappeared, forgotten like a fragment of a dream.

When Iris calmed down enough to stand, Foxx helped her to her feet. Seth ran to join them and wrapped her in another hug. Declan took her hand on the opposite side of Seth, and Asher and Foxx stood in front of them with their backs to Mr. Magpie's limp form.

"We need to get him down and bury him properly," Asher said.

"No, you can't!" Seth cried. "The soldiers told us if they came back and he had been taken down, they would put someone else up there. They said he needed to stay there to remind us what happens if we stand against the King and Queen."

Declan frowned. "I bet they did."

Asher asked, "Who said that, Seth? One of the soldiers?"

Seth thought for a moment. "It was something like dragon, I think."

"Dagon?" Declan guessed.

"That's it, yes."

Declan clenched the fingers of his free hand and shared a furious look with Asher. Both knew Dagon Wraith and the kind of attributes he glorified in himself.

"There was someone else with him. He grabbed my shirt." Seth's hand slid up to touch the back of his neck, remembering what it had felt like to have the soldier's hand clutching his collar. Iris' eyes lit with outrage, and Declan felt her grip tighten, adding fuel to his own inner fire.

Asher crouched so he stood eye level with Seth. Extending a hand to him, he said, "I feel like we haven't officially met. My name is Asher."

Seth looked from Asher's face to his calloused hand. Cautiously, he accepted the handshake. "Hello Asher, I'm Seth."

"Wonderful to meet you, lad. I'm only sorry it's during such sad times."

Seth nodded and pulled his hand away, letting it fall to his side.

"But here's the thing, Seth. I kind of have a little secret." Asher held his thumb and index finger together to display how little. "Everyone here already knows, but you haven't heard it yet. Do you want to? Can I trust you to keep it for me?"

Seth tilted his head before looking up at Iris, who offered him an encouraging smile. Since her cheeks were red and puffy from crying, Seth realized it must be a pretty good secret if she was still able to smile while feeling so distraught. He nodded again.

Asher squared Seth's shoulders to his own. "The truth is, though I answer to Asher, my full name is Prince Alexander Asher Aldrich." Seth's eyes widened, his eyebrows disappearing beneath his hair as he took a step closer to Iris. "You don't have to be afraid. I'm on your side. On their side." He glanced up at Iris and Foxx before whispering, "Who wouldn't be, right?" Seth grinned shyly. "So, because I am the Prince, I have the authority to declare that this man be taken down and proper buried. If anyone has a problem with that, they will have to answer to me."

Seth again looked up at Iris to see teeth peeking through her smile. She confirmed what Asher said to be true, and he looked back at the Prince with a heavy sigh of relief.

Asher put a finger to his lips. "But remember, you can't tell anyone while I'm here, okay? Once I'm gone, if anyone says anything about Mr. Magpie, you can tell them the Prince of Arkaemor came through town and took him down himself, all right?"

Seth smiled and held his thumb in the air. "Okay, Prince Alexan… er… Asher." Asher rubbed the top of his head, scrambling his hair. Suddenly, Seth looked worried. "Can I tell Rossnetta? I don't like keeping secrets from her."

Asher chuckled and agreed. Then he rose and looked at Declan. "Dec, you want to help me?"

Declan asked Iris, "Are you going to be okay?"

She nodded and slid an arm over Seth's shoulder. "We're going back to Rossnetta's."

Foxx kissed her sister's cheek. "I'm going to stay and help them." Unsurprised, Iris felt a sense of relief in her sister's returned strength.

Asher said, "Foxx, you don't—"

"Are you seriously going to try and stop me?" Foxx put her hand on her hip and raised her eyebrows.

He ran his hand through his hair. "Nope, definitely not."

"I'll walk Iris and Seth back and see if Rossnetta has a shovel," Declan said. Iris glimpsed Mr. Magpie's body one last time, hoping to burn the image into her brain so she would never forget why they were fighting—what they were fighting for. Then Declan pulled her and Seth back toward town.

Without acknowledging each other, Asher and Foxx turned back to Mr. Magpie and watched as the last fragment of the sun disappeared from the sky behind him.

CHAPTER 42

A NEW ADDITION

They set up camp outside of town near the grave they'd dug for Mr. Magpie. Rossnetta and Seth joined them around the fire, bringing with them a tray of mugs, a kettle, and her jar of tea leaves.

Though an air of sorrow hung heavily over them, like the humidity of the rainforest after a storm, they tried to enjoy their time together. Seth and Rossnetta told stories about Mr. Magpie and the happenings in Kesken Ala, and Foxx and Iris shared a few exciting tales from their journey so far. They talked until the waxing moon climbed high into the sky.

Seth and Rossnetta turned in first, despite Seth's groggy protests about not being even a little bit tired. Iris and Declan went next, laying face to face on a blanket not far from the fire with their fingers intertwined between them.

Asher and Foxx stayed awake a while longer, sitting on opposite sides of the flames. Sharing the trait of overthinking, it seemed unlikely either of them would get much sleep, and neither had yet given in to the temptation to try. The flames popped and sizzled between them, shooting glowing embers into the darkness above.

Pulling himself from the inner worries plaguing his thoughts, Asher summoned enough courage to ask, "How are you?"

To his surprise, she looked down at her hands and replied honestly. "Sorrowful about Mr. Magpie. Filled with a sweltering rage like I've never felt before. Nervous about getting to the

Monastery and what we might find there." As well as a hundred other things she'd been obsessively chronicling in a cycle of truths and emotions.

"I understand."

His words needlessly irritated her, and she mumbled, "Of course you do." Several silent minutes passed before she looked at him. "This is where all the magic happens, isn't it?"

His brow creased. "What do you mean?"

She smiled unwittingly to herself and stared down at a stone she played with between her fingers. It was smooth and coated in the red clay of the desert. "You and me beneath the moon, baring our souls to one another."

During their travels together, Iris had often gone to bed first, leaving Asher and Foxx to spend most of their nights together by the fireside. Sometimes she would read and he would write. Other times they would sit in silence, lost in their own musings but comforted by each other's presence. Either way, whether wandering in thoughts or conversation, they would sit by the fire, bonding effortlessly without really even noticing it happening.

"I love our late night conversations." He held her gaze across the fire, watching the amber glow dance against her olive skin.

After a long moment, she averted her eyes. "Or I guess I should say: me baring my soul and you lying through your teeth." She sat up straighter and dropped the stone, placing her hands on her knees to prevent them from fidgeting.

The warmth spawned by her sentiment disappeared as quickly as it had come. Asher sighed and pushed hair out of his face. "That's fair, I guess." It wasn't true, but it made sense that she saw it that way. He had bared his soul on several occasions, and if she took the time to look back through her memories, he thought she would be able to see the truths he'd shared amongst the evasions.

"You guess?"

His eyes met hers again, and the ferocious wrath she'd been masking—containing—was alight within them. Still, he didn't look away. "Not everything was a deception, Foxx."

"But how can I be sure, Asher? When it feels like every second of it was a manipulation? A lie to trick us into doing exactly what you needed us to do. Congratulations! You've got all seven keys and are ready to fulfill your destiny." She swallowed, forcing saliva past the burning lump in her throat. Her fingers hadn't warmed since they'd found Mr. Magpie, and she rubbed the tips of them together, hoping the friction would melt the icy chill.

"Is that the issue?" This sparked his attention. If he only needed to prove their bond was as real for him as it had been for her, maybe she could move past this. "You think I somehow conned you into loving me? That I feel nothing?"

Her heart toppled into her stomach at his easy use of the word *love*. It spilled out in fragmented pieces, littering the sand with shattered memories. "You forced me to feel things for you. You charmed me to orchestrate the outcome you desired despite the fact that I fought against you from day one. How did you choose me anyway? Wouldn't Iris have satisfied your needs just as well? I'm sure wooing her would have been far easier. Or was the challenge a contributing factor?"

His temperature rose, and he fought to keep his anger in check. "Now you're just being hurtful."

"How am I to know what was real and what was part of some master plan to be a hero?"

A jolt of anger boiled his blood, and he snapped, "That's really what you think of me, Foxxglove? You think I want to be the bloody hero? You think *that's* what's important? I don't want this, Foxx! This life! I never wanted to be king. I never wanted any of it."

"How am I supposed to believe a word you say, Asher? Oh, I'm sorry, *Prince Alexander*." She spat the title as if it were rotten mushrooms in her mouth, dirty and dry, impossible to swallow, and clinging to her tongue. "I don't even know who you are!"

Growling in frustration and spectacularly failing in his attempt not to raise his voice, he yelled back, "Yes, Foxx, you do! You know exactly who I am. Better than most, I'd wager. You're just blinded by your stubborn pride, and you aren't paying attention." He'd felt her anger before, but he hadn't anticipated the hatred he'd see in her eyes.

"Fine, then." Seething, she stood with the intention of storming off, but Asher was already on his feet in front of her.

"Fine? That's all you have to say to me? You're going to insult me and have that be the end of it? I'm sorry, Foxx. You know I'm sorry. I never meant to hurt you. You know me, Foxxglove. You do. I never meant for things to turn out this way. I never expected I'd—" Asher let out a breath of air and sucked his lips between his teeth.

Looking down at her fingers, Foxx sighed. Her boiling fury

suddenly faded to exhaustion, as if she'd already given up the fight and was ready to sit the next round out. Her shoulders slumped with another exhale, and her eyes burned with suppressed tears. "What do you want from me, Asher?"

Asher clasped her hands in his own. Foxx didn't pull away. "You know what I want, love?" His husky voice, thick with emotion, made her heart hurt. "I want to go back to that moment in the rain before everything changed."

She searched his eyes, and despite her mistrust, she could sense the truth in this statement. He did long for that moment, as she'd spent so many hours yearning for the same thing: when he'd wrapped his arms around her, caressed the scar that marred her face, and called her stunning. When he'd made her feel things she'd never felt before.

But it didn't matter. It didn't change anything. "I don't think I know how to do that." For a heavy moment, she mourned the loss of a life unlived; a path not taken; the abrupt and unfair halt of a love story never told, as if the back of the book had been torn away, robbing the reader's chance to find out if the prince and princess got to live happily ever after.

He scowled at her stubbornness. "So it's over then? Just like that? Six years of my life searching for you, Foxxglove. Do you get that? Six years. And now I finally have you, and I'm supposed to let you go, after everything?" Releasing one of her hands, he gestured to the space between them. "You really think you're capable of walking away from this?"

Foxx's anger instantly reignited with a vengeance. "Don't challenge my capabilities, Asher. I already told you, and you agreed. Allies—not friends. And certainly not anything else." She ripped her hand from his grasp. "Not ever."

Then she stomped toward her bedroll and laid down facing away from him, doing her best to keep her body frozen so as not to reveal her sobs, and hoping desperately that when she finally fell to pieces, he wouldn't still be watching.

Asher stood by the fire for a long while, his feet rooted to the spot as he watched the flames dance. Then he sighed with a heavy heart and laid down on his own roll, feeling like the battle hadn't even begun, and he'd already lost.

C

The next morning, Iris was startled awake by a dark shadow hanging over her. She squealed and bolted upright, elbowing Declan's cheek in her momentum. Seth stood next to them, staring at her innocently. "Sorry, Iris! I didn't mean to scare you." Then he looked at Declan rubbing his sore face. "Sorry, Declan."

"It's all right, buddy. You really know how to wake a guy up, huh?" Declan wiped sleep from his eyes as he joined Iris in a seated position. Seth smiled, and his head shrank into his shoulders like a turtle shying morosely into its shell. "Don't worry, it's not the first time Iris has blackened my eye, just the first time it happened accidentally." He chuckled and nudged her. Iris lifted her hands to cover her pink cheeks as Seth's brows rose in surprise.

Foxx and Asher heard the conversation and stirred. When Asher saw Seth, he rolled onto his back and stared up at the sky. Foxx sat up. "Merry morning, Seth. Did you come to see us off?"

"Actually—" Seth paused, leaning back on the heels of his feet. "No."

"No?" Iris yawned, lifting her arms into a stretch.

Seth positioned himself equal distance from all of them and placed his hands together in his lap. "I am coming with you!" The company exchanged looks of surprise. Asher sat up.

Foxx asked, "What do you mean, Seth?"

"Okay, listen." Seth cleared his throat, trying to make his voice sound as manly and mature as possible. "You have to let me come with you. Ms. Rossnetta already agreed to let me, and I can't stay in Kesken Ala anymore, and I can be brave, I promise, and I will learn to fight, and I won't get in the way, I promise, and I already packed a bag, see? And I know a little about hunting and trapping, and Mr. —he was teaching me how to cook, and I promise I won't get in the way. Please let me come. I can't..." He paused again, trying to keep his emotions at bay and display an aura of strength. "It's too hard to be here. First my mother, and then... Well, you know. It's been three months, and I thought it would get easier, but it hasn't. It's worse every day." He looked at each of them with the saddest eyes a little boy could muster. "Please?"

The group stared at him with dumbfounded faces. Foxx began to speak but stopped herself with another uncertain gasp. She looked at Iris, who appeared to be commiserating with the boy's speech, which Foxx thought was not a good sign.

"Seth, would you mind letting us discuss it before we give you an answer?" Asher could feel Foxx's eyes on him, but kept his focus on Seth. With a glum expression, Seth dropped his head, nodding as he looked down at the sand. "It's a big decision. Give us a few moments, all right?" The boy agreed and moved to sit next to the extinguished fire pit.

Asher, Foxx, Iris, and Declan rose from their bedrolls and walked several paces away so they would be out of Seth's earshot. "So, what do we think?" Asher intertwined his fingers and stretched them out in front of him.

"You can't be serious." Foxx looked shocked they were even discussing it. "He's a child. We can't bring him with us."

"It would be another mouth to feed," Declan pointed out in agreement. "Someone else to look after."

"It will be dangerous!" Foxx said, since that was the most important defense.

Asher said, "It's dangerous everywhere. We don't know how bad things are going to get before the end. Kesken Ala won't be the exception. I think the death of Mr. Magpie proves that." Internally, he cursed himself for disagreeing with Foxx again, but he also sympathized with Seth, knowing all too well how painful and deeply rooted the need to escape could feel.

"No, it proves that when people are around us, they die." Foxx felt a piercing ache in her chest as she admitted the fear aloud.

Asher said her name, but she kept her eyes on the landscape in the distance. He had known she would be feeling that way: blaming herself and stacking all of the responsibility on her own shoulders. "Mr. Magpie helped you and Iris because he saw something good in you and wanted to be a part of it. You can't blame yourself for his decisions, and you certainly can't blame yourself for the cruel measures of the Legion."

"Since you seem so enlightened on the subject, Asher, what exactly *can* I blame myself for?" Foxx crossed her arms and glared at him.

Though he could think of several unhelpful responses to that question, he kept them to himself. "I'm just saying, yes, he was killed because of his connection to you, and before this war is over, that may be true of others as well, but that doesn't make it your fault. Showing you kindness was Mr. Magpie's choice, perhaps the very last important decision he ever made. How dare you take that from him and taint it with your own self-loathing?"

Iris' mouth dropped open, stupefied by Asher's harsh and direct assertion. Her eyes snapped back and forth between them as she wondered what Foxx might say. Iris hadn't considered it from Asher's perspective, but she thought he did have a valid point. "I don't think Mr. Magpie would take back his actions if he had known the outcome. In fact, I'm almost sure he wouldn't have. It's pretty obvious that Seth doesn't blame us for what happened to Mr. Magpie. Neither does Rossnetta. They see the enemy for who she is —a wicked and vicious Queen."

"I think it's important we remember who the real enemy is too and not let disagreements divide us," Asher said.

Foxx was astounded. She looked at Declan, hoping he would be a voice of reason, but he seemed tongue-tied as well, unsure which side to stand on.

Iris added, "And I think Asher made another good point. Nowhere is safe. If he's with us, we can protect him."

Declan finally relented. "Iris won't be able to focus on anything she's doing if she's worrying about him stuck here unprotected." Iris smiled and reached for his hand.

"He's too young!" Foxx exclaimed.

"He isn't much younger than I was when we first left home."

"That was different, Iris. We didn't have a choice. He will be safe here with Rossnetta."

"He isn't safe anywhere, Foxx. None of us are." Iris tilted her head, pleading with her sister to back down. "And you can bet if the Queen gets a whiff of our connection to him, she will come here and find even more awful ways to use our family to hurt us."

Declan scuffed the stubble on his jaw. "She may already know. Us being here may have put him at risk."

Foxxglove put her hands on her hips and took a step back, somehow feeling claustrophobic in the boundless desert. "I can't believe I am hearing this."

"I think the only way to decide is to vote," Asher said.

"I think it's pretty clear most of us already agree." Iris met her sister's eyes again, willing her to change her mind. "Come on, Foxxglove. I want you to be on board with this. He needs us." She looked over her shoulder at Seth. Foxx criss-crossed her fingers together on top of her head as she looked from Iris to Declan and then to Asher.

"I'll watch out for him," he promised.

Foxx felt something rude on the tip of her tongue, but she didn't set it free. "Fine." Then she turned away from all of them, smothering the tightening panic in her chest.

Iris beamed and spun back to Seth with a big smile and two thumbs up.

"I can come?" Seth sat up on his knees. "Really?"

Asher and Iris walked over to him. "You can come, but you have to make sure you listen to everything we say. That's very important, because we can't protect you if you don't follow instructions. Do you think you can do that?"

Seth stood up, his back straight as a rod, and flung his hand into a salute. "I promise, sir, Prince, sir!" They both laughed, and Seth ran over to hug them.

Asher patted him on the head. "All right, let's get things cleaned up and get moving. We still have a two day hike through the desert before we reach the Monastery." Seth nodded in agreement and began rolling up Iris' bedroll for her.

Foxx stared out over the open desert, watching long shadows shrink across the terrain.

Declan approached her, stopping at her side and folding his arms as he took in the view. After a quiet moment, he exhaled. "They're right, you know. Mr. Magpie wouldn't want either of you to blame yourselves."

"How could you possibly know that, Declan? You never met him."

"I know because, from what you've both told me anyway, it sounds like he was a good man, and good men aren't afraid to do what's right, regardless of the consequences."

Foxx released a breath and willed her anger to fizzle away. Her temper ignited so easily now and with such ferocity. She imagined it had something to do with ice crystals on her fingers and all the confusing words Sirena had spoken about the darkness inside spilling over like a boiling pot. She looked down at her hands, but saw nothing amiss. Had she imagined it? Was she beginning to lose her mind, like her mother?

Out of control emotions promote out of control mistakes.

That's what her mother had always taught her, but lately, she felt herself losing the grip on her controlled demeanor. How many mistakes might it take before she regained some semblance of the woman she used to be? Had something inside of her shifted so drastically that she would never find her way back? The face of the Konungr flashed into her thoughts, startling her so her eyebrows pinched together.

Declan broke through her introspection. "I know if it had been me, I wouldn't want you blaming yourself." She turned to look at him, and he matched her. "Everything will work out how it's meant to, Foxx. Some of us will live, and some of us will die. As long as Sirena is taken out in the process, then it doesn't matter. No cost is too great to see that outcome achieved."

"No cost?" she echoed, feeling a pain in her heart she didn't understand and the continued reflection of Vali Kirkavall's infectious smile blazing through her mind's eye.

Declan nodded. "Whatever it takes."

C

Foxx, Asher, and Declan returned to town to fill their bags with food and water for the journey. Iris and Seth crossed the barrier into Metsa Sateen to gather flowers for Mr. Magpie's grave, and Seth picked some yellow birds of paradise as a parting gift for Rossnetta.

They met at Rossnetta's house, and Seth set the flowers in a vase on the table. Then they all walked to Mr. Magpie's gravesite, and Asher spoke a short eulogy over him. Though he hadn't known the man personally, Foxx and Iris had shared enough for him to make it honorable. Iris said a few words, too, but cut herself short when she began to cry.

Rossnetta also shed tears, though she'd had three months to grieve already. Foxx didn't cry at all. Her rage was nearly palpable, despite her unrelenting endeavor to suffocate it. Asher noticed, but after their conversation the previous night, he didn't dare attempt to comfort her. He didn't speak to her at all, except when explicitly necessary.

Seth hugged Rossnetta for a very long time, asking over and over if she was absolutely sure she would be alright without him. She assured him she would be, and he promised to come see her when he could.

Rossnetta hugged the rest of them, kissing their cheeks as if they were her own children. Then, with bittersweet emotions, she stood on the outskirts of town, waving at them until they disappeared into the mid-morning desert.

C

The first day was long and hot, as was to be expected in the territory of the Grim Wilds. Foxx had not missed the dry heat, but Iris seemed pleased to have returned to the sandy plains. Their journey had started in the Wilds, and it seemed fitting they should find themselves back there to finish it. The map they'd discovered in their father's desk had led them to the correct place all along. Looking back over the past four and half months, it seemed unbelievable they'd learned and experienced so much: a whole world of adventure, new friendships, and knowledge of things they had never thought possible.

They traveled all through the day and camped the first night on a flat rock formation high off the ground. Exhausted from the hiking and the heat, they all went to bed early. When the sun rose, they were off again.

Seth did a great job keeping pace with everyone. As they traveled, they told him more about their journey so far. They shared how Asher had saved them from the nieda and told him about the children of Ataraxia. They described in great detail the remarkable city of Petrichor, and from how marvelous they made it sound, he hoped to be able to see it for himself someday.

Iris recounted her leap into the gorgeous lagoon, and Declan chimed in to share how she'd saved the day by climbing the roots, injured and bleeding, and shooting the beast dead. Seth found this fascinating and totally believable because of how awesome and brave he knew Iris to be.

Then they told him more about Jericho and the dragon and the soldiers in purple and gray, the Reko Raptors and Hector, and the Mad King and his beautiful wife. They promised to let him experience barrier jumping as soon as the opportunity presented itself.

When they explained the plan to find Pyhä-ki and kill the Queen, he was intrigued by the thought of such a great and noble adventure. Unsurprisingly, he was up for whatever they wanted to do without displaying a single smidgen of fear.

On their luncheon break, he and Asher sparred with swords. Seth told them he'd been practicing with sticks since Iris saved him from the bullies, whom he was pleased to report had been nothing but kind to him, and possibly a little scared, since she threatened them. Declan pulled Iris close and kissed her cheek after hearing the story of how she valiantly took on a couple of ten year olds to save her little friend.

Foxx decided, despite the obvious insanity and danger of bringing a child along with them, she was glad to have him there as a distraction. With everyone's focus on him, it was much easier to avoid focusing on each other. At times, she would catch Asher glancing at her, though he always looked away the moment their eyes met.

Seth's presence didn't seem to deter Iris and Declan from growing closer. Foxx thought it was nice, but worrisome, though she assumed her fears only stemmed from her obvious trust issues, and possibly the fact that he'd once kidnapped them. He'd done much to prove himself since then, however, and Iris seemed delighted, so Foxx decided to be happy for her. Plus, she liked Declan. His stiff and reserved demeanor had blossomed effortlessly into one of easygoing peacefulness. Most importantly, he was good to Iris. She thought she must have been wrong under the falls when she'd predicted he would choose Orion in the end and felt glad of it.

They arrived at the sand-covered Monastery before sunset. Asher peeked his head through the door as Iris, Foxx, Declan, and Seth passed around a skin of water.

When Iris had her fill, she joined Asher. "Yep, it looks as creepy as I remember."

"We should probably get going, shouldn't we?" Declan looked up at the cloudy sky.

Foxx agreed. "It's going to get dark soon, and it seems like a storm might be brewing."

Seth joined Asher and Iris by the door and looked down into the eerie, shadow-filled room. "Are you sure it's safe?" He stifled a gulp.

Iris put a hand on his shoulder. "Foxx and I were here a few months ago, and it was fine. Come on." She crawled through the space between the doorframe and the sand dune and slid until she hit the ground on the other side. The table with the skull carving stood at the center of the room, as it had before. Turning around, she called to Seth, "See? Totally safe." He looked skeptical, but Asher helped him through the hole, and he slid down into her arms.

Foxx stepped up next to Declan, who loitered on the far side of the building watching the sun fall. Opal, crimson, and salmon were smeared across the sky. "It's really beautiful isn't it?"

"Very."

She looked sideways at him. "Are you all right?"

He met her inspection with a smile. "Yes, fine. I… I don't know how to explain it."

"I think I understand." She returned her gaze to the glowing sky. Then she spoke his name again, and he said, "Yeah?"

"I'm really glad you're here with us. I know we had a rough start, but Iris seems really happy with you. I appreciate you taking care of her, more than you know, and I'm sorry for misjudging you."

His face flushed. "It's fine." Looking once more up into the choppy sky, he said, "We should get moving. It would be nice to be in and out before this storm hits."

She agreed and followed him, ducking down to peer inside. Asher, Iris, and Seth waited at the bottom of the dune. With one last glance at Declan, Foxx asked, "Ready?"

He nodded. "After you."

CHAPTER 43

IN BETWEEN

Crawling through the hole, Foxx slid down into the dusty room. It was darker than she'd realized, and her eyes needed time to adjust. Declan slid in behind her, and she offered him a hand. They blinked as they scanned the room for the others. A spark of fire illuminated the space, blinding their nearly adapted vision, and Foxx held up a hand to block the shine.

"That's better." Asher held his torch out so it brightened the entirety of the room. He and Iris stood in front of the corridor with Seth, though Seth soon ventured to the center of the room where the light had revealed a carving on the table. Foxx and Declan joined Asher and Iris by the corridor.

"So this is it, huh?" Foxx gazed into the darkness, feeling the same reluctance she'd felt at the black walls. For a brief moment, she considered running back up the sand mound and fleeing into the desert. "I honestly don't remember seeing this doorway here."

"We stood right here, in this exact spot." Iris took a step closer to the entrance, stopping next to her sister and pointing at the ground. Foxx shrugged, and Iris shook her head in disbelief.

"That's the power of the illusion. It makes sense you don't remember, but we all see it now, right?" Asher looked back at Declan, who nodded, then at Seth, who said, "I see it, but this carving is much more interesting to look at." He ran his fingers down the groove of the skull.

Iris looked over her shoulder at him and chuckled. Then something else caught her eye, and she crossed the room to the eastern wall. "The painting of Lacuna Kaput is gone."

Foxx tilted her head. "How can that be?"

Declan said, "It was probably stolen by scavengers."

Iris tucked her hair behind her ear and folded her arms as if combating a chill. "That makes me sad." Foxx agreed.

"Let's focus on the task at hand." Asher tapped the doorframe.

"This is definitely the spot. I feel that horrible pressure to look away." Declan let his head fall from side to side as he rolled his shoulders, trying to relax away the unease.

Foxx put a hand on either side of the frame and leaned her head inside. The feeling of dread grew, and her stomach felt fluttery, like she might be falling. She looked back at Asher, then at her sister. "Are you sure you're ready for this?"

Iris smirked and returned to them. "*Ready*? Define your terms."

"Are you prepared for what we might find through here? However horrible it might be." Foxx thought of the very real possibility that they were about to come face to face with their father's corpse. She had no idea what to expect of the In-Between, but she wondered if her father could have survived being trapped there for so long. He'd been a soldier, so perhaps he would be fine, but they wouldn't know for sure until they braved the corridor.

"I'm ready." Iris hugged her sister around her shoulders with a single arm.

"Do you want me to go first?" Asher asked.

Foxx shook her head but didn't turn to look at him, finding herself transfixed by the mysterious hallway of darkness. She saw patches of color and movement within the pitch but thought it must be her eyes playing tricks. "No. I'll go first. Should I take the torch?"

"You can't carry a lit torch through a barrier. I suspect this will be the same."

Nodding, Foxx took a single step into the corridor and stretched her hands out to either side so the tips of her fingers grazed the walls. When nothing monumental happened, she took a second step, then a third. At first, nothing felt out of the ordinary, but after her fifth step, she felt a presence similar to a barrier take her breath away.

Jumping from Cordillera to the Grim Wilds had taken longer than she'd grown accustomed to, and she guessed the hallway might be the same. She pressed on, expecting to soon be released from the suffocation. Her panic grew with each passing step as the lack of air persisted. Stopping to look over her shoulder, she realized she could no longer see her sister or the others in the entranceway behind her. She croaked out Iris' name, but no response came. Her nerves tingled with anxious electricity that cooled her fingertips as they glided against the wall.

Iris and Asher had been certain the corridor was one of the Creator's seven doorways to the In-Between. If the Queen had spelled the entrances to prevent people from finding them, it was logical to think she would have made it a terrifying experience to endure in the hopes that anyone attempting to find the In-Between would grow too afraid and turn back.

Fear crawled up her spine like a creeping insect, sending prickling needles throughout her limbs. Picking up the pace, she latched on to her courage and continued through the dense shadow.

Just when she thought she couldn't hold her breath a moment longer, the end of the invisible barrier slid over her face, and a surge of muggy oxygen forced its way into her lungs. She dropped to her knees, wheezing and groping for air.

Moments later, Iris emerged and fell next to her. Together, they dragged themselves forward in the grass, crawling on their hands and knees and striving to get out of the way so the others wouldn't tumble over them when they arrived. Iris flung her pack from her shoulders and rolled onto her back. Foxx mirrored her action, removing her bag and bow, and lifting her hands high above her head. Gasping for air, they let their chests rise and fall as their breathing normalized.

Seth stumbled through next, followed closely by Asher, and then Declan.

"What in the world was that?" Iris gasped.

"Horrible." Seth coughed and rolled onto his side.

"A really thick barrier," Asher answered through a scratchy throat. He reached for Declan, touching his arm to see if he was all right.

"I hope we don't have to go back the same way." Seth sounded like he might cry.

One by one, their breathing settled. Foxx was the first to pull herself to her feet. She extended an arm to her sister, who accepted it gratefully and allowed Foxx to help her up. They took in the surrounding area, spinning in a circle so they could see everything.

Behind them stood the black hallway. Large, gray bricks covered in moss surrounded the frame, and ivy spilled down around it.

A patch of grass lay at their feet, encircled by a forest of tropical trees like the ones growing in Metsa Sateen. An aroma of dampness and humidity, made more prevalent by the light breeze whistling through the leaves, enveloped their nostrils. Aside from the tune of the wind, the mysterious realm was impossibly silent. Not the call of a bird or the chirping of a cricket could be heard, a stark variation from the rainforest territory, despite the perceptible similarities.

"This place feels bizarre," Iris said.

Once everyone made it to their feet, they followed the path that stretched out opposite the door. The ground grew wetter with each passing step, squishing beneath their boots. Eventually, they stood in a thin layer of water.

"It's a swamp." Seth pointed ahead where the trees began to thin, growing further apart and allowing them a better view of the scenery.

Asher agreed. "I think you're right, Seth. We shouldn't go too deep into the water. Be on the lookout for higher ground."

Before the water level reached their ankles, the path began to rise at a slight incline, morphing into a walkway of stone bricks. Three steps led to a bridge that spanned a stagnant pool of water, and from the bridge, they got an elevated view of the marshland surrounding them on either side. The trees cleared enough for them to see the sky, which was midnight blue and splattered with glistening specks of light. Though pigments of magenta and cerulean painted the galaxy in spectacular artistry, they saw no moon.

On the other side of the bridge stood a decorated wall surrounded by the same bricks that held the corridor behind them and an awning held up by two stone pillars. The massive roots of a kapok tree cascaded over the structure like the legs of a giant spider spinning its prey into a cocoon. The tree had grown directly above the decorated wall, and its roots created a blockade preventing anyone from traveling around or over it, marking the end of the road. The roots slid down into the swampy water where patches of lime algae, lily pads, and all other manner of water dwelling plants adorned the surface. Out in the bog, will-o'-the-wisps levitated above the water's surface, hoping to mislead them, luring them into the swamp and away from the enchanting door.

When Foxx glimpsed the symbols on the wall, she sucked in a breath. "I've been here before."

"Don't be daft, you can't have." Asher immediately regretted his words.

Shooting him a glare, she said through her teeth, "Don't call me *daft*. I saw it during the storm. After the Queen spoke to me." She looked at Iris. At the mens' questioning expressions, she said, "I'll explain later."

Declan crossed the platform to look out over the water. "This isn't what I expected the In-Between to look like. I'm not sure what I expected, but it definitely wasn't this."

Asher approached the wall to get a better view of the crescent moon carved into it. It rose to his full height and stretched about a *syli* wide. Inside the crescent, seven symbols identical to the stone keys were laid out in a circular pattern, with the Cordilleran moon at its center. Asher ran his finger down a crack in the middle. "I think these are the doors."

Foxx and Iris joined him. "They are. They opened in my vision. Right here." When she pointed to the crack, her fingers accidentally brushed his, and she cringed away.

Iris asked, "Where do the keys go?"

"Over here." Declan stood beside a stone table at the edge of the platform. The others approached it to find a replica of the door's design: a crescent moon circling seven symbols, each recessed as if an object of the same size could fit perfectly inside.

Asher's face lit up as he ran his fingers over the shapes. "This is where the keys go. It's all real. Actually, properly real!" Seth touched each of the carved out hollows, running his fingers along the insides of them as Asher had done.

"You had doubts?" Iris asked.

"Only slightly."

"Foxxglove?" A voice from behind shocked them from their skins. They whipped around to find a man with a long, shabby beard and dirty clothing staring at them. "Foxxglove, is that you?"

Foxx froze, observing the strangely familiar man. She took a step toward him, and Asher reached for her arm. Yanking it away, she whispered, "Father?"

"No way," Declan uttered.

"Daddy?" Tears pooled in Iris' eyes.

"Foxxglove, it's me, honey. It's me." His voice was rough, the voice of someone who hadn't spoken for a very long time. Stepping closer, Foxx examined his face. He was filthy, as only a man who'd spent six years in a swamp could be. His hair had grown thin and gray, but his face didn't seem to have aged a single day.

He touched her cheek. "When did you have time to grow so?"

"You've been gone a long time, Father." A tear rolled from her eye onto his fingers, and she put her hand atop his.

His eyes lingered on her scar as he grazed it. "No." He took a step back and shook his head. "No, it can't be. I've only just arrived. I was trying to get into Celestelvyra, but I couldn't figure out how to get the doors open. I've been trying to find a way to open them so I could come back to you."

Iris stepped up to join them. "Daddy?"

Turning to face her, he smiled. "My baby, look at you!" Tears filled his eyes.

Hovering near Iris in distrust, Declan swallowed the heaviness blocking his throat.

The noise drew Sawyer's attention. "Declan? What on earth are you doing here?"

"Good to see you, Lieutenant." It occurred to him immediately that he and Orion had been foolish to imagine they could have turned Sawyer over to the Queen. Not just because of the state they found him in, but because he was their lieutenant, a man they trusted and respected deeply. "I'm glad to see you're all right."

Again, Sawyer shook his head in confusion. "I don't understand. What's happening? How ever did you find me?"

Iris threw her arms around him, unable to hold back the tears bursting free.

Foxx wrapped her arms around both of them and squeezed. "We found you. We finally found you."

After a long embrace, he pulled away and used his grimy hands to wipe his face, smearing the dirt that soiled his skin. "I don't understand. Explain to me please, how did you grow so much?"

Foxx and Iris shared a glance. "You've been gone more than six years, Father. We've been looking for you." He tilted his head, trying to interpret her words as if she'd spoken them in a different language.

Asher left Seth by the table and walked over to them, extending his hand. "Lieutenant Belamour. Brilliant to see you again."

Sawyer's eyes grew huge. "Alexander! Why, you've grown, too!

What are you doing here? Are you the one who brought my girls to me? Amaryllis always said you would look after them." He leaned closer and spoke behind his fingers. "To be honest, I didn't believe her. But here you are!"

"He came with us, Daddy. He helped us find you. We couldn't have done it without him." Iris gave Asher's hand a squeeze.

Sawyer dug around in his pants pocket, retrieving an empty crystal vial cut into the shape of an arrowhead with a cork on top. "I believe this belongs to you, Your Highness. It's why you're here, isn't it?"

"The Artifact," Foxx breathed.

"Thank you, Lieutenant. It is indeed." Asher gave him a slight bow and slipped the vial into his pocket. Despite Sawyer's state, he felt grateful they hadn't needed to loot the vial off his corpse.

Suddenly, Sawyer's face went dark. He looked at Foxx and groaned. "Your mother. She's..." Foxx nodded, and Iris wiped away more tears. "Sirena. It was Sirena! I came here because... Oh, my sweet Amaryllis." His shadowed features transformed into rage. "Where is Sirena? Is she still alive?" He turned to Asher and grabbed his shirt with both hands. "Well? Is she?"

"She's alive, all right."

A spark of fear ricocheted through the group as they spun to see Queen Sirena standing before them in a sparkling, scarlet dress that hugged her all the way to her knees.

Foxx felt her presence like a touchable aura that emanated from where she stood. Pressure began to build behind her eyes and against her temples, and she wondered if the sensation might be the result of Sirena trying to invade her thoughts. Momentarily light-headed, she squinted and wiped her brow, regaining control quickly and pushing back against the foreign force. The pressure ebbed, seemingly shielded despite its persistence.

On either side of Sirena knelt two men. One Foxx recognized right away as Orion. She heard Iris inhale a sharp breath at her back. With hands tied behind him, Orion's head hung forward so his hair draped over his face. His clothing was drenched in blood, so much blood that it didn't make sense for his heart to remain beating.

The other man didn't look familiar to her. Though not as bloody as Orion, he wasn't in great shape, either. His blood looked fresher. Some had dried across his skin or stiffened the fabric of his shirt, but in comparison to the bruises covering Orion, it was clear the second man hadn't been a captive nearly as long. Foxx mentally calculated the number of days since the attack on Jericho and wondered if Sirena had captured him then and had been torturing him ever since.

Neither man looked conscious. They sat upright on their knees, hovering as if in a trance.

Seth ducked behind the stone table, hoping to go unnoticed. Declan shifted to block the Queen's view of him. Foxx took a protective step in front of Sawyer, and Iris moved to join her, but Asher cut her off, placing himself next to Foxx with Iris behind him.

"Mother, what are you doing here?"

"Mother, mother, mother. Oh, what an exhausting word it is. Why anyone would willingly choose to be a mother, I will never understand." Viewing Sawyer's head sticking out behind Foxx and Asher, she cried, "Sawyer, fabulous to see you again, darling! You've no idea the time and resources I've spent searching for you all these years. Who would have thought you've been under my nose this entire time?"

He growled at her, enraged. In his reality, the Queen had murdered his wife days ago, and the unbridled fury, even in his bedraggled state, was formidable.

"Mother, why are you here?" Asher shifted his body so he stood closer to Foxx, unsure what his mother planned to do or how she'd managed to show up at the exact right moment. Had the corridor been a trap, ready to alert her the moment someone passed through? If so, wouldn't she have known Sawyer's location all this time?

Sirena gagged. "When are you going to get it, Alexander? I would think it pretty obvious by now." Her cackle was vicious.

"What is obvious?" To Asher's surprise, Foxx grabbed his hand and squeezed. She'd questioned the truth since Declan told them about the mysteriously improbable birth of the Prince and Princess. Asher glanced at her from the corner of his eye, but he feared taking his attention from the Queen for too long and decided to accept Foxx's comfort. He squeezed back and readjusted his grip.

"You're continuous whining of *mother, mother, mother.*" Taking a step closer to him, Sirena leaned forward and put a single hand next to her lips as if sharing a secret. "I am an immortal, my dear, one of the great numinae, if you weren't certain. And numinae cannot bear children. I'm sure you've heard this, haven't you? It must be some-where in that book you worship so dearly."

Confusion rocked him, swirling in his stomach like a spoiled piece of meat. "But I tho…"

"Well, you thought wrong, sweetie. You must have come across that information with all of the tedious research you've been doing." She tisked and shook her head with disapproval. Asher felt like he'd been kicked in the gut, though he remained motionless, trying with effort to wash the bewilderment from his face. "I killed your little tramp of a mother as soon as she pushed out your disgusting sister." Sirena's face contorted with pleasure at the memory.

Asher's distress transformed into anger at the insult to his sister and the murder of the birth mother he'd never had the opportunity to know. His mind raked through the new information, generating a million questions he may never learn the answers to. He and Avaline were nearly ten years apart, so where had his mother been when he was growing up? Had she lived in the castle? Had he known her without realizing who she was?

Sirena broke through his internal monologue. "Now we can get on to threatening each other like proper enemies, don't you think? With all of this family business out of the way."

"You—" He stepped toward her, but Foxx held him taut, trig-gering another teeth-baring grin from the Queen.

She jeered in a sing-song voice. "That's right, Foxxglove. Protect your lover from the big, bad witch. It's your life's purpose, after all. Isn't it?"

"What do you want?" Asher demanded, refusing to be pulled in deeper to the Queen's fallacies and mind games.

The Queen gestured to the doorway of Celestelvyra. "I want to stop you from entering the Sacred Realm, of course. A little bird whispered in my ear that you've collected all the keys." She wiggled her finger at him scoldingly. "Very naughty, Alexander. Though if it's true and they are on your person right now, perhaps you've also been extremely helpful and made my task of searching for them all the more easier."

"Okay, you have us here. What happens now?" Foxx felt eager to get things moving. It was pretty obvious they were all about to die, quite possibly in incredibly gruesome ways. If Asher was to be believed, Sirena couldn't be killed without Pyhä-ki, and since they'd yet to make it through the doors, it seemed impossible to think they should somehow succeed in doing so with her now there, guarding them.

"Hmm, a very good question, Foxxglove. So clever, as always. I can see why the tales of old speak so highly of you. What does happen next?" Tapping the bottom of her chin, Sirena asked, "Alexander? Thoughts?"

Iris glimpsed Seth behind the stone table and considered moving to protect him. She tried to think as Foxx would, analyzing the entire scene. Glancing sideways at her father, she found him still looking a chaotic mixture of disoriented fury.

They were all stuck out in the open, surrounded on either side by a swamp. Though they'd seen no signs of wildlife, there was no telling what kind of creatures may be lurking in the depths of the murky water guarding the gates to Celestelvyra.

In front of her, Asher adjusted his posture, drawing her attention. She realized he probably still had the keys in one of the outer pockets of his pack and wondered if she could retrieve them inconspicuously. It would be a tricky maneuver while the Queen stared directly at him, but if Sirena shifted her focus elsewhere, she may have a chance.

If she failed and was caught, Sirena would take the keys and murder them all.

In fact, it occurred to her that the Queen could end it now. She could kill them this instant, search their corpses, and claim the keys for herself. So why didn't she?

Foxx was thinking the same thing. She hadn't let go of Asher's hand, worried he might charge the Queen in some foolish attempt to distract her so the rest of them could get away. Declan guarded Seth. Her father stood at her back, but she didn't suspect he would be much help in his current condition. Iris' brain was calculating something, a fact made visible in the crinkle atop the bridge of her nose. Foxx found it concerning and hoped she didn't need to shield both Asher and her sister from sacrificing themselves.

Keeping them both in her peripherals, she tried to figure out the Queen's plan, her end game. If she intended to kill them all, then what could she be waiting for? Sirena was cunning, intentional, so if the goal was to hoard the keys so no one could ever again unlock the doors to Celestelvyra, there seemed no plausible reason for her to waste time talking.

"If you aren't my mother then who is?" Asher noticed Foxx's intense premeditations and decided to keep Sirena talking while a plan materialized. "What about my father?"

The Queen sighed as though she'd never been so annoyed. "Pollux is your father, yes. Had to get rid of the woman though. I couldn't have her causing any more trouble for me, now could I?"

"But who—"

"Enough, Alexander. I have tired of this. I am here to follow through with my end of the deal, and then I shall be off. I will even let you and your precious Belamours live again, as was an unfortunate requirement of the arrangement. Though I suppose you're no threat to me without those keys in your pocket."

Foxx's brows knit together. "What deal?"

The Queen laughed, pleased to find no one but herself in on the secret. "The deal I made prior to coming here this evening, Foxxglove." She pointed to the men on either side of her. "These two in exchange for the keys. And your safety, of course." She dipped her head as if bowing respectfully, but her expression showed her malice. "Isn't that right, little bird?" Her eyes flashed to Declan with a wicked grin. Air fled from Iris' lungs as she gaped at him, but the Queen prattled on. "Though he must have caught me on a good day, because I have no idea why I agreed to let the rest of you live. Oh well. Something to look forward to. With ancient prophecies in the works, it's generally safer not to interfere if possible. To be honest, I'm quite intrigued to see how this all plays out now that I hold the keys. Whatever will you do without the ability to slay the Immortal Queen?"

Iris kept her eyes on Declan. Asher's flickered back and forth between him and the Queen.

Palms in the air, Declan said, "It's not what you think."

Sirena took several steps toward him and ran a long fingernail across his chest, ogling his lean, muscular body as she circled behind him. His eyes were on fire with rage at her unwelcomed touch, but he didn't push her away.

Words poured from her as sweet as poisonous honey as she whispered into his ear, loud enough for the others to overhear. "Look at her over there, Silas. You have absolutely shattered her heart. Your sweet, little Iris. It's a tragedy, really. You know, based on my time with Orion, I had thought it he who would end up at her side. Oh, how he cried out her name. Though, I suppose now that you've ruthlessly betrayed her, that path is still possible." His face grew red with fury as Sirena leaned in closer, sniffing the sweat of his neck and humming with delight. Then she spoke viciously through her teeth. "Now, you're going to cooperate and give me what we agreed upon, or I am going to gut her with my bare hands while you watch. Is that clear?"

"You can't break our bargain," Declan growled.

"I'm the Queen of Arkaemor, darling. I can do anything I want." She rested her hand on his left shoulder and spoke to the others from behind his right. "Now, you have your brute of a friend, you have your brother. Give me what is mine."

Iris' eyes grew impossibly wider in response to the word *brother*. She couldn't deny it now. Declan had betrayed them. He stared at her, guilt and remorse written all over his face.

Asher said, "You can't have them. I don't care what Declan promised you. They aren't his to give."

Sirena strode out around Declan and stood next to him. "Don't be angry, Alexander. You have no idea what this poor boy has been through." Looking at Declan, she spoke to him like a wounded child. "It's been a hard life, hasn't it, Silas?"

Asher swore. "Stop. Leave him alone."

Sawyer slammed his body between Foxx and Asher, pushing them out of the way as he charged the Queen, howling a wild battle cry. When he reached her, she grabbed both sides of his head and stopped him in his tracks. "Stupid man. I've waited years for this, and you've played right into my hands." Then she snapped his neck with an echoing crack before allowing his body to crumple to the ground in a dead heap.

Iris and Foxx screamed. Foxx tried to run to him, but Asher held her back.

Sirena spoke over their shouts. "So much tragedy. Abandoned by your mother. Lied to by Alexander. Betrayed by your friend. And now losing your father when you've only just gotten him back."

"You witch!" Foxx's throat swelled with agony as she fought against Asher's restraints. In her mind, she snarled, *I'll kill you, Sirena. No matter what it takes. I swear it. I will not stop until you're little more than a horrible memory.*

Sirena cackled. *Learning so quickly, aren't you? I'm impressed.* "Make all the threats you want, but the only way to end me is through those doors, Foxxglove. And you're never getting through them."

Foxx felt the tips of her fingers grow cold as she shoved Asher away from her. Her bow slipped from her shoulder into her hand. A scream burst from her as she released the arrow, hitting the Queen straight through the heart. The impact had Sirena stumbling backward.

"You can't kill me with an arrow!" She laughed wildly and yanked it from her chest as another landed below her shoulder.

Iris fought through the anguish of losing her father and took advantage of the opportunity to grab the keys from Asher's bag. She sprinted to the stone table and began placing the keys in their correct hollows. As she inserted them, they sank into the stone and melded flush with the surface as if they'd been there all along. Seth stood to help.

Asher pulled his rifle and aimed it at Sirena. Foxx nocked another arrow as they both sidestepped in the direction of the door.

The Queen screamed with rage and ripped the second arrow free. "That was not very nice, Foxxglove." Her hands rose to her sides and filled with crackling smoke, like miniature storm clouds. Keeping her eyes on Foxx, she shot black lightning toward Iris. Declan jumped in front of it, taking the shot to his right shoulder. He cried out in pain and grabbed the wound. Something like black ink spread out from beneath it, darkening his clothes and bringing him to his knees.

Then the clinking and grinding of gears drew their attention to the doors behind them. The crack at the center of the wall displaying the seven symbols and the crescent moon split open, revealing a set of doors.

Grabbing Seth's hand, Iris dragged him toward the entrance of Celestelvyra. She looked back to see if Declan followed, but he was clutching the table, trying to stand.

Asher shot Sirena once in the heart and once in the head. Blood spilled down her face and soaked her dress from both wounds. She faltered long enough for them to race for the door. Declan looked from the doorway to Orion and Johnathan, still unconscious and on their knees.

The Queen made the decision for him. She yanked him up by his shoulder and slammed her stiletto blade up under his ribcage. He clutched the wound and gasped as blood spilled from his lips. His eyes met Iris' through the closing doors, and he hoped she could feel his remorse.

Iris' hands covered her mouth as she dropped to the ground.

Sirena pulled the blade free and pushed him over. Then she ran for the doors, but by the time she reached them, they'd closed tight. She wailed with rage, running to the table holding the keys and trying to remove them, but they'd forged with the stone and wouldn't budge. She slammed her hands on the flat surface and yowled again. Racing back to the doors, she pounded them with her fists and shouted, "Elohim! You cannot keep me locked out forever!"

Lightning cracked above her in the night sky and moments later, a thunderous boom shook the entire swamp. She flinched and covered her ears before releasing another howling shriek. Bending over Sawyer's felled corpse, she searched his pockets for the Artifact, finding nothing. Then she walked up to Orion and shot him with a burst of black lightning. He hardly moved, as if he hadn't felt it. She screamed again. "I don't have the keys, and so the bargain is terminated. Let me take him!"

Another peal of thunder rattled the sky.

Sirena growled at the expanse. "Fine! Have it your way. They can rot here for all I care." She stomped between Orion and Johnathan and smacked both of them across the face with the backs of her hands, snapping them out of their trance. They tumbled to the ground as she stormed off the platform and followed the path back toward the hallway barrier.

The swamp settled into silence, but for the shallow breathing of two wounded soldiers on the brink of awakening, about to find themselves trapped in a place they had never been before.

EPILOGUE

I ris curled over her knees as tears streamed down her face. Foxx sat against the door, at a loss for words. Asher lay on his back with his eyes closed, trying to breathe. Seth sat in the corner of the door, unsure what to do with the inconsolable adults.

It was a long while until everyone calmed down enough to function. Iris sat up and wiped her tears before joining Seth, wrapping her arm around his shoulder to comfort him. Asher had risen to a seated position and was watching Foxx. He said her name, but she didn't respond. A minute later, he tried again, and she gazed at him blankly.

"I'm sorry, did you say something?"

"What can I do?" he asked. She sighed and rested her head back against the door, ignoring his question.

"We won't be able to get back, will we?" Seth wondered out loud. "We don't have the keys."

"We'll figure it out," Iris assured him.

Asher agreed and rose to his feet to look around. Rather than being inside a building, they were beneath an awning. The wall behind them was a mirror image to what they'd seen on the opposite side of the doors.

He stepped out from under the roof into the lush grass and saw what lay before them. Then he turned back around to find the same tree draping its roots down around the entrance and into the ground.

"Listen," he said, addressing everyone. "I want you all to look at me so I know you are paying attention." Iris and Seth lifted their eyes to him straight away, but Foxx resisted. He called her name, and she lifted her head from the door. "Everything that happened back there, the whole heinous event was… insane. Absolutely awful. For all of us. We shall definitely need to work through many of those traumas at some point, but can we do something else first?"

"What?" Seth asked.

"Everybody stand up. Come on, come on." He waved his arms, motioning for them to rise. Begrudgingly, they did as they were told. "Now, look." He coaxed them to move away from the doorway and observe what lay before them. They stepped from beneath the structure surrounding the door and out into the light, and the tiniest spark of joy came to life in each of their hearts.

They were in a garden. The most glorious garden any of them had ever seen. They saw trees, berry bushes, flowers, and birds. A path stretched out in front of them, leading somewhere unknown, but undoubtedly even more stunning than what they could already see. Their eyes widened with amazement as they took it all in. Grinning, Asher held his arm out in presentation. "Welcome, my friends, to the Sacred Realm of Celestelvyra."

C

These are the things I look back on years later
as I try to decipher
how I got this way.

What led me here?
Why does it all hurt so much *all the time?*
Nothing   fills   the   void,
Nothing curbs the screaming inside.
Nothing silences the whispers.

unfinished

jessica pietro

About the Author

Jessica Pietro has been enchanted by fantasy worlds her entire life. Though she dabbled in writing, she never anticipated being a published author.

In 2019, she started selling artwork and teaching under the name *Vellichor and More.* In 2021, she began writing *The Great King and the Seer.*

Not only is she passionate about art and stories, she also enjoys adventuring, board games, studying her bible, anime, gardening, music, hot beverages, camping, and spending time with her family.

Jessica resides in Pennsylvania, with her husband, their son, and their kitties. Find out more about her by connecting with her on social media.

Links to all of her sites can be found here:

www.vellichorandmore.com

C

Reviews are always appreciated and are truly imperative to any author's success. Please take a moment to rate and review this book on Amazon, Goodreads, and anywhere else books are sold online.

Thank you so much for reading!

Kainos International

Jessica Pietro is very passionate about Kainos International, a missions organization focused on the rescue and rehabilitation of victims from the horrific world of sex-trafficking. With the Holy Spirit's leading, she has decided to donate all royalties from her first book, Seeking Elvyra, to this ministry.

"Kainos" [καινός]
is a Greek word that means
"completely new."

Kainos International is a beacon of hope and change, dedicated to breaking the cycle of commercial sex exploitation. Taking steps toward prevention, intervention, and rehabilitation, Kainos empowers survivors to heal, grow, and help others. Kainos began as a major presence in Germany, where they work out of four different locations offering sanctuary and learning centers for those who have suffered. They visit brothels and clubs, where victims of forced prostitution are hidden in plain sight, to build relationships and trust. Along the way, they convey a message of hope in Christ and an opportunity for a new life of freedom.

Their continued expansion into advocacy work alongside survivors in the United States and internationally further solidifies their commitment to making a lasting impact. Partnering with churches around the U.S. allows even more opportunities for education and change and paves the way for more victims to be rescued from a life of slavery.

To learn more about Kainos International and to join in their noble cause, please visit their website at www.kainos-international.org or contact them at hello@kainos-international.org.

> "Human trafficking is among the world's fastest growing criminal enterprises and is estimated to be a $150 billion-a-year global industry. It is a form of modern day slavery that profits from the exploitation of our most vulnerable populations." *Bonta, Rob. Office of the Attorney General. https://oag.ca.gov/human-trafficking*

Together, we can make a difference and create a world where survivors of the sex-trafficking industry can find healing and hope.

Thank you for supporting this ministry.

www.ingramcontent.com/pod-product-compliance
Lightning Source LLC
Chambersburg PA
CBHW032059310726

48972CB00001B/27